THE WORLD OVER

THE WORLD OVER

W. SOMERSET MAUGHAM

The Collected Stories

VOLUME TWO

THE REPRINT SOCIETY LONDON

FIRST PUBLISHED 1951
THIS EDITION PUBLISHED BY THE REPRINT SOCIETY
BY ARRANGEMENT WITH WM HEINEMANN LTD 1954
SECOND IMPRESSION 1954

PRINTED IN GREAT BRITAIN BY RICHARD CLAY AND COMPANY, LTD.,
BUNGAY, SUFFOLK

Contents

VOLUME TWO

Sanatorium

FOR the first six weeks that Ashenden was at the sanatorium he stayed in bed. He saw nobody but the doctor who visited him morning and evening, the nurses who looked after him and the maid who brought him his meals. He had contracted tuberculosis of the lungs and since at the time there were reasons that made it difficult for him to go to Switzerland the specialist he saw in London had sent him up to a sanatorium in the north of Scotland. At last the day came that he had been patiently looking forward to when the doctor told him he could get up; and in the afternoon his nurse, having helped him to dress, took him down to the verandah, placed cushions behind him, wrapped him up in rugs and left him to enjoy the sun that was streaming down from a cloudless sky. It was midwinter. The sanatorium stood on the top of a hill and from it you had a spacious view of the snow-clad country. There were people lying all along the verandah in deck-chairs, some chatting with their neighbours and some reading. Every now and then one would have a fit of coughing and you noticed that at the end of it he looked anxiously at his handkerchief. Before the nurse left Ashenden she turned with a kind of professional briskness to the man who was lying in the next chair.

"I want to introduce Mr. Ashenden to you," she said. And then to Ashenden: "This is Mr. McLeod. He and Mr. Campbell have been here longer than anyone else."

On the other side of Ashenden was lying a pretty girl, with red hair and bright blue eyes; she had on no make-up, but her lips were very red and the colour on her cheeks was high. It emphasised the astonishing whiteness of her skin. It was lovely even when you realised that its delicate texture was due to illness. She wore a fur coat and was wrapped up in rugs, so that you could see nothing of her body, but her face was extremely thin, so thin that it made her nose, which wasn't really large, look a trifle prominent. She gave Ashenden a friendly look, but did not speak, and Ashenden, feeling rather shy among all those strange people, waited to be spoken to.

"First time they've let you get up, is it?" said McLeod.

"Yes."

"Where's your room?"

Ashenden told him.

"Small. I know every room in the place. I've been here for

731

seventeen years. I've got the best room here and so I damned well ought to have. Campbell's been trying to get me out of it, he wants it himself, but I'm not going to budge; I've got a right to it, I came here six months before he did."

McLeod, lying there, gave you the impression that he was immensely tall; his skin was stretched tight over his bones, his cheeks and temples hollow, so that you could see the formation of his skull under it; and in that emaciated face, with its great bony nose, the eyes were preternaturally large.

"Seventeen years is a long time," said Ashenden, because he could think of nothing else to say.

"Time passes very quickly. I like it here. At first, after a year or two, I went away in the summer, but I don't any more. It's my home now. I've got a brother and two sisters; but they're married and now they've got families; they don't want me. When you've been here a few years and you go back to ordinary life, you feel a bit out of it, you know. Your pals have gone their own ways and you've got nothing in common with them any more. It all seems an awful rush. Much ado about nothing, that's what it is. It's noisy and stuffy. No, one's better off here. I shan't stir again till they carry me out feet first in my coffin."

The specialist had told Ashenden that if he took care of himself for a reasonable time he would get well, and he looked at McLeod with curiosity.

"What do you do with yourself all day long?" he asked.

"Do? Having T.B. is a whole-time job, my boy. There's my temperature to take and then I weigh myself. I don't hurry over my dressing. I have breakfast, I read the papers and go for a walk. Then I have my rest. I lunch and play bridge. I have another rest and then I dine. I play a bit more bridge and I go to bed. They've got quite a decent library here, we get all the new books, but I don't really have much time for reading. I talk to people. You meet all sorts here, you know. They come and they go. Sometimes they go because they think they're cured, but a lot of them come back, and sometimes they go because they die. I've seen a lot of people out and before I go I expect to see a lot more."

The girl sitting on Ashenden's other side suddenly spoke.

"I should tell you that few persons can get a heartier laugh out of a hearse than Mr. McLeod," she said.

McLeod chuckled.

"I don't know about that, but it wouldn't be human nature if I didn't say to myself: Well, I'm just as glad it's him and not me they're taking for a ride."

It-occurred to him that Ashenden didn't know the pretty girl, so he introduced him.

"By the way, I don't think you've met Mr. Ashenden—Miss Bishop. She's English, but not a bad girl."

"How long have *you* been here?" asked Ashenden.

"Only two years. This is my last winter. Dr. Lennox says I shall be all right in a few months and there's no reason why I shouldn't go home."

"Silly, I call it," said McLeod. "Stay where you're well off, that's what I say."

At that moment a man, leaning on a stick, came walking slowly along the verandah.

"Oh, look, there's Major Templeton," said Miss Bishop, a smile lighting up her blue eyes; and then, as he came up: "I'm glad to see you up again."

"Oh, it was nothing. Only a bit of a cold. I'm quite all right now."

The words were hardly out of his mouth when he began to cough. He leaned heavily on his stick. But when the attack was over he smiled gaily.

"Can't get rid of this damned cough," he said. "Smoking too much. Dr. Lennox says I ought to give it up, but it's no good—I can't."

He was a tall fellow, good-looking in a slightly theatrical way, with a dusky, sallow face, fine very dark eyes and a neat black moustache. He was wearing a fur coat with an Astrakhan collar. His appearance was smart and perhaps a trifle showy. Miss Bishop made Ashenden known to him. Major Templeton said a few civil words in an easy, cordial way, and then asked the girl to go for a stroll with him; he had been ordered to walk to a certain place in the wood behind the sanatorium and back again. McLeod watched them as they sauntered off.

"I wonder if there's anything between those two," he said. "They do say Templeton was a devil with the girls before he got ill."

"He doesn't look up to much in that line just now," said Ashenden.

"You never can tell. I've seen a lot of rum things here in my day. I could tell you no end of stories if I wanted to."

"You evidently do, so why don't you?"

McLeod grinned.

"Well, I'll tell you one. Three or four years ago there was a woman here who was pretty hot stuff. Her husband used to come

and see her every other week-end, he was crazy about her, used to
fly up from London; but Dr. Lennox was pretty sure she was carrying on with somebody here, but he couldn't find out who. So one
night when we'd all gone to bed he had a thin coat of paint put
down just outside her room and next day he had everyone's slippers
examined. Neat, wasn't it? The fellow whose slippers had paint on
them got the push. Dr. Lennox has to be particular, you know.
He doesn't want this place to get a bad name."

"How long has Templeton been here?"

"Three or four months. He's been in bed most of the time.
He's for it all right. Ivy Bishop'll be a damned fool if she gets
stuck on him. She's got a good chance of getting well. I've seen
so many of them, you know, I can tell. When I look at a fellow I
make up my mind at once whether he'll get well or whether he won't,
and if he won't I can make a pretty shrewd guess how long he'll last.
I'm very seldom mistaken. I give Templeton about two years
myself."

McLeod gave Ashenden a speculative look and Ashenden, knowing what he was thinking, though he tried to be amused, could not
help feeling somewhat concerned. There was a twinkle in McLeod's
eyes. He plainly knew what was passing though Ashenden's mind.

"You'll get all right. I wouldn't have mentioned it if I hadn't
been pretty sure of that. I don't want Dr. Lennox to hoof me out
for putting the fear of God into his bloody patients."

Then Ashenden's nurse came to take him back to bed. Even
though he had only sat out for an hour, he was tired, and was glad
to find himself once more between the sheets. Dr. Lennox came
in to see him in the course of the evening. He looked at his temperature chart.

"That's not so bad," he said.

Dr. Lennox was small, brisk and genial. He was a good enough
doctor, an excellent business man, and an enthusiastic fisherman.
When the fishing season began he was inclined to leave the care of
his patients to his assistants; the patients grumbled a little, but
were glad enough to eat the young salmon he brought back to vary
their meals. He was fond of talking, and now, standing at the end
of Ashenden's bed, he asked him, in his broad Scots, whether he
had got into conversation with any of the patients that afternoon.
Ashenden told him the nurse had introduced him to McLeod. Dr.
Lennox laughed.

"The oldest living inhabitant. He knows more about the sanatorium and its inmates than I do. How he gets his information I
haven't an idea, but there's not a thing about the private lives of

anyone under this roof that he doesn't know. There's not an old maid in the place with a keener nose for a bit of scandal. Did he tell you about Campbell?"

"He mentioned him."

"He hates Campbell, and Campbell hates him. Funny, when you come to think of it, those two men, they've been here for seventeen years and they've got about one sound lung between them. They loathe the sight of one another. I've had to refuse to listen to the complaints about one another that they come to me with. Campbell's room is just below McLeod's and Campbell plays the fiddle. It drives McLeod wild. He says he's been listening to the same tunes for fifteen years, but Campbell says McLeod doesn't know one tune from another. McLeod wants me to stop Campbell playing, but I can't do that, he's got a perfect right to play so long as he doesn't play in the silence hours. I've offered to change McLeod's room, but he won't do that. He says Campbell only plays to drive him out of the room because it's the best in the house, and he's damned if he's going to have it. It's queer, isn't it, that two middle-aged men should think it worth while to make life hell for one another? Neither can leave the other alone. They have their meals at the same table, they play bridge together; and not a day passes without a row. Sometimes I've threatened to turn them both out if they don't behave like sensible fellows. That keeps them quiet for a bit. They don't want to go. They've been here so long, they've got no one any more who gives a damn for them, and they can't cope with the world outside. Campbell went away for a couple of months' holiday some years ago. He came back after a week; he said he couldn't stand the racket, and the sight of so many people in the streets scared him."

It was a strange world into which Ashenden found himself thrown when, his health gradually improving, he was able to mix with his fellow patients. One morning Dr. Lennox told him he could thenceforward lunch in the dining-room. This was a large, low room, with great window space; the windows were always wide open and on fine days the sun streamed in. There seemed to be a great many people and it took him some time to sort them out. They were of all kinds, young, middle-aged and old. There were some, like McLeod and Campbell, who had been at the sanatorium for years and expected to die there. Others had only been there for a few months. There was one middle-aged spinster called Miss Atkin who had been coming every winter for a long time and in the summer went to stay with friends and relations. She had nothing much the matter with her any more, and might just as well have stayed away altogether, but she liked the life. Her long residence had given her a sort of position, she was honorary librarian and hand in glove with the matron. She was always ready to gossip with you, but you were soon warned that everything you said was passed on. It was useful to Dr. Lennox to know that his patients were getting on well together and were happy, that they did nothing imprudent and followed his instructions. Little escaped Miss Atkin's sharp eyes, and from her it went to the matron, and so to Dr. Lennox. Because she had been coming for so many years, she sat at the same table as McLeod and Campbell, together with an old general who had been put there on account of his rank. The table was in no way different from any other, and it was not more advantageously placed, but because the oldest residents sat there it was looked upon as the most desirable place to sit, and several elderly women were bitterly resentful because Miss Atkin, who went away for four or five months every summer, should be given a place there while they who spent the whole year in the sanatorium sat at other tables. There was an old Indian Civilian who had been at the sanatorium longer than anyone but McLeod and Campbell; he was a man who in his day had ruled a province, and he was waiting irascibly for either McLeod or Campbell to die so that he might take his place at the first table. Ashenden made the acquaintance of Campbell. He was a long, big-boned fellow with a bald head, so thin that you wondered how his limbs held together; and when he sat crumpled in an arm-chair he gave you the uncanny impression of a mannikin in a puppet-show. He was brusque, touchy and bad-tempered. The first thing he asked Ashenden was:

"Are you fond of music?"

"Yes."

"No one here cares a damn for it. I play the violin. But if you like it, come to my room one day and I'll play to you."

"Don't you go," said McLeod, who heard him. "It's torture."

"How can you be so rude?" cried Miss Atkin. "Mr. Campbell plays very nicely."

"There's no one in this beastly place that knows one note from another," said Campbell.

With a derisive chuckle McLeod walked off. Miss Atkin tried to smooth things down.

"You mustn't mind what McLeod said."

"Oh, I don't. I'll get back on him all right."

He played the same tune over and over again all that afternoon. McLeod banged on the floor, but Campbell went on. He sent a message by a maid to say that he had a headache and would Mr.

Campbell mind not playing; Campbell replied that he had a perfect right to play and if McLeod didn't like it he could lump it. When next they met high words passed.

Ashenden was put at a table with the pretty Miss Bishop, with Templeton, and with a London man, an accountant, called Henry Chester. He was a stocky, broad-shouldered, wiry little fellow, and the last person you would ever have thought would be attacked by T.B. It had come upon him as a sudden and unexpected blow. He was a perfectly ordinary man, somewhere between thirty and forty, married, with two children. He lived in a decent suburb. He went up to the City every morning and read the morning paper; he came down from the City every evening and read the evening paper. He had no interests except his business and his family. He liked his work; he made enough money to live in comfort, he put by a reasonable sum every year, he played golf on Saturday afternoon and on Sunday, he went every August for a three weeks' holiday to the same place on the east coast; his children would grow up and marry, then he would turn his business over to his son and retire with his wife to a little house in the country where he could potter about till death claimed him at a ripe old age. He asked nothing more from life than that, and it was a life that thousands upon thousands of his fellow-men lived with satisfaction. He was the average citizen. Then this thing happened. He had caught cold playing golf, it had gone to his chest, and he had had a cough that he couldn't shake off. He had always been strong and healthy, and had no opinion of doctors; but at last at his wife's persuasion he had consented to see one. It was a shock to him, a fearful shock, to learn that there was tubercle in both his lungs and that his only chance of life was to go immediately to a sanatorium. The specialist he saw then told him that he might be able to go back to work in a couple of years, but two years had passed and Dr. Lennox advised him not to think of it for at least a year more. He showed him the bacilli in his sputum, and in an X-ray photograph the actively diseased patches in his lungs. He lost heart. It seemed to him a cruel and unjust trick that fate had played upon him. He could have understood it if he had led a wild life, if he had drunk too much, played around with women or kept late hours. He would have deserved it then. But he had done none of these things. It was monstrously unfair. Having no resources in himself, no interest in books, he had nothing to do but think of his health. It became an obsession. He watched his symptoms anxiously. They had to deprive him of a thermometer because he took his temperature a dozen times a day. He got it into his head that the doctors were taking his case too indifferently, and in order to force their attention used every method he could devise to make the thermometer register a temperature that would alarm; and when his tricks were foiled he grew sulky and querulous. But he was by nature a jovial, friendly creature, and when he forgot himself he talked and laughed gaily; then on a sudden he remembered that he was a sick man and you would see in his eyes the fear of death.

At the end of every month his wife came up to spend a day or two in a lodging-house near-by. Dr. Lennox did not much like the visits that relatives paid the patients; it excited and unsettled them. It was moving to see the eagerness with which Henry Chester looked forward to his wife's arrival; but it was strange to notice that once she had come he seemed less pleased than one would have expected. Mrs. Chester was a pleasant, cheerful little woman, not pretty, but neat, as commonplace as her husband, and you only had to look at her to know that she was a good wife and mother, a careful housekeeper, a nice, quiet body who did her duty and interfered with nobody. She had been quite happy in the dull, domestic life they had led for so many years, her only dissipation a visit to the pictures, her great thrill the sales in the big London shops; and it had never occurred to her that it was monotonous. It completely satisfied her. Ashenden liked her. He listened with interest while she prattled about her children and her house in the suburbs, her neighbours and her trivial occupations. On one occasion he met her in the road. Chester for some reason connected with his treatment had stayed in and she was alone. Ashenden suggested that they should walk together. They talked for a little of indifferent things. Then she suddenly asked him how he thought her husband was.

"I think he seems to be getting on all right."

"I'm so terribly worried."

"You must remember it's a slow, long business. One has to have patience."

They walked on a little and then he saw she was crying.

"You mustn't be unhappy about him," said Ashenden gently.

"Oh, you don't know what I have to put up with when I come here. I know I ought not to speak about it, but I must. I can trust you, can't I?"

"Of course."

"I love him. I'm devoted to him. I'd do anything in the world I could for him. We've never quarrelled, we've never even differed about a single thing. He's beginning to hate me and it breaks my heart."

"Oh, I can't believe that. Why, when you're not here he talks of you all the time. He couldn't talk more nicely. He's devoted to you."

"Yes, that's when I'm not here. It's when I'm here, when he sees me well and strong, that it comes over him. You see, he resents it so terribly that he's ill and I'm well. He's afraid he's going to die and he hates me because I'm going to live. I have to be on my guard all the time; almost everything I say, if I speak of the children, if I speak of the future, exasperates him, and he says bitter, wounding things. When I speak of something I've had to do to the house or a servant I've had to change it irritates him beyond endurance. He complains that I treat him as if he didn't count any more. We used to be so united, and now I feel there's a great wall of antagonism between us. I know I shouldn't blame him, I know it's only his illness, he's a dear good man really, and kindness itself, normally he's the easiest man in the world to get on with; and now I simply dread coming here and I go with relief. He'd be terribly sorry if I had T.B. but I know that in his heart of hearts it would be a relief. He could forgive me, he could forgive fate, if he thought I was going to die too. Sometimes he tortures me by talking about what I shall do when he's dead, and when I get hysterical and cry out to him to stop, he says I needn't grudge him a little pleasure when he'll be dead so soon and I can go on living for years and years and have a good time. Oh, it's so frightful to think that this love we've had for one another all these years should die in this sordid miserable way."

Mrs. Chester sat down on a stone by the roadside and gave way to passionate weeping. Ashenden looked at her with pity, but could find nothing to say that might comfort her. What she had told him did not come quite as a surprise.

"Give me a cigarette," she said at last. "I mustn't let my eyes get all red and swollen, or Henry'll know I've been crying and he'll think I've had bad news about him. Is death so horrible? Do we all fear death like that?"

"I don't know," said Ashenden.

"When my mother was dying she didn't seem to mind a bit. She knew it was coming and she even made little jokes about it. But she was an old woman."

Mrs. Chester pulled herself together and they set off again. They walked for a while in silence.

"You won't think any the worse of Henry for what I've told you?" she said at last.

"Of course not."

"He's been a good husband and a good father. I've never known a better man in my life. Until this illness I don't think an unkind or ungenerous thought ever passed through his head."

The conversation left Ashenden pensive. People often said he had a low opinion of human nature. It was because he did not always judge his fellows by the usual standards. He accepted, with a smile, a tear or a shrug of the shoulders, much that filled others with dismay. It was true that you would never have expected that good-natured, commonplace little chap to harbour such bitter and unworthy thoughts; but who has ever been able to tell to what depths man may fall or to what heights rise? The fault lay in the poverty of his ideals. Henry Chester was born and bred to lead an average life, exposed to the normal vicissitudes of existence, and when an unforeseeable accident befell him he had no means of coping with it. He was like a brick made to take its place with a million others in a huge factory, but by chance with a flaw in it so that it is inadequate to its purpose. And the brick too, if it had a mind, might cry: What have I done that I cannot fulfil my modest end, but must be taken away from all these other bricks that support me and thrown on the dust-heap? It was no fault of Henry Chester's that he was incapable of the conceptions that might have enabled him to bear his calamity with resignation. It is not everyone who can find solace in art or thought. It is the tragedy of our day that these humble souls have lost their faith in God, in whom lay hope, and their belief in a resurrection that might bring them the happiness that has been denied them on earth; and have found nothing to put in their place.

There are people who say that suffering ennobles. It is not true. As a general rule it makes man petty, querulous and selfish; but here in this sanatorium there was not much suffering. In certain stages of tuberculosis the slight fever that accompanies it excites rather than depresses, so that the patient feels alert and, upborne by hope, faces the future blithely; but for all that the idea of death haunts the subconscious. It is a sardonic theme song that runs through a sprightly operetta. Now and again the gay, melodious arias, the dance measures, deviate strangely into tragic strains that throb menacingly down the nerves; the petty interests of every day, the small jealousies and trivial concerns are as nothing; pity and terror make the heart on a sudden stand still and the awfulness of death broods as the silence that precedes a tropical storm broods over the tropical jungle. After Ashenden had been for some time at the sanatorium there came a boy of twenty. He was in the navy, a sub-lieutenant in a submarine, and he had what they used to call in novels galloping consumption. He was a tall, good-looking youth, with curly brown hair, blue eyes and a very sweet smile. Ashenden saw him two or three times lying on the terrace in the sun and passed the time of day with him. He was a cheerful lad. He talked of musical shows and film stars; and he read the paper for the football results and the boxing news. Then he was put to bed and Ashenden saw him no more. His relations were sent for and in two months he was dead. He died uncomplaining. He understood what was happening to him as little as an animal. For a day or two there was the same malaise in the sanatorium as there is in a prison when a man has been hanged; and then, as though by universal consent, in obedience to an instinct of self-preservation, the boy was put out of mind: life, with its three meals a day, its golf on the miniature course, its regulated exercise, its prescribed rests, its quarrels and jealousies, its scandal-mongering and petty vexations, went on as before. Campbell, to the exasperation of McLeod, continued to play the prize-song and "Annie Laurie" on his fiddle. McLeod continued to boast of his bridge and gossip about other people's health and morals. Miss Atkin continued to backbite. Henry Chester continued to complain that the doctors gave him insufficient attention and railed against fate because, after the model life he had led, it had played him such a dirty trick. Ashenden continued to read, and with amused tolerance to watch the vagaries of his fellow-creatures.

He became intimate with Major Templeton. Templeton was perhaps a little more than forty years of age. He had been in the Grenadier Guards, but had resigned his commission after the war. A man of ample means, he had since then devoted himself entirely to pleasure. He raced in the racing season, shot in the shooting season and hunted in the hunting season. When this was over he went to Monte Carlo. He told Ashenden of the large sums he had made and lost at baccarat. He was very fond of women and if his stories could be believed they were very fond of him. He loved good food and good drink. He knew by their first names the head waiters of every restaurant in London where you ate well. He belonged to half a dozen clubs. He had led for years a useless, selfish, worthless life, the sort of life which maybe it will be impossible for anyone to live in the future, but he had lived it without misgiving and had enjoyed it. Ashenden asked him once what he would do if he had his time over again and he answered that he would do exactly what he had done. He was an amusing talker, gay and pleasantly ironic, and he dealt with the surface of things, which was all he knew, with a light, easy and assured touch. He

always had a pleasant word for the dowdy spinsters in the sanatorium and a joking one for the peppery old gentlemen, for he
combined good manners with a natural kindliness. He knew his
way about the superficial world of the people who have more
money than they know what to do with as well as he knew his way
about Mayfair. He was the kind of man who would always have
been willing to take a bet, to help a friend and to give a tenner to a
rogue. If he had never done much good in the world he had never
done much harm. He amounted to nothing. But he was a more
agreeable companion than many of more sterling character and of
more admirable qualities. He was very ill now. He was dying
and he knew it. He took it with the same easy, laughing nonchalance as he had taken all the rest. He'd had a thundering good
time, he regretted nothing, it was rotten tough luck getting T.B.
but to hell with it, no one can live for ever, and when you came to
think of it, he might have been killed in the war or broken his
bloody neck in a point-to-point. His principle all through life
had been, when you've made a bad bet, pay up and forget about it.
He'd had a good run for his money and he was ready to call it a day.
It had been a damned good party while it lasted, but every party's
got to come to an end, and next day it doesn't matter much if you
went home with the milk or if you left while the fun was in full swing.

Of all those people in the sanatorium he was probably from the
moral standpoint the least worthy, but he was the only one who
genuinely accepted the inevitable with unconcern. He snapped his
fingers in the face of death, and you could choose whether to call
his levity unbecoming or his insouciance gallant.

The last thing that ever occurred to him when he came to the
sanatorium was that he might fall more deeply in love there than
he had ever done before. His amours had been numerous, but
they had been light; he had been content with the politely mercenary
love of chorus girls and with ephemeral unions with women of
easy virtue whom he met at house parties. He had always taken
care to avoid any attachment that might endanger his freedom.
His only aim in life had been to get as much fun out of it as possible,
and where sex was concerned he found every advantage and no
inconvenience in ceaseless variety. But he liked women. Even
when they were quite old he could not talk to them without a
caress in his eyes and a tenderness in his voice. He was prepared to
do anything to please them. They were conscious of his interest
in them and were agreeably flattered, and they felt, quite mis-
takenly, that they could trust him never to let them down. He once
said a thing that Ashenden thought showed insight:

"You know, any man can get any woman he wants if he tries hard enough, there's nothing in that, but once he's got her, only a man who thinks the world of women can get rid of her without humiliating her."

It was simply from habit that he began to make love to Ivy Bishop. She was the prettiest and the youngest girl in the sanatorium. She was in point of fact not so young as Ashenden had first thought her, she was twenty-nine, but for the last eight years she had been wandering from one sanatorium to another, in Switzerland, England and Scotland, and the sheltered invalid life had preserved her youthful appearance so that you might easily have taken her for twenty. All she knew of the world she had learnt in these establishments, so that she combined rather curiously extreme innocence with extreme sophistication. She had seen a number of love affairs run their course. A good many men, of various nationalities, had made love to her; she accepted their attentions with self-possession and humour, but she had at her disposal plenty of firmness when they showed an inclination to go too far. She had a force of character unexpected in anyone who looked so flower-like, and when it came to a show-down knew how to express her meaning in plain, cool and decisive words. She was quite ready to have a flirtation with George Templeton. It was a game she understood, and though always charming to him, it was with a bantering lightness that showed quite clearly that she had summed him up and had no mind to take the affair more seriously than he did. Like Ashenden, Templeton went to bed every evening at six and dined in his room, so that he saw Ivy only by day. They went for little walks together, but otherwise were seldom alone. At lunch the conversation between the four of them, Ivy, Templeton, Henry Chester and Ashenden, was general, but it was obvious that it was for neither of the two men that Templeton took so much trouble to be entertaining. It seemed to Ashenden that he was ceasing to flirt with Ivy to pass the time, and that his feeling for her was growing deeper and more sincere; but he could not tell whether she was conscious of it nor whether it meant anything to her. Whenever Templeton hazarded a remark that was more intimate than the occasion warranted she countered it with an ironic one that made them all laugh. But Templeton's laugh was rueful. He was no longer content to have her take him as a play-boy. The more Ashenden knew Ivy Bishop the more he liked her. There was something pathetic in her sick beauty, with that lovely transparent skin, the thin face in which the eyes were so large and so wonderfully blue; and there was something pathetic in her plight, for like so many others in the sanatorium she seemed to be alone in the world.

Her mother led a busy social life, her sisters were married; they took but a perfunctory interest in the young woman from whom they had been separated now for eight years. They corresponded, they came to see her occasionally, but there was no longer very much between them. She accepted the situation without bitterness. She was friendly with everyone and prepared always to listen with sympathy to the complaints and the distress of all and sundry. She went out of her way to be nice to Henry Chester and did what she could to cheer him.

"Well, Mr. Chester," she said to him one day at lunch, "it's the end of the month, your wife will be coming to-morrow. That's something to look forward to."

"No, she's not coming this month," he said quietly, looking down at his plate.

"Oh, I am sorry. Why not? The children are all right, aren't they?"

"Dr. Lennox thinks it's better for me that she shouldn't come."

There was a silence. Ivy looked at him with troubled eyes.

"That's tough luck, old man," said Templeton in his hearty way. "Why didn't you tell Lennox to go to hell?"

"He must know best," said Chester.

Ivy gave him another look and began to talk of something else.

Looking back, Ashenden realised that she had at once suspected the truth. For next day he happened to walk with Chester.

"I'm awfully sorry your wife isn't coming," he said. "You'll miss her visit dreadfully."

"Dreadfully."

He gave Ashenden a sidelong glance. Ashenden felt that he had something he wanted to say, but could not bring himself to say it. He gave his shoulders an angry shrug.

"It's my fault if she's not coming. I asked Lennox to write and tell her not to. I couldn't stick it any more. I spend the whole month looking forward to her coming and then when she's here I hate her. You see, I resent so awfully having this filthy disease. She's strong and well and full of beans. It maddens me when I see the pain in her eyes. What does it matter to her really? Who cares if you're ill? They pretend to care, but they're jolly glad it's you and not them. I'm a swine, aren't I?"

Ashenden remembered how Mrs. Chester had sat on a stone by the side of the road and wept.

"Aren't you afraid you'll make her very unhappy, not letting her come?"

"She must put up with that. I've got enough with my own un-happiness without bothering with hers."

Ashenden did not know what to say and they walked on in silence. Suddenly Chester broke out irritably.

"It's all very well for you to be disinterested and unselfish, you're going to live. I'm going to die, and God damn it, I don't want to die. Why should I? It's not fair."

Time passed. In a place like the sanatorium where there was little to occupy the mind it was inevitable that soon everyone should know that George Templeton was in love with Ivy Bishop. But it was not so easy to tell what her feelings were. It was plain that she liked his company, but she did not seek it, and indeed it looked as though she took pains not to be alone with him. One or two of the middle-aged ladies tried to trap her into some com-promising admission, but ingenuous as she was, she was easily a match for them. She ignored their hints and met their straight questions with incredulous laughter. She succeeded in exasperating them.

"She can't be so stupid as not to see that he's mad about her."

"She has no right to play with him like that."

"I believe she's just as much in love with him as he is with her."

"Dr. Lennox ought to tell her mother."

No one was more incensed than McLeod.

"Too ridiculous. After all, nothing can come of it. He's riddled with T.B. and she's not much better."

Campbell on the other hand was sardonic and gross.

"I'm all for their having a good time while they can. I bet there's a bit of hanky-panky going on if one only knew, and I don't blame 'em."

"You cad," said McLeod.

"Oh, come off it. Templeton isn't the sort of chap to play bumble-puppy bridge with a girl like that unless he's getting something out of it, and she knows a thing or two, I bet."

Ashenden, who saw most of them, knew them better than any of the others. Templeton at last had taken him into his confidence. He was rather amused at himself.

"Rum thing at my time of life, falling in love with a decent girl. Last thing I'd ever expected of myself. And it's no good denying it, I'm in it up to the neck; if I were a well man I'd ask her to marry me to-morrow. I never knew a girl could be as nice as that. I've always thought girls, decent girls, I mean, damned bores. But she isn't a bore, she's as clever as she can stick. And pretty too. My God, what a skin! And that hair: but it isn't any of that

that's bowled me over like a row of ninepins. D'you know what's got me? Damned ridiculous when you come to think of it. An old rip like me. Virtue. Makes me laugh like a hyena. Last thing I've ever wanted in a woman, but there it is, no getting away from it, she's good, and it makes me feel like a worm. Surprise you, I suppose?"

"Not a bit," said Ashenden. "You're not the first rake who's fallen to innocence. It's merely the sentimentality of middle age."

"Dirty dog," laughed Templeton.

"What does she say to it?"

"Good God, you don't suppose I've told her. I've never said a word to her that I wouldn't have said before anyone else. I may be dead in six months, and besides, what have I got to offer a girl like that?"

Ashenden by now was pretty sure that she was just as much in love with Templeton as he was with her. He had seen the flush that coloured her cheeks when Templeton came into the dining-room and he had noticed the soft glance she gave him now and then when he was not looking at her. There was a peculiar sweetness in her smile when she listened to him telling some of his old experiences. Ashenden had the impression that she basked comfortably in his love as the patients on the terrace, facing the snow, basked in the hot sunshine; but it might very well be that she was content to leave it at that, and it was certainly no business of his to tell Templeton what perhaps she had no wish that he should know.

Then an incident occurred to disturb the monotony of life. Though McLeod and Campbell were always at odds they played bridge together because, till Templeton came, they were the best players in the sanatorium. They bickered incessantly, their post-mortems were endless, but after so many years each knew the other's game perfectly and they took a keen delight in scoring off one another. As a rule Templeton refused to play with them; though a fine player, he preferred to play with Ivy Bishop, and McLeod and Campbell were agreed on this, that she ruined the game. She was the kind of player who, having made a mistake that lost the rubber, would laugh and say: Well, it only made the difference of a trick. But one afternoon, since Ivy was staying in her room with a headache, Templeton consented to play with Campbell and McLeod. Ashenden was the fourth. Though it was the end of March there had been heavy snow for several days, and they played, in a verandah open on three sides to the wintry air, in fur coats and caps, with mittens on their hands. The stakes were too small for a gambler like Templeton to take the game seriously and his bidding was overbold, but he played so much better than the other three that he generally managed to make his contract or at least to come near it. But there was much doubling and redoubling. The cards ran high, so that an inordinate number of small slams were bid; it was a tempestuous game, and McLeod and Campbell lashed one another with their tongues. Half-past five arrived and the last rubber was started, for at six the bell rang to send everyone to rest. It was a hard-fought rubber, with sets on both sides, for McLeod and Campbell were opponents and each was determined that the other should not win. At ten minutes to six it was game all and the last hand was dealt. Templeton was McLeod's partner and Ashenden Campbell's. The bidding started with two clubs from McLeod; Ashenden said nothing; Templeton showed that he had substantial help, and finally McLeod called a grand slam. Campbell doubled and McLeod redoubled. Hearing this, the players at other tables who had broken off gathered round and the hands were played in deadly silence to a little crowd of onlookers. McLeod's face was white with excitement and there were beads of sweat on his brow. His hands trembled. Campbell was very grim. McLeod had to take two finesses and they both came off. He finished with a squeeze and got the last of the thirteen tricks. There was a burst of applause from the onlookers. McLeod, arrogant in victory, sprang to his fet. He shook his clenched fits at Campbell.

"Play that off on your blasted fiddle," he shouted. "Grand slam doubled and redoubled. I've wanted to get it all my life and now I've got it. By God. By God."

He gasped. He staggered forward and fell across the table. A stream of blood poured from his mouth. The doctor was sent for. Attendants came. He was dead.

He was buried two days later, early in the morning so that the patients should not be disturbed by the sight of a funeral. A relation in black came from Glasgow to attend it. No one had liked him. No one regretted him. At the end of a week so far as one could tell, he was forgotten. The Indian Civilian took his place at the principal table and Campbell moved into the room he had so long wanted.

"Now we shall have peace," said Dr. Lennox to Ashenden. "When you think that I've had to put up with the quarrels and complaints of those two men for years and years. . . . Believe me, one has to have patience to run a sanatorium. And to think that after all the trouble he's given me he had to end up like that and scare all those people out of their wits."

"It was a bit of a shock, you know," said Ashenden.

"He was a worthless fellow and yet some of the women have been quite upset about it. Poor little Miss Bishop cried her eyes out."

"I suspect that she was the only one who cried for him and not for herself."

But presently it appeared that there was one person who had not forgotten him. Campbell went about like a lost dog. He wouldn't play bridge. He wouldn't talk. There was no doubt about it, he was moping for McLeod. For several days he remained in his room, having his meals brought to him, and then went to Dr. Lennox and said he didn't like it as well as his old one and wanted to be moved back. Dr. Lennox lost his temper, which he rarely did, and told him he had been pestering him to give him that room for years and now he could stay there or get out of the sanatorium. He returned to it and sat there gloomily brooding.

"Why don't you play your violin," the matron asked him at length. "I haven't heard you play for a fortnight."

"I haven't."

"Why not?"

"It's no fun any more. I used to get a kick out of playing because I knew it maddened McLeod. But now nobody cares if I play or not. I shall never play again."

Nor did he for all the rest of the time that Ashenden was at the sanatorium. It was strange, now that McLeod was dead life had lost its savour for him. With no one to quarrel with, no one to infuriate, he had lost his incentive and it was plain that it would not be long before he followed his enemy to the grave.

But on Templeton McLeod's death had another effect, and one which was soon to have unexpected consequences. He talked to Ashenden about it in his cool, detached way.

"Grand, passing out like that in his moment of triumph. I can't make out why everyone got in such a state about it. He'd been here for years, hadn't he?"

"Eighteen, I believe."

"I wonder if it's worth it. I wonder if it's not better to have one's fling and take the consequences."

"I suppose it depends on how much you value life."

"But is this life?"

Ashenden had no answer. In a few months he could count on being well, but you only had to look at Templeton to know that he was not going to recover. The death-look was on his face.

"D'you know what I've done?" asked Templeton. "I've asked Ivy to marry me."

' Ashenden was startled.

"What did she say?"

"Bless her little heart, she said it was the most ridiculous idea she'd ever heard in her life and I was crazy to think of such a thing."

"You must admit she was right."

"Quite. But she's going to marry me."

"It's madness."

"I dare say it is; but anyhow, we're going to see Lennox and ask him what he thinks about it."

The winter had broken at last; there was still snow on the hills, but in the valleys it was melted and on the lower slopes the birch-trees were in bud all ready to burst into delicate leaf. The enchantment of spring was in the air. The sun was hot. Everyone felt alert and some felt happy. The old stagers who came only for the winter were making their plans to go south. Templeton and Ivy went to see Dr. Lennox together. They told him what they had in mind. He examined them; they were X-rayed and various tests were taken. Dr. Lennox fixed a day when he would tell them the results and in the light of this discuss their proposal. Ashenden saw them just before they went to keep the appointment. They were anxious, but did their best to make a joke of it. Dr. Lennox showed them the results of his examinations and explained to them in plain language what their condition was.

"All that's very fine and large," said Templeton then, "but what we want to know is whether we can get married."

"It would be highly imprudent."

"We know that, but does it matter?"

"And criminal if you had a child."

"We weren't thinking of having one," said Ivy.

"Well, then I'll tell you in very few words how the matter stands. Then you must decide for yourselves."

Templeton gave Ivy a little smile and took her hand. The doctor went on.

"I don't think Miss Bishop will ever be strong enough to lead a normal life, but if she continues to live as she has been doing for the last eight years . . ."

"In sanatoriums?"

"Yes. There's no reason why she shouldn't live very comfortably, if not to a ripe old age, as long as any sensible person wants to live. The disease is quiescent. If she marries, if she attempts to live an ordinary life, the foci of infection may very well light up again, and what the results of that may be no one can foretell.

So far as you are concerned, Templeton, I can put it even more shortly. You've seen the X-ray photos yourself. Your lungs are riddled with tubercle. If you marry you'll be dead in six months."

"And if I don't how long can I live?"

The doctor hesitated.

"Don't be afraid. You can tell me the truth."

"Two or three years."

"Thank you, that's all we wanted to know."

They went as they had come, hand in hand; Ivy was crying softly. No one knew what they said to one another; but when they came into luncheon they were radiant. They told Ashenden and Chester that they were going to be married as soon as they could get a licence. Then Ivy turned to Chester.

"I should so much like your wife to come up for my wedding. D'you think she would?"

"You're not going to be married here?"

"Yes. Our respective relations will only disapprove, so we're not going to tell them until it's over. We shall ask Dr. Lennox to give me away."

She looked mildly at Chester, waiting for him to speak, for he had not answered her. The other two men watched him. His voice shook a little when he spoke.

"It's very kind of you to want her. I'll write and ask her."

When the news spread among the patients, though everyone congratulated them, most of them privately told one another that it was very injudicious; but when they learnt, as sooner or later everything that happened in the sanatorium was learnt, that Dr. Lennox had told Templeton that if he married he would be dead in six months, they were awed to silence. Even the dullest were moved at the thought of these two persons who loved one another so much that they were prepared to sacrifice their lives. A spirit of kindliness and good will descended on the sanatorium: people who hadn't been speaking spoke to one another again; others forgot for a brief space their own anxieties. Everyone seemed to share in the happiness of the happy pair. And it was not only the spring that filled those sick hearts with new hope, the great love that had taken possession of the man and the girl seemed to spread its effulgence on all that came near them. Ivy was quietly blissful; the excitement became her and she looked younger and prettier. Templeton seemed to walk on air. He laughed and joked as if he hadn't a care in the world. You would have said that he looked forward to long years of uninterrupted felicity. But one day he confided in Ashenden.

"This isn't a bad place, you know," he said. "Ivy's promised me that when I hand in my checks she'll come back here. She knows the people and she won't be so lonely."

"Doctors are often mistaken," said Ashenden. "If you live reasonably I don't see why you shouldn't go on for a long time yet."

"I'm only asking for three months. If I can only have that it'll be worth it."

Mrs. Chester came up for two days before the wedding. She had not seen her husband for several months and they were shy with one another. It was easy to guess that when they were alone they felt awkward and constrained. Yet Chester did his best to shake off the depression that was now habitual and at all events at meal-times showed himself the jolly, hearty little fellow that he must have been before he fell ill. On the eve of the wedding day they all dined together, Templeton and Ashenden both sitting up for dinner; they drank champagne and stayed up till ten joking, laughing and enjoying themselves. The wedding took place next morning in the kirk. Ashenden was best man. Everyone in the sanatorium who could stand on his feet attended it. The newly married couple were setting out by car immediately after lunch. Patients, doctors and nurses assembled to see them off. Someone had tied an old shoe on the back of the car, and as Templeton and his wife came out of the door of the sanatorium rice was flung over them. A cheer was raised as they drove away, as they drove away to love and death. The crowd separated slowly. Chester and his wife went silently side by side. After they had gone a little way he shyly took her hand. Her heart seemed to miss a beat. With a sidelong glance she saw that his eyes were wet with tears.

"Forgive me, dear," he said. "I've been very unkind to you."

"I knew you didn't mean it," she faltered.

"Yes, I did. I wanted you to suffer because I was suffering. But not any more. All this about Templeton and Ivy Bishop— I don't know how to put it, it's made me see everything differently. I don't mind dying any more. I don't think death's very important, not so important as love. And I want you to live and be happy. I don't grudge you anything any more and I don't resent anything. I'm glad now it's me that must die and not you. I wish for you everything that's good in the world. I love you."

Lord Mountdrago

DR. AUDLIN looked at the clock on his desk. It was twenty minutes to six. He was surprised that his patient was late, for Lord Mountdrago prided himself on his punctuality; he had a sententious way of expressing himself which gave the air of an epigram to a commonplace remark, and he was in the habit of saying that punctuality is a compliment you pay to the intelligent and a rebuke you administer to the stupid. Lord Mountdrago's appointment was for five-thirty.

There was in Dr. Audlin's appearance nothing to attract attention. He was tall and spare, with narrow shoulders and something of a stoop; his hair was grey and thin; his long, sallow face deeply lined. He was not more than fifty, but he looked older. His eyes, pale-blue and rather large, were weary. When you had been with him for a while you noticed that they moved very little; they remained fixed on your face, but so empty of expression were they that it was no discomfort. They seldom lit up. They gave no clue to his thoughts nor changed with the words he spoke. If you were of an observant turn it might have struck you that he blinked much less often than most of us. His hands were on the large side, with long, tapering fingers; they were soft, but firm, cool but not clammy. You could never have said what Dr. Audlin wore unless you had made a point of looking. His clothes were dark. His tie was black. His dress made his sallow lined face paler, and his pale eyes more wan. He gave you the impression of a very sick man.

Dr. Audlin was a psycho-analyst. He had adopted the profession by accident and practised it with misgiving. When the war broke out he had not been long qualified and was getting experience at various hospitals; he offered his services to the authorities, and after a time was sent out to France. It was then that he discovered his singular gift. He could allay certain pains by the touch of his cool, firm hands, and by talking to them often induce sleep in men who were suffering from sleeplessness. He spoke slowly. His voice had no particular colour, and its tone did not alter with the words he uttered, but it was musical, soft and lulling. He told the men that they must rest, that they mustn't worry, that they must sleep; and rest stole into their jaded bodies, tranquillity pushed their anxieties away, like a man finding a place for himself

on a crowded bench, and slumber fell on their tired eyelids like
the light rain of spring upon the fresh-turned earth. Dr. Audlin
found that by speaking to men with that low, monotonous voice
of his, by looking at them with his pale, quiet eyes, by stroking
their weary foreheads with his long firm hands, he could soothe
their perturbations, resolve the conflicts that distracted them and
banish the phobias that made their lives a torment. Sometimes he
effected cures that seemed miraculous. He restored speech to a
man who, after being buried under the earth by a bursting shell,
had been struck dumb, and he gave back the use of his limbs to
another who had been paralysed after a crash in a plane. He could
not understand his powers; he was of a sceptical turn, and though
they say that in circumstances of this kind the first thing is to
believe in yourself, he never quite succeeded in doing that; and
it was only the outcome of his activities, patent to the most incredulous observer, that obliged him to admit that he had some
faculty, coming from he knew not where, obscure and uncertain,
that enabled him to do things for which he could offer no explanation. When the war was over he went to Vienna and studied there,
and afterwards to Zurich; and then settled down in London to
practise the art he had so strangely acquired. He had been practising
now for fifteen years, and had attained, in the speciality he followed,
a distinguished reputation. People told one another of the amazing
things he had done, and though his fees were high, he had as many
patients as he had time to see. Dr. Audlin knew that he had achieved
some very extraordinary results; he had saved men from suicide,
others from the lunatic asylum, he had assuaged griefs that embittered useful lives, he had turned unhappy marriages into happy
ones, he had eradicated abnormal instincts and thus delivered not a
few from a hateful bondage, he had given health to the sick in
spirit; he had done all this, and yet at the back of his mind remained
the suspicion that he was little more than a quack.

It went against his grain to exercise a power that he could not
understand, and it offended his honesty to trade on the faith of
the people he treated when he had no faith in himself. He was
rich enough now to live without working, and the work exhausted
him; a dozen times he had been on the point of giving up practice.
He knew all that Freud and Jung and the rest of them had written.
He was not satisfied; he had an intimate conviction that all their
theory was hocus-pocus, and yet there the results were, incomprehensible, but manifest. And what had he not seen of human nature
during the fifteen years that patients had been coming to his dingy
back room in Wimpole Street? The revelations that had been

poured into his ears, sometimes only too willingly, sometimes with shame, with reservations, with anger, had long ceased to surprise him. Nothing could shock him any longer. He knew by now that men were liars, he knew how extravagant was their vanity; he knew far worse than that about them; but he knew that it was not for him to judge or to condemn. But year by year as these terrible confidences were imparted to him his face grew a little greyer, its lines a little more marked and his pale eyes more weary. He seldom laughed, but now and again when for relaxation he read a novel he smiled. Did their authors really think the men and women they wrote of were like that? If they only knew how much more complicated they were, how much more unexpected, what irreconcilable elements co-existed within their souls and what dark and sinister contentions afflicted them!

It was a quarter to six. Of all the strange cases he had been called upon to deal with Dr. Audlin could remember none stranger than that of Lord Mountdrago. For one thing the personality of his patient made it singular. Lord Mountdrago was an able and a distinguished man. Appointed Secretary for Foreign Affairs when still under forty, now after three years in office he had seen his policy prevail. It was generally acknowledged that he was the ablest politician in the Conservative Party and only the fact that his father was a peer, on whose death he would no longer be able to sit in the House of Commons, made it impossible for him to aim at the premiership. But if in these democratic times it is out of the question for a Prime Minister of England to be in the House of Lords, there was nothing to prevent Lord Mountdrago from continuing to be Secretary for Foreign Affairs in successive Conservative administrations and so for long directing the foreign policy of his country.

Lord Mountdrago had many good qualities. He had intelligence and industry. He was widely travelled, and spoke several languages fluently. From early youth he had specialised in foreign affairs, and had conscientiously made himself acquainted with the political and economic circumstances of other countries. He had courage, insight and determination. He was a good speaker, both on the platform and in the House, clear, precise and often witty. He was a brilliant debater and his gift of repartee was celebrated. He had a fine presence: he was a tall, handsome man, rather bald and somewhat too stout, but this gave him solidity and an air of maturity that were of service to him. As a young man he had been something of an athlete and had rowed in the Oxford boat, and he was known to be one of the best shots in England. At twenty-four he had married a girl of eighteen whose father was a duke and her mother a great

American heiress, so that she had both position and wealth, and by her he had had two sons. For several years they had lived privately apart, but in public united, so that appearances were saved, and no other attachment on either side had given the gossips occasion to whisper. Lord Mountdrago indeed was too ambitious, too hard-working, and it must be added too patriotic, to be tempted by any pleasures that might interfere with his career. He had, in short, a great deal to make him a popular and successful figure. He had unfortunately great defects.

He was a fearful snob. You would not have been surprised at this if his father had been the first holder of the title. That the son of an ennobled lawyer, a manufacturer or a distiller should attach an inordinate importance to his rank is understandable. The earldom held by Lord Mountdrago's father was created by Charles II, and the barony held by the first Earl dated from the Wars of the Roses. For three hundred years the successive holders of the title had allied themselves with the noblest families of England. But Lord Mountdrago was as conscious of his birth as a *nouveau riche* is conscious of his money. He never missed an opportunity of impressing it upon others. He had beautiful manners when he chose to display them, but this he did only with people whom he regarded as his equals. He was coldly insolent to those whom he looked upon as his social inferiors. He was rude to his servants and insulting to his secretaries. The subordinate officials in the government offices to which he had been successively attached feared and hated him. His arrogance was horrible. He knew that he was a great deal cleverer than most of the persons he had to do with, and never hesitated to apprise them of the fact. He had no patience with the infirmities of human nature. He felt himself born to command and was irritated with people who expected him to listen to their arguments or wished to hear the reasons for his decisions. He was immeasurably selfish. He looked upon any service that was rendered him as a right due to his rank and intelligence and therefore deserving of no gratitude. It never entered his head that he was called upon to do anything for others. He had many enemies: he despised them. He knew no one who merited his assistance, his sympathy or his compassion. He had no friends. He was distrusted by his chiefs, because they doubted his loyalty; he was unpopular with his party, because he was over-bearing and discourteous; and yet his merit was so great, his patriotism so evident, his intelligence so solid and his management of affairs so brilliant that they had to put up with him. And what made it possible to do this was that on occasion he could be enchanting; when he was with persons whom he considered his equals, or whom he wished to captivate, in the company of foreign dignitaries or women of distinction, he could be gay, witty and debonair; his manners then reminded you that in his veins ran the same blood as had run in the veins of Lord Chesterfield; he could tell a story with point, he could be natural, sensible and even profound. You were surprised at the extent of his knowledge and the sensitiveness of his taste. You thought him the best company in the world, you forgot that he had insulted you the day before and was quite capable of cutting you dead the next.

Lord Mountdrago almost failed to become Dr. Audlin's patient. A secretary rang up the doctor and told him that his lordship, wishing to consult him, would be glad if he would come to his house at ten o'clock on the following morning. Dr. Audlin answered that he was unable to go to Lord Mountdrago's house, but would be pleased to give him an appointment at his consulting-room at five o'clock on the next day but one. The secretary took the message and presently rang back to say that Lord Mountdrago insisted on seeing Dr. Audlin in his own house and the doctor could fix his own fee. Dr. Audlin replied that he only saw patients in his consulting-room and expressed his regret that unless Lord Mountdrago was prepared to come to him he could not give him his attention. In a quarter of an hour a brief message was delivered to him that his lordship would come not next day but one, but next day, at five.

When Lord Mountdrago was then shown in he did not come forward, but stood at the door and insolently looked the doctor up and down. Dr. Audlin perceived that he was in a rage; he gazed at him, silently, with still eyes. He saw a big heavy man, with greying hair, receding on the forehead so that it gave nobility to his brow, a puffy face with bold regular features and an expression of haughtiness. He had somewhat the look of one of the Bourbon sovereigns of the eighteenth century.

"It seems that it is as difficult to see you as a Prime Minister, Dr. Audlin. I'm an extremely busy man."

"Won't you sit down?" said the doctor.

His face showed no sign that Lord Mountdrago's speech in any way affected him. Dr. Audlin sat in his chair at the desk. Lord Mountdrago still stood and his frown darkened.

"I think I should tell you that I am His Majesty's Secretary for Foreign Affairs," he said acidly.

"Won't you sit down?" the doctor repeated.

Lord Mountdrago made a gesture, which might have suggested that he was about to turn on his heel and stalk out of the room;

but if that was his intention he apparently thought better of it. He
seated himself. Dr. Audlin opened a large book and took up his
pen. He wrote without looking at his patient.

"How old are you?"

"Forty-two."

"Are you married?"

"Yes."

"How long have you been married?"

"Eighteen years."

"Have you any children?"

"I have two sons."

Dr. Audlin noted down the facts as Lord Mountdrago abruptly
answered his questions. Then he leaned back in his chair and
looked at him. He did not speak; he just looked, gravely, with pale
eyes that did not move.

"Why have you come to see me?" he asked at length.

"I've heard about you. Lady Canute is a patient of yours, I
understand. She tells me you've done her a certain amount of
good."

Dr. Audlin did not reply. His eyes remained fixed on the other's
face, but they were so empty of expression that you might have
thought he did not even see him.

"I can't do miracles," he said at length. Not a smile, but the
shadow of a smile flickered in his eyes. "The Royal College of
Physicians would not approve of it if I did."

Lord Mountdrago gave a brief chuckle. It seemed to lessen his
hostility. He spoke more amiably.

"You have a very remarkable reputation. People seem to believe
in you."

"Why have you come to me?" repeated Dr. Audlin.

Now it was Lord Mountdrago's turn to be silent. It looked as
though he found it hard to answer. Dr. Audlin waited. At last Lord
Mountdrago seemed to make an effort. He spoke.

"I'm in perfect health. Just as a matter of course I had myself
examined by my own doctor the other day, Sir Augustus Fitzherbert, I daresay you've heard of him, and he tells me I have the
physique of a man of thirty. I work hard, but I'm never tired,
and I enjoy my work. I smoke very little and I'm an extremely
moderate drinker. I take a sufficiency of exercise and I lead a
regular life. I am a perfectly sound, normal, healthy man. I quite
expect you to think it very silly and childish of me to consult
you."

Dr. Audlin saw that he must help him.

B

"I don't know if I can do anything to help you. I'll try. You're distressed?"

Lord Mountdrago frowned.

"The work that I'm engaged in is important. The decisions I am called upon to make can easily affect the welfare of the country and even the peace of the world. It is essential that my judgment should be balanced and my brain clear. I look upon it as my duty to eliminate any cause of worry that may interfere with my usefulness."

Dr. Audlin had never taken his eyes off him. He saw a great deal. He saw behind his patient's pompous manner and arrogant pride an anxiety that he could not dispel.

"I asked you to be good enough to come here because I know by experience that it's easier for someone to speak openly in the dingy surroundings of a doctor's consulting-room than in his accustomed surroundings."

"They're certainly dingy," said Lord Mountdrago acidly. He paused. It was evident that this man who had so much self-assurance, so quick and decided a mind that he was never at a loss, at this moment was embarrassed. He smiled in order to show the doctor that he was at his ease, but his eyes betrayed his disquiet. When he spoke again it was with unnatural heartiness.

"The whole thing's so trivial that I can hardly bring myself to bother you with it. I'm afraid you'll just tell me not to be a fool and waste your valuable time."

"Even things that seem very trivial may have their importance. They can be a symptom of a deep-seated derangement. And my time is certainly at your disposal."

Dr. Audlin's voice was low and grave. The monotone in which he spoke was strangely soothing. Lord Mountdrago at length made up his mind to be frank.

"The fact is I've been having some very tiresome dreams lately. I know it's silly to pay any attention to them, but—well, the honest truth is that I'm afraid they've got on my nerves."

"Can you describe any of them to me?"

Lord Mountdrago smiled, but the smile that tried to be careless was only rueful.

"They're so idiotic, I can hardly bring myself to narrate them."

"Never mind."

"Well, the first I had was about a month ago. I dreamt that I was at a party at Connemara House. It was an official party. The King and Queen were to be there and of course decorations were

worn. I was wearing my ribbon and my star. I went into a sort of
cloakroom they have to take off my coat. There was a little man
there called Owen Griffiths, who's a Welsh Member of Parliament,
and to tell you the truth, I was surprised to see him. He's very
common, and I said to myself: 'Really, Lydia Connemara is going
too far, whom will she ask next?' I thought he looked at me rather
curiously, but I didn't take any notice of him; in fact I cut the
little bounder and walked upstairs. I suppose you've never been
there?"

"Never."

"No, it's not the sort of house you'd ever be likely to go to. It's a
rather vulgar house, but it's got a very fine marble staircase, and
the Connemaras were at the top receiving their guests. Lady Connemara gave me a look of surprise when I shook hands with her, and
began to giggle; I didn't pay much attention, she's a very silly, ill-
bred woman and her manners are no better than those of her
ancestor whom King Charles II made a duchess. I must say the
reception rooms at Connemara House are stately. I walked through,
nodding to a number of people and shaking hands; then I saw the
German Ambassador talking with one of the Austrian Archdukes.
I particularly wanted to have a word with him, so I went up and
held out my hand. The moment the Archduke saw me he burst
into a roar of laughter. I was deeply affronted. I looked him up and
down sternly, but he only laughed the more. I was about to speak
to him rather sharply, when there was a sudden hush and I realised
that the King and Queen had come. Turning my back on the
Archduke, I stepped forward and then, quite suddenly, I noticed
that I hadn't got any trousers on. I was in short silk drawers, and I
wore scarlet sock-suspenders. No wonder Lady Connemara had
giggled; no wonder the Archduke had laughed! I can't tell you what
that moment was. An agony of shame. I awoke in a cold sweat.
Oh, you don't know the relief I felt to find it was only a dream."

"It's the kind of dream that's not so very uncommon," said Dr.
Audlin.

"I dare say not. But an odd thing happened next day. I was in
the lobby of the House of Commons, when that fellow Griffiths
walked slowly past me. He deliberately looked down at my legs
and then he looked me full in the face and I was almost certain he
winked. A ridiculous thought came to me. He'd been there the
night before and seen me make that ghastly exhibition of myself
and was enjoying the joke. But of course I knew that was impossible
because it was only a dream. I gave him an icy glare and he walked
on. But he was grinning his head off."

Lord Mountdrago took his handkerchief out of his pocket and wiped the palms of his hands. He was making no attempt now to conceal his perturbation. Dr. Audlin never took his eyes off him. "Tell me another dream."

"It was the night after, and it was even more absurd than the first one. I dreamt that I was in the House. There was a debate on foreign affairs which not only the country, but the world, had been looking forward to with the gravest concern. The government had decided on a change in their policy which vitally affected the future of the Empire. The occasion was historic. Of course the House was crowded. All the ambassadors were there. The galleries were packed. It fell to me to make the important speech of the evening. I had prepared it carefully. A man like me has enemies, there are a lot of people who resent my having achieved the position I have at an age when even the cleverest men are content with situations of relative obscurity, and I was determined that my speech should not only be worthy of the occasion, but should silence my detractors. It excited me to think that the whole world was hanging on my lips. I rose to my feet. If you've ever been in the House you'll know how members chat to one another during a debate, rustle papers and turn over reports. The silence was the silence of the grave when I began to speak. Suddenly I caught sight of that odious little bounder on one of the benches opposite, Griffiths the Welsh member; he put out his tongue at me. I don't know if you've ever heard a vulgar music-hall song called *A Bicycle Made for Two*. It was very popular a great many years ago. To show Griffiths how completely I despised him I began to sing it. I sang the first verse right through. There was a moment's surprise, and when I finished they cried 'Hear, hear,' on the opposite benches. I put up my hand to silence them and sang the second verse. The House listened to me in stony silence and I felt the song wasn't going down very well. I was vexed, for I have a good baritone voice, and I was determined that they should do me justice. When I started the third verse the members began to laugh; in an instant the laughter spread; the ambassadors, the strangers in the Distinguished Strangers' Gallery, the ladies in the Ladies' Gallery, the reporters, they shook, they bellowed, they held their sides, they rolled in their seats; everyone was overcome with laughter except the ministers on the Front Bench immediately behind me. In that incredible, in that unprecedented uproar, they sat petrified. I gave them a glance, and suddenly the enormity of what I had done fell upon me. I had made myself the laughing-stock of the whole world. With misery

I realised that I should have to resign. I woke and knew it was only a dream."

Lord Mountdrago's grand manner had deserted him as he narrated this, and now having finished he was pale and trembling. But with an effort he pulled himself together. He forced a laugh to his shaking lips.

"The whole thing was so fantastic that I couldn't help being amused. I didn't give it another thought, and when I went into the House on the following afternoon I was feeling in very good form. The debate was dull, but I had to be there, and I read some documents that required my attention. For some reason I chanced to look up and I saw that Griffiths was speaking. He has an unpleasant Welsh accent and an unprepossessing appearance. I couldn't imagine that he had anything to say that it was worth my while to listen to, and I was about to return to my papers when he quoted two lines from *A Bicycle Made for Two*. I couldn't help glancing at him and I saw that his eyes were fixed on me with a grin of bitter mockery. I faintly shrugged my shoulders. It was comic that a scrubby little Welsh member should look at me like that. It was an odd coincidence that he should quote two lines from that disastrous song I'd sung all through in my dream. I began to read my papers again, but I don't mind telling you that I found it difficult to concentrate on them. I was a little puzzled. Owen Griffiths had been in my first dream, the one at Connemara House, and I'd received a very definite impression afterwards that he knew the sorry figure I'd cut. Was it a mere coincidence that he had just quoted those two lines? I asked myself if it was possible that he was dreaming the same dreams as I was. But of course the idea was preposterous and I determined not to give it a second thought."

There was a silence. Dr. Audlin looked at Lord Mountdrago and Lord Mountdrago looked at Dr. Audlin.

"Other people's dreams are very boring. My wife used to dream occasionally and insist on telling me her dreams next day with circumstantial detail. I found it maddening."

Dr. Audlin faintly smiled.

"You're not boring me."

"I'll tell you one more dream I had a few days later. I dreamt that I went into a public-house at Limehouse. I've never been to Limehouse in my life and I don't think I've ever been in a public-house since I was at Oxford, and yet I saw the street and the place I went into as exactly as if I were at home there. I went into a room, I don't know whether they call it the saloon bar or the private bar; there was a fireplace and a large leather arm-chair on one side of it, and on the other a small sofa; a bar ran the whole length of the room and over it you could see into the public bar. Near the door was a round marble-topped table and two arm-chairs beside it. It was a Saturday night and the place was packed. It was brightly lit, but the smoke was so thick that it made my eyes smart. I was dressed like a rough, with a cap on my head and a handkerchief round my neck. It seemed to me that most of the people there were drunk. I thought it rather amusing. There was a gramophone going, or the radio, I don't know which, and in front of the fireplace two women were doing a grotesque dance. There was a little crowd round them, laughing, cheering and singing. I went up to have a look and some man said to me: ''Ave a drink, Bill?' There were glasses on the table full of a dark liquid which I understand is called brown ale. He gave me a glass and not wishing to be conspicuous I drank it. One of the women who were dancing broke away from the other and took hold of the glass. ' 'Ere, what's the idea?' she said. 'That's my beer you're putting away.' 'Oh, I'm so sorry,' I said, 'this gentle-man offered it me and I very naturally thought it was his to offer.' 'All right, mate,' she said, 'I don't mind. You come an' 'ave a dance with me.' Before I could protest she'd caught hold of me and we were dancing together. And then I found myself sitting in the arm-chair with the woman on my lap and we were sharing a glass of beer. I should tell you that sex has never played any great part in my life. I married young because in my position it was desirable that I should marry, but also in order to settle once for all the question of sex. I had the two sons I had made up my mind to have, and then I put the whole matter on one side. I've always been too busy to give much thought to that kind of thing, and living so much in the public eye as I do it would have been madness to do anything that might give rise to scandal. The greatest asset a politician can have is a blameless record as far as women are concerned. I have no patience with the men who smash up their careers for women. I only despise them. The woman I had on my knees was drunk; she wasn't pretty and she wasn't young: in fact, she was just a blowsy old prostitute. She filled me with disgust, and yet when she put her mouth to mine and kissed me, though her breath stank of beer and her teeth were decayed, though I loathed myself, I wanted her—I wanted her with all my soul. Suddenly I heard a voice. 'That's right, old boy, have a good time.' I looked up and there was Owen Griffiths. I tried to spring out of the chair, but that horrible woman wouldn't let me. 'Don't you pay no attention to 'im,' she said, ' 'e's only one of them nosyparkers.' 'You go to it,' he said. 'I know Moll. She'll give you your money's worth all right.' You know, I wasn't so much annoyed at his seeing me in that absurd situation as angry that he should address me as 'old boy'. I pushed the woman aside and stood up and faced him. 'I don't know you and I don't want to know you,' I said. 'I know you all right,' he said. 'And my advice to you, Molly, is, see that you get your money, he'll bilk you if he can.' There was a bottle of beer standing on the table close by. Without a word I seized it by the neck and hit him over the head with it as hard as I could. I made such a violent gesture that it woke me up."

"A dream of that sort is not incomprehensible," said Dr. Audlin. "It is the revenge nature takes on persons of unimpeachable character."

"The story's idiotic. I haven't told it to you for its own sake. I've told it you for what happened next day. I wanted to look up something in a hurry and I went into the library of the House. I got the book and began reading. I hadn't noticed when I sat down that Griffiths was sitting in a chair close by me. Another of the Labour members came in and went up to him. 'Hullo, Owen,' he said to him, 'you're looking pretty dicky to-day.' 'I've got an awful headache,' he answered. 'I feel as if I'd been cracked over the head with a bottle.' "

Now Lord Mountdrago's face was grey with anguish.

"I knew then that the idea I'd had and dismissed as preposterous was true. I knew that Griffiths was dreaming my dreams and that he remembered them as well as I did."

"It may also have been a coincidence."

"When he spoke he didn't speak to his friend, he deliberately spoke to me. He looked at me with sullen resentment."

"Can you offer any suggestion why this same man should come into your dreams?"

"None."

Dr. Audlin's eyes had not left his patient's face and he saw that he lied. He had a pencil in his hand and he drew a straggling line or two on his blotting-paper. It often took a long time to get people to tell the truth, and yet they knew that unless they told it he could do nothing for them.

"The dream you've just described to me took place just over three weeks ago. Have you had any since?"

"Every night."

"And does this man Griffiths come into them all?"

"Yes."

The doctor drew more lines on his blotting-paper. He wanted

the silence, the drabness, the dull light of that little room to have its effect on Lord Mountdrago's sensibility. Lord Mountdrago threw himself back in his chair and turned his head away so that he should not see the other's grave eyes.

"Dr. Audlin, you must do something for me. I'm at the end of my tether. I shall go mad if this goes on. I'm afraid to go to sleep. Two or three nights I haven't. I've sat up reading and when I felt drowsy put on my coat and walked till I was exhausted. But I must have sleep. With all the work I have to do I must be at concert pitch; I must be in complete control of all my faculties. I need rest; sleep brings me none. I no sooner fall asleep than my dreams begin, and he's always there, that vulgar little cad, grinning at me, mocking me, despising me. It's a monstrous persecution. I tell you, doctor, I'm not the man of my dreams; it's not fair to judge me by them. Ask anyone you like. I'm an honest, upright, decent man. No one can say anything against my moral character either private or public. My whole ambition is to serve my country and maintain its greatness. I have money, I have rank, I'm not exposed to many of the temptations of lesser men, so that it's no credit to me to be incorruptible; but this I can claim, that no honour, no personal advantage, no thought of self would induce me to swerve by a hair's breadth from my duty. I've sacrificed everything to become the man I am. Greatness is my aim. Greatness is within my reach and I'm losing my nerve. I'm not the mean, despicable, cowardly, lewd creature that horrible little man sees. I've told you three of my dreams; they're nothing; that man has seen me do things that are so beastly, so horrible, so shameful, that even if my life depended on it I wouldn't tell them. And he remembers them. I can hardly meet the derision and disgust I see in his eyes and I even hesitate to speak because I know my words can seem to him nothing but utter humbug. He's seen me do things that no man with any self-respect would do, things for which men are driven out of the society of their fellows and sentenced to long terms of imprisonment; he's heard the foulness of my speech; he's seen me not only ridiculous, but revolting. He despises me and he no longer pretends to conceal it. I tell you that if you can't do something to help me I shall either kill myself or kill him."

"I wouldn't kill him if I were you," said Dr. Audlin, coolly, in that soothing voice of his. "In this country the consequences of killing a fellow-creature are awkward."

"I shouldn't be hanged for it, if that's what you mean. Who would know that I'd killed him? That dream of mine has shown me how. I told you, the day after I'd hit him over the head with a beer-bottle he had such a headache that he couldn't see straight. He said so himself. That shows that he can feel with his waking body what happens to his body asleep. It's not with a bottle I shall hit him next time. One night, when I'm dreaming, I shall find myself with a knife in my hand or a revolver in my pocket, I must because I want to so intensely, and then I shall seize my opportunity. I'll stick him like a pig; I'll shoot him like a dog. In the heart. And then I shall be free of this fiendish persecution."

Some people might have thought that Lord Mountdrago was mad; after all the years during which Dr. Audlin had been treating the diseased souls of men he knew how thin a line divides those whom we call sane from those whom we call insane. He knew how often in men who to all appearance were healthy and normal, who were seemingly devoid of imagination, and who fulfilled the duties of common life with credit to themselves and with benefit to their fellows, when you gained their confidence, when you tore away the mask they wore to the world, you found not only hideous abnormality, but kinks so strange, mental extravagances so fantastic, that in that respect you could only call them lunatic. If you put them in an asylum not all the asylums in the world would be large enough. Anyhow, a man was not certifiable because he had strange dreams and they had shattered his nerve. The case was singular, but it was only an exaggeration of others that had come under Dr. Audlin's observation; he was doubtful, however, whether the methods of treatment that he had so often found efficacious would here avail.

"Have you consulted any other member of my profession?" he asked.

"Only Sir Augustus. I merely told him that I suffered from nightmares. He said I was overworked and recommended me to go for a cruise. That's absurd. I can't leave the Foreign Office just now when the international situation needs constant attention. I'm indispensable, and I know it. On my conduct at the present juncture my whole future depends. He gave me sedatives. They had no effect. He gave me tonics. They were worse than useless. He's an old fool."

"Can you give any reason why it should be this particular man who persists in coming into your dreams?"

"You asked me that question before. I answered it."

That was true. But Dr. Audlin had not been satisfied with the answer.

"Just now you talked of persecution. Why should Owen Griffiths want to persecute you?"

"I don't know."

Lord Mountdrago's eyes shifted a little. Dr. Audlin was sure that he was not speaking the truth.

"Have you ever done him an injury?"

"Never."

Lord Mountdrago made no movement, but Dr. Audlin had a queer feeling that he shrank into his skin. He saw before him a large, proud man who gave the impression that the questions put to him were an insolence, and yet for all that, behind that façade, was something shifting and startled that made you think of a frightened animal in a trap. Dr. Audlin leaned forward and by the power of his eyes forced Lord Mountdrago to meet them.

"Are you quite sure?"

"Quite sure. You don't seem to understand that our ways lead along different paths. I don't wish to harp on it, but I must remind you that I am a Minister of the Crown and Griffiths is an obscure member of the Labour Party. Naturally there's no social connection between us; he's a man of very humble origin, he's not the sort of person I should be likely to meet at any of the houses I go to; and politically our respective stations are so far separated that we could not possibly have anything in common."

"I can do nothing for you unless you tell me the complete truth."

Lord Mountdrago raised his eyebrows. His voice was rasping.

"I'm not accustomed to having my word doubted, Dr. Audlin. If you're going to do that I think to take up any more of your time can only be a waste of mine. If you will kindly let my secretary know what your fee is he will see that a cheque is sent to you."

For all the expression that was to be seen on Dr. Audlin's face you might have thought that he simply had not heard what Lord Mountdrago said. He continued to look steadily into his eyes and his voice was grave and low.

"Have you done anything to this man that *he* might look upon as an injury?"

Lord Mountdrago hesitated. He looked away, and then, as though there were in Dr. Audlin's eyes a compelling force that he could not resist, looked back. He answered sulkily:

"Only if he was a dirty, second-rate little cad."

"But that is exactly what you've described him to be."

Lord Mountdrago sighed. He was beaten. Dr. Audlin knew that the sigh meant he was going at last to say what he had till then held back. Now he had no longer to insist. He dropped his eyes and began again drawing vague geometrical figures on his blotting-paper. The silence lasted two or three minutes.

"I'm anxious to tell you everything that can be of any use to you. If I didn't mention this before, it's only because it was so unimportant that I didn't see how it could possibly have anything to do with the case. Griffiths won a seat at the last election and he began to make a nuisance of himself almost at once. His father's a miner, and he worked in a mine himself when he was a boy; he's been a schoolmaster in the board schools and a journalist. He's the half-baked, conceited intellectual, with inadequate knowledge, ill-considered ideas and impracticable plans, that compulsory education has brought forth from the working-classes. He's a scrawny, grey-faced man, who looks half-starved, and he's always very slovenly in appearance; heaven knows members nowadays don't bother much about their dress, but his clothes are an outrage to the dignity of the House. They're ostentatiously shabby, his collar's never clean and his tie's never tied properly; he looks as if he hadn't had a bath for a month and his hands are filthy. The Labour Party have two or three fellows on the Front Bench who've got a certain ability, but the rest of them don't amount to much. In the kingdom of the blind the one-eyed man is king: because Griffiths is glib and has a lot of superficial information on a number of subjects, the Whips on his side began to put him up to speak whenever there was a chance. It appeared that he fancied himself on foreign affairs, and he was continually asking me silly, tiresome questions. I don't mind telling you that I made a point of snubbing him as soundly as I thought he deserved. From the beginning I hated the way he talked, his whining voice and his vulgar accent; he had nervous mannerisms that intensely irritated me. He talked rather shyly, hesitatingly, as though it were torture to him to speak and yet he was forced to by some inner passion, and often he used to say some very disconcerting things. I'll admit that now and again he had a sort of tub-thumping eloquence. It had a certain influence over the ill-regulated minds of the members of his party. They were impressed by his earnestness and they weren't, as I was, nauseated by his sentimentality. A certain sentimentality is the common coin of political debate. Nations are governed by self-interest, but they prefer to believe that their aims are altruistic, and the politician is justified if with fair words and fine phrases he can persuade the electorate that the hard bargain he is driving for his country's advantage tends to the good of humanity. The mistake people like Griffiths make is to take these fair words and fine phrases at their face value. He's a crank, and a noxious crank. He calls himself an idealist. He has at his tongue's end all the tedious blather that the intelligentsia have been boring us with for years. Non-resistance.

The brotherhood of man. You know the hopeless rubbish. The worst of it was that it impressed not only his own party, it even shook some of the sillier, more sloppy-minded members of ours. I heard rumours that Griffiths was likely to get office when a Labour Government came in; I even heard it suggested that he might get the Foreign Office. The notion was grotesque but not impossible. One day I had occasion to wind up a debate on foreign affairs which Griffiths had opened. He'd spoken for an hour. I thought it a very good opportunity to cook his goose, and by God, sir, I cooked it. I tore his speech to pieces. I pointed out the faultiness of his reasoning and emphasised the deficiency of his knowledge. In the House of Commons the most devastating weapon is ridicule: I mocked him; I bantered him; I was in good form that day and the House rocked with laughter. Their laughter excited me and I excelled myself. The Opposition sat glum and silent, but even some of them couldn't help laughing once or twice; it's not intolerable, you know, to see a colleague, perhaps a rival, made a fool of. And if ever a man was made a fool of I made a fool of Griffiths. He shrank down in a seat, I saw his face go white, and presently he buried it in his hands. When I sat down I'd killed him. I'd destroyed his prestige for ever; he had no more chance of getting office when a Labour Government came in than the policeman at the door. I heard afterwards that his father, the old miner, and his mother had come up from Wales, with various supporters of his in the constituency, to watch the triumph they expected him to have. They had seen only his utter humiliation. He'd won the constituency by the narrowest margin. An incident like that might very easily lose him his seat. But that was no business of mine."

"Should I be putting it too strongly if I said you had ruined his career?" asked Dr. Audlin.

"I don't suppose you would."

"That is a very serious injury you've done him."

"He brought it on himself."

"Have you never felt any qualms about it?"

"I think perhaps if I'd known that his father and mother were there I might have let him down a little more gently."

There was nothing further for Dr. Audlin to say, and he set about treating his patient in such a manner as he thought might avail. He sought by suggestion to make him forget his dreams when he awoke; he sought to make him sleep so deeply that he would not dream. He found Lord Mountdrago's resistance impossible to break down. At the end of an hour he dismissed him. Since then he had seen Lord Mountdrago half a dozen times. He had done him no good. The frightful dreams continued every night to harass the unfortunate man, and it was clear that his general condition was growing rapidly worse. He was worn out. His irritability was uncontrollable. Lord Mountdrago was angry because he received no benfit from his treatment, and yet continued it, not only because it seemed his only hope, but because it was a relief to him to have someone with whom he could talk openly. Dr. Audlin came to the conclusion at last that there was only one way in which Lord Mountdrago could achieve deliverance, but he knew him well enough to be assured that of his own free will he would never, never take it. If Lord Mountdrago was to be saved from the breakdown that was threatening he must be induced to take a step that must be abhorrent to his pride of birth and his self-complacency. Dr. Audlin was convinced that to delay was impossible. He was treating his patient by suggestion, and after several visits found him more susceptible to it. At length he managed to get him into a condition of somnolence. With his low, soft, monotonous voice he soothed his tortured nerves. He repeated the same words over and over again. Lord Mountdrago lay quite still, his eyes closed; his breathing was regular, and his limbs were relaxed. Then Dr. Audlin in the same quiet tone spoke the words he had prepared.

"You will go to Owen Griffiths and say that you are sorry that you caused him that great injury. You will say that you will do whatever lies in your power to undo the harm that you have done him."

The words acted on Lord Mountdrago like the blow of a whip across his face. He shook himself out of his hypnotic state and sprang to his feet. His eyes blazed with passion and he poured forth upon Dr. Audlin a stream of angry vituperation such as even he had never heard. He swore at him. He cursed him. He used language of such obscenity that Dr. Audlin, who had heard every sort of foul word, sometimes from the lips of chaste and distinguished women, was surprised that he knew it.

"Apologise to that filthy little Welshman? I'd rather kill myself."

"I believe it to be the only way in which you can regain your balance."

Dr. Audlin had not often seen a man presumably sane in such a condition of uncontrollable fury. He grew red in the face and his eyes bulged out of his head. He did really foam at the mouth. Dr. Audlin watched him coolly, waiting for the storm to wear itself out, and presently he saw that Lord Mountdrago, weakened by the strain to which he had been subjected for so many weeks, was exhausted.

"Sit down," he said then, sharply.

Lord Mountdrago crumpled up into a chair.

"Christ, I feel all in. I must rest a minute and then I'll go."

For five minutes perhaps they sat in complete silence. Lord Mountdrago was a gross, blustering bully, but he was also a gentleman. When he broke the silence he had recovered his self-control.

"I'm afraid I've been very rude to you. I'm ashamed of the things I've said to you and I can only say you'd be justified if you refused to have anything more to do with me. I hope you won't do that. I feel that my visits to you do help me. I think you're my only chance."

"You mustn't give another thought to what you said. It was of no consequence."

"But there's one thing you mustn't ask me to do, and that is to make excuses to Griffiths."

"I've thought a great deal about your case. I don't pretend to understand it, but I believe that your only chance of release is to do what I proposed. I have a notion that we're none of us one self, but many, and one of the selves in you has risen up against the injury you did Griffiths and has taken on the form of Griffiths in your mind and is punishing you for what you cruelly did. If I were a priest I should tell you that it is your conscience that has adopted the shape and lineaments of this man to scourge you to repentance and persuade you to reparation."

"My conscience is clear. It's not my fault if I smashed the man's career. I crushed him like a slug in my garden. I regret nothing."

It was on these words that Lord Mountdrago had left him. Reading through his notes, while he waited, Dr. Audlin considered how best he could bring his patient to the state of mind that, now that his usual methods of treatment had failed, he thought alone could help him. He glanced at his clock. It was six. It was strange that Lord Mountdrago did not come. He knew he had intended to because his secretary had rung up that morning to say that he would be with him at the usual hour. He must have been detained by pressing work. This notion gave Dr. Audlin something else to think of: Lord Mountdrago was quite unfit to work and in no condition to deal with important matters of state. Dr. Audlin wondered whether it behoved him to get in touch with someone in authority, the Prime Minister or the Permanent Under-Secretary for Foreign Affairs, and impart to him his conviction that Lord Mountdrago's mind was so unbalanced that it was dangerous to leave affairs of moment in his hands. It was a ticklish thing to do.

He might cause needless trouble and get roundly snubbed for his pains. He shrugged his shoulders.

"After all," he reflected, "the politicians have made such a mess of the world during the last five-and-twenty years, I don't suppose it makes much odds if they're mad or sane."

He rang the bell.

"If Lord Mountdrago comes now will you tell him that I have another appointment at six-fifteen and so I'm afraid I can't see him."

"Very good, sir."

"Has the evening paper come yet?"

"I'll go and see."

In a moment the servant brought it in. A huge headline ran across the front page: Tragic Death of Foreign Minister.

"My God!" cried Dr. Audlin.

For once he was wrenched out of his wonted calm. He was shocked, horribly shocked, and yet he was not altogether surprised. The possibility that Lord Mountdrago might commit suicide had occurred to him several times, for that it was suicide he could not doubt. The paper said that Lord Mountdrago had been waiting in a Tube station, standing on the edge of the platform, and as the train came in was seen to fall on the rail. It was supposed that he had had a sudden attack of faintness. The paper went on to say that Lord Mountdrago had been suffering for some weeks from the effects of overwork, but had felt it impossible to absent himself while the foreign situation demanded his unremitting attention. Lord Mountdrago was another victim of the strain that modern politics placed upon those who played the more important parts in it. There was a neat little piece about the talents and industry, the patriotism and vision, of the deceased statesman, followed by various surmises upon the Prime Minister's choice of his successor. Dr. Audlin read all this. He had not liked Lord Mountdrago. The chief emotion that his death caused in him was dissatisfaction with himself because he had been able to do nothing for him.

Perhaps he had done wrong in not getting into touch with Lord Mountdrago's doctor. He was discouraged, as always when failure frustrated his conscientious efforts, and repulsion seized him for the theory and practice of this empiric doctrine by which he earned his living. He was dealing with dark and mysterious forces that it was perhaps beyond the powers of the human mind to understand. He was like a man blindfold trying to feel his way to he knew not whither. Listlessly he turned the pages of the paper. Suddenly he gave a great start, and an exclamation once more was forced from his lips. His eyes had fallen on a small paragraph near the bottom of a column. Sudden Death of an M.P., he read. Mr. Owen Griffiths, member for so-and-so, had been taken ill in Fleet Street that afternoon and when he was brought to Charing Cross Hospital life was found to be extinct. It was supposed that death was due to natural causes, but an inquest would be held. Dr. Audlin could hardly believe his eyes. Was it possible that the night before Lord Mountdrago had at last in his dream found himself possessed of the weapon, knife or gun, that he had wanted, and had killed his tormentor, and had that ghostly murder, in the same way as the blow with the bottle had given him a racking headache on the following day, taken effect a certain number of hours later on the waking man? Or was it, more mysterious and more frightful, that when Lord Mountdrago sought relief in death, the enemy he had so cruelly wronged, unappeased, escaping from his own mortality, had pursued him to some other sphere there to torment him still? It was strange. The sensible thing was to look upon it merely as an odd coincidence. Dr. Audlin rang the bell.

"Tell Mrs. Milton that I'm sorry I can't see her this evening. I'm not well."

It was true; he shivered as though of an ague. With some kind of spiritual sense he seemed to envisage a bleak, a horrible void. The dark night of the soul engulfed him, and he felt a strange, primeval terror of he knew not what.

The Social Sense

I DO not like long-standing engagements. How can you tell whether on a certain day three or four weeks ahead you will wish to dine with a certain person? The chances are that in the interval something will turn up that you would much sooner do and so long a notice presages a large and formal party. But what help is there? The date has been fixed thus far away so that the guests bidden may be certainly disengaged and it needs a very adequate excuse to prevent your refusal from seeming churlish. You accept, and for a month the engagement hangs over you with gloomy menace. It interferes with your cherished plans. It disorganises your life. There is really only one way to cope with the situation and that is to put yourself off at the last moment. But it is one that I have never had the courage or the want of scruple to adopt.

It was with a faint sense of resentment then that one June evening towards half-past eight I left my lodging in Half Moon Street to walk round the corner to dine with the Macdonalds. I liked them. Many years ago I made up my mind not to eat the food of persons I disliked or despised, and though I have on this account enjoyed the hospitality of far fewer people than I otherwise should have done I still think the rule a good one. The Macdonalds were nice, but their parties were a toss-up. They suffered from the delusion that if they asked six persons to dine with them who had nothing in the world to say to one another the party would be a failure, but if they multiplied it by three and asked eighteen it must be a success. I arrived a little late, which is almost inevitable when you live so near the house you are going to that it is not worth while to take a taxi, and the room into which I was shown was filled with people. I knew few of them and my heart sank as I saw myself laboriously making conversation through a long dinner with two total strangers. It was a relief to me when I saw Thomas and Mary Warton come in and an unexpected pleasure when I found on going in to dinner that I had been placed next to Mary.

Thomas Warton was a portrait-painter who at one time had had considerable success, but he had never fulfilled the promise of his youth and had long ceased to be taken seriously by the critics. He made an adequate income, but at the Private View of the Royal Academy no one gave more than a passing glance at the dull but conscientious portraits of fox-hunting squires and prosperous merchants which with unfailing regularity he sent to the annual exhibition. One would have liked to admire his work because he was an amiable and kindly man. If you happened to be a writer he was so genuinely enthusiastic over anything you had done, so charmed with any success you might have had, that you wished your conscience would allow you to speak with decent warmth of his own productions. It was impossible and you were driven to the last refuge of the portrait-painter's friend.

"It looks as if it were a marvellous likeness," you said.

Mary Warton had been in her day a well-known concert singer and she had still the remains of a lovely voice. She must in her youth have been very handsome. Now, at fifty-three, she had a haggard look. Her features were rather mannish and her skin was weather-beaten; but her short grey hair was thick and curly and her fine eyes were bright with intelligence. She dressed picturesquely rather than fashionably and she had a weakness for strings of beads and fantastic ear-rings. She had a blunt manner, a quick sense of human folly and a sharp tongue, so that many people did not like her. But no one could deny that she was clever. She was not only an accomplished musician, but she was a great reader and she was passionately interested in painting. She had a very rare feeling for art. She liked the modern, not from pose but from natural inclination, and she had bought for next to nothing the pictures of unknown painters who later became famous. You heard at her house the most recent and difficult music and no poet or novelist in Europe could offer the world something new and strange without her being ready to fight on his behalf the good fight against the philistines. You might say she was a highbrow; she was; but her taste was almost faultless, her judgment sound and her enthusiasm honest.

No one admired her more than Thomas Warton. He had fallen in love with her when she was still a singer and had pestered her to marry him. She had refused him half a dozen times and I had a notion that she had married him in the end with hesitation. She thought that he would become a great painter and when he turned out to be no more than a decent craftsman, without originality or imagination, she felt that she had been cheated. She was mortified by the contempt with which the connoisseurs regarded him. Thomas Warton loved his wife. He had the greatest respect for her judgment and would sooner have had a word of praise from her than columns of eulogy in all the papers in London. She was too honest to say what did not think. It wounded him bitterly that she held his work in such poor esteem, and though he pretended to make a joke of it you could see that at heart he resented her outspoken comments. Sometimes his long, horse-like face grew red with the anger he tried to control and his eyes dark with hatred. It was notorious among their friends that the couple did not get on. They had the distressing habit of fripping in public. Warton never spoke to others of Mary but with admiration, but she was less discreet and her confidants knew how exasperating she found him. She admitted his goodness, his generosity, his unselfishness; she admitted them ungrudgingly; but his defects were of the sort that make a man hard to live with, for he was narrow, argumentative and conceited. He was not an artist and Mary Warton cared more for art than for anything in the world. It was a matter on which she could not compromise. It blinded her to the fact that the faults in Warton that maddened her were due in large part to his hurt feelings. She wounded him continually and he was dogmatic and intolerant in self-protection. There cannot be anything much worse than to be despised by the one person whose approval is all in all to you; and though Thomas Warton was intolerable it was impossible not to feel sorry for him. But if I have given the impression that Mary was a discontented, rather tiresome, pretentious woman I have been unjust to her. She was a loyal friend and a delightful companion. You could talk to her of any subject under the sun. Her conversation was humorous and witty. Her vitality was immense.

She was sitting now on the left hand of her host and the talk around her was general. I was occupied with my next-door neighbour, but I guessed by the laughter with which Mary's sallies were greeted that she was at her brilliant best. When she was in the vein no one could approach her.

"You're in great form to-night," I remarked, when at last she turned to me.

"Does it surprise you?"

"No, it's what I expect of you. No wonder people tumble over one another to get you to their houses. You have the inestimable gift of making a party go."

"I do my little best to earn my dinner."

"By the way, how's Manson? Someone told me the other day that he was going into a nursing-home for an operation. I hope it's nothing serious."

Mary paused for a moment before answering, but she still smiled brightly.

"Haven't you seen the paper to-night?"

"No, I've been playing golf. I only got home in time to jump into a bath and change."

"He died at two o'clock this afternoon." I was about to make an exclamation of horrified surprise, but she stopped me. "Take care. Tom is watching me like a lynx. They're all watching me. They all know I adored him, but they none of them know for certain if he was my lover, even Tom doesn't know; they want to see how I'm taking it. Try to look as if you were talking of the Russian Ballet."

At that moment someone addressed her from the other side of the table, and throwing back her head a little with a gesture that was habitual with her, a smile on her large mouth, she flung at the speaker so quick and apt an answer that everyone round her burst out laughing. The talk once more became general and I was left to my consternation.

I knew, everyone knew, that for five and twenty years there had existed between Gerrard Manson and Mary Warton a passionate attachment. It had lasted so long that even the more strait-laced of their friends, if ever they had been shocked by it, had long since learnt to accept it with tolerance. They were middle-aged people, Manson was sixty and Mary not much younger, and it was absurd that at their age they should not do what they liked. You met them sometimes sitting in a retired corner of an obscure restaurant or walking together in the Zoo and you wondered why they still took care to conceal an affair that was nobody's business but their own. But of course there was Thomas. He was insanely jealous of Mary. He made many violent scenes and indeed, at the end of one tempestuous period, not so very long ago, he forced her to promise never to see Manson again. Of course she broke the promise, and though she knew that Thomas suspected this, she took precautions to prevent him from discovering it for a fact.

It was hard on Thomas. I think he and Mary would have jogged on well enough together and she would have resigned herself to the fact that he was a second-rate painter if her intercourse with Manson had not embittered her judgment. The contrast between her husband's mediocrity and her lover's brilliance was too galling.

"With Tom I feel as if I were stifling in a closed room full of dusty knick-knacks," she told me. "With Gerrard I breathe the pure air of the mountain tops."

"Is it possible for a woman to fall in love with a man's mind?" I asked in a pure spirit of enquiry.

"What else is there in Gerrard?"

That, I admit, was a poser. For my part I thought, nothing; but the sex is extraordinary and I was quite ready to believe that Mary saw in Gerrard Manson a charm and a physical attractiveness to which most people were blind. He was a shrivelled little man, with a pale intellectual face, faded blue eyes behind his spectacles, and a high dome of shiny bald head. He had none of the appearance of a romantic lover. On the other hand he was certainly a very subtle critic and a felicitous essayist. I resented somewhat his contemptuous attitude towards English writers unless they were safely dead and buried; but this was only to his credit with the intelligentsia, who are ever ready to believe that there can be no good in what is produced in their own country, and with them his influence was great. On one occasion I told him that one had only to put a commonplace in French for him to mistake it for an epigram and he had thought well enough of the joke to use it as his own in one of his essays. He reserved such praise as he was willing to accord his contemporaries to those who wrote in a foreign tongue. The exasperating thing was that no one could deny that he was himself a brilliant writer. His style was exquisite. His knowledge was vast. He could be profound without pomposity, amusing without frivolity, and polished without affectation. His slightest article was readable. His essays were little masterpieces. For my part I did not find him a very agreeable companion. Perhaps I did not get the best out of him. Though I knew him a great many years I never heard him say an amusing thing. He was not talkative and when he made a remark it was oracular. The prospect of spending an evening alone with him would have filled me with dismay. It never ceased to puzzle me that this dull and mannered little man should be able to write with so much grace, wit and gaiety.

It puzzled me even more that a gallant and vivacious creature like Mary Warton should have cherished for him so consuming a passion. These things are inexplicable and there was evidently something in that odd, crabbed, irascible creature that appealed to women. His wife adored him. She was a fat, frowsy boring person. She had led Gerrard a dog's life, but had always refused to give him his freedom. She swore to kill herself if he left her and since she was unbalanced and hysterical he was never quite certain that she would not carry out her threat. One day, when I was having tea with Mary, I saw that she was distraught and nervous and when I asked her what was the matter she burst into tears. She had been lunching with Manson and had found him shattered after a terrific scene with his wife.

"We can't go on like this," Mary cried. "It's ruining his life. It's ruining all our lives."

"Why don't you take the plunge?"

"What do you mean?"

"You've been lovers so long, you know the best and the worst of one another by now; you're getting old and you can't count on many more years of life; it seems a pity to waste a love that has endured so long. What good are you doing to Mrs. Manson or to Tom? Are they happy because you two are making yourselves miserable?"

"No."

"Then why don't you chuck everything and just go off together and let come what may?"

Mary shook her head.

"We've talked that over endlessly. We've talked it over for a quarter of a century. It's impossible. For years Gerrard couldn't on account of his daughters. Mrs. Manson may have been a very fond mother, but she was a very bad one, and there was no one to see the girls were properly brought up but Gerrard. And now that they're married off he's set in his habits. What should we do? Go to France or Italy? I couldn't tear Gerrard away from his surroundings. He'd be wretched. He's too old to make a fresh start. And besides, though Thomas nags me and makes scenes and we frip and get on one another's nerves, he loves me. When it came to the point I simply shouldn't have the heart to leave him. He'd be lost without me."

"It's a situation without an issue. I'm dreadfully sorry for you."

On a sudden Mary's haggard, weather-beaten face was lit by a smile that broke on her large red mouth; and upon my word at that moment she was beautiful.

"You need not be. I was rather low a little while ago, but now I've had a good cry I feel better. Notwithstanding all the pain, all the unhappiness this affair has caused me, I wouldn't have missed it for all the world. For those few moments of ecstasy my love has brought me I would be willing to live all my life over again. And I think he'd tell you the same thing. Oh, it's been so infinitely worth while."

I could not help but be moved.

"There's no doubt about it," I said. "That's love all right."

"Yes, it's love, and we've just got to go through with it. There's no way out."

And now with this tragic suddenness the way out had come. I turned a little to look at Mary and she, feeling my eyes upon her, turned too. There was a smile on her lips.

"Why did you come here to-night? It must be awful for you."

She shrugged her shoulders.

"What could I do? I read the news in the evening paper while I was dressing. He'd asked me not to ring up the nursing-home on account of his wife. It's death to me. Death. I had to come.

We'd been engaged for a month. What excuse could I give Tom? I'm not supposed to have seen Gerrard for two years. Do you know that for twenty years we've written to one another every day?" Her lower lip trembled a little, but she bit it and for a moment her face was twisted to a strange grimace; then with a smile she pulled herself together. "He was everything I had in the world, but I couldn't let the party down, could I? He always said I had a social sense."

"Happily we shall break up early and you can go home."

"I don't want to go home. I don't want to be alone. I daren't cry because my eyes will get red and swollen, and we've got a lot of people lunching with us to-morrow. Will you come, by the way? I want an extra man. I must be in good form; Tom expects to get a commission for a portrait out of it."

"By George, you've got courage."

"D'you think so? I'm heartbroken, you know. I suppose that's what makes it easier for me. Gerrard would have liked me to put a good face on it. He would have appreciated the irony of the situation. It's the sort of thing he always thought the French novelists described so well."

The Verger

THERE had been a christening that afternoon at St. Peter's, Neville Square, and Albert Edward Foreman still wore his verger's gown. He kept his new one, its folds as full and stiff as though it were made not of alpaca but of perennial bronze, for funerals and weddings (St. Peter's, Neville Square, was a church much favoured by the fashionable for these ceremonies) and now he wore only his second-best. He wore it with complacence, for it was the dignified symbol of his office, and without it (when he took it off to go home) he had the disconcerting sensation of being somewhat insufficiently clad. He took pains with it; he pressed it and ironed it himself. During the sixteen years he had been verger of this church he had had a succession of such gowns, but he had never been able to throw them away when they were worn out and the complete series, neatly wrapped up in brown paper, lay in the bottom drawers of the wardrobe in his bedroom.

The verger busied himself quietly, replacing the painted wooden cover on the marble font, taking away a chair that had been brought for an infirm old lady, and waited for the vicar to have finished in the vestry so that he could tidy up in there and go home. Presently he saw him walk across the chancel, genuflect in front of the high altar and come down the aisle; but he still wore his cassock.

"What's he 'anging about for?" the verger said to himself. "Don't 'e know I want my tea?"

The vicar had been but recently appointed, a red-faced energetic man in the early forties, and Albert Edward still regretted his predecessor, a clergyman of the old school who preached leisurely sermons in a silvery voice and dined out a great deal with his more aristocratic parishioners. He liked things in church to be just so, but he never fussed; he was not like this new man who wanted to have his finger in every pie. But Albert Edward was tolerant. St. Peter's was in a very good neighbourhood and the parishioners were a very nice class of people. The new vicar had come from the East End and he couldn't be expected to fall in all at once with the discreet ways of his fashionable congregation.

"All this 'ustle," said Albert Edward. "But give 'im time, he'll learn."

When the vicar had walked down the aisle so far that he could address the verger without raising his voice more than was becoming in a place of worship he stopped.

"Foreman, will you come into the vestry for a minute. I have something to say to you."

"Very good, sir."

The vicar waited for him to come up and they walked up the church together.

"A very nice christening, I thought, sir. Funny 'ow the baby stopped cryin' the moment you took him."

"I've noticed they very often do," said the vicar, with a little smile. "After all I've had a good deal of practice with them."

It was a source of subdued pride to him that he could nearly always quiet a whimpering infant by the manner in which he held it and he was not unconscious of the amused admiration with which mothers and nurses watched him settle the baby in the crook of his surpliced arm. The verger knew that it pleased him to be complimented on his talent.

The vicar preceded Albert Edward into the vestry. Albert Edward was a trifle surprised to find the two churchwardens there. He had not seen them come in. They gave him pleasant nods.

"Good-afternoon, my lord. Good-afternoon, sir," he said to one after the other.

They were elderly men, both of them, and they had been church-wardens almost as long as Albert Edward had been verger. They were sitting now at a handsome refectory table that the old vicar had brought many years before from Italy and the vicar sat down in the vacant chair between them. Albert Edward faced them, the table between him and them, and wondered with slight uneasiness what was the matter. He remembered still the occasion on which the organist had got into trouble, and the bother they had all had to hush things up. In a church like St. Peter's, Neville Square, they couldn't afford a scandal. On the vicar's red face was a look of resolute benignity, but the others bore an expression that was slightly troubled.

"He's been naggin' them, he 'as," said the verger to himself. "He's jockeyed them into doin' something, but they don't 'alf like it. That's what it is, you mark my words."

But his thoughts did not appear on Albert Edward's clean-cut and distinguished features. He stood in a respectful but not obsequious attitude. He had been in service before he was appointed to his ecclesiastical office, but only in very good houses, and his deportment was irreproachable. Starting as a page-boy in the household of a merchant-prince, he had risen by due degrees from the position of fourth to first footman, for a year he had been single-handed butler to a widowed peeress and, till the vacancy occurred at St. Peter's, butler with two men under him in the house of a retired ambassador. He was tall, spare, grave and dignified. He looked, if not like a duke, at least like an actor of the old school who specialised in dukes' parts. He had tact, firmness and self-assurance. His character was unimpeachable.

The vicar began briskly.

"Foreman, we've got something rather unpleasant to say to you. You've been here a great many years and I think his lordship and the general agree with me that you've fulfilled the duties of your office to the satisfaction of everybody concerned."

The two churchwardens nodded.

"But a most extraordinary circumstance came to my knowledge the other day and I felt it my duty to impart it to the churchwardens. I discovered to my astonishment that you could neither read nor write."

The verger's face betrayed no sign of embarrassment.

"The last vicar knew that, sir," he replied. "He said it didn't make no difference. He always said there was a great deal too much education in the world for 'is taste."

"It's the most amazing thing I ever heard," cried the general. "Do you mean to say that you've been verger of this church for sixteen years and never learned to read or write?"

"I went into service when I was twelve, sir. The cook in the first place tried to teach me once, but I didn't seem to 'ave the knack for it, and then what with one thing and another I never seemed to 'ave the time. I've never really found the want of it. I think a lot of these young fellows waste a rare lot of time readin' when they might be doin' something useful."

"But don't you want to know the news?" said the other church-warden. "Don't you ever want to write a letter?"

"No, me lord, I seem to manage very well without. And of late years now they've all these pictures in the papers I get to know what's goin' on pretty well. Me wife's quite a scholar and if I want to write a letter she writes it for me. It's not as if I was a bettin' man."

The two churchwardens gave the vicar a troubled glance and then looked down at the table.

"Well, Foreman, I've talked the matter with these gentlemen and they quite agree with me that the situation is impossible. At a church like St. Peter's, Neville Square, we cannot have a verger who can neither read nor write."

Albert Edward's thin, sallow face reddened and he moved uneasily on his feet, but he made no reply.

"Understand me, Foreman, I have no complaint to make against you. You do your work quite satisfactorily; I have the highest opinion both of your character and of your capacity; but we haven't the right to take the risk of some accident that might happen owing to your lamentable ignorance. It's a matter of prudence as well as of principle."

"But couldn't you learn, Foreman?" asked the general.

"No, sir, I'm afraid I couldn't, not now. You see, I'm not as young as I was and if I couldn't seem able to get the letters in me 'ead when I was a nipper I don't think there's much chance of it now."

"We don't want to be harsh with you, Foreman," said the vicar. "But the churchwardens and I have quite made up our minds. We'll give you three months, and if at the end of that time you cannot read and write I'm afraid you'll have to go."

Albert Edward had never liked the new vicar. He'd said from the beginning that they'd made a mistake when they gave him St. Peter's. He wasn't the type of man they wanted with a classy congregation like that. And now he straightened himself a little. He knew his value and he wasn't going to allow himself to be put upon.

"I'm very sorry, sir, I'm afraid it's no good. I'm too old a dog to learn new tricks. I've lived a good many years without knowin' 'ow to read and write, and without wishin' to praise myself, self-praise is no recommendation, I don't mind sayin' I've done my duty in that state of life in which it 'as pleased a merciful providence to place me, and if I *could* learn now I don't know as I'd want to."

"In that case, Foreman, I'm afraid you must go."

"Yes, sir, I quite understand. I shall be 'appy to 'and in my resignation as soon as you've found somebody to take my place."

But when Albert Edward with his usual politeness had closed the church door behind the vicar and the two churchwardens he could not sustain the air of unruffled dignity with which he had borne the blow inflicted upon him and his lips quivered. He walked slowly back to the vestry and hung up on its proper peg his verger's gown. He sighed as he thought of all the grand funerals and smart weddings it had seen. He tied everything up, put on his coat, and hat in hand walked down the aisle. He locked the church door behind him. He strolled across the square, but deep in his sad thoughts he did not take the street that led him home, where a nice strong cup of tea awaited him; he took the wrong turning. He walked slowly along. His heart was heavy. He did not know what he should do with himself. He did not fancy the notion of going back to domestic service;

after being his own master for so many years, for the vicar and churchwardens could say what they liked, it was he that had run St. Peter's, Neville Square, he could scarcely demean himself by accepting a situation. He had saved a tidy sum, but not enough to live on without doing something, and life seemed to cost more every year. He had never thought to be troubled with such questions. The vergers of St. Peter's, like the popes of Rome, were there for life. He had often thought of the pleasant reference the vicar would make in his sermon at evensong the first Sunday after his death to the long and faithful service and the exemplary character of their late verger, Albert Edward Foreman. He sighed deeply. Albert Edward was a non-smoker and a total abstainer, but with a certain latitude; that is to say he liked a glass of beer with his dinner and when he was tired he enjoyed a cigarette. It occurred to him now that one would comfort him and since he did not carry them he looked about him for a shop where he could buy a packet of Gold Flakes. He did not at once see one and walked on a little. It was a long street, with all sorts of shops in it, but there was not a single one where you could buy cigarettes.

"That's strange," said Albert Edward.

To make sure he walked right up the street again. No, there was no doubt about it. He stopped and looked reflectively up and down.

"I can't be the only man as walks along this street and wants a fag," he said. "I shouldn't wonder but what a fellow might do very well with a little shop here. Tobacco and sweets, you know."

He gave a sudden start.

"That's an idea," he said. "Strange 'ow things come to you when you least expect it."

He turned, walked home, and had his tea.

"You're very silent this afternoon, Albert," his wife remarked.

"I'm thinkin'," he said.

He considered the matter from every point of view and next day he went along the street and by good luck found a little shop to let that looked as though it would exactly suit him. Twenty-four hours later he had taken it and when a month after that he left St. Peter's, Neville Square, for ever, Albert Edward Foreman set up in business as a tobacconist and newsagent. His wife said it was a dreadful come-down after being verger of St. Peter's, but he answered that you had to move with the times, the church wasn't what it was, and 'enceforward he was going to render unto Cæsar what was Cæsar's. Albert Edward did very well. He did so well that in a year or so it struck him that he might take a second shop and put a manager in. He looked for another long street that hadn't got a tobacconist in it and when he found it, and a shop to let, took it and stocked it. This was a success too. Then it occurred to him that if he could run two he could run half a dozen, so he began walking about London, and whenever he found a long street that had no tobacconist and a shop to let he took it. In the course of ten years he had acquired no less than ten shops and he was making money hand over fist. He went round to all of them himself every Monday, collected the week's takings and took them to the bank.

One morning when he was there paying in a bundle of notes and a heavy bag of silver the cashier told him that the manager would like to see him. He was shown into an office and the manager shook hands with him.

"Mr. Foreman, I wanted to have a talk to you about the money you've got on deposit with us. D'you know exactly how much it is?"

"Not within a pound or two, sir; but I've got a pretty rough idea."

"Apart from what you paid in this morning it's a little over thirty thousand pounds. That's a very large sum to have on deposit and I should have thought you'd do better to invest it."

"I wouldn't want to take no risk, sir. I know it's safe in the bank."

"You needn't have the least anxiety. We'll make you out a list of absolutely gilt-edged securities. They'll bring you in a better rate of interest than we can possibly afford to give you."

A troubled look settled on Mr. Foreman's distinguished face. "I've never 'ad anything to do with stocks and shares and I'd 'ave to leave it all in your 'ands," he said.

The manager smiled. "We'll do everything. All you'll have to do next time you come in is just to sign the transfers."

"I could do that all right," said Albert uncertainly. "But 'ow should I know what I was signin'?"

"I suppose you can read," said the manager a trifle sharply.

Mr. Foreman gave him a disarming smile.

"Well, sir, that's just it. I can't. I know it sounds funny-like, but there it is, I can't read or write, only me name, an' I only learnt to do that when I went into business."

The manager was so surprised that he jumped up from his chair.

"That's the most extraordinary thing I ever heard."

"You see, it's like this, sir, I never 'ad the opportunity until it was too late and then some'ow I wouldn't. I got obstinate-like."

The manager stared at him as though he were a prehistoric monster.

"And do you mean to say that you've built up this important business and amassed a fortune of thirty thousand pounds without being able to read or write? Good God, man, what would you be now if you had been able to?"

"I can tell you that, sir," said Mr. Foreman, a little smile on his still aristocratic features. "I'd be verger of St. Peter's, Neville Square."

Appearance and Reality

I DO not vouch for the truth of this story, but it was told me by a professor of French literature at an English university, and he was a man of too high a character, I think, to have told it to me unless it were true. His practice was to draw the attention of his students to three French writers who in his opinion combined the qualities that are the mainsprings of the French character. By reading them, he said, you could learn so much about the French people that, if he had the power, he would not trust such of our rulers as have to deal with the French nation to enter upon their offices till they had passed a pretty stiff examination on their works. They are Rabelais, with his *gauloiserie*, which may be described as the ribaldry that likes to call a spade something more than a bloody shovel; La Fontaine, with his *bon sens*, which is just horse sense; and finally Corneille, with his *panache*. This is translated in the dictionaries as the plume, the plume the knight at arms wore on his helmet, but metaphorically it seems to signify dignity and bravado, display and heroism, vainglory and pride. It was *le panache* that made the French gentlemen at Fontenoy say to the officers of King George II, fire first, gentlemen; it was *le panache* that wrung from Cambronne's bawdy lips at Waterloo the phrase: the guard dies but never surrenders; and it is *le panache* that urges an indigent French poet, awarded the Nobel prize, with a splendid gesture to give it all away. My professor was not a frivolous man and to his mind the story I am about to tell brought out so distinctly the three master qualities of the French that it had a high educational value.

I have called it Appearance and Reality. This is the title of what I suppose may be looked upon as the most important philosophical work that my country (right or wrong) produced in the nineteenth century. It is stiff, but stimulating reading. It is written in excellent English, with considerable humour, and even though the lay reader is unlikely to follow with understanding some of its very subtle arguments he has nevertheless the thrilling sensation of walking a spiritual tight-rope over a metaphysical abyss, and he ends the book with a comfortable feeling that nothing matters a hang anyway. There is no excuse for my making use of the title of so celebrated a book except that it so admirably suits my story. Though Lisette was a philosopher only in the sense in which we are all philosophers, that she exercised thought in dealing with the problems of existence, her feeling for reality was so strong and her sympathy for appearance so genuine that she might almost claim to have established that reconciliation of irreconcilables at which the philosophers have for so many centuries been aiming. Lisette was French, and she passed several hours of every working day dressing and undressing herself at one of the most expensive and fashionable establishments in Paris. A pleasant occupation for a young woman who was well aware that she had a lovely figure. She was in short a mannequin. She was tall enough to be able to wear a train with elegance and her hips were so slim that in sports clothes she could bring the scent of heather to your nostrils. Her long legs enabled her to wear pyjamas with distinction, and her slim waist, her little breasts, made the simplest bathing dress a ravishment. She could wear anything. She had a way of huddling herself in a chinchilla coat that made the most sensible persons admit that chinchilla was worth all the money it cost. Fat women, gross women, stumpy women, bony women, shapeless women, old women, plain women, sat in the spacious armchairs and because Lisette looked so sweet bought the clothes that so admirably suited her. She had large brown eyes, a large red mouth and a very clear but slightly freckled skin. It was difficult for her to preserve that haughty, sullen and coldly indifferent demeanour that appears to be essential to the mannequin as she sails in with deliberate steps, turns round slowly and, with an air of contempt for the universe equalled only by the camel's, sails out. There was the suspicion of a twinkle in Lisette's large brown eyes and her red lips seemed to tremble as though on the smallest provocation they would break into a smile. It was the twinkle that attracted the attention of Monsieur Raymond Le Sueur.

He was sitting in a spurious Louis XVI chair by the side of his wife (in another) who had induced him to come with her to see the private view of the spring fashions. This was a proof of Monsieur Le Sueur's amiable disposition, for he was an extremely busy man who, one would have thought, had many more important things to do than to sit for an hour and watch a dozen beautiful young women parade themselves in a bewildering variety of costumes. He could not have thought that any of them could possibly make his wife other than she was, and she was a tall, angular woman of fifty, with features considerably larger than life-size. He had not indeed married her for her looks, and she had never, even in the first delirious days of their honeymoon, imagined that he had. He had married her in order to combine the flourishing steel works of which she was the heiress with his equally flourishing manufactory of locomotives. The marriage had been a success. She had provided him with a son who could play tennis nearly as well as a professional, dance quite as well as a gigolo, and hold his own at bridge with any of the experts; and a daughter whom he had been able to dower sufficiently to marry to a very nearly authentic prince. He had reason to be proud of his children. By perseverance and a reasonable integrity he had prospered sufficiently to gain the controlling interest in a sugar refinery, a movie company, a firm that built motor-cars and a newspaper; and finally he had been able to spend enough money to persuade the free and independent electorate of a certain district to send him to the Senate. He was a man of a dignified presence, a pleasing corpulence and a sanguine complexion, with a neat grey beard cut square, a bald head and a roll of fat at the back of his neck. You had no need to look at the red button that adorned his black coat to surmise that he was a person of consequence. He was a man who made up his mind quickly and when his wife left the dressmaker's to go and play bridge he parted from her, saying that for the sake of exercise he would walk to the Senate, where his duty to his country called him. He did not however go as far as this, but contented himself with taking his exercise up and down a back street into which he rightly surmised the young ladies of the dressmaker's establishment would emerge at the close of business hours. He had barely waited for a quarter of an hour when the appearance of a number of women in groups, some young and pretty, some not so young and far from pretty, apprised him that the moment for which he had been waiting was come, and in two or three minutes Lisette tripped into the street. The Senator was well aware that his appearance and his age made it unlikely that young women would find him attractive at first sight, but he had found that his wealth and his position counterbalanced these disadvantages. Lisette had a companion with her, which would possibly have embarrassed a man of less importance, but did not cause the Senator to hesitate for an instant; he went up to her, raising his hat politely but not so much as to show how bald he was, and bade her good evening.

"*Bon soir, Mademoiselle,*" he said with an ingratiating smile.

She gave him the shortest possible look and, her full red lips just trembling with a smile, stiffened; she turned her head away and breaking into conversation with her friend, walked on with a very good assumption of supreme indifference. Far from disconcerted, the Senator turned round and followed the two girls at a distance of a few yards. They walked along the little back street, turned into the boulevard and at the Place de la Madeleine took a bus. The Senator was well satisfied. He had drawn a number of correct conclusions. The fact that she was obviously going home with a girl friend proved

C

that she had no accredited admirer. The fact that she had turned away when he had accosted her showed that she was discreet and modest and well behaved, which he liked young women to be when they were pretty; and her coat and skirt, the plain black hat and the rayon stockings proclaimed that she was poor and therefore virtuous. In those clothes she looked just as attractive as in the splendid garments he had seen her wearing before. He had a funny little feeling in his heart. He had not had that peculiar sensation, pleasurable and yet oddly painful, for several years, but he recognised it at once.

"It's love, by blue," he muttered.

He had never expected to feel it again, and squaring his shoulders he walked on with a confident step. He walked to the offices of a private detective and there left instructions that enquiries should be made about a young person called Lisette, who worked as a mannequin at such and such an address; and then, remembering that at the Senate they were discussing the American Debt, took a cab to the impressive building, entered the library, where there was an arm-chair he very much liked, and had a pleasant nap. The information he had asked for reached him three days later. It was cheap at the price. Mademoiselle Lisette Larion lived with a widowed aunt in a two-roomed apartment in the district of Paris known as the Batignolles. Her father, a wounded hero of the great war, had a *bureau de tabac* in a small country town in the south-west of France. The rent of the flat was two thousand francs. She led a regular life, but was fond of going to the pictures, was not known to have a lover, and was nineteen years old. She was well spoken of by the concierge of the apartments and well liked by her companions at the shop. Obviously she was a very respectable young woman and the Senator could not but think that she was eminently suited to solace the leisure moments of a man who wanted relaxation from the cares of state and the exacting pressure of Big Business.

It is unnecessary to relate in detail the steps that Monsieur Le Sueur took to achieve the end he had in view. He was too important and too busy to occupy himself with the matter personally, but he had a confidential secretary who was very clever at dealing with electors who had not made up their minds how to vote, and who certainly knew how to put before a young woman who was honest but poor the advantages that might ensue if she were lucky enough to secure the friendship of such a man as his employer. The confidential secretary paid the widowed aunt, Madame Saladin by name, a visit and told her that Monsieur Le Sueur, always abreast of the time, had lately begun to take an interest in films and was indeed about to engage in the production of a picture. (This shows how much a clever brain can make use of a fact that an ordinary person would have passed over as insignificant.) Monsieur Le Sueur had been struck by the appearance of Mademoiselle Lisette at the dressmaker's and the brilliant way she wore her clothes, and it had occurred to him that she might very well suit a part he had it in mind for her to play. (Like all intelligent people the Senator always stuck as close to the truth as he could.) The confidential secretary then invited Madame Saladin and her niece to a dinner where they could make one another's further acquaintance and the Senator could judge whether Mademoiselle Lisette had the aptitude for the screen that he suspected. Madame Saladin said she would ask her niece, but for her part seemed to think the suggestion quite reasonable.

When Madame Saladin put the proposition before Lisette and explained the rank, dignity and importance of their generous host, that young person shrugged her pretty shoulders disdainfully.

"*Cette vieille carpe*," she said, of which the not quite literal translation is: that old trout.

"What does it matter if he's an old trout if he gives you a part?" said Madame Saladin.

"*Et ta sœur*," said Lisette.

This phrase, which of course means: and your sister, and sounds harmless enough, and even pointless, is a trifle vulgar and is used by well-brought-up young women, I think, only if they want to shock. It expresses the most forcible unbelief, and the only correct translation into the vernacular is too coarse for my chaste pen.

"Anyhow we should get a slap-up dinner," said Madame Saladin. "After all, you're not a child any more."

"Where did he say we should dine?"

"The Château de Madrid. Everyone knows it's the most expensive restaurant in the world."

There is no reason why it should not be. The food is very good, the cellar is famous, and its situation makes it on a fine evening of early summer an enchanting place to eat at. A very pretty dimple appeared on Lisette's cheek and a smile on her large red mouth. She had perfect teeth.

"I can borrow a dress from the shop," she murmured.

A few days later the Senator's confidential secretary fetched them in a taxi and drove Madame Saladin and her engaging niece to the Bois de Boulogne. Lisette looked ravishing in one of the firm's most successful models and Madame Saladin extremely respectable in her own black satin and a hat that Lisette had made for the occasion. The secretary introduced the ladies to Monsieur Le Sueur, who greeted them with the benign dignity of the politician who is behaving graciously to the wife and daughter of a valued constituent; and this is exactly what in his asute way he thought people at adjacent tables who knew him would imagine his guests to be. The dinner passed off very agreeably, and less than a month later Lisette moved into a charming little flat at a convenient distance both from her place of business and from the Senate. It was decorated in the modern style by a fashionable upholsterer. Monsieur Le Sueur wished Lisette to continue to work. It suited him very well that she should have something to do during the hours that he was obliged to devote to affairs, for it would keep her out of mischief, and he very well knew that a woman who has nothing to do all day spends much more money than one who has an occupation. An intelligent man thinks of these things.

But extravagance was a vice to which Lisette was strange. The Senator was fond and generous. It was a source of satisfaction to him that Lisette began very soon to save money. She ran her apartment with thrift and bought her clothes at trade prices, and every month sent a certain sum home to her heroic father, who purchased little plots of land with it. She continued to lead a quiet and modest life and Monsieur Le Sueur was pleased to learn from the concierge, who had a son she wanted to place in a government office, that Lisette's only visitors were her aunt and one or two girls from the shop.

The Senator had never been happier in his life. It was very satisfactory to him to think that even in this world a good action had its reward, for was it not from pure kindness that he had accompanied his wife to the dressmaker's on that afternoon when they were discussing the American Debt at the Senate and thus seen for the first time the charming Lisette? The more he knew her the more he doted on her. She was a delightful companion. She was gay and debonair. Her intelligence was respectable and she could listen cleverly when he discussed business matters or affairs of state with her. She rested him when he was weary and cheered him when he was depressed. She was glad to see him when he came, and he came frequently, generally from five till seven, and sorry when he went away. She gave him the impression that he was not only her lover but her friend. Sometimes they dined together in her apartment, and the well-appointed meal, the genial comfort, gave him a keen appreciation of the charm of domesticity. His friends told the Senator he looked twenty years younger. He felt it. He was conscious of his good fortune. He could not but feel, however, that after a life of honest toil and public service it was only his due.

It was thus a shock to him, after things had been proceeding so happily for nearly two years, on coming back to Paris early one

Sunday morning unexpectedly after a visit to his constituency which was to last over the week-end, when he let himself into the apartment with his latchkey, thinking since it was the day of rest to find Lisette in bed, to discover her having breakfast in her bedroom *tête-à-tête* with a young gentleman he had never seen before who was wearing his (the Senator's) brand new pyjamas. Lisette was surprised to see him. Indeed she gave a distinct start.

"*Tiens*," she said. "Where have you sprung from? I didn't expect you till to-morrow."

"The Ministry has fallen," he answered mechanically. "I have been sent for. I am to be offered the Ministry of the Interior." But that was not what he wanted to say at all. He gave the gentleman who was wearing his pyjamas a furious look. "Who is that young man?" he cried.

Lisette's large red mouth broke into a most alluring smile.

"My lover," she answered.

"Do you think I'm a fool?" shouted the Senator. "I know he's your lover."

"Why do you ask then?"

Monsieur Le Sueur was a man of action. He went straight up to Lisette and smacked her hard on her right cheek with his left hand and then smacked her hard on the left cheek with his right hand.

"Brute," screamed Lisette.

He turned to the young man, who had watched this scene of violence with some embarrassment, and, drawing himself to his full height, flung out his arm and with a dramatic finger pointed to the door.

"Get out," he cried. "Get out."

One would have thought, such was the commanding aspect of a man who was accustomed to sway a crowd of angry tax-payers and who could dominate with his frown an annual meeting of disappointed shareholders, that the young man would have made a bolt for the door; but he stood his ground, irresolutely it is true, but he stood his ground; he gave Lisette an appealing look and slightly shrugged his shoulders.

"What are you waiting for?" shouted the Senator. "Do you want me to use force?"

"He can't go out in his pyjamas," said Lisette.

"They're not his pyjamas, they're my pyjamas."

"He's waiting for his clothes."

Monsieur Le Sueur looked round and on the chair behind him, flung down in a disorderly fashion, was a variety of masculine garments. The Senator gave the young man a look of contempt.

"You may take your clothes, Monsieur," he said with cold disdain.

The young man picked them up in his arms, gathered up the shoes that were lying about the floor, and quickly left the room. Monsieur Le Sueur had a considerable gift of oratory. Never had he made better use of it than now. He told Lisette what he thought of her. It was not flattering. He painted her ingratitude in the blackest colours. He ransacked an extensive vocabulary in order to find opprobrious names to call her. He called all the powers of heaven to witness that never had a woman repaid with such gross deception an honest man's belief in her. In short he said everything that anger, wounded vanity and disappointment suggested to him. Lisette did not seek to defend herself. She listened in silence, looking down and mechanically crumbling the roll which the Senator's appearance had prevented her from finishing. He flung an irritated glance at her plate.

"I was so anxious that you should be the first to hear my great news that I came straight here from the station. I was expecting to have my *petit déjeuner* with you, sitting at the end of your bed."

"My poor dear, haven't you had your breakfast? I'll order some for you at once."

"I don't want any."

"Nonsense. With the great responsibility you are about to assume you must keep up your strength."

She rang and when the maid came told her to bring in hot coffee. It was brought and Lisette poured it out. He would not touch it. She buttered a roll. He shrugged his shoulders and began to eat. Meanwhile he uttered a few remarks on the perfidy of women. She remained silent.

"At all events it is something," he said, "that you have not the effrontery to attempt to excuse yourself. You know that I am not a man who can be ill-used with impunity. The soul of generosity when people behave well to me I am pitiless when they behave badly. The very moment I have drunk my coffee I shall leave this apartment for ever."

Lisette sighed.

"I will tell you now that I had prepared a surprise for you. I had made up my mind to celebrate the second anniversary of our union by settling a sum of money on you sufficient to give you a modest independence if anything happened to me."

"How much?" asked Lisette sombrely.

"A million francs."

She sighed again. Suddenly something soft hit the Senator on the back of the head and he gave a start.

"What is that?" he cried.

"He's returning your pyjamas."

The young man had opened the door, flung the pyjamas at the Senator's head, and quickly closed it again. The Senator disengaged himself from the silk trousers that clung round his neck.

"What a way to return them! It is obvious that your friend has no education."

"Of course he has not your distinction," murmured Lisette.

"And has he my intelligence?"

"Oh, no."

"Is he rich?"

"Penniless."

"Then, name of a name, what is it you see in him?"

"He's young," smiled Lisette.

The Senator looked down at his plate and a tear rose in his eyes and rolled down his cheek into the coffee. Lisette gave him a kindly look.

"My poor friend, one can't have everything in this life," she said.

"I knew I was not young. But my situation, my fortune, my vitality. I thought it made up. There are women who only like men of a certain age. There are celebrated actresses who look upon it as an honour to be the little friend of a Minister. I am too well brought up to throw your origins in your face, but the fact remains that you are a mannequin and I took you out of an apartment of which the rent is only two thousand francs a year. It was a step up for you."

"The daughter of poor but honest parents, I have no reason to be ashamed of my origins, and it is not because I have earned my living in a humble sphere that you have the right to reproach me."

"Do you love this boy?"

"Yes."

"And not me?"

"You too. I love you both, but I love you differently. I love you because you are so distinguished and your conversation is instructive and interesting. I love you because you are kind and generous. I love him because his eyes are so big and his hair waves and he dances divinely. It's very natural."

"You know that in my position I cannot take you to places where they dance and I daresay when he's as old as I am he'll have no more hair than I have."

"That may well be true," Lisette agreed, but she did not think it much mattered.

"What will your aunt, the respectable Madame Saladin, say to you when she hears what you have done?"

"It will not be exactly a surprise to her."

"Do you mean to say that worthy woman countenances your conduct? *O tempora, o mores!* How long then has this been going on?"

"Since I first went to the shop. He travels for a big silk firm in Lyons. He came in one day with his samples. We liked the look of one another."

"But your aunt was there to defend you from the temptations to which a young girl is exposed in Paris. She should never have allowed you to have anything to do with this young man."

"I did not ask her permission."

"It is enough to bring the grey hairs of your poor father to the grave. Had you no thought of that wounded hero whose services to his country have been rewarded with a licence to sell tobacco? Do you forget that as Minister of the Interior the department is under my control? I should be within my rights if I revoked the licence on account of your flagrant immorality."

"I know you are too great a gentleman to do a dastardly thing like that."

He waved his hand in an impressive, though perhaps too dramatic a manner.

"Don't be afraid, I will never stoop so low as to revenge myself on one who has deserved well of his country for the misdeeds of a creature my sense of dignity forces me to despise."

He went on with his interrupted breakfast. Lisette did not speak and there was silence between them. But his appetite satisfied, his mood changed; he began to feel sorry for himself rather than angry with her, and with a strange ignorance of woman's heart he thought to arouse Lisette's remorse by exhibiting himself as an object of pity.

"It is hard to break a habit to which one has grown accustomed. It was a relief and a solace to me to come here when I could snatch a moment from my many occupations. Will you regret me a little, Lisette?"

"Of course."

He gave a deep sigh.

"I should never have thought you capable of so much deception."

"It is the deception that rankles," she murmured thoughtfully. "Men are funny in that way. They cannot forgive being made fools of. It is because they are so vain. They attach importance to things that are of no consequence."

"Do you call it a matter of no consequence that I should find you having breakfast with a young man wearing my pyjamas?"

"If he were my husband and you were my lover you would think it perfectly natural."

"Obviously. For then I should be deceiving him and my honour would be secure."

"In short, I have only to marry him to make the situation perfectly regular."

For a moment he did not understand. Then her meaning flashed across his clever brain and he gave her a quick look. Her lovely eyes had the twinkle he always found so alluring and on her large red mouth was the suspicion of a roguish smile.

"Do not forget that as a member of the Senate I am by all the traditions of the Republic the authorised mainstay of morality and good behaviour."

"Does that weigh very heavily with you?"

He stroked his handsome square beard with a composed and dignified gesture.

"Not a row of beans," he replied, but the expression he used had a Gallic breadth that would perhaps have given his more conservative supporters something of a shock.

"Would he marry you?" he asked.

"He adores me. Of course he would marry me. If I told him I had a *dot* of a million francs he would ask nothing better."

Monsieur Le Sueur gave her another look. When in a moment of anger he told her it had been his intention to settle a million francs on her he had exaggerated a good deal in the desire to make her see how much her treachery was costing her. But he was not the man to draw back when his dignity was concerned.

"It is much more than a young man in his position of life could aspire to. But if he adores you he would be always at your side."

"Didn't I tell you that he was a commercial traveller? He can only come to Paris for the week-end."

"That of course is a horse of another colour," said the Senator. "It would naturally be a satisfaction to him to know that during his absence I should be there to keep an eye on you."

"A considerable satisfaction," said Lisette.

To facilitate the conversation she rose from her seat and made herself comfortable on the Senator's knees. He pressed her hand tenderly.

"I am very fond of you, Lisette," he said. "I should not like you to make a mistake. Are you sure he will make you happy?"

"I think so."

"I will have proper enquiries made. I would never consent to your marrying anyone not of exemplary character and unimpeachable morality. For all our sakes we must make quite sure about this young man whom we are preparing to bring into our lives."

Lisette raised no objection. She was aware that the Senator liked to do things with order and method. He now prepared to leave her. He wanted to break his important news to Madame Le Sueur, and he had to get in touch with various persons in the parliamentary group to which he belonged.

"There is only one more thing," he said, as he bade Lisette an affectionate farewell, "if you marry I must insist on your giving up your work. The place of a wife is the home, and it is against all my principles that a married woman should take the bread out of a man's mouth."

Lisette reflected that a strapping young man would look rather funny walking round the room, with his hips swaying, to show off the latest models, but she respected the Senator's principles.

"It shall be as you wish, darling," she said.

The enquiries he made were satisfactory and the marriage took place on a Saturday morning as soon as the legal formalities were completed. Monsieur Le Sueur, Minister of the Interior, and Madame Saladin were witnesses. The bridegroom was a slim young man with a straight nose, fine eyes and black waving hair brushed straight back from his forehead. He looked more like a tennis-player than a traveller in silk. The Mayor, impressed by the august presence of the Minister of the Interior, made according to French practice a speech which he sought to render eloquent. He began by telling the married couple what presumably they knew already. He informed the bridegroom that he was the son of worthy parents and was engaged in an honourable profession. He congratulated him on entering the bonds of matrimony at an age when many young men thought only of their pleasures. He reminded the bride that her father was a hero of the great war, whose glorious wounds had been rewarded by a concession to sell tobacco, and he told her that she had earned a decent living since her arrival in Paris in an establishment that was one of the glories of French taste and luxury. The Mayor was of a literary turn and he briefly mentioned various celebrated lovers of fiction, Romeo and Juliet whose short but legitimate union had been interrupted by a regrettable misunderstanding, Paul and Virginia who had met her death at sea rather than sacrifice her modesty by taking off her clothes, and finally Daphnis and Chloe who had not consummated their marriage till it was sanctioned by the legitimate authority. He was so moving that Lisette shed a few tears. He paid a compliment to Madame Saladin whose example and precept had preserved her young and beautiful niece from the dangers that are likely to befall a young girl alone in a great city, and finally he congratulated the happy pair on the honour that the Minister of the Interior had done them in consenting to be a witness at the ceremony. It was a testimony to their own probity that this captain of industry and eminent statesman should find time to perform a humble office to persons in their modest sphere, and it proved not only the excellence of his heart but his lively sense of duty. His action showed that he appreciated the importance of early marriage, affirmed the security of the family and emphasised the desirability of producing offspring to increase the power, influence and consequence of the fair land of France. A very good speech indeed.

The wedding breakfast was held at the Château de Madrid, which had sentimental associations for Monsieur Le Sueur. It has been mentioned already that among his many interests the Minister (as we must now call him) was interested in a firm of motor-cars. His wedding present to the bridegroom was a very nice two-seater of his own manufacture, and in this, when lunch was over, the young couple started off for their honeymoon. This could only last over the week-end since the young man had to get back to his work, which would take him to Marseilles, Toulon and Nice. Lisette kissed her aunt and she kissed Monsieur Le Sueur.

"I shall expect you at five on Monday," she whispered to him.

"I shall be there," he answered.

They drove away and for a moment Monsieur Le Sueur and Madame Saladin looked at the smart yellow roadster.

"As long as he makes her happy," sighed Madame Saladin, who was not used to champagne at lunch and felt unreasonably melancholy.

"If he does not make her happy he will have me to count with," said Monsieur Le Sueur impressively.

His car drove up.

"*Au revoir, chère Madame.* You will get a bus at the Avenue de Neuilly."

He stepped into his car and as he thought of the affairs of state that awaited his attention he sighed with content. It was evidently much more fitting to his situation that his mistress should be, not just a little mannequin in a dressmaker's shop, but a respectable married woman.

The Three Fat Women of Antibes

ONE was called Mrs. Richman and she was a widow. The second was called Mrs. Sutcliffe; she was American and she had divorced two husbands. The third was called Miss Hickson and she was a spinster. They were all in the comfortable forties and they were all well off. Mrs. Sutcliffe had the odd first name of Arrow. When she was young and slender she had liked it well enough. It suited her and the jests it occasioned though too often repeated were very flattering; she was not disinclined to believe that it suited her character too: it suggested directness, speed and purpose. She liked it less now that her delicate features had grown muzzy with fat, that her arms and shoulders were so substantial and her hips so massive. It was increasingly difficult to find dresses to make her look as she liked to look. The jests her name gave rise to now were made behind her back and she very well knew that they were far from obliging. But she was by no means resigned to middle age. She still wore blue to bring out the colour of her eyes and, with the help of art, her fair hair had kept its lustre. What she liked about Beatrice Richman and Frances Hickson was that they were both so much fatter than she, it made her look quite slim; they were both of them older and much inclined to treat her as a little young thing. It was not disagreeable. They were good-natured women and they chaffed her pleasantly about her beaux; they had both given up the thought of that kind of nonsense, indeed Miss Hickson had never given it a moment's consideration, but they were sympathetic to her flirtations. It was understood that one of these days Arrow would make a third man happy.

"Only you mustn't get any heavier, darling," said Mrs. Richman.

"And for goodness' sake make certain of his bridge," said Miss Hickson.

They saw for her a man of about fifty, but well-preserved and of distinguished carriage, an admiral on the retired list and a good golfer, or a widower without encumbrances, but in any case with a substantial income. Arrow listened to them amiably, and kept to herself the fact that this was not at all her idea. It was true that she would have liked to marry again, but her fancy turned to a dark slim Italian with flashing eyes and a sonorous title or to a Spanish don of noble lineage; and not a day more than thirty. There were times when, looking at herself in her mirror, she was certain she did not look any more than that herself.

They were great friends, Miss Hickson, Mrs. Richman and Arrow Sutcliffe. It was their fat that had brought them together and bridge that had cemented their alliance. They had met first at Carlsbad, where they were staying at the same hotel and were treated by the same doctor who used them with the same ruthlessness. Beatrice Richman was enormous. She was a handsome woman, with fine eyes, rouged cheeks and painted lips. She was very well content to be a widow with a handsome fortune. She adored her food. She liked bread and butter, cream, potatoes and suet puddings, and for eleven months of the year she ate pretty well everything she had a mind to, and for one month went to Carlsbad to reduce. But every year she grew fatter. She upbraided the doctor, but got no sympathy from him. He pointed out to her various plain and simple facts.

"But if I'm never to eat a thing I like, life isn't worth living," she expostulated.

He shrugged his disapproving shoulders. Afterwards she told Miss Hickson that she was beginning to suspect he wasn't so clever as she had thought. Miss Hickson gave a great guffaw. She was that sort of woman. She had a deep bass voice, a large flat sallow face from which twinkled little bright eyes; she walked with a slouch, her hands in her pockets, and when she could do so without exciting attention smoked a long cigar. She dressed as like a man as she could.

"What the deuce should I look like in frills and furbelows?" she said. "When you're as fat as I am you may just as well be comfortable."

She wore tweeds and heavy boots and whenever she could went about bareheaded. But she was as strong as an ox and boasted that few men could drive a longer ball than she. She was plain of speech, and she could swear more variously than a stevedore. Though her name was Frances she preferred to be called Frank. Masterful, but with tact, it was her jovial strength of character that held the three together. They drank their waters together, had their baths at the same hour, they took their strenuous walks together, pounded about the tennis court with a professional to make them run, and ate at the same table their sparse and regulated meals. Nothing impaired their good humour but the scales, and when one or other of them weighed as much on one day as she had the day before neither Frank's coarse jokes, the *bonhomie* of Beatrice nor Arrow's pretty kittenish ways sufficed to dispel the gloom. Then drastic measures were resorted to, the culprit went to bed for twenty-four hours and nothing passed her lips but the doctor's famous vegetable soup which tasted like hot water in which a cabbage had been well rinsed.

Never were three women greater friends. They would have been independent of anyone else if they had not needed a fourth at bridge. They were fierce, enthusiastic players and the moment the day's cure was over they sat down at the bridge table. Arrow, feminine as she was, played the best game of the three, a hard, brilliant game, in which she showed no mercy and never conceded a point or failed to take advantage of a mistake. Beatrice was solid and reliable. Frank was dashing; she was a great theorist, and had all the authorities at the tip of her tongue. They had long arguments over the rival systems. They bombarded one another with Culbertson and Sims. It was obvious that not one of them ever played a card without fifteen good reasons, but it was also obvious from the subsequent conversation that there were fifteen equally good reasons why she should not have played it. Life would have been perfect, even with the prospect of twenty-four hours of that filthy soup when the doctor's rotten (Beatrice) bloody (Frank) lousy (Arrow) scales pretended one hadn't lost an ounce in two days, if only there had not been this constant difficulty of finding someone to play with them who was in their class.

It was for this reason that on the occasion with which this narrative deals Frank invited Lena Finch to come and stay with them at Antibes. They were spending some weeks there on Frank's suggestion. It seemed absurd to her, with her common sense, that immediately the cure was over Beatrice who always lost twenty pounds should by giving way to her ungovernable appetite put it all on again. Beatrice was weak. She needed a person of strong will to watch her diet. She proposed then that on leaving Carlsbad they should take a house at Antibes, where they could get plenty of exercise—everyone knew that nothing slimmed you like swimming —and as far as possible could go on with the cure. With a cook of their own they could at least avoid things that were obviously fattening. There was no reason why they should not all lose several pounds more. It seemed a very good idea. Beatrice knew what was good for her, and she could resist temptation well enough if temptation was not put right under her nose. Besides, she liked gambling, and a flutter at the Casino two or three times a week would pass the time very pleasantly. Arrow adored Antibes, and she would be looking her best after a month at Carlsbad. She could just pick and choose among the young Italians, the passionate Spaniards, the gallant Frenchmen, and the long-limbed English who sauntered about all day in bathing trunks and gay-coloured dressing-gowns. The plan worked very well. They had a grand time. Two days a week they ate nothing but hard-boiled eggs and raw tomatoes and they mounted the scales every morning with light hearts. Arrow got down to eleven stone and felt just like a girl; Beatrice and Frank by standing in a certain way just avoided the thirteen. The machine they had bought registered kilogrammes, and they got extraordinarily clever at translating these in the twinkling of an eye to pounds and ounces.

But the fourth at bridge continued to be the difficulty. This person played like a fool, the other was so slow that it drove you frantic, one was quarrelsome, another was a bad loser, a third was next door to a crook. It was strange how hard it was to find exactly the player you wanted.

One morning when they were sitting in pyjamas on the terrace overlooking the sea, drinking their tea (without milk or sugar) and eating a rusk prepared by Dr. Hudebert and guaranteed not to be fattening, Frank looked up from her letters.

"Lena Finch is coming down to the Riviera," she said.

"Who's she?" asked Arrow.

"She married a cousin of mine. He died a couple of months ago and she's just recovering from a nervous breakdown. What about asking her to come here for a fortnight?"

"Does she play bridge?" asked Beatrice.

"You bet your life she does," boomed Frank in her deep voice. "And a damned good game too. We should be absolutely independent of outsiders."

"How old is she?" asked Arrow.

"Same age as I am."

"That sounds all right."

It was settled. Frank, with her usual decisiveness, stalked out as soon as she had finished her breakfast to send a wire, and three days later Lena Finch arrived. Frank met her at the station. She was in deep but not obtrusive mourning for the recent death of her husband. Frank had not seen her for two years. She kissed her warmly and took a good look at her.

"You're very thin, darling," she said.

Lena smiled bravely.

"I've been through a good deal lately. I've lost a lot of weight."

Frank sighed, but whether from sympathy with her cousin's sad loss, or from envy, was not obvious.

Lena was not, however, unduly depressed, and after a quick bath

was quite ready to accompany Frank to Eden Roc. Frank introduced the stranger to her two friends and they sat down in what
was known as the Monkey House. It was an enclosure covered
with glass overlooking the sea, with a bar at the back, and it was
crowded with chattering people in bathing costumes, pyjamas or
dressing-gowns, who were seated at the tables having drinks.
Beatrice's soft heart went out to the lorn widow, and Arrow, seeing
that she was pale, quite ordinary to look at and probably forty-
eight, was prepared to like her very much. A waiter approached
them.

"What will you have, Lena dear?" Frank asked.

"Oh, I don't know, what you all have, a dry Martini or a White
Lady."

Arrow and Beatrice gave her a quick look. Everyone knows how
fattening cocktails are.

"I daresay you're tired after your journey," said Frank kindly.

She ordered a dry Martini for Lena and a mixed lemon and orange
juice for herself and her two friends.

"We find alcohol isn't very good in all this heat," she explained.

"Oh, it never affects me at all," Lena answered airily. "I like
cocktails."

Arrow went very slightly pale under her rouge (neither she nor
Beatrice ever wet their faces when they bathed and they thought it
absurd of Frank, a woman of her size, to pretend she liked diving)
but she said nothing. The conversation was gay and easy, they all
said the obvious things with gusto, and presently they strolled back
to the villa for luncheon.

In each napkin were two little antifat rusks. Lena gave a bright
smile as she put them by the side of her plate.

"May I have some bread?" she asked.

The grossest indecency would not have fallen on the ears of
those three women with such a shock. Not one of them had eaten
bread for ten years. Even Beatrice, greedy as she was, drew the
line there. Frank, the good hostess, recovered herself first.

"Of course, darling," she said and turning to the butler asked him
to bring some.

"And some butter," said Lena in that pleasant easy way of hers.

There was a moment's embarrassed silence.

"I don't know if there's any in the house," said Frank, "but I'll
enquire. There may be some in the kitchen."

"I adore bread and butter, don't you?" said Lena, turning to
Beatrice.

Beatrice gave a sickly smile and an evasive reply. The butler brought a long crisp roll of French bread. Lena slit it in two and plastered it with the butter which was miraculously produced. A grilled sole was served.

"We eat very simply here," said Frank. "I hope you won't mind."

"Oh, no, I like my food very plain," said Lena as she took some butter and spread it over her fish. "As long as I can have bread and butter and potatoes and cream I'm quite happy."

The three friends exchanged a glance. Frank's great sallow face sagged a little and she looked with distaste at the dry, insipid sole on her plate. Beatrice came to the rescue.

"It's such a bore, we can't get cream here," she said. "It's one of the things one has to do without on the Riviera."

"What a pity," said Lena.

The rest of the luncheon consisted of lamb cutlets, with the fat carefully removed so that Beatrice should not be led astray, and spinach boiled in water, with stewed pears to end up with. Lena tasted her pears and gave the butler a look of enquiry. The resourceful man understood her at once and though powdered sugar had never been served at that table before handed her without a moment's hesitation a bowl of it. She helped herself liberally. The other three pretended not to notice. Coffee was served and Lena took three lumps of sugar in hers.

"You have a very sweet tooth," said Arrow in a tone which she struggled to keep friendly.

"We think saccharine so much more sweetening," said Frank, as she put a tiny tablet of it into her coffee.

"Disgusting stuff," said Lena.

Beatrice's mouth drooped at the corners, and she gave the lump sugar a yearning look.

"Beatrice," boomed Frank sternly.

Beatrice stifled a sigh, and reached for the saccharine.

Frank was relieved when they could sit down to the bridge table. It was plain to her that Arrow and Beatrice were upset. She wanted them to like Lena and she was anxious that Lena should enjoy her fortnight with them. For the first rubber Arrow cut with the new-comer.

"Do you play Vanderbilt or Culbertson?" she asked her.

"I have no conventions," Lena answered in a happy-go-lucky way, "I play by the light of nature."

"I play strict Culbertson," said Arrow acidly.

The three fat women braced themselves to the fray. No conventions indeed! They'd learn her. When it came to bridge even Frank's family feeling was forgotten and she settled down with the same determination as the others to trim the stranger in their midst. But the light of nature served Lena very well. She had a natural gift for the game and great experience. She played with imagination, quickly, boldly, and with assurance. The other players were in too high a class not to realise very soon that Lena knew what she was about, and since they were all thoroughly good-natured, generous women, they were gradually mollified. This was real bridge. They all enjoyed themselves. Arrow and Beatrice began to feel more kindly towards Lena, and Frank, noticing this, heaved a fat sigh of relief. It was going to be a success.

After a couple of hours they parted, Frank and Beatrice to have a round of golf, and Arrow to take a brisk walk with a young Prince Roccamare whose acquaintance she had lately made. He was very sweet and young and good-looking. Lena said she would rest.

They met again just before dinner.

"I hope you've been all right, Lena dear," said Frank. "I was rather conscience-stricken at leaving you with nothing to do all this time."

"Oh, don't apologise. I had a lovely sleep and then I went down to Juan and had a cocktail. And d'you know what I discovered? You'll be so pleased. I found a dear little tea-shop where they've got the most beautiful thick fresh cream. I've ordered half a pint to be sent every day. I thought it would be my little contribution to the household."

Her eyes were shining. She was evidently expecting them to be delighted.

"How very kind of you," said Frank, with a look that sought to quell the indignation that she saw on the faces of her two friends. "But we never eat cream. In this climate it makes one so bilious."

"I shall have to eat it all myself then," said Lena cheerfully.

"Don't you ever think of your figure?" Arrow asked with icy deliberation.

"The doctor said I must eat."

"Did he say you must eat bread and butter and potatoes and cream?"

"Yes. That's what I thought you meant when you said you had simple food."

"You'll get simply enormous," said Beatrice.

Lena laughed gaily.

"No, I shan't. You see, nothing ever makes me fat. I've always eaten everything I wanted to and it's never had the slightest effect on me."

The stony silence that followed this speech was only broken by the entrance of the butler.

"*Mademoiselle est servie,*" he announced.

They talked the matter over late that night, after Lena had gone to bed, in Frank's room. During the evening they had been furiously cheerful, and they had chaffed one another with a friendliness that would have taken in the keenest observer. But now they dropped the mask. Beatrice was sullen, Arrow was spiteful and Frank was unmanned.

"It's not very nice for me to sit there and see her eat all the things I particularly like," said Beatrice plaintively.

"It's not very nice for any of us," Frank snapped back.

"You should never have asked her here," said Arrow.

"How was I to know?" cried Frank.

"I can't help thinking that if she really cared for her husband she would hardly eat so much," said Beatrice. "He's only been buried two months. I mean, I think you ought to show some respect for the dead."

"Why can't she eat the same as we do?" asked Arrow viciously. "She's a guest."

"Well, you heard what she said. The doctor told her she must eat."

"Then she ought to go to a sanatorium."

"It's more than flesh and blood can stand, Frank," moaned Beatrice.

"If I can stand it you can stand it."

"She's your cousin, she's not our cousin," said Arrow. "I'm not going to sit there for fourteen days and watch that woman make a hog of herself."

"It's so vulgar to attach all this importance to food," Frank boomed, and her voice was deeper than ever. "After all the only thing that counts really is spirit."

"Are you calling *me* vulgar, Frank?" asked Arrow with flashing eyes.

"No, of course she isn't," interrupted Beatrice.

"I wouldn't put it past you to go down in the kitchen when we're all in bed and have a good square meal on the sly."

Frank sprang to her feet.

"How dare you say that, Arrow! I'd never ask anybody to do what I'm not prepared to do myself. Have you known me all these years and do you think me capable of such a mean thing?"

"How is it you never take off any weight then?"

Frank gave a gasp and burst into a flood of tears.

"What a cruel thing to say! I've lost pounds and pounds."

She wept like a child. Her vast body shook and great tears splashed on her mountainous bosom.

"Darling, I didn't mean it," cried Arrow.

She threw herself on her knees and enveloped what she could of Frank in her own plump arms. She wept and the mascara ran down her cheeks.

"D'you mean to say I don't look thinner?" Frank sobbed. "After all I've gone through."

"Yes, dear, of course you do," cried Arrow through her tears. "Everybody's noticed it."

Beatrice, though naturally of a placid disposition, began to cry gently. It was pathetic. Indeed, it would have been a hard heart that failed to be moved by the sight of Frank, that lion-hearted woman, crying her eyes out. Presently, however, they dried their tears and had a little brandy and water, which every doctor had told them was the least fattening thing they could drink, and then they felt much better. They decided that Lena should have the nourishing food that had been ordered her and they made a solemn resolution not to let it disturb their equanimity. She was certainly a first-rate bridge-player and after all it was only for a fortnight. They would do whatever they could to make her stay enjoyable. They kissed one another warmly and separated for the night feeling strangely uplifted. Nothing should interfere with the wonderful friendship that had brought so much happiness into their three lives.

But human nature is weak. You must not ask too much of it. They ate grilled fish while Lena ate macaroni sizzling with cheese and butter; they ate grilled cutlets and boiled spinach while Lena ate *pâté de foie gras*; twice a week they ate hard-boiled eggs and raw tomatoes, while Lena ate peas swimming in cream and potatoes cooked in all sorts of delicious ways. The chef was a good chef and leapt at the opportunity afforded him to send up one dish more rich, tasty and succulent than the other.

"Poor Jim," sighed Lena, thinking of her husband, "he loved French cooking."

The butler disclosed the fact that he could make half a dozen kinds of cocktail and Lena informed them that the doctor had recommended her to drink burgundy at luncheon and champagne at dinner. The three fat women persevered. They were gay, chatty and even hilarious (such is the natural gift that women have for deception) but Beatrice grew limp and forlorn, and Arrow's tender blue eyes acquired a steely glint. Frank's deep voice grew more raucous. It was when they played bridge that the strain showed itself. They had always been fond of talking over their hands, but their discussions had been friendly. Now a distinct bitterness crept in and sometimes one pointed out a mistake to another with quite unnecessary frankness. Discussion turned to argument and argument to altercation. Sometimes the session ended in angry silence. Once Frank accused Arrow of deliberately letting her down. Two or three times Beatrice, the softest of the three, was reduced to tears. On another occasion Arrow flung down her cards and swept out of the room in a pet. Their tempers were getting frayed. Lena was the peacemaker.

"I think it's such a pity to quarrel over bridge," she said. "After all, it's only a game."

It was all very well for her. She had had a square meal and half a bottle of champagne. Besides, she had phenomenal luck. She was winning all their money. The score was put down in a book after each session, and hers mounted up day after day with unfailing regularity. Was there no justice in the world? They began to hate one another. And though they hated her too they could not resist confiding in her. Each of them went to her separately and told her how detestable the others were. Arrow said she was sure it was bad for her to see so much of women so much older than herself. She had a good mind to sacrifice her share of the lease and go to Venice for the rest of the summer. Frank told Lena that with her masculine mind it was too much to expect that she could be satisfied with anyone so frivolous as Arrow and so frankly stupid as Beatrice.

"I must have intellectual conversation," she boomed. "When you have a brain like mine you've got to consort with your intellectual equals."

Beatrice only wanted peace and quiet.

"Really I hate women," she said. "They're so unreliable; they're so malicious."

By the time Lena's fortnight drew to its close the three fat women were barely on speaking terms. They kept up appearances before Lena, but when she was not there made no pretences. They had got past quarrelling. They ignored one another, and when this was not possible treated each other with icy politeness.

Lena was going to stay with friends on the Italian Riviera and Frank saw her off by the same train as that by which she had arrived. She was taking away with her a lot of their money.

"I don't know how to thank you," she said, as she got into the carriage. "I've had a wonderful visit."

If there was one thing that Frank Hickson prided herself on more than on being a match for any man it was that she was a gentlewoman, and her reply was perfect in its combination of majesty and graciousness.

"We've all enjoyed having you here, Lena," she said. "It's been a real treat."

But when she turned away from the departing train she heaved such a vast sigh of relief that the platform shook beneath her. She flung back her massive shoulders and strode home to the villa.

"Ouf!" she roared at intervals. "Ouf!"

She changed into her one-piece bathing-suit, put on her espa-drilles and a man's dressing-gown (no nonsense about it) and went to Eden Roc. There was still time for a bathe before luncheon. She passed through the Monkey House, looking about her to say good morning to anyone she knew, for she felt on a sudden at peace with mankind, and then stopped dead still. She could not believe her eyes. Beatrice was sitting at one of the tables, by herself; she wore the pyjamas she had bought at Molyneux's a day or two before, she had a string of pearls round her neck, and Frank's quick eyes saw that she had just had her hair waved; her cheeks, her eyes, her lips were made up. Fat, nay vast, as she was, none could deny that she was an extremely handsome woman. But what was she doing? With the slouching gait of the Neanderthal man which was Frank's characteristic walk she went up to Beatrice. In her black bathing-dress Frank looked like the huge cetacean which the Japanese catch in the Torres Straits and which the vulgar call a sea-cow.

"Beatrice, what are you doing?" she cried in her deep voice.

It was like the roll of thunder in the distant mountains. Beatrice looked at her coolly.

"Eating," she answered.

"Damn it, I can see you're eating."

In front of Beatrice was a plate of *croissants* and a plate of butter, a pot of strawberry jam, coffee and a jug of cream. Beatrice was spreading butter thick on the delicious hot bread, covering this with jam, and then pouring the thick cream over all.

"You'll kill yourself," said Frank.

"I don't care," mumbled Beatrice with her mouth full.

"You'll put on pounds and pounds."

"Go to hell!"

She actually laughed in Frank's face. My God, how good those *croissants* smelt!

"I'm disappointed in you, Beatrice. I thought you had more character."

"It's your fault. That blasted woman. You would have her down. For a fortnight I've watched her gorge like a hog. It's more than flesh and blood can stand. I'm going to have one square meal if I bust."

The tears welled up to Frank's eyes. Suddenly she felt very weak and womanly. She would have liked a strong man to take her on his knee and pet her and cuddle her and call her little baby names. Speechless she sank down on a chair by Beatrice's side. A waiter came up. With a pathetic gesture she waved towards the coffee and *croissants*.

"I'll have the same," she sighed.

She listlessly reached out her hand to take a roll, but Beatrice snatched away the plate.

"No, you don't," she said. "You wait till you get your own."

Frank called her a name which ladies seldom apply to one another in affection. In a moment the waiter brought her *croissants*, butter, jam and coffee.

"Where's the cream, you fool?" she roared like a lioness at bay.

She began to eat. She ate gluttonously. The place was beginning to fill up with bathers coming to enjoy a cocktail or two after having done their duty by the sun and the sea. Presently Arrow strolled along with Prince Roccamare. She had on a beautiful silk wrap which she held tightly round her with one hand in order to look as slim as possible and she bore her head high so that he should not see her double chin. She was laughing gaily. She felt like a girl. He had just told her (in Italian) that her eyes made the blue of the Mediterranean look like pea-soup. He left her to go into the men's room to brush his sleek black hair and they arranged to meet in five minutes for a drink. Arrow walked on to the women's room to put a little more rouge on her cheeks and a little more red on her lips. On her way she caught sight of Frank and Beatrice. She stopped. She could hardly believe her eyes.

"My God!" she cried. "You beasts. You hogs." She seized a chair. "Waiter."

Her appointment went clean out of her head. In the twinkling of an eye the waiter was at her side.

"Bring me what these ladies are having," she ordered.

Frank lifted her great heavy head from her plate.

"Bring me some *pâté de foie gras*," she boomed.

"Frank!" cried Beatrice.

"Shut up."

"All right. I'll have some too."

The coffee was brought and the hot rolls and cream and the *pâté de foie gras* and they set to. They spread the cream on the *pâté* and they ate it. They devoured great spoonfuls of jam. They crunched the delicious crisp bread voluptuously. What was love to Arrow then? Let the Prince keep his palace in Rome and his castle in the Apennines. They did not speak. What they were about was much too serious. They ate with solemn, ecstatic fervour.

"I haven't eaten potatoes for twenty-five years," said Frank in a far-off brooding tone.

"Waiter," cried Beatrice, "bring fried potatoes for three."

"*Très bien, Madame.*"

The potatoes were brought. Not all the perfumes of Arabia smelt so sweet. They ate them with their fingers.

"Bring me a dry Martini," said Arrow.

"You can't have a dry Martini in the middle of a meal, Arrow," said Frank.

"Can't I? You wait and see."

"All right then. Bring me a double dry Martini," said Frank.

"Bring three double dry Martinis," said Beatrice.

They were brought and drunk at a gulp. The women looked at one another and sighed. The misunderstandings of the last fortnight dissolved and the sincere affection each had for the other welled up again in their hearts. They could hardly believe that they had ever contemplated the possibility of severing a friendship that had brought them so much solid satisfaction. They finished the potatoes.

"I wonder if they've got any chocolate éclairs," said Beatrice.

"Of course they have."

And of course they had. Frank thrust one whole into her huge mouth, swallowed it and seized another, but before she ate it she looked at the other two and plunged a vindictive dagger into the heart of the monstrous Lena.

"You can say what you like, but the truth is she played a damned rotten game of bridge, really."

"Lousy," agreed Arrow.

But Beatrice suddenly thought she would like a meringue.

The Facts of Life

IT was Henry Garnet's habit on leaving the city of an afternoon to drop in at his club and play bridge before going home to dinner. He was a pleasant man to play with. He knew the game well and you could be sure that he would make the best of his cards. He was a good loser; and when he won was more inclined to ascribe his success to his luck than to his skill. He was indulgent, and if his partner made a mistake could be trusted to find an excuse for him. It was surprising then on this occasion to hear him telling his partner with unnecessary sharpness that he had never seen a hand worse played; and it was more surprising still to see him not only make a grave error himself, an error of which you would never have thought him capable, but when his partner, not unwilling to get a little of his own back, pointed it out, insist against all reason and with considerable heat that he was perfectly right. But they were all old friends, the men he was playing with, and none of them took his ill-humour very seriously. Henry Garnet was a broker, a partner in a firm of repute, and it occurred to one of them that something had gone wrong with some stock he was interested in.

"How's the market to-day?" he asked.

"Booming. Even the suckers are making money."

It was evident that stocks and shares had nothing to do with Henry Garnet's vexation; but something was the matter; that was evident too. He was a hearty fellow, who enjoyed excellent health; he had plenty of money; he was fond of his wife and devoted to his children. As a rule he had high spirits, and he laughed easily at the nonsense they were apt to talk while they played; but to-day he sat glum and silent. His brows were crossly puckered and there was a sulky look about his mouth. Presently, to ease the tension, one of the others mentioned a subject upon which they all knew Henry Garnet was glad to speak.

"How's your boy, Henry? I see he's done pretty well in the tournament."

Henry Garnet's frown grew darker.

"He's done no better than I expected him to."

"When does he come back from Monte?"

"He got back last night."

"Did he enjoy himself?"

"I suppose so; all I know is that he made a damned fool of himself."

"Oh. How?"

"I'd rather not talk about it if you don't mind."

The three men looked at him with curiosity. Henry Garnet scowled at the green baize.

"Sorry, old boy. Your call."

The game proceeded in a strained silence. Garnet got his bid, and when he played his cards so badly that he went three down not a word was said. Another rubber was begun and in the second game Garnet denied a suit.

"Having none?" his partner asked him.

Garnet's irritability was such that he did not even reply, and when at the end of the hand it appeared that he had revoked, and that his revoke cost the rubber, it was not to be expected that his partner should let his carelessness go without remark.

"What the devil's the matter with you, Henry?" he said. "You're playing like a fool."

Garnet was disconcerted. He did not so much mind losing a big rubber himself, but he was sore that his inattention should have made his partner lose too. He pulled himself together.

"I'd better not play any more. I thought a few rubbers would calm me, but the fact is I can't give my mind to the game. To tell you the truth I'm in a hell of a temper."

They all burst out laughing.

"You don't have to tell us that, old boy. It's obvious."

Garnet gave them a rueful smile.

"Well, I bet you'd be in a temper if what's happened to me had happened to you. As a matter of fact I'm in a damned awkward situation, and if any of you fellows can give me any advice how to deal with it I'd be grateful."

"Let's have a drink and you tell us all about it. With a K.C., a Home Office official and an eminent surgeon—if we can't tell you how to deal with a situation, nobody can."

The K.C. got up and rang the bell for a waiter.

"It's about that damned boy of mine," said Henry Garnet.

Drinks were ordered and brought. And this is the story that Henry Garnet told them.

The boy of whom he spoke was his only son. His name was Nicholas and of course he was called Nicky. He was eighteen. The Garnets had two daughters besides, one of sixteen and the other of twelve, but however unreasonable it seemed, for a father is generally supposed to like his daughters best, and though he did

all he could not to show his preference, there was no doubt that
the greater share of Henry Garnet's affection was given to his son.
He was kind, in a chaffing, casual way, to his daughters, and gave
them handsome presents on their birthdays and at Christmas; but
he doted on Nicky. Nothing was too good for him. He thought
the world of him. He could hardly take his eyes off him. You could
not blame him, for Nicky was a son that any parent might have
been proud of. He was six foot two, lithe but muscular, with broad
shoulders and a slim waist, and he held himself gallantly erect;
he had a charming head, well placed on the shoulders, with pale
brown hair that waved slightly, blue eyes with long dark lashes
under well-marked eyebrows, a full red mouth and a tanned,
clean skin. When he smiled he showed very regular and very white
teeth. He was not shy, but there was a modesty in his demeanour
that was attractive. In social intercourse he was easy, polite and
quietly gay. He was the offspring of nice, healthy, decent parents,
he had been well brought up in a good home, he had been sent to a
good school, and the general result was as engaging a specimen of
young manhood as you were likely to find in a long time. You felt
that he was as honest, open and virtuous as he looked. He had
never given his parents a moment's uneasiness. As a child he was
seldom ill and never naughty. As a boy he did everything that was
expected of him. His school reports were excellent. He was wonderfully popular, and he ended his career, with a creditable number of
prizes, as head of the school and captain of the football team.
But this was not all. At the age of fourteen Nicky had developed an
unexpected gift for lawn tennis. This was a game that his father
not only was fond of, but played very well, and when he discerned
in the boy the promise of a tennis-player he fostered it. During the
holidays he had him taught by the best professionals and by the
time he was sixteen he had won a number of tournaments for boys
of his age. He could beat his father so badly that only parental
affection reconciled the older player to the poor show he put up.
At eighteen Nicky went to Cambridge and Henry Garnet conceived
the ambition that before he was through with the university he
should play for it. Nicky had all the qualifications for becoming a
great tennis-player. He was tall, he had a long reach, he was quick
on his feet and his timing was perfect. He realised instinctively
where the ball was coming and, seemingly without hurry, was
there to take it. He had a powerful serve, with a nasty break that
made it difficult to return, and his forehand drive, low, long and
accurate, was deadly. He was not so good on the backhand and his
volleying was wild, but all through the summer before he went to

Cambridge Henry Garnet made him work on these points under the best teacher in England. At the back of his mind, though he did not even mention it to Nicky, he cherished a further ambition, to see his son play at Wimbledon, and who could tell, perhaps be chosen to represent his country in the Davis Cup. A great lump came into Henry Garnet's throat as he saw in fancy his son leap over the net to shake hands with the American champion whom he had just defeated, and walk off the court to the deafening plaudits of the multitude.

As an assiduous frequenter of Wimbledon Henry Garnet had a good many friends in the tennis world, and one evening he found himself at a City dinner sitting next to one of them, a Colonel Brabazon, and in due course began talking to him of Nicky and what chance there might be of his being chosen to play for his university during the following season.

"Why don't you let him go down to Monte Carlo and play in the spring tournament there?" said the Colonel suddenly.

"Oh, I don't think he's good enough for that. He's not nineteen yet, he only went to Cambridge last October; he wouldn't stand a chance against all those cracks."

"Of course, Austin and von Cramm and so on would knock spots off him, but he might snatch a game or two; and if he got up against some of the smaller fry there's no reason why he shouldn't win two or three matches. He's never been up against any of the first-rate players and it would be wonderful practice for him. He'd learn a lot more than he'll ever learn in the seaside tournaments you enter him for."

"I wouldn't dream of it. I'm not going to let him leave Cambridge in the middle of a term. I've always impressed upon him that tennis is only a game and it mustn't interfere with work."

Colonel Brabazon asked Garnet when the term ended.

"That's all right. He'd only have to cut about three days. Surely that could be arranged. You see, two of the men we were depending on have let us down, and we're in a hole. We want to send as good a team as we can. The Germans are sending their best players and so are the Americans."

"Nothing doing, old boy. In the first place Nicky's not good enough, and secondly, I don't fancy the idea of sending a kid like that to Monte Carlo without anyone to look after him. If I could get away myself I might think of it, but that's out of the question."

"I shall be there. I'm going as the non-playing captain of the English team. I'll keep an eye on him."

"You'll be busy, and besides, it's not a responsibility I'd like to ask you to take. He's never been abroad in his life, and to tell you the truth, I shouldn't have a moment's peace all the time he was there."

They left it at that and presently Henry Garnet went home. He was so flattered by Colonel Brabazon's suggestion that he could not help telling his wife.

"Fancy his thinking Nicky's as good as that. He told me he'd seen him play and his style was fine. He only wants more practice to get into the first flight. We shall see the kid playing in the semi-finals at Wimbledon yet, old girl."

To his surprise Mrs. Garnet was not so much opposed to the notion as he would have expected.

"After all the boy's eighteen. Nicky's never got into mischief yet and there's no reason to suppose he will now."

"There's his work to be considered; don't forget that. I think it would be a very bad precedent to let him cut the end of term."

"But what can three days matter? It seems a shame to rob him of a chance like that. I'm sure he'd jump at it if you asked him."

"Well, I'm not going to. I haven't sent him to Cambridge just to play tennis. I know he's steady, but it's silly to put temptation in his way. He's much too young to go to Monte Carlo by himself."

"You say he won't have a chance against these crack players, but you can't tell."

Henry Garnet sighed a little. On the way home in the car it had struck him that Austin's health was uncertain and that von Cramm had his off-days. Supposing, just for the sake of argument, that Nicky had a bit of luck like that—then there would be no doubt that he would be chosen to play for Cambridge. But of course that was all nonsense.

"Nothing doing, my dear. I've made up my mind and I'm not going to change it."

Mrs. Garnet held her peace. But next day she wrote to Nicky, telling him what had happened, and suggested to him what she would do in his place if, wanting to go, he wished to get his father's consent. A day or two later Henry Garnet received a letter from his son. He was bubbling over with excitement. He had seen his tutor, who was a tennis-player himself, and the Provost of his college, who happened to know Colonel Brabazon, and no objection would be made to his leaving before the end of term; they both thought it an opportunity that shouldn't be missed. He didn't see what harm he could come to, and if only, just this once, his father would stretch a point, well, next term, he promised faithfully, he'd work like blazes. It was a very pretty letter. Mrs. Garnet watched her husband read it at the breakfast table; she was undisturbed by the frown on his face. He threw it over to her.

"I don't know why you thought it necessary to tell Nicky something I told you in confidence. It's too bad of you. Now you've thoroughly unsettled him."

"I'm sorry. I thought it would please him to know that Colonel Brabazon had such a high opinion of him. I don't see why one should only tell people the disagreeable things that are said about them. Of course I made it quite clear that there could be no question of his going."

"You've put me in an odious position. If there's anything I hate it's for the boy to look upon me as a spoil-sport and a tyrant."

"Oh, he'll never do that. He may think you rather silly and unreasonable, but I'm sure he'll understand that it's only for his own good that you're being so unkind."

"Christ," said Henry Garnet.

His wife had a great inclination to laugh. She knew the battle was won. Dear, oh dear, how easy it was to get men to do what you wanted. For appearance sake Henry Garnet held out for forty-eight hours, but then he yielded, and a fortnight later Nicky came to London. He was to start for Monte Carlo next morning, and after dinner, when Mrs. Garnet and her elder daughter had left them, Henry took the opportunity to give his son some good advice.

"I don't feel quite comfortable about letting you go off to a place like Monte Carlo at your age practically by yourself," he finished, "but there it is and I can only hope you'll be sensible. I don't want to play the heavy father, but there are three things especially that I want to warn you against: one is gambling, don't gamble; the second is money, don't lend anyone money; and the third is women, don't have anything to do with women. If you don't do any of those three things you can't come to much harm, so remember them well."

"All right, father," Nicky smiled.

"That's my last word to you. I know the world pretty well and believe me, my advice is sound."

"I won't forget it. I promise you."

"That's a good chap. Now let's go up and join the ladies."

Nicky beat neither Austin nor von Cramm in the Monte Carlo tournament, but he did not disgrace himself. He snatched an unexpected victory over a Spanish player and gave one of the Austrians a closer match than anyone had thought possible. In the mixed doubles he got into the semi-final. His charm conquered everyone and he vastly enjoyed himself. It was generally allowed that he showed promise, and Colonel Brabazon told him that when he was a little older and had had more practice with first-class players he would be a credit to his father. The tournament came to an end and the day following he was to fly back to London. Anxious to play his best he had lived very carefully, smoking little and drinking nothing, and going to bed early; but on his last evening he thought he would like to see something of the life in Monte Carlo of which he had heard so much. An official dinner was given to the tennis-players and after dinner with the rest of them he went into the Sporting Club. It was the first time he had been there. Monte Carlo was very full and the rooms were crowded. Nicky had never before seen roulette played except in the pictures; in a maze he stopped at the first table he came to; chips of different sizes were scattered over the green cloth in what looked like a hopeless muddle; the croupier gave the wheel a sharp turn and with a flick threw in the little white ball. After what seemed an endless time the ball stopped and another croupier with a broad, indifferent gesture raked in the chips of those who had lost.

Presently Nicky wandered over to where they were playing *trente et quarante*, but he couldn't understand what it was all about and he thought it dull. He saw a crowd in another room and sauntered in. A big game of baccara was in progress and he was immediately conscious of the tension. The players were protected from the thronging bystanders by a brass rail; they sat round the table, nine on each side, with the dealer in the middle and the croupier facing him. Big money was changing hands. The dealer was a member of the Greek Syndicate. Nicky looked at his impassive face. His eyes were watchful, but his expression never changed whether he won or lost. It was a terrifying, strangely impressive sight. It gave Nicky, who had been thriftily brought up, a peculiar thrill to see someone risk a thousand pounds on the turn of a card and when he lost make a little joke and laugh. It was all terribly exciting. An acquaintance came up to him.

"Been doing any good?" he asked.

"I haven't been playing."

"Wise of you. Rotten game. Come and have a drink."

"All right."

While they were having it Nicky told his friend that this was the first time he had ever been in the rooms.

"Oh, but you must have one little flutter before you go. It's idiotic to leave Monte without having tried your luck. After all it won't hurt you to lose a hundred francs or so."

"I don't suppose it will, but my father wasn't any too keen on my coming at all and one of the three things he particularly advised me not to do was to gamble."

But when Nicky left his companion he strolled back to one of the tables where they were playing roulette. He stood for a while looking at the losers' money being raked-in by the croupier and the money that was won paid out to the winners. It was impossible to deny that it was thrilling. His friend was right, it did seem silly to leave Monte without putting something on the table just once. It would be an experience, and at his age you had to have all the experience you could get. He reflected that he hadn't promised his father not to gamble, he'd promised him not to forget his advice. It wasn't quite the same, was it? He took a hundred-franc note out of his pocket and rather shyly put it on number eighteen. He chose it because that was his age. With a wildly beating heart he watched the wheel turn; the little white ball whizzed about like a small demon of mischief; the wheel went round more slowly, the little white ball hesitated, it seemed about to stop, it went on again; Nicky could hardly believe his eyes when it fell into number eighteen. A lot of chips were passed over to him and his hands trembled as he took them. It seemed to amount to a lot of money. He was so confused that he never thought of putting anything on the following round; in fact he had no intention of playing any more, once was enough; and he was surprised when eighteen again came up. There was only one chip on it.

"By George, you've won again," said a man who was standing near to him.

"Me? I hadn't got anything on."

"Yes, you had. Your original stake. They always leave it on unless you ask for it back. Didn't you know?"

Another packet of chips was handed over to him. Nicky's head reeled. He counted his gains: seven thousand francs. A queer sense of power seized him; he felt wonderfully clever. This was the easiest way of making money that he had ever heard of. His frank charming face was wreathed in smiles. His bright eyes met those of a woman standing by his side. She smiled.

"You're in luck," she said.

She spoke English, but with a foreign accent.

"I can hardly believe it. It's the first time I've ever played."

"That explains it. Lend me a thousand francs, will you? I've lost everything I've got. I'll give it you back in half an hour."

"All right."

She took a large red chip from his pile and with a word of

thanks disappeared. The man who had spoken to him before grunted.

"You'll never see that again."

Nicky was dashed. His father had particularly advised him not to lend anyone money. What a silly thing to do! And to somebody he'd never seen in his life. But the fact was, he felt at that moment such a love for the human race that it had never occurred to him to refuse. And that big red chip, it was almost impossible to realise that it had any value. Oh well, it didn't matter, he still had six thousand francs, he'd just try his luck once or twice more and if he didn't win he'd go home. He put a chip on sixteen, which was his elder sister's age, but it didn't come up; then on twelve, which was his younger sister's, and that didn't come up either; he tried various numbers at random, but without success. It was funny, he seemed to have lost his knack. He thought he would try just once more and then stop; he won. He had made up all his losses and had something over. At the end of an hour, after various ups and downs, having experienced such thrills as he had never known in his life, he found himself with so many chips that they would hardly go in his pockets. He decided to go. He went to the changers' office and he gasped when twenty thousand-franc notes were spread out before him. He had never had so much money in his life. He put it in his pocket and was turning away when the woman to whom he had lent the thousand francs came up to him.

"I've been looking for you everywhere," she said. "I was afraid you'd gone. I was in a fever, I didn't know what you'd think of me. Here's your thousand francs and thank you so much for the loan."

Nicky, blushing scarlet, stared at her with amazement. How he had misjudged her! His father had said, don't gamble; well, he had, and he'd made twenty thousand francs; and his father had said, don't lend anyone money; well, he had, he'd lent quite a lot to a total stranger, and she'd returned it. The fact was that he wasn't nearly such a fool as his father thought: he'd had an instinct that he could lend her the money with safety, and you see, his instinct was right. But he was so obviously taken aback that the little lady was forced to laugh.

"What is the matter with you?" she asked.

"To tell you the truth I never expected to see the money back."

"What did you take me for? Did you think I was a—cocotte?"

Nicky reddened to the roots of his wavy hair.

"No, of course not."

"Do I look like one?"

D

"Not a bit."

She was dressed very quietly, in black, with a string of gold beads round her neck; her simple frock showed off a neat, slight figure; she had a pretty little face and a trim head. She was made up, but not excessively, and Nicky supposed that she was not more than three or four years older than himself. She gave him a friendly smile.

"My husband is in the administration in Morocco, and I've come to Monte Carlo for a few weeks because he thought I wanted a change."

"I was just going," said Nicky because he couldn't think of anything else to say.

"Already!"

"Well, I've got to get up early to-morrow. I'm going back to London by air."

"Of course. The tournament ended to-day, didn't it? I saw you play, you know, two or three times."

"Did you? I don't know why you should have noticed me."

"You've got a beautiful style. And you looked very sweet in your shorts."

Nicky was not an immodest youth, but it did cross his mind that perhaps she had borrowed that thousand francs in order to scrape acquaintance with him.

"Do you ever go to the Knickerbocker?" she asked.

"No. I never have."

"Oh, but you mustn't leave Monte Carlo without having been there. Why don't you come and dance a little? To tell you the truth, I'm starving with hunger and I should adore some bacon and eggs."

Nicky remembered his father's advice not to have anything to do with women, but this was different; you had only to look at the pretty little thing to know at once that she was perfectly respectable. Her husband was in what corresponded, he supposed, to the Civil Service. His father and mother had friends who were Civil Servants and they and their wives sometimes came to dinner. It was true that the wives were neither so young nor so pretty as this one, but she was just as ladylike as they were. And after winning twenty thousand francs he thought it wouldn't be a bad idea to have a little fun.

"I'd love to go with you," he said. "But you won't mind if I don't stay very long. I've left instructions at my hotel that I'm to be called at seven."

"We'll leave as soon as ever you like."

Nicky found it very pleasant at the Knickerbocker. He ate his bacon and eggs with appetite. They shared a bottle of champagne. They danced, and the little lady told him he danced beautifully. He knew he danced pretty well, and of course she was easy to dance with. As light as a feather. She laid her cheek against his and when their eyes met there was in hers a smile that made his heart go pit-a-pat. A coloured woman sang in a throaty, sensual voice. The floor was crowded.

"Have you ever been told that you're very good-looking?" she asked.

"I don't think so," he laughed. "Gosh," he thought, "I believe she's fallen for me."

Nicky was not such a fool as to be unaware that women often liked him, and when she made that remark he pressed her to him a little more closely. She closed her eyes and a faint sigh escaped her lips.

"I suppose it wouldn't be quite nice if I kissed you before all these people," he said.

"What do you think they would take me for?"

It began to grow late and Nicky said that really he thought he ought to be going.

"I shall go too," she said. "Will you drop me at my hotel on your way?"

Nicky paid the bill. He was rather surprised at its amount, but with all that money he had in his pocket he could afford not to care, and they got into a taxi. She snuggled up to him and he kissed her. She seemed to like it.

"By Jove," he thought, "I wonder if there's anything doing."

It was true that she was a married woman, but her husband was in Morocco, and it certainly did look as if she'd fallen for him. Good and proper. It was true also that his father had warned him to have nothing to do with women, but, he reflected again, he hadn't actually promised he wouldn't, he'd only promised not to forget his advice. Well, he hadn't; he was bearing it in mind that very minute. But circumstances alter cases. She was a sweet little thing; it seemed silly to miss the chance of an adventure when it was handed to you like that on a tray. When they reached the hotel he paid off the taxi.

"I'll walk home," he said. "The air will do me good after the stuffy atmosphere of that place."

"Come up a moment," she said. "I'd like to show you the photo of my little boy."

"Oh, have you got a little boy?" he exclaimed, a trifle dashed.

"Yes, a sweet little boy."

He walked upstairs after her. He didn't in the least want to see the photograph of her little boy, but he thought it only civil to pretend he did. He was afraid he'd made a fool of himself; it occurred to him that she was taking him up to look at the photograph in order to show him in a nice way that he'd made a mistake. He'd told her he was eighteen.

"I suppose she thinks I'm just a kid."

He began to wish he hadn't spent all that money on champagne at the night-club.

But she didn't show him the photograph of her little boy after all. They had no sooner got into her room than she turned to him, flung her arms round his neck, and kissed him full on the lips. He had never in all his life been kissed so passionately.

"Darling," she said.

For a brief moment his father's advice once more crossed Nicky's mind and then he forgot it.

Nicky was a light sleeper and the least sound was apt to wake him. Two or three hours later he awoke and for a moment could not imagine where he was. The room was not quite dark, for the door of the bathroom was ajar, and the light in it had been left on. Suddenly he was conscious that someone was moving about the room. Then he remembered. He saw that it was his little friend, and he was on the point of speaking when something in the way she was behaving stopped him. She was walking very cautiously, as though she were afraid of waking him; she stopped once or twice and looked over at the bed. He wondered what she was after. He soon saw. She went over to the chair on which he had placed his clothes and once more looked in his direction. She waited for what seemed to him an interminable time. The silence was so intense that Nicky thought he could hear his own heart beating. Then, very slowly, very quietly, she took up his coat, slipped her hand into the inside pocket and drew out all those beautiful thousand-franc notes that Nicky had been so proud to win. She put the coat back and placed some other clothes on it so that it should look as though it had not been disturbed, then, with the bundle of notes in her hand, for an appreciable time stood once more stock-still. Nicky had repressed an instinctive impulse to jump up and grab her, it was partly surprise that had kept him quiet, partly the notion that he was in a strange hotel, in a foreign country, and if he made a row he didn't know what might happen. She looked at him. His eyes were partly closed and he was sure that she thought he was asleep. In the silence she could hardly fail to hear his regular breathing. When she had reassured herself that her movements had not disturbed him she stepped, with infinite caution, across the room. On a small table in the window a cineraria was growing in a pot. Nicky watched her now with his eyes wide open. The plant was evidently placed quite loosely in the pot, for taking it by the stalks she lifted it out; she put the banknotes in the bottom of the pot and replaced the plant. It was an excellent hiding-place. No one could have guessed that anything was concealed under that richly-flowering plant. She pressed the earth down with her fingers and then, very slowly, taking care not to make the smallest noise, crept across the room, and slipped back into bed.

"Chéri," she said, in a caressing voice.

Nicky breathed steadily, like a man immersed in deep sleep. The little lady turned over on her side and disposed herself to slumber. But though Nicky lay so still his thoughts worked busily. He was extremely indignant at the scene he had just witnessed, and to himself he spoke his thoughts with vigour.

"She's nothing but a damned tart. She and her dear little boy and her husband in Morocco. My eye! She's a rotten thief, that's what she is. Took me for a mug. If she thinks she's going to get away with anything like that, she's mistaken."

He had already made up his mind what he was going to do with the money he had so cleverly won. He had long wanted a car of his own, and had thought it rather mean of his father not to have given him one. After all, a feller doesn't always want to drive about in the family bus. Well, he'd just teach the old man a lesson and buy one himself. For twenty thousand francs, two hundred pounds roughly, he could get a very decent second-hand car. He meant to get the money back, but just then he didn't quite know how. He didn't like the idea of kicking up a row, he was a stranger in an hotel he knew nothing of; it might very well be that the beastly woman had friends there, he didn't mind facing anyone in a fair fight, but he'd look pretty foolish if someone pulled a gun on him. He reflected besides, very sensibly, that he had no proof the money was his. If it came to a showdown and she swore it was hers, he might very easily find himself hauled off to a police-station. He really didn't know what to do. Presently by her regular breathing he knew that the little lady was asleep. She must have fallen asleep with an easy mind, for she had done her job without a hitch. It infuriated Nicky that she should rest so peacefully while he lay awake worried to death. Suddenly an idea occurred to him. It was such a good one that it was only by the exercise of all his self-control that he prevented himself from jumping out of bed and carrying it out at once. Two could play at her game. She'd stolen his money; well, he'd steal it back again, and they'd be all square. He made up his mind to wait quite quietly until he was sure that deceitful woman was sound asleep. He waited for what seemed to him a very long time. She did not stir. Her breathing was as regular as a child's.

"Darling," he said at last.

No answer. No movement. She was dead to the world. Very slowly, pausing after every movement, very silently, he slipped out of bed. He stood still for a while, looking at her to see whether he had disturbed her. Her breathing was as regular as before. During the time he was waiting he had taken note carefully of the furniture in the room so that in crossing it he should not knock against a chair or a table and make a noise. He took a couple of steps and waited, he took a couple of steps more; he was very light on his feet and made no sound as he walked; he took fully five minutes to get to the window, and here he waited again. He started, for the bed slightly creaked, but it was only because the sleeper turned in her sleep. He forced himself to wait till he had counted one hundred. She was sleeping like a log. With infinite care he seized the cineraria by the stalks and gently pulled it out of the pot; he put his other hand in, his heart beat nineteen to the dozen as his fingers touched the notes, his hand closed on them and he slowly drew them out. He replaced the plant and in his turn carefully pressed down the earth. While he was doing all this he had kept one eye on the form lying in the bed. It remained still. After another pause he crept softly to the chair on which his clothes were lying. He first put the bundle of notes in his coat pocket and then proceeded to dress. It took him a good quarter of an hour, because he could afford to make no sound. He had been wearing a soft shirt with his dinner jacket, and he congratulated himself on this, because it was easier to put on silently than a stiff one. He had some difficulty in tying his tie without a looking-glass, but he very wisely reflected that it didn't really matter if it wasn't tied very well. His spirits were rising. The whole thing now began to seem rather a lark. At length he was completely dressed except for his shoes, which he took in his hand; he thought he would put them on when he got into the passage. Now he had to cross the room to get to the door. He reached it so quietly that he could not have disturbed the lightest sleeper. But the door had to be unlocked. He turned the key very slowly; it creaked.

"Who's that?"

The little woman suddenly sat up in bed. Nicky's heart jumped
to his mouth. He made a great effort to keep his head.

"It's only me. It's six o'clock and I've got to go. I was trying
not to wake you."

"Oh, I forgot."

She sank back on to the pillow.

"Now that you're awake I'll put on my shoes."

He sat down on the edge of the bed and did this.

"Don't make a noise when you go out. The hotel people don't
like it. Oh, I'm so sleepy."

"You go right off to sleep again."

"Kiss me before you go." He bent down and kissed her. "You're
a sweet boy and a wonderful lover. *Bon voyage.*"

Nicky did not feel quite safe till he got out of the hotel. The
dawn had broken. The sky was unclouded, and in the harbour
the yachts and the fishing-boats lay motionless on the still water.
On the quay fishermen were getting ready to start on their day's
work. The streets were deserted. Nicky took a long breath of the
sweet morning air. He felt alert and well. He also felt as pleased
as Punch. With a swinging stride, his shoulders well thrown back,
he walked up the hill and along the gardens in front of the Casino
—the flowers in that clear light had a dewy brilliance that was
delicious—till he came to his hotel. Here the day had already
begun. In the hall porters with mufflers round their necks and
berets on their heads were busy sweeping. Nicky went up to his
room and had a hot bath. He lay in it and thought with satisfaction
that he was not such a mug as some people might think. After his
bath he did his exercises, dressed, packed and went down to breakfast. He had a grand appetite. No continental breakfast for him!
He had grape-fruit, porridge, bacon and eggs, rolls fresh from the
oven, so crisp and delicious they melted in your mouth, marmalade
and three cups of coffee. Though feeling perfectly well before, he
felt better after that. He lit the pipe he had recently learnt to
smoke, paid his bill and stepped into the car that was waiting to
take him to the aerodrome on the other side of Cannes. The road
as far as Nice ran over the hills and below him was the blue sea and
the coast-line. He couldn't help thinking it damned pretty. They
passed through Nice, so gay and friendly in the early morning, and
presently they came to a long stretch of straight road that ran by
the sea. Nicky had paid his bill, not with the money he had won
the night before, but with the money his father had given him; he
had changed a thousand francs to pay for supper at the Knickerbocker, but that deceitful little woman had returned him the

thousand francs he had lent her, so that he still had twenty thousand-franc notes in his pocket. He thought he would like to have a look at them. He had so nearly lost them that they had a double value for him. He took them out of his hip-pocket into which for safety's sake he had stuffed them when he put on the suit he was travelling in, and counted them one by one. Something very strange had happened to them. Instead of there being twenty notes as there should have been there were twenty-six. He couldn't understand it at all. He counted them twice more. There was no doubt about it; somehow or other he had twenty-six thousand francs instead of the twenty he should have had. He couldn't make it out. He asked himself if it was possible that he had won more at the Sporting Club than he had realised. But no, that was out of the question; he distinctly remembered the man at the desk laying the notes out in four rows of five, and he had counted them himself. Suddenly the explanation occurred to him; when he had put his hand into the flower-pot, after taking out the cineraria, he had grabbed everything he felt there. The flower-pot was the little hussy's money-box and he had taken out not only his own money, but her savings as well. Nicky leant back in the car and burst into a roar of laughter. It was the funniest thing he had ever heard in his life. And when he thought of her going to the flower-pot some time later in the morning when she awoke, expecting to find the money she had so cleverly got away with, and finding, not only that it wasn't there, but that her own had gone too, he laughed more than ever. And so far as he was concerned there was nothing to do about it; he neither knew her name, nor the name of the hotel to which she had taken him. He couldn't return her money even if he wanted to.

"It serves her damned well right," he said.

This then was the story that Henry Garnet told his friends over the bridge-table, for the night before, after dinner when his wife and daughter had left them to their port, Nicky had narrated it in full.

"And you know what infuriates me is that he's so damned pleased with himself. Talk of a cat swallowing a canary. And d'you know what he said to me when he'd finished? He looked at me with those innocent eyes of his and said: 'You know, father, I can't help thinking there was something wrong about the advice you gave me. You said, don't gamble; well, I did, and I made a packet; you said, don't lend money; well, I did, and I got it back; and you said, don't have anything to do with women; well, I did, and I made six thousand francs on the deal.' "

It didn't make it any better for Henry Garnet that his three companions burst out laughing.

"It's all very well for you fellows to laugh, but you know, I'm in a damned awkward position. The boy looked up to me, he respected me, he took whatever I said as gospel truth, and now, I saw it in his eyes, he just looks upon me as a drivelling old fool. It's no good my saying one swallow doesn't make a summer; he doesn't see that it was just a fluke, he thinks the whole thing was due to his own cleverness. It may ruin him."

"You do look a bit of a damned fool, old man," said one of the others. "There's no denying that, is there?"

"I know I do, and I don't like it. It's so dashed unfair. Fate has no right to play one tricks like that. After all, you must admit that my advice was good."

"Very good."

"And the wretched boy ought to have burnt his fingers. Well, he hasn't. You're all men of the world, you tell me how I'm to deal with the situation now."

But they none of them could.

"Well, Henry, if I were you I wouldn't worry," said the lawyer. "My belief is that your boy's born lucky, and in the long run that's better than to be born clever or rich."

Gigolo and Gigolette

THE bar was crowded. Sandy Westcott had had a couple of cocktails and he was beginning to feel hungry. He looked at his watch. He had been asked to dinner at half-past nine and it was nearly ten. Eva Barrett was always late and he would be lucky if he got anything to eat by ten-thirty. He turned to the barman to order another cocktail and caught sight of a man who at that moment came up to the bar.

"Hullo, Cotman," he said. "Have a drink?"

"I don't mind if I do, sir."

Cotman was a nice-looking fellow, of thirty perhaps, short, but with so good a figure that he did not look it, very smartly dressed in a double-breasted dinner jacket, a little too much waisted, and a butterfly tie a good deal too large. He had a thick mat of black, wavy hair, very sleek and shiny, brushed straight back from his forehead, and large flashing eyes. He spoke with great refinement, but with a Cockney accent.

"How's Stella?" asked Sandy.

"Oh, she's all right. Likes to have a lay-down before the show, you know. Steadies the old nerves, she says."

"I wouldn't do that stunt of hers for a thousand pounds."

"I don't suppose you would. No one can do it but her, not from that height, I mean, and only five foot of water."

"It's the most sick-making thing I've ever seen."

Cotman gave a little laugh. He took this as a compliment. Stella was his wife. Of course she did the trick and took the risk, but it was he who had thought of the flames, and it was the flames that had taken the public fancy and made the turn the huge success it was. Stella dived into a tank from the top of a ladder sixty feet high, and as he said, there were only five feet of water in the tank. Just before she dived they poured enough petrol on to cover the surface and he set it alight; the flames soared up and she dived straight into them.

"Paco Espinel tells me it's the biggest draw the Casino has ever had," said Sandy.

"I know. He told me they'd served as many dinners in July as they generally do in August. And that's you, he says to me."

"Well, I hope you're making a packet."

"Well, I can't exactly say that. You see, we've got our contract and naturally we didn't know it was going to be a riot, but Mr. Espinel's talking of booking us for next month, and I don't mind telling you he's not going to get us on the same terms or anything like it. Why, I had a letter from an agent only this morning saying they wanted us to go to Deauville."

"Here are my people," said Sandy.

He nodded to Cotman and left him. Eva Barrett sailed in with the rest of her guests. She had gathered them together downstairs. It was a party of eight.

"I knew we should find you here, Sandy," she said. "I'm not late, am I?"

"Only half an hour."

"Ask them what cocktails they want and then we'll dine."

While they were standing at the bar, emptying now, for nearly everyone had gone down to the terrace for dinner, Paco Espinel passed through and stopped to shake hands with Eva Barrett. Paco Espinel was a young man who had run through his money and now made his living by arranging the turns with which the Casino sought to attract visitors. It was his duty to be civil to the rich and great. Mrs. Chaloner Barrett was an American widow of vast wealth; she not only entertained expensively, but also gambled. And after all, the dinners and suppers and the two cabaret shows that accompanied them were only provided to induce people to lose their money at the tables.

"Got a good table for me, Paco?" said Eva Barrett.

"The best." His eyes, fine, dark Argentine eyes, expressed his admiration of Mrs. Barrett's opulent, ageing charms. This also was business. "You've seen Stella?"

"Of course. Three times. It's the most terrifying thing I've ever seen."

"Sandy comes every night."

"I want to be in at the death. She's bound to kill herself one of these nights and I don't want to miss that if I can help it."

Paco laughed.

"She's been such a success, we're going to keep her on another month. All I ask is that she shouldn't kill herself till the end of August. After that she can do as she likes."

"Oh, God, have I got to go on eating trout and roast chicken every night till the end of August?" cried Sandy.

"You brute, Sandy," said Eva Barrett. "Come on, let's go in to dinner. I'm starving."

Paco Espinel asked the barman if he'd seen Cotman. The barman said he'd had a drink with Mr. Westcott.

"Oh, well, if he comes in here again, tell him I want a word with him."

Mrs. Barrett paused at the top of the steps that led down to the terrace long enough for the Press representative, a little haggard woman with an untidy head, to come up with her note-book. Sandy whispered the names of the guests. It was a representative Riviera party. There was an English Lord and his Lady, long and lean both of them, who were prepared to dine with anyone who would give them a free meal. They were certain to be as tight as drums before midnight. There was a gaunt Scotch woman, with a face like a Peruvian mask that has been battered by the storms of ten centuries, and her English husband. Though a broker by profession, he was bluff, military and hearty. He gave you an impression of such integrity that you were almost more sorry for him than for yourself when the good thing he had put you on to as a special favour turned out to be a dud. There was an Italian countess who was neither Italian nor a countess, but played a beautiful game of bridge, and there was a Russian prince who was ready to make Mrs. Barrett a princess and in the meantime sold champagne, motor-cars and Old Masters on commission. A dance was in progress and Mrs. Barrett, waiting for it to end, surveyed with a look which her short upper lip made scornful the serried throng on the dance floor. It was a gala night and the dining tables were crowded together. Beyond the terrace the sea was calm and silent. The music stopped and the head waiter, affably smiling, came up to guide her to her table. She swept down the steps with majestic gait.

"We shall have quite a good view of the dive," she said as she sat down.

"I like to be next door to the tank," said Sandy, "so that I can see her face."

"Is she pretty?" asked the Countess.

"It's not that. It's the expression of her eyes. She's scared to death every time she does it."

"Oh, I don't believe that," said the City gentleman, Colonel Goodhart by name, though no one had ever discovered how he came by the title. "I mean, the whole bally stunt's only a trick. There's no danger really, I mean."

"You don't know what you're talking about. Diving from that height in as little water as that, she's got to turn like a flash the moment she touches the water. And if she doesn't do it right she's bound to dash her head against the bottom and break her back."

"That's just what I'm telling you, old boy," said the Colonel, "it's a trick. I mean, there's no argument."

"If there's no danger there's nothing to it, anyway," said Eva Barrett. "It's over in a minute. Unless she's risking her life it's the biggest fraud of modern times. Don't say we've come to see this over and over again and it's only a fake."

"Pretty well everything is. You can take my word for that."

"Well, you ought to know," said Sandy.

If it occurred to the Colonel that this might be a nasty dig he admirably concealed it. He laughed.

"I don't mind saying I know a thing or two," he admitted. "I mean, I've got my eyes peeled all right. You can't put much over on me."

The tank was on the far left of the terrace, and behind it, supported by stays, was an immensely tall ladder at the top of which was a tiny platform. After two or three dances more, when Eva Barrett's party were eating asparagus, the music stopped and the lights were lowered. A spot was turned on the tank. Cotman was visible in the brilliance. He ascended half a dozen steps so that he was on a level with the top of the tank.

"Ladies and gentlemen," he cried out, in a loud clear voice, "you are now going to see the most marvellous feat of the century. Madam Stella, the greatest diver in the world, is about to dive from a height of sixty feet into a lake of flames five foot deep. This is a feat that has never been performed before, and Madam Stella is prepared to give one hundred pounds to anyone who will attempt it. Ladies and gentlemen, I have the honour to present Madam Stella."

A little figure appeared at the top of the steps that led on to the terrace, ran quickly up to the tank, and bowed to the applauding audience. She wore a man's silk dressing-gown and on her head a bathing-cap. Her thin face was made up as if for the stage. The Italian countess looked at her through her *face-à-main.*

"Not pretty," she said.

"Good figure," said Eva Barrett. "You'll see."

Stella slipped out of her dressing-gown and gave it to Cotman. He went down the steps. She stood for a moment and looked at the crowd. They were in darkness and she could only see vague white faces and white shirt-fronts. She was small, beautifully made, with legs long for her body and slim hips. Her bathing-costume was very scanty.

"You're quite right about the figure, Eva," said the Colonel. "Bit undeveloped, of course, but I know you girls think that's quite the thing."

Stella began to climb the ladder and the spot-light followed her. It seemed an incredible height. An attendant poured petrol on the surface of the water. Cotman was handed a flaming torch. He watched Stella reach the top of the ladder and settle herself on the platform.

"Ready?" he cried.

"Yes."

"Go," he shouted.

And as he shouted he seemed to plunge the burning torch into the water. The flames sprang up, leaping high, and really terrifying to look at. At the same moment Stella dived. She came down like a streak of lightning and plunged through the flames, which subsided a moment after she had reached the water. A second later she was at the surface and jumped out to a roar, a storm of applause. Cotman wrapped the dressing-gown round her. She bowed and bowed. The applause went on. Music struck up. With a final wave of the hand she ran down the steps and between the tables to the door. The lights went up and the waiters hurried along with their neglected service.

Sandy Westcott gave a sigh. He did not know whether he was disappointed or relieved.

"Top hole," said the English peer.

"It's a bally fake," said the Colonel, with his British pertinacity. "I bet you anything you like."

"It's over so quickly," said her English ladyship. "I mean, you don't get your money's worth really."

Anyhow it wasn't her money. That it never was. The Italian countess leaned forward. She spoke fluent English, but with a strong accent.

"Eva, my darling, who are those extraordinary people at the table near the door under the balcony?"

"Packet of fun, aren't they?" said Sandy. "I simply haven't been able to take my eyes off them."

Eva Barrett glanced at the table the Countess indicated, and the Prince, who sat with his back to it, turned round to look.

"They can't be true," cried Eva. "I must ask Angelo who they are."

Mrs. Barrett was the sort of woman who knew the head waiters of all the principal restaurants in Europe by their first names. She told the waiter who was at that moment filling her glass to send Angelo to her.

It was certainly an odd pair. They were sitting by themselves at a small table. They were very old. The man was big and stout, with a mass of white hair, great bushy white eyebrows and an enormous white moustache. He looked like the late King Humbert of Italy, but much more like a king. He sat bolt upright. He wore full evening dress, with a white tie and a collar that has been out of fashion for hard on thirty years. His companion was a little old lady in a black satin ball dress, cut very low and tight at the waist. Round her neck were several chains of coloured beads. She wore what was obviously a wig, and a very ill-fitting one at that; it was very elaborate, all curls and sausages, and raven black. She was outrageously made-up, bright blue under the eyes and on the eyelids, the eyebrows heavily black, a great patch of very pink rouge on each cheek and the lips a livid scarlet. The skin hung loosely on her face in deep wrinkles. She had large bold eyes and they darted eagerly from table to table. She was taking everything in, and every other minute called the old man's attention to someone or other. The appearance of the couple was so fantastic in that fashionable crowd, the men in dinner jackets, the women in thin, pale-coloured frocks, that many eyes were turned on them. The staring did not seem to incommode the old lady. When she felt certain persons were looking at her she raised her eyebrows archly, smiled and rolled her eyes. She seemed on the point of acknowledging applause.

Angelo hurried up to the good customer that Eva Barrett was.

"You wished to see me, my lady?"

"Oh, Angelo, we're simply dying to know who those absolutely marvellous people are at the next table to the door."

Angelo gave a look and then assumed a deprecating air. The expression of his face, the movement of his shoulders, the turn of his spine, the gesture of his hands, probably even the twiddle of his toes, all indicated a half-humorous apology.

"You must overlook them, my lady." He knew of course that Mrs. Barrett had no right to be thus addressed, just as he knew that the Italian countess was neither Italian nor a countess and that the English lord never paid for a drink if anyone else would pay for it, but he also knew that to be thus addressed did not displease her. "They begged me to give them a table because they wanted to see Madame Stella do her dive. They were in the profession themselves once. I know they're not the sort of people one expects to see dining here, but they made such a point of it I simply hadn't the heart to refuse."

"But I think they're a perfect scream. I adore them."

"I've known them for many years. The man indeed is a compatriot of mine." The head waiter gave a condescending little laugh. "I told them I'd give them a table on the condition that they didn't dance. I wasn't taking any risks, my lady."

"Oh, but I should have loved to see them dance."

"One has to draw the line somewhere, my lady," said Angelo gravely.

He smiled, bowed again and withdrew.

"Look," cried Sandy, "they're going."

The funny old couple were paying their bill. The old man got up and put round his wife's neck a large white, but not too clean, feather boa. She rose. He gave her his arm, holding himself very erect, and she, small in comparison, tripped out beside him. Her black satin dress had a long train, and Eva Barrett (who was well over fifty) screamed with joy.

"Look, I remember my mother wearing a dress like that when I was in the school-room."

The comic pair walked, still arm in arm, through the spacious rooms of the Casino till they came to the door. The old man addressed a commissionaire.

"Be so good as to direct me to the artistes' dressing-rooms. We wish to pay our respects to Madame Stella."

The commissionaire gave them a look and summed them up. They were not people with whom it was necessary to be very polite.

"You won't find her there."

"She has not gone? I thought she gave a second performance at two?"

"That's true. They might be in the bar."

"It won't 'urt us just to go an' 'ave a look, Carlo," said the old lady.

"Right-o, my love," he answered with a great roll of the R.

They walked slowly up the great stairs and entered the bar. It was empty but for the deputy-barman and a couple sitting in two arm-chairs in the corner. The old lady released her husband's arm and tripped up with outstretched hands.

"'Ow are you, dear? I felt I just 'ad to come and congratulate you, bein' English, same as you are. And in the profession meself. It's a grand turn, my dear, it deserves to be a success." She turned to Cotman. "And this is your 'usband?"

Stella got out of her arm-chair and a shy smile broke on her lips as she listened with some confusion to the voluble old lady.

"Yes, that's Syd."

"Pleased to meet you," he said.

"And this is mine," said the old lady, with a little dig of the elbow in the direction of the tall white-haired man. "Mr. Penezzi. 'E's a count really, and I'm the Countess Penezzi by rights, but when we retired from the profession we dropped the title."

"Will you have a drink?" said Cotman.

"No, you 'ave one with us," said Mrs. Penezzi, sinking into an arm-chair. "Carlo, you order."

The barman came, and after some discussion three bottles of beer were ordered. Stella would not have anything.

"She never has anything till after the second show," explained Cotman.

Stella was slight and small, about twenty-six, with light brown hair, cut short and waved, and grey eyes. She had reddened her lips, but wore little rouge on her face. Her skin was pale. She was not very pretty, but she had a neat little face. She wore a very simple evening frock of white silk. The beer was brought and Mr. Penezzi, evidently not very talkative, took a long swig.

"What was your line?" asked Syd Cotman, politely.

Mrs. Penezzi gave him a rolling glance of her flashing, made-up eyes and turned to her husband.

"Tell 'em who I am, Carlo," she said.

"The 'uman cannon-ball," he announced.

Mrs. Penezzi smiled brightly and with a quick, birdlike glance looked from one to the other. They stared at her in dismay.

"Flora," she said. "The 'uman cannon-ball."

She so obviously expected them to be impressed that they did not quite know what to do. Stella gave her Syd a puzzled look. He came to the rescue.

"It must have been before our time."

"Naturally it was before your time. Why, we retired from the profession definitely the year poor Queen Victoria died. It made quite a sensation when we did too. But you've 'eard of me, of course." She saw the blank look on their faces; her tone changed a little. "But I was the biggest draw in London. At the Old Aquarium, that was. All the swells came to see me. The Prince of Wales and I don't know who all. I was the talk of the town. Isn't that true, Carlo?"

"She crowded the Aquarium for a year."

"It was the most spectacular turn they'd ever 'ad there. Why, only a few years ago I went up and introduced meself to Lady de Bathe. Lily Langtry, you know. She used to live down 'ere. She remembered me perfectly. She told me she'd seen me ten times."

"What did you do?" asked Stella.

"I was fired out of a cannon. Believe me, it was a sensation.

And after London I went all over the world with it. Yes, my dear, I'm an old woman now and I won't deny it. Seventy-eight Mr. Penezzi is and I shall never see seventy again, but I've 'ad me portrait on every 'oardin' in London. Lady de Bathe said to me: My dear, you was as celebrated as I was. But you know what the public is, give 'em a good thing and they go mad over it, only they want change; 'owever good it is, they get sick of it and then they won't go and see it any more. It'll 'appen to you, my dear, same as it 'appened to me. It comes to all of us. But Mr. Penezzi always 'ad 'is 'ead screwed on 'is shoulders the right way. Been in the business since 'e was so 'igh. Circus, you know. Ringmaster. That's 'ow I first knew 'im. I was in a troupe of acrobacks. Trapeze act, you know. 'E's a fine-lookin' man now, but you should 'ave seen 'im then, in 'is Russian boots, and ridin' breeches, and a tight-fittin' coat with frogs all down the front of it, crackin' 'is long whip as 'is 'orses galloped round the ring, the 'andsomest man I ever see in my life."

Mr. Penezzi did not make any remark, but thoughtfully twisted his immense white moustache.

"Well, as I was tellin' you, 'e was never one to throw money about and when the agents couldn't get us bookin's any more 'e said, let's retire. And 'e was quite right, after 'avin' been the biggest star in London, we couldn't go back to circus work any more, I mean, Mr. Penezzi bein' a count really, 'e 'ad 'is dignity to think of, so we come down 'ere and we bought a 'ouse and started a pension. It always 'ad been Mr. Penezzi's ambition to do something like that. Thirty-five years we been 'ere now. We 'aven't done so badly not until the last two or three years, and the slump came, though visitors are very different from what they was when we first started, the things they want, electric light and runnin' water in their bedrooms and I don't know what all. Give them a card, Carlo. Mr. Penezzi does the cookin' 'imself, and if ever you want a real 'ome, you'll know where to find it. I like professional people and we'd 'ave a rare lot to talk about, you and me, dearie. Once a professional always a professional, I say."

At that moment the head barman came back from his supper. He caught sight of Syd.

"Oh, Mr. Cotman, Mr. Espinel was looking for you, wants to see you particularly."

"Oh, where is he?"

"You'll find him around somewhere."

"We'll be going," said Mrs. Penezzi, getting up. "Come and 'ave lunch with us one day, will you? I'd like to show you my old photographs and me press cuttin's. Fancy you not 'avin' 'eard of the 'uman cannon-ball. Why, I was as well known as the Tower of London."

Mrs. Penezzi was not vexed at finding that these young people had never even heard of her. She was simply amused.

They bade one another good-bye, and Stella sank back again into her chair.

"I'll just finish my beer," said Syd, "and then I'll go and see what Paco wants. Will you stay here, ducky, or would you like to go to your dressing-room?"

Stella's hands were tightly clenched. She did not answer. Syd gave her a look and then quickly glanced away.

"Perfect riot, that old girl," he went on, in his hearty way. "Real figure of fun. I suppose it's true what she said. It's difficult to believe, I must say. Fancy 'er drawing all London, what, forty year ago? And the funny thing is, her thinking anybody remembered. Seemed as though she simply couldn't understand us not having heard of her even."

He gave Stella another glance, from the corner of his eye so that she should not see he was looking at her, and he saw she was crying. He faltered. The tears were rolling down her pale face. She made no sound.

"What's the matter, darling?"

"Syd, I can't do it again to-night," she sobbed.

"Why on earth not?"

"I'm afraid."

He took her hand.

"I know you better than that," he said. "You're the bravest little woman in the world. Have a brandy, that'll pull you together."

"No, that'd only make it worse."

"You can't disappoint your public like that."

"That filthy public. Swine who eat too much and drink too much. A pack of chattering fools with more money than they know what to do with. I can't stick them. What do they care if I risk my life?"

"Of course, it's the thrill they come for, there's no denying that," he replied uneasily. "But you know and I know, there's no risk, not if you keep your nerve."

"But I've lost my nerve, Syd. I shall kill myself."

She had raised her voice a little, and he looked round quickly at the barman. But the barman was reading the *Eclaireur de Nice* and paying no attention.

"You don't know what it looks like from up there, the top of the ladder, when I look down at the tank. I give you my word, to-night I thought I was going to faint. I tell you I can't do it again to-night, you've got to get me out of it, Syd."

"If you funk it to-night it'll be worse to-morrow."

"No, it won't. It's having to do it twice kills me. The long wait and all that. You go and see Mr. Espinel and tell him I can't give two shows a night. It's more than my nerves'll stand."

"He'll never stand for that. The whole supper trade depends on you. It's only to see you they come in then at all."

"I can't help it, I tell you I can't go on."

He was silent for a moment. The tears still streamed down her pale little face, and he saw that she was quickly losing control of herself. He had felt for some days that something was up and he had been anxious. He had tried not to give her an opportunity to talk. He knew obscurely that it was better for her not to put into words what she felt. But he had been worried. For he loved her.

"Anyhow Espinel wants to see me," he said.

"What about?"

"I don't know. I'll tell him you can't give the show more than once a night and see what he says. Will you wait here?"

"No, I'll go along to the dressing-room."

Ten minutes later he found her there. He was in great spirits and his step was jaunty. He burst open the door.

"I've got grand news for you, honey. They're keeping us on next month at twice the money."

He sprang forward to take her in his arms and kiss her, but she pushed him away.

"Have I got to go on again to-night?"

"I'm afraid you must. I tried to make it only one show a night, but he wouldn't hear of it. He says it's quite essential you should do the supper turn. And after all, for double the money, it's worth it."

She flung herself down on the floor and this time burst into a storm of tears.

"I can't, Syd, I can't. I shall kill myself."

He sat down on the floor and raised her head and took her in his arms and petted her.

"Buck up, darling. You can't refuse a sum like that. Why, it'll keep us all the winter and we shan't have to do a thing. After all there are only four more days to the end of July and then it's only August."

"No, no, no. I'm frightened. I don't want to die, Syd. I love you."

"I know you do, darling, and I love you. Why, since we married I've never looked at another woman. We've never had money like this before and we shall never get it again. You know what these things are, we're a riot now, but we can't expect it to go on for ever. We've got to strike while the iron's hot."

"D'you want me to die, Syd?"

"Don't talk so silly. Why, where should I be without you? You mustn't give way like this. You've got your self-respect to think of. You're famous all over the world."

"Like the human cannon-ball was," she cried with a laugh of fury.

"That damned old woman," he thought.

He knew that was the last straw. Bad luck, Stella taking it like that.

"That was an eye-opener to me," she went on. "What do they come and see me over and over again for? On the chance they'll see me kill myself. And a week after I'm dead they'll have forgotten even my name. That's what the public is. When I looked at that painted old hag I saw it all. Oh, Syd, I'm so miserable." She threw her arms round his neck and pressed her face to his. "Syd, it's no good, I can't do it again."

"To-night, d'you mean? If you really feel like that about it, I'll tell Espinel you've had a fainting fit. I daresay it'll be all right just for once."

"I don't mean to-night, I mean never."

She felt him stiffen a little.

"Syd dear, don't think I'm being silly. It's not just to-day, it's been growing on me. I can't sleep at night thinking of it, and when I do drop off I see myself standing at the top of the ladder and looking down. To-night I could hardly get up it, I was trembling so, and when you lit the flames and said go, something seemed to be holding me back. I didn't even know I'd jumped. My mind was a blank till I found myself on the platform and heard them clapping. Syd, if you loved me you wouldn't want me to go through such torture."

He sighed. His own eyes were wet with tears. For he loved her devotedly.

"You know what it means," he said. "The old life. Marathons and all."

"Anything's better than this."

The old life. They both remembered it. Syd had been a dancing gigolo since he was eighteen, he was very good-looking in his dark Spanish way and full of life, old women and middle-aged women were glad to pay to dance with him, and he was never out of work. He had drifted from England to the Continent and there he had stayed, going from hotel to hotel, to the Riviera in the winter, to watering-places in France in the summer. It wasn't a bad life they led, there were generally two or three of them together, the men, and they shared a room in cheap lodgings. They didn't have to get up till late and they only dressed in time to go to the hotel at twelve to dance with stout women who wanted to get their weight down. Then they were free till five, when they went to the hotel again and sat at a table, the three of them together, keeping a sharp eye open for anyone who looked a likely client. They had their regular customers. At night they went to the restaurant and the house provided them with quite a decent meal. Between the courses they danced. It was good money. They generally got fifty or a hundred francs from anyone they danced with. Sometimes a rich woman, after dancing a good deal with one of them for two or three nights, would give him as much as a thousand francs. Sometimes a middle-aged woman would ask one to spend a night with her, and he would get two hundred and fifty francs for that. There was always the chance of a silly old fool losing her head, and then there were platinum and sapphire rings, cigarette-cases, clothes and a wrist-watch to be got. One of Syd's friends had married one of them, who was old enough to be his mother, but she gave him a car and money to gamble with, and they lived in a beautiful villa at Biarritz. Those were the good days when everybody had money to burn. The slump came and hit the gigolos hard. The hotels were empty, and the clients didn't seem to want to pay for the pleasure of dancing with a nice-looking young fellow. Often and often Syd passed a whole day without earning the price of a drink, and more than once a fat old girl who weighed a ton had had the nerve to give him ten francs. His expenses didn't go down, for he had to be smartly dressed or the manager of the hotel made remarks, washing cost a packet, and you'd be surprised the amount of linen he needed; then shoes, those floors were terribly hard on shoes, and they had to look new. He had his room to pay for and his lunch.

It was then he met Stella. It was at Evian, and the season was disastrous. She was a swimming instructress. She was Australian, and a beautiful diver. She gave exhibitions every morning and afternoon. At night she was engaged to dance at the hotel. They dined together at a little table in the restaurant apart from the guests, and when the band began to play they danced together to induce the customers to come on to the floor. But often no one followed them and they danced by themselves. Neither of them got anything much in the way of paying partners. They fell in love with one another, and at the end of the season got married.

They had never regretted it. They had gone through hard times. Even though for business reasons (elderly ladies didn't so much like the idea of dancing with a married man when his wife was there) they concealed their marriage, it was not so easy to get an hotel job for the pair of them and Syd was far from being able to earn enough to keep Stella, even in the most modest pension, without working. The gigolo business had gone to pot. They went to Paris and learnt a dancing act, but the competition was fearful and cabaret engagements were very hard to get. Stella was a good ballroom dancer, but the rage was for acrobats, and however much they practised she never managed to do anything startling. The public was sick of the apache turn. They were out of a job for weeks at a time. Syd's wrist-watch, his gold cigarette-case, his platinum ring, all went up the spout. At last they found themselves in Nice reduced to such straits that Syd had to pawn his evening clothes. It was a castastrophe. They were forced to enter for the Marathon that an enterprising manager was starting. Twenty-four hours a day they danced, resting every hour for fifteen minutes. It was frightful. Their legs ached, their feet were numb. For long periods they were unconscious of what they were doing. They just kept time to the music, exerting themselves as little as possible. They made a little money, people gave them sums of a hundred francs, or two hundred, to encourage them, and sometimes to attract attention they roused themselves to give an exhibition dance. If the public was in a good humour this might bring in a decent sum. They grew terribly tired. On the eleventh day Stella fainted and had to give up. Syd went on by himself, moving, moving without pause, grotesquely, without a partner. That was the worst time they ever had. It was the final degradation. It had left with them a recollection of horror and misery.

But it was then that Syd had his inspiration. It had come to him while he was slowly going round the hall by himself. Stella always said she could dive in a saucer. It was just a trick.

"Funny how ideas come," he said afterwards. "Like a flash of lightning."

He suddenly remembered having seen a boy set fire to some petrol that had been spilt on the pavement, and the sudden blaze-up. For of course it was the flames on the water and the spectacular dive into them that had caught the public fancy. He stopped dancing there and then; he was too excited to go on. He talked it over with Stella, and she was enthusiastic. He wrote to an agent who was a friend of his; everyone liked Syd, he was a nice little man, and the agent put up the money for the apparatus. He got them an engagement at a circus in Paris, and the turn was a success. They were made. Engagements followed here and there. Syd bought himself an entire outfit of new clothes, and the climax came when they got a booking for the summer casino on the coast. It was no exaggeration of Syd's when he said that Stella was a riot.

"All our troubles are over, old girl," he said fondly. "We can put a bit by now for a rainy day, and when the public's sick of this I'll just think of something else."

And now, without warning, at the top of their boom, Stella wanted to chuck it. He didn't know what to say to her. It broke his heart to see her so unhappy. He loved her more now even than when he had married her. He loved her because of all they'd gone through together; after all, for five days once they'd had nothing to eat but a hunk of bread each and a glass of milk, and he loved her because she'd taken him out of all that; he had good clothes to wear again and his three meals a day. He couldn't look at her; the anguish in her clear grey eyes was more than he could bear. Timidly she stretched out her hand and touched his. He gave a deep sigh.

"You know what it means, honey. Our connection in the hotels has gone west, and the business is finished, anyway. What there is'll go to people younger than us. You know what these old women are as well as I do; it's a boy they want, and besides, I'm not tall enough really. It didn't matter so much when I was a kid. It's no good saying I don't look my age because I do."

"Perhaps we can get into pictures."

He shrugged his shoulders. They'd tried that before when they were down and out.

"I wouldn't mind what I did. I'd serve in a shop."

"D'you think jobs can be had for the asking?"

She began to cry again.

"Don't, honey. It breaks my heart."

"We've got a bit put by."

"I know we have. Enough to last us six months. And then it'll mean starvation. First popping the bits and pieces, and then the clothes'll have to go, same as they did before. And then dancing in lowdown joints for our supper and fifty francs a night. Out of a job for weeks together. And Marathons whenever we hear of one. And how long will the public stand for them?"

"I know you think I'm unreasonable, Syd."

He turned and looked at her now. There were tears in her eyes. He smiled, and the smile he gave her was charming and tender.

"No, I don't, ducky. I want to make you happy. After all, you're all I've got. I love you."

He took her in his arms and held her. He could feel the beating of her heart. If Stella felt like that about it, well, he must just make the best of it. After all, supposing she were killed? No, no, let her chuck it and be damned to the money. She made a little movement.

"What is it, honey?"

She released herself and stood up. She went over to the dressing-table.

"I expect it's about time for me to be getting ready," she said.

He started to his feet.

"You're not going to do a show to-night?"

"To-night, and every night till I kill myself. What else is there? I know you're right, Syd. I can't go back to all that other, stinking rooms in fifth-rate hotels and not enough to eat. Oh, that Marathon. Why did you bring that up? Being tired and dirty for days at a time and then having to give up because flesh and blood just couldn't stand it. Perhaps I can go on another month and then there'll be enough to give you a chance of looking round."

"No, darling, I can't stand for that. Chuck it. We'll manage somehow. We starved before; we can starve again."

She slipped out of her clothes, and for a moment stood naked⹁ but for her stockings, looking at herself in the glass. She gave her reflection a hard smile.

"I mustn't disappoint my public," she sniggered.

The Happy Couple

I DON'T know that I very much liked Landon. He was a member of a club I belonged to, and I had often sat next to him at lunch. He was a judge at the Old Bailey, and it was through him I was able to get a privileged seat in court when there was an interesting trial that I wanted to attend. He was an imposing figure on the bench in his great full-bottomed wig, his red robes and his ermine tippet; and with his long, white face, thin lips and pale blue eyes, a somewhat terrifying one. He was just, but harsh; and sometimes it made me uncomfortable to hear the bitter scolding he gave a convicted prisoner whom he was about to sentence to a long term of imprisonment. But his acid humour at the lunch-table and his willingness to discuss the cases he had tried made him sufficiently good company for me to disregard the slight malaise I felt in his presence. I asked him once whether he did not feel a certain uneasiness of mind after he had sent a man to the gallows. He smiled as he sipped his glass of port.

"Not at all. The man's had a fair trial; I've summed up as fairly as I could, and the jury has found him guilty. When I condemn him to death, I sentence him to a punishment he richly deserves; and when the court rises, I put the case out of my head. Nobody but a sentimental fool would do anything else."

I knew he liked to talk to me, but I never thought he looked upon me as anything but a club acquaintance, so I was not a little surprised when one day I received a telegram from him saying that he was spending his vacation on the Riviera, and would like to stay with me for two or three days on his way to Italy. I wired that I should be glad to see him. But it was with a certain trepidation that I met him at the station.

On the day of his arrival, to help me out, I asked Miss Gray, a neighbour and an old friend of mine, to dinner. She was of mature age, but charming, and she had a flow of lively conversation which I knew nothing could discourage. I gave them a very good dinner, and though I had no port to offer the judge, I was able to provide him with a good bottle of Montrachet and an even better bottle of Mouton Rothschild. He enjoyed them both; and I was glad of that, because when I had offered him a cocktail, he had refused with indignation.

"I have never understood," he said, "how people presumably

civilised can indulge in a habit that is not only barbarous but disgusting."

I may state that this did not deter Miss Gray and me from having a couple of dry Martinis, though it was with impatience and distaste that he watched us drink them.

But the dinner was a success. The good wine and Miss Gray's sprightly chatter combined to give Landon a geniality I had never before seen in him. It was plain to me that notwithstanding his austere appearance he liked feminine society; and Miss Gray in a becoming dress, with her neat head only just touched with grey and her delicate features, her sparkling eyes, was still alluring. After dinner the judge, with some old brandy still further to mellow him, let himself go, and for a couple of hours held us entranced while he told us of celebrated trials in which he had been concerned. I was not surprised therefore that when Miss Gray asked us to lunch with her next day, Landon, even before I could answer, accepted with alacrity.

"A very nice woman," he said when she had left us. "And a head on her shoulders. She must have been very pretty as a girl. She's not bad now. Why isn't she married?"

"She always says nobody asked her."

"Stuff and nonsense! Women ought to marry. Too many of these women about who want their independence. I have no patience with them."

Miss Gray lived in a little house facing the sea at St. Jean, which is a couple of miles from my own house at Cap Ferrat. We drove down next day at one and were shown into her sitting-room.

"I have a surprise for you," she said to me, as we shook hands. "The Craigs are coming."

"You've got to know them at last."

"Well, I thought it was too absurd that we should live next door to one another, and bathe from the same beach every day and not speak. So I forced myself on them, and they've promised to come to lunch to-day. I wanted you to meet them, to see what you make of them." She turned to Landon. "I hope you don't mind."

But he was on his best behaviour.

"I'm sure I shall be delighted to meet any friends of yours, Miss Gray," he said.

"But they're not friends of mine. I've seen a lot of them, but I never spoke to them till yesterday. It'll be a treat for them to meet an author and a celebrated judge."

I had heard a good deal of the Craigs from Miss Gray during the previous three weeks. They had taken the cottage next to hers, and at first she feared they would be a nuisance. She liked her own company and did not want to be bothered with the trivialities of social intercourse. But she very quickly discovered that the Craigs were as plainly disinclined to strike up an acquaintance with her as she with them. Though in that little place they could not but meet two or three times a day, the Craigs never by so much a glance gave an indication that they had ever seen her before. Miss Gray told me she thought it very tactful of them to make no attempt to intrude upon her privacy, but I had an idea that she was not affronted, a little puzzled rather, that they apparently wanted to know her as little as she wanted to know them. I had guessed some time before that she would not be able to resist making the first advance. On one occasion, while we were walking, we passed them, and I was able to have a good look at them. Craig was a handsome man, with a red, honest face, a grey moustache and thick strong grey hair. He held himself well, and there was a bluff heartiness of manner about him that suggested a broker who had retired on a handsome fortune. His wife was a woman hard of visage, tall and of masculine appearance, with dull, fair hair too elaborately dressed, a large nose, a large mouth and a weather-beaten skin. She was not only plain but grim. Her clothes, pretty, flimsy and graceful, sat oddly upon her, for they would better have suited a girl of eighteen, and Mrs. Craig was certainly forty. Miss Gray told me they were well cut and expensive. I thought he looked commonplace and she looked disagreeable, and I told Miss Gray she was lucky that they were obviously disposed to keep themselves to themselves.

"There's something rather sweet about them," she answered.

"What?"

"They love one another. And they adore the baby."

For they had a child that was not more than a year old; and from this Miss Gray had concluded that they had not long been married. She liked to watch them with their baby. A nurse took it out every morning in a pram, but before this, father and mother spent an ecstatic quarter of an hour teaching it to walk. They stood a few yards apart and urged the child to flounder from one to the other; and each time it tumbled into the parental arms it was lifted up and rapturously embraced. And when finally it was tucked up in the smart pram, they hung over it with charming baby talk and watched it out of sight as though they couldn't bear to let it go.

Miss Gray used often to see them walking up and down the lawn of their garden arm in arm; they did not talk, as though they were so happy to be together that conversation was unnecessary; and it warmed her heart to observe the affection which that dour, unsympathetic woman so obviously felt for her tall, handsome husband. It was a pretty sight to see Mrs. Craig brush an invisible speck of dust off his coat, and Miss Gray was convinced that she purposely made holes in his socks in order to have the pleasure of darning them. And it looked as though he loved her as much as she loved him. Every now and then he would give her a glance, and she would look up at him and smile, and he gave her cheek a little pat. Because they were no longer young, their mutual devotion was peculiarly touching.

I never knew why Miss Gray had never married; I felt as certain as the judge that she had had plenty of chances; and I asked myself, when she talked to me about the Craigs, whether the sight of this matrimonial felicity didn't give her a slight pang. I suppose complete happiness is very rare in this world, but these two people seemed to enjoy it, and it may be that Miss Gray was so strangely interested in them only because she could not quite suppress the feeling in her heart that by remaining single she had missed something.

Because she didn't know what their first names were, she called them Edwin and Angelina. She made up a story about them. She told it to me one day; and when I ridiculed it, she was quite short with me. This, as far as I can remember, is how it went: They had fallen in love with one another years before—perhaps twenty years—when Angelina, a young girl then, had the fresh grace of her teens and Edwin was a brave youth setting out joyously on the journey of life. And since the gods, who are said to look upon young love with kindliness, nevertheless do not bother their heads with practical matters, neither Edwin nor Angelina had a penny. It was impossible for them to marry, but they had courage, hope and confidence. Edwin made up his mind to go out to South America or Malaya or where you like, make his fortune and return to marry the girl who had patiently waited for him. It couldn't take more than two or three years, five at the utmost; and what is that, when you're twenty and the whole of life is before you? Meanwhile of course Angelina would live with her widowed mother.

But things didn't pan out according to schedule. Edwin found it more difficult than he had expected to make a fortune; in fact, he found it hard to earn enough money to keep body and soul together, and only Angelina's love and her tender letters gave him the heart to continue the struggle. At the end of five years he was

not much better off than when he started. Angelina would willingly
have joined him and shared his poverty, but it was impossible for
her to leave her mother, bed-ridden as she was, poor thing, and
there was nothing for them to do but have patience. And so the
years passed slowly, and Edwin's hair grew grey, and Angelina
became grim and haggard. Hers was the harder lot, for she could
do nothing but wait. The cruel glass showed such charms as she
had possessed slipping away from her one by one; and at last she
discovered that youth, with a mocking laugh and a pirouette, had
left her for good. Her sweetness turned sour from long tending
of a querulous invalid; her mind was narrowed by the society
of the small town in which she lived. Her friends married and had
children, but she remained a prisoner to duty.

She wondered if Edwin still loved her. She wondered if he
would ever come back. She often despaired. Ten years went
by, and fifteen, and twenty. Then Edwin wrote to say that his
affairs were settled, and he had made enough money for them to
live upon in comfort, and if she were still willing to marry him,
he would return at once. By a merciful interposition of providence,
Angelina's mother chose that very moment to abandon a world
in which she had made herself a thorough nuisance. But when
after so long a separation they met, Angelina saw with dismay that
Edwin was as young as ever. It's true his hair was grey, but it
infinitely became him. He had always been good-looking, but now
he was a very handsome man in the flower of his age. She felt
as old as the hills. She was conscious of her narrowness, her terrible
provincialism, compared with the breadth he had acquired by
his long sojourn in foreign countries. He was gay and breezy as
of old, but her spirit was crushed. The bitterness of life had warped
her soul. It seemed monstrous to bind that alert and active man to
her by a promise twenty years old, and she offered him his release.
He went deathly pale.

"Don't you care for me any more?" he cried brokenly.

And she realised on a sudden—oh, the rapture, oh, the relief!
—that to him she was just the same as she had ever been. He had
thought of her always as she was; her portrait had been, as it were,
stamped on his heart, so that now, when the real woman stood
before him, she was, to him, still eighteen.

So they were married.

"I don't believe a word of it," I said when Miss Gray had brought
her story to its happy ending.

"I insist on your believing it," she said. "I'm convinced it's true,
and I haven't the smallest doubt that they'll live happily together

to a ripe old age." Then she made a remark that I thought rather shrewd. "Their love is founded on an illusion, perhaps; but since it has to them all the appearance of reality, what does it matter?"

While I have told you this idyllic story of Miss Gray's invention, the three of us, our hostess, Landon and myself, waited for the Craigs to come.

"Have you ever noticed that if people live next door to you, they're invariably late?" Miss Gray asked the judge.

"No, I haven't," he answered acidly. "I'm always punctual myself, and I expect other people to be punctual."

"I suppose it's no good offering you a cocktail?"

"None whatever, madam."

"But I have some sherry that they tell me isn't bad."

The judge took the bottle out of her hands and looked at the label. A faint smile broke on his thin lips.

"This is a civilised drink, Miss Gray. With your permission I will help myself. I never knew a woman yet who knew how to pour out a glass of wine. One should hold a woman by the waist, but a bottle by the neck."

While he was sipping the old sherry with every sign of satisfaction, Miss Gray glanced out of the window.

"Oh, that's why the Craigs are late. They were waiting for the baby to come back."

I followed her eyes and saw that the nurse had just pushed the pram past Miss Gray's house on her way home. Craig took the baby out of the pram and lifted it high in the air. The baby, trying to tug at his moustache, crowed gleefully. Mrs. Craig stood by, watching, and the smile on her face made her harsh features almost pleasant. The window was open, and we heard her speak.

"Come along, darling," she said, "we're late."

He put the baby back in the pram, and they came up to the door of Miss Gray's house and rang the bell. The maid showed them in. They shook hands with Miss Gray, and because I was standing near, she introduced me to them. Then she turned to the judge.

"And this is Sir Edward Landon—Mr. and Mrs. Craig."

One would have expected the judge to move forward with an outstretched hand, but he remained stock-still. He put his eyeglass up to his eye, that eyeglass that I had on more than one occasion seen him use with devastating effect in court, and stared at the newcomers.

"Gosh, what a dirty customer," I said to myself.

He let the glass drop from his eye.

"How do you do," he said. "Am I mistaken in thinking that we've met before?"

The question turned my eyes to the Craigs. They stood side by side close to one another, as though they had drawn together for mutual protection. They did not speak. Mrs. Craig looked terrified. Craig's red face was darkened by a purple flush, and his eyes appeared almost to start out of his head. But that only lasted a second.

" I don't think so," he said in a rich, deep voice. "Of course I've heard of you, Sir Edward."

"More people know Tom Fool than Tom Fool knows," said he.

Miss Gray meanwhile had been giving the cocktail-shaker a shake, and now she handed cocktails to her two guests. She had noticed nothing. I didn't know what it all meant; in fact, I wasn't sure it meant anything. The incident, if incident there was, passed so quickly that I was half inclined to think that I had read into the strangers' momentary embarrassment on being introduced to a celebrated man something for which there was no foundation. I set about making myself pleasant. I asked them how they liked the Riviera and if they were comfortable in their house. Miss Gray joined in, and we chatted, as one does with strangers, of commonplace things. They talked easily and pleasantly. Mrs. Craig said how much they enjoyed the bathing and complained of the difficulty of getting fish at the seaside. I was aware that the judge did not join in the conversation, but looked down at his feet as though he were unconscious of the company.

Lunch was announced. We went into the dining-room. We were only five, and it was a small round table, so the conversation could not be anything but general. I must confess that it was carried on chiefly by Miss Gray and myself. The judge was silent, but he often was, for he was a moody creature, and I paid no attention. I noticed that he ate the omelette with good appetite, and when it was passed round again took a second helping. The Craigs struck me as a little shy, but that didn't surprise me, and as the second course was produced they began to talk more freely. It didn't strike me that they were very amusing people; they didn't seem interested in very much besides their baby, the vagaries of the two Italian maids they had, and an occasional flutter at Monte Carlo; and I couldn't help thinking that Miss Gray had erred in making their acquaintance. Then suddenly something happened: Craig rose abruptly from his chair and fell headlong to the floor. We jumped up. Mrs. Craig threw herself down, over her husband, and took his head in her hands.

"It's all right, George," she cried in an agonised tone. "It's all right!"

"Put his head down," I said. "He's only fainted."

I felt his pulse and could feel nothing. I said he had fainted, but I wasn't sure it wasn't a stroke. He was the sort of heavy, plethoric man who might easily have one. Miss Gray dipped her napkin into water and dabbed his forehead. Mrs. Craig seemed distraught. Then I noticed that Landon had remained quietly sitting in his chair.

"If he's fainted, you're not helping him to recover by crowding round him," he said acidly.

Mrs. Craig turned her head and gave him a look of bitter hatred.

"I'll ring up the doctor," said Miss Gray.

"No, I don't think that's necessary," I said. "He's coming to."

I could feel his pulse growing stronger, and in a minute or two he opened his eyes. He gasped when he realised what had happened, and tried to struggle to his feet.

"Don't move," I said. "Lie still a little longer."

I got him to drink a glass of brandy, and the colour came back to his face.

"I feel all right now," he said.

"We'll get you into the next room, and you can lie on the sofa for a bit."

"No, I'd sooner go home. It's only a step."

He got up from the floor.

"Yes, let's go back," said Mrs. Craig. She turned to Miss Gray. "I'm so sorry; he's never done anything like this before."

They were determined to go, and I thought myself it was the best thing for them to do.

"Put him to bed and keep him there, and he'll be as right as rain to-morrow."

Mrs. Craig took one of his arms and I took the other; Miss Gray opened the door, and though still a bit shaky, he was able to walk. When we arrived at the Craigs' home, I offered to go in and help undress him; but they would neither of them hear of it. I went back to Miss Gray's and found them at dessert.

"I wonder why he fainted," Miss Gray was saying. "All the windows are open, and it's not particularly hot to-day."

"I wonder," said the judge.

I noticed that his thin pale face bore an expression of some complacency. We had our coffee; and then, since the judge and I were going to play golf, we got into the car and drove up the hill to my house.

E

"How did Miss Gray get to know these people?" Landon asked
me. "They struck me as rather second-rate. I shouldn't have
thought they were very much her mark."

"You know women. She likes her privacy, and when they
settled in next door, she was quite decided that she wouldn't have
anything to do with them; but when she discovered that they didn't
want to have anything to do with her, she couldn't rest till she'd
made their acquaintance."

I told him the story she had invented about her neighbours.
He listened with an expressionless face.

"I'm afraid your friend Miss Gray is a sentimental donkey,
my dear fellow," he said when I had come to an end. "I tell you,
women ought to marry. She'd soon have had all that nonsense
knocked out of her if she'd had half a dozen brats."

"What do you know about the Craigs?" I asked.

He gave me a frigid glance.

"I? Why should I know anything about them? I thought they
were very ordinary people."

I wish I knew how to describe the strong impression he gave me,
both by the glacial austerity of his look and by the rasping finality
of his tone, that he was not prepared to say anything more. We
finished the drive in silence.

Landon was well on in his sixties, and he was the kind of golfer
who never hits a long ball but is never off the straight, and he was
a deadly putter, so, though he gave me strokes, he beat me hand-
somely. After dinner I took him in to Monte Carlo, where he
finished the evening by winning a couple of thousand francs at the
roulette table. These successive events put him into a remarkably
good humour.

"A very pleasant day," he said when we parted for the night.
"I've thoroughly enjoyed it."

I spent the next morning at work, and we did not meet till
lunch. We were just finishing when I was called to the telephone.

When I came back, my guest was drinking a second cup of
coffee.

"That was Miss Gray," I said.

"Oh? What had she to say?"

"The Craigs have done a bolt. They disappeared last night.
The maids live in the village; and when they came this morning,
they found the house empty. They'd skipped—the Craigs, the
nurse and the baby—and taken their luggage with them. They left
money on the table for the maids' wages, the rent to the end of
their tenancy and the tradesmen's bills."

The judge said nothing. He took a cigar from the box, examined it carefully and then lit it with deliberation.

"What have you got to say about that?" I asked.

"My dear fellow, are you obliged to use these American phrases? Isn't English good enough for you?"

"Is that an American phrase? It expresses exactly what I mean. You can't imagine I'm such a fool as not to have noticed that you and the Craigs had met before; and if they've vanished into thin air like figments of the imagination, it's a fairly reasonable conclusion that the circumstances under which you met were not altogether pleasant."

The judge gave a little chuckle, and there was a twinkle in his cold blue eyes.

"That was a very good brandy you gave me last night," he said. "It's against my principles to drink liqueurs after lunch, but it's a very dull man who allows his principles to enslave him, and for once I think I should enjoy one."

I sent for the brandy and watched the judge while he poured himself out a generous measure. He took a sip with obvious satisfaction.

"Do you remember the Wingford murder?" he asked me.

"No."

"Perhaps you weren't in England at the time. Pity—you might have come to the trial. You'd have enjoyed it. It caused a lot of excitement; the papers were full of it.

"Miss Wingford was a rich spinster of mature age who lived in the country with a companion. She was a healthy woman for her age; and when she died rather suddenly, her friends were surprised. Her physician, a fellow called Brandon, signed the certificate and she was duly buried. The will was read, and it appeared that she had left everything she had, something between sixty and seventy thousand pounds, to her companion. The relations were very sore, but there was nothing they could do about it. The will had been drawn up by her lawyer and witnessed by his clerk and Dr. Brandon.

"But Miss Wingford had a maid who had been with her for thirty years and had always understood that she would be remembered in the will; she claimed that Miss Wingford had promised to leave her well provided for, and when she found that she wasn't even mentioned, she flew into a passion. She told the nephew and the two nieces who had come down for the funeral that she was sure Miss Wingford had been poisoned, and she said that if they didn't go to the police, she'd go herself. Well, they didn't do that, but they went to see Dr. Brandon. He laughed. He said that Miss Wingford had had a weak heart and he'd been treating her for years. She died just as he had always expected her to die, peacefully in her sleep; and he advised them not to pay any attention to what the maid said. She had always hated the companion, a Miss Starling, and been jealous of her. Dr. Brandon was highly respected; he had been Miss Wingford's doctor for a long time, and the two nieces, who'd stayed with her often, knew him well. He was not profiting by the will, and there seemed no reason to doubt his word, so the family thought there was nothing to do but make the best of a bad job and went back to London.

"But the maid went on talking; she talked so much that at last the police, much against their will, I must admit, were obliged to take notice, and an order to exhume the body was made. There was an inquest, and it was found that Miss Wingford had died from an overdose of veronal. The coroner's jury found that it had been administered by Miss Starling, and she was arrested. A detective was sent down from Scotland Yard, and he got together some unexpected evidence. It appeared that there'd been a good deal of gossip about Miss Starling and Dr. Brandon. They'd been seen a lot together in places in which there was no reason for them to be except that they wanted to be together, and the general impression in the village was that they were only waiting for Miss Wingford to die to get married. That put a very different complexion on the case. To make a long story short, the police got enough evidence in their opinion to justify them in arresting the doctor and charging him and Miss Starling with the murder of the old lady."

The judge took another sip of brandy.

"The case came up for trial before me. The case for the prosecution was that the accused were madly in love with one another and had done the poor old lady to death so that they could marry on the fortune Miss Starling had wheedled her employer into leaving her. Miss Wingford always had a cup of cocoa when she went to bed, which Miss Starling prepared for her; and the counsel for the prosecution claimed that it was in this that Miss Starling had dissolved the tablets that caused Miss Wingford's death. The accused elected to give evidence on their own behalf, and they made a miserable showing in the witness-box. They lied their heads off. Though witnesses testified they had seen them walking together at night with their arms round one another's waists, though Brandon's maid testified she had seen them kissing one another in the doctor's house, they swore they were no more than friends. And oddly enough, medical evidence proved that Miss Starling was *virgo intacta*.

"Brandon admitted that he had given Miss Wingford a bottle of veronal tablets because she complained of sleeplessness, but declared he had warned her never to take more than one, and then only when absolutely necessary. The defence sought to prove that she had taken the tablets either by accident or because she wanted to commit suicide. That didn't hold water for a moment. Miss Wingford was a jolly, normal old lady who thoroughly enjoyed life; and her death occurred two days before the expected arrival of an old friend for a week's visit. She hadn't complained to the maid of sleeping badly—in fact, her maid had always thought her a very good sleeper. It was impossible to believe that she had accidentally taken a sufficient number of tablets to kill herself. Personally, I had no doubt that it was a put-up job between the doctor and the companion. The motive was obvious and sufficient. I summed up and I hope summed up fairly; but it was my duty to put the facts before the jury, and to my mind the facts were damning. The jury filed out. I don't suppose you know that when you are sitting on the bench, you somehow get the feeling of the court. You have to be on your guard against it, to be sure it doesn't influence you. I never had it more strongly than on that day that there wasn't a soul in court who wasn't convinced that those two people had committed the crime with which they were charged. I hadn't the shadow of a doubt that the jury would bring in a verdict of guilty. Juries are incalculable. They were out for three hours, and when they came back I knew at once that I was mistaken. In a murder case, when a jury is going to bring in a verdict of guilty they won't look at the prisoner; they look away. I noticed that three or four of the jurymen glanced at the two prisoners in the dock. They brought in a verdict of not guilty. The real names of Mr. and Mrs. Craig are Dr. and Mrs. Brandon. I'm just as certain as I am that I'm sitting here that they committed between them a cruel and heartless murder and richly deserved to be hanged."

"What do you think made the jury find them not guilty?"

"I've asked myself that; and do you know the only explanation I can give? The fact that it was conclusively proved that they had never been lovers. And if you come to think of it, that's one of the most curious features of the whole case. That woman was prepared to commit murder to get the man she loved, but she wasn't prepared to have an illicit love affair with him."

"Human nature is very odd, isn't it?"

"Very," said Landon, helping himself to another glass of brandy.

The Voice of the Turtle

FOR some time I could not make up my mind if I liked Peter Melrose or not. He had had a novel published that had caused some stir among the rather dreary but worthy people who are always on the lookout for new talent. Elderly gentlemen with nothing much to do but go to luncheon parties praised it with girlish enthusiasm, and wiry little women who didn't get on with their husbands thought it showed promise. I read a few reviews. They contradicted one another freely. Some of the critics claimed that with this first novel the author had sprung into the front rank of English novelists: others reviled it. I did not read it. I have learnt by experience that when a book makes a sensation it is just as well to wait a year before you read it. It is astonishing how many books then you need not read at all. But it chanced that one day I met Peter Melrose. With some misgiving I had accepted an invitation to a sherry party. It was in the top flat of a converted house in Bloomsbury, and I was a trifle out of breath when I had climbed four flights of stairs. My hostesses were two women, much over life-size, in early middle life, the sort of women who know all about the insides of motor-cars and like a good tramp in the rain, but very feminine for all that, fond of eating out of paper bags. The drawing-room, which they called "our workshop", though being of independent means neither had ever done a stroke of work in her life, was large and bare, furnished with rustless-steel chairs, which looked as though they could with difficulty support the very substantial weight of their owners, glass-topped tables and a vast divan covered with zebra-skin. On the walls were bookshelves, and pictures by the better-known English imitators of Cézanne, Braque and Picasso. In the shelves, besides a number of "curious" books of the eighteenth century (for pornography is ageless) there were only the works of living authors, mostly first editions, and it was indeed to sign some of my own that I had been asked to the party.

It was quite small. There was but one other woman, who might have been a younger sister of my hostesses, for, though stout, she was not quite so stout, though tall, not quite so tall, and though hearty, not quite so hearty. I did not catch her name, but she answered to that of Boofuls. The only man besides myself was Peter Melrose. He was quite young, twenty-two or twenty-three, of the middle height, but with an ungainly figure that made him look squat. He had a reddish skin that seemed to fit over the bones of his face too tightly, a rather large semitic nose, though he was not a Jew, and alert green eyes under bushy eyebrows. His brown hair, cut very short, was scurfy. He was dressed in the brown Norfolk jacket and grey flannel trousers that are worn by the art students who wander hatless along King's Road, Chelsea. An uncouth young man. Nor was there much to attract in his manner. He was self-assertive, disputatious and intolerant. He had a hearty contempt for his fellow-writers which he expressed with zest. The satisfaction he gave me by his breezy attacks on reputations which for my part I considered exaggerated, but prudently held my tongue about, was only lessened by the conviction that no sooner was my back turned than he would tear my own to shreds. He talked well. He was amusing and sometimes witty. I should have laughed at his sallies more easily if those three ladies had not been so unreasonably convulsed by them. They roared with laughter at what he said, whether it was funny or whether it was inept. He said many silly things, for he talked without stopping, but he also said some very clever ones. He had a point of view, crude and not so original as he thought, but sincere. But the most striking thing about him was his eager, impetuous vitality; it was like a hot flame that burnt him with an unendurable fury. It even shed a glow on those about him. He had something, if only that, and when I left it was with a slight sense of curiosity at what would come of him. I did not know if he had talent; so many young things can write a clever novel—that means nothing; but it seemed to me that as a man he was not quite like everybody else. He was the sort of person who at thirty, when time had softened his asperity and experience had taught him that he was not quite so intelligent as he thought, would turn into an interesting and agreeable fellow. But I never expected to see him again.

It was with surprise that I received two or three days later a copy of his novel with a very flattering dedication. I read it. It was obviously autobiographical. The scene was a small town in Sussex, and the characters of the upper middle class that strives to keep up appearances on an inadequate income. The humour was rather brutal and rather vulgar. It grated on me, for it consisted chiefly of mockery at people because they were old and poor. Peter Melrose did not know how hard those misfortunes are to bear, and that the efforts made to cope with them are more deserving of sympathy than of derision. But there were descriptions of places, little pictures of a room or impressions of the countryside, which were excellently done. They showed tenderness and a sense of the spiritual beauty of material things. The book was written easily, without affectation, and with a pleasant feeling for the sound of words. But what made it indeed somewhat remarkable, so that I understood why it had attracted attention, was the passion that quivered in the love story of which the plot, such as it was, consisted. It was, as is the modern fashion, more than a trifle coarse and, again in the modern fashion, it tailed off vaguely, without any particular result, so that everything was left in the end pretty much as it had been in the beginning; but you did get the impression of young love, idealistic and yet vehemently sexual; it was so vivid and so deeply felt that it took your breath away. It seemed to throb on the printed page like the pulse of life. It had no reticence. It was absurd, scandalous and beautiful. It was like a force of nature. That was passion all right. There is nothing, anywhere, so moving and so awe-inspiring.

I wrote to Peter Melrose and told him what I thought of his book, then suggested that we might lunch together. He rang me up next day and we made a date.

I found him unaccountably shy when we sat down opposite one another at a table in a restaurant. I gave him a cocktail. He talked glibly enough, but I could not help seeing that he was ill at ease. I gained the impression that his self-assurance was a pose assumed to conceal, from himself, maybe, a diffidence that tortured him. His manners were brusque and awkward. He would say a rude thing and then laugh nervously to cover his own embarrassment. Though he pretended to be so sure of himself he wanted all the time to be reassured by you. By irritating you, by saying the things he thought would annoy, he tried to force from you some admission, tacit it might be, that he was as wonderful as he longed to think himself. He wanted to despise the opinion of his fellows, and nothing was more important to him. I thought him rather an odious young man, but I did not mind that. It is very natural that clever young men should be rather odious. They are conscious of gifts that they do not know how to use. They are exasperated with the world that will not recognise their merit. They have something to give, and no hand is stretched out to receive it. They are impatient for the fame they regard as their due. No, I do not mind odious young men; it is when they are charming that I button up the pockets of my sympathy.

Peter Melrose was extremely modest about his book. He blushed through his reddish skin when I praised what I liked in it, and accepted my strictures with a humility that was almost embarrassing.

He had made very little money out of it, and his publishers were giving him a small monthly allowance in advance of royalties on the next one. This he had just started, but he wanted to get away to write it in peace, and knowing I lived on the Riviera he asked me if I could tell him of a quiet place where he could bathe and live cheaply. I suggested that he should come and spend a few days with me so that he could look about till he found something to suit him. His green eyes sparkled when I proposed this and he flushed.

"Shouldn't I be an awful nuisance?"

"No. I shall be working. All I can offer you is three meals a day and a room to sleep in. It'll be very dull, but you can do exactly what you like."

"It sounds grand. May I let you know if I decide to come?"

"Of course."

We separated, and a week or two later I went home. This was in May. Early in June I received a letter from Peter Melrose asking if I really meant what I said when I invited him to spend a few days with me, whether he might arrive on such and such a date. Well, at the time I had meant it, but now, a month later, I remembered that he was an arrogant and ill-bred youth, whom I had seen but twice and wasn't in the least interested in, and I didn't mean it any longer. It seemed to me very likely that he would be bored stiff. I lived a very quiet life and saw few people. And I thought it would be a great strain on my nerves if he were as rude as I knew he could be, and I as his host felt it behoved me to keep my temper. I saw myself driven beyond endurance, and ringing the bell to have his clothes packed and the car brought round to take him away within half an hour. But there was nothing to do about it. It would save him the cost of board and lodging to spend a short period with me, and if he was tired and unhappy as he said in his letter it might be that it would do him good. I sent him a wire and shortly afterwards he arrived.

He looked very hot and grubby in his grey flannel trousers and brown tweed coat when I met him at the station, but after a swim in the pool he changed into white shorts and a Cochet shirt. He looked then quite absurdly young. He had never been out of England before. He was excited. It was touching to see his delight. He seemed, amid those unaccustomed surroundings, to lose his sense of himself, and he was simple, boyish and modest. I was agreeably surprised. In the evening, after dinner, sitting in the garden, with only the croaking of the little green frogs to break the silence, he began talking to me of his novel. It was a romantic story about a young writer and a celebrated prima donna. The theme was reminiscent of Ouida, the last thing I should have expected this hard-boiled youth to write, and I was tickled; it was odd how the fashion completed the circle and returned generation after generation to the same themes. I had no doubt that Peter Melrose would treat it in a very modern way, but there it was, the same old story as had entranced sentimental readers in the three-volume novels of the eighties. He proposed to set it in the beginning of the Edwardian era, which to the young has already acquired the fantastic, far-away feeling of a past age. He talked and talked. He was not unpleasant to listen to. He had no notion that he was putting into fiction his own day-dreams, the comic and touching day-dreams of a rather unattractive, obscure young man who sees himself beloved, to the admiration of the whole world, by an incredibly beautiful, celebrated and magnificent woman. I always enjoyed the novels of Ouida and Peter's idea did not at all displease me. With his charming gift of description, his vivid, ingenuous way of looking at material things, fabrics, pieces of furniture, walls, trees, flowers, and his power of representing the passion of life, the passion of love, that thrilled every fibre of his own uncouth body, I had a notion that he might well produce something exuberant, absurd and poetical. But I asked him a question.

"Have you ever known a prima donna?"

"No, but I've read all the autobiographies and memoirs that I could find. I've gone into it pretty thoroughly. Not only the obvious things, you know, but I've hunted around in all sorts of byways to get the revealing touch or the suggestive anecdote."

"And have you got what you wanted?"

"I think so."

He began to describe his heroine to me. She was young and beautiful, wilful it is true and with a quick temper, but magnanimous. A woman on the grand scale. Music was her passion; there was music not only in her voice, but in her gestures and in her inmost thoughts. She was devoid of envy, and her appreciation of art was such that when another singer had done her an injury she forgave her when she heard her sing a role beautifully. She was of a wonderful generosity, and would give away everything she possessed when a story of misfortune touched her soft heart. She was a great lover, prepared to sacrifice the world for the man she loved. She was intelligent and well-read. She was tender, unselfish and disinterested. In fact she was much too good to be true.

"I think you'd better meet a prima donna," I said at last.

"How can I?"

"Have you ever heard of La Falterona?"

"Of course I have. I've read her memoirs."

"She lives just along the coast. I'll ring her up and ask her to dinner."

"Will you really? It would be wonderful."

"Don't blame me if you don't find her quite what you expect."

"It's the truth I want."

Everyone has heard of La Falterona. Not even Melba had a greater reputation. She had ceased now to sing in opera, but her voice was still lovely, and she could fill a concert hall in any part of the world. She went for long tours every winter, and in summer rested in a villa by the sea. On the Riviera people are neighbours if they live thirty miles from one another, and for some years I had seen a good deal of La Falterona. She was a woman of ardent temperament, and she was celebrated not only for her singing, but for her love affairs: she never minded talking about them, and I had often sat entranced for hours while with the humour which to me was her most astonishing characteristic she regaled me with lurid tales of royal or very opulent adorers. I was satisfied that there was at least a measure of truth in them. She had been married, for short periods, three or four times, and in one of these unions had annexed a Neapolitan prince. Thinking that to be known as La Falterona was grander than any title, she did not use his name (to which indeed she had no right, since after divorcing him she had married somebody else); but her silver, her cutlery and her dinner-service were heavily decorated with a coat of arms and a crown, and her servants invariably addressed her as *madame la princesse*. She claimed to be a Hungarian, but her English was perfect; she spoke it with a slight accent (when she remembered), but with an intonation suggestive, I had been told, of Kansas City. This she explained by saying that her father was a political exile who had fled to America when she was no more than a child; but she did not seem quite sure whether he was a distinguished scientist who had got into trouble for his liberal views, or a Magyar of high rank who had brought down on his head the imperial wrath because he had had a love affair with an Archduchess. It depended on whether she was just an artist among artists, or a great lady among persons of noble birth.

With me she was not natural, for that she could never have been if she had tried, but franker than with anyone else. She had a natural and healthy contempt for the arts. She genuinely looked upon the whole thing as a gigantic bluff, and deep down in her heart was an amused sympathy for all the people who were able to put it over on the public. I will admit that I looked forward to the encounter between Peter Melrose and La Falterona with a good deal of sardonic amusement.

She liked coming to dine with me because she knew the food was good. It was the only meal she ate in the day, for she took great care of her figure, but she liked that one to be succulent and ample. I asked her to come at nine, knowing that was the earliest hour she dreamt of eating, and ordered dinner for half past. She turned up at a quarter to ten. She was dressed in apple-green satin, cut very low in front, with no back at all, and she wore a string of huge pearls, a number of expensive-looking rings, and on her left arm diamond and emerald bracelets from the wrist to the elbow. Two or three of them were certainly real. On her raven-black hair was a thin circlet of diamonds. She could not have looked more splendid if she had been going to a ball at Stafford House in the old days. We were in white ducks.

"How grand you are," I said. "I told you it wasn't a party."

She flashed a look of her magnificent black eyes at Peter.

"Of course it's a party. You told me your friend was a writer of talent. I am only an interpreter." She ran one finger down her flashing bracelets. "This is the homage I pay to the creative artist."

I did not utter the vulgar monosyllable that rose to my lips, but offered her what I knew was her favourite cocktail. I was privileged to call her Maria, and she always called me Master. This she did, first because she knew it made me feel a perfect fool, and secondly because, though she was in point of fact not more than two or three years younger than I, it made it quite clear that we belonged to different generations. Sometimes, however, she also called me you dirty swine. This evening she certainly might very well have passed for thirty-five. She had those rather large features which somehow do not seem to betray age. On the stage she was a beautiful woman, and even in private life, notwithstanding her big nose, large mouth and fleshy face, a good-looking one. She wore a brown make-up, with dark rouge, and her lips were vividly scarlet. She looked very Spanish and, I suspected, felt it, for her accent at the beginning of dinner was quite Sevillian. I wanted her to talk so that Peter should get his money's worth, and I knew there was but one subject in the world that she could talk about. She was in point of fact a stupid woman who had acquired a line of glib chatter which made people on first meeting her think she was as brilliant as she looked; but it was merely a performance she gave, and you soon discovered that she not only did not know what she was talking about, but was not in the least interested in it. I do not think she had ever read a book in her life. Her knowledge of what was going on in the world was confined to what she was able to gather by looking at the pictures in the illustrated press. Her passion for music was complete bunkum. Once at a concert to which I went with her she slept all through the Fifth Symphony, and I was charmed to hear her during the interval telling people that Beethoven stirred her so much that she hesitated to come and hear him, for with those glorious themes singing through her head, it meant that she wouldn't sleep a wink all night. I could well believe she would lie awake, for she had had so sound a nap during the Symphony that it could not but interfere with her night's rest.

But there was one subject in which her interest never failed. She pursued it with indefatigable energy. No obstacle prevented her from returning to it; no chance word was so remote that she could not use it as a stepping-stone to come back to it, and in effecting this she displayed a cleverness of which one would never have thought her capable. On this subject she could be witty, vivacious, philosophic, tragic and inventive. It enabled her to exhibit all the resources of her ingenuity. There was no end to its ramifications, and no limit to its variety. This subject was herself. I gave her an opening at once and then all I had to do was to make suitable interjections. She was in great form. We were dining on the terrace and a full moon was obligingly shining on the sea in front of us. Nature, as though she knew what was proper to the occasion, had set just the right scene. The view was framed by two tall black cypresses, and all round us on the terrace the orange trees in full flower exhaled their heady perfume. There was no wind, and the candles on the table flamed with a steady softness. It was a light that exactly suited La Falterona. She sat between us, eating heartily and thoroughly appreciating the champagne, and she was enjoying herself. She gave the moon a glance. On the sea was a broad pathway of silver.

"How beautiful nature is," she said. "My God, the scenery one has to play in. How can they expect one to sing? You know, really, the sets at Covent Garden are a disgrace. The last time I sang Juliet I just told them I wouldn't go on unless they did something about the moon."

Peter listened to her in silence. He ate her words. She was better value than I had dared to hope. She got a little tight not only on the champagne but on her own loquaciousness. To listen to her you would have thought she was a meek and docile creature against whom the whole world was in conspiracy. Her life had been one long bitter struggle against desperate odds. Managers treated her vilely, impresarios played foul tricks on her, singers combined to ruin her, critics bought by the money of her enemies wrote scandalous things about her, lovers for whom she had sacrificed everything used her with base ingratitude; and yet, by the miracle of her genius and her quick wits, she had discomfited them all. With joyous glee, her eyes flashing, she told us how she had defeated their machinations and what disaster had befallen the wretches who had stood in her way. I wondered how she had the nerve to tell the disgraceful stories she told. Without the smallest consciousness of what she was doing she showed herself vindictive and envious, hard as nails, incredibly vain, cruel, selfish, scheming and mercenary. I stole a glance now and then at Peter. I was tickled at the confusion he must be experiencing when he compared his ideal picture of the prima donna with the ruthless reality. She was a woman without a heart. When at last she left us I turned to Peter with a smile.

"Well," I said, "at all events you've got some good material."

"I know, and it all fits in so beautifully," he said with enthusiasm.

"Does it?" I exclaimed, taken aback.

"She's exactly like my woman. She'll never believe that I'd sketched out the main lines of the character before I'd ever seen her."

I stared at him in amazement.

"The passion for art. The disinterestedness. She has that same nobility of soul that I saw in my mind's eye. The small-minded, the curious, the vulgar put every obstacle in her way and she sweeps them all aside by the greatness of her purpose and the purity of her ends." He gave a little happy laugh. "Isn't it wonderful how nature copies art? I swear to you, I've got her to the life."

I was about to speak; I held my tongue; though I shrugged a spiritual shoulder I was touched. Peter had seen in her what he was determined to see. There was something very like beauty in his illusion. In his own way he was a poet. We went to bed, and two or three days later, having found a pension to his liking, he left me.

In course of time his book appeared, and like most second novels by young people it had but a very moderate success. The critics had overpraised his first effort and now were unduly censorious. It is of course a very different thing to write a novel about yourself and the people you have known from childhood and to write one about persons of your own invention. Peter's was too long. He had allowed his gift for word-painting to run away with him, the humour was still rather vulgar; but he had reconstructed the period with skill, and the romantic story had that same thrill of real passion which in his first book had so much impressed me.

After the dinner at my house I did not see La Falterona for more than a year. She went for a long tour in South America and did not come down to the Riviera till late in the summer. One night she asked me to dine with her. We were alone but for her companion-secretary, an Englishwoman, Miss Glaser by name, whom La Falterona bullied and ill-treated, hit and swore at, but whom she could not do without. Miss Glaser was a haggard person of fifty, with grey hair and a sallow, wrinkled face. She was a queer creature. She knew everything there was to be known about La Falterona. She both adored and hated her. Behind her back she could be extremely funny at her expense, and the imitation she gave in secret of the great singer with her admirers was the most richly comic thing I have ever heard. But she watched over her like a mother. It was she who, sometimes by wheedling, sometimes by sheer plainness of speech, caused La Falterona to behave herself something like a human being. It was she who had written the singer's exceedingly inaccurate memoirs.

La Falterona wore pale-blue satin pyjamas (she liked satin) and, presumably to rest her hair, a green silk wig; except for a few rings, a pearl necklace, a couple of bracelets and a diamond brooch at her waist, she wore no jewellery. She had much to tell me of her triumphs in South America. She talked on and on. She had never been in more superb voice and the ovations she had received were unparalleled. The concert halls were sold out for every performance, and she had made a packet.

"Is it true or is it not true, Glaser?" cried Maria with a strong South American accent.

"Most of it," said Miss Glaser.

La Falterona had the objectionable habit of addressing her companion by her surname. But it must long since have ceased to annoy the poor woman, so there was not much point in it.

"Who was the man we met in Buenos Ayres?"

"Which man?"

"You fool, Glaser. You remember perfectly. The man I was married to once."

"Pepe Zapata," Miss Glaser replied without a smile.

"He was broke. He had the impudence to ask me to give him back a diamond necklace he'd given me. He said it had belonged to his mother."

"It wouldn't have hurt you to give it him," said Miss Glaser. "You never wear it."

"Give it him back?" cried La Falterona, and her astonishment was such that she spoke the purest English. "Give it him back? You're crazy."

She looked at Miss Glaser as though she expected her there and then to have an attack of acute mania. She got up from the table, for we had finished our dinner.

"Let us go outside," she said. "If I hadn't the patience of an angel I'd have sacked that woman long ago."

La Falterona and I went out, but Miss Glaser did not come with us. We sat on the verandah. There was a magnificent cedar in the garden, and its dark branches were silhouetted against the starry sky. The sea, almost at our feet, was marvellously still. Suddenly La Falterona gave a start.

"I almost forgot. Glaser, you fool," she shouted, "why didn't you remind me?" And then again to me: "I'm furious with you."

"I'm glad you didn't remember till after dinner," I answered.

"That friend of yours and his book."

I didn't immediately grasp what she was talking about.

"What friend and what book?"

"Don't be so stupid. An ugly little man with a shiny face and a bad figure. He wrote a book about me."

"Oh! Peter Melrose. But it's not about you."

"Of course it is. Do you take me for a fool? He had the impudence to send it me."

"I hope you had the decency to acknowledge it."

"Do you think I have the time to acknowledge all the books twopenny-halfpenny authors send me? I expect Glaser wrote to him. You had no right to ask me to dinner to meet him. I came to oblige you, because I thought you liked me for myself, I didn't know I was just being made use of. It's awful that one can't trust one's oldest friends to behave like gentlemen. I'll never dine with you again so long as I live. Never, never, never."

She was working herself into one of her tantrums, so I interrupted her before it was too late.

"Come off it, my dear," I said. "In the first place the character of the singer in that book, which I suppose is the one you're referring to . . ."

"You don't suppose I'm referring to the charwoman, do you?"

"Well, the character of the singer was roughed out before he'd even seen you, and besides, it isn't in the least like you."

"How d'you mean, it's not like me? All my friends have recognised me. I mean, it's the most obvious portrait."

"Mary," I expostulated.

"My name is Maria and no one knows it better than you, and if you can't call me Maria you can call me Madame Falterona or Princess."

I paid no attention to this.

"Did you read the book?"

"Of course I read it. When everyone told me it was about me."

"But the boy's heroine, the prima donna, is twenty-five."

"A woman like me is ageless."

"She's musical to her finger-tips, gentle as a dove, and a miracle of unselfishness; she's frank, loyal and disinterested. Is that the opinion you have of yourself?"

"And what is *your* opinion of me?"

"Hard as nails, absolutely ruthless, a born intriguer and as self-centred as they make 'em."

She then called me a name which a lady does not habitually apply to a gentleman who, whatever his faults, has never had his legitimacy called in question. But though her eyes flashed I could see that she was not in the least angry. She accepted my description of her as complimentary.

"And what about the emerald ring? Are you going to deny that I told him that?"

The story of the emerald ring was this: La Falterona was having a passionate love affair with the Crown Prince of a powerful state and he had made her a present of an emerald of immense value. One night they had a quarrel, high words passed, and some reference being made to the ring she tore it off her finger and flung it in the fire. The Crown Prince, being a man of thrifty habit, with a cry of consternation, threw himself on his knees and began raking out the coals till he recovered the ring. The Falterona watched him scornfully as he grovelled on the floor. She didn't give much away herself, but she could not bear economy in others. She finished the story with these splendid words:

"After that I *couldn't* love him."

The incident was picturesque and had taken Peter's fancy. He had used it very neatly.

"I told you both about that in the greatest confidence and I've never told it to a soul before. It's a scandalous breach of confidence to have put it into a book. There are no excuses either for him or for you."

"But I've heard you tell the story dozens of times. And it was told me by Florence Montgomerie about herself and the Crown Prince Rudolf. It was one of her favourite stories too. Lola Montez used to tell it about herself and the King of Bavaria. I have little doubt that Nell Gwyn told it about herself and Charles II. It's one of the oldest stories in the world."

She was taken aback, but only for an instant.

"I don't see anything strange in its having happened more than once. Everyone knows that women are passionate and that men are as mean as cat's-meat. I could show you the emerald if you liked. I had to have it reset, of course."

"With Lola Montez it was pearls," I said ironically. "I believe they were considerably damaged."

"Pearls?" She gave that brilliant smile of hers. "Have I ever told you about Benjy Riesenbaum and the pearls? You might make a story out of it."

Benjy Riesenbaum was a person of great wealth, and it was common knowledge that for a long time he had been the Falterona's lover. In fact it was he who had bought her the luxurious little villa in which we were now sitting.

"He'd given me a very handsome string in New York. I was singing at the Metropolitan, and at the end of the season we travelled back to Europe together. You never knew him, did you?"

"No."

"Well, he wasn't bad in some ways, but he was insanely jealous. We had a row on the boat because a young Italian officer was paying me a good deal of attention. Heaven knows, I'm the easiest woman in the world to get on with, but I will not be bullied by any man. After all, I have my self-respect to think of. I told him where he got off, if you understand what I mean, and he slapped my face. On deck if you please. I don't mind telling you I was mad. I tore the string of pearls off my neck and flung it in the sea. 'They cost fifty thousand dollars,' he gasped. He went white. I drew myself up to my full height. 'I only valued them because I loved you,' I said. And I turned on my heel."

"You were a fool," I said.

"I wouldn't speak to him for twenty-four hours. At the end of that time I had him eating out of my hand. When we got to Paris the first thing he did was to go to Cartier's and buy me another just as good."

She began to giggle.

"Did you say I was a fool? I'd left the real string in the bank in New York, because I knew I was going back next season. It was an imitation one that I threw in the sea."

She started to laugh, and her laugh was rich and joyous and like a child's. That was the sort of trick that thoroughly appealed to her. She chortled with glee.

"What fools men are," she gasped. "And you, you thought I'd throw a real string into the sea."

She laughed and laughed. At last she stopped. She was excited.

"I want to sing. Glaser, play an accompaniment."

A voice came from the drawing-room.

"You can't sing after all that food you walloped down."

"Shut up, you old cow. Play something, I tell you."

There was no reply, but in a moment Miss Glaser began to play the opening bars of one of Schumann's songs. It was no strain on the voice, and I guessed that Miss Glaser knew what she was doing when she chose it. La Falterona began to sing, in an undertone, but as she heard the sounds come from her lips and found that they were clear and pure she let herself go. The song finished. There was silence. Miss Glaser had heard that La Falterona was in magnificent voice, and she sensed that she wished to sing again. The prima donna was standing in the window, with her back to the lighted room, and she looked out at the darkly shining sea. The cedar made a lovely pattern against the sky. The night was soft and balmy. Miss Glaser played a couple of bars. A cold shiver ran down my spine. La Falterona gave a little start as she recognised the music, and I felt her gather herself together.

> " *Mild und leise wie er lächelt*
> *Wie das Auge er öffnet.*"

It was Isolde's death song. She had never sung in Wagner, fearing the strain on her voice, but this, I suppose, she had often sung in concerts. It did not matter now that instead of an orchestral accompaniment she had only the thin tinkle of a piano. The notes of the heavenly melody fell upon the still air and travelled over the water. In that too romantic scene, in that starry night, the effect was shattering. La Falterona's voice, even now, was exquisite in its quality, mellow and crystalline; and she sang with wonderful emotion, so tenderly, with such tragic, beautiful anguish that my heart melted within me. I had a most awkward lump in my throat when she finished, and looking at her I saw that tears were streaming down her face. I did not want to speak. She stood quite still looking out at that ageless sea.

What a strange woman! I thought then that I would sooner have her as she was, with her monstrous faults, than as Peter Melrose saw her, a pattern of all the virtues. But then people blame me because I rather like people who are a little worse than is reasonable. She was hateful, of course, but she was irresistible.

The Lion's Skin

A GOOD many people were shocked when they read that Captain
Forestier had met his death in a forest fire when trying to save
his wife's dog, which had been accidentally shut up in the house.
Some said they never knew he had it in him; others said it was
exactly what they would have expected of him, but of these some
meant it in one way and some in another. After the tragic occurrence
Mrs. Forestier found shelter in the villa of some people called Hardy,
whose acquaintance she and her husband had but lately made.
Captain Forestier had not liked them, at any rate he had not liked
Fred Hardy, but she felt that if he had lived through that terrible
night he would have changed his mind. He would have realised
how much good there was in Hardy notwithstanding his reputation,
and like the great gentleman he was he would not have hesitated
to admit that he had been mistaken. Mrs. Forestier did not know
how she could ever have kept her reason after the loss of the man
who wa everything in the world to her but for the Hardys' wonderful
kindness. In her immense distress their unfailing sympathy had
been her only consolation. They, who had been almost eye-witnesses
of her husband's great sacrifice, knew as did no one else how wonderful he had been. She could never forget the words dear Fred Hardy
had used when he was breaking the dreadful news to her. It was
these words that had enabled her not only to bear the frightful
disaster, but to face the desolate future with the courage with
which she well knew that brave man, that gallant gentleman, whom
she had loved so well, would have wished her to face it.

Mrs. Forestier was a very nice woman. Kindly people often
say that of a woman when they can say nothing about her, and it
has come to be looked upon as cold praise. I do not mean it as
such. Mrs. Forestier was neither charming, beautiful nor intelligent;
on the contrary she was absurd, homely and foolish; yet the more
you knew her, the more you liked her, and when asked why, you
found yourself forced to repeat that she was a very nice woman.
She was as tall as the average man; she had a large mouth and a
great hooked nose, pale-blue short-sighted eyes and big ugly hands.
Her skin was lined and weather-beaten, but she made up heavily,
and her hair, which she wore long, was dyed golden, tightly
marcelled and elaborately dressed. She did everything she could to
counteract the aggressive masculinity of her appearance, and

succeeded only in looking like a vaudeville artist doing a female impersonation. Her voice was a woman's voice, but you were always expecting her, at the end of the number as it were, to break into a deep bass, and tearing off that golden wig, discover a man's bald pate. She spent a great deal of money on her clothes, which she got from the most fashionable dressmakers in Paris, but though a woman of fifty she had an unfortunate taste for choosing dresses that looked exquisite on pretty little mannequins in the flower of their youth. She always wore a great quantity of rich jewels. Her movements were awkward and her gestures clumsy. If she went into a drawing-room where there was a valuable piece of jade she managed to sweep it on the floor; if she lunched with you and you had a set of glasses you treasured she was almost certain to smash one of them to atoms.

Yet this ungainly exterior sheltered a tender, romantic and idealistic soul. It took you some time to discover this, for when first you knew her you took her for a figure of fun, and then when you knew her better (and had suffered from her clumsiness) she exasperated you; but when you did discover it, you thought yourself very stupid not to have known it all the time, for then it looked out at you through those pale-blue, near-sighted eyes, rather shyly, but with a sincerity that only a fool could miss. Those dainty muslins and spring-like organdies, those virginal silks, clothed not the uncouth body but the fresh, girlish spirit. You forgot that she broke your china and looked like a man dressed up as a woman, you saw her as she saw herself, as indeed she really was if reality were visible, as a dear little thing with a heart of gold. When you came to know her you found her as simple as a child; she was touchingly grateful for any attention you paid her; her own kindness was infinite, you could ask her to do anything for you, however tiresome, and she would do it as though by giving her the opportunity to put herself out you rendered her a service. She had a rare capacity for disinterested love. You knew that never an unkind nor a malicious thought had once passed through her head. And having granted all that you said over again that Mrs. Forestier was a very nice woman.

Unfortunately she was also a damned fool. This you discovered when you met her husband. Mrs. Forestier was American and Captain Forestier was English. Mrs. Forestier was born in Portland, Oregon, and had never been to Europe till the war of 1914, when, her first husband having recently died, she joined a hospital unit and came to France. She was not rich by American standards, but by our English ones in affluent circumstances. From the way

the Forestiers lived I should guess that she had something like
thirty thousand dollars a year. Except that she undoubtedly gave
the wrong medicines to the wrong men, put on their bandages
so that they were worse than useless, and broke every utensil that
was breakable, I am sure that she was an admirable nurse. I do not
think she ever found work too revolting for her to do it without
hesitation; she certainly never spared herself and was surely never
out of temper; I have a notion that many a poor wretch had cause
to bless the tenderness of her heart, and it may be that not a few
took the last bitter step into the unknown with more courage
because of the loving-kindness of her golden soul. It was during
the last year of the war that Captain Forestier came under her care,
and soon after peace was declared they married. They settled down
in a handsome villa on the hills behind Cannes, and in a short
time became conspicuous in the social life of the Riviera. Captain
Forestier played bridge well and was a keen golfer. He was not a
bad tennis-player either. He had a sailing boat, and in the summer
the Forestiers gave very nice parties between the islands. After
seventeen years of marriage Mrs. Forestier still adored her good-
looking husband, and you were unlikely to know her long without
being told in that slow Western drawl of hers the full story of their
courtship.

"It was a case of love at first sight," she said. "He was brought
in when I happened to be off duty, and when I came on and
found him lying in one of my beds, oh, my dear, I felt such a
pang in my heart, for a moment I thought I'd been overworking
and had strained it. He was the handsomest man I'd ever seen in
my life."

"Was he badly wounded?"

"Well, he wasn't exactly wounded. You know, it's a most
extraordinary thing, he went all through the war, he was under
fire for months at a time, and of course he risked his life twenty
times a day, he's one of those men who simply doesn't know what
fear is; but he never even got a scratch. He had carbuncles."

It seemed an unromantic ailment on which to start a passionate
attachment. Mrs. Forestier was a trifle prudish, and though Captain
Forestier's carbuncles greatly interested her she always found it a
little difficult to tell you exactly where they were.

"They were right down at the bottom of his back, even farther
really, and he hated to have me dress them. Englishmen are
curiously modest, I've noticed that over and over again, and it
mortified him terribly. You'd have thought being on those terms,
if you know what I mean, from our first acquaintance it would have

made us more intimate. But somehow it didn't. He was very stand-offish with me. When I used to get to his bed on my round I was so breathless and my heart beat so I couldn't make out what was the matter with me. I'm not naturally a clumsy woman, I never drop things or break anything; but you wouldn't believe it, when I had to give Robert his medicine I used to drop the spoon and break the glass, I couldn't imagine what he must be thinking of me."

It was almost impossible not to laugh when Mrs. Forestier told you this. She smiled rather sweetly.

"I suppose it sounds very absurd to you, but you see I'd never felt that way before. When I married my first husband—well, he was a widower with grown-up children, he was a fine man and one of the most prominent citizens in the state, but somehow it was different."

"And how did you eventually discover that you were in love with Captain Forestier?"

"Well, I don't ask you to believe me, I know it sounds funny, but the fact is that one of the other nurses told me, and as soon as she did of course I knew it was true. I was terribly upset at first. You see, I knew nothing about him. Like all Englishmen he was very reserved and for all I knew he had a wife and half a dozen children."

"How did you find out he hadn't?"

"I asked him. The moment he told me he was a bachelor I made up my mind that by hook or by crook I was going to marry him. He suffered agonies, poor darling; you see, he had to lie on his face almost all the time, lying on his back was torture, and as to sitting down—well, of course he couldn't even think of that. But I don't believe his agonies were worse than mine. Men like clinging silks and soft, fluffy things, you know what I mean, and I was at such a disadvantage in my nurse's uniform. The matron, one of those New England spinsters, couldn't bear make-up, and in those days I didn't make-up anyway; my first husband never liked it; and then my hair wasn't as pretty as it is now. He used to look at me with those wonderful blue eyes of his, and I felt he must be thinking I looked a perfect sight. He was very low and I thought I ought to do all I could to cheer him up, so whenever I had a few minutes to spare I'd go and talk to him. He said he couldn't bear the thought of a strong, husky chap like he was lying in bed week after week while all his pals were in the trenches. You couldn't talk to him without realising that he was one of those men who never feel the joy of life so intensely as when the bullets are whistling all round them, and the next moment may be their last. Danger was a stimulant to him. I don't mind telling you that when I used to write down his temperature on the chart I added a point or two so that the doctors should think him a little worse than he was. I knew he was doing his damnedest to get them to discharge him, and I thought it only fair to him to make sure that they wouldn't. He used to look at me thoughtfully while I talked away and I know he looked forward to our little chats. I told him that I was a widow and had no one dependent on me, and I told him that I was thinking of settling down in Europe after the war. Gradually he thawed a little. He didn't say much about himself, but he began to chaff me, he had a great sense of humour, you know, and sometimes I really began to think he rather liked me. At last they reported him fit for duty. To my surprise he asked me to dine with him on his last evening. I managed to get leave from the matron and we drove in to Paris. You can't imagine how handsome he looked in his uniform. I've never seen anyone look so distinguished. Aristocratic to his finger-tips. Somehow or other he wasn't in such good spirits as I'd expected. He'd been crazy to get back to the front.

" 'Why are you so down to-night?' I asked him. 'After all, you've got your wish at last.'

" 'I know I have,' he said. 'If for all that I'm a bit blue, can't you guess why?'

"I simply dared not think what he meant. I thought I'd better make a little joke.

" 'I'm not very good at guessing,' I said, with a laugh. 'If you want me to know you'd better tell me.'

"He looked down and I could see he was nervous.

" 'You've been most awfully good to me,' he said. 'I can never begin to thank you for all your kindness. You're the grandest woman I've ever known.'

"It upset me terribly to hear him say that. You know how funny Englishmen are; he'd never paid me a compliment before.

" 'I've only done what any competent nurse would have,' I said.

" 'Shall I ever see you again?' he said.

" 'That's up to you,' I said.

"I hoped he didn't hear the tremble in my voice.

" 'I hate leaving you,' he said.

"I really could hardly speak.

" 'Need you?' I said.

" 'So long as my King and Country want me I am at their service.' "

When Mrs. Forestier reached this point her pale blue eyes filled with tears.

" 'But the war can't last for ever,' I said.

" 'When the war ends,' he answered, 'supposing a bullet hasn't put an end to me, I shan't have a penny. I don't even know how I shall set about earning my living. You're a very rich woman; I'm a pauper.'

" 'You're an English gentleman,' I said.

" 'Will that matter very much when the world has been made safe for democracy?' he said bitterly.

"I was just crying my eyes out by then. Everything he said was so beautiful. Of course I saw what he meant. He didn't think it honourable to ask me to marry him. I felt he'd sooner die than let me think he was after my money. He was a fine man. I knew that I wasn't worthy of him, but I saw that if I wanted him I must go out and get him myself.

" 'It's no good pretending I'm not crazy about you, because I am,' I said.

" 'Don't make it harder for me,' he said hoarsely.

"I thought I should die, I loved him so much when he said that. It told me all I wanted to know. I stretched out my hand.

" 'Will you marry me, Robert?' I said, very simply.

" 'Eleanor,' he said.

"It was then he told me that he'd loved me from the first day he ever saw me. At first he hadn't taken it seriously, he thought I was just a nurse and perhaps he'd have an affair with me, and then when he found out that I wasn't that sort of woman and had a certain amount of money, he made up his mind that he must conquer his love. You see, he thought that marriage was quite out of the question."

Probably nothing flattered Mrs. Forestier more than the idea that Captain Forestier had wanted to have a slap and tickle with her. It was certain that no one else had ever made dishonourable proposals to her, and though Forestier hadn't either, the conviction that he had entertained the notion was a never-failing source of satisfaction to her. When they were married Eleanor's relations, hard-bitten Western people, had suggested that her husband should go to work rather than live on her money, and Captain Forestier was all for it. The only stipulation he made was this:

"There are some things a gentleman can't do, Eleanor. Anything else I'll do gladly. God knows, I don't attach any importance to that sort of thing, but if one's a sahib one can't help it, and damn it all, especially in these days, one does owe something to one's class."

Eleanor thought he had done enough in risking his life for his country in one bloody battle after another during four long years, but she was too proud of him to let it be said that he was a fortune-hunter who had married her for her money, and she made up her mind not to object if he found something to do that was worth his while. Unfortunately, the only jobs that offered were not very important. But he did not turn them down on his own responsibility.

"It's up to you, Eleanor," he told her. "You've only got to say the word and I'll take it. It would make my poor old governor turn in his grave to see me do it, but that can't be helped. My first duty is to you."

Eleanor wouldn't hear of it, and gradually the idea of his working was dropped. The Forestiers lived most of the year in their villa on the Riviera. They seldom went to England; Robert said it was no place for a gentleman since the war, and all the good fellows, white men every one of them, that he used to go about with when he was "one of the boys", had been killed. He would have liked to spend his winters in England, three days a week with the Quorn, that was the life for a man, but poor Eleanor, she would be so out of it in that hunting set, he couldn't ask her to make the sacrifice. Eleanor was prepared to make any sacrifice, but Captain Forestier shook his head. He wasn't as young as he had been, and his hunting days were over. He was quite satisfied to breed Sealyhams and raise Buff Orpingtons. They had a good deal of land; the house stood on the top of a hill, on a plateau, surrounded on three sides by forest, and in front they had a garden. Eleanor said he was never so happy as when he was walking round the estate in an old tweed suit with the kennel-man, who also looked after the chickens. It was then you saw in him all those generations of country squires that he had behind him. It touched and amused Eleanor to see the long talks he had with the kennel-man about the Buff Orpingtons; it was for all the world as if he were discussing the pheasants with his head keeper: and he fussed over the Sealyhams as much as if they had been the pack of hounds you couldn't help feeling he would have been so much more at home with. Captain Forestier's great-grandfather had been one of the bucks of the Regency. It was he who had ruined the family so that the estates had to be sold. They had a wonderful old place in Shropshire, they'd had it for centuries, and Eleanor, even though it no longer belonged to them, would have liked to go and see it; but Captain Forestier said it would be too painful to him and would never take her.

The Forestiers entertained a good deal. Captain Forestier was a connoisseur of wines and was proud of his cellar.

"His father was well known to have the best palate in England," said Eleanor, "and he's inherited it."

Most of their friends were Americans, French and Russians. Robert found them on the whole more interesting than the English, and Eleanor liked everybody he liked. Robert did not think the English quite up to their mark. Most of the people he had known in the old days belonged to the shooting, hunting, and fishing set; they, poor devils, were all broke now, and though, thank God, he wasn't a snob, he didn't half like the idea of his wife getting herself mixed up with a lot of *nouveaux riches* no one had ever heard of. Mrs. Forestier was not nearly so particular, but she respected his prejudices and admired his exclusiveness.

"Of course he has his whims and fancies," she said, "but I think it's only loyal on my part to defer to them. When you know the sort of people he comes from you can't help seeing how natural it is he should have them. The only time I've ever seen him vexed in all the years we've been married was when once a gigolo came up to me in the Casino and asked me to dance. Robert nearly knocked him down. I told him the poor little thing was only doing his job, but he said he wasn't going to have a damned swine like that even asking his wife to dance."

Captain Forestier had high moral standards. He thanked God that he wasn't narrow-minded, but one had to draw the line somewhere; and just because he lived on the Riviera he didn't see why he should hob-nob with drunks, wastrels and perverts. He had no indulgence for sexual irregularities and would not allow Eleanor to frequent women of doubtful reputation.

"You see," said Eleanor, "he's a man of complete integrity; he's the cleanest man I've ever known; and if sometimes he seems a little intolerant you must always remember that he never asks of others what he isn't prepared to do himself. After all, one can't help admiring a man whose principles are so high and who's prepared to stick to them at any cost."

When Captain Forestier told Eleanor that such and such a man, whom you met everywhere, and who you thought was rather pleasant, wasn't a pukka sahib, she knew it was no good insisting. She knew that in her husband's judgment that finished him, and she was prepared to abide by it. After nearly twenty years of marriage she was sure of one thing, if of no other, and this was that Robert Forestier was the perfect type of an English gentleman.

"And I don't know that God has ever created anything finer than that," she said.

The trouble was that Captain Forestier was almost too perfect a type of the English gentleman. He was at forty-five (he was two or three years younger than Eleanor) still a very handsome man, with his wavy, abundant grey hair, and his handsome moustache; he had the weather-beaten, healthy, tanned skin of a man who is much in the open air. He was tall, lean and broad-shouldered. He looked every inch a soldier. He had a bluff, hearty way with him and a loud, frank laugh. In his conversation, in his manner, in his dress he was so typical that you could hardly believe it. He was so much of a country gentleman that he made you think rather of an actor giving a marvellous performance of the part. When you saw him walking along the Croisette, a pipe in his mouth, in plus-fours and just the sort of tweed coat he would have worn on the moors, he looked so like an English sportsman that it gave you quite a shock. And his conversation, the way he dogmatised, the platitudinous inanity of his statements, his amiable, well-bred stupidity, were all so characteristic of the retired officer that you could hardly help thinking he was putting it on.

When Eleanor heard that the house at the bottom of their hill had been taken by a Sir Frederick and Lady Hardy she was much pleased. It would be nice for Robert to have as a near neighbour someone of his own class. She made enquiries about them from her friends in Cannes. It appeared that Sir Frederick had lately come into the baronetcy on the death of an uncle and was come to the Riviera for two or three years while he was paying off the death duties. He was said to have been very wild in his youth, he was well on in the fifties when he came to Cannes, but now he was respectably married, to a very nice little woman, and had two small boys. It was a pity that Lady Hardy had been an actress, for Robert was apt to be a little stuffy about actresses, but everyone said that she was very well-mannered and ladylike, and you would never have guessed she had been on the stage. The Forestiers met her first at a tea-party to which Sir Frederick did not go, and Robert acknowledged that she seemed a very decent sort of person; so Eleanor, wishing to be neighbourly, invited them both to luncheon. A day was arranged. The Forestiers had asked a good many people to meet them, and the Hardys were rather late. Eleanor took an immediate fancy to Sir Frederick. He looked much younger than she expected, he hadn't a white hair on his close-cropped head; indeed there was about him something boyish that was rather attractive. He was slightly built, not as tall as she was;

and he had bright friendly eyes and a ready smile. She noticed that he wore the same Guards tie that Robert sometimes wore; he was not nearly so well-dressed as Robert, who always looked as though he had stepped out of a show-window, but he wore his old clothes as though it didn't much matter what one wore. Eleanor could quite believe he had been a trifle wild as a young man. She was not inclined to blame him.

"I must introduce my husband to you," she said.

She called him. Robert was talking to some of the other guests on the terrace, and hadn't noticed the Hardys come in. He came forward and in his affable, hearty way, with a grace that always charmed Eleanor, shook hands with Lady Hardy. Then he turned to Sir Frederick. Sir Frederick gave him a puzzled look.

"Haven't we met before?" he said.

Robert looked at him coolly.

"I don't think so."

"I could have sworn I knew your face."

Eleanor felt her husband stiffen and at once realised that something was going wrong. Robert laughed.

"It sounds terribly rude, but to the best of my belief I've never set eyes on you in my life. We may have run across one another in the war. One met such hosts of fellers, then, didn't one? Will you have a cocktail, Lady Hardy?"

During luncheon Eleanor noticed that Hardy kept looking at Robert. He was evidently trying to place him. Robert was busy with the women on either side of him and did not catch the glances. He was making efforts to entertain his neighbours; and his loud, ringing laugh rang through the room. He was a wonderful host. Eleanor had always admired his sense of social duty; however dull the women were he was sitting next to he gave them of his best. But when their guests had gone Robert's gaiety dropped from him like a cloak from his shoulders. She had a feeling that he was upset.

"Was the princess very boring?" she asked kindly.

"She's a malignant old cat, but otherwise she was all right."

"Funny that Sir Frederick thought he knew you."

"I've never set eyes on him in my life. But I know all about him. I wouldn't have more to do with him than you can help if I were you, Eleanor. I don't think he's quite our mark."

"But it's one of the oldest baronetcies in England. We looked it out in *Who's Who*."

"He's a disreputable scamp. I didn't dream that the Captain Hardy," Robert corrected himself, "the Fred Hardy I used to know about in the old days was now Sir Frederick. I would never have allowed you to ask him to my house."

"Why, Robert? I'm bound to tell you that I thought him very attractive."

For once Eleanor thought her husband rather unreasonable.

"A great many women have found him so, and a pretty penny it's cost them."

"You know how people talk. One really can't believe everything one hears."

He took one of her hands in his and looked earnestly into her eyes.

"Eleanor, you know I'm not the sort of chap to say anything against another chap behind his back, and I'd rather not tell you what I know about Hardy; I can only ask you to take my word for it that he isn't a proper person for you to know."

This was an appeal to which Eleanor was incapable of turning a deaf ear. It thrilled her to know that Robert placed such confidence in her; he knew that in a crisis he had only to call on her loyalty and she would not fail him.

"No one can be better aware than I, Robert," she answered gravely, "of your perfect integrity; I know that if you could tell me you would, but even if you wanted to now I wouldn't let you; it would look as if I had less confidence in you than you have in me. I am willing to abide by your judgment. I promise you that the Hardys shall never darken these doors again."

But Eleanor often lunched out without Robert, when he was playing golf, and so frequently met the Hardys. She was very stiff with Sir Frederick, because if Robert disapproved of him, she must too; but he either did not notice or did not care. He went out of his way to be nice to her and she found him easy to get on with. It was difficult to dislike a man who plainly thought that no woman was better than she should be, but very sweet for all that, and who had such delightful manners. It might be that he was an improper man for her to know, but she couldn't help liking the look in his brown eyes. It was a mocking look, which put you on your guard, and yet so caressing that you could not think he meant you harm. But the more Eleanor heard about him, the more she realised how right Robert was. He was an unprincipled rascal. They mentioned the names of women who had sacrificed everything for his sake and whom he had thrown aside without ceremony the moment he was tired of them. He seemed to have settled down now, and to be devoted to his wife and children; but can the leopard change his spots? It was only too probable that Lady Hardy had more to put up with than anyone suspected.

Fred Hardy was a bad lot. Pretty women, *chemin de fer*, and an unlucky knack for backing the wrong horse had landed him in the bankruptcy court by the time he was twenty-five, and he had been forced to resign his commission. He had seen no shame then in allowing women no longer in their first youth, who found his charm irresistible, to supply his wants. But the war came, he rejoined his regiment, and got a D.S.O. Then he went out to Kenya, where he found occasion to become co-respondent in a notorious divorce case; he left Kenya over some trouble with a cheque. His ideas of honesty were lax. It was unsafe to buy a car or a horse off him, and you did much better to keep away from the champagnes he warmly recommended to you. When with his persuasive charm he put before you a speculation by which you and he would make a fortune, you could only be sure that whatever he made out of it you would make nothing. He was in turn a motor-salesman, an outside broker, a commission agent and an actor. Were there any justice in the world he should have ended if not in gaol at least in the gutter. But by one of fate's monstrous tricks, having at last inherited his baronetcy and an adequate income, having married when well over forty a pretty, clever wife to whom were in due course born two healthy and handsome children, the future offered him affluence, position and respectability. He had never taken life any more seriously than he took women, and life had been as kind to him as women. If he thought of his past it was with complacency; he had had a good time, he had enjoyed his ups and downs; and now, with good health and a clear conscience, he was prepared to settle down as a country gentleman, damn it, bring up the kids as kids should be brought up; and when the old buffer who sat for his constituency pegged out, by George, go into Parliament himself.

"I could tell them a thing or two they don't know," he said.

He was probably right, but he did not stop to reflect that perhaps they were not things they much wanted to know.

One afternoon, about sunset, Fred Hardy went into one of the bars on the Croisette. He was a sociable creature and did not care to drink alone, so he looked around to see if there were anyone he knew. He caught sight of Robert, who had been playing golf and was waiting there for Eleanor.

"Hulloa, Bob, what about having a tiddly?"

Robert gave a start. No one on the Riviera called him Bob. When he saw who it was he answered stiffly:

"I've got a drink, thanks."

"Have another. My old lady don't approve of my drinking

between meals, but when I can manage to get away from her I generally slip in and have one about this time. I don't know what you think about it, but my feeling is that God made six o'clock for man to have a drink at."

He flung himself into a great leather arm-chair next to the one Robert was sitting in and called a waiter. He gave Robert his good-natured, engaging smile.

"A lot of water has passed under the bridges since first we met, old boy, hasn't it?"

Robert, frowning a little, shot a look at him which an observer might have described as wary.

"I don't know exactly what you mean. To the best of my belief we met for the first time three or four weeks ago when you and your wife were good enough to come and have lunch with us."

"Come off it, Bob. I knew I'd seen you before. I was puzzled at first and then it flashed across me. You were the car-washer at that garage off Bruton Street where I used to keep my car."

Captain Forestier gave a hearty laugh.

"I'm sorry, but you've made a mistake. I never heard anything so ridiculous."

"I've got a damned good memory and I never forget a face. I bet you haven't forgotten me either. Many's the half-crown I've given you for fetching the car away from my flat when I didn't want to be bothered to bring it round to the garage myself."

"You're talking absolute rot. I'd never seen you in my life till you came to my house."

Hardy grinned cheerfully.

"You know I've always been a Kodak-fiend. I've got albums of snaps that I've taken at one time and another. Would it surprise you to learn that I've found a snap of you standing by a two-seater I'd just bought? A damned good-looking fellow you were in those days even though you had overalls on and your face was none too clean. Of course you've broadened out, your hair's grey and you've got a moustache, but it's the same chap. Unmistakably."

Captain Forestier looked at him coolly.

"You must have been misled by an accidental resemblance. It was somebody else you gave your half-crowns to."

"Well, where were you then, if you weren't a car-washer at the Bruton Garage between 1913 and 1914?"

"I was in India."

"With your regiment?" asked Fred Hardy with another grin.

"I was shooting."

"You liar."

Robert flushed deeply.

"This isn't quite the place to choose for a scrap, but if you think I'm going to stay here to be insulted by a drunken swine like you, you're mistaken."

"Wouldn't you like to hear what else I know about you? You know how things come back to one, and I've remembered quite a lot."

"I'm not in the least interested. I tell you that you're making an absolute mistake. You're confusing me with somebody else."

But he made no attempt to go.

"You were a bit of a slacker even in those days. I remember once, when I was going into the country early, I'd told you to have my car washed by nine and it wasn't ready, so I kicked up a row and old Thompson told me then your father had been a pal of his and he'd taken you on out of charity because you were down and out. Your father had been a wine waiter at one of the clubs, White's or Brooks's, I forget which, and you'd been a page-boy there yourself. You enlisted in the Coldstream Guards, if I remember right, and some chap bought you out and made you his valet."

"It's too fantastic," said Robert scornfully.

"And I remember, when I was home on leave once and went to the garage, old Thompson told me you'd enlisted in the A.S.C. You weren't going to take any more risks than you could help, were you? You've been drawing the long bow a bit, haven't you, with all those stories I hear of your gallantry in the trenches? I suppose you did get a commission, or is that a fake too?"

"Of course I got a commission."

"Well, a lot of funny people did in those days, but you know, old boy, if it was in the A.S.C. I wouldn't wear a Guards tie if I were you."

Captain Forestier instinctively put his hand up to his tie, and Fred Hardy, watching him with his mocking eyes, was pretty sure that notwithstanding his tan he went white.

"It's no business of yours what tie I wear."

"Don't get snotty, old boy. There's no reason to get up on your hind legs. I've got the goods on you, but I'm not going to give you away, so why don't you come clean?"

"I've got nothing to come clean about. I tell you it's all an absurd mistake. And I should tell you that if I find that you've been spreading these lying stories about me, I shall immediately start proceedings for slander."

"Stow it, Bob. I'm not going to spread any stories. You don't

F

think I care? I think the whole thing's rather a lark. I've got no ill-feeling towards you. I've been a bit of an adventurer myself; I admire you for carrying off such a stupendous bluff. Starting as a page-boy and then being a trooper, a valet and a car-washer; and here you are, a fine gentleman, with a grand house, entertaining all the big bugs of the Riviera, winning golf tournaments, vice-president of the Sailing Club, and I don't know what all. You're It in Cannes and no mistake. It's stupendous. I've done some pretty rum things in my day, but the nerve you must have; old boy, I take off my hat to you."

"I wish I deserved your compliments. I don't. My father was in the Indian cavalry and I was at least born a gentleman. I may not have had a very distinguished career, but I certainly have nothing to be ashamed of."

"Oh, come off it, Bob. I shan't split, you know, not even to my old lady. I never tell women anything that they don't know already. Believe me, I'd have got into even worse scrapes than I have if I hadn't made a rule of that. I should have thought you'd be glad to have someone around that you could be yourself with. Isn't it a strain never to let up? Silly of you to keep me at arm's length. I haven't got anything on you, old boy. It's true I'm a bart and a landed proprietor now, but I've been in some pretty tight places in my time, and it's a wonder to me that I've kept out of gaol."

"It's a wonder to a good many other people."

Fred Hardy broke into a guffaw.

"That's one on me, old boy. All the same, if you don't mind my saying so, I think it was a bit thick your telling your wife I wasn't a proper person for her to associate with."

"I never said anything of the sort."

"Oh yes, you did. She's a grand old girl, but a bit garrulous, or am I mistaken?"

"I'm not prepared to discuss my wife with a man like you," said Captain Forestier, coldly.

"Oh, don't be so damned gentlemanly with me, Bob. We're a couple of bums and that's all there is to it. We could have some grand times together if you'd only have a little sense. You're a liar, a humbug and a cheat, but you seem to be very decent to your wife, and that's something in your favour. She just dotes upon you, doesn't she? Funny, women are. She's a very nice woman, Bob."

Robert's face grew red, he clenched his fist and half rose from his chair.

"Damn you, stop talking about my wife. If you mention her name again I swear I'll knock you down."

"Oh no, you won't. You're too great a gentleman to hit a feller smaller than yourself."

Hardy had said these words mockingly, watching Robert, and quite ready to dodge if that great fist struck out; he was astounded at their effect. Robert sank back into his chair and unclenched his fist.

"You're right. But only a mean hound would trade on it."

The reply was so theatrical that Fred Hardy began to chuckle, but then he saw that the man meant it. He was deadly serious. Fred Hardy was no fool; he could hardly have lived for twenty-five years on his wits in tolerable comfort unless he had had them all about him. And now, in amazement, staring at that heavy powerful man, who looked so like the typical English sportsman, sunk back in the chair, he had a sudden flash of comprehension. He was no common swindler who had got hold of a silly woman to keep him in luxury and idleness. She was only a means to a greater end. He had been captivated by an ideal and in pursuit of it had stuck at nothing. Perhaps the notion had come to him when he was a page-boy in a smart club; the members, with their lounging ease, their casual manner, may have seemed very wonderful to him; and afterwards as a trooper, as a valet, as a car-washer, the many men he ran across, belonging to a different world and seen through a haze of hero-worship, had filled him perhaps with admiration and envy. He wanted to be like them. He wanted to be one of them. That was the ideal that haunted his dreams. He wanted—it was grotesque, it was pathetic—he wanted to be a gentleman. The war, with the commission it brought him, gave him his chance. Eleanor's money provided the means. That wretched fellow had spent twenty years pretending to be something the only value of which was that it wasn't a pretence. That was grotesque too; that was pathetic. Without meaning to, Fred Hardy uttered the thought that passed through his head.

"Poor old chap," he said.

Forestier looked at him quickly. He could not understand what those words meant nor the tone in which they were said. He flushed.

"What d'you mean by that?"

"Nothing. Nothing."

"I don't think we need continue this conversation. Apparently there's nothing I can say to persuade you that you're mistaken. I can only repeat that there's not a word of truth in it. I am not the fellow you think I am."

"All right, old boy, have it your own way."

Forestier called the waiter.

"D'you want me to pay for your drink?" he asked icily.

"Yes, old boy."

Forestier somewhat grandly gave the waiter a note and told him to keep the change, then without a word, without giving Fred Hardy another look, stalked out of the bar.

They did not meet again till the night on which Robert Forestier lost his life.

The winter passed into spring, and the gardens on the Riviera were ablaze with colour. The hillsides were primly gay with wild flowers. The spring passed into summer. In the towns along the Riviera the streets were hot with a bright, eager heat that made the blood run faster; and women walked about in great straw hats and pyjamas. The beaches were crowded. Men in trunks and women almost naked lay in the sun. In the evening the bars on the Croisette were thronged by a restless, chattering crowd as many-coloured as the flowers of spring. It had not rained for weeks. There had been several forest fires along the coast, and Robert Forestier in his hearty, joking way had several times said that they would stand a pretty thin chance if they had a fire in their woods. One or two people had advised him to cut down some of the trees at the back of his house; but he couldn't bear to: they had been in poor condition when the Forestiers bought the place, but now that the dead wood had been cut away year by year, that they had been given air and kept clean of pests, they were magnificent.

"Why, it would be like having my leg chopped off to cut one of 'em down. They must be the best part of a hundred years old."

On the fourteenth of July the Forestiers went over to a gala dinner at Monte Carlo, and they gave their staff leave to go to Cannes. It was the national holiday, and in Cannes they danced in the open air under the plane trees, there were fireworks, and from far and near the people came in to have a good time. The Hardys had sent their servants out too, but they were sitting at home, and their two little boys were in bed. Fred was playing patience and Lady Hardy was working at a piece of tapestry to cover a chair. Suddenly there was a ring of the bell and a loud knocking on the door.

"Who the devil's that?"

Hardy went to the door and found a boy who told him that fire had broken out in the Forestiers' woods. Some men had gone up from the village and were fighting it, but they needed all the help they could get, and would he come.

"Of course I'll come." He hurried back to his wife and told her.

"Wake the kids and let them come up and see the fun. By George, after all this drought it'll be a blaze."

He bolted out. The boy told him they had telephoned to the police station and they were going to send along the soldiers. Someone was trying to get through to Monte Carlo and let Captain Forestier know.

"It'll take him an hour to get here," said Hardy.

As they ran they saw the glow in the sky, and when they came to the top of the hill, the leaping flames. There was no water and the only thing was to try to beat them out. Already a number of men were at work. Hardy joined them. But you had no sooner beat out the flames in one bush than another began to crackle and before you could look had turned into a fiery torch. The heat was terrific, and the workers, unable to support it, were slowly driven back. A breeze was blowing, and the sparks were carried from tree to bush. After weeks of drought everything was as dry as tinder, and the moment a spark fell the tree, the bush, went up in flames. If it had not been terrifying, it would have been awe-inspiring to see a great fir-tree, sixty feet high, blazing like match-wood. The fire roared like the fire in a factory furnace. The best way to put a stop to it was by cutting down trees and brushwood, but the men were few, and but two or three had axes. The only hope was in the troops, who were used to dealing with the forest fires, and the troops did not come.

"Unless they get here soon we shall never save the house," said Hardy.

He caught sight of his wife, who had come up with the two boys, and waved to them. Already he was black with grime, and the sweat was pouring down his face. Lady Hardy ran up.

"Oh, Fred, the dogs and the chickens."

"By George, yes."

The kennels and the chicken-run were at the back of the house, in a clearing that had been cut in the woods, and the wretched animals were already frantic with terror. Hardy let them out and they rushed to safety. They could only be left to shift for themselves. They must be rounded up later. The blaze could be seen now from far away. But the troops did not come, and the small body of helpers were powerless against the advancing flames.

"If those damned soldiers don't get here soon the house is for it," said Hardy. "I think we'd better get what we can out of it."

It was a stone house, but there were wooden verandahs all round it, and they would burn like kindling. The Forestiers' servants had come by now. He got them together, his wife gave a hand,

and the two boys; they carried out on to the lawn in front such things as were portable, linen and silver, clothes, ornaments, pictures, pieces of furniture. At last the troops came, two lorry-loads of them, and set about systematically digging trenches and felling trees. There was an officer in charge and Hardy, pointing out the danger to the house, begged him first of all to cut down the trees that surrounded it.

"The house must look after itself," he said. "I've got to prevent the fire spreading beyond the hill."

The lights of a car were seen speeding along the winding road, and a few minutes later Forestier and his wife sprang out of it.

"Where are the dogs?" he cried.

"I've let them out," said Hardy.

"Oh, it's you."

At first in that filthy fellow, his face begrimed with soot and sweat, he had not recognised Fred Hardy. He frowned angrily.

"I thought the house might catch. I've got everything out I could."

Forestier looked at the blazing forest.

"Well, that's the end of my trees," he said.

"The soldiers are working on the side of the hill. They're trying to save the next property. We'd better go along and see if we can save anything."

"I'll go. You needn't," Forestier cried irritably.

On a sudden Eleanor gave an anguished cry.

"Oh, look. The house."

From where they stood they could see a verandah at the back suddenly burst into flames.

"That's all right, Eleanor. The house can't burn. It'll only get the woodwork. Take my coat; I'm going along to help the soldiers."

He took off his dinner jacket and handed it to his wife.

"I'll come with you," said Hardy. "Mrs. Forestier, you'd better go along to where your things are. I think we've got everything out that's valuable."

"Thank heaven, I was wearing most of my jewellery."

Lady Hardy was a woman of sense.

"Mrs. Forestier, let's get the servants together and carry what we can down to our house."

The two men walked towards where the soldiers were at work.

"It's very decent of you to have got that stuff out of my house," said Robert, stiffly.

"Not at all," answered Fred Hardy.

They had not gone far when they heard somebody calling. They looked round and vaguely saw a woman running after them.

"*Monsieur, Monsieur.*"

They stopped and the woman, her arms outstretched, rushed up. It was Eleanor's maid. She was distraught.

"*La petite Judy.* Judy. I shut her up when we went out. She's on heat. I put her in the servants' bathroom."

"My God!" cried Forestier.

"What is it?"

"Eleanor's dog. I must save her at any cost."

He turned round and started to run back to the house. Hardy caught hold of his arm to hold him.

"Don't be a damned fool, Bob. The house is burning. You can't go into it."

Forestier struggled to release himself.

"Let me go, damn you. D'you think I'm going to let a dog be burned alive?"

"Oh, shut up. This is no time for play-acting!"

Forestier shook Hardy off, but Hardy sprang on him and seized him round the middle. Forestier with his clenched fist hit Hardy in the face as hard as he could. Hardy staggered, releasing his hold, and Forestier hit him again; Hardy fell to the ground.

"You rotten bounder. I'll show you how a gentleman behaves."

Fred Hardy picked himself up slowly and felt his face. It hurt him.

"God, the black eye I'm going to have to-morrow." He was shaken and a trifle dazed. The maid suddenly broke into a storm of hysterical tears. "Shut up, you slut," he cried crossly. "And don't say a word to your mistress."

Forestier was nowhere to be seen. It was more than an hour before they were able to get at him. They found him lying on the landing outside the bathroom, dead, with the dead Sealyham in his arms. Hardy looked at him for a long time before speaking.

"You fool," he muttered between his teeth, angrily. "You damned fool!"

That imposture of his had paid him out at last. Like a man who cherishes a vice till it gets a stranglehold on him so that he is its helpless slave, he had lied so long that he had come to believe his own lies. Bob Forestier had pretended for so many years to be a gentleman that in the end, forgetting that it was all a fake, he had found himself driven to act as in that stupid, conventional brain of his he thought a gentleman must act. No longer knowing the difference between sham and real, he had sacrificed his life to a

spurious heroism. But Fred Hardy had to break the news to Mrs.
Forestier. She was with his wife, in their villa at the bottom of the
hill, and she still thought that Robert was with the soldiers cutting
down trees and clearing the brushwood. He told her as gently as he
could, but he had to tell her, and he had to tell her everything.
At first it seemed as though she could not grasp the sense of what
he said.

"Dead?" she cried. "Dead? My Robert?"

Then Fred Hardy, the rip, the cynic, the unscrupulous ruffian,
took her hands in his and said the words that alone enabled her to
bear her anguish.

"Mrs. Forestier, he was a very gallant gentleman."

The Unconquered

HE came back into the kitchen. The man was still on the floor, lying where he had hit him, and his face was bloody. He was moaning. The woman had backed against the wall and was staring with terrified eyes at Willi, his friend, and when he came in she gave a gasp and broke into loud sobbing. Willi was sitting at the table, his revolver in his hand, with a half empty glass of wine beside him. Hans went up to the table, filled his glass and emptied it at a gulp.

"You look as though you'd had trouble, young fellow," said Willi with a grin.

Han's face was blood-stained and you could see the gashes of five sharp finger-nails. He put his hand gingerly to his cheek.

"She'd have scratched my eyes out if she could, the bitch. I shall have to put some iodine on. But she's all right now. You go along."

"I don't know. Shall I? It's getting late."

"Don't be a fool. You're a man, aren't you? What if it is getting late? We lost our way."

It was still light and the westering sun streamed into the kitchen windows of the farm-house. Willi hesitated a moment. He was a little fellow, dark and thin-faced, a dress designer in civil life, and he didn't want Hans to think him a cissy. He got up and went towards the door through which Hans had come. When the woman saw what he was going to do she gave a shriek and sprang forward.

"*Non, Non,*" she cried.

With one step Hans was in front of her. He seized her by the shoulders and flung her violently back. She tottered and fell. He took Willi's revolver.

"Stop still, both of you," he rasped in French, but with his guttural German accent. He nodded his head towards the door. "Go on. I'll look after them."

Willi went out, but in a moment was back again.

"She's unconscious."

"Well, what of it?"

"I can't. It's no good."

"Stupid, that's what you are. *Ein Weibchen.* A woman."

Willi flushed.

"We'd better be getting on our way."

Hans shrugged a scornful shoulder.

"I'll just finish the bottle of wine and then we'll go."

He was feeling at ease and it would have been pleasant to linger. He had been on the job since morning and after so many hours on his motor-cycle his limbs ached. Luckily they hadn't far to go, only to Soissons—ten or fifteen kilometres. He wondered if he'd have the luck to get a bed to sleep in. Of course all this wouldn't have happened if the girl hadn't been a fool. They had lost their way, he and Willi, they had stopped a peasant working in a field and he had deliberately misled them, and they found themselves on a side road. When they came to the farm they stopped to ask for a direction. They'd asked very politely, for orders were to treat the French population well as long as they behaved themselves. The door was opened for them by the girl and she said she didn't know the way to Soissons, so they pushed in; then the woman, her mother, Hans guessed, told them. The three of them, the farmer, his wife and daughter, had just finished supper and there was a bottle of wine on the table. It reminded Hans that he was as thirsty as the devil. The day had been swelter-ing and he hadn't had a drink since noon. He asked them for a bottle of wine and Willi had added that they would pay them well for it. Willi was a good little chap, but soft. After all, they were the victors. Where was the French army? In headlong flight. And the English, leaving everything behind, had scuttled like rabbits back to their island. The conquerors took what they wanted, didn't they? But Willi had worked at a Paris dressmaker's for two years. It's true he spoke French well, that's why he had his present job, but it had done something to him. A decadent people. It did a German no good to live among them.

The farmer's wife put a couple of bottles of wine on the table and Willi took twenty francs out of his pocket and gave it to her. She didn't even say thank you. Hans's French wasn't as good as Willi's, but he could make himself understood, and he and Willi spoke it together all the time. Willi corrected his mistakes. It was because Willi was so useful to him in this way that he had made him his friend, and he knew that Willi admired him. He admired him because he was so tall, slim and broad-shouldered, because his curly hair was so fair and his eyes so blue. He never lost an opportunity to practise his French, and he tried to talk now, but those three French people wouldn't meet him half-way. He told them that he was a farmer's son himself and when the war was over was going back to the farm. He had been sent to school in

Munich because his mother wanted him to go into business, but his heart wasn't in it, and so after matriculating he had gone to an agricultural college.

"You came here to ask your way and now you know it," said the girl. "Drink up your wine and go."

He had hardly looked at her before. She wasn't pretty, but she had fine dark eyes and a straight nose. Her face was very pale. She was plainly dressed, but somehow she didn't look quite like what she evidently was. There was a sort of distinction about her. Ever since the war started he'd heard fellows talk about the French girls. They had something the German girls hadn't. Chic, Willi said it was, but when he asked him just what he meant by that Willi could only say that you had to see it to understand. Of course he'd heard others say that they were mercenary and hard as nails. Well, they'd be in Paris in a week and he'd find out for himself. They said the High Command had already arranged for houses for the men to go to.

"Finish your wine and let's go," said Willi.

But Hans was feeling comfortable and didn't want to be hurried.

"You don't look like a farmer's daughter," he said to the girl.

"And so what?" she answered.

"She's a teacher," said her mother.

"Then you've had a good education." She shrugged her shoulders, but he went on good-humouredly in his bad French. "You ought to understand that this is the best thing that has ever happened to the French people. We didn't declare war. You declared war. And now we're going to make France a decent country. We're going to put order into it. We're going to teach you to work. You'll learn obedience and discipline."

She clenched her fists and looked at him, her eyes black with hatred. But she did not speak.

"You're drunk, Hans," said Willi.

"I'm as sober as a judge. I'm only telling them the truth and they may just as well know it at once."

"He's right," she cried out, unable any longer to contain herself. "You're drunk. Now go. Go."

"Oh, you understand German, do you? All right, I'll go. But you must give me a kiss first."

She took a step back to avoid him, but he seized her wrist.

"Father," she cried. "Father."

The farmer flung himself on the German. Hans let go of her and with all his might hit him in the face. He crumpled up on the floor. Then, before she could escape him, he caught the girl in his arms. She gave him a swinging blow on the cheek. . . . He chuckled grimly.

"Is that how you take it when a German soldier wants to kiss you? You'll pay for this."

With his great strength he pinioned her arms and was dragging her out of the door, but her mother rushed at him and catching him by the clothes tried to pull him away. With one arm holding the girl close to him, with the flat of his other hand he gave the woman a great push and she staggered back to the wall.

"Hans, Hans," cried Willi.

"Shut up, damn you."

He put his hands over the girl's mouth to stop her shrieking and carried her out of the room. That was how it had happened and you had to admit that she'd brought it on herself. She shouldn't have slapped him. If she'd given him the kiss he'd asked for he'd have gone away. He gave a glance at the farmer still lying where he had fallen and he could hardly help laughing at his funny face. There was a smile in his eyes when he looked at the woman cowering against the wall. Was she afraid it was her turn next? Not likely. He remembered a French proverb.

"*C'est le premier pas qui coûte*. There's nothing to cry about, old woman. It had to come sooner or later." He put his hand to his hip pocket and pulled out a wallet. "Look, here's a hundred francs so that mademoiselle can buy herself a new dress. There's not much left of that one." He placed the note on the table and put his helmet back on his head. "Let's go."

They slammed the door behind them and got on their motor-cycles. The woman went into the parlour. Her daughter was lying on the divan. She was lying as he had left her and she was weeping bitterly.

Three months later Hans found himself in Soissons again. He had been in Paris with the conquering army and had ridden through the Arc de Triomphe on his motor-cycle. He had advanced with the army first to Tours and then to Bordeaux. He'd seen very little fighting. The only French soldiers he'd seen were prisoners. The campaign had been the greatest spree he could ever have imagined. After the armistice he had spent a month in Paris. He'd sent picture postcards to his family in Bavaria and bought them all presents. Willi, because he knew the city like the palm of his hand, had stayed on, but he and the rest of his unit were sent to Soissons to join the force that was holding it. It was a nice little town and he was comfortably billeted. Plenty to eat and champagne for less than a mark a bottle in German money. When he was ordered to proceed there it had occurred to him that it would be fun to go and have a look at the girl he'd had. He'd take her a pair of silk stockings to show there was no ill-feeling. He had a good bump of locality and he thought he would be able to find the farm without difficulty. So one afternoon, when he had nothing to do, he put the silk stockings in his pocket and got on his machine. It was a lovely autumn day, with hardly a cloud in the sky, and it was pretty, undulating country that he rode through. It had been fine and dry for so long that, though it was September, not even the restless poplars gave sign that the summer was drawing to an end. He took one wrong turning, which delayed him, but for all that he got to the place he sought in less than half an hour. A mongrel dog barked at him as he walked up to the door. He did not knock, but turned the handle and stepped in. The girl was sitting at the table peeling potatoes. She sprang to her feet when she saw the uniformed man.

"What d'you want?" Then she recognised him. She backed to the wall, clutching the knife in her hands. "It's you. *Cochon*."

"Don't get excited. I'm not going to hurt you. Look. I've brought you some silk stockings."

"Take them away and take yourself off with them."

"Don't be silly. Drop that knife. You'll only get hurt if you try to be nasty. You needn't be afraid of me."

"I'm not afraid of you," she said.

She let the knife fall to the floor. He took off his helmet and sat down. He reached out with his foot and drew the knife towards him.

"Shall I peel some of your potatoes for you?" She did not answer. He bent down for the knife and then took a potato out of the bowl and went to work on it. Her face hard, her eyes hostile, she stood against the wall and watched him. He smiled at her disarmingly. "Why do you look so cross? I didn't do you much harm, you know. I was excited, we all were, they'd talked of the invincible French army and the Maginot line . . ." he finished the sentence with a chuckle. "And the wine went to my head. You might have fared worse. Women have told me that I'm not a bad-looking fellow."

She looked him up and down scornfully.

"Get out of here."

"Not until I choose."

"If you don't go my father will go to Soissons and complain to the general."

"Much he'll care. Our orders are to make friends with the population. What's your name?"

"That's not your business."

There was a flush in her cheeks now and her angry eyes were blazing. She was prettier than he remembered her. He hadn't done so badly. She had a refinement that suggested the city-dweller rather than the peasant. He remembered her mother saying she was a teacher. Because she was almost a lady it amused him to torment her. He felt strong and healthy. He passed his hand through his curly blond hair, and giggled when he thought that many girls would have jumped at the chance she had had. His face was so deeply tanned by the summer that his eyes were startlingly blue.

"Where are your father and mother?"

"Working in the fields."

"I'm hungry. Give me a bit of bread and cheese and a glass of wine. I'll pay."

She gave a harsh laugh.

"We haven't seen cheese for three months. We haven't enough bread to stay our hunger. The French took our horses a year ago and now the Boches have taken our cows, our pigs, our chickens, everything."

"Well, they paid you for them."

"Can we eat the worthless paper they gave us?"

She began to cry.

"Are you hungry?"

"Oh, no," she answered bitterly, "we can eat like kings on potatoes and bread and turnips and lettuce. To-morrow my father's going to Soissons to see if he can buy some horse meat."

"Listen, Miss. I'm not a bad fellow. I'll bring you a cheese, and I think I can get hold of a bit of ham."

"I don't want your presents. I'll starve before I touch the food you swine have stolen from us."

"We'll see," he said good-humouredly.

He put on his hat, got up, and with an *Au revoir, mademoiselle*, walked out.

He wasn't supposed to go joy-riding round the country and he had to wait to be sent on an errand before he was able to get to the farm again. It was ten days later. He walked in as unceremoniously as before and this time he found the farmer and his wife in the kitchen. It was round about noon and the woman was stirring a pot on the stove. The man was seated at table. They gave him a glance when he came in, but there was no surprise in it. Their daughter had evidently told them of his visit. They did not speak. The woman went on with her cooking, and the man, a surly look on his face, stared at the oil-cloth on the table. But it required more than this to disconcert the good-humoured Hans.

"*Bonjour, la compagnie*," he said cheerfully. "I've brought you a present."

He undid the package he had with him and set out a sizable piece of gruyère cheese, a piece of pork and a couple of tins of sardines. The woman turned round and he smiled when he saw the light of greed in her eyes. The man looked at the foodstuff sullenly. Hans gave him his sunny grin.

"I'm sorry we had a misunderstanding the first time I came here. But you shouldn't have interfered."

At that moment the girl came in.

"What are you doing here?" she cried harshly. Then her eyes fell on the things he had brought. She swept them together and flung them at him. "Take them away. Take them."

But her mother sprang forward.

"Annette, you're crazy."

"I won't take his presents."

"It's our own food that they've stolen from us. Look at the sardines. They're Bordeaux sardines."

She picked the things up. Hans looked at the girl with a mocking smile in his light blue eyes.

"Annette's your name, is it? A pretty name. Do you grudge your parents a little food? You said you hadn't had cheese for three months. I couldn't get any ham; I did the best I could."

The farmer's wife took the lump of meat in her hands and pressed it to her bosom. You felt that she could have kissed it. Tears ran down Annette's cheeks.

"The shame of it," she groaned.

"Oh, come now, there's no shame in a bit of gruyère and a piece of pork."

Hans sat down and lit a cigarette. Then he passed the packet over to the old man. The farmer hesitated for a moment, but the temptation was too strong for him; he took one and handed back the packet.

"Keep it," said Hans. "I can get plenty more." He inhaled the smoke and blew a cloud of it from his nostrils. "Why can't we be friends? What's done can't be undone. War is war, and, well, you know what I mean. I know Annette's an educated girl and I want her to think well of me. I expect we shall be in Soissons for quite a while and I can bring you something now and then to help out. You know, we do all we can to make friends with the townspeople, but they won't let us. They won't even look at us when we pass them in the street. After all, it was an accident, what happened that time I came here with Willi. You needn't be afraid of me. I'll respect Annette as if she was my own sister."

"Why do you want to come here? Why can't you leave us alone?" asked Annette.

He really didn't know. He didn't like to say that he wanted a little human friendship. The silent hostility that surrounded them all at Soissons got on his nerves so that sometimes he wanted to go up to a Frenchman who looked at him as if he wasn't there and knock him down, and sometimes it affected him so that he was almost inclined to cry. It would be nice if he had some place to go where he was welcome. He spoke the truth when he said he had no desire for Annette. She wasn't the sort of woman he fancied. He liked women to be tall and full-breasted, blue-eyed and fair-haired like himself; he liked them to be strong and hefty and well-covered. That refinement which he couldn't account for, that thin fine nose and those dark eyes, the long pale face—there was something intimidating about the girl, so that if he hadn't been excited by the great victories of the German armies, if he hadn't been so tired and yet so elated, if he hadn't drunk all that wine on an empty stomach, it would never have crossed his mind that he could have anything to do with her.

For a fortnight after that Hans couldn't get away. He'd left the food at the farm and he had no doubt that the old people had wolfed it. He wondered if Annette had eaten it too; he wouldn't have been surprised to discover that the moment his back was turned she had set to with the others. These French people, they couldn't resist getting something for nothing. They were weak and decadent. She hated him, yes, God, how she hated him, but pork was pork and cheese was cheese. He thought of her quite a lot. It tantalised him that she should have such a loathing for him. He was used to being liked by women. It would be funny if one of these days she fell in love with him. He'd been her first lover and he'd heard the students at Munich over their beer saying that it was her first lover a woman loved, after that it was love. When he'd set his mind on getting a girl he'd never failed yet. Hans laughed to himself and a sly look came into his eyes.

At last he got his chance to go to the farm. He got hold of cheese and butter, sugar, a tin of sausages, and some coffee, and set off on his motor-cycle. But that time he didn't see Annette. She and her father were at work in the fields. The old woman was in the yard and her face lit up when she saw the parcel he was bringing. She led him into the kitchen. Her hands trembled a little as she untied the string and when she saw what he had brought her eyes filled with tears.

"You're very good," she said.

"May I sit down?" he asked politely.

"Of course." She looked out of the window and Hans guessed that she wanted to make sure that Annette was not coming. "Can I offer you a glass of wine?"

"I'd be glad of it."

He was sharp enough to see that her greed for food had made her, if not friendly to him, at least willing to come to terms with him. That look out of the window made them almost fellow conspirators.

"Did you like the pork?" he asked.

"It was a treat."

"I'll try to bring you some more next time I come. Did Annette like it?"

"She wouldn't touch a thing you'd left. She said she'd rather starve."

"Silly."

"That's what I said to her. As long as the food is there, I said, there's nothing to be gained by not eating it."

They chatted quite amicably while Hans sipped his wine. He discovered that she was called Madame Périer. He asked her whether there were any other members of the family. She sighed. No, they'd had a son, but he'd been mobilised at the beginning of the war and he'd died. He hadn't been killed, he'd got pneumonia and died in the hospital at Nancy.

"I'm sorry," said Hans.

"Perhaps he's better off than if he'd lived. He was like Annette in many ways. He could never have borne the shame of defeat." She sighed again. "Oh, my poor friend, we've been betrayed."

"Why did you want to fight for the Poles? What were they to you?"

"You're right. If we had let your Hitler take Poland he would have left us alone."

When Hans got up to go he said he would come again soon.

"I shan't forget the pork."

Then Hans had a lucky break; he was given a job that took him twice a week to a town in the vicinity so that he was able to get to the farm much oftener. He took care never to come without bringing something. But he made no headway with Annette. Seeking to ingratiate himself with her, he used the simple wiles that he had discovered went down with women; but they only excited her derision. Thin-lipped and hard, she looked at him as though he were dirt. On more than one occasion she made him so angry that he would have liked to take her by the shoulders and shake the life out of her. Once he found her alone, and when she got up to go he barred her passage.

"Stop where you are. I want to talk to you."

"Talk. I am a woman and defenceless."

"What I want to say is this: for all I know I may be here for a long time. Things aren't going to get easier for you French, they're going to get harder. I can be useful to you. Why don't you be reasonable like your father and mother?"

It was true that old Périer had come round. You couldn't say that he was cordial, he was indeed cold and gruff, but he was civil. He had even asked Hans to bring him some tobacco, and when he wouldn't accept payment for it had thanked him. He was pleased to hear the news of Soissons and grabbed the paper that Hans brought him. Hans, a farmer's son, could talk about the farm as one who knew. It was a good farm, not too big and not too small, well watered, for a sizable brook ran through it, and well wooded, with arable land and pasture. Hans listened with understanding sympathy when the old man bewailed himself because without labour, without fertilisers, his stock taken from him, it was all going to rack and ruin.

"You ask me why I can't be reasonable like my father and mother," said Annette.

She pulled her dress tight and showed herself to him. He couldn't believe his eyes. What he saw caused such a convulsion in his soul as he had never known. The blood rushed to his cheeks.

"You're pregnant."

She sank back on her chair and leaning her head on her hands began to weep as though her heart would break.

"The shame of it. The shame."

He sprang towards her to take her in his arms.

"My sweet," he cried.

But she sprang to her feet and pushed him away.

"Don't touch me. Go away. Go away. Haven't you done me enough harm already?"

She flung out of the room. He waited by himself for a few minutes. He was bewildered. His thoughts in a whirl, he rode slowly back to Soissons, and when he went to bed he couldn't get to sleep for hours. He could think of nothing but Annette and her swollen body. She had been unbearably pathetic as she sat there at the table crying her eyes out. It was his child she bore in her womb. He began to feel drowsy, and then with a start he was once more wide awake, for suddenly it came to him, it came to him with the shattering suddenness of gun-fire: he was in love with her. It was such a surprise, such a shock that he couldn't cope with it. Of course he'd thought of her a lot, but never in that way, he'd thought it would be a great joke if he made her fall in love with him, it would be a triumph if the time came when she offered what he had taken by force; but not for a moment had it occurred to him that she was anything to him but a woman like another. She wasn't his type. She wasn't very pretty. There was nothing to her. Why should he have all of a sudden this funny feeling for her? It wasn't a pleasant feeling either, it was a pain. But he knew what it was all right; it was love, and it made him feel happier than he had ever felt in his life. He wanted to take her in his arms, he wanted to pet her, he wanted to kiss those tear-stained eyes of hers. He didn't desire her, he thought, as a man desires a woman, he wanted to comfort her, he wanted her to smile at him—strange, he had never seen her smile, he wanted to see her eyes—fine eyes they were, beautiful eyes—soft with tenderness.

For three days he could not leave Soissons and for three days, three days and three nights, he thought of Annette and the child she would bear. Then he was able to go to the farm. He wanted to see Madame Périer by herself, and luck was with him, for he met her on the road some way from the house. She had been gathering sticks in the wood and was going home with a great bundle on her back. He stopped his motor-cycle. He knew that the friendliness she showed him was due only to the provisions he brought with him, but he didn't care; it was enough that she was mannerly, and that she was prepared to be so as long as she could get something out of him. He told her he wanted to talk to her and asked her to put her bundle down. She did as he bade. It was a grey, cloudy day, but not cold.

"I know about Annette," he said.

She started.

"How did you find out? She was set on your not knowing."

"She told me."

"That was a pretty job of work you did that evening."

"I didn't know. Why didn't you tell me sooner?"

She began to talk, not bitterly, not blaming him even, but as though it were a misfortune of nature, like a cow dying in giving birth to a calf or a sharp spring frost nipping the fruit trees and ruining the crop, a misfortune that human kind must accept with resignation and humility. After that dreadful night Annette had been in bed for days with a high fever. They thought she was going out of her mind. She would scream for hours on end. There were no doctors to be got. The village doctor had been called to the colours. Even in Soissons there were only two doctors left, old men both of them, and how could they get to the farm even if it had been possible to send for them? They weren't allowed to leave the town. Even when the fever went down Annette was too ill to leave her bed, and when she got up she was so weak, so pale, it was pitiful. The shock had been terrible, and when a month went by, and another month, without her being unwell she paid no attention. She had always been irregular. It was Madame Périer who first suspected that something was wrong. She questioned Annette. They were terrified, both of them, but they weren't certain and they said nothing to Périer. When the third month came it was impossible to doubt any longer. Annette was pregnant.

They had an old Citroën in which before the war Madame Périer had taken the farm produce into the market at Soissons two mornings a week, but since the German occupation they had had nothing to sell that made the journey worth while. Petrol was almost unobtainable. But now they got it out and drove into town. The only cars to be seen were the military cars of the Germans. German soldiers lounged about. There were German signs in the streets, and on public buildings proclamations in French signed by the Officer Commanding. Many shops were closed. They went to the old doctor they knew, and he confirmed their suspicions. But he was a devout Catholic and would not help them. When they wept he shrugged his shoulders.

"You're not the only one," he said. "*Il faut souffrir.*"

They knew about the other doctor too and went to see him. They rang the bell and for a long time no one answered. At last the door was opened by a sad-faced woman in black, but when they asked to see the doctor she began to cry. He had been arrested by the Germans because he was a freemason, and was held as a hostage. A bomb had exploded in a café frequented by German officers and two had been killed and several wounded. If the guilty were not handed over before a certain date he was to be shot. The woman seemed kindly and Madame Périer told her of their trouble.

"The brutes," she said. She looked at Annette with compassion. "My poor child."

She gave them the address of a midwife in the town and told them to say that they had come from her. The midwife gave them some medicine. It made Annette so ill that she thought she was going to die, but it had no further effect. Annette was still pregnant.

That was the story that Madame Périer told Hans. For a while he was silent.

"It's Sunday to-morrow," he said then. "I shall have nothing to do. I'll come and we'll talk. I'll bring something nice."

"We have no needles. Can you bring some?"

"I'll try."

She hoisted the bundle of sticks on her back and trudged down the road. Hans went back to Soissons. He dared not use his motor-cycle, so next day he hired a push-bike. He tied his parcel of food on the carrier. It was a larger parcel than usual because he had put a bottle of champagne into it. He got to the farm when the gathering darkness made it certain that they would all be home from work. It was warm and cosy in the kitchen when he walked in. Madame Périer was cooking and her husband was reading a *Paris-Soir*. Annette was darning stockings.

"Look, I've brought you some needles," he said, as he undid his parcel. "And here's some material for you, Annette."

"I don't want it."

"Don't you?" he grinned. "You'll have to begin making things for the baby."

"That's true, Annette," said her mother, "and we have nothing." Annette did not look up from her sewing. Madame Périer's greedy eyes ran over the contents of the parcel. "A bottle of champagne."

Hans chuckled.

"I'll tell you what that's for presently. I've had an idea." He hesitated for a moment, then drew up a chair and sat down facing Annette. "I don't know quite how to begin. I'm sorry for what I did that night, Annette. It wasn't my fault, it was the circumstances. Can't you forgive me?"

She threw him a look of hatred.

"Never. Why don't you leave me alone? Isn't it enough that you've ruined my life?"

"Well, that's just it. Perhaps I haven't. When I knew you were going to have a baby it had a funny effect on me. It's all different now. It's made me so proud."

"Proud?" she flung at him viciously.

"I want you to have the baby, Annette. I'm glad you couldn't get rid of it."

"How dare you say that?"

"But listen to me. I've been thinking of nothing else since I knew. The war will be over in six months. We shall bring the English to their knees in the spring. They haven't got a chance. And then I shall be demobilised and I'll marry you."

"You? Why?"

He blushed under his tan. He could not bring himself to say it in French, so he said it in German. He knew she understood it.

"*Ich liebe dich.*"

"What does he say?" asked Madame Périer.

"He says he loves me."

Annette threw back her head and broke into a peal of harsh laughter. She laughed louder and louder and she couldn't stop and tears streamed from her eyes. Madame Périer slapped her sharply on both cheeks.

"Don't pay any attention," she said to Hans. "It's hysteria. Her condition, you know."

Annette gasped. She gained control over herself.

"I brought the bottle of champagne to celebrate our engagement," said Hans.

"That's the bitterest thing of all," said Annette, "that we were beaten by fools, by such fools."

Hans went on speaking in German.

"I didn't know I loved you till that day when I found out that you were going to have a baby. It came like a clap of thunder, but I think I've loved you all the time."

"What does he say?" asked Madame Périer.

"Nothing of importance."

He fell back into French. He wanted Annette's parents to hear what he had to say.

"I'd marry you now, only they wouldn't let me. And don't think I'm nothing at all. My father's well-to-do and we're well thought of in our commune. I'm the eldest son and you'd want for nothing."

"Are you a Catholic?" asked Madame Périer.

"Yes, I'm a Catholic."

"That's something."

"It's pretty, the country where we live and the soil's good. There's not better farming land between Munich and Innsbruck, and it's our own. My grandfather bought it after the war of '70. And we've got a car and a radio, and we're on the telephone."

Annette turned to her father.

"He has all the tact in the world, this gentleman," she cried ironically. She eyed Hans. "It would be a nice position for me, the foreigner from the conquered country with a child born out of wedlock. It offers me a chance of happiness, doesn't it? A fine chance."

Périer, a man of few words, spoke for the first time.

"No. I don't deny that it's a fine gesture you're making. I went through the last war and we all did things we wouldn't have done in peace time. Human nature is human nature. But now that our son is dead, Annette is all we have. We can't let her go."

"I thought you might feel that way," said Hans, "and I've got my answer to that. I'll stay here."

Annette gave him a quick look.

"What do you mean?" asked Madame Périer.

"I've got another brother. He can stay and help my father. I like this country. With energy and initiative a man could make a good thing of your farm. When the war's over a lot of Germans will be settling here. It's well known that you haven't got enough men in France to work the land you've got. A fellow gave us a lecture the other day at Soissons. He said that a third of the farms were left uncultivated because there aren't the men to work them."

Périer and his wife exchanged glances and Annette saw that they were wavering. That was what they'd wanted since their son had died, a son-in-law who was strong and hefty and could take over when they grew too old to do more than potter about.

"That changes the case," said Madame Périer. "It's a proposition to consider."

"Hold your tongue," cried Annette roughly. She leant forward and fixed her burning eyes on the German. "I'm engaged to a teacher who worked in the boys' school in the town where I taught, we were to be married after the war. He's not strong and big like you, or handsome; he's small and frail. His only beauty is the intelligence that shines in his face, his only strength is the greatness of his soul. He's not a barbarian, he's civilised; he has a thousand years of civilisation behind him. I love him. I love him with all my heart and soul."

Hans's face grew sullen. It had never occurred to him that Annette might care for anyone else.

"Where is he now?"

"Where do you suppose he is? In Germany. A prisoner and starving. While you eat the fat of our land. How many times have I got to tell you that I hate you? You ask me to forgive you. Never. You want to make reparation. You fool." She threw her head back and there was a look of intolerable anguish on her face. "Ruined. Oh, he'll forgive me. He's tender. But I'm tortured by the thought that one day the suspicion may come to him that perhaps I hadn't been forced—that perhaps I'd given myself to you for butter and cheese and silk stockings. I shouldn't be the only one. And what would our life be with that child between us, your child, a German child? Big like you, and blond like you, and blue-eyed like you. Oh, my God, why do I have to suffer this?"

She got up and went swiftly out of the kitchen. For a minute the three were left in silence. Hans looked ruefully at his bottle of champagne. He sighed and rose to his feet. When he went out Madame Périer accompanied him.

"Did you mean it when you said you would marry her?" she asked him, speaking in a low voice.

"Yes. Every word. I love her."

"And you wouldn't take her away? You'd stay here and work on the farm?"

"I promise you."

"Evidently my old man can't last for ever. At home you'd have to share with your brother. Here you'd share with nobody."

"There's that too."

"We never were in favour of Annette marrying that teacher, but our son was alive then and he said, if she wants to marry him, why shouldn't she? Annette was crazy about him. But now that our son's dead, poor boy, it's different. Even if she wanted to, how could she work the farm alone?"

"It would be a shame if it was sold. I know how one feels about one's own land."

They had reached the road. She took his hand and gave it a little squeeze.

"Come again soon."

Hans knew that she was on his side. It was a comfort to him to think that as he rode back to Soissons. It was a bother that Annette was in love with somebody else. Fortunately he was a prisoner; long before he was likely to be released the baby would be born. That might change her: you could never tell with a woman. Why, in his village there'd been a woman who was so much in love with her husband that it had been a joke, and then she had a baby and after that she couldn't bear the sight of him. Well, why shouldn't the contrary happen too? And now that he'd offered to marry her she must see that he was a decent sort of fellow. God, how pathetic she'd looked with her head flung back, and how well she'd spoken! What language! An actress on the stage couldn't have expressed herself better, and yet it had all sounded so natural. You had to admit that, these French people knew how to talk. Oh, she was clever. Even when she lashed him with that bitter tongue it was a joy to listen to her. He hadn't had a bad education himself, but he couldn't hold a candle to her. Culture, that's what she had.

"I'm a donkey," he said out loud as he rode along. She'd said he was big and strong and handsome. Would she have said that if it hadn't meant something to her? And she'd talked of the baby having fair hair and blue eyes like his own. If that didn't mean that his colouring had made an impression on her he was a Dutchman. He chuckled. "Give me time. Patience, and let nature go to work."

The weeks went by. The C.O. at Soissons was an elderly, easy-going fellow and in view of what the spring had in store for them he was content not to drive his men too hard. The German papers told them that England was being wrecked by the Luftwaffe and the people were in a panic. Submarines were sinking British ships by the score and the country was starving. Revolution was imminent. Before summer it would be all over and the Germans would be masters of the world. Hans wrote home and told his parents that he was going to marry a French girl and with her a fine farm. He proposed that his brother should borrow money to buy him out of his share of the family property so that he could increase the size of his own holding while land, owing to the war and the exchange, could still be bought for a song. He went over the farm with Périer. The old man listened quietly when Hans told him his ideas: the farm would have to be restocked and as a German he would have a pull; the motor tractor was old, he would get a fine new one from Germany, and a motor plough. To make a farm pay you had to take advantage of modern inventions. Madame Périer told him afterwards that her husband had said he wasn't a bad lad and seemed to know a lot. She was very friendly with him now and insisted that he should share their mid-day meal with them on Sundays. She translated his name into French and called him Jean. He was always ready to give a hand, and as time went on and Annette could do less and less it was useful to have a man about who didn't mind doing a job of work.

Annette remained fiercely hostile. She never spoke to him except to answer his direct questions and as soon as it was possible went to her own room. When it was so cold that she couldn't stay there she sat by the side of the kitchen stove, sewing or reading, and took no more notice of him than if he hadn't been there. She was in radiant health. There was colour in her cheeks and in Hans's eyes she was beautiful. Her approaching maternity had given her a strange dignity and he was filled with exultation when he gazed upon her. Then one day when he was on his way to the

farm he saw Madame Périer in the road waving to him to stop.
He put his brakes on hard.

"I've been waiting for an hour. I thought you'd never come.
You must go back. Pierre is dead."

"Who's Pierre?"

"Pierre Gavin. The teacher Annette was going to marry."

Hans's heart leapt. What luck! Now he'd have his chance.

"Is she upset?"

"She's not crying. When I tried to say something she bit my
head off. If she saw you to-day she's capable of sticking a knife
into you."

"It's not my fault if he died. How did you hear?"

"A prisoner, a friend of his, escaped through Switzerland and
he wrote to Annette. We got the letter this morning. There
was a mutiny in the camp because they weren't given enough to
eat, and the ringleaders were shot. Pierre was one of them."

Hans was silent. He could only think it served the man right.
What did they think that a prison camp was—the Ritz?

"Give her time to get over the shock," said Madame Périer.
"When she's calmer I'll talk to her. I'll write you a letter when
you can come again."

"All right. You will help me, won't you?"

"You can be sure of that. My husband and I, we're agreed.
We talked it over and we came to the conclusion that the only
thing to do was to accept the situation. He's no fool, my husband,
and he says the best chance for France now is to collaborate.
And take it all in all I don't dislike you. I shouldn't wonder if
you didn't make Annette a better husband than that teacher. And
with the baby coming and all."

"I want it to be a boy," said Hans.

"It's going to be a boy. I know for certain. I've seen it in the
coffee grounds and I've put out the cards. The answer is a boy
every time."

"I almost forgot, here are some papers for you," said Hans, as
he turned his cycle and prepared to mount.

He handed her three numbers of *Paris-Soir*. Old Périer read
every evening. He read that the French must be realistic and
accept the new order that Hitler was going to create in Europe.
He read that the German submarines were sweeping the sea. He
read that the General Staff had organised to the last detail the
campaign that would bring England to her knees and that the
Americans were too unprepared, too soft and too divided to come
to her help. He read that France must take the heaven-sent

opportunity and by loyal collaboration with the Reich regain her honoured position in the new Europe. And it wasn't Germans who wrote it all; it was Frenchmen. He nodded his head with approval when he read that the plutocrats and the Jews would be destroyed and the poor man in France would at last come into his own. They were quite right, the clever fellows who said that France was essentially an agricultural country and its backbone was its industrious farmers. Good sense, that was.

One evening, when they were finishing their supper, ten days after the news had come of Pierre Gavin's death, Madame Périer, by arrangement with her husband, said to Annette:

"I wrote a letter to Hans a few days ago telling him to come here to-morrow."

"Thank you for the warning. I shall stay in my room."

"Oh, come, daughter, the time has passed for foolishness. You must be realistic. Pierre is dead. Hans loves you and wants to marry you. He's a fine-looking fellow. Any girl would be proud of him as a husband. How can we restock the farm without his help? He's going to buy a tractor and a plough with his own money. You must let bygones be bygones."

"You're wasting your breath, Mother. I earned my living before, I can earn my living again. I hate him. I hate his vanity and his arrogance. I could kill him: his death wouldn't satisfy me. I should like to torture him as he's tortured me. I think I should die happy if I could find a way to wound him as he's wounded me."

"You're being very silly, my poor child."

"Your mother's right, my girl," said Périer. "We've been defeated and we must accept the consequences. We've got to make the best arrangement we can with the conquerors. We're cleverer than they are and if we play our cards well we shall come out on top. France was rotten. It's the Jews and the plutocrats who ruined the country. Read the papers and you'll see for yourself!"

"Do you think I believe a word in that paper? Why do you think he brings it to you except that it's sold to the Germans? The men who write in it—traitors, traitors. Oh God, may I live to see them torn to pieces by the mob. Bought, bought every one of them—bought with German money. The swine."

Madame Périer was getting exasperated.

"What have you got against the boy? He took you by force— yes, he was drunk at the time. It's not the first time that's happened to a woman and it won't be the last time. He hit your father and he bled like a pig, but does your father bear him malice?"

"It was an unpleasant incident, but I've forgotten it," said Périer.

Annette burst into harsh laughter.

"You should have been a priest. You forgive injuries with a spirit truly Christian."

"And what is there wrong about that?" asked Madame Périer angrily. "Hasn't he done everything he could to make amends? Where would your father have got his tobacco all these months if it hadn't been for him? If we haven't gone hungry it's owing to him."

"If you'd had any pride, if you'd had any sense of decency, you'd have thrown his presents in his face."

"You've profited by them, haven't you?"

"Never. Never."

"It's a lie and you know it. You've refused to eat the cheese he brought and the butter and the sardines. But the soup you've eaten, you know I put the meat in it that he brought; and the salad you ate to-night, if you didn't have to eat it dry, it's because he brought me oil."

Annette sighed deeply. She passed her hand over her eyes.

"I know. I tried not to, I couldn't help myself, I was so hungry. Yes, I knew his meat went into the soup and I ate it. I knew the salad was made with his oil. I wanted to refuse it; I had such a longing for it, it wasn't I that ate it, it was a ravenous beast within me."

"That's neither here nor there. You ate it."

"With shame. With despair. They broke our strength first with their tanks and their planes, and now when we're defenceless they're breaking our spirit by starving us."

"You get nowhere by being theatrical, my girl. For an educated woman you have really no sense. Forget the past and give a father to your child, to say nothing of a good workman for the farm who'll be worth two hired men. That is sense."

Annette shrugged her shoulders wearily and they lapsed into silence. Next day Hans came. Annette gave him a sullen look, but neither spoke nor moved. Hans smiled.

"Thank you for not running away," he said.

"My parents asked you to come and they've gone down to the village. It suits me because I want to have a definite talk with you. Sit down."

He took off his coat and his helmet and drew a chair to the table.

"My parents want me to marry you. You've been clever; with

your presents, with your promises, you've got round them. They believe all they read in the papers you bring them. I want to tell you that I will never marry you. I wouldn't have thought it possible that I could hate a human being as I hate you."

"Let me speak in German. You understand enough to know what I'm saying."

"I ought to. I taught it. For two years I was governess to two little girls in Stuttgart."

He broke into German, but she went on speaking French.

"It's not only that I love you, I admire you. I admire your distinction and your grace. There's something about you I don't understand. I respect you. Oh, I can see that you don't want to marry me now even if it were possible. But Pierre is dead."

"Don't speak of him," she cried violently. "That would be the last straw."

"I only want to tell you that for your sake I'm sorry he died."

"Shot in cold blood by his German jailers."

"Perhaps in time you'll grieve for him less. You know, when someone you love dies, you think you'll never get over it, but you do. Won't it be better then to have a father for your child?"

"Even if there were nothing else do you think I could ever forget that you are a German and I'm a Frenchwoman? If you weren't as stupid as only a German can be you'd see that that child must be a reproach to me as long as I live. Do you think I have no friends? How could I ever look them in the face with the child I had with a German soldier? There's only one thing I ask you: leave me alone with my disgrace. Go, go—for God's sake go and never come again."

"But he's my child too. I want him."

"You?" she cried in astonishment. "What can a by-blow that you got in a moment of savage drunkenness mean to you?"

"You don't understand. I'm so proud and so happy. It was when I knew you were going to have a baby that I knew I loved you. At first I couldn't believe it; it was such a surprise to me. Don't you see what I mean? That child that's going to be born means everything in the world to me. Oh, I don't know how to put it; it's put feelings in my heart that I don't understand myself."

She looked at him intently and there was a strange gleam in her eyes. You would have said it was a look of triumph. She gave a short laugh.

"I don't know whether I more loathe the brutality of you Germans or despise your sentimentality."

He seemed not to have heard what she said.

"I think of him all the time."

"You've made up your mind it'll be a boy?"

"I know it'll be a boy. I want to hold him in my arms and I want to teach him to walk. And then when he grows older I'll teach him all I know. I'll teach him to ride and I'll teach him to shoot. Are there fish in your brook? I'll teach him to fish. I'm going to be the proudest father in the world."

She stared at him with hard, hard eyes. Her face was set and stern. An idea, a terrible idea was forming itself in her mind. He gave her a disarming smile.

"Perhaps when you see how much I love our boy, you'll come to love me too. I'll make you a good husband, my pretty."

She said nothing. She merely kept on gazing at him sullenly.

"Haven't you one kind word for me?" he said.

She flushed. She clasped her hands tightly together.

"Others may despise me. I will never do anything that can make me despise myself. You are my enemy and you will always be my enemy. I only live to see the deliverance of France. It'll come, perhaps not next year or the year after, perhaps not for thirty years, but it'll come. The rest of them can do what they like, I will never come to terms with the invaders of my country. I hate you and I hate this child that you've given me. Yes, we've been defeated. Before the end comes you'll see that we haven't been conquered. Now go. My mind's made up and nothing on God's earth can change it."

He was silent for a minute or two.

"Have you made arrangements for a doctor? I'll pay all the expenses."

"Do you suppose we want to spread our shame through the whole countryside? My mother will do all that's necessary."

"But supposing there's an accident?"

"And supposing you mind your own business!"

He sighed and rose to his feet. When he closed the door behind him she watched him walk down the pathway that led to the road. She realised with rage that some of the things he said had aroused in her heart a feeling that she had never felt for him before.

"O God, give me strength," she cried.

Then, as he walked along, the dog, an old dog they'd had for years, ran up to him barking angrily. He had tried for months to make friends with the dog, but it had never responded to his advances; when he tried to pat it, it backed away growling and showing its teeth. And now as the dog ran towards him, irritably giving way to his feeling of frustration, Hans gave it a savage, brutal kick and the dog was flung into the bushes and limped yelping away.

"The beast," she cried. "Lies, lies, lies. And I was weak enough to be almost sorry for him."

There was a looking-glass hanging by the side of the door and she looked at herself in it. She drew herself up and smiled at her reflection. But rather than a smile it was a fiendish grimace.

It was now March. There was a bustle of activity in the garrison at Soissons. There were inspections and there was intensive training. Rumour was rife. There was no doubt they were going somewhere, but the rank and file could only guess where. Some thought they were being got ready at last for the invasion of England, others were of opinion that they would be sent to the Balkans, and others again talked of the Ukraine. Hans was kept busy. It was not till the second Sunday afternoon that he was able to get out to the farm. It was a cold grey day, with sleet that looked as though it might turn to snow falling in sudden windy flurries. The country was grim and cheerless.

"You!" cried Madame Périer when he went in. "We thought you were dead."

"I couldn't come before. We're off any day now. We don't know when."

"The baby was born this morning. It's a boy."

Hans's heart gave a great leap in his breast. He flung his arms round the old woman and kissed her on both cheeks.

"A Sunday child, he ought to be lucky. Let's open the bottle of champagne. How's Annette?"

"She's as well as can be expected. She had a very easy time. She began to have pains last night and by five o'clock this morning it was all over."

Old Périer was smoking his pipe sitting as near the stove as he could get. He smiled quietly at the boy's enthusiasm.

"One's first child, it has an effect on one," he said.

"He has quite a lot of hair and it's as fair as yours; and blue eyes just like you said he'd have," said Madame Périer. "I've never seen a lovelier baby. He'll be just like his papa."

"Oh, my God, I'm so happy," cried Hans. "How beautiful the world is! I want to see Annette."

"I don't know if she'll see you. I don't want to upset her on account of the milk."

"No, no, don't upset her on my account. If she doesn't want to see me it doesn't matter. But let me see the baby just for a minute."

"I'll see what I can do. I'll try to bring it down."

Madame Périer went out and they heard her heavy tread clumping up the stairs. But in a moment they heard her clattering down again. She burst into the kitchen.

"They're not there. She isn't in her room. The baby's gone."

Périer and Hans cried out and without thinking what they were doing all three of them scampered upstairs. The harsh light of the winter afternoon cast over the shabby furniture, the iron bed, the cheap wardrobe, the chest of drawers, a dismal squalor. There was no one in the room.

"Where is she?" screamed Madame Périer. She ran into the narrow passage, opening doors, and called the girl's name. "Annette, Annette. Oh, what madness!"

"Perhaps in the sitting-room."

They ran downstairs to the unused parlour. An icy air met them as they opened the door. They opened the door of a store-room.

"She's gone out. Something awful has happened."

"How could she have got out?" asked Hans, sick with anxiety.

"Through the front door, you fool."

Périer went up to it and looked.

"That's right. The bolt's drawn back."

"Oh, my God, my God, what madness," cried Madame Périer. "It'll kill her."

"We must look for her," said Hans. Instinctively, because that was the way he always went in and out, he ran back into the kitchen and the others followed him. "Which way?"

"The brook," the old woman gasped.

He stopped as though turned to stone with horror. He stared at the old woman aghast.

"I'm frightened," she cried. "I'm frightened."

Hans flung open the door, and as he did so Annette walked in. She had nothing on but her nightdress and a flimsy rayon dressing-gown. It was pink, with pale blue flowers. She was soaked, and her hair, dishevelled, clung damply to her head and hung down her shoulders in bedraggled wisps. She was deathly white. Madame Périer sprang towards her and took her in her arms.

"Where have you been? Oh, my poor child, you're wet through. What madness!"

But Annette pushed her away. She looked at Hans.

"You've come at the right moment, you."

"Where's the baby?" cried Madame Périer.

"I had to do it at once. I was afraid if I waited I shouldn't have the courage."

"Annette, what have you done?"

"I've done what I had to do. I took it down to the brook and held it under water till it was dead."

Hans gave a great cry, the cry of an animal wounded to death; he covered his face with his hands, and staggering like a drunken man flung out of the door. Annette sank into a chair, and leaning her forehead on her two fists burst into passionate weeping.

G

In a Strange Land

I AM of a roving disposition; but I travel not to see imposing monuments, which indeed somewhat bore me, nor beautiful scenery, of which I soon tire; I travel to see men. I avoid the great. I would not cross the road to meet a president or a king; I am content to know the writer in the pages of his book and the painter in his picture; but I have journeyed a hundred leagues to see a missionary of whom I had heard a strange story and I have spent a fortnight in a vile hotel in order to improve my acquaintance with a billiard-marker. I should be inclined to say that I am not surprised to meet any sort of person were it not that there is one sort that I am constantly running against and that never fails to give me a little shock of amused astonishment. This is the elderly Englishwoman, generally of adequate means, who is to be found living alone, up and down the world, in unexpected places. You do not wonder when you hear of her living in a villa on a hill outside a small Italian town, the only Englishwoman in the neighbourhood, and you are almost prepared for it when a lonely hacienda is pointed out to you in Andalusia and you are told that there has dwelt for many years an English lady. But it is more surprising when you hear that the only white person in a Chinese city is an Englishwoman, not a missionary, who lives there none knows why; and there is another who inhabits an island in the South Seas and a third who has a bungalow on the outskirts of a large village in the centre of Java. They live solitary lives, these women, without friends, and they do not welcome the stranger. Though they may not have seen one of their own race for months they will pass you on the road as though they did not see you, and if, presuming on your nationality, you should call, as likely as not they will decline to see you; but if they do, they will give you a cup of tea from a silver teapot and on a plate of old Worcester you will find Scotch scones. They will talk to you politely, as though they were entertaining you in a Kentish vicarage, but when you take your leave will show no particular desire to continue the acquaintance. One wonders in vain what strange instinct it is that has driven them to separate themselves from their kith and kin and thus to live apart from all their natural interests in an alien land. Is it romance they have sought or freedom?

But of all these Englishwomen whom I have met or perhaps only heard of (for as I have said they are difficult of access) the one who

remains most vividly in my memory is an elderly person who lived
in Asia Minor. I had arrived after a tedious journey at a little town
from which I proposed to make the ascent of a celebrated mountain
and I was taken to a rambling hotel that stood at its foot. I arrived
late at night and signed my name in the book. I went up to my room.
It was cold and I shivered as I undressed, but in a moment there was
a knock at the door and the dragoman came in.

"Signora Niccolini's compliments," he said.

To my astonishment he handed me a hot-water bottle. I took it
with grateful hands.

"Who is Signora Niccolini?" I asked.

"She is the proprietor of this hotel," he answered.

I sent her my thanks and he withdrew. The last thing I expected
in a scrubby hotel in Asia Minor kept by an old Italian woman was
a beautiful hot-water bottle. There is nothing I like more (if we
were not all sick to death of the war I would tell you the story of how
six men risked their lives to fetch a hot-water bottle from a château
in Flanders that was being bombarded); and next morning, so that
I might thank her in person, I asked if I might see the Signora
Niccolini. While I waited for her I racked my brains to think what
hot-water bottle could possibly be in Italian. In a moment she came
in. She was a little stout woman, not without dignity, and she wore
a black apron trimmed with lace and a small black lace cap. She
stood with her hands crossed. I was astonished at her appearance
for she looked exactly like a housekeeper in a great English house.

"Did you wish to speak to me, sir?"

She was an Englishwoman and in those few words I surely recognised the trace of a cockney accent.

"I wanted to thank you for the hot-water bottle," I replied in
some confusion.

"I saw by the visitors' book that you were English, sir, and I
always send up a 'ot-water bottle to English gentlemen."

"Believe me, it was very welcome."

"I was for many years in the service of the late Lord Ormskirk,
sir. He always used to travel with a 'ot-water bottle. Is there anything else, sir?"

"Not at the moment, thank you."

She gave me a polite little nod and withdrew. I wondered how on
earth it came about that a funny old Englishwoman like that should
be the landlady of a hotel in Asia Minor. It was not easy to make her
acquaintance, for she knew her place, as she would herself have put
it, and she kept me at a distance. It was not for nothing that she had
been in service in a noble English family. But I was persistent and I

induced her at last to ask me to have a cup of tea in her own little parlour. I learnt that she had been lady's-maid to a certain Lady Ormskirk, and Signor Niccolini (for she never alluded to her deceased husband in any other way) had been his lordship's chef. Signor Niccolini was a very handsome man and for some years there had been an "understanding" between them. When they had both saved a certain amount of money they were married, retired from service, and looked about for a hotel. They had bought this one on an advertisement because Signor Niccolini thought he would like to see something of the world. That was nearly thirty years ago and Signor Niccolini had been dead for fifteen. His widow had not once been back to England. I asked her if she was never homesick.

"I don't say as I wouldn't like to go back on a visit, though I expect I'd find many changes. But my family didn't like the idea of me marrying a foreigner and I 'aven't spoken to them since. Of course there are many things here that are not the same as what they 'ave at 'ome, but it's surprising what you get used to. I see a lot of life. I don't know as I should care to live the humdrum life they do in a place like London."

I smiled. For what she said was strangely incongruous with her manner. She was a pattern of decorum. It was extraordinary that she could have lived for thirty years in this wild and almost barbaric country without its having touched her. Though I knew no Turkish and she spoke it with ease I was convinced that she spoke it most incorrectly and with a cockney accent. I suppose she had remained the precise, prim English lady's-maid, knowing her place, through all these vicissitudes because she had no faculty of surprise. She took everything that came as a matter of course. She looked upon everyone who wasn't English as a foreigner and therefore as someone, almost imbecile, for whom allowance must be made. She ruled her staff despotically—for did she not know how an upper servant in a great house should exercise his authority over the under servants?—and everything about the hotel was clean and neat.

"I do my best," she said, when I congratulated her on this, standing, as always when she spoke to me, with her hands respectfully crossed. "Of course one can't expect foreigners to 'ave the same ideas what we 'ave, but as his lordship used to say to me, what we've got to do, Parker, he said to me, what we've got to do in this life is to make the best of our raw material."

But she kept her greatest surprise for the eve of my departure.

"I'm glad you're not going before you've seen my two sons, sir."

"I didn't know you had any."

"They've been away on business, but they've just come back.

You'll be surprised when you've seen them. I've trained them with me own 'ands so to speak, and when I'm gone they'll carry on the 'otel between them."

In a moment two tall, swarthy, strapping young fellows entered the hall. Her eyes lit up with pleasure. They went up to her and took her in their arms and gave her resounding kisses.

"They don't speak English, sir, but they understand a little, and of course they speak Turkish like natives, and Greek and Italian."

I shook hands with the pair and then Signora Niccolini said something to them and they went away.

"They're handsome fellows, Signora," I said. "You must be very proud of them."

"I am, sir, and they're good boys, both of them. They've never give me a moment's trouble from the day they was born and they're the very image of Signor Niccolini."

"I must say no one would think they had an English mother."

"I'm not exactly their mother, sir. I've just sent them along to say 'ow do you do to 'er."

I dare say I looked a little confused.

"They're the sons that Signor Niccolini 'ad by a Greek girl that used to work in the 'otel, and 'aving no children of me own I adopted them."

I sought for some remark to make.

"I 'ope you don't think that there's any blame attaches to Signor Niccolini," she said, drawing herself up a little. "I shouldn't like you to think that, sir." She folded her hands again and with a mixture of pride, primness and satisfaction added the final word: "Signor Niccolini was a very full-blooded man."

The Taipan

No one knew better than he that he was an important person. He was number one in not the least important branch of the most important English firm in China. He had worked his way up through solid ability and he looked back with a faint smile at the callow clerk who had come out to China thirty years before. When he remembered the modest home he had come from, a little red house in a long row of little red houses, in Barnes, a suburb which, aiming desperately at the genteel, achieves only a sordid melancholy, and compared it with the magnificent stone mansion, with its wide verandahs and spacious rooms, which was at once the office of the company and his own residence, he chuckled with satisfaction. He had come a long way since then. He thought of the high tea to which he sat down when he came home from school (he was at St. Paul's), with his father and mother and his two sisters, a slice of cold meat, a great deal of bread and butter and plenty of milk in his tea, everybody helping himself, and then he thought of the state in which now he ate his evening meal. He always dressed and whether he was alone or not he expected the three boys to wait at table. His number one boy knew exactly what he liked and he never had to bother himself with the details of housekeeping; but he always had a set dinner with soup and fish, entrée, roast, sweet and savoury, so that if he wanted to ask anyone in at the last moment he could. He liked his food and he did not see why when he was alone he should have less good a dinner than when he had a guest.

He had indeed gone far. That was why he did not care to go home now, he had not been to England for ten years, and he took his leave in Japan or Vancouver, where he was sure of meeting old friends from the China coast. He knew no one at home. His sisters had married in their own station, their husbands were clerks and their sons were clerks; there was nothing between him and them; they bored him. He satisfied the claims of relationship by sending them every Christmas a piece of fine silk, some elaborate embroidery, or a case of tea. He was not a mean man and as long as his mother lived he had made her an allowance. But when the time came for him to retire he had no intention of going back to England, he had seen too many men do that and he knew how often it was a failure; he meant to take a house near the race-course in Shanghai: what with bridge and his ponies and golf he expected to get through the rest of his life very comfortably. But he had a good many years before he need think of retiring. In another five or six Higgins would be going home and then he would take charge of the head office in Shanghai. Meanwhile he was very happy where he was, he could save money, which you couldn't do in Shanghai, and have a good time into the bargain. This place had another advantage over Shanghai: he was the most prominent man in the community and what he said went. Even the consul took care to keep on the right side of him. Once a consul and he had been at loggerheads and it was not he who had gone to the wall. The taipan thrust out his jaw pugnaciously as he thought of the incident.

But he smiled, for he felt in an excellent humour. He was walking back to his office from a capital luncheon at the Hong-Kong and Shanghai Bank. They did you very well there. The food was first-rate and there was plenty of liquor. He had started with a couple of cocktails, then he had some excellent sauterne and he had finished up with two glasses of port and some fine old brandy. He felt good. And when he left he did a thing that was rare with him; he walked. His bearers with his chair kept a few paces behind him in case he felt inclined to slip into it, but he enjoyed stretching his legs. He did not get enough exercise these days. Now that he was too heavy to ride it was difficult to get exercise. But if he was too heavy to ride he could still keep ponies, and as he strolled along in the balmy air he thought of the spring meeting. He had a couple of griffins that he had hopes of and one of the lads in his office had turned out a fine jockey (he must see they didn't sneak him away, old Higgins in Shanghai would give a pot of money to get him over there) and he ought to pull off two or three races. He flattered himself that he had the finest stable in the city. He pouted his broad chest like a pigeon. It was a beautiful day, and it was good to be alive.

He paused as he came to the cemetery. It stood there, neat and orderly, as an evident sign of the community's opulence. He never passed the cemetery without a little glow of pride. He was pleased to be an Englishman. For the cemetery stood in a place, valueless when it was chosen, which with the increase of the city's affluence was now worth a great deal of money. It had been suggested that the graves should be moved to another spot and the land sold for building, but the feeling of the community was against it. It gave the taipan a sense of satisfaction to think that their dead rested on the most valuable site on the island. It showed that there were things they cared for more than money. Money be blowed! When it came to "the things that mattered" (this was a favourite phrase with the taipan), well, one remembered that money wasn't everything.

And now he thought he would take a stroll through. He looked at the graves. They were neatly kept and the pathways were free from weeds. There was a look of prosperity. And as he sauntered along he read the names on the tombstones. Here were three side by side; the captain, the first mate, and the second mate of the barque *Mary Baxter*, who had all perished together in the typhoon of 1908. He remembered it well. There was a little group of two missionaries, their wives and children, who had been massacred during the Boxer troubles. Shocking thing that had been! Not that he took 'much stock in missionaries; but, hang it all, one couldn't have these damned Chinese massacring them. Then he came to a cross with a name on it he knew. Good chap, Edward Mulock, but he couldn't stand his liquor, drank himself to death, poor devil, at twenty-five; the taipan had known a lot of them do that; there were several more neat crosses with a man's name on them and the age, twenty-five, twenty-six, or twenty-seven; it was always the same story: they had come out to China; they had never seen so much money before, they were good fellows and they wanted to drink with the rest: they couldn't stand it, and there they were in the cemetery. You had to have a strong head and a fine constitution to drink drink for drink on the China coast. Of course it was very sad, but the taipan could hardly help a smile when he thought how many of those young fellows he had drunk underground. And there was a death that had been useful, a fellow in his own firm, senior to him and a clever chap too: if that fellow had lived he might not have been taipan now. Truly the ways of fate were inscrutable. Ah, and here was little Mrs. Turner, Violet Turner, she had been a pretty little thing, he had had quite an affair with her; he had been devilish cut up when she died. He looked at her age on the tombstone. She'd be no chicken if she were alive now. And as he thought of all those dead people a sense of satisfaction spread through him. He had beaten them all. They were dead and he was alive, and by George he'd scored them off. His eyes collected in one picture all those crowded graves and he smiled scornfully. He very nearly rubbed his hands.

"No one ever thought I was a fool," he muttered.

He had a feeling of good-natured contempt for the gibbering dead. Then, as he strolled along, he came suddenly upon two coolies digging a grave. He was astonished, for he had not heard that anyone in the community was dead.

"Who the devil's that for?" he said aloud.

The coolies did not even look at him, they went on with their work, standing in the grave, deep down, and they shovelled up heavy clods of earth. Though he had been so long in China he knew no

Chinese, in his day it was not thought necessary to learn the damned language, and he asked the coolies in English whose grave they were digging. They did not understand. They answered him in Chinese and he cursed them for ignorant fools. He knew that Mrs. Broome's child was ailing and it might have died, but he would certainly have heard of it, and besides, that wasn't a child's grave, it was a man's and a big man's too. It was uncanny. He wished he hadn't gone into that cemetery; he hurried out and stepped into his chair. His good-humour had all gone and there was an uneasy frown on his face. The moment he got back to his office he called to his number two:

"I say, Peters, who's dead, d'you know?"

But Peters knew nothing. The taipan was puzzled. He called one of the native clerks and sent him to the cemetery to ask the coolies. He began to sign his letters. The clerk came back and said the coolies had gone and there was no one to ask. The taipan began to feel vaguely annoyed: he did not like things to happen of which he knew nothing. His own boy would know, his boy always knew everything, and he sent for him; but the boy had heard of no death in the community.

"I knew no one was dead," said the taipan irritably. "But what's the grave for?"

He told the boy to go to the overseer of the cemetery and find out what the devil he had dug a grave for when no one was dead.

"Let me have a whisky and soda before you go," he added, as the boy was leaving the room.

He did not know why the sight of the grave had made him uncomfortable. But he tried to put it out of his mind. He felt better when he had drunk the whisky, and he finished his work. He went upstairs and turned over the pages of *Punch*. In a few minutes he would go to the club and play a rubber or two of bridge before dinner. But it would ease his mind to hear what his boy had to say and he waited for his return. In a little while the boy came back and he brought the overseer with him.

"What are you having a grave dug for?" he asked the overseer point-blank. "Nobody's dead."

"I no dig glave," said the man.

"What the devil do you mean by that? There were two coolies digging a grave this afternoon."

The two Chinese looked at one another. Then the boy said they had been to the cemetery together. There was no new grave there.

The taipan only just stopped himself from speaking.

"But damn it all, I saw it myself," were the words on the tip of his tongue.

But he did not say them. He grew very red as he choked them down. The two Chinese looked at him with their steady eyes. For a moment his breath failed him.

"All right. Get out," he gasped.

But as soon as they were gone he shouted for the boy again, and when he came, maddeningly impassive, he told him to bring some whisky. He rubbed his sweating face with a handkerchief. His hand trembled when he lifted the glass to his lips. They could say what they liked, but he had seen the grave. Why, he could hear still the dull thud as the coolies threw the spadefuls of earth on the ground above them. What did it mean? He could feel his heart beating. He felt strangely ill at ease. But he pulled himself together. It was all nonsense. If there was no grave there it must have been an hallucination. The best thing he could do was to go to the club, and if he ran across the doctor he would ask him to give him a look over.

Everyone in the club looked just the same as ever. He did not know why he should have expected them to look different. It was a comfort. These men, living for many years with one another lives that were methodically regulated, had acquired a number of little idiosyncrasies—one of them hummed incessantly while he played bridge, another insisted on drinking beer through a straw—and these tricks which had so often irritated the taipan now gave him a sense of security. He needed it, for he could not get out of his head that strange sight he had seen; he played bridge very badly; his partner was censorious, and the taipan lost his temper. He thought the men were looking at him oddly. He wondered what they saw in him that was unaccustomed.

Suddenly he felt he could not bear to stay in the club any longer. As he went out he saw the doctor reading *The Times* in the reading-room, but he could not bring himself to speak to him. He wanted to see for himself whether that grave was really there and stepping into his chair he told his bearers to take him to the cemetery. You couldn't have an hallucination twice, could you? And besides, he would take the overseer in with him and if the grave was not there he wouldn't see it, and if it was he'd give the overseer the soundest thrashing he'd ever had. But the overseer was nowhere to be found. He had gone out and taken the keys with him. When the taipan found he could not get into the cemetery he felt suddenly exhausted. He got back into his chair and told his bearers to take him home. He would lie down for half an hour before dinner. He was tired out. That was it. He had heard that people had hallucinations when they were tired. When his boy came in to put out his clothes for dinner it was only by an effort of will that he got up. He had a strong inclination not to dress that evening, but he resisted it: he made it a rule to dress, he had dressed every evening for twenty years and it would never do to break his rule. But he ordered a bottle of champagne with his dinner and that made him feel more comfortable. Afterwards he told the boy to bring him the best brandy. When he had drunk a couple of glasses of this he felt himself again. Hallucinations be damned! He went to the billiard-room and practised a few difficult shots. There could not be much the matter with him when his eye was so sure. When he went to bed he sank immediately into a sound sleep.

But suddenly he awoke. He had dreamed of that open grave and the coolies digging leisurely. He was sure he had seen them. It was absurd to say it was an hallucination when he had seen them with his own eyes. Then he heard the rattle of the night-watchman going his rounds. It broke upon the stillness of the night so harshly that it made him jump out of his skin. And then terror seized him. He felt a horror of the winding multitudinous streets of the Chinese city, and there was something ghastly and terrible in the convoluted roofs of the temples with their devils grimacing and tortured. He loathed the smells that assaulted his nostrils. And the people. Those myriads of blue-clad coolies, and the beggars in their filthy rags, and the merchants and the magistrates, sleek, smiling, and inscrutable, in their long black gowns. They seemed to press upon him with menace. He hated the country. China. Why had he ever come? He was panic-stricken now. He must get out. He would not stay another year, another month. What did he care about Shanghai?

"Oh, my God," he cried, "if I were only safely back in England."

He wanted to go home. If he had to die he wanted to die in England. He could not bear to be buried among all these yellow men, with their slanting eyes and their grinning faces. He wanted to be buried at home, not in that grave he had seen that day. He could never rest there. Never. What did it matter what people thought? Let them think what they liked. The only thing that mattered was to get away while he had the chance.

He got out of bed and wrote to the head of the firm and said he had discovered he was dangerously ill. He must be replaced. He could not stay longer than was absolutely necessary. He must go home at once.

They found the letter in the morning clenched in the taipan's hand. He had slipped down between the desk and the chair. He was stone dead.

The Consul

MR. PETE was in a state of the liveliest exasperation. He had been in the consular service for more than twenty years and he had had to deal with all manner of vexatious people, officials who would not listen to reason, merchants who took the British Government for a debt-collecting agency, missionaries who resented as gross injustice any attempt at fair play; but he never recollected a case which had left him more completely at a loss. He was a mild-mannered man, but for no reason he flew into a passion with his writer and he very nearly sacked the Eurasian clerk because he had wrongly spelt two words in a letter placed before him for his official signature. He was a conscientious man and he could not persuade himself to leave his office before the clock struck four, but the moment it did he jumped up and called for his hat and stick. Because his boy did not bring them at once he abused him roundly. They say that the consuls all grow a little odd; and the merchants who can live for thirty-five years in China without learning enough of the language to ask their way in the street say that it is because they have to study Chinese; and there was no doubt that Mr. Pete was decidedly odd. He was a bachelor and on that account had been sent to a series of posts which by reason of their isolation were thought unsuited to married men. He had lived so much alone that his natural tendency to eccentricity had developed to an extravagant degree, and he had habits which surprised the stranger. He was very absent-minded. He paid no attention to his house, which was always in great disorder, nor to his food; his boys gave him to eat what they liked and for everything he had made him pay through the nose. He was untiring in his efforts to suppress the opium traffic, but he was the only person in the city who did not know that his servants kept opium in the consulate itself, and a busy traffic in the drug was openly conducted at the back door of the compound. He was an ardent collector and the house provided for him by the government was filled with the various things which he had collected one after the other, pewter, brass, carved wood; these were his more legitimate enterprises; but he also collected stamps, birds' eggs, hotel labels, and postmarks: he boasted that he had a collection of postmarks which was unequalled in the Empire. During his long sojourning in lonely places he had read a great deal, and though he was no sinologue he had a greater knowledge of China, its history, literature, and people, than most of his

928

colleagues; but from his wide reading he had acquired not toleration but vanity. He was a man of a singular appearance. His body was small and frail and when he walked he gave you the idea of a dead leaf dancing before the wind; and then there was something extraordinarily odd in the small Tyrolese hat, with a cock's feather in it, very old and shabby, which he wore perched rakishly on the side of his large head. He was exceedingly bald. You saw that his eyes, blue and pale, were weak behind the spectacles, and a drooping, ragged, dingy moustache did not hide the peevishness of his mouth. And now, turning out of the street in which was the consulate, he made his way on to the city wall, for there only in the multitudinous city was it possible to walk with comfort.

He was a man who took his work hardly, worrying himself to death over every trifle, but as a rule a walk on the wall soothed and rested him. The city stood in the midst of a great plain and often at sundown from the wall you could see in the distance the snow-capped mountains, the mountains of Tibet; but now he walked quickly, looking neither to the right nor to the left, and his fat spaniel frisked about him unobserved. He talked to himself rapidly in a low monotone. The cause of his irritation was a visit that he had that day received from a lady who called herself Mrs. Yü and whom he with a consular passion for precision insisted on calling Miss Lambert. This in itself sufficed to deprive their intercourse of amenity. She was an Englishwoman married to a Chinese. She had arrived two years before with her husband from England, where he had been studying at the University of London; he had made her believe that he was a great personage in his own country and she had imagined herself to be coming to a gorgeous palace and a position of consequence. It was a bitter surprise when she found herself brought to a shabby Chinese house crowded with people: there was not even a foreign bed in it, nor a knife and fork: everything seemed to her very dirty and smelly. It was a shock to find that she had to live with her husband's father and mother and he told her that she must do exactly what his mother bade her; but in her complete ignorance of Chinese it was not till she had been two or three days in the house that she realised that she was not her husband's only wife. He had been married as a boy before he left his native city to acquire the knowledge of the barbarians. When she bitterly upbraided him for deceiving her he shrugged his shoulders. There was nothing to prevent a Chinese from having two wives if he wanted them and, he added with some disregard to truth, no Chinese woman looked upon it as a hardship. It was upon making this discovery that she paid her first visit to the consul. He had already heard of her arrival—

in China everyone knows everything about everyone—and he received her without surprise. Nor had he much sympathy to show her. That a foreign woman should marry a Chinese at all filled him with indignation, but that she should do so without making proper enquiries vexed him like a personal affront. She was not at all the sort of woman whose appearance led you to imagine that she would be guilty of such a folly. She was a solid, thick-set, young person, short, plain, and matter-of-fact. She was cheaply dressed in a tailor-made suit and she wore a tam-o'-shanter. She had bad teeth and a muddy skin. Her hands were large and red and ill-cared for. You could tell that she was not unused to hard work. She spoke English with a cockney whine.

"How did you meet Mr. Yü?" asked the consul frigidly.

"Well, you see, it's like this," she answered. "Dad was in a very good position, and when he died mother said: 'Well, it seems a waste to keep all these rooms empty, I'll put a card in the window.'"

The consul interrupted her.

"He had lodgings with you?"

"Well, they weren't exactly lodgings," she said.

"Shall we say apartments then?" replied the consul, with his thin, slightly vain smile.

That was generally the explanation of these marriages. Then because he thought her a very foolish vulgar woman he explained bluntly that according to English law she was not married to Yü and that the best thing she could do was to go back to England at once. She began to cry and his heart softened a little to her. He promised to put her in charge of some missionary ladies who would look after her on the long journey, and indeed, if she liked, he would see if meanwhile she could not live in one of the missions. But while he talked Miss Lambert dried her tears.

"What's the good of going back to England?" she said at last. "I 'aven't got nowhere to go to."

"You can go to your mother."

"She was all against my marrying Mr. Yü. I should never hear the last of it if I was to go back now."

The consul began to argue with her, but the more he argued the more determined she became, and at last he lost his temper.

"If you like to stay here with a man who isn't your husband it's your own look-out, but I wash my hands of all responsibility."

Her retort had often rankled.

"Then you've got no cause to worry," she said, and the look on her face returned to him whenever he thought of her.

That was two years ago and he had seen her once or twice since then. It appeared that she got on very badly both with her mother-in-law and with her husband's other wife, and she had come to the consul with preposterous questions about her rights according to Chinese law. He repeated his offer to get her away, but she remained steadfast in her refusal to go, and their interview always ended in the consul's flying into a passion. He was almost inclined to pity the rascally Yü who had to keep the peace between three warring women. According to his English wife's account he was not unkind to her. He tried to act fairly by both his wives. Miss Lambert did not improve. The consul knew that ordinarily she wore Chinese clothes, but when she came to see him she put on European dress. She was become extremely blowsy. Her health suffered from the Chinese food she ate and she was beginning to look wretchedly ill. But really he was shocked when she had been shown into his office that day. She wore no hat and her hair was dishevelled. She was in a highly hysterical state.

"They're trying to poison me," she screamed and she put before him a bowl of some foul-smelling food. "It's poisoned," she said. "I've been ill for the last ten days, it's only by a miracle I've escaped."

She gave him a long story, circumstantial and probable enough to convince him: after all, nothing was more likely than that the Chinese women should use familiar methods to get rid of an intruder who was hateful to them.

"Do they know you've come here?"

"Of course they do; I told them I was going to show them up."

Now at last was the moment for decisive action. The consul looked at her in his most official manner.

"Well, you must never go back there. I refuse to put up with your nonsense any longer. I insist on your leaving this man who isn't your husband."

But he found himself helpless against the woman's insane obstinacy. He repeated all the arguments he had used so often, but she would not listen, and as usual he lost his temper. It was then, in answer to his final, desperate question, that she had made the remark which had entirely robbed him of his calm.

"But what on earth makes you stay with the man?" he cried.

She hesitated for a moment and a curious look came into her eyes.

"There's something in the way his hair grows on his forehead that I can't help liking," she answered.

The consul had never heard anything so outrageous. It really was the last straw. And now while he strode along, trying to walk off his anger, though he was not a man who often used bad language he really could not restrain himself, and he said fiercely:

"Women are simply bloody."

A Friend in Need

For thirty years now I have been studying my fellow-men. I do not know very much about them. I should certainly hesitate to engage a servant on his face, and yet I suppose it is on the face that for the most part we judge the persons we meet. We draw our conclusions from the shape of the jaw, the look in the eyes, the contour of the mouth. I wonder if we are more often right than wrong. Why novels and plays are so often untrue to life is because their authors, perhaps of necessity, make their characters all of a piece. They cannot afford to make them self-contradictory, for then they become incomprehensible, and yet self-contradictory is what most of us are. We are a haphazard bundle of inconsistent qualities. In books on logic they will tell you that it is absurd to say that yellow is tubular or gratitude heavier than air; but in that mixture of incongruities that makes up the self yellow may very well be a horse and cart and gratitude the middle of next week. I shrug my shoulders when people tell me that their first impressions of a person are always right. I think they must have small insight or great vanity. For my own part I find that the longer I know people the more they puzzle me: my oldest friends are just those of whom I can say that I don't know the first thing about them.

These reflections have occurred to me because I read in this morning's paper that Edward Hyde Burton had died at Kobe. He was a merchant and he had been in business in Japan for many years. I knew him very little, but he interested me because once he gave me a great surprise. Unless I had heard the story from his own lips I should never have believed that he was capable of such an action. It was more startling because both in appearance and manner he suggested a very definite type. Here if ever was a man all of a piece. He was a tiny little fellow, not much more than five feet four in height, and very slender, with white hair, a red face much wrinkled, and blue eyes. I suppose he was about sixty when I knew him. He was always neatly and quietly dressed in accordance with his age and station.

Though his offices were in Kobe Burton often came down to Yokohama. I happened on one occasion to be spending a few days there, waiting for a ship, and I was introduced to him at the British Club. We played bridge together. He played a good game and a generous one. He did not talk very much, either then or later when we were having drinks, but what he said was sensible. He had a quiet, dry humour. He seemed to be popular at the club and afterwards, when he had gone, they described him as one of the best. It happened that we were both staying at the Grand Hotel and next day he asked me to dine with him. I met his wife, fat, elderly and smiling, and his two daughters. It was evidently a united and affectionate family. I think the chief thing that struck me about Burton was his kindliness. There was something very pleasing in his mild blue eyes. His voice was gentle; you could not imagine that he could possibly raise it in anger; his smile was benign. Here was a man who attracted you because you felt in him a real love for his fellows. He had charm. But there was nothing mawkish in him: he liked his game of cards and his cocktail, he could tell with point a good and spicy story, and in his youth he had been something of an athlete. He was a rich man and he had made every penny himself. I suppose one thing that made you like him was that he was so small and frail; he aroused your instincts of protection. You felt that he could not bear to hurt a fly.

One afternoon I was sitting in the lounge of the Grand Hotel. This was before the earthquake and they had leather arm-chairs there. From the windows you had a spacious view of the harbour with its crowded traffic. There were great liners on their way to Vancouver and San Francisco or to Europe by way of Shanghai, Hong-Kong and Singapore; there were tramps of all nations, battered and sea-worn, junks with their high sterns and great coloured sails, and innumerable sampans. It was a busy, exhilarating scene, and yet, I know not why, restful to the spirit. Here was romance and it seemed that you had but to stretch out your hand to touch it.

Burton came into the lounge presently and caught sight of me. He seated himself in the chair next to mine.

"What do you say to a little drink?"

He clapped his hands for a boy and ordered two gin fizzes. As the boy brought them a man passed along the street outside and seeing me waved his hand.

"Do you know Turner?" said Burton as I nodded a greeting.

"I've met him at the club. I'm told he's a remittance man."

"Yes, I believe he is. We have a good many here."

"He plays bridge well."

"They generally do. There was a fellow here last year, oddly enough a namesake of mine, who was the best bridge-player I ever met. I suppose you never came across him in London. Lenny Burton he called himself. I believe he'd belonged to some very good clubs."

"No, I don't believe I remember the name."

"He was quite a remarkable player. He seemed to have an instinct about the cards. It was uncanny. I used to play with him a lot. He was in Kobe for some time."

Burton sipped his gin fizz.

"It's rather a funny story," he said. "He wasn't a bad chap. I liked him. He was always well-dressed and smart-looking. He was handsome in a way with curly hair and pink-and-white cheeks. Women thought a lot of him. There was no harm in him, you know, he was only wild. Of course he drank too much. Those sort of fellows always do. A bit of money used to come in for him once a quarter and he made a bit more by card-playing. He won a good deal of mine, I know that."

Burton gave a kindly chuckle. I knew from my own experience that he could lose money at bridge with a good grace. He stroked his shaven chin with his thin hand; the veins stood out on it and it was almost transparent.

"I suppose that is why he came to me when he went broke, that and the fact that he was a namesake of mine. He came to see me in my office one day and asked me for a job. I was rather surprised. He told me that there was no more money coming from home and he wanted to work. I asked him how old he was.

" 'Thirty-five,' he said.

" 'And what have you been doing hitherto?' I asked him.

" 'Well, nothing very much,' he said.

"I couldn't help laughing.

" 'I'm afraid I can't do anything for you just yet,' I said. 'Come back and see me in another thirty-five years, and I'll see what I can do.'

"He didn't move. He went rather pale. He hesitated for a moment and then he told me that he had had bad luck at cards for some time. He hadn't been willing to stick to bridge, he'd been playing poker, and he'd got trimmed. He hadn't a penny. He'd pawned everything he had. He couldn't pay his hotel bill and they wouldn't give him any more credit. He was down and out. If he couldn't get something to do he'd have to commit suicide.

"I looked at him for a bit. I could see now that he was all to pieces. He'd been drinking more than usual and he looked fifty. The girls wouldn't have thought so much of him if they'd seen him then.

" 'Well, isn't there anything you can do except play cards?' I asked him.

" 'I can swim,' he said.

" 'Swim!'

"I could hardly believe my ears; it seemed such an insane answer to give.

" 'I swam for my university.'

"I got some glimmering of what he was driving at. I've known too many men who were little tin gods at their university to be impressed by it.

" 'I was a pretty good swimmer myself when I was a young man,' I said.

"Suddenly I had an idea."

Pausing in his story, Burton turned to me.

"Do you know Kobe?" he asked.

"No," I said, "I passed through it once, but I only spent a night there."

"Then you don't know the Shioya Club. When I was a young man I swam from there round the beacon and landed at the creek of Tarumi. It's over three miles and it's rather difficult on account of the currents round the beacon. Well, I told my young name-sake about it and I said to him that if he'd do it I'd give him a job.

"I could see he was rather taken aback.

" 'You say you're a swimmer,' I said.

" 'I'm not in very good condition,' he answered.

"I didn't say anything. I shrugged my shoulders. He looked at me for a moment and then he nodded.

" 'All right,' he said. 'When do you want me to do it?'

"I looked at my watch. It was just after ten.

" 'The swim shouldn't take you much over an hour and a quarter. I'll drive round to the creek at half-past twelve and meet you. I'll take you back to the club to dress and then we'll have lunch to-gether.'

" 'Done,' he said.

"We shook hands. I wished him good luck and he left me. I had a lot of work to do that morning and I only just managed to get to the creek at Tarumi at half-past twelve. But I needn't have hurried; he never turned up."

"Did he funk it at the last moment?" I asked.

"No, he didn't funk it. He started all right. But of course he'd ruined his constitution by drink and dissipation. The currents round the beacon were more than he could manage. We didn't get the body for about three days."

I didn't say anything for a moment or two. I was a trifle shocked. Then I asked Burton a question.

"When you made him that offer of a job, did you know he'd be drowned?"

He gave a little mild chuckle, and he looked at me with those kind and candid blue eyes of his. He rubbed his chin with his hand.

"Well, I hadn't got a vacancy in my office at the moment."

The Round Dozen

I LIKE Elsom. It is a seaside resort in the South of England, not very far from Brighton, and it has something of the late Georgian charm of that agreeable town. But it is neither bustling nor garish. Ten years ago, when I used to go there not infrequently, you might still see here and there an old house, solid and pretentious in no unpleasing fashion (like a decayed gentlewoman of good family whose discreet pride in her ancestry amuses rather than offends you), which was built in the reign of the First Gentleman in Europe and where a courtier of fallen fortunes may well have passed his declining years. The main street had a lackadaisical air and the doctor's motor seemed a trifle out of place. The housewives did their housekeeping in a leisurely manner. They gossiped with the butcher as they watched him cut from his great joint of South Down a piece of the best end of the neck, and they asked amiably after the grocer's wife as he put half a pound of tea and a packet of salt into their string bag. I do not know whether Elsom was ever fashionable: it certainly was not so then; but it was respectable and cheap. Elderly ladies, maiden and widowed, lived there, Indian Civilians and retired soldiers: they looked forward with little shudders of dismay to August and September which would bring holiday-makers; but did not disdain to let them their houses and on the proceeds spend a few worldly weeks in a Swiss pension. I never knew Elsom at that hectic time when the lodging-houses were full and young men in blazers sauntered along the front, when Pierrots performed on the beach and in the billiard-room at the Dolphin you heard the click of balls till eleven at night. I only knew it in winter. Then in every house on the sea-front, stucco houses with bow-windows built a hundred years ago, there was a sign to inform you that apartments were to let; and the guests of the Dolphin were waited on by a single waiter and the boots. At ten o'clock the porter came into the smoking-room and looked at you in so marked a manner that you got up and went to bed. Then Elsom was a restful place and the Dolphin a very comfortable inn. It was pleasing to think that the Prince Regent drove over with Mrs. Fitzherbert more than once to drink a dish of tea in its coffee-room. In the hall was a framed letter from Mr. Thackeray ordering a sitting-room and two bedrooms overlooking the sea and giving instructions that a fly should be sent to the station to meet him.

One November, two or three years after the war, having had a bad attack of influenza, I went down to Elsom to regain my strength. I arrived in the afternoon and when I had unpacked my things went for a stroll on the front. The sky was overcast and the calm sea grey and cold. A few seagulls flew close to the shore. Sailing-boats, their masts taken down for the winter, were drawn up high on the shingly beach and the bathing-huts stood side by side in a long, grey and tattered row. No one was sitting on the benches that the town council had put here and there, but a few people were trudging up and down for exercise. I passed an old colonel with a red nose who stamped along in plus-fours followed by a terrier, two elderly women in short skirts and stout shoes and a plain girl in a tam-o'-shanter. I had never seen the front so deserted. The lodging-houses looked like bedraggled old maids waiting for lovers who would never return, and even the friendly Dolphin seemed wan and desolate. My heart sank. Life on a sudden seemed very drab. I returned to the hotel, drew the curtains of my sitting-room, poked the fire and with a book sought to dispel my melancholy. But I was glad enough when it was time to dress for dinner. I went into the coffee-room and found the guests of the hotel already seated. I gave them a casual glance. There was one lady of middle age by herself and there were two elderly gentlemen, golfers probably, with red faces and baldish heads, who ate their food in moody silence. The only other persons in the room were a group of three who sat in the bow-window, and they immediately attracted my surprised attention. The party consisted of an old gentleman and two ladies, one of whom was old and probably his wife, while the other was younger and possibly his daughter. It was the old lady who first excited my interest. She wore a voluminous dress of black silk and a black lace cap; on her wrists were heavy gold bangles and round her neck a substantial gold chain from which hung a large gold locket; at her neck was a large gold brooch. I did not know that anyone still wore jewellery of that sort. Often, passing second-hand jewellers and pawnbrokers, I had lingered for a moment to look at these strangely old-fashioned articles, so solid, costly and hideous, and thought, with a smile in which there was a tinge of sadness, of the women long since dead who had worn them. They suggested the period when the bustle and the flounce were taking the place of the crinoline and the pork-pie hat was ousting the poke-bonnet. The British people liked things solid and good in those days. They went to church on Sunday morning and after church walked in the Park. They gave dinner-parties of twelve courses where the master of the house carved the beef and the chickens, and after dinner the ladies who could play favoured the company with Mendelssohn's *Songs without Words* and the gentleman with the fine baritone voice sang an old English ballad.

The younger woman had her back turned to me and at first I could see only that she had a slim and youthful figure. She had a great deal of brown hair which seemed to be elaborately arranged. She wore a grey dress. The three of them were chatting in low tones and presently she turned her head so that I saw her profile. It was astonishingly beautiful. The nose was straight and delicate, the line of the cheek exquisitely modelled; I saw then that she wore her hair after the manner of Queen Alexandra. The dinner proceeded to its close and the party got up. The old lady sailed out of the room, looking neither to the right nor to the left, and the young one followed her. Then I saw with a shock that she was old. Her frock was simple enough, the skirt was longer than was at that time worn, and there was something slightly old-fashioned in the cut, I dare say the waist was more clearly indicated than was then usual, but it was a girl's frock. She was tall, like a heroine of Tennyson's, slight, with long legs and a graceful carriage. I had seen the nose before, it was the nose of a Greek goddess, her mouth was beautiful, and her eyes were large and blue. Her skin was of course a little tight on the bones and there were wrinkles on her forehead and about her eyes, but in youth it must have been lovely. She reminded you of those Roman ladies with features of an exquisite regularity whom Alma-Tadema used to paint, but who, notwithstanding their antique dress, were so stubbornly English. It was a type of cold perfection that one had not seen for five-and-twenty years. Now it is as dead as the epigram. I was like an archæologist who finds some long-buried statue and I was thrilled in so unexpected a manner to hit upon this survival of a past era. For no day is so dead as the day before yesterday.

The gentleman rose to his feet when the two ladies left, and then resumed his chair. A waiter brought him a glass of heavy port. He smelt it, sipped it, and rolled it round his tongue. I observed him. He was a little man, much shorter than his imposing wife, well-covered without being stout, with a fine head of curling grey hair. His face was much wrinkled and it bore a faintly humorous expression. His lips were tight and his chin was square. He was, according to our present notions, somewhat extravagantly dressed. He wore a black velvet jacket, a frilled shirt with a low collar and a large black tie, and very wide evening trousers. It gave you vaguely the effect of costume. Having drunk his port with deliberation, he got up and sauntered out of the room.

When I passed through the hall, curious to know who these singular people were, I glanced at the visitors' book. I saw written in an angular feminine hand, the writing that was taught to young ladies in modish schools forty years or so ago, the names: Mr. and Mrs. Edwin St. Clair and Miss Porchester. Their address was given as 68, Leinster Square, Bayswater, London. These must be the names and this the address of the persons who had so much interested me. I asked the manageress who Mr. St. Clair was and she told me that she believed he was something in the City. I went into the billiard-room and knocked the balls about for a little while and then on my way upstairs passed through the lounge. The two red-faced gentlemen were reading the evening paper and the elderly lady was dozing over a novel. The party of three sat in a corner. Mrs. St. Clair was knitting, Miss Porchester was busy with embroidery, and Mr. St. Clair was reading aloud in a discreet but resonant tone. As I passed I discovered that he was reading *Bleak House*.

I read and wrote most of the next day, but in the afternoon I went for a walk and on my way home I sat down for a little on one of those convenient benches on the sea-front. It was not quite so cold as the day before and the air was pleasant. For want of anything better to do I watched a figure advancing towards me from a distance. It was a man and as he came nearer I saw that it was rather a shabby little man. He wore a thin black greatcoat and a somewhat battered bowler. He walked with his hands in his pockets and looked cold. He gave me a glance as he passed by, went on a few steps, hesitated, stopped and turned back. When he came up once more to the bench on which I sat he took a hand out of his pocket and touched his hat. I noticed that he wore shabby black gloves, and surmised that he was a widower in straitened circumstances. Or he might have been a mute recovering, like myself, from influenza.

"Excuse me, sir," he said, "but could you oblige me with a match?"

"Certainly."

He sat down beside me and while I put my hand in my pocket for matches he hunted in his for cigarettes. He took out a small packet of Gold Flake and his face fell.

"Dear, dear, how very annoying! I haven't got a cigarette left."

"Let me offer you one," I replied, smiling.

I took out my case and he helped himself.

"Gold?" he asked, giving the case a tap as I closed it. "Gold? That's a thing I never could keep. I've had three. All stolen."

His eyes rested in a melancholy way on his boots, which were sadly in need of repair. He was a wizened little man with a long thin nose and pale-blue eyes. His skin was sallow and he was much lined. I could not tell what his age was; he might have been five-and-thirty or he might have been sixty. There was nothing remarkable about him except his insignificance. But though evidently poor he was neat and clean. He was respectable and he clung to respectability. No, I did not think he was a mute, I thought he was a solicitor's clerk who had lately buried his wife and been sent to Elsom by an indulgent employer to get over the first shock of his grief.

"Are you making a long stay, sir?" he asked me.

"Ten days or a fortnight."

"Is this your first visit to Elsom, sir?"

"I have been here before."

"I know it well, sir. I flatter myself there are very few seaside resorts that I have not been to at one time or another. Elsom is hard to beat, sir. You get a very nice class of people here. There's nothing noisy or vulgar about Elsom, if you understand what I mean. Elsom has very pleasant recollections for me, sir. I knew Elsom well in bygone days. I was married in St. Martin's Church, sir."

"Really," I said feebly.

"It was a very happy marriage, sir."

"I'm very glad to hear it," I returned.

"Nine months, that one lasted," he said reflectively.

Surely the remark was a trifle singular. I had not looked forward with any enthusiasm to the probability which I so clearly foresaw that he would favour me with an account of his matrimonial experiences, but now I waited if not with eagerness at least with curiosity for a further observation. He made none. He sighed a little. At last I broke the silence.

"There don't seem to be very many people about," I remarked.

"I like it so. I'm not one for crowds. As I was saying just now, I reckon I've spent a good many years at one seaside resort after the other, but I never came in the season. It's the winter I like."

"Don't you find it a little melancholy?"

He turned towards me and placed his black-gloved hand for an instant on my arm.

"It is melancholy. And because it's melancholy a little ray of sunshine is very welcome."

The remark seemed to me perfectly idiotic and I did not answer. He withdrew his hand from my arm and got up.

"Well, I mustn't keep you, sir. Pleased to have made your acquaintance."

He took off his dingy hat very politely and strolled away. It was beginning now to grow chilly and I thought I would return to the Dolphin. As I reached its broad steps a landau drove up, drawn by two scraggy horses, and from it stepped Mr. St. Clair. He wore a hat that looked like the unhappy result of a union between a bowler and a top-hat. He gave his hand to his wife and then to his niece. The porter carried in after them rugs and cushions. As Mr. St. Clair paid the driver I heard him tell him to come at the usual time next day and I understood that the St. Clairs took a drive every afternoon in a landau. It would not have surprised me to learn that none of them had ever been in a motor-car.

The manageress told me that they kept very much to themselves and sought no acquaintance among the other persons staying at the hotel. I rode my imagination on a loose rein. I watched them eat three meals a day. I watched Mr. and Mrs. St. Clair sit at the top of the hotel steps in the morning. He read *The Times* and she knitted. I suppose Mrs. St. Clair had never read a paper in her life, for they never took anything but *The Times* and Mr. St. Clair of course took it with him every day to the City. At about twelve Miss Porchester joined them.

"Have you enjoyed your walk, Eleanor?" asked Mrs. St. Clair.

"It was very nice, Aunt Gertrude," answered Miss Porchester.

And I understood that just as Mrs. St. Clair took "her drive" every afternoon Miss Porchester took "her walk" every morning.

"When you have come to the end of your row, my dear," said Mr. St. Clair, with a glance at his wife's knitting, "we might go for a constitutional before luncheon."

"That will be very nice," answered Mrs. St. Clair. She folded up her work and gave it to Miss Porchester. "If you're going upstairs, Eleanor, will you take my work?"

"Certainly, Aunt Gertrude."

"I dare say you're a little tired after your walk, my dear."

"I shall have a little rest before luncheon."

Miss Porchester went into the hotel and Mr. and Mrs. St. Clair walked slowly along the sea-front, side by side, to a certain point, and then walked slowly back.

When I met one of them on the stairs I bowed and received an unsmiling, polite bow in return, and in the morning I ventured upon a good-day, but there the matter ended. It looked as though I should never have a chance to speak to any of them. But presently I thought that Mr. St. Clair gave me now and then a glance, and thinking he had heard my name I imagined, perhaps vainly, that he looked at me with curiosity. And a day or two after that I was sitting in my room when the porter came in with a message.

"Mr. St. Clair presents his compliments and could you oblige him with the loan of *Whitaker's Almanack*."

I was astonished.

"Why on earth should he think that I have a *Whitaker's Almanack*?"

"Well, sir, the manageress told him you wrote."

I could not see the connection.

"Tell Mr. St. Clair that I'm very sorry that I haven't got a *Whitaker's Almanack*, but if I had I would very gladly lend it to him."

Here was my opportunity. I was by now filled with eagerness to know these fantastic persons more closely. Now and then in the heart of Asia I have come upon a lonely tribe living in a little village among an alien population. No one knows how they came there or why they settled in that spot. They live their own lives, speak their own language, and have no communication with their neighbours. No one knows whether they are the descendants of a band that was left behind when their nation swept in a vast horde across the continent or whether they are the dying remnant of some great people that in that country once held empire. They are a mystery. They have no future and no history. This odd little family seemed to me to have something of the same character. They were of an era that is dead and gone. They reminded me of persons in one of those leisurely, old-fashioned novels that one's father read. They belonged to the 'eighties and they had not moved since then. How extraordinary it was that they could have lived through the last forty years as though the world stood still! They took me back to my childhood and I recollected people who are long since dead. I wonder if it is only distance that gives me the impression that they were more peculiar than anyone is now. When a person was described then as "quite a character", by heaven, it meant something.

So that evening after dinner I went into the lounge and boldly addressed Mr. St. Clair.

"I'm so sorry I haven't got a *Whitaker's Almanack*," I said, "but if I have any other book that can be of service to you I shall be delighted to lend it to you."

Mr. St. Clair was obviously startled. The two ladies kept their eyes on their work. There was an embarrassed hush.

"It does not matter at all, but I was given to understand by the manageress that you were a novelist."

I racked my brain. There was evidently some connection between my profession and *Whitaker's Almanack* that escaped me.

"In days gone by Mr. Trollope used often to dine with us in Leinster Square and I remember him saying that the two most useful books to a novelist were the Bible and *Whitaker's Almanack*."

"I see that Thackeray once stayed in this hotel," I remarked, anxious not to let the conversation drop.

"I never very much cared for Mr. Thackeray, though he dined more than once with my wife's father, the late Mr. Sargent Saunders.

He was too cynical for me. My niece has not read *Vanity Fair* to this day."

Miss Porchester blushed slightly at this reference to herself. A waiter brought in the coffee and Mrs. St. Clair turned to her husband.

"Perhaps, my dear, this gentleman would do us the pleasure to have his coffee with us."

Although not directly addressed I answered promptly:

"Thank you very much."

I sat down.

"Mr. Trollope was always my favourite novelist," said Mr. St. Clair. "He was so essentially a gentleman. I admire Charles Dickens. But Charles Dickens could never draw a gentleman. I am given to understand that young people nowadays find Mr. Trollope a little slow. My niece, Miss Porchester, prefers the novels of Mr. William Black."

"I'm afraid I've never read any," I said.

"Ah, I see that you are like me; you are not up to date. My niece once persuaded me to read a novel by a Miss Rhoda Broughton, but I could not manage more than a hundred pages of it."

"I did not say I liked it, Uncle Edwin," said Miss Porchester, defending herself, with another blush, "I told you it was rather fast, but everybody was talking about it."

"I'm quite sure it is not the sort of book your Aunt Gertrude would have wished you to read, Eleanor."

"I remember Miss Broughton telling me once that when she was young people said her books were fast and when she was old they said they were slow, and it was very hard since she had written exactly the same sort of book for forty years."

"Oh, did you know Miss Broughton?" asked Miss Porchester, addressing me for the first time. "How very interesting! And did you know Ouida?"

"My dear Eleanor, what will you say next! I'm quite sure you've never read anything by Ouida."

"Indeed, I have, Uncle Edwin. I've read *Under Two Flags* and I liked it very much."

"You amaze and shock me. I don't know what girls are coming to nowadays."

"You always said that when I was thirty you gave me complete liberty to read anything I liked."

"There is a difference, my dear Eleanor, between liberty and licence," said Mr. St. Clair, smiling a little in order not to make his reproof offensive, but with a certain gravity.

I do not know if in recounting this conversation I have managed to convey the impression it gave me of a charming and old-fashioned air. I could have listened all night to them discussing the depravity of an age that was young in the eighteen-eighties. I would have given a good deal for a glimpse of their large and roomy house in Leinster Square. I should have recognised the suite covered in red brocade that stood stiffly about the drawing-room, each piece in its appointed place; and the cabinets filled with Dresden china would have brought me back my childhood. In the dining-room, where they habitually sat, for the drawing-room was used only for parties, was a Turkey carpet and a vast mahogany sideboard "groaning" with silver. On the walls were the pictures that had excited the admiration of Mrs. Humphry Ward and her uncle Matthew in the Academy of eighteen-eighty.

Next morning, strolling through a pretty lane at the back of Elsom, I met Miss Porchester, who was taking "her walk". I should have liked to go a little way with her, but felt certain that it would embarrass this maiden of fifty to saunter alone with a man even of my respectable years. She bowed as I passed her and blushed. Oddly enough, a few yards behind her I came upon the funny shabby little man in black gloves with whom I had spoken for a few minutes on the front. He touched his old bowler hat.

"Excuse me, sir, but could you oblige me with a match?" he said.

"Certainly," I retorted, "but I'm afraid I have no cigarettes on me."

"Allow me to offer you one of mine," he said, taking out the paper case. It was empty. "Dear, dear, I haven't got one either. What a curious coincidence!"

He went on and I had a notion that he a little hastened his steps. I was beginning to have my doubts about him. I hoped he was not going to bother Miss Porchester. For a moment I thought of walking back, but I did not. He was a civil little man and I did not believe he would make a nuisance of himself to a single lady.

I saw him again that very afternoon. I was sitting on the front. He walked towards me with little, halting steps. There was something of a wind and he looked like a dried leaf being driven before it. This time he did not hesitate, but sat down beside me.

"We meet again, sir. The world is a small place. If it will not inconvenience you perhaps you will allow me to rest a few minutes. I am a wee bit tired."

"This is a public bench, and you have just as much right to sit on it as I."

I did not wait for him to ask me for a match, but at once offered him a cigarette.

"How very kind of you, sir! I have to limit myself to so many cigarettes a day, but I enjoy those I smoke. As one grows older the pleasures of life diminish, but my experience is that one enjoys more those that remains."

"That is a very consoling thought."

"Excuse me, sir, but am I right in thinking that you are the well-known author?"

"I am an author," I replied. "But what made you think it?"

"I have seen your portrait in the illustrated papers. I suppose you don't recognise me?"

I looked at him again, a weedy little man in neat but shabby black clothes, with a long nose and watery blue eyes.

"I'm afraid I don't."

"I dare say I've changed," he sighed. "There was a time when my photograph was in every paper in the United Kingdom. Of course, those press photographs never do you justice. I give you my word, sir, that if I hadn't seen my name underneath I should never have guessed that some of them were meant for me."

He was silent for a while. The tide was out and beyond the shingle of the beach was a strip of yellow mud. The breakwaters were half buried in it like the backbones of prehistoric beasts.

"It must be a wonderfully interesting thing to be an author, sir. I've often thought I had quite a turn for writing myself. At one time and another I've done a rare lot of reading. I haven't kept up with it much lately. For one thing my eyes are not so good as they used to be. I believe I could write a book if I tried."

"They say anybody can write one," I answered.

"Not a novel, you know. I'm not much of a one for novels; I prefer histories and that-like. But memoirs. If anybody was to make it worth my while I wouldn't mind writing my memoirs."

"It's very fashionable just now."

"There are not many people who've had the experiences I've had in one way and another. I did write to one of the Sunday papers about it some little while back, but they never answered my letter."

He gave me a long, appraising look. He had too respectable an air to be about to ask me for half a crown.

"Of course you don't know who I am, sir, do you?"

"I honestly don't."

He seemed to ponder for a moment, then he smoothed down his black gloves on his fingers, looked for a moment at a hole in one of them, and then turned to me not without self-consciousness.

"I am the celebrated Mortimer Ellis," he said.

"Oh?"

I did not know what other ejaculation to make, for to the best of my belief I had never heard the name before. I saw a look of disappointment come over his face, and I was a trifle embarrassed.

"Mortimer Ellis," he repeated. "You're not going to tell me you don't know."

"I'm afraid I must. I'm very often out of England."

I wondered to what he owed his celebrity. I passed over in my mind various possibilities. He could never have been an athlete, which alone in England gives a man real fame, but he might have been a faith-healer or a champion billiard-player. There is of course no one so obscure as a Cabinet Minister out of office and he might have been the President of the Board of Trade in a defunct administration. But he had none of the look of a politician.

"That's fame for you," he said bitterly. "Why, for weeks I was the most talked-about man in England. Look at me. You must have seen my photograph in the papers. Mortimer Ellis."

"I'm sorry," I said, shaking my head.

He paused a moment to give his disclosure effectiveness.

"I am the well-known bigamist."

Now what are you to reply when a person who is practically a stranger to you informs you that he is a well-known bigamist? I will confess that I have sometimes had the vanity to think that I am not as a rule at a loss for a retort, but here I found myself speechless.

"I've had eleven wives, sir," he went on.

"Most people find one about as much as they can manage."

"Ah, that's want of practice. When you've had eleven there's very little you don't know about women."

"But why did you stop at eleven?"

"There now, I knew you'd say that. The moment I set eyes on you I said to myself, he's got a clever face. You know, sir, that's the thing that always grizzles me. Eleven does seem a funny number, doesn't it? There's something unfinished about it. Now three anyone might have, and seven's all right, they say nine's lucky, and there's nothing wrong with ten. But eleven! That's the one thing I regret. I shouldn't have minded anything if I could have brought it up to the Round Dozen."

He unbuttoned his coat and from an inside pocket produced a bulging and very greasy pocket-book. From this he took a large bundle of newspaper cuttings; they were worn and creased and dirty. But he spread out two or three.

"Now just you look at those photographs. I ask you, are they like me? It's an outrage. Why, you'd think I was a criminal to look at them."

The cuttings were of imposing length. In the opinion of sub-editors Mortimer Ellis had obviously been a news item of value. One was headed, A Much Married Man; another, Heartless Ruffian Brought to Book; a third, Contemptible Scoundrel Meets his Waterloo.

"Not what you would call a good press," I murmured.

"I never pay any attention to what the newspapers say," he answered, with a shrug of his thin shoulders. "I've known too many journalists myself for that. No, it's the judge I blame. He treated me shocking and it did him no good, mind you; he died within the year."

I ran my eyes down the report I held.

"I see he gave you five years."

"Disgraceful, I call it, and see what it says." He pointed to a place with his forefinger. " 'Three of his victims pleaded for mercy to be shown to him.' That shows what they thought of me. And after that he gave me five years. And just look what he called me, a heartless scoundrel—me, the best-hearted man that ever lived—a pest of society and a danger to the public. Said he wished he had the power to give me the cat. I don't so much mind his giving me five years, though you'll never get me to say it wasn't excessive, but I ask you, had he the right to talk to me like that? No, he hadn't, and I'll never forgive him, not if I live to be a hundred."

The bigamist's cheeks flushed and his watery eyes were filled for a moment with fire. It was a sore subject with him.

"May I read them?" I asked him.

"That's what I gave them you for. I want you to read them, sir. And if you can read them without saying that I'm a much wronged man, well, you're not the man I took you for."

As I glanced through one cutting after another I saw why Mortimer Ellis had so wide an acquaintance with the seaside resorts of England. They were his hunting-ground. His method was to go to some place when the season was over and take apartments in one of the empty lodging-houses. Apparently it did not take him long to make acquaintance with some woman or other, widow or spinster, and I noticed that their ages at the time were between thirty-five and fifty. They stated in the witness-box that they had met him first on the sea-front. He generally proposed marriage to them within a fortnight of this and they were married shortly after. He induced them in one way or another to entrust him with their savings and in a few months, on the pretext that he had to go to London on

H

business, he left them never to return. Only one had ever seen him again till, obliged to give evidence, they saw him in the dock. They were women of a certain respectability; one was the daughter of a doctor and another of a clergyman; there was a lodging-house keeper, there was the widow of a commercial traveller, and there was a retired dressmaker. For the most part, their fortunes ranged from five hundred to a thousand pounds, but whatever the sum the misguided women were stripped of every penny. Some of them told really pitiful stories of the destitution to which they had been reduced. But they all acknowledged that he had been a good husband to them. Not only had three actually pleaded for mercy to be shown him, but one said in the witness-box that, if he was willing to come, she was ready to take him back. He noticed that I was reading this.

"And she'd have worked for me," he said, "there's no doubt about that. But I said, better let bygones be bygones. No one likes a cut off the best end of the neck better than I do, but I'm not much of a one for cold roast mutton, I will confess."

It was only by an accident that Mortimer Ellis did not marry his twelfth wife and so achieve the Round Dozen which I understand appealed to his love of symmetry. For he was engaged to be married to a Miss Hubbard—"two thousand pounds she had, if she had a penny, in war-loan," he confided to me—and the banns had been read, when one of his former wives saw him, made enquiries, and communicated with the police. He was arrested on the very day before his twelfth wedding.

"She was a bad one, she was," he told me. "She deceived me something cruel."

"How did she do that?"

"Well, I met her at Eastbourne, one December it was, on the pier, and she told me in course of conversation that she'd been in the millinery business and had retired. She said she'd made a tidy bit of money. She wouldn't say exactly how much it was, but she gave me to understand it was something like fifteen hundred pounds. And when I married her, would you believe it, she hadn't got three hundred. And that's the one who gave me away. And mind you, I'd never blamed her. Many a man would have cut up rough when he found out he'd been made a fool of. I never showed her that I was disappointed even, I just went away without a word."

"But not without the three hundred pounds, I take it."

"Oh come, sir, you must be reasonable," he returned in an injured tone. "You can't expect three hundred pounds to last for ever and I'd been married to her four months before she confessed the truth."

"Forgive my asking," I said, "and pray don't think my question suggests a disparaging view of your personal attractions, but—why did they marry you?"

"Because I asked them," he answered, evidently very much surprised at my enquiry.

"But did you never have any refusals?"

"Very seldom. Not more than four or five in the whole course of my career. Of course I didn't propose till I was pretty sure of my ground and I don't say I didn't draw a blank sometimes. You can't expect to click every time, if you know what I mean, and I've often wasted several weeks making up to a woman before I saw there was nothing doing."

I surrendered myself for a time to my reflections. But I noticed presently that a broad smile spread over the mobile features of my friend.

"I understand what you mean," he said. "It's my appearance that puzzles you. You don't know what it is they see in me. That's what comes of reading novels and going to the pictures. You think what women want is the cowboy type, or the romance of old Spain touch, flashing eyes, an olive skin, and a beautiful dancer. You make me laugh."

"I'm glad," I said.

"Are you a married man, sir?"

"I am. But I only have one wife."

"You can't judge by that. You can't generalise from a single instance, if you know what I mean. Now, I ask you, what would you know about dogs if you'd never had anything but one bullterrier?"

The question was rhetorical and I felt sure did not require an answer. He paused for an effective moment and went on.

"You're wrong, sir. You're quite wrong. They may take a fancy to a good-looking young fellow, but they don't want to marry him. They don't really care about looks."

"Douglas Jerrold, who was as ugly as he was witty, used to say that if he was given ten minutes' start with a woman he could cut out the handsomest man in the room."

"They don't want wit. They don't want a man to be funny; they think he's not serious. They don't want a man who's too handsome; they think he's not serious either. That's what they want, they want a man who's serious. Safety first. And then—attention. I may not be handsome and I may not be amusing, but believe me, I've got what every woman wants. Poise. And the proof is, I've made every one of my wives happy."

"It certainly is much to your credit that three of them pleaded for mercy to be shown to you and that one was willing to take you back."

"You don't know what an anxiety that was to me all the time I was in prison. I thought she'd be waiting for me at the gate when I was released and I said to the Governor: For God's sake, sir, smuggle me out so as no one can see me."

He smoothed his gloves again over his hands and his eye once more fell upon the hole in the first finger.

"That's what comes of living in lodgings, sir. How's a man to keep himself neat and tidy without a woman to look after him? I've been married too often to be able to get along without a wife. There are men who don't like being married. I can't understand them. The fact is, you can't do a thing really well unless you've got your heart in it, and I like being a married man. It's no difficulty to me to do the little things that women like and that some men can't be bothered with. As I was saying just now, it's attention a woman wants. I never went out of the house without giving my wife a kiss and I never came in without giving her another. And it was very seldom I came in without bringing her some chocolates or a few flowers. I never grudged the expense."

"After all, it was her money you were spending," I interposed.

"And what if it was? It's not the money that you've paid for a present that signifies, it's the spirit you give it in. That's what counts with women. No, I'm not one to boast, but I will say this of myself, I am a good husband."

I looked desultorily at the reports of the trial which I still held.

"I'll tell you what surprises me," I said. "All these women were very respectable, of a certain age, quiet, decent persons. And yet they married you without any enquiry after the shortest possible acquaintance."

He put his hand impressively on my arm.

"Ah, that's what you don't understand, sir. Women have got a craving to be married. It doesn't matter how young they are or how old they are, if they're short or tall, dark or fair, they've all got one thing in common: they want to be married. And mind you, I married them in church. No woman feels really safe unless she's married in church. You say I'm no beauty, well, I never thought I was, but if I had one leg and a hump on my back I could find any number of women who'd jump at the chance of marrying me. It's a mania with them. It's a disease. Why, there's hardly one of them who wouldn't have accepted me the second time I saw her only I like to make sure of my ground before I commit myself. When it all came out there was a rare to-do because I'd married eleven times. Eleven times? Why, it's nothing, it's not even a Round Dozen. I could have married thirty times if I'd wanted to. I give you my word, sir, when I consider my opportunities, I'm astounded at my moderation."

"You told me you were very fond of reading history."

"Yes, Warren Hastings said that, didn't he? It struck me at the time I read it. It seemed to fit me like a glove."

"And you never found these constant courtships a trifle monotonous?"

"Well, sir, I think I've got a logical mind, and it always gave me a rare lot of pleasure to see how the same effects followed on the same causes, if you know what I mean. Now, for instance, with a woman who'd never been married before I always passed myself off as a widower. It worked like a charm. You see, a spinster likes a man who knows a thing or two. But with a widow I always said I was a bachelor: a widow's afraid a man who's been married before knows too much."

I gave him back his cuttings; he folded them up neatly and replaced them in his greasy pocket-book.

"You know, sir, I always think I've been misjudged. Just see what they say about me: a pest of society, unscrupulous villain, contemptible scoundrel. Now just look at me. I ask you, do I look that sort of man? You know me, you're a judge of character, I've told you all about myself: do you think me a bad man?"

"My acquaintance with you is very slight," I answered with what I thought considerable tact.

"I wonder if the judge, I wonder if the jury, I wonder if the public ever thought about my side of the question. The public booed me when I was taken into the court and the police had to protect me from their violence. Did any of them think what I'd done for these women?"

"You took their money."

"Of course I took their money. I had to live the same as anybody has to live. But what did I give them in exchange for their money?"

This was another rhetorical question and though he looked at me as though he expected an answer I held my tongue. Indeed I did not know the answer. His voice was raised and he spoke with emphasis. I could see that he was serious.

"I'll tell you what I gave them in exchange for their money. Romance. Look at this place." He made a wide, circular gesture that embraced the sea and the horizon. "There are a hundred places in England like this. Look at that sea and that sky; look at these lodging-houses; look at that pier and the front. Doesn't it make your heart sink? It's dead as mutton. It's all very well for you who come down here for a week or two because you're run down. But think of all those women who live here from one year's end to another. They haven't a chance. They hardly know anyone. They've just got enough money to live on and that's all. I wonder if you know how terrible their lives are. Their lives are just like the front, a long, straight, cemented walk that goes on and on from one seaside resort to another. Even in the season there's nothing for them. They're out of it. They might as well be dead. And then I come along. Mind you, I never made advances to a woman who wouldn't have gladly acknowledged to thirty-five. And I give them love. Why, many of them had never known what it was to have a man do them up be-hind. Many of them had never known what it was to sit on a bench in the dark with a man's arm round their waist. I bring them change and excitement. I give them a new pride in themselves. They were on the shelf and I come along quite quietly and I deliberately take them down. A little ray of sunshine in those drab lives, that's what I was. No wonder they jumped at me, no wonder they wanted me to go back to them. The only one who gave me away was the milliner; she said she was a widow, my private opinion is that she'd never been married at all. You say I did the dirty on them; why, I brought happiness and glamour into eleven lives that never thought they had even a dog's chance of it again. You say I'm a villain and a scoundrel, you're wrong. I'm a philanthropist. Five years, they gave me; they should have given me the medal of the Royal Humane Society."

He took out his empty packet of Gold Flake and looked at it with a melancholy shake of the head. When I handed him my cigarette case he helped himself without a word. I watched the spectacle of a good man struggling with his emotion.

"And what did I get out of it, I ask you?" he continued presently. "Board and lodging and enough to buy cigarettes. But I never was able to save, and the proof is that now, when I'm not so young as I was, I haven't got half a crown in my pocket." He gave me a sidelong glance. "It's a great come-down for me to find myself in this position. I've always paid my way and I've never asked a friend for a loan in all my life. I was wondering, sir, if you could oblige me with a trifle. It's humiliating to me to have to suggest it, but the fact is, if you could oblige me with a pound it would mean a great deal to me."

Well, I had certainly had a pound's worth of entertainment out of the bigamist and I dived for my pocket-book.

"I shall be very glad," I said.

He looked at the notes I took out.

"I suppose you couldn't make it two, sir?"

"I think I could."

I handed him a couple of pound notes and he gave a little sigh as he took them.

"You don't know what it means to a man who's used to the comforts of home life not to know where to turn for a night's lodging."

"But there is one thing I should like you to tell me," I said. "I shouldn't like you to think me cynical, but I had a notion that women on the whole take the maxim, 'It is more blessed to give than to receive,' as applicable exclusively to our sex. How did you persuade these respectable, and no doubt thrifty, women to entrust you so confidently with all their savings?"

An amused smile spread over his undistinguished features.

"Well, sir, you know what Shakespeare said about ambition o'er-leaping itself. That's the explanation. Tell a woman you'll double her capital in six months if she'll give it you to handle and she won't be able to give you the money quick enough. Greed, that's what it is. Just greed."

It was a sharp sensation, stimulating to the appetite (like hot sauce with ice cream), to go from this diverting ruffian to the respectability, all lavender bags and crinolines, of the St. Clairs and Miss Porchester. I spent every evening with them now. No sooner had the ladies left him than Mr. St. Clair sent his compliments to my table and asked me to drink a glass of port with him. When we had finished it we went into the lounge and drank coffee. Mr. St. Clair enjoyed his glass of old brandy. The hour I thus spent with them was so exquisitely boring that it had for me a singular fascination. They were told by the manageress that I had written plays.

"We used often to go to the theatre when Sir Henry Irving was at the Lyceum," said Mr. St. Clair. "I once had the pleasure of meeting him. I was taken to supper at the Garrick Club by Sir Everard Millais and I was introduced to Mr. Irving, as he then was."

"Tell him what he said to you, Edwin," said Mrs. St. Clair.

Mr. St. Clair struck a dramatic attitude and gave not at all a bad imitation of Henry Irving.

" 'You have the actor's face, Mr. St. Clair,' he said to me. 'If you ever think of going on the stage, come to me and I will give you a part.' " Mr. St. Clair resumed his natural manner. "It was enough to turn a young man's head."

"But it didn't turn yours," I said.

"I will not deny that if I had been otherwise situated I might have allowed myself to be tempted. But I had my family to think of. It would have broken my father's heart if I had not gone into the business."

"What is that?" I asked.

"I am a tea merchant, sir. My firm is the oldest in the City of London. I have spent forty years of my life in combating to the best of my ability the desire of my fellow-countrymen to drink Ceylon tea instead of the China tea which was universally drunk in my youth."

I thought it charmingly characteristic of him to spend a lifetime in persuading the public to buy something they didn't want rather than something they did.

"But in his younger days my husband did a lot of amateur acting and he was thought very clever," said Mrs. St. Clair.

"Shakespeare, you know, and sometimes *The School for Scandal*. I would never consent to act trash. But that is a thing of the past. I had a gift, perhaps it was a pity to waste it, but it's too late now. When we have a dinner-party I sometimes let the ladies persuade me to recite the great soliloquies of Hamlet. But that is all I do."

Oh! Oh! Oh! I thought with shuddering fascination of those dinner-parties and wondered whether I should ever be asked to one of them. Mrs. St. Clair gave me a little smile, half shocked, half prim.

"My husband was very Bohemian as a young man," she said.

"I sowed my wild oats. I knew quite a lot of painters and writers, Wilkie Collins, for instance, and even men who wrote for the papers. Watts painted a portrait of my wife, and I bought a picture of Millais. I knew a number of the pre-Raphaelites."

"Have you a Rossetti?" I asked.

"No. I admired Rossetti's talent, but I could not approve of his private life. I would never buy a picture by an artist whom I should not care to ask to dinner at my house."

My brain was reeling when Miss Porchester, looking at her watch, said: "Are you not going to read to us to-night, Uncle Edwin?"

I withdrew.

It was while I was drinking a glass of port with Mr. St. Clair one evening that he told me the sad story of Miss Porchester. She was engaged to be married to a nephew of Mrs. St. Clair, a barrister, when it was discovered that he had had an intrigue with the daughter of his laundress.

"It was a terrible thing," said Mr. St. Clair. "A terrible thing. But of course my niece took the only possible course. She returned him his ring, his letters and his photograph, and said that she could never marry him. She implored him to marry the young person he had wronged and said she would be a sister to her. It broke her heart. She has never cared for anyone since."

"And did he marry the young person?"

Mr. St. Clair shook his head and sighed.

"No, we were greatly mistaken in him. It has been a sore grief to my dear wife to think that a nephew of hers should behave in such a dishonourable manner. Some time later we heard that he was engaged to a young lady in a very good position with ten thousand pounds of her own. I considered it my duty to write to her father and put the facts before him. He answered my letter in a most insolent fashion. He said he would much rather his son-in-law had a mistress before marriage than after."

"What happened then?"

"They were married and now my wife's nephew is one of His Majesty's Judges of the High Court, and his wife is My Lady. But we've never consented to receive them. When my wife's nephew was knighted Eleanor suggested that we should ask them to dinner, but my wife said that he should never darken our doors and I upheld her."

"And the laundress's daughter?"

"She married in her own class and has a public-house at Canterbury. My niece, who has a little money of her own, did everything for her and is godmother to her eldest child."

Poor Miss Porchester. She had sacrificed herself on the altar of Victorian morality and I am afraid the consciousness that she had behaved beautifully was the only benefit she had got from it.

"Miss Porchester is a woman of striking appearance," I said. "When she was younger she must have been perfectly lovely. I wonder she never married somebody else."

"Miss Porchester was considered a great beauty. Alma-Tadema admired her so much that he asked her to sit as a model for one of his pictures, but of course we couldn't very well allow that." Mr. St. Clair's tone conveyed that the suggestion had deeply outraged his sense of decency. "No, Miss Porchester never cared for anyone but her cousin. She never speaks of him and it is now thirty years since they parted, but I am convinced that she loves him still. She is a true woman, my dear sir, one life, one love, and though perhaps I regret that she has been deprived of the joys of marriage and motherhood I am bound to admire her fidelity."

But the heart of woman is incalculable and rash is the man who thinks she will remain in one stay. Rash, Uncle Edwin. You have known Eleanor for many years, for when, her mother having fallen

into a decline and died, you brought the orphan to your comfortable and even luxurious house in Leinster Square, she was but a
child; but what, when it comes down to brass tacks, Uncle Edwin,
do you really know of Eleanor?

It was but two days after Mr. St. Clair had confided to me the
touching story which explained why Miss Porchester had remained
a spinster that, coming back to the hotel in the afternoon after a
round of golf, the manageress came up to me in an agitated manner.

"Mr. St. Clair's compliments and will you go up to number
twenty-seven the moment you come in."

"Certainly. But why?"

"Oh, there's a rare upset. They'll tell you."

I knocked at the door. I heard a "Come in, come in," which
reminded me that Mr. St. Clair had played Shakespearean parts in
probably the most refined amateur dramatic company in London.
I entered and found Mrs. St. Clair lying on the sofa with a handkerchief soaked in eau-de-Cologne on her brow and a bottle of smelling-
salts in her hand. Mr. St. Clair was standing in front of the fire in
such a manner as to prevent anyone else in the room from obtaining
any benefit from it.

"I must apologise for asking you to come up in this unceremonious
fashion, but we are in great distress, and we thought you might be
able to throw some light on what has happened."

His perturbation was obvious.

"What *has* happened?"

"Our niece, Miss Porchester, has eloped. This morning she sent
in a message to my wife that she had one of her sick headaches.
When she has one of her sick headaches she likes to be left absolutely
alone and it wasn't till this afternoon that my wife went to see if
there was anything she could do for her. The room was empty. Her
trunk was packed. Her dressing-case with silver fittings was gone.
And on the pillow was a letter telling us of her rash act."

"I'm very sorry," I said. " I don't know exactly what I can do."

"We were under the impression that you were the only gentleman
at Elsom with whom she had any acquaintance."

His meaning flashed across me.

"I haven't eloped with her," I said. "I happen to be a married
man."

"I see you haven't eloped with her. At the first moment we
thought perhaps . . . but if it isn't you, who is it?"

"I'm sure I don't know."

"Show him the letter, Edwin," said Mrs. St. Clair from the sofa.

"Don't move, Gertrude. It will bring on your lumbago."

Miss Porchester had "her" sick headaches and Mrs. St. Clair had "her" lumbago. What had Mr. St. Clair? I was willing to bet a fiver that Mr. St. Clair had "his" gout. He gave me the letter and I read it with an air of decent commiseration.

Dearest Uncle Edwin and Aunt Gertrude,
   When you receive this I shall be far away. I am going to be married this morning to a gentleman who is very dear to me. I know I am doing wrong in running away like this, but I was afraid you would endeavour to set obstacles in the way of my marriage and since nothing would induce me to change my mind I thought it would save us all much unhappiness if I did it without telling you anything about it. My fiancé is a very retiring man, owing to his long residence in tropical countries not in the best of health, and he thought it much better that we should be married quite privately. When you know how radiantly happy I am I hope you will forgive me. Please send my box to the luggage office at Victoria Station.

Your loving niece,
Eleanor.

"I will never forgive her," said Mr. St. Clair as I returned him the letter. "She shall never darken my doors again. Gertrude, I forbid you ever to mention Eleanor's name in my hearing."

Mrs. St. Clair began to sob quietly.

"Aren't you rather hard?" I said. "Is there any reason why Miss Porchester shouldn't marry?"

"At her age," he answered angrily. "It's ridiculous. We shall be the laughing-stock of everyone in Leinster Square. Do you know how old she is? She's fifty-one."

"Fifty-four," said Mrs. St. Clair through her sobs.

"She's been the apple of my eye. She's been like a daughter to us. She's been an old maid for years. I think it's positively improper for her to think of marriage."

"She was always a girl to us, Edwin," pleaded Mrs. St. Clair.

"And who is this man she's married? It's the deception that rankles. She must have been carrying on with him under our very noses. She does not even tell us his name. I fear the very worst."

Suddenly I had an inspiration. That morning after breakfast I had gone out to buy myself some cigarettes and at the tobacconist's I ran across Mortimer Ellis. I had not seen him for some days.

"You're looking very spruce," I said.

His boots had been repaired and were neatly blacked, his hat was brushed, he was wearing a clean collar and new gloves. I thought he had laid out my two pounds to advantage.

"I have to go to London this morning on business," he said.

I nodded and left the shop.

I remembered that a fortnight before, walking in the country, I had met Miss Porchester and, a few yards behind, Mortimer Ellis. Was it possible that they had been walking together and he had fallen back as they caught sight of me? By heaven, I saw it all.

"I think you said that Miss Porchester had money of her own," I said.

"A trifle. She has three thousand pounds."

Now I was certain. I looked at them blankly. Suddenly Mrs. St. Clair, with a cry, sprang to her feet.

"Edwin, Edwin, supposing he doesn't marry her?"

Mr. St. Clair at this put his hand to his head and in a state of collapse sank into a chair.

"The disgrace would kill me," he groaned.

"Don't be alarmed," I said. "He'll marry her all right. He always does. He'll marry her in church."

They paid no attention to what I said. I suppose they thought I'd suddenly taken leave of my senses. I was quite sure now. Mortimer Ellis had achieved his ambition after all. Miss Porchester completed the Round Dozen.

Jane

I REMEMBER very well the occasion on which I first saw Jane Fowler. It is indeed only because the details of the glimpse I had of her then are so clear that I trust my recollection at all, for, looking back, I must confess that I find it hard to believe that it has not played me a fantastic trick. I had lately returned to London from China and was drinking a dish of tea with Mrs. Tower. Mrs. Tower had been seized with the prevailing passion for decoration; and with the ruthlessness of her sex had sacrificed chairs in which she had comfortably sat for years, tables, cabinets, ornaments on which her eyes had dwelt in peace since she was married, pictures that had been familiar to her for a generation; and delivered herself into the hands of an expert. Nothing remained in her drawing-room with which she had any association, or to which any sentiment was attached; and she had invited me that day to see the fashionable glory in which she now lived. Everything that could be pickled was pickled and what couldn't be pickled was painted. Nothing matched, but everything harmonised.

"Do you remember that ridiculous drawing-room suite that I used to have?" asked Mrs. Tower.

The curtains were sumptuous yet severe; the sofa was covered with Italian brocade; the chair on which I sat was in *petit point*. The room was beautiful, opulent without garishness and original without affectation; yet to me it lacked something; and while I praised with my lips I asked myself why I so much preferred the rather shabby chintz of the despised suite, the Victorian watercolours that I had known so long, and the ridiculous Dresden china that had adorned the chimney-piece. I wondered what it was that I missed in all these rooms that the decorators were turning out with a profitable industry. Was it heart? But Mrs. Tower looked about her happily.

"Don't you like my alabaster lamps?" she said. "They give such a soft light."

"Personally I have a weakness for a light that you can see by," I smiled.

"It's so difficult to combine that with a light that you can't be too much seen by," laughed Mrs. Tower.

I had no notion what her age was. When I was quite a young man she was a married woman a good deal older than I, but now

she treated me as her contemporary. She constantly said that she
made no secret of her age, which was forty, and then added with a
smile that all women took five years off. She never sought to conceal
the fact that she dyed her hair (it was a very pretty brown with
reddish tints), and she said she did this because hair was hideous
while it was going grey; as soon as hers was white she would cease
to dye it.

"Then they'll say what a young face I have."

Meanwhile it was painted, though with discretion, and her eyes
owed not a little of their vivacity to art. She was a handsome
woman, exquisitely gowned, and in the sombre glow of the alabaster
lamps did not look a day more than the forty she gave herself.

"It is only at my dressing-table that I can suffer the naked bright-
ness of a thirty-two-candle electric bulb," she added with smiling
cynicism. "There I need it to tell me first the hideous truth and then
to enable me to take the necessary steps to correct it."

We gossiped pleasantly about our common friends and Mrs.
Tower brought me up to date in the scandal of the day. After
roughing it here and there it was very agreeable to sit in a comfortable chair, the fire burning brightly on the hearth, charming tea-
things set out on a charming table, and talk with this amusing,
attractive woman. She treated me as a prodigal returned from his
husks and was disposed to make much of me. She prided herself
on her dinner-parties; she took no less trouble to have her guests
suitably assorted than to give them excellent food; and there
were few persons who did not look upon it as a treat to be bidden
to one of them. Now she fixed a date and asked me whom I would
like to meet.

"There's only one thing I must tell you. If Jane Fowler is still
here I shall have to put it off."

"Who is Jane Fowler?" I asked.

Mrs. Tower gave a rueful smile.

"Jane Fowler is my cross."

"Oh!"

"Do you remember a photograph that I used to have on the
piano before I had my room done, of a woman in a tight dress with
tight sleeves and a gold locket, with her hair drawn back from a
broad forehead and her ears showing and spectacles on a rather
blunt nose? Well, that was Jane Fowler."

"You had so many photographs about the room in your un-
regenerate days," I said, vaguely.

"It makes me shudder to think of them. I've made them into a
huge brown-paper parcel and hidden them in an attic."

"Well, who is Jane Fowler?" I asked again, smiling.

"She's my sister-in-law. She was my husband's sister and she married a manufacturer in the North. She's been a widow for many years, and she's very well-to-do."

"And why is she your cross?"

"She's worthy, she's dowdy, she's provincial. She looks twenty years older than I do and she's quite capable of telling anyone she meets that we were at school together. She has an overwhelming sense of family affection and because I am her only living connection she's devoted to me. When she comes to London it never occurs to her that she should stay anywhere but here—she thinks it would hurt my feelings—and she'll pay me visits of three or four weeks. We sit here and she knits and reads. And sometimes she insists on taking me to dine at Claridge's and she looks like a funny old charwoman and everyone I particularly don't want to be seen by is sitting at the next table. When we are driving home she says she loves giving me a little treat. With her own hands she makes me tea-cosies that I am forced to use when she is here and doilies and centrepieces for the dining-room table."

Mrs. Tower paused to take breath.

"I should have thought a woman of your tact would find a way to deal with a situation like that."

"Ah, but don't you see, I haven't a chance. She's so immeasurably kind. She has a heart of gold. She bores me to death, but I wouldn't for anything let her suspect it."

"And when does she arrive?"

"To-morrow."

But the answer was hardly out of Mrs. Tower's mouth when the bell rang. There were sounds in the hall of a slight commotion and in a minute or two the butler ushered in an elderly lady.

"Mrs. Fowler," he announced.

"Jane," cried Mrs. Tower, springing to her feet. "I wasn't expecting you to-day."

"So your butler has just told me. I certainly said to-day in my letter."

Mrs. Tower recovered her wits.

"Well, it doesn't matter. I'm very glad to see you whenever you come. Fortunately I'm doing nothing this evening."

"You mustn't let me give you any trouble. If I can have a boiled egg for my dinner that's all I shall want."

A faint grimace for a moment distorted Mrs. Tower's handsome features. A boiled egg!

"Oh, I think we can do a little better than that."

I chuckled inwardly when I recollected that the two ladies were contemporaries. Mrs. Fowler looked a good fifty-five. She was a rather big woman; she wore a black straw hat with a wide brim and from it a black lace veil hung over her shoulders, a cloak that oddly combined severity with fussiness, a long black dress, voluminous as though she wore several petticoats under it, and stout boots. She was evidently short-sighted, for she looked at you through large gold-rimmed spectacles.

"Won't you have a cup of tea?" asked Mrs. Tower.

"If it wouldn't be too much trouble. I'll take off my mantle."

She began by stripping her hands of the black gloves she wore, and then took off her cloak. Round her neck was a solid gold chain from which hung a large gold locket in which I felt certain was a photograph of her deceased husband. Then she took off her hat and placed it neatly with her gloves and cloak on the sofa corner. Mrs. Tower pursed her lips. Certainly those garments did not go very well with the austere but sumptuous beauty of Mrs. Tower's redecorated drawing-room. I wondered where on earth Mrs. Fowler had found the extraordinary clothes she wore. They were not old and the materials were expensive. It was astounding to think that dressmakers still made things that had not been worn for a quarter of a century. Mrs. Fowler's grey hair was very plainly done, showing all her forehead and her ears, with a parting in the middle. It had evidently never known the tongs of Monsieur Marcel. Now her eyes fell on the tea-table with its teapot of Georgian silver and its cups in old Worcester.

"What have you done with the tea-cosy I gave you last time I came up, Marion?" she asked. "Don't you use it?"

"Yes, I used it every day, Jane," answered Mrs. Tower glibly. "Unfortunately we had an accident with it a little while ago. It got burnt."

"But the last one I gave you got burnt."

"I'm afraid you'll think us very careless."

"It doesn't really matter," smiled Mrs. Fowler. "I shall enjoy making you another. I'll go to Liberty's to-morrow and buy some silks."

Mrs. Tower kept her face bravely.

"I don't deserve it, you know. Doesn't your vicar's wife need one?"

"Oh, I've just made her one," said Mrs. Fowler brightly.

I noticed that when she smiled she showed white, small and regular teeth. They were a real beauty. Her smile was certainly very sweet.

But I felt it high time for me to leave the two ladies to themselves, so I took my leave.

Early next morning Mrs. Tower rang me up and I heard at once from her voice that she was in high spirits.

"I've got the most wonderful news for you," she said. "Jane is going to be married."

"Nonsense."

"Her fiancé is coming to dine here to-night to be introduced to me and I want you to come too."

"Oh, but I shall be in the way."

"No, you won't. Jane suggested herself that I should ask you. Do come."

She was bubbling over with laughter.

"Who is he?"

"I don't know. She tells me he's an architect. Can you imagine the sort of man Jane would marry?"

I had nothing to do and I could trust Mrs. Tower to give me a good dinner.

When I arrived Mrs. Tower, very splendid in a tea-gown a little too young for her, was alone.

"Jane is putting the finishing touches to her appearance. I'm longing for you to see her. She's all in a flutter. She says he adores her. His name is Gilbert and when she speaks of him her voice gets all funny and tremulous. It makes me want to laugh."

"I wonder what he's like."

"Oh, I'm sure I know. Very big and massive, with a bald head and an immense gold chain across an immense tummy. A large, fat, clean-shaven, red face and a booming voice."

Mrs. Fowler came in. She wore a very stiff black silk dress with a wide skirt and a train. At the neck it was cut into a timid V and the sleeves came down to the elbows. She wore a necklace of diamonds set in silver. She carried in her hands a long pair of black gloves and a fan of black ostrich feathers. She managed (as so few people do) to look exactly what she was. You could never have thought her anything in the world but the respectable relict of a North-country manufacturer of ample means.

"You've really got a quite pretty neck, Jane," said Mrs. Tower with a kindly smile.

It was indeed astonishingly young when you compared it with her weather-beaten face. It was smooth and unlined and the skin was white. And I noticed then that her head was very well placed on her shoulders.

"Has Marion told you my news?" she said, turning to me with

that really charming smile of hers as if we were already old friends.

"I must congratulate you," I said.

"Wait to do that till you've seen my young man."

"I think it's too sweet to hear you talk of your young man," smiled Mrs. Tower.

Mrs. Fowler's eyes certainly twinkled behind her preposterous spectacles.

"Don't expect anyone too old. You wouldn't like me to marry a decrepit old gentleman with one foot in the grave, would you?"

This was the only warning she gave us. Indeed there was no time for any further discussion, for the butler flung open the door and in a loud voice announced:

"Mr. Gilbert Napier."

There entered a youth in a very well-cut dinner jacket. He was slight, not very tall, with fair hair in which there was a hint of a natural wave, clean-shaven and blue-eyed. He was not particularly good-looking, but he had a pleasant, amiable face. In ten years he would probably be wizened and sallow; but now, in extreme youth, he was fresh and clean and blooming. For he was certainly not more than twenty-four. My first thought was that this was the son of Jane Fowler's fiancé (I had not known he was a widower) come to say that his father was prevented from dining by a sudden attack of gout. But his eyes fell immediately on Mrs. Fowler, his face lit up, and he went towards her with both hands outstretched. Mrs. Fowler gave him hers, a demure smile on her lips, and turned to her sister-in-law.

"This is my young man, Marion," she said.

He held out his hand.

"I hope you'll like me, Mrs. Tower," he said. "Jane tells me you're the only relation she has in the world."

Mrs. Tower's face was wonderful to behold. I saw then to admiration how bravely good breeding and social usage could combat the instincts of the natural woman. For the astonishment and then the dismay that for an instant she could not conceal were quickly driven away, and her face assumed an expression of affable welcome. But she was evidently at a loss for words. It was not unnatural if Gilbert felt a certain embarrassment and I was too busy preventing myself from laughing to think of anything to say. Mrs. Fowler alone kept perfectly calm.

"I know you'll like him, Marion. There's no one enjoys good food more than he does." She turned to the young man. "Marion's dinners are famous."

"I know," he beamed.

Mrs. Tower made some quick rejoinder and we went downstairs. I shall not soon forget the exquisite comedy of that meal. Mrs. Tower could not make up her mind whether the pair of them were playing a practical joke on her or whether Jane by wilfully concealing her fiancé's age had hoped to make her look foolish. But then Jane never jested and she was incapable of doing a malicious thing. Mrs. Tower was amazed, exasperated and perplexed. But she had recovered her self-control, and for nothing would she have forgotten that she was a perfect hostess whose duty it was to make her party go. She talked vivaciously; but I wondered if Gilbert Napier saw how hard and vindictive was the expression of her eyes behind the mask of friendliness that she turned to him. She was measuring him. She was seeking to delve into the secret of his soul. I could see that she was in a passion, for under her rouge her cheeks glowed with an angry red.

"You've got a very high colour, Marion," said Jane, looking at her amiably through her great round spectacles.

"I dressed in a hurry. I dare say I put on too much rouge."

"Oh, is it rouge? I thought it was natural. Otherwise I shouldn't have mentioned it." She gave Gilbert a shy little smile. "You know, Marion and I were at school together. You would never think it to look at us now, would you? But of course I've lived a very quiet life."

I do not know what she meant by these remarks; it was almost incredible that she had made them in complete simplicity; but anyhow they goaded Mrs. Tower to such a fury that she flung her own vanity to the winds. She smiled brightly.

"We shall neither of us see fifty again, Jane," she said.

If the observation was meant to discomfit the widow it failed.

"Gilbert says I mustn't acknowledge to more than forty-nine for his sake," she answered blandly.

Mrs. Tower's hands trembled slightly, but she found a retort.

"There is of course a certain disparity of age between you," she smiled.

"Twenty-seven years," said Jane. "Do you think it's too much? Gilbert says I'm very young for my age. I told you I shouldn't like to marry a man with one foot in the grave."

I was really obliged to laugh and Gilbert laughed too. His laughter was frank and boyish. It looked as though he were amused at everything Jane said. But Mrs. Tower was almost at the end of her tether and I was afraid that unless relief came she would for once forget that she was a woman of the world. I came to the rescue as best I could.

"I suppose you're very busy buying your trousseau," I said.

"No. I wanted to get my things from the dressmaker in Liverpool I've been to ever since I was first married. But Gilbert won't let me. He's very masterful, and of course he has wonderful taste."

She looked at him with a little affectionate smile, demurely, as though she were a girl of seventeen.

Mrs. Tower went quite pale under her make-up.

"We're going to Italy for our honeymoon. Gilbert has never had a chance of studying Renaissance architecture and of course it's important for an architect to see things for himself. And we shall stop in Paris on the way and get my clothes there."

"Do you expect to be away long?"

"Gilbert has arranged with his office to stay away for six months. It will be such a treat for him, won't it? You see, he's never had more than a fortnight's holiday before."

"Why not?" asked Mrs. Tower in a tone that no effort of will could prevent from being icy.

"He's never been able to afford it, poor dear."

"Ah!" said Mrs. Tower, and into the exclamation put volumes.

Coffee was served and the ladies went upstairs. Gilbert and I began to talk in the desultory way in which men talk who have nothing whatever to say to one another; but in two minutes a note was brought in to me by the butler. It was from Mrs. Tower and ran as follows:

"Come upstairs quickly and then go as soon as you can. Take him with you. Unless I have it out with Jane at once I shall have a fit."

I told a facile lie.

"Mrs. Tower has a headache and wants to go to bed. I think if you don't mind we'd better clear out."

"Certainly," he answered.

We went upstairs and five minutes later were on the doorstep. I called a taxi and offered the young man a lift.

"No, thanks,'" he answered. "I'll just walk to the corner and jump on a bus."

Mrs. Tower sprang to the fray as soon as she heard the front-door close behind us.

"Are you crazy, Jane?" she cried.

"Not more than most people who don't habitually live in a lunatic asylum, I trust," Jane answered blandly.

"May I ask why you're going to marry this young man?" asked Mrs. Tower with formidable politeness.

"Partly because he won't take no for an answer. He's asked me five times. I grew positively tired of refusing him."

"And why do you think he's so anxious to marry you?"

"I amuse him."

Mrs. Tower gave an exclamation of annoyance.

"He's an unscrupulous rascal. I very nearly told him so to his face."

"You would have been wrong, and it wouldn't have been very polite."

"He's penniless and you're rich. You can't be such a besotted fool as not to see that he's marrying you for your money."

Jane remained perfectly composed. She observed her sister-in-law's agitation with detachment.

"I don't think he is, you know," she replied. "I think he's very fond of me."

"You're an old woman, Jane."

"I'm the same age as you are, Marion," she smiled.

"I've never let myself go. I'm very young for my age. No one would think I was more than forty. But even I wouldn't dream of marrying a boy twenty years younger than myself."

"Twenty-seven," corrected Jane.

"Do you mean to tell me that you can bring yourself to believe that it's possible for a young man to care for a woman old enough to be his mother?"

"I've lived very much in the country for many years. I dare say there's a great deal about human nature that I don't know. They tell me there's a man called Freud, an Austrian, I believe . . ."

But Mrs. Tower interrupted her without any politeness at all.

"Don't be ridiculous, Jane. It's so undignified. It's so ungraceful. I always thought you were a sensible woman. Really you're the last person I should ever have thought likely to fall in love with a boy."

"But I'm not in love with him. I've told him that. Of course I like him very much or I wouldn't think of marrying him. I thought it only fair to tell him quite plainly what my feelings were towards him."

Mrs. Tower gasped. The blood rushed to her head and her breathing oppressed her. She had no fan, but she seized the evening paper and vigorously fanned herself with it.

"If you're not in love with him why do you want to marry him?"

"I've been a widow a very long time and I've led a very quiet life. I thought I'd like a change."

"If you want to marry just to be married why don't you marry a man of your own age?"

"No man of my own age has asked me five times. In fact no man of my own age has asked me at all."

Jane chuckled as she answered. It drove Mrs. Tower to the final pitch of frenzy.

"Don't laugh, Jane. I won't have it. I don't think you can be right in your mind. It's dreadful."

It was altogether too much for her and she burst into tears. She knew that at her age it was fatal to cry, her eyes would be swollen for twenty-four hours and she would look a sight. But there was no help for it. She wept. Jane remained perfectly calm. She looked at Marion through her large spectacles and reflectively smoothed the lap of her black silk dress.

"You're going to be so dreadfully unhappy," Mrs. Tower sobbed, dabbing her eyes cautiously in the hope that the black on her lashes would not smudge.

"I don't think so, you know," Jane answered in those equable, mild tones of hers, as if there were a little smile behind the words. "We've talked it over very thoroughly. I always think I'm a very easy person to live with. I think I shall make Gilbert very happy and comfortable. He's never had anyone to look after him properly. We're only marrying after mature consideration. And we've decided that if either of us wants his liberty the other will place no obstacles in the way of his getting it."

Mrs. Tower had by now recovered herself sufficiently to make a cutting remark.

"How much has he persuaded you to settle on him?"

"I wanted to settle a thousand a year on him, but he wouldn't hear of it. He was quite upset when I made the suggestion. He says he can earn quite enough for his own needs."

"He's more cunning than I thought," said Mrs. Tower acidly.

Jane paused a little and looked at her sister-in-law with kindly but resolute eyes.

"You see, my dear, it's different for you," she said. "You've never been so very much a widow, have you?"

Mrs. Tower looked at her. She blushed a little. She even felt slightly uncomfortable. But of course Jane was much too simple to intend an innuendo. Mrs. Tower gathered herself together with dignity.

"I'm so upset that I really must go to bed," she said. "We'll resume the conversation to-morrow morning."

"I'm afraid that won't be very convenient, dear. Gilbert and I are going to get the licence to-morrow morning."

Mrs. Tower threw up her hands in a gesture of dismay, but she found nothing more to say.

The marriage took place at a registrar's office. Mrs. Tower and I were the witnesses. Gilbert in a smart blue suit looked absurdly young and he was obviously nervous. It is a trying moment for any man. But Jane kept her admirable composure. She might have been in the habit of marrying as frequently as a woman of fashion. Only a slight colour on her cheeks suggested that beneath her calm was some faint excitement. It is a thrilling moment for any woman. She wore a very full dress of silvery grey velvet in the cut of which I recognised the hand of the dressmaker in Liverpool (evidently a widow of unimpeachable character) who had made her gowns for so many years; but she had so far succumbed to the frivolity of the occasion as to wear a large picture hat covered with blue ostrich feathers. Her gold-rimmed spectacles made it extraordinarily grotesque. When the ceremony was over the registrar (somewhat taken aback, I thought, by the difference of age between the pair he was marrying) shook hands with her, tendering his strictly official congratulations; and the bridegroom, blushing slightly, kissed her. Mrs. Tower, resigned but implacable, kissed her; and the bride looked at me expectantly. It was evidently fitting that I should kiss her too. I did. I confess that I felt a little shy as we walked out of the registrar's office past loungers who waited cynically to see the bridal pair, and it was with relief that I stepped into Mrs. Tower's car. We drove to Victoria Station, for the happy couple were to go over to Paris by the two o'clock train, and Jane had insisted that the wedding-breakfast should be eaten at the station restaurant. She said it always made her nervous not to be on the platform in good time. Mrs. Tower, present only from a strong sense of family duty, was able to do little to make the party go off well; she ate nothing (for which I could not blame her, since the food was execrable, and anyway I hate champagne at luncheon) and talked in a strained voice. But Jane went through the menu conscientiously.

"I always think one should make a hearty meal before starting out on a journey," she said.

We saw them off, and I drove Mrs. Tower back to her house.

"How long do you give it?" she said. "Six months?"

"Let's hope for the best," I smiled.

"Don't be so absurd. There can be no 'best'. You don't think he's marrying her for anything but her money, do you? Of course it can't last. My only hope is that she won't have to go through as much suffering as she deserves."

I laughed. The charitable words were spoken in such a tone as to leave me in small doubt of Mrs. Tower's meaning.

"Well, if it doesn't last you'll have the consolation of saying: 'I told you so'," I said.

"I promise you I'll never do that."

"Then you'll have the satisfaction of congratulating yourself on your self-control in not saying: 'I told you so'."

"She's old and dowdy and dull."

"Are you sure she's dull?" I said. "It's true she doesn't say very much, but when she says anything it's very much to the point."

"I've never heard her make a joke in my life."

I was once more in the Far East when Gilbert and Jane returned from their honeymoon and this time I remained away for nearly two years. Mrs. Tower was a bad correspondent and though I sent her an occasional picture-postcard I received no news from her. But I met her within a week of my return to London; I was dining out and found that I was seated next to her. It was an immense party, I think we were four-and-twenty, like the blackbirds in the pie, and, arriving somewhat late, I was too confused by the crowd in which I found myself to notice who was there. But when we sat down, looking round the long table I saw that a good many of my fellow-guests were well known to the public from their photographs in the illustrated papers. Our hostess had a weakness for the persons technically known as celebrities and this was an unusually brilliant gathering. When Mrs. Tower and I had exchanged the conventional remarks that two people make when they have not seen one another for a couple of years I asked about Jane.

"She's very well," said Mrs. Tower with a certain dryness.

"How has the marriage turned out?"

Mrs. Tower paused a little and took a salted almond from the dish in front of her.

"It appears to be quite a success."

"You were wrong then?"

"I said it wouldn't last and I still say it won't last. It's contrary to human nature."

"Is she happy?"

"They're both happy."

"I suppose you don't see very much of them."

"At first I saw quite a lot of them. But now . . ." Mrs. Tower pursed her lips a little. "Jane is becoming very grand."

"What *do* you mean?" I laughed.

"I think I should tell you that she's here to-night."

"Here?"

I was startled. I looked round the table again. Our hostess was a delightful and an entertaining woman, but I could not imagine that she would be likely to invite to a dinner such as this the elderly and dowdy wife of an obscure architect. Mrs. Tower saw my perplexity and was shrewd enough to see what was in my mind. She smiled thinly.

"Look on the left of our host."

I looked. Oddly enough the woman who sat there had by her fantastic appearance attracted my attention the moment I was ushered into the crowded drawing-room. I thought I noticed a gleam of recognition in her eye, but to the best of my belief I had never seen her before. She was not a young woman, for her hair was iron-grey; it was cut very short and clustered thickly round her well-shaped head in tight curls. She made no attempt at youth, for she was conspicuous in that gathering by using neither lipstick, rouge nor powder. Her face, not a particularly handsome one, was red and weather-beaten; but because it owed nothing to artifice had a naturalness that was very pleasing. It contrasted oddly with the whiteness of her shoulders. They were really magnificent. A woman of thirty might have been proud of them. But her dress was extraordinary. I had not often seen anything more audacious. It was cut very low, with short skirts, which were then the fashion, in black and yellow; it had almost the effect of fancy-dress and yet so became her that though on anyone else it would have been outrageous, on her it had the inevitable simplicity of nature. And to complete the impression of an eccentricity in which there was no pose and of an extravagance in which there was no ostentation she wore, attached by a broad black ribbon, a single eyeglass.

"You're not going to tell me *that* is your sister-in-law," I gasped.

"That is Jane Napier," said Mrs. Tower icily.

At that moment she was speaking. Her host was turned towards her with an anticipatory smile. A baldish white-haired man, with a sharp, intelligent face, who sat on her left, was leaning forward eagerly, and the couple who sat opposite, ceasing to talk with one another, listened intently. She said her say and they all, with a sudden movement, threw themselves back in their chairs and burst into vociferous laughter. From the other side of the table

a man addressed Mrs. Tower: I recognised a famous statesman.

"Your sister-in-law has made another joke, Mrs. Tower," he
said.

Mrs. Tower smiled.

"She's priceless, isn't she?"

"Let me have a long drink of champagne and then for heaven's
sake tell me all about it," I said.

Well, this is how I gathered it had all happened. At the beginning
of their honeymoon Gilbert took Jane to various dressmakers in
Paris and he made no objection to her choosing a number of "gowns"
after her own heart; but he persuaded her to have a "frock" or two
made according to his own design. It appeared that he had a
knack for that kind of work. He engaged a smart French maid.
Jane had never had such a thing before. She did her own mending
and when she wanted "doing up" was in the habit of ringing for the
housemaid. The dresses Gilbert had devised were very different from
anything she had worn before; but he had been careful not to go too
far too quickly, and because it pleased him she persuaded herself,
though not without misgivings, to wear them in preference to those
she had chosen herself. Of course she could not wear them with the
voluminous petticoats she had been in the habit of using, and these,
though it cost her an anxious moment, she discarded.

"Now if you please," said Mrs. Tower, with something very like
a sniff of disapproval, "she wears nothing but thin silk tights. It's
a wonder to me she doesn't catch her death of cold at her age."

Gilbert and the French maid taught her how to wear her clothes,
and, unexpectedly enough, she was very quick at learning. The
French maid was in raptures over Madame's arms and shoulders.
It was a scandal not to show anything so fine.

"Wait a little, Alphonsine," said Gilbert. "The next lot of clothes
I design for Madame we'll make the most of her."

The spectacles of course were dreadful. No one could look really
well in gold-rimmed spectacles. Gilbert tried some with tortoise-
shell rims. He shook his head.

"They'd look all right on a girl," he said. "You're too old to
wear spectacles, Jane." Suddenly he had an inspiration. "By George,
I've got it. You must wear an eyeglass."

"Oh, Gilbert, I couldn't."

She looked at him and his excitement, the excitement of the artist,
made her smile. He was so sweet to her she wanted to do what she
could to please him.

"I'll try," she said.

When they went to an optician and, suited with the right size, she placed an eyeglass jauntily in her eye Gilbert clapped his hands. There and then, before the astonished shopman, he kissed her on both cheeks.

"You look wonderful," he cried.

So they went down to Italy and spent happy months studying Renaissance and Baroque architecture. Jane not only grew accustomed to her changed appearance, but found she liked it. At first she was a little shy when she went into the dining-room of an hotel and people turned round to stare at her, no one had ever raised an eyelid to look at her before, but presently she found that the sensation was not disagreeable. Ladies came up to her and asked her where she got her dress.

"Do you like it?" she answered demurely. "My husband designed it for me."

"I should like to copy it if you don't mind."

Jane had certainly for many years lived a very quiet life, but she was by no means lacking in the normal instincts of her sex. She had her answer ready.

"I'm so sorry, but my husband's very particular and he won't hear of anyone copying my frocks. He wants me to be unique."

She had an idea that people would laugh when she said this, but they didn't; they merely answered:

"Oh, of course I quite understand. You *are* unique."

But she saw them making mental notes of what she wore, and for some reason this quite "put her about". For once in her life that she wasn't wearing what everybody else did, she reflected, she didn't see why everybody else should want to wear what she did.

"Gilbert," she said, quite sharply for her, "next time you're designing dresses for me I wish you'd design things that people *can't* copy."

"The only way to do that is to design things that only you can wear."

"Can't you do that?"

"Yes, if you'll do something for me."

"What is it?"

"Cut off your hair."

I think this was the first time that Jane jibbed. Her hair was long and thick and as a girl she had been quite vain of it; to cut it off was a very drastic proceeding. This really was burning her boats behind her. In her case it was not the first step that cost so much, it was the last; but she took it ("I know Marion will think

me a perfect fool, and I shall never be able to go to Liverpool again,"
she said), and when they passed through Paris on their way home
Gilbert led her (she felt quite sick, her heart was beating so fast)
to the best hairdresser in the world. She came out of his shop
with a jaunty, saucy, impudent head of crisp grey curls. Pygmalion
had finished his fantastic masterpiece: Galatea was come to life.

"Yes," I said, "but that isn't enough to explain why Jane is here
to-night amid this crowd of duchesses, Cabinet Ministers and suchlike; nor why she is sitting on one side of her host with an Admiral
of the Fleet on the other."

"Jane is a humorist," said Mrs. Tower. "Didn't you see them all
laughing at what she said?"

There was no doubt now of the bitterness in Mrs. Tower's heart.

"When Jane wrote and told me they were back from their honeymoon I thought I must ask them both to dinner. I didn't much like
the idea, but I felt it had to be done. I knew the party would be
deadly and I wasn't going to sacrifice any of the people who really
mattered. On the other hand I didn't want Jane to think I hadn't
any nice friends. You know I never have more than eight, but on
this occasion I thought it would make things go better if I had
twelve. I'd been too busy to see Jane until the evening of the
party. She kept us all waiting a little—that was Gilbert's cleverness
—and at last she sailed in. You could have knocked me down with
a feather. She made the rest of the women look dowdy and provincial. She made me feel like a painted old trollop."

Mrs. Tower drank a little champagne.

"I wish I could describe the frock to you. It would have been
quite impossible on anyone else; on her it was perfect. And the
eyeglass! I'd known her for thirty-five years and I'd never seen her
without spectacles."

"But you knew she had a good figure."

"How should I? I'd never seen her except in the clothes you
first saw her in. Did *you* think she had a good figure? She seemed
not to be unconscious of the sensation she made but to take it as
a matter of course. I thought of my dinner and I heaved a sigh of
relief. Even if she was a little heavy in hand, with that appearance
it didn't so very much matter. She was sitting at the other end of
the table and I heard a good deal of laughter, I was glad to think
that the other people were playing up well; but after dinner I was
a good deal taken aback when no less than three men came up to
me and told me that my sister-in-law was priceless, and did I
think she would allow them to call on her? I didn't quite know
whether I was standing on my head or my heels. Twenty-four

hours later our hostess of to-night rang me up and said she had heard my sister-in-law was in London and she was priceless and would I ask her to luncheon to meet her? She has an infallible instinct, that woman: in a month everyone was talking about Jane. I am here to-night, not because I've known our hostess for twenty years and have asked her to dinner a hundred times, but because I'm Jane's sister-in-law."

Poor Mrs. Tower. The position was galling, and though I could not help being amused, for the tables were turned on her with a vengeance, I felt that she deserved my sympathy.

"People never can resist those who make them laugh," I said, trying to console her.

"She never makes *me* laugh."

Once more from the top of the table I heard a guffaw and guessed that Jane had said another amusing thing.

"Do you mean to say that you are the only person who doesn't think her funny?" I asked, smiling.

"Had it struck *you* that she was a humorist?"

"I'm bound to say it hadn't."

"She says just the same things as she's said for the last thirty-five years. I laugh when I see everyone else does because I don't want to seem a perfect fool, but I am not amused."

"Like Queen Victoria," I said.

It was a foolish jest and Mrs. Tower was quite right sharply to tell me so. I tried another tack.

"Is Gilbert here?" I asked, looking down the table.

"Gilbert was asked because she won't go out without him, but to-night he's at a dinner of the Architects' Institute or whatever it's called."

"I'm dying to renew my acquaintance with her."

"Go and talk to her after dinner. She'll ask you to her Tuesdays."

"Her Tuesdays?"

"She's at home every Tuesday evening. You'll meet there everyone you ever heard of. They're the best parties in London. She's done in one year what I've failed to do in twenty."

"But what you tell me is really miraculous. How has it been done?"

Mrs. Tower shrugged her handsome but adipose shoulders.

"I shall be glad if you'll tell me," she replied.

After dinner I tried to make my way to the sofa on which Jane was sitting, but I was intercepted and it was not till a little later that my hostess came up to me and said:

"I must introduce you to the star of my party. Do you know

Jane Napier? She's priceless. She's much more amusing than your comedies."

I was taken up to the sofa. The admiral who had been sitting beside her at dinner was with her still. He showed no sign of moving and Jane, shaking hands with me, introduced me to him.

"Do you know Sir Reginald Frobisher?"

We began to chat. It was the same Jane as I had known before, perfectly simple, homely and unaffected, but her fantastic appearance certainly gave a peculiar savour to what she said. Suddenly I found myself shaking with laughter. She had made a remark, sensible and to the point, but not in the least witty, which her manner of saying and the bland look she gave me through her eyeglass made perfectly irresistible. I felt light-hearted and buoyant. When I left her she said to me:

"If you've got nothing better to do, come and see us on Tuesday evening. Gilbert will be so glad to see you."

"When he's been a month in London he'll know that he *can* have nothing better to do," said the admiral.

So, on Tuesday but rather late, I went to Jane's. I confess I was a little surprised at the company. It was quite a remarkable collection of writers, painters and politicians, actors, great ladies and great beauties: Mrs. Tower was right, it was a grand party; I had seen nothing like it in London since Stafford House was sold. No particular entertainment was provided. The refreshments were adequate without being luxurious. Jane in her quiet way seemed to be enjoying herself; I could not see that she took a great deal of trouble with her guests, but they seemed to like being there and the gay, pleasant party did not break up till two in the morning. After that I saw much of her. I not only went often to her house, but seldom went out to luncheon or to dinner without meeting her. I am an amateur of humour and I sought to discover in what lay her peculiar gift. It was impossible to repeat anything she said, for the fun, like certain wines, would not travel. She had no gift for epigram. She never made a brilliant repartee. There was no malice in her remarks nor sting in her rejoinders. There are those who think that impropriety, rather than brevity, is the soul of wit; but she never said a thing that could have brought a blush to a Victorian cheek. I think her humour was unconscious and I am sure it was unpremeditated. It flew like a butterfly from flower to flower, obedient only to its own caprice and pursuivant of neither method nor intention. It depended on the way she spoke and on the way she looked. Its subtlety gained by the flaunting and extravagant appearance that Gilbert had achieved for her; but her appearance was only an element in it. Now of course she was the fashion and people laughed if she but opened her mouth. They no longer wondered that Gilbert had married a wife so much older than himself. They saw that Jane was a woman with whom age did not count. They thought him a devilish lucky young fellow. The admiral quoted Shakespeare to me: "Age cannot wither her, nor custom stale her infinite variety." Gilbert was delighted with her success. As I came to know him better I grew to like him. It was quite evident that he was neither a rascal nor a fortune-hunter. He was not only immensely proud of Jane but genuinely devoted to her. His kindness to her was touching. He was a very unselfish and sweet-tempered young man.

"Well, what do you think of Jane now?" he said to me once, with boyish triumph.

"I don't know which of you is more wonderful," I said. "You or she."

"Oh, I'm nothing."

"Nonsense. You don't think I'm such a fool as not to see that it's you, and you only, who've made Jane what she is."

"My only merit is that I saw what was there when it wasn't obvious to the naked eye," he answered.

"I can understand your seeing that she had in her the possibility of that remarkable appearance, but how in the world have you made her into a humorist?"

"But I always thought the things she said a perfect scream. She was always a humorist."

"You're the only person who ever thought so."

Mrs. Tower, not without magnanimity, acknowledged that she had been mistaken in Gilbert. She grew quite attached to him. But notwithstanding appearances she never faltered in her opinion that the marriage could not last. I was obliged to laugh at her.

"Why, I've never seen such a devoted couple," I said.

"Gilbert is twenty-seven now. It's just the time for a pretty girl to come along. Did you notice the other evening at Jane's that pretty little niece of Sir Reginald's? I thought Jane was looking at them both with a good deal of attention, and I wondered to myself."

"I don't believe Jane fears the rivalry of any girl under the sun."

"Wait and see," said Mrs. Tower.

"You gave it six months."

"Well, now I give it three years."

When anyone is very positive in an opinion it is only human

nature to wish him proved wrong. Mrs. Tower was really too cocksure. But such a satisfaction was not mine, for the end that she had always and confidently predicted to the ill-assorted match did in point of fact come. Still, the fates seldom give us what we want in the way we want it, and though Mrs. Tower could flatter herself that she had been right, I think after all she would sooner have been wrong. For things did not happen at all in the way she expected.

One day I received an urgent message from her and fortunately went to see her at once. When I was shown into the room Mrs. Tower rose from her chair and came towards me with the stealthy swiftness of a leopard stalking his prey. I saw that she was excited.

"Jane and Gilbert have separated," she said.

"Not really? Well, you were right after all."

Mrs. Tower looked at me with an expression I could not understand.

"Poor Jane," I muttered.

"Poor Jane," she repeated, but in tones of such derision that I was dumbfounded.

She found some difficulty in telling me exactly what had occurred. Gilbert had left her a moment before she leaped to the telephone to summon me. When he entered the room, pale and distraught, she saw at once that something terrible had happened. She knew what he was going to say before he said it.

"Marion, Jane has left me."

She gave him a little smile and took his hand.

"I knew you'd behave like a gentleman. It would have been dreadful for her for people to think that *you* had left her."

"I've come to you because I knew I could count on your sympathy."

"Oh, I don't blame you, Gilbert," said Mrs. Tower, very kindly. "It was bound to happen."

He sighed.

"I suppose so. I couldn't hope to keep her always. She was too wonderful and I'm a perfectly commonplace fellow."

Mrs. Tower patted his hand. He was really behaving beautifully.

"And what is going to happen now?"

"Well, she's going to divorce me."

"Jane always said she'd put no obstacle in your way if ever you wanted to marry a girl."

"You don't think it's likely I should ever be willing to marry anyone else after being Jane's husband," he answered.

Mrs. Tower was puzzled.

"Of course you mean that *you've* left Jane."

"I? That's the last thing I should ever do."

"Then why is she divorcing you?"

"She's going to marry Sir Reginald Frobisher as soon as the decree is made absolute."

Mrs. Tower positively screamed. Then she felt so faint that she had to get her smelling salts.

"After all you've done for her?"

"I've done nothing for her."

"Do you mean to say you're going to allow yourself to be made use of like that?"

"We arranged before we married that if either of us wanted his liberty the other should put no hindrance in the way."

"But that was done on your account. Because you were twenty-seven years younger than she was."

"Well, it's come in very useful for her," he answered bitterly.

Mrs. Tower expostulated, argued and reasoned; but Gilbert insisted that no rules applied to Jane, and he must do exactly what she wanted. He left Mrs. Tower prostrate. It relieved her a good deal to give me a full account of this interview. It pleased her to see that I was as surprised as herself and if I was not so indignant with Jane as she was she ascribed that to the criminal lack of morality incident to my sex. She was still in a state of extreme agitation when the door was opened and the butler showed in—Jane herself. She was dressed in black and white as no doubt befitted her slightly ambiguous position, but in a dress so original and fantastic, in a hat so striking, that I positively gasped at the sight of her. But she was as ever bland and collected. She came forward to kiss Mrs. Tower, but Mrs. Tower withdrew herself with icy dignity.

"Gilbert has been here," she said.

"Yes, I know," smiled Jane. "I told him to come and see you. I'm going to Paris to-night and I want you to be very kind to him while I am away. I'm afraid just at first he'll be rather lonely and I shall feel more comfortable if I can count on your keeping an eye on him."

Mrs. Tower clasped her hands.

"Gilbert has just told me something that I can hardly bring myself to believe. He tells me that you're going to divorce him to marry Reginald Frobisher."

"Don't you remember, before I married Gilbert you advised me to marry a man of my own age? The admiral is fifty-three."

"But, Jane, you owe everything to Gilbert," said Mrs. Tower

I

indignantly. "You wouldn't exist without him. Without him to design your clothes, you'll be nothing."

"Oh, he's promised to go on designing my clothes," Jane answered blandly.

"No woman could want a better husband. He's always been kindness itself to you."

"Oh, I know he's been sweet."

"How *can* you be so heartless?"

"But I was never in love with Gilbert," said Jane. "I always told him that. I'm beginning to feel the need of the companionship of a man of my own age. I think I've probably been married to Gilbert long enough. The young have no conversation." She paused a little and gave us both a charming smile. "Of course I shan't lose sight of Gilbert. I've arranged that with Reginald. The admiral has a niece that would just suit him. As soon as we're married we'll ask them to stay with us at Malta—you know that the admiral is to have the Mediterranean Command—and I shouldn't be at all surprised if they fell in love with one another."

Mrs. Tower gave a little sniff.

"And have you arranged with the admiral that if you want your liberty neither should put any hindrance in the way of the other?"

"I suggested it," Jane answered with composure. "But the admiral says he knows a good thing when he sees it and he won't want to marry anyone else, and if anyone wants to marry me—he has eight twelve-inch guns on his flagship and he'll discuss the matter at short range." She gave us a look through her eyeglass which even the fear of Mrs. Tower's wrath could not prevent me from laughing at. "I think the admiral's a very passionate man."

Mrs. Tower indeed gave me an angry frown.

"I never thought you funny, Jane," she said. "I never understood why people laughed at the things you said."

"I never thought I was funny myself, Marion," smiled Jane, showing her bright, regular teeth. "I am glad to leave London before too many people come round to our opinion."

"I wish you'd tell me the secret of your astonishing success," I said.

She turned to me with that bland, homely look I knew so well.

"You know, when I married Gilbert and settled in London and people began to laugh at what I said no one was more surprised than I was. I'd said the same things for thirty years and no one ever saw anything to laugh at. I thought it must be my clothes or my bobbed hair or my eyeglass. Then I discovered it was because

I spoke the truth. It was so unusual that people thought it humorous. One of these days someone else will discover the secret and when people habitually tell the truth of course there'll be nothing funny in it."

"And why am I the only person not to think it funny?" asked Mrs. Tower.

Jane hesitated a little as though she were honestly searching for a satisfactory explanation.

"Perhaps you don't know the truth when you see it, Marion dear," she answered in her mild good-natured way.

It certainly gave her the last word. I felt that Jane would always have the last word. She *was* priceless.

Footprints in the Jungle

THERE is no place in Malaya that has more charm than Tanah Merah. It lies on the sea and the sandy shore is fringed with casuarinas. The government offices are still in the old Raad Huis that the Dutch built when they owned the land, and on the hill stand the grey ruins of the fort by aid of which the Portuguese maintained their hold over the unruly natives. Tanah Merah has a history and in the vast labyrinthine houses of the Chinese merchants, backing on the sea so that in the cool of the evening they may sit in their loggias and enjoy the salt breeze, families dwell that have been settled in the country for three centuries. Many have forgotten their native language and hold intercourse with one another in Malay and pidgin English. The imagination lingers here gratefully, for in the Federated Malay States the only past is within the memory for the most part of the fathers of living men.

Tanah Merah was for long the busiest mart of the Middle East and its harbour was crowded with shipping when the clipper and the junk still sailed the China seas. But now it is dead. It has the sad and romantic air of all places that have once been of importance and live now on the recollection of a vanished grandeur. It is a sleepy little town and strangers that come to it, losing their native energy, insensibly drop into its easy and lethargic ways. Successive rubber booms bring it no prosperity and the ensuing slumps hasten its decay.

The European quarter is very silent. It is trim and neat and clean. The houses of the white men—government servants and agents of companies—stand round an immense padang, agreeable and roomy bungalows shaded by great cassias, and the padang is vast and green and well cared for, like the lawn of a cathedral close, and indeed there is in the aspect of this corner of Tanah Merah something quiet and delicately secluded that reminds you of the precincts of Canterbury.

The club faces the sea; it is a spacious but shabby building; it has an air of neglect and when you enter you feel that you intrude. It gives you the impression that it is closed really, for alterations and repairs, and that you have taken indiscreet advantage of an open door to go where you are not wanted. In the morning you may find there a couple of planters who have come in from their estates on business and are drinking a gin-sling before starting back again; and latish in the afternoon a lady or two may perhaps be seen looking with a furtive air through old numbers of the *Illustrated London News*. At nightfall a few men saunter in and sit about the billiard-room watching the play and drinking sukus. But on Wednesdays there is a little more animation. On that day the gramophone is set going in the large room upstairs and people come in from the surrounding country to dance. There are sometimes no less than a dozen couples and it is even possible to make up two tables of bridge.

It was on one of these occasions that I met the Cartwrights. I was staying with a man called Gaze who was head of the police and he came into the billiard-room, where I was sitting, and asked me if I would make up a four. The Cartwrights were planters and they came in to Tanah Merah on Wednesdays because it gave their girl a chance of a little fun. They were very nice people, said Gaze, quiet and unobtrusive, and played a very pleasant game of bridge. I followed Gaze into the card-room and was introduced to them. They were already seated at a table and Mrs. Cartwright was shuffling the cards. It inspired me with confidence to see the competent way in which she did it. She took half the pack in each hand, and her hands were large and strong, deftly inserted the corners of one half under the corners of the other, and with a click and a neat bold gesture cascaded the cards together.

It had all the effect of a conjuring trick. The card-player knows that it can be done perfectly only after incessant practice. He can be fairly sure that anyone who can so shuffle a pack of cards loves cards for their own sake.

"Do you mind if my husband and I play together?" asked Mrs. Cartwright. "It's no fun for us to win one another's money."

"Of course not."

We cut for deal and Gaze and I sat down.

Mrs. Cartwright drew an ace and while she dealt, quickly and neatly, chatted with Gaze of local affairs. But I was aware that she took stock of me. She looked shrewd, but good-natured.

She was a woman somewhere in the fifties (though in the East, where people age quickly, it is difficult to tell their ages), with white hair very untidily arranged, and a constant gesture with her was an impatient movement of the hand to push back a long wisp of hair that kept falling over her forehead. You wondered why she did not, by the use of a hairpin or two, save herself so much trouble. Her blue eyes were large, but pale and a little tired; her face was lined and sallow; I think it was her mouth that gave it the expression which I felt was characteristic of caustic but tolerant irony. You saw that here was a woman who knew her mind and was never afraid to speak it. She was a chatty player (which some people object to strongly, but which does not disconcert me, for I do not see why you should behave at the card-table as though you were at a memorial service) and it was soon apparent that she had an effective knack of badinage. It was pleasantly acid, but it was amusing enough to be offensive only to a fool. If now and then she uttered a remark so sarcastic that you wanted all your sense of humour to see the fun in it, you could not but quickly see that she was willing to take as much as she gave. Her large, thin mouth broke into a dry smile and her eyes shone brightly when by a lucky chance you brought off a repartee that turned the laugh against her.

I thought her a very agreeable person. I liked her frankness. I liked her quick wit. I liked her plain face. I never met a woman who obviously cared so little how she looked. It was not only her head that was untidy, everything about her was slovenly; she wore a high-necked silk blouse, but for coolness had unbuttoned the top buttons and showed a gaunt and withered neck; the blouse was crumpled and none too clean, for she smoked innumerable cigarettes and covered herself with ash. When she got up for a moment to speak to somebody I saw that her blue skirt was rather ragged at the hem and badly needed a brush, and she wore heavy, low-heeled boots. But none of this mattered. Everything she wore was perfectly in character.

And it was a pleasure to play bridge with her. She played very quickly, without hesitation, and she had not only knowledge but flair. Of course she knew Gaze's game, but I was a stranger and she soon took my measure. The team-work between her husband and herself was admirable; he was sound and cautious, but knowing him, she was able to be bold with assurance and brilliant with safety. Gaze was a player who founded a foolish optimism on the hope that his opponents would not have the sense to take advantage of his errors, and the pair of us were no match for the Cartwrights. We lost one rubber after another, and there was nothing to do but smile and look as if we liked it.

"I don't know what's the matter with the cards," said Gaze at last, plaintively. "Even when we have every card in the pack we go down."

"It can't be anything to do with your play," answered Mrs. Cartwright, looking him full in the face with those pale blue eyes of hers, "it must be bad luck pure and simple. Now if you hadn't had your hearts mixed up with your diamonds in that last hand you'd have saved the game."

Gaze began to explain at length how the misfortune, which had cost us dear, occurred, but Mrs. Cartwright, with a deft flick of the hand, spread out the cards in a great circle so that we should cut for deal. Cartwright looked at the time.

"This will have to be the last, my dear," he said.

"Oh, will it?" She glanced at her watch and then called to a young man who was passing through the room. "Oh, Mr. Bullen, if you're going upstairs tell Olive that we shall be going in a few minutes." She turned to me. "It takes us the best part of an hour to get back to the estate and poor Theo has to be up at the crack of dawn."

"Oh, well, we only come in once a week," said Cartwright, "and it's the one chance Olive gets of being gay and abandoned."

I thought Cartwright looked tired and old. He was a man of middle height, with a bald, shiny head, a stubbly grey moustache, and gold-rimmed spectacles. He wore white ducks and a black-and-white tie. He was rather neat and you could see he took much more pains with his clothes than his untidy wife. He talked little, but it was plain that he enjoyed his wife's caustic humour and sometimes he made quite a neat retort. They were evidently very good friends. It was pleasing to see so solid and tolerant an affection between two people who were almost elderly and must have lived together for so many years.

It took but two hands to finish the rubber and we had just ordered a final gin and bitters when Olive came down.

"Do you really want to go already, Mumsey?" she asked.

Mrs. Cartwright looked at her daughter with fond eyes.

"Yes, darling. It's nearly half-past eight. It'll be ten before we get our dinner."

"Damn our dinner," said Olive, gaily.

"Let her have one more dance before we go," suggested Cartwright.

"Not one. You must have a good night's rest."

Cartwright looked at Olive with a smile.

"If your mother has made up her mind, my dear, we may just as well give in without any fuss."

"She's a determined woman," said Olive, lovingly stroking her mother's wrinkled cheek.

Mrs. Cartwright patted her daughter's hand, and kissed it.

Olive was not very pretty, but she looked extremely nice. She was nineteen or twenty, I suppose, and she had still the plumpness of her age; she would be more attractive when she had fined down a little. She had none of the determination that gave her mother's

face so much character, but resembled her father; she had his
dark eyes and slightly aquiline nose, and his look of rather weak
good nature. It was plain that she was strong and healthy. Her
cheeks were red and her eyes bright. She had a vitality that he had
long since lost. She seemed to be the perfectly normal English
girl, with high spirits, a great desire to enjoy herself, and an excellent
temper.

When we separated, Gaze and I set out to walk to his house.

"What did you think of the Cartwrights?" he asked me.

"I liked them. They must be a great asset in a place like this."

"I wish they came oftener. They live a very quiet life."

"It must be dull for the girl. The father and mother seem very
well satisfied with one another's company."

"Yes, it's been a great success."

"Olive is the image of her father, isn't she?"

Gaze gave me a sidelong glance.

"Cartwright isn't her father. Mrs. Cartwright was a widow when
he married her. Olive was born four months after her father's
death."

"Oh!"

I drew out the sound in order to put in it all I could of surprise,
interest and curiosity. But Gaze said nothing and we walked the
rest of the way in silence. The boy was waiting at the door as we
entered the house and after a last gin pahit we sat down to dinner.

At first Gaze was inclined to be talkative. Owing to the restric-
tion of the output of rubber there had sprung up a considerable
activity among the smugglers and it was part of his duty to circum-
vent their knavishness. Two junks had been captured that day
and he was rubbing his hands over his success. The go-downs
were full of confiscated rubber and in a little while it was going to
be solemnly burnt. But presently he fell into silence and we finished
without a word. The boys brought in coffee and brandy and we
lit our cheroots. Gaze leaned back in his chair. He looked at me
reflectively and then looked at his brandy. The boys had left the
room and we were alone.

"I've known Mrs. Cartwright for over twenty years," he said
slowly. "She wasn't a bad-looking woman in those days. Always
untidy, but when she was young it didn't seem to matter so much.
It was rather attractive. She was married to a man called Bronson.
Reggie Bronson. He was a planter. He was manager of an estate
up in Selantan and I was stationed at Alor Lipis. It was a much
smaller place than it is now; I don't suppose there were more than
twenty people in the whole community, but they had a jolly little

club, and we used to have a very good time. I remember the first
time I met Mrs. Bronson as though it was yesterday. There were
no cars in those days and she and Bronson had ridden in on their
bicycles. Of course then she didn't look so determined as she
looks now. She was much thinner, she had a nice colour, and her
eyes were very pretty—blue, you know—and she had a lot of dark
hair. If she'd only taken more trouble with herself she'd have
been rather stunning. As it was she was the best-looking woman
there."

I tried to construct in my mind a picture of what Mrs. Cartwright—Mrs. Bronson as she was then—looked like from what
she was now and from Gaze's not very graphic description. In the
solid woman, with her well-covered bones, who sat rather heavily
at the bridge-table, I tried to see a slight young thing with buoyant
movements and graceful, easy gestures. Her chin now was square
and her nose decided, but the roundness of youth must have masked
this: she must have been charming with a pink-and-white skin and
her hair, carelessly dressed, brown and abundant. At that period
she wore a long skirt, a tight waist and a picture hat. Or did
women in Malaya still wear the topees that you see in old numbers
of the illustrated papers?

"I hadn't seen her for—oh, nearly twenty years," Gaze went on.
"I knew she was living somewhere in the F.M.S., but it was a
surprise when I took this job and came here to run across her in the
club just as I had up in Selantan so many years before. Of course
she's an elderly woman now and she's changed out of all recognition.
It was rather a shock to see her with a grown-up daughter, it made
me realise how the time had passed; I was a young fellow when I
met her last and now, by Jingo, I'm due to retire on the age limit
in two or three years. Bit thick, isn't it?"

Gaze, a rueful grin on his ugly face, looked at me with faint
indignation, as though I could help the hurrying march of the years
as they trod upon one another's heels.

"I'm no chicken myself," I replied.

"You haven't lived out East all your life. It ages one before
one's time. One's an elderly man at fifty and at fifty-five one's
good for nothing but the scrap-heap."

But I did not want Gaze to wander off into a disquisition on old
age.

"Did you recognise Mrs. Cartwright when you saw her again?"
I asked.

"Well, I did and I didn't. At the first glance I thought I knew
her, but couldn't quite place her. I thought perhaps she was

someone I'd met on board ship when I was going on leave and had known only by sight. But the moment she spoke I remembered at once. I remembered the dry twinkle in her eyes and the crisp sound of her voice. There was something in her voice that seemed to mean: You're a bit of a damned fool, my lad, but you're not a bad sort and upon my soul I rather like you."

"That's a good deal to read into the sound of a voice," I smiled.

"She came up to me in the club and shook hands with me. 'How do you do, Major Gaze? Do you remember me?' she said.

" 'Of course I do.'

" 'A lot of water has passed under the bridge since we met last. We're none of us as young as we were. Have you seen Theo?'

"For a moment I couldn't think whom she meant. I suppose I looked rather stupid, because she gave a little smile, that chaffing smile that I knew so well, and explained.

" 'I married Theo, you know. It seemed the best thing to do. I was lonely and he wanted it.'

" 'I heard you married him,' I said. 'I hope you've been very happy.'

" 'Oh, very. Theo's a perfect duck. He'll be here in a minute. He'll be so glad to see you.'

"I wondered. I should have thought I was the last man Theo would wish to see. I shouldn't have thought she would wish it very much either. But women are funny."

"Why shouldn't she wish to see you?" I asked.

"I'm coming to that later," said Gaze. "Then Theo turned up. I don't know why I call him Theo; I never called him anything but Cartwright, I never thought of him as anything but Cartwright. Theo was a shock. You know what he looks like now; I remembered him as a curly-headed youngster, very fresh and clean-looking, he was always neat and dapper, he had a good figure and he held himself well, like a man who's used to taking a lot of exercise. Now I come to think of it he wasn't bad-looking, not in a big, massive way, but graceful, you know, and lithe. When I saw this bowed, cadaverous, bald-headed old buffer with spectacles I could hardly believe my eyes. I shouldn't have known him from Adam. He seemed pleased to see me, at least, interested; he wasn't effusive, but he'd always been on the quiet side and I didn't expect him to be.

" 'Are you surprised to find us here?' he asked me.

" 'Well, I hadn't the faintest notion where you were.'

" 'We've kept track of your movements more or less. We've seen your name in the paper every now and then. You must come out one day and have a look at our place. We've been settled there a good many years, and I suppose we shall stay there till we go home for good. Have you ever been back to Alor Lipis?'

" 'No, I haven't,' I said.

" 'It was a nice little place. I'm told it's grown. I've never been back.'

" 'It hasn't got the pleasantest recollections for us,' said Mrs. Cartwright.

"I asked them if they'd have a drink and we called the boy. I dare say you noticed that Mrs. Cartwright likes her liquor; I don't mean that she gets tight or anything like that, but she drinks her stengah like a man. I couldn't help looking at them with a certain amount of curiosity. They seemed perfectly happy; I gathered that they hadn't done at all badly, and I found out later that they were quite well off. They had a very nice car, and when they went on leave they denied themselves nothing. They were on the best of terms with one another. You know how jolly it is to see two people who've been married a great many years obviously better pleased with their own company than anyone else's. Their marriage had evidently been a great success. And they were both of them devoted to Olive and very proud of her, Theo especially."

"Although she was only his step-daughter?" I said.

"Although she was only his step-daughter," answered Gaze. "You'd think that she would have taken his name. But she hadn't. She called him Daddy, of course, he was the only father she'd ever known, but she signed her letters, Olive Bronson."

"What was Bronson like, by the way?"

"Bronson? He was a great big fellow, very hearty, with a loud voice and a bellowing laugh, beefy, you know, and a fine athlete. There was not very much to him, but he was as straight as a die. He had a red face and red hair. Now I come to think of it I remember that I never saw a man sweat as much as he did. Water just poured off him, and when he played tennis he always used to bring a towel on the court with him."

"It doesn't sound very attractive."

"He was a handsome chap. He was always fit. He was keen on that. He hadn't much to talk about but rubber and games, tennis, you know, and golf and shooting; and I don't suppose he read a book from year's end to year's end. He was the typical public-school boy. He was about thirty-five when I first knew him, but he had the mind of a boy of eighteen. You know how many fellows when they come out East seem to stop growing."

I did indeed. One of the most disconcerting things to the traveller is to see stout, middle-aged gentlemen, with bald heads, speaking

and acting like schoolboys. You might almost think that no idea
has entered their heads since they first passed through the Suez
Canal. Though married and the fathers of children, and perhaps in
control of a large business, they continue to look upon life from the
standpoint of the sixth form.

"But he was no fool," Gaze went on. "He knew his work from
A to Z. His estate was one of the best managed in the country
and he knew how to handle his labour. He was a damned good
sort, and if he did get on your nerves a little you couldn't help
liking him. He was generous with his money, and always ready
to do anybody a good turn. That's how Cartwright happened to
turn up in the first instance."

"Did the Bronsons get on well together?"

"Oh, yes, I think so. I'm sure they did. He was good-natured
and she was very jolly and gay. She was very outspoken, you know.
She can be damned amusing when she likes even now, but there's
generally a sting lurking in the joke; when she was a young woman
and married to Bronson it was just pure fun. She had high spirits
and liked having a good time. She never cared a hang what she
said, but it went with her type, if you understand what I mean;
there was something so open and frank and careless about her
that you didn't care what she said to you. They seemed very
happy.

"Their estate was about five miles from Alor Lipis. They had
a trap and they used to drive in most evenings about five. Of course
it was a very small community and men were in the majority.
There were only about six women. The Bronsons were a god-send.
They bucked things up the moment they arrived. We used to
have very jolly times in that little club. I've often thought of them
since and I don't know that on the whole I've ever enjoyed myself
more than I did when I was stationed there. Between six and eight-
thirty the club at Alor Lipis twenty years ago was about as lively
a place as you could find between Aden and Yokohama.

"One day Mrs. Bronson told us that they were expecting a friend
to stay with them and a few days later they brought Cartwright
along. It appeared that he was an old friend of Bronson's, they'd
been at school together, Marlborough, or some place like that,
and they'd first come out East on the same ship. Rubber had taken
a toss and a lot of fellows had lost their jobs. Cartwright was one
of them. He'd been out of work for the greater part of a year
and he hadn't anything to fall back on. In those days planters
were even worse paid than they are now and a man had to be very
lucky to put by something for a rainy day. Cartwright had gone to

Singapore. They all go there when there's a slump, you know. It's awful then, I've seen it; I've known of planters sleeping in the street because they hadn't the price of a night's lodging. I've known them stop strangers outside the Europe and ask for a dollar to get a meal, and I think Cartwright had had a pretty rotten time.

"At last he wrote to Bronson and asked him if he couldn't do something for him. Bronson asked him to come and stay till things got better, at least it would be free board and lodging, and Cartwright jumped at the chance, but Bronson had to send him the money to pay his railway fare. When Cartwright arrived at Alor Lipis he hadn't ten cents in his pocket. Bronson had a little money of his own, two or three hundred a year, I think, and though his salary had been cut, he'd kept his job, so that he was better off than most planters. When Cartwright came Mrs. Bronson told him that he was to look upon the place as his home and stay as long as he liked."

"It was very nice of her, wasn't it?" I remarked.

"Very."

Gaze lit himself another cheroot and filled his glass. It was very still and but for the occasional croak of the chik-chak the silence was intense. We seemed to be alone in the tropical night and heaven only knows how far from the habitations of men. Gaze did not speak for so long that at last I was forced to say something.

"What sort of a man was Cartwright at that time?" I asked. "Younger, of course, and you told me rather nice-looking; but in himself?"

"Well, to tell you the truth, I never paid much attention to him. He was pleasant and unassuming. He's very quiet now, as I dare say you noticed; well, he wasn't exactly lively then. But he was perfectly inoffensive. He was fond of reading and he played the piano rather nicely. You never minded having him about, he was never in the way, but you never bothered very much about him. He danced well and the women rather liked that, but he also played billiards quite decently and he wasn't bad at tennis. He fell into our little groove very naturally. I wouldn't say that he ever became wildly popular, but everybody liked him. Of course we were sorry for him, as one is for a man who's down and out, but there was nothing we could do, and, well, we just accepted him and then forgot that he hadn't always been there. He used to come in with the Bronsons every evening and pay for his drinks like everyone else, I suppose Bronson had lent him a bit of money for current expenses, and he was always very civil. I'm rather vague about him, because really he didn't make any particular impression on me; in the East one meets such a lot of people, and he seemed very much like anybody else. He did everything he could to get something to do, but he had no luck; the fact is, there were no jobs going, and sometimes he seemed rather depressed about it. He was with the Bronsons for over a year. I remember his saying to me once:

" 'After all I can't live with them for ever. They've been most awfully good to me, but there are limits.'

" 'I should think the Bronsons would be very glad to have you,' I said. 'It's not particularly gay on a rubber estate, and as far as your food and drink go, it must make precious little difference if you're there or not.' "

Gaze stopped once more and looked at me with a sort of hesitation. "What's the matter?" I asked.

"I'm afraid I'm telling you this story very badly," he said. "I seem to be just rambling on. I'm not a damned novelist, I'm a policeman, and I'm just telling you the facts as I saw them at the time; and from my point of view all the circumstances are important; it's important, I mean, to realise what sort of people they were."

"Of course. Fire away."

"I remember someone, a woman, I think it was, the doctor's wife, asking Mrs. Bronson if she didn't get tired sometimes of having a stranger in the house. You know, in places like Alor Lipis there isn't very much to talk about, and if you didn't talk about your neighbours there'd be nothing to talk about at all.

" 'Oh, no,' she said, 'Theo's no trouble.' She turned to her husband, who was sitting there mopping his face. 'We like having him, don't we?'

" 'He's all right,' said Bronson.

" 'What does he do with himself all day long?'

" 'Oh, I don't know,' said Mrs. Bronson. 'He walks round the estate with Reggie sometimes, and he shoots a bit. He talks to me.'

" 'He's always glad to make himself useful,' said Bronson. 'The other day when I had a go of fever, he took over my work and I just lay in bed and had a good time.' "

"Hadn't the Bronsons any children?" I asked.

"No," Gaze answered. "I don't know why, they could well have afforded it."

Gaze leant back in his chair. He took off his glasses and wiped them. They were very strong and hideously distorted his eyes. Without them he wasn't so homely. The chik-chak on the ceiling gave its strangely human cry. It was like the cackle of an idiot child.

"Bronson was killed," said Gaze suddenly.

"Killed?"

"Yes, murdered. I shall never forget that night. We'd been playing tennis, Mrs. Bronson and the doctor's wife, Theo Cartwright and I; and then we played bridge. Cartwright had been off his game and when we sat down at the bridge-table Mrs. Bronson said to him: 'Well, Theo, if you play bridge as rottenly as you played tennis we shall lose our shirts.'

"We'd just had a drink, but she called the boy and ordered another round.

" 'Put that down your throat,' she said to him, 'and don't call without top honours and an outside trick.'

"Bronson hadn't turned up, he'd cycled in to Kabulong to get the money to pay his coolies their wages and was to come along to the club when he got back. The Bronsons' estate was nearer Alor Lipis than it was to Kabulong, but Kabulong was a more important place commercially, and Bronson banked there.

" 'Reggie can cut in when he turns up,' said Mrs. Bronson.

" 'He's late, isn't he?' said the doctor's wife.

" 'Very. He said he wouldn't get back in time for tennis, but would be here for a rubber. I have a suspicion that he went to the club at Kabulong instead of coming straight home and is having drinks, the ruffian.'

" 'Oh, well, he can put away a good many without their having much effect on him,' I laughed.

" 'He's getting fat, you know. He'll have to be careful.'

"We sat by ourselves in the card-room and we could hear the crowd in the billiard-room talking and laughing. They were all on the merry side. It was getting on to Christmas Day and we were all letting ourselves go a little. There was going to be a dance on Christmas Eve.

"I remembered afterwards that when we sat down the doctor's wife asked Mrs. Bronson if she wasn't tired.

" 'Not a bit,' she said. 'Why should I be?'

"I didn't know why she flushed.

" 'I was afraid the tennis might have been too much for you,' said the doctor's wife.

" 'Oh, no,' answered Mrs. Bronson, a trifle abruptly, I thought, as though she didn't want to discuss the matter.

"I didn't know what they meant, and indeed it wasn't till later that I remembered the incident.

"We played three or four rubbers and still Bronson didn't turn up.

" 'I wonder what's happened to him,' said his wife. 'I can't think why he should be so late.'

"Cartwright was always silent, but this evening he had hardly opened his mouth. I thought he was tired and asked him what he'd been doing.

" 'Nothing very much,' he said. 'I went out after tiffin to shoot pigeon.'

" 'Did you have any luck?' I asked.

" 'Oh, I got half a dozen. They were very shy.'

"But now he said: 'If Reggie got back late, I dare say he thought it wasn't worth while to come here. I expect he's had a bath and when we get in we shall find him asleep in his chair.'

" 'It's a good long ride from Kabulong,' said the doctor's wife.

" 'He doesn't take the road, you know,' Mrs. Bronson explained. 'He takes the short cut through the jungle.'

" 'Can he get along on his bicycle?' I asked.

" 'Oh, yes, it's a very good track. It saves about a couple of miles.'

"We had just started another rubber when the bar-boy came in and said there was a police-sergeant outside who wanted to speak to me.

" 'What does he want?' I asked.

"The boy said he didn't know, but he had two coolies with him.

" 'Curse him,' I said. 'I'll give him hell if I find he's disturbed me for nothing.'

"I told the boy I'd come and I finished playing the hand. Then I got up.

" 'I won't be a minute,' I said. 'Deal for me, will you?' I added to Cartwright.

"I went out and found the sergeant with two Malays waiting for me on the steps. I asked him what the devil he wanted. You can imagine my consternation when he told me that the Malays had come to the police-station and said there was a white man lying dead on the path that led through the jungle to Kabulong. I immediately thought of Bronson.

" 'Dead?' I cried.

" 'Yes, shot. Shot through the head. A white man with red hair.'

"Then I knew it was Reggie Bronson, and indeed, one of them naming his estate said he'd recognised him as the man. It was an awful shock. And there was Mrs. Bronson in the card-room waiting impatiently for me to sort my cards and make a bid. For a moment I really didn't know what to do. I was frightfully upset. It was dreadful to give her such a terrible and unexpected blow without a word of preparation, but I found myself quite unable to think of any way to soften it. I told the sergeant and the coolies to wait and went back into the club. I tried to pull myself together. As I entered the card-room Mrs. Bronson said: 'You've been an awful long time.' Then she caught sight of my face. 'Is anything the matter?' I saw her clench her fists and go white. You'd have thought she had a presentiment of evil.

" 'Something dreadful has happened,' I said, and my throat was all closed up so that my voice sounded even to myself hoarse and uncanny. 'There's been an accident. Your husband's been wounded.'

"She gave a long gasp, it was not exactly a scream, it reminded me oddly of a piece of silk torn in two.

" 'Wounded?'

"She leapt to her feet and with her eyes starting from her head stared at Cartwright. The effect on him was ghastly, he fell back in his chair and went as white as death.

" 'Very, very badly, I'm afraid,' I added.

"I knew that I must tell her the truth, and tell it then, but I couldn't bring myself to tell it all at once.

" 'Is he,' her lips trembled so that she could hardly form the words, 'is he—conscious?'

"I looked at her for a moment without answering. I'd have given a thousand pounds not to have to.

" 'No, I'm afraid he isn't.'

"Mrs. Bronson stared at me as though she were trying to see right into my brain.

" 'Is he dead?'

"I thought the only thing was to get it out and have done with it.

" 'Yes, he was dead when they found him.'

"Mrs. Bronson collapsed into her chair and burst into tears.

" 'Oh, my God,' she muttered. 'Oh, my God.'

"The doctor's wife went to her and put her arms round her. Mrs. Bronson with her face in her hands swayed to and fro weeping hysterically. Cartwright, with that livid face, sat quite still, his mouth open, and stared at her. You might have thought he was turned to stone.

" 'Oh, my dear, my dear,' said the doctor's wife, 'you must try and pull yourself together.' Then, turning to me: 'Get her a glass of water and fetch Harry.'

"Harry was her husband and he was playing billiards. I went in and told him what had happened.

" 'A glass of water be damned,' he said. 'What she wants is a good long peg of brandy.'

"We took it in to her and forced her to drink it and gradually the violence of her emotion exhausted itself. In a few minutes the doctor's wife was able to take her into the ladies' lavatory to wash her face. I'd made up my mind now what had better be done. I could see that Cartwright wasn't good for much; he was all to pieces. I could understand that it was a fearful shock to him, for after all Bronson was his greatest friend and had done everything in the world for him.

" 'You look as though you'd be all the better for a drop of brandy yourself, old man,' I said to him.

"He made an effort.

" 'It's shaken me, you know,' he said. 'I . . . I didn't . . .' He stopped as though his mind was wandering; he was still fearfully pale; he took out a packet of cigarettes and struck a match, but his hand was shaking so that he could hardly manage it.

" 'Yes, I'll have a brandy.'

" 'Boy,' I shouted, and then to Cartwright: 'Now, are you fit to take Mrs. Bronson home?'

" 'Oh, yes,' he answered.

" 'That's good. The doctor and I will go along with the coolies and some police to where the body is.'

" 'Will you bring him back to the bungalow?' asked Cartwright.

" 'I think he'd better be taken straight to the mortuary,' said the doctor before I could answer. 'I shall have to do a P.M.'

"When Mrs. Bronson, now so much calmer that I was amazed, came back, I told her what I suggested. The doctor's wife, kind woman, offered to go with her and spend the night at the bungalow, but Mrs. Bronson wouldn't hear of it. She said she would be perfectly all right, and when the doctor's wife insisted—you know how bent some people are on forcing their kindness on those in trouble—she turned on her almost fiercely.

" 'No, no, I must be alone,' she said. 'I really must. And Theo will be there.'

"They got into the trap. Theo took the reins and they drove off. We started after them, the doctor and I, while the sergeant and the coolies followed. I had sent my seis to the police-station with instructions to send two men to the place where the body was lying. We soon passed Mrs. Bronson and Cartwright.

" 'All right?' I called.

" 'Yes,' he answered.

"For some time the doctor and I drove without saying a word; we were both of us deeply shocked. I was worried as well. Somehow or other I'd got to find the murderers and I foresaw that it would be no easy matter.

" 'Do you suppose it was gang robbery?' said the doctor at last.

"He might have been reading my thoughts.

" 'I don't think there's a doubt of it,' I answered. 'They knew he'd gone into Kabulong to get the wages and lay in wait for him on the way back. Of course he should never have come alone through the jungle when everyone knew he had a packet of money with him.'

" 'He'd done it for years,' said the doctor. 'And he's not the only one.'

" 'I know. The question is, how we're going to get hold of the fellows that did it.'

" 'You don't think the two coolies who say they found him could have had anything to do with it?'

" 'No. They wouldn't have the nerve. I think a pair of Chinks might think out a trick like that, but I don't believe Malays would. They'd be much too frightened. Of course we'll keep an eye on them. We shall soon see if they seem to have any money to fling about.'

" 'It's awful for Mrs. Bronson,' said the doctor. 'It would have been bad enough at any time, but now she's going to have a baby . . .'

" 'I didn't know that,' I said, interrupting him.

" 'No, for some reason she wanted to keep it dark. She was rather funny about it, I thought.'

"I recollected then that little passage between Mrs. Bronson and the doctor's wife. I understood why that good woman had been so anxious that Mrs. Bronson should not overtire herself.

" 'It's strange her having a baby after being married so many years.'

" 'It happens, you know. But it was a surprise to her. When first she came to see me and I told her what was the matter she fainted, and then she began to cry. I should have thought she'd be as pleased as Punch. She told me that Bronson didn't like children and he'd be awfully bored at the idea, and she made me promise to say nothing about it till she had had a chance of breaking it to him gradually.'

"I reflected for a moment.

" 'He was the kind of breezy, hearty cove whom you'd expect to be as keen as mustard on having kids.'

" 'You never can tell. Some people are very selfish and just don't want the bother.'

" 'Well, how did he take it when she did tell him? Wasn't he rather bucked?'

" 'I don't know that she ever told him. Though she couldn't have waited much longer; unless I'm very much mistaken she ought to be confined in about five months.'

" 'Poor devil,' I said. 'You know, I've got a notion that he'd have been most awfully pleased to know.'

"We drove in silence for the rest of the way and at last came to the point at which the short cut to Kabulong branched off from the road. Here we stopped and in a minute or two my trap, in which were the police-sergeant and the two Malays, came up. We took the head-lamps to light us on our way. I left the doctor's seis to look after the ponies and told him that when the policemen came they were to follow the path till they found us. The two coolies, carrying the lamps, walked ahead and we followed them. It was a fairly broad track, wide enough for a small cart to pass, and before the road was built it had been the highway between Kabulong and Alor Lipis. It was firm to the foot and good walking. The surface here and there was sandy and in places you could see quite plainly the mark of a bicycle wheel. It was the track Bronson had left on his way to Kabulong.

"We walked twenty minutes, I should think, in single file, and on a sudden the coolies, with a cry, stopped sharply. The sight had come upon them so abruptly that notwithstanding they were expecting it they were startled. There, in the middle of the pathway lit dimly by the lamps the coolies carried, lay Bronson; he'd fallen over his bicycle and lay across it in an ungainly heap. I was too shocked to speak, and I think the doctor was, too. But in our silence the din of the jungle was deafening; those damned cicadas and the bull-frogs were making enough row to wake the dead. Even under ordinary circumstances the noise of the jungle at night is uncanny; because you feel that at that hour there should be utter silence it has an odd effect on you, that ceaseless and invisible uproar that beats upon your nerves. It surrounds you and hems you in. But just then, believe me, it was terrifying. That poor fellow lay dead and all round him the restless life of the jungle pursued its indifferent and ferocious course.

"He was lying face downwards. The sergeant and the coolies looked at me as though awaiting an order. I was a young fellow then and I'm afraid I felt a little frightened. Though I couldn't see the face I had no doubt that it was Bronson, but I felt that I ought to turn the body over to make sure. I suppose we all have our little squeamishnesses; you know, I've always had a horrible distaste for touching dead bodies. I've had to do it fairly often now, but it still makes me feel slightly sick.

" 'It's Bronson, all right,' I said.

"The doctor—by George, it was lucky for me he was there—the doctor bent down and turned the head. The sergeant directed the lamp on the dead face.

" 'My God, half his head's been shot away,' I cried.

" 'Yes.'

"The doctor stood up straight and wiped his hands on the leaves of a tree that grew beside the path.

" 'Is he quite dead?' I asked.

" 'Oh, yes. Death must have been instantaneous. Whoever shot him must have fired at pretty close range.'

" 'How long has he been dead, d'you think?'

" 'Oh, I don't know, several hours.'

" 'He would have passed here about five o'clock, I suppose, if he was expecting to get to the club for a rubber at six.'

" 'There's no sign of any struggle,' said the doctor.

" 'No, there wouldn't be. He was shot as he was riding along.'

"I looked at the body for a little while. I couldn't help thinking how short a time ago it was since Bronson, noisy and loud-voiced, had been so full of hearty life.

" 'You haven't forgotten that he had the coolies' wages on him,' said the doctor.

" 'No, we'd better search him.'

" 'Shall we turn him over?'

" 'Wait a minute. Let us just have a look at the ground first.'

"I took the lamp and as carefully as I could looked all about me. Just where he had fallen the sandy pathway was trodden and confused; there were our footprints and the footprints of the coolies who had found him. I walked two or three paces and then saw quite clearly the mark of his bicycle wheels; he had been riding straight and steadily. I followed it to the spot where he had fallen, to just before that, rather, and there saw very distinctly the prints on each side of the wheels of his heavy boots. He had evidently stopped there and put his feet to the ground, then he'd started off again, there was a great wobble of the wheel, and he'd crashed.

" 'Now let's search him,' I said.

"The doctor and the sergeant turned the body over and one of the coolies dragged the bicycle away. They laid Bronson on his back. I supposed he would have had the money partly in notes and partly in silver. The silver would have been in a bag attached to the bicycle and a glance told me that it was not there. The notes he would have put in a wallet. It would have been a good thick bundle. I felt him all over, but there was nothing; then I turned out the pockets, they were all empty except the right trouser pocket, in which there was a little small change.

" 'Didn't he always wear a watch?' asked the doctor.

" 'Yes, of course he did.'

"I remembered that he wore the chain through the buttonhole in the lapel of his coat and the watch and some seals and things in his handkerchief pocket. But watch and chain were gone.

" 'Well, there's not much doubt now, is there?' I said.

"It was clear that he had been attacked by gang robbers who knew he had money on him. After killing him they had stripped him of everything. I suddenly remembered the footprints that proved that for a moment he had stood still. I saw exactly how it had been done. One of them had stopped him on some pretext and then, just as he started off again, another, slipping out of the jungle behind him, had emptied the two barrels of a gun into his head.

" 'Well,' I said to the doctor, 'it's up to me to catch them, and I'll tell you what, it'll be a real pleasure to me to see them hanged.'

"Of course there was an inquest. Mrs. Bronson gave evidence, but she had nothing to say that we didn't know already. Bronson had left the bungalow about eleven, he was to have tiffin at Kabulong and was to be back between five and six. He asked her not to wait for him, he said he would just put the money in the safe and come straight to the club. Cartwright confirmed this. He had lunched alone with Mrs. Bronson and after a smoke had gone out with a gun to shoot pigeon. He had got in about five, a little before perhaps, had a bath and changed to play tennis. He was shooting not far from the place where Bronson was killed, but never heard a shot. That, of course, meant nothing; what with the cicadas and the frogs and the other sounds of the jungle, he would have had to be very near to hear anything; and besides, Cartwright was probably back in the bungalow before Bronson was killed. We traced Bronson's movements. He had lunched at the club, he had got money at the bank just before it closed, had gone back to the club and had one more drink, and then started off on his bicycle. He had crossed the river by the ferry; the ferryman remembered distinctly seeing him, but was positive that no one else with a bicycle had crossed. That looked as though the murderers were not following, but lying in wait for him. He rode along the main road for a couple of miles and then took the path which was a short cut to his bungalow.

"It looked as though he had been killed by men who knew his habits, and suspicion, of course, fell immediately on the coolies of his estate. We examined them all—pretty carefully—but there was not a scrap of evidence to connect any of them with the crime. In fact, most of them were able satisfactorily to account for their actions and those who couldn't seemed to me for one reason and another out of the running. There were a few bad characters among the Chinese at Alor Lipis and I had them looked up. But somehow I didn't think it was the work of the Chinese; I had a feeling that Chinese would have used revolvers and not a shotgun. Anyhow, I could find out nothing there. So then we offered a reward of a thousand dollars to anyone who could put us in the way of discovering the murderers. I thought there were a good many people to whom it would appeal to do a public service and at the same time earn a tidy sum. But I knew that an informer would take no risks, he wouldn't want to tell what he knew till he knew he could tell it safely, and I armed myself with patience. The reward had brightened the interest of my police and I knew they would use every means they had to bring the criminals to trial. In a case like this they could do more than I.

"But it was strange, nothing happened; the reward seemed to tempt no one. I cast my net a little wider. There were two or three kampongs along the road and I wondered if the murderer were there; I saw the headmen, but got no help from them. It was not that they would tell me nothing, I was sure they had nothing to tell. I talked to the bad hats, but there was absolutely nothing to connect them with the murder. There was not the shadow of a clue.

" 'Very well, my lads,' I said to myself, as I drove back to Alor Lipis, 'there's no hurry; the rope won't spoil by keeping.'

"The scoundrels had got away with a considerable sum, but money is no good unless you spend it. I felt I knew the native temperament enough to be sure that the possession of it was a constant temptation. The Malays are an extravagant race, and a race of gamblers, and the Chinese are gamblers, too; sooner or later someone would start flinging his money about, and then I should want to know where it came from. With a few well-directed questions I thought I could put the fear of God into the fellow and then, if I knew my business, it shouldn't be hard to get a full confession.

"The only thing now was to sit down and wait till the hue and cry had died down and the murderers thought the affair was forgotten. The itch to spend those ill-gotten dollars would grow more and more intolerable till at last it could be resisted no longer. I would go about my business, but I meant never to relax my watch, and one day, sooner or later, my time must come.

"Cartwright took Mrs. Bronson down to Singapore. The company Bronson had worked for asked him if he would care to take Bronson's place, but he said, very naturally, that he didn't like the idea of it; so they put another man in and told Cartwright that he could have the job that Bronson's successor had vacated. It was the management of the estate that Cartwright lives on now. He moved in at once. Four months after this Olive was born at Singapore, and a few months later, when Bronson had been dead just over a year, Cartwright and Mrs. Bronson were married. I was surprised; but on thinking it over I couldn't help confessing that it was very natural. After the trouble Mrs. Bronson had leant much on Cartwright and he had arranged everything for her; she must have been lonely, and rather lost, and I dare say she was grateful for his kindness, he did behave like a brick; and so far as he was concerned I imagined he was sorry for her, it was a dreadful position for a woman, she had nowhere to go, and all they'd gone through must have been a tie between them. There was every reason for them to marry and it was probably the best thing for them both.

"It looked as though Bronson's murderers would never be caught, for that plan of mine didn't work; there was no one in the district who spent more money than he could account for, and if anyone had that hoard buried away under his floor he was showing a self-control that was superhuman. A year had passed and to all intents and purposes the thing was forgotten. Could anyone be so prudent as after so long not to let a little money dribble out? It was incredible. I began to think that Bronson had been killed by a couple of wandering Chinese who had got away, to Singapore perhaps, where there would be small chance of catching them. At last I gave it up. If you come to think of it, as a rule, it's just those crimes, crimes of robbery, in which there is least chance of getting the culprit; for there's nothing to attach suspicion to him, and if he's caught it can only be by his own carelessness. It's different with crimes of passion or vengeance, then you can find out who had a motive to put the victim out of the way.

"It's no use grizzling over one's failures, and bringing my common sense to bear I did my best to put the matter out of my mind.

No one likes to be beaten, but beaten I was and I had to put as good a face on it as I could. And then a Chinaman was caught trying to pawn poor Bronson's watch.

"I told you that Bronson's watch and chain had been taken, and of course Mrs. Bronson was able to give us a fairly accurate description of it. It was a half-hunter, by Benson, there was a gold chain, three or four seals and a sovereign purse. The pawnbroker was a smart fellow and when the Chinaman brought the watch he recognised it at once. On some pretext he kept the man waiting and sent for a policeman. The man was arrested and immediately brought to me. I greeted him like a long-lost brother. I was never so pleased to see anyone in my life. I have no feeling about criminals, you know; I'm rather sorry for them, because they're playing a game in which their opponents hold all the aces and kings; but when I catch one it gives me a little thrill of satisfaction, like bringing off a neat finesse at bridge. At last the mystery was going to be cleared up, for if the Chinaman hadn't done the thing himself we were pretty sure through him to trace the murderers. I beamed on him.

"I asked him to account for his possession of the watch. He said he had bought it from a man he didn't know. That was very thin. I explained the circumstances briefly and told him he would be charged with murder. I meant to frighten him and I did. He said then that he'd found the watch.

"'Found it?' I said. 'Fancy that. Where?'

"His answer staggered me; he said he'd found it in the jungle; I laughed at him; I asked him if he thought watches were likely to be left lying about in the jungle; then he said he'd been coming along the pathway that led from Kabulong to Alor Lipis, and had gone into the jungle and caught sight of something gleaming and there was the watch. That was odd. Why should he have said he found the watch just there? It was either true or excessively astute. I asked him where the chain and the seals were, and he produced them immediately. I'd got him scared, and he was pale and shaking; he was a knock-kneed little fellow and I should have been a fool not to see that I hadn't got hold of the murderer there. But his terror suggested that he knew something.

"I asked him when he'd found the watch.

"'Yesterday,' he said.

"I asked him what he was doing on the short-cut from Kabulong to Alor Lipis. He said he'd been working in Singapore and had gone to Kabulong because his father was ill, and that he himself had come to Alor Lipis to work. A friend of his father, a carpenter by trade, had given him a job. He gave me the name of the man with whom he had worked in Singapore and the name of the man who had engaged him at Alor Lipis. All he said seemed plausible and could so easily be verified that it was hardly likely to be false. Of course it occurred to me that if he had found the watch as he said, it must have been lying in the jungle for more than a year. It could hardly be in very good condition; I tried to open it, but couldn't. The pawnbroker had come to the police-station and was waiting in the next room. Luckily he was also something of a watch-maker. I sent for him and asked him to look at the watch; when he opened it he gave a little whistle, the works were thick with rust.

" 'This watch no good,' he said, shaking his head. 'Him never go now.'

"I asked him what had put it in such a state, and without a word from me he said that it had been long exposed to wet. For the moral effect I had the prisoner put in a cell and I sent for his employer. I sent a wire to Kabulong and another to Singapore. While I waited I did my best to put two and two together. I was inclined to believe the man's story true; his fear might be ascribed to no more guilt than consisted in his having found something and tried to sell it. Even quite innocent persons are apt to be nervous when they're in the hands of the police; I don't know what there is about a policeman, people are never very much at their ease in his company. But if he really had found the watch where he said, someone had thrown it there. Now that was funny. Even if the murderers had thought the watch a dangerous thing to possess, one would have expected them to melt down the gold case; that would be a very simple thing for any native to do; and the chain was of so ordinary a pattern they could hardly have thought it possible to trace that. There were chains like it in every jeweller's shop in the country. Of course there was the possibility that they had plunged into the jungle and having dropped the watch in their hurry had been afraid to go back and look for it. I didn't think that very likely: the Malays are used to keeping things tucked away in their sarongs, and the Chinese have pockets in their coats. Besides, the moment they got into the jungle they knew there was no hurry; they probably waited and divided the swag then and there.

"In a few minutes the man I had sent for came to the police-station and confirmed what the prisoner had said, and in an hour I got an answer from Kabulong. The police had seen his father, who told them that the boy had gone to Alor Lipis to get a job with a carpenter. So far everything he had said seemed true. I had him brought in again, and told him I was going to take him to the place where he said he had found the watch and he must show me the exact spot. I handcuffed him to a policeman, though it was hardly necessary, for the poor devil was shaking with fright, and took a couple of men besides. We drove out to where the track joined the road and walked along it; within five yards of the place where Bronson was killed the Chinaman stopped.

" 'Here,' he said.

"He pointed to the jungle and we followed him in. We went in about ten yards and he pointed to a chink between two large boulders and said that he found the watch there. It could only have been by the merest chance that he noticed it, and if he really had found it there it looked very much as though someone had put it there to hide it."

Gaze stopped and gave me a reflective look.

"What would you have thought then?" he asked.

"I don't know," I answered.

"Well, I'll tell you what I thought. I thought that if the watch was there the money might be there, too. It seemed worth while having a look. Of course, to look for something in the jungle makes looking for a needle in a bundle of hay a drawing-room pastime. I couldn't help that. I released the Chinaman, I wanted all the help I could get, and set him to work. I set my three men to work, and I started in myself. We made a line—there were five of us—and we searched from the road; for fifty yards on each side of the place at which Bronson was murdered and for a hundred yards in we went over the ground foot by foot. We routed among dead leaves and peered in bushes, we looked under boulders and in the hollow of trees. I knew it was a foolish thing to do, for the chances against us were a thousand to one; my only hope was that anyone who had just committed a murder would be rattled and if he wanted to hide anything would hide it quickly; he would choose the first obvious hiding-place that offered itself. That is what he had done when he hid the watch. My only reason for looking in so circumscribed an area was that as the watch had been found so near the road, the person who wanted to get rid of the things must have wanted to get rid of them quickly.

"We worked on. I began to grow tired and cross. We were sweating like pigs. I had a maddening thirst and nothing in the world to drink. At last I came to the conclusion that we must give it up as a bad job, for that day at least, when suddenly the Chinaman—he must have had sharp eyes, that young man—uttered a guttural cry. He stooped down and from under the winding root of a tree drew out a messy, mouldering, stinking thing. It was a pocket-book that had been out in the rain for a year, that had been eaten by ants and beetles and God knows what, that was sodden and foul, but it was a pocket-book all right, Bronson's, and inside were the shapeless, mushed-up, fetid remains of the Singapore notes he had got from the bank at Kabulong. There was still the silver and I was convinced that it was hidden somewhere about, but I wasn't going to bother about that. I had found out something very important; whoever had murdered Bronson had made no money out of it.

"Do you remember my telling you that I'd noticed the print of Bronson's feet on each side of the broad line of the pneumatic tyre, where he had stopped, and presumably spoken to someone? He was a heavy man and the prints were well marked. He hadn't just put his feet on the soft sand and taken them off, but must have stopped at least for a minute or two. My explanation was that he had stopped to chat with a Malay or a Chinaman, but the more I thought of it the less I liked it. Why the devil should he? Bronson wanted to get home, and though a jovial chap, he certainly was not hail-fellow-well-met with the natives. His relations towards them were those of master and servants. Those footprints had always puzzled me. And now the truth flashed across me. Whoever had murdered Bronson hadn't murdered him to rob and if he'd stopped to talk with someone it could only be with a friend. I knew at last who the murderer was."

I have always thought the detective story a most diverting and ingenious variety of fiction, and have regretted that I never had the skill to write one, but I have read a good many, and I flatter myself it is rarely that I have not solved the mystery before it was disclosed to me; and now for some time I had foreseen what Gaze was going to say, but when at last he said it I confess that it gave me, notwithstanding, somewhat of a shock.

"The man he met was Cartwright. Cartwright was pigeon-shooting. He stopped and asked him what sport he had had, and as he rode on Cartwright raised his gun and discharged both barrels into his head. Cartwright took the money and the watch in order to make it look like the work of gang robbers and hurriedly hid them in the jungle, then made his way along the edge till he got to the road, went back to the bungalow, changed into his tennis things and drove with Mrs. Bronson to the club.

"I remembered how badly he'd played tennis, and how he'd collapsed when, in order to break the news more gently to Mrs. Bronson, I said Bronson was wounded and not dead. If he was only wounded he might have been able to speak. By George, I bet that was a bad moment. The child was Cartwright's. Look at Olive: why, you saw the likeness yourself. The doctor had said that Mrs. Bronson was upset when he told her she was going to have a baby and made him promise not to tell Bronson. Why? Because Bronson knew that he couldn't be the father of the child."

"Do you think that Mrs. Bronson knew what Cartwright had done?" I asked.

"I'm sure of it. When I look back on her behaviour that evening at the club I am convinced of it. She was upset, but not because Bronson was killed; she was upset because I said he was wounded; on my telling her that he was dead when they found him she burst out crying, but from relief. I know that woman. Look at that square chin of hers and tell me that she hasn't got the courage of the devil. She has a will of iron. She made Cartwright do it. She planned every detail and every move. He was completely under her influence; he is now."

"But do you mean to tell me that neither you nor anyone else ever suspected that there was anything between them?"

"Never. Never."

"If they were in love with one another and knew that she was going to have a baby, why didn't they just bolt?"

"How could they? It was Bronson who had the money; she hadn't a bean and neither had Cartwright. He was out of a job. Do you think he would have got another with that story round his neck? Bronson had taken him in when he was starving and he'd stolen his wife from him. They wouldn't have had a dog's chance. They couldn't afford to let the truth come out, their only chance was to get Bronson out of the way, and they got him out of the way."

"They might have thrown themselves on his mercy."

"Yes, but I think they were ashamed. He'd been so good to them, he was such a decent chap, I don't think they had the heart to tell him the truth. They preferred to kill him."

There was a moment's silence while I reflected over what Gaze said.

"Well, what did you do about it?" I asked.

"Nothing. What was there to do? What was the evidence? That the watch and notes had been found? They might easily have been hidden by someone who was afterwards afraid to come and get them. The murderer might have been quite content to get away with the silver. The footprints? Bronson might have stopped to light a cigarette or there might have been a tree-trunk across the path and he waited while the coolies he met there by chance moved it away. Who could prove that the child that a perfectly decent, respectable woman had had four months after her husband's death was not his child? No jury would have convicted Cartwright. I held my tongue and the Bronson murder was forgotten."

"I don't suppose the Cartwrights have forgotten," I suggested.

"I shouldn't be surprised. Human memory is astonishingly short and if you want my professional opinion I don't mind telling you that I don't believe remorse for a crime ever sits very heavily on a man when he's absolutely sure he'll never be found out."

I thought once more of the pair I had met that afternoon, the thin, elderly, bald man with gold-rimmed spectacles, and that white-haired untidy woman with her frank speech and kindly, caustic smile. It was almost impossible to imagine that in the distant past they had been swayed by so turbulent a passion, for that alone made their behaviour explicable, that it had brought them in the end to such a pass that they could see no other issue than a cruel and cold-blooded murder.

"Doesn't it make you feel a little uncomfortable to be with them?" I asked Gaze. "For, without wishing to be censorious, I'm bound to say that I don't think they can be very nice people."

"That's where you're wrong. They are very nice people; they're about the pleasantest people here. Mrs. Cartwright is a thoroughly good sort and a very amusing woman. It's my business to prevent crime and to catch the culprit when crime is committed, but I've known far too many criminals to think that on the whole they're worse than anybody else. A perfectly decent fellow may be driven by circumstances to commit a crime and if he's found out he's punished; but he may very well remain a perfect decently fellow. Of course society punishes him if he breaks its laws, and it's quite right, but it's not always his actions that indicate the essential man. If you'd been a policeman as long as I have, you'd know it's not what people do that really matters, it's what they are. Luckily a policeman has nothing to do with their thoughts, only with their deeds; if he had, it would be a very different, a much more difficult matter."

Gaze flicked the ash from his cheroot and gave me his wry, sardonic, but agreeable smile.

"I'll tell you what, there's one job I *shouldn't* like," he said.

"What is that?" I asked.

"God's, at the Judgment Day," said Gaze. "No, sir."

The Door of Opportunity

THEY got a first-class carriage to themselves. It was lucky, because they were taking a good deal in with them, Alban's suit-case and a hold-all, Anne's dressing-case and her hat-box. They had two trunks in the van, containing what they wanted immediately, but all the rest of their luggage Alban had put in the care of an agent who was to take it up to London and store it till they had made up their minds what to do. They had a lot, pictures and books, curios that Alban had collected in the East, his guns and saddles. They had left Sondurah for ever. Alban, as was his way, tipped the porter generously and then went to the bookstall and bought papers. He bought the *New Statesman* and the *Nation*, and the *Tatler* and the *Sketch*, and the last number of the *London Mercury*. He came back to the carriage and threw them on the seat.

"It's only an hour's journey," said Anne.

"I know, but I wanted to buy them. I've been starved so long. Isn't it grand to think that to-morrow morning we shall have to-morrow's *Times*, and the *Express* and the *Mail*?"

She did not answer and he turned away, for he saw coming towards them two persons, a man and his wife, who had been fellow-passengers from Singapore.

"Get through the Customs all right?" he cried to them cheerily.

The man seemed not to hear, for he walked straight on, but the woman answered.

"Yes, they never found the cigarettes."

She saw Anne, gave her a friendly little smile, and passed on. Anne flushed.

"I was afraid they'd want to come in here," said Alban. "Let's have the carriage to ourselves if we can."

She looked at him curiously.

"I don't think you need worry," she answered. "I don't think anyone will come in."

He lit a cigarette and lingered at the carriage door. On his face was a happy smile. When they had passed through the Red Sea and found a sharp wind in the Canal, Anne had been surprised to see how much the men who had looked presentable enough in the white ducks in which she had been accustomed to see them, were changed when they left them off for warmer clothes. They looked like nothing on earth then. Their ties were awful and their shirts all wrong. They wore grubby flannel trousers and shabby old golf-coats that had too obviously been bought off the nail, or blue serge suits that betrayed the provincial tailor. Most of the passengers had got off at Marseilles, but a dozen or so, either because after a long period in the East they thought the trip through the Bay would do them good, or, like themselves, for economy's sake, had gone all the way to Tilbury, and now several of them walked along the platform. They wore solar topees or double-brimmed terais, and heavy greatcoats, or else shapeless soft hats or bowlers, not too well brushed, that looked too small for them. It was a shock to see them. They looked suburban and a trifle second-rate. But Alban had already a London look. There was not a speck of dust on his smart greatcoat, and his black Homburg hat looked brand-new. You would never have guessed that he had not been home for three years. His collar fitted closely round his neck and his foulard tie was neatly tied. As Anne looked at him she could not but think how good-looking he was. He was just under six feet tall, and slim, and he wore his clothes well, and his clothes were well cut. He had fair hair, still thick, and blue eyes and the faintly yellow skin common to men of that complexion after they have lost the pink-and-white freshness of early youth. There was no colour in his cheeks. It was a fine head, well set on rather a long neck, with a somewhat prominent Adam's apple; but you were more impressed with the distinction than with the beauty of his face. It was because his features were so regular, his nose so straight, his brow so broad that he photographed so well. Indeed, from his photographs you would have thought him extremely handsome. He was not that, perhaps because his eyebrows and his eyelashes were pale, and his lips thin, but he looked very intellectual. There was refinement in his face and a spirituality that was oddly moving. That was how you thought a poet should look; and when Anne became engaged to him she told her girl friends who asked her about him that he looked like Shelley. He turned to her now with a little smile in his blue eyes. His smile was very attractive.

"What a perfect day to land in England!"

It was October. They had steamed up the Channel on a grey sea under a grey sky. There was not a breath of wind. The fishing boats seemed to rest on the placid water as though the elements had for ever forgotten their old hostility. The coast was incredibly green, but with a bright cosy greenness quite unlike the luxuriant, vehement verdure of Eastern jungles. The red towns they passed here and there were comfortable and homelike. They seemed to welcome the exiles with a smiling friendliness. And when they

drew into the estuary of the Thames they saw the rich levels of
Essex and in a little while Chalk Church on the Kentish shore,
lonely in the midst of weather-beaten trees, and beyond it the
woods of Cobham. The sun, red in a faint mist, set on the marshes,
and night fell. In the station the arc-lamps shed a light that spotted
the darkness with cold hard patches. It was good to see the porters
lumbering about in their grubby uniforms and the stationmaster
fat and important in his bowler hat. The stationmaster blew a
whistle and waved his arm. Alban stepped into the carriage and
seated himself in the corner opposite to Anne. The train started.

"We're due in London at six-ten," said Alban. "We ought to
get to Jermyn Street by seven. That'll give us an hour to bath and
change and we can get to the Savoy for dinner by eight-thirty.
A bottle of pop to-night, my pet, and a slap-up dinner." He gave a
chuckle. "I heard the Strouds and the Maundys arranging to meet
at the Trocadero Grill-Room."

He took up the papers and asked if she wanted any of them.
Anne shook her head.

"Tired?" he smiled.

"No."

"Excited?"

In order not to answer she gave a little laugh. He began to look
at the papers, starting with the publishers' advertisements, and
she was conscious of the intense satisfaction it was to him to feel
himself through them once more in the middle of things. They
had taken in those same papers in Sondurah, but they arrived six
weeks old, and though they kept them abreast of what was going
on in the world that interested them both, they emphasised their
exile. But these were fresh from the press. They smelt different.
They had a crispness that was almost voluptuous. He wanted to
read them all at once. Anne looked out of the window. The
country was dark, and she could see little but the lights of their
carriage reflected on the glass, but very soon the town encroached
upon it, and then she saw little sordid houses, mile upon mile of
them, with a light in a window here and there, and the chimneys
made a dreary pattern against the sky. They passed through
Barking and East Ham and Bromley—it was silly that the name
on the platform as they went through the station should give her
such a tremor—and then Stepney. Alban put down his papers.

"We shall be there in five minutes now."

He put on his hat and took down from the racks the things the
porter had put in them. He looked at her with shining eyes and
his lips twitched. She saw that he was only just able to control

K

his emotion. He looked out of the window, too, and they passed over brightly lighted thoroughfares, close packed with tram-cars, buses and motor-vans, and they saw the streets thick with people. What a mob! The shops were all lit up. They saw the hawkers with their barrows at the kerb.

"London," he said.

He took her hand and gently pressed it. His smile was so sweet that she had to say something. She tried to be facetious.

"Does it make you feel all funny inside?"

"I don't know if I want to cry or if I want to be sick."

Fenchurch Street. He lowered the window and waved his arm for a porter. With a grinding of brakes the train came to a standstill. A porter opened the door and Alban handed him out one package after another. Then in his polite way, having jumped out, he gave his hand to Anne to help her down to the platform. The porter went to fetch a barrow and they stood by the pile of their luggage. Alban waved to two passengers from the ship who passed them. The man nodded stiffly.

"What a comfort it is that we shall never have to be civil to those awful people any more," said Alban lightly.

Anne gave him a quick glance. He was really incomprehensible. The porter came back with his barrow, the luggage was put on and they followed him to collect their trunks. Alban took his wife's arm and pressed it.

"The smell of London. By God, it's grand."

He rejoiced in the noise and the bustle, and the crowd of people who jostled them; the radiance of the arc-lamps and the black shadows they cast, sharp but full-toned, gave him a sense of elation. They got out into the street and the porter went off to get them a taxi. Alban's eyes glittered as he looked at the buses and the policemen trying to direct the confusion. His distinguished face bore a look of something like inspiration. The taxi came. Their luggage was stowed away and piled up beside the driver, Alban gave the porter half-a-crown, and they drove off. They turned down Gracechurch Street and in Cannon Street were held up by a block in the traffic. Alban laughed out loud.

"What's the matter?" said Anne.

"I'm so excited."

They went along the Embankment. It was relatively quiet there. Taxis and cars passed them. The bells of the trams were music in his ears. At Westminster Bridge they cut across Parliament Square and drove through the green silence of St. James's Park. They had engaged a room at a hotel just off Jermyn Street. The reception clerk took them upstairs and a porter brought up their luggage. It was a room with twin beds and a bathroom.

"This looks all right," said Alban. "It'll do us till we can find a flat or something."

He looked at his watch.

"Look here, darling, we shall only fall over one another if we try to unpack together. We've got oodles of time and it'll take you longer to get straight and dress than me. I'll clear out. I want to go to the club and see if there's any mail for me. I've got my dinner jacket in my suit-case and it'll only take me twenty minutes to have a bath and dress. Does that suit you?"

"Yes. That's all right."

"I'll be back in an hour."

"Very well."

He took out of his pocket the little comb he always carried and passed it through his long fair hair. Then he put on his hat. He gave himself a glance in the mirror.

"Shall I turn on the bath for you?"

"No, don't bother."

"All right. So long."

He went out.

When he was gone Anne took her dressing-case and her hat-box and put them on the top of her trunk. Then she rang the bell. She did not take off her hat. She sat down and lit a cigarette. When a servant answered the bell she asked for the porter. He came. She pointed to the luggage.

"Will you take those things and leave them in the hall for the present. I'll tell you what to do with them presently."

"Very good, ma'am."

She gave him a florin. He took the trunk out and the other packages and closed the door behind him. A few tears slid down Anne's cheeks, but she shook herself; she dried her eyes and powdered her face. She needed all her calm. She was glad that Alban had conceived the idea of going to his club. It made things easier and gave her a little time to think them out.

Now that the moment had come to do what she had for weeks determined, now that she must say the terrible things she had to say, she quailed. Her heart sank. She knew exactly what she meant to say to Alban, she had made up her mind about that long ago, and had said the very words to herself a hundred times, three or four times a day every day of the long journey from Singapore, but she was afraid that she would grow confused. She dreaded an argument. The thought of a scene made her feel slightly sick.

It was something at all events to have an hour in which to collect herself. He would say she was heartless and cruel and unreasonable. She could not help it.

"No, no, no," she cried aloud.

She shuddered with horror. And all at once she saw herself again in the bungalow, sitting as she had been sitting when the whole thing started. It was getting on towards tiffin time and in a few minutes Alban would be back from the office. It gave her pleasure to reflect that it was an attractive room for him to come back to, the large verandah which was their parlour, and she knew that though they had been there eighteen months he was still alive to the success she had made of it. The jalousies were drawn now against the midday sun and the mellowed light filtering through them gave an impression of cool silence. Anne was house-proud, and though they were moved from district to district according to the exigencies of the Service and seldom stayed anywhere very long, at each new post she started with new enthusiasm to make their house cosy and charming. She was very modern. Visitors were surprised because there were no knick-knacks. They were taken aback by the bold colour of her curtains and could not at all make out the tinted reproductions of pictures by Marie Laurencin and Gauguin in silvered frames which were placed on the walls with such cunning skill. She was conscious that few of them quite approved and the good ladies of Port Wallace and Pemberton thought such arrangements odd, affected and out of place; but this left her calm. They would learn. It did them good to get a bit of a jolt. And now she looked round the long, spacious verandah with the complacent sigh of the artist satisfied with his work. It was gay. It was bare. It was restful. It refreshed the spirit and gently excited the fancy. Three immense bowls of yellow cannas completed the colour scheme. Her eyes lingered for a moment on the book-shelves filled with books; that was another thing that disconcerted the colony, all the books they had, and strange books too, heavy they thought them for the most part; and she gave them a little affectionate look as though they were living things. Then she gave the piano a glance. A piece of music was still open on the rack, it was something of Debussy, and Alban had been playing it before he went to the office.

Her friends in the colony had condoled with her when Alban was appointed D.O. at Daktar, for it was the most isolated district in Sondurah. It was connected with the town which was the head-quarters of the Government neither by telegraph nor telephone. But she liked it. They had been there for some time and she hoped they would remain till Alban went home on leave in another twelve months. It was as large as an English county, with a long coast-line, and the sea was dotted with little islands. A broad, winding river ran through it and on each side of this stretched hills densely covered with virgin forest. The station, a good way up the river, consisted of a row of Chinese shops and a native village nestling amid coconut trees, the District Office, the D.O.'s bungalow, the clerk's quarters and the barracks. Their only neighbours were the manager of a rubber estate a few miles up the river and the manager and his assistant, Dutchmen both, of a timber camp on one of the river's tributaries. The rubber estate's launch went up and down twice a month and was their only means of regular communication with the outside world. But though they were lonely they were not dull. Their days were full. Their ponies waited for them at dawn and they rode while the day was still fresh and in the bridle-paths through the jungle lingered the mystery of the tropical night. They came back, bathed, changed and had breakfast, and Alban went to the office. Anne spent the morning writing letters and working. She had fallen in love with the country from the first day she arrived in it and had taken pains to master the common language spoken. Her imagination was inflamed by the stories she heard of love and jealousy and death. She was told romantic tales of a time that was only just past. She sought to steep herself in the lore of those strange people. Both she and Alban read a great deal. They had for the country a considerable library and new books came from London by nearly every mail. Little that was noteworthy escaped them. Alban was fond of playing the piano. For an amateur he played very well. He had studied rather seriously, and he had an agreeable touch and a good ear; he could read music with ease, and it was always a pleasure to Anne to sit by him and follow the score when he tried something new. But their great delight was to tour the district. Sometimes they would be away for a fortnight at a time. They would go down the river in a prahu and then sail from one little island to another, bathe in the sea, and fish, or else row upstream till it grew shallow and the trees on either bank were so close to one another that you only saw a slim strip of sky between. Here the boatmen had to pole and they would spend the night in a native house. They bathed in a river pool so clear that you could see the sand shining silver at the bottom; and the spot was so lovely, so peaceful and remote, that you felt you could stay there for ever. Sometimes, on the other hand, they would tramp for days along the jungle paths, sleeping under canvas, and notwithstanding the mosquitoes that tormented them and the leeches that sucked their blood, enjoy every moment. Whoever slept so well as on a camp bed? And then there was the gladness of getting back, the delight in the comfort of the well-ordered establishment, the mail that had arrived with letters from home and all the papers, and the piano.

Alban would sit down to it then, his fingers itching to feel the keys, and in what he played, Stravinsky, Ravel, Darius Milhaud, she seemed to feel that he put in something of his own, the sounds of the jungle at night, dawn over the estuary, the starry nights and the crystal clearness of the forest pools.

Sometimes the rain fell in sheets for days at a time. Then Alban worked at Chinese. He was learning it so that he could communicate with the Chinese of the country in their own language, and Anne did the thousand-and-one things for which she had not had time before. Those days brought them even more closely together; they always had plenty to talk about, and when they were occupied with their separate affairs they were pleased to feel in their bones that they were near to one another. They were wonderfully united. The rainy days that shut them up within the walls of the bungalow made them feel as if they were one body in face of the world.

On occasion they went to Port Wallace. It was a change, but Anne was always glad to get home. She was never quite at her ease there. She was conscious that none of the people they met liked Alban. They were very ordinary people, middle-class and suburban and dull, without any of the intellectual interests that made life so full and varied to Alban and her, and many of them were narrow-minded and ill-natured; but since they had to pass the better part of their lives in contact with them, it was tiresome that they should feel so unkindly towards Alban. They said he was conceited. He was always very pleasant with them, but she was aware that they resented his cordiality. When he tried to be jovial they said he was putting on airs, and when he chaffed them they thought he was being funny at their expense.

Once they stayed at Government House, and Mrs. Hannay, the Governor's wife, who liked her, talked to her about it. Perhaps the Governor had suggested that she should give Anne a hint.

"You know, my dear, it's a pity your husband doesn't try to be more come-hither with people. He's very intelligent; don't you think it would be better if he didn't let others see he knows it quite so clearly? My husband said to me only yesterday: Of course I know Alban Torel is the cleverest young man in the Service, but he does manage to put my back up more than anyone

I know. I am the Governor, but when he talks to me he always gives me the impression that he looks upon me as a damned fool."

The worst of it was that Anne knew how low an opinion Alban had of the Governor's parts.

"He doesn't mean to be superior," Anne answered, smiling. "And he really isn't in the least conceited. I think it's only because he has a straight nose and high cheek-bones."

"You know, they don't like him at the club. They call him Powder-Puff Percy."

Anne flushed. She had heard that before and it made her very angry. Her eyes filled with tears.

"I think it's frightfully unfair."

Mrs. Hannay took her hand and gave it an affectionate little squeeze.

"My dear, you know I don't want to hurt your feelings. Your husband can't help rising very high in the Service. He'd make things so much easier for himself if he were a little more human. Why doesn't he play football?"

"It's not his game. He's always only too glad to play tennis."

"He doesn't give that impression. He gives the impression that there's no one here who's worth his while to play with."

"Well, there isn't," said Anne, stung.

Alban happened to be an extremely good tennis-player. He had played a lot of tournaments in England and Anne knew that it gave him a grim satisfaction to knock those beefy, hearty men all over the court. He could make the best of them look foolish. He could be maddening on the tennis court and Anne was aware that sometimes he could not resist the temptation.

"He does play to the gallery, doesn't he?" said Mrs. Hannay.

"I don't think so. Believe me, Alban has no idea he isn't popular. As far as I can see he's always pleasant and friendly with everybody."

"It's then he's most offensive," said Mrs. Hannay dryly.

"I know people don't like us very much," said Anne, smiling a little. "I'm very sorry, but really I don't know what we can do about it."

"Not you, my dear," cried Mrs. Hannay. "Everybody adores you. That's why they put up with your husband. My dear, who could help liking you?"

"I don't know why they should adore me," said Anne.

But she did not say it quite sincerely. She was deliberately playing the part of the dear little woman and within her she bubbled with amusement. They disliked Alban because he had such an air of distinction, and because he was interested in art and literature; they did not understand these things and so thought them unmanly; and they disliked him because his capacity was greater than theirs. They disliked him because he was better bred than they. They thought him superior; well, he was superior, but not in the sense they meant. They forgave her because she was an ugly little thing. That was what she called herself, but she wasn't that, or if she was it was with an ugliness that was most attractive. She was like a little monkey, but a very sweet little monkey and very human. She had a neat figure. That was her best point. That and her eyes. They were very large, of a deep brown, liquid and shining; they were full of fun, but they could be tender on occasion with a charming sympathy. She was dark, her frizzy hair was almost black, and her skin was swarthy; she had a small fleshy nose, with large nostrils, and much too big a mouth. But she was alert and vivacious. She could talk with a show of real interest to the ladies of the colony about their husbands and their servants and their children in England, and she could listen appreciatively to the men who told her stories that she had often heard before. They thought her a jolly good sort. They did not know what clever fun she made of them in private. It never occurred to them that she thought them narrow, gross and pretentious. They found no glamour in the East because they looked at it vulgarly with material eyes. Romance lingered at their threshold and they drove it away like an importunate beggar. She was aloof. She repeated to herself Landor's line:

"Nature I loved, and next to nature, art."

She reflected on her conversation with Mrs. Hannay, but on the whole it left her unconcerned. She wondered whether she should say anything about it to Alban; it had always seemed a little odd to her that he should be so little aware of his unpopularity; but she was afraid that if she told him of it he would become self-conscious. He never noticed the coldness of the men at the club. He made them feel shy and therefore uncomfortable. His appearance there caused a sort of awkwardness, but he, happily insensible, was breezily cordial to all and sundry. The fact was that he was strangely unconscious of other people. She was in a class by herself, she and a little group of friends they had in London, but he could never quite realise that the people of the colony, the government officials and the planters and their wives, were human beings. They were to him like pawns in a game. He laughed with them, chaffed them, and was amiably tolerant of them; with a chuckle Anne told herself that he was rather like the master of a preparatory school taking little boys out on a picnic and anxious to give them a good time.

She was afraid it wasn't much good telling Alban. He was incapable of the dissimulation which, she happily realised, came so easily to her. What was one to do with these people? The men had come out to the colony as lads from second-rate schools, and life had taught them nothing. At fifty they had the outlook of hobbledehoys. Most of them drank a great deal too much. They read nothing worth reading. Their ambition was to be like everybody else. Their highest praise was to say that a man was a damned good sort. If you were interested in the things of the spirit you were a prig. They were eaten up with envy of one another and devoured by petty jealousies. And the women, poor things, were obsessed by petty rivalries. They made a circle that was more provincial than any in the smallest town in England. They were prudish and spiteful. What did it matter if they did not like Alban? They would have to put up with him because his ability was so great. He was clever and energetic. They could not say that he did not do his work well. He had been successful in every post he had occupied. With his sensitiveness and his imagination he understood the native mind and he was able to get the natives to do things that no one in his position could. He had a gift for languages, and he spoke all the local dialects. He not only knew the common tongue that most of the government officials spoke, but was acquainted with the niceties of the language and on occasion could make use of a ceremonial speech that flattered and impressed the chiefs. He had a gift for organisation. He was not afraid of responsibility. In due course he was bound to be made a Resident. Alban had some interest in England; his father was a brigadier-general killed in the war, and though he had no private means he had influential friends. He spoke of them with pleasant irony.

"The great advantage of democratic government," he said, "is that merit, with influence to back it, can be pretty sure of receiving its due reward."

Alban was so obviously the ablest man in the Service that there seemed no reason why he should not eventually be made Governor. Then, thought Anne, his air of superiority, of which they complained, would be in place. They would accept him as their master and he would know how to make himself respected and obeyed. The position she foresaw did not dazzle her. She accepted it as a right. It would be fun for Alban to be Governor and for her to be the Governor's wife. And what an opportunity! They were sheep, the government servants and the planters; when Government House was the seat of culture they would soon fall into line. When the best way to the Governor's favour was to be intelligent, intelligence would become the fashion. She and Alban would cherish the native arts and collect carefully the memorials of a vanished past. The country would make an advance it had never dreamed of. They would develop it, but along lines of order and beauty. They would instil into their subordinates a passion for that beautiful land and a loving interest in these romantic races. They would make them realise what music meant. They would cultivate literature. They would create beauty. It would be the golden age.

Suddenly she heard Alban's footstep. Anne awoke from her day-dream. All that was far away in the future. Alban was only a District Officer yet and what was important was the life they were living now. She heard Alban go into the bath-house and splash water over himself. In a minute he came in. He had changed into a shirt and shorts. His fair hair was still wet.

"Tiffin ready?" he asked.

"Yes."

He sat down at the piano and played the piece that he had played in the morning. The silvery notes cascaded coolly down the sultry air. You had an impression of a formal garden with great trees and elegant pieces of artificial water and of leisurely walks bordered with pseudo-classical statues. Alban played with a peculiar delicacy. Lunch was announced by the head boy. He rose from the piano. They walked into the dining-room hand in hand. A punkah lazily fanned the air. Anne gave the table a glance. With its bright-coloured tablecloth and the amusing plates it looked very gay.

"Anything exciting at the office this morning?" she asked.

"No, nothing much. A buffalo case. Oh, and Prynne has sent along to ask me to go up to the estate. Some coolies have been damaging the trees and he wants me to come along and look into it."

Prynne was manager of the rubber estate up the river and now and then they spent a night with him. Sometimes when he wanted a change he came down to dinner and slept at the D.O.'s bungalow. They both liked him. He was a man of five-and-thirty, with a red face, with deep furrows in it, and very black hair. He was quite uneducated, but cheerful and easy, and being the only Englishman within two days' journey they could not but be friendly with him. He had been a little shy of them at first. News spreads quickly in the East and long before they arrived in the district he heard that they were highbrows. He did not know what he would make of them. He probably did not know that he had charm, which makes up for many more commendable qualities, and Alban with his almost feminine sensibilities was peculiarly susceptible to this. He found Alban much more human than he expected, and of course Anne was stunning. Alban played ragtime for him, which he would not have done for the Governor, and played dominoes with him. When Alban was making his first tour of the district with Anne, and suggested that they would like to spend a couple of nights on the estate, he had thought it as well to warn him that he lived with a native woman and had two children by her. He would do his best to keep them out of Anne's sight, but he could not send them away, there was nowhere to send them. Alban laughed.

"Anne isn't that sort of woman at all. Don't dream of hiding them. She loves children."

Anne quickly made friends with the shy, pretty little native woman and soon was playing happily with the children. She and the girl had long confidential chats. The children took a fancy to her. She brought them lovely toys from Port Wallace. Prynne, comparing her smiling tolerance with the disapproving acidity of the other white women of the colony, described himself as knocked all of a heap. He could not do enough to show his delight and gratitude.

"If all highbrows are like you," he said, "give me highbrows every time."

He hated to think that in another year they would leave the district for good and the chances were that, if the next D.O. was married, his wife would think it dreadful that, rather than live alone, he had a native woman to live with him and, what was more, was much attached to her.

But there had been a good deal of discontent on the estate of late. The coolies were Chinese and infected with communist ideas. They were disorderly. Alban had been obliged to sentence several of them for various crimes to terms of imprisonment.

"Prynne tells me that as soon as their term is up he's going to send them all back to China and get Javanese instead," said Alban. "I'm sure he's right. They're much more amenable."

"You don't think there's going to be any serious trouble?"

"Oh, no. Prynne knows his job and he's a pretty determined fellow. He wouldn't put up with any nonsense and with me and our policemen to back him up I don't imagine they'll try any monkey tricks." He smiled. "The iron hand in the velvet glove."

The words were barely out of his mouth when a sudden shouting arose. There was a commotion and the sound of steps. Loud voices and cries.

"Tuan, Tuan."

"What the devil's the matter?"

Alban sprang from his chair and went swiftly on to the verandah. Anne followed him. At the bottom of the steps was a group of natives. There was the sergeant, and three or four policemen, boatmen and several men from the kampong.

"What is it?" called Alban.

Two or three shouted back in answer. The sergeant pushed others aside and Alban saw lying on the ground a man in a shirt and khaki shorts. He ran down the steps. He recognised the man as the assistant manager of Prynne's estate. He was a half-caste. His shorts were covered with blood and there was clotted blood all over one side of his face and head. He was unconscious.

"Bring him up here," called Anne.

Alban gave an order. The man was lifted up and carried on to the verandah. They laid him on the floor and Anne put a pillow under his head. She sent for water and for the medicine-chest in which they kept things for emergency.

"Is he dead?" asked Alban.

"No."

"Better try to give him some brandy."

The boatmen brought ghastly news. The Chinese coolies had risen suddenly and attacked the manager's office. Prynne was killed and the assistant manager, Oakley by name, had escaped only by the skin of his teeth. He had come upon the rioters when they were looting the office, he had seen Prynne's body thrown out of the window, and had taken to his heels. Some of the Chinese saw him and gave chase. He ran for the river and was wounded as he jumped into the launch. The launch managed to put off before the Chinese could get on board and they had come down-stream for help as fast as they could go. As they went they saw flames rising from the office buildings. There was no doubt that the coolies had burned down everything that would burn.

Oakley gave a groan and opened his eyes. He was a little, dark-skinned man, with flattened features and thick coarse hair. His great native eyes were filled with terror.

"You're all right," said Anne. "You're quite safe."

He gave a sigh and smiled. Anne washed his face and swabbed it with antiseptics. The wound on his head was not serious.

"Can you speak yet?" said Alban.

"Wait a bit," she said. "We must look at his leg."

Alban ordered the sergeant to get the crowd out of the verandah. Anne ripped up one leg of the shorts. The material was clinging to the coagulated wound.

"I've been bleeding like a pig," said Oakley.

It was only a flesh wound. Alban was clever with his fingers, and though the blood began to flow again they stanched it. Alban put on a dressing and a bandage. The sergeant and a policeman lifted Oakley on to a long chair. Alban gave him a brandy and soda, and soon he felt strong enough to speak. He knew no more than the boatmen had already told. Prynne was dead and the estate was in flames.

"And the girl and the children?" asked Anne.

"I don't know."

"Oh, Alban."

"I must turn out the police. Are you sure Prynne is dead?"

"Yes, sir. I saw him."

"Have the rioters got fire-arms?"

"I don't know, sir."

"How d'you mean, you don't know?" Alban cried irritably. "Prynne had a gun, hadn't he?"

"Yes, sir."

"There must have been more on the estate. You had one, didn't you? The head overseer had one."

The half-caste was silent. Alban looked at him sternly.

"How many of those damned Chinese are there?"

"A hundred and fifty."

Anne wondered that he asked so many questions. It seemed waste of time. The important thing was to collect coolies for the transport up-river, prepare the boats and issue ammunition to the police.

"How many policemen have you got, sir?" asked Oakley.

"Eight and the sergeant."

"Could I come too? That would make ten of us. I'm sure I shall be all right now I'm bandaged."

"I'm not going," said Alban.

"Alban, you must," cried Anne. She could not believe her ears.

"Nonsense. It would be madness. Oakley's obviously useless. He's sure to have a temperature in a few hours. He'd only be in the way. That leaves nine guns. There are a hundred and fifty

Chinese and they've got fire-arms and all the ammunition in the world."

"How d'you know?"

"It stands to reason they wouldn't have started a show like this unless they had. It would be idiotic to go."

Anne stared at him with open mouth. Oakley's eyes were puzzled.

"What are you going to do?"

"Well, fortunately we've got the launch. I'll send it to Port Wallace with a request for reinforcements."

"But they won't be here for two days at least."

"Well, what of it? Prynne's dead and the estate burned to the ground. We couldn't do any good by going up now. I shall send a native to reconnoitre so that we can find out exactly what the rioters are doing." He gave Anne his charming smile. "Believe me, my pet, the rascals won't lose anything by waiting a day or two for what's coming to them."

Oakley opened his mouth to speak, but perhaps he hadn't the nerve. He was a half-caste assistant manager and Alban, the D.O., represented the power of the Government. But the man's eyes sought Anne's and she thought she read in them an earnest and personal appeal.

"But in two days they're capable of committing the most frightful atrocities," she cried. "It's quite unspeakable what they may do."

"Whatever damage they do they'll pay for. I promise you that."

"Oh, Alban, you can't sit still and do nothing. I beseech you to go yourself at once."

"Don't be so silly. I can't quell a riot with eight policemen and a sergeant. I haven't got the right to take a risk of that sort. We'd have to go in boats. You don't think we could get up unobserved. The lalang along the banks is perfect cover and they could just take pot shots at us as we came along. We shouldn't have a chance."

"I'm afraid they'll only think it weakness if nothing is done for two days, sir," said Oakley.

"When I want your opinion I'll ask for it," said Alban acidly. "So far as I can see when there was danger the only thing you did was to cut and run. I can't persuade myself that your assistance in a crisis would be very valuable."

The half-caste reddened. He said nothing more. He looked straight in front of him with troubled eyes.

"I'm going down to the office," said Alban. "I'll just write a short report and send it down the river by launch at once."

He gave an order to the sergeant, who had been standing all this time stiffly at the top of the steps. He saluted and ran off.

Alban went into a little hall they had to get his topee. Anne swiftly followed him.

"Alban, for God's sake listen to me a minute," she whispered.

"I don't want to be rude to you, darling, but I am pressed for time. I think you'd much better mind your own business."

"You can't do nothing, Alban. You must go. Whatever the risk."

"Don't be such a fool," he said angrily.

He had never been angry with her before. She seized his hand to hold him back.

"I tell you I can do no good by going."

"You don't know. There's the woman and Prynne's children. We must do something to save them. Let me come with you. They'll kill them."

"They've probably killed them already."

"Oh, how can you be so callous! If there's a chance of saving them it's your duty to try."

"It's my duty to act like a reasonable human being. I'm not going to risk my life and my policemen's for the sake of a native woman and her half-caste brats. What sort of a damned fool do you take me for?"

"They'll say you were afraid."

"Who?"

"Everyone in the colony."

He smiled disdainfully.

"If you only knew what a complete contempt I have for the opinion of everyone in the colony."

She gave him a long searching look. She had been married to him for eight years and she knew every expression of his face and every thought in his mind. She stared into his blue eyes as if they were open windows. She suddenly went quite pale. She dropped his hand and turned away. Without another word she went back on to the verandah. Her ugly little monkey face was a mask of horror.

Alban went to his office, wrote a brief account of the facts, and in a few minutes the motor launch was pounding down the river.

The next two days were endless. Escaped natives brought them news of happenings on the estate. But from their excited and terrified stories it was impossible to get an exact impression of the truth. There had been a good deal of bloodshed. The head over-seer had been killed. They brought wild tales of cruelty and outrage. Anne could hear nothing of Prynne's woman and the two children. She shuddered when she thought of what might have been their fate. Alban collected as many natives as he could. They were armed with spears and swords. He commandeered boats. The situation was serious, but he kept his head. He felt that he had done all that was possible and nothing remained but for him to carry on normally. He did his official work. He played the piano a great deal. He rode with Anne in the early morning. He appeared to have forgotten that they had had the first serious difference of opinion in the whole of their married life. He took it that Anne had accepted the wisdom of his decision. He was as amusing, cordial and gay with her as he had always been. When he spoke of the rioters it was with grim irony: when the time came to settle matters a good many of them would wish they had never been born.

"What'll happen to them?" asked Anne.

"Oh, they'll hang." He gave a shrug of distaste. "I hate having to be present at executions. It always makes me feel rather sick."

He was very sympathetic to Oakley, whom they had put to bed and whom Anne was nursing. Perhaps he was sorry that in the exasperation of the moment he had spoken to him offensively, and he went out of his way to be nice to him.

Then on the afternoon of the third day, when they were drinking their coffee after luncheon, Alban's quick ears caught the sound of a motor boat approaching. At the same moment a policeman ran up to say that the government launch was sighted.

"At last," cried Alban.

He bolted out of the house. Anne raised one of the jalousies and looked out at the river. Now the sound was quite loud and in a moment she saw the boat come round the bend. She saw Alban on the landing-stage. He got into a prahu and as the launch dropped her anchor he went on board. She told Oakley that the reinforcements had come.

"Will the D.O. go up with them when they attack?" he asked her.

"Naturally," said Anne coldly.

"I wondered."

Anne felt a strange feeling in her heart. For the last two days she had had to exercise all her self-control not to cry. She did not answer. She went out of the room.

A quarter of an hour later Alban returned to the bungalow with the captain of constabulary who had been sent with twenty Sikhs to deal with the rioters. Captain Stratton was a little red-faced man with a red moustache and bow legs, very hearty and dashing, whom she had met often at Port Wallace.

"Well, Mrs. Torel, this is a pretty kettle of fish," he cried, as he shook hands with her, in a loud jolly voice. "Here I am, with my army all full of pep and ready for a scrap. Up, boys, and at 'em. Have you got anything to drink in this benighted place?"

"Boy," she cried, smiling.

"Something long and cool and faintly alcoholic, and then I'm ready to discuss the plan of campaign."

His breeziness was very comforting. It blew away the sullen apprehension that had seemed ever since the disaster to brood over the lost peace of the bungalow. The boy came in with a tray and Stratton mixed himself a stengah. Alban put him in possession of the facts. He told them clearly, briefly and with precision.

"I must say I admire you," said Stratton. "In your place I should never have been able to resist the temptation to take my eight cops and have a whack at the blighters myself."

"I thought it was a perfectly unjustifiable risk to take."

"Safety first, old boy, eh, what?" said Stratton jovially. "I'm jolly glad you didn't. It's not often we get the chance of a scrap. It would have been a dirty trick to keep the whole show to yourself."

Captain Stratton was all for steaming straight up the river and attacking at once, but Alban pointed out to him the inadvisability of such a course. The sound of the approaching launch would warn the rioters. The long grass at the river's edge offered them cover and they had enough guns to make a landing difficult. It seemed useless to expose the attacking force to their fire. It was silly to forget that they had to face a hundred and fifty desperate men and it would be easy to fall into an ambush. Alban expounded his own plan. Stratton listened to it. He nodded now and then. The plan was evidently a good one. It would enable them to take the rioters on the rear, surprise them, and in all probability finish the job without a single casualty. He would have been a fool not to accept it.

"But why didn't you do that yourself?" asked Stratton.

"With eight men and a sergeant?"

Stratton did not answer.

"Anyhow it's not a bad idea and we'll settle on it. It gives us plenty of time, so with your permission, Mrs. Torel, I'll have a bath."

They set out at sunset, Captain Stratton and his twenty Sikhs, Alban with his policemen and the natives he had collected. The night was dark and moonless. Trailing behind them were the dugouts that Alban had gathered together and into which after a certain distance they proposed to transfer their force. It was important that no sound should give warning of their approach. After they had gone for about three hours by launch they took to the dug-outs and in them silently paddled up-stream. They reached the border of the vast estate and landed. Guides led them along a path so narrow that they had to march in single file. It had been long unused and the going was heavy. They had twice to ford a stream. The path led them circuitously to the rear of the coolie lines, but they did not wish to reach them till nearly dawn and presently Stratton gave the order to halt. It was a long cold wait. At last the night seemed to be less dark; you did not see the trunks of the trees, but were vaguely sensible of them against its darkness. Stratton had been sitting with his back to a tree. He gave a whispered order to a sergeant and in a few minutes the column was once more on the march. Suddenly they found themselves on a road. They formed fours. The dawn broke and in the ghostly light the surrounding objects were wanly visible. The column stopped on a whispered order. They had come in sight of the coolie lines. Silence reigned in them. The column crept on again and again halted. Stratton, his eyes shining, gave Alban a smile.

"We've caught the blighters asleep."

He lined up his men. They inserted cartridges in their guns. He stepped forward and raised his hand. The carbines were pointed at the coolie lines.

"Fire."

There was a rattle as the volley of shots rang out. Then suddenly there was a tremendous din and the Chinese poured out, shouting and waving their arms, but in front of them, to Alban's utter bewilderment, bellowing at the top of his voice and shaking his fist at them, was a white man.

"Who the hell's that?" cried Stratton.

A very big, very fat man, in khaki trousers and a singlet, was running towards them as fast as his fat legs would carry him and as he ran shaking both fists at them and yelling:

"*Smerige flikkers! Verlockte ploerten!*"

"My God, it's Van Hasseldt," said Alban.

This was the Dutch manager of the timber camp which was situated on a considerable tributary of the river about twenty miles away.

"What the hell do you think you're doing?" he puffed as he came up to them.

"How the hell did you get here?" asked Stratton in turn.

He saw that the Chinese were scattering in all directions and gave his men instructions to round them up. Then he turned again to Van Hasseldt.

"What's it mean?"

"Mean? Mean?" shouted the Dutchman furiously. "That's what I want to know. You and your damned policemen. What do you mean by coming here at this hour in the morning and firing a damned volley? Target practice? You might have killed me. Idiots!"

"Have a cigarette," said Stratton.

"How did you get here, Van Hasseldt?" asked Alban again, very much at sea. "This is the force they've sent from Port Wallace to quell the riot."

"How did I get here? I walked. How did you think I got here? Riot be damned. I quelled the riot. If that's what you came for you can take your damned policemen home again. A bullet came within a foot of my head."

"I don't understand," said Alban.

"There's nothing to understand," spluttered Van Hasseldt, still fuming. "Some coolies came to my estate and said the Chinks had killed Prynne and burned the bally place down, so I took my assistant and my head overseer and a Dutch friend I had staying with me and came over to see what the trouble was."

Captain Stratton opened his eyes wide.

"Did you just stroll in as if it was a picnic?" he asked.

"Well, you don't think after all the years I've been in this country I'm going to let a couple of hundred Chinks put the fear of God into me? I found them all scared out of their lives. One of them had the nerve to pull a gun on me and I blew his bloody brains out. And the rest surrendered. I've got the leaders tied up. I was going to send a boat down to you this morning to come up and get them."

Stratton stared at him for a minute and then burst into a shout of laughter. He laughed till the tears ran down his face. The Dutchman looked at him angrily, then began to laugh too; he laughed with the big belly laugh of a very fat man and his coils of fat heaved and shook. Alban watched them sullenly. He was very angry.

"What about Prynne's girl and the kids?" he asked.

"Oh, they got away all right."

It just showed how wise he had been not to let himself be influenced by Anne's hysteria. Of course the children had come to no harm. He never thought they would.

Van Hasseldt and his little party started back for the timber

camp, and as soon after as possible Stratton embarked his twenty
Sikhs and leaving Alban with his sergeant and his policemen to
deal with the situation departed for Port Wallace. Alban gave
him a brief report for the Governor. There was much for him to
do. It looked as though he would have to stay for a considerable
time; but since every house on the estate had been burned to the
ground and he was obliged to instal himself in the coolie lines he
thought it better that Anne should not join him. He sent her a
note to that effect. He was glad to be able to reassure her of the
safety of poor Prynne's girl. He set to work at once to make his
preliminary enquiry. He examined a host of witnesses. But a
week later he received an order to go to Port Wallace at once.
The launch that brought it was to take him and he was able to see
Anne on the way down for no more than an hour. Alban was a
trifle vexed.

"I don't know why the Governor can't leave me to get things
straight without dragging me off like this. It's extremely inconvenient."

"Oh, well, the Government never bothers very much about the
convenience of its subordinates, does it?" smiled Anne.

"It's just red-tape. I would offer to take you along, darling,
only I shan't stay a minute longer than I need. I want to get my
evidence together for the Sessions Court as soon as possible. I think in
a country like this it's very important that justice should be prompt."

When the launch came in to Port Wallace one of the harbour
police told him that the harbour-master had a chit for him. It
was from the Governor's secretary and informed him that His
Excellency desired to see him as soon as convenient after his arrival.
It was ten in the morning. Alban went to the club, had a bath and
shaved, and then in clean ducks, his hair neatly brushed, he called
a rickshaw and told the boy to take him to the Governor's office.
He was at once shown in to the secretary's room. The secretary
shook hands with him.

"I'll tell H.E. you're here," he said. "Won't you sit down?"

The secretary left the room and in a little while came back.

"H.E. will see you in a minute. Do you mind if I get on with my
letters?"

Alban smiled. The secretary was not exactly come-hither. He
waited, smoking a cigarette, and amused himself with his own
thoughts. He was making a good job of the preliminary enquiry.
It interested him. Then an orderly came in and told Alban that
the Governor was ready for him. He rose from his seat and followed
him into the Governor's room.

"Good-morning, Torel."

"Good-morning, sir."

The Governor was sitting at a large desk. He nodded to Alban and motioned to him to take a seat. The Governor was all grey. His hair was grey, his face, his eyes; he looked as though the tropical suns had washed the colour out of him; he had been in the country for thirty years and had risen one by one through all the ranks of the Service; he looked tired and depressed. Even his voice was grey. Alban liked him because he was quiet; he did not think him clever, but he had an unrivalled knowledge of the country, and his great experience was a very good substitute for intelligence. He looked at Alban for a full moment without speaking and the odd idea came to Alban that he was embarrassed. He very nearly gave him a lead.

"I saw Van Hasseldt yesterday," said the Governor suddenly.

"Yes, sir?"

"Will you give me your account of the occurrences at the Alud Estate and of the steps you took to deal with them."

Alban had an orderly mind. He was self-possessed. He marshalled his facts well and was able to state them with precision. He chose his words with care and spoke them fluently.

"You had a sergeant and eight policemen. Why did you not immediately go to the scene of the disturbance?"

"I thought the risk was unjustifiable."

A thin smile was outlined on the Governor's grey face.

"If the officers of this Government had hesitated to take unjustifiable risks it would never have become a province of the British Empire."

Alban was silent. It was difficult to talk to a man who spoke obvious nonsense.

"I am anxious to hear your reasons for the decision you took."

Alban gave them coolly. He was quite convinced of the rightness of his action. He repeated, but more fully, what he had said in the first place to Anne. The Governor listened attentively.

"Van Hasseldt, with his manager, a Dutch friend of his, and a native overseer, seems to have coped with the situation very efficiently," said the Governor.

"He had a lucky break. That doesn't prevent him from being a damned fool. It was madness to do what he did."

"Do you realise that by leaving a Dutch planter to do what you should have done yourself, you have covered the Government with ridicule?"

"No, sir."

"You've made yourself a laughing-stock in the whole colony."

Alban smiled.

"My back is broad enough to bear the ridicule of persons to whose opinion I am entirely indifferent."

"The utility of a government official depends very largely on his prestige, and I'm afraid his prestige is likely to be inconsiderable when he lies under the stigma of cowardice."

Alban flushed a little.

"I don't quite know what you mean by that, sir."

"I've gone into the matter very carefully. I've seen Captain Stratton, and Oakley, poor Prynne's assistant, and I've seen Van Hasseldt. I've listened to your defence."

"I didn't know that I was defending myself, sir."

"Be so good as not to interrupt me. I think you committed a grave error of judgment. As it turns out, the risk was very small, but whatever it was, I think you should have taken it. In such matters promptness and firmness are essential. It is not for me to conjecture what motive led you to send for a force of constabulary and do nothing till they came. I am afraid, however, that I consider that your usefulness in the Service is no longer very great."

Alban looked at him with astonishment.

"But would you have gone under the circumstances?" he asked him.

"I should."

Alban shrugged his shoulders.

"Don't you believe me?" rapped out the Governor.

"Of course I believe you, sir. But perhaps you will allow me to say that if you had been killed the colony would have suffered an irreparable loss."

The Governor drummed on the table with his fingers. He looked out of the window and then looked again at Alban. When he spoke it was not unkindly.

"I think you are unfitted by temperament for this rather rough-and-tumble life, Torel. If you'll take my advice you'll go home. With your abilities I feel sure that you'll soon find an occupation much better suited to you."

"I'm afraid I don't understand what you mean, sir."

"Oh, come, Torel, you're not stupid. I'm trying to make things easy for you. For your wife's sake as well as for your own I do not wish you to leave the colony with the stigma of being dismissed from the Service for cowardice. I'm giving you the opportunity of resigning."

"Thank you very much, sir. I'm not prepared to avail myself

of the opportunity. If I resign I admit that I committed an error and that the charge you make against me is justified. I don't admit it."

"You can please yourself. I have considered the matter very carefully and I have no doubt about it in my mind. I am forced to discharge you from the Service. The necessary papers will reach you in due course. Meanwhile you will return to your post and hand over to the officer appointed to succeed you on his arrival."

"Very good, sir," replied Alban, a twinkle of amusement in his eyes. "When do you desire me to return to my post?"

"At once."

"Have you any objection to my going to the club and having tiffin before I go?"

The Governor looked at him with surprise. His exasperation was mingled with an unwilling admiration.

"Not at all. I'm sorry, Torel, that this unhappy incident should have deprived the Government of a servant whose zeal has always been so apparent and whose tact, intelligence and industry seemed to point him out in the future for very high office."

"Your Excellency does not read Schiller, I suppose. You are probably not acquainted with his celebrated line: *mit der Dummheit kämpfen die Götter selbst vergebens.*"

"What does it mean?"

"Roughly: Against stupidity the gods themselves battle in vain."

"Good-morning."

With his head in the air, a smile on his lips, Alban left the Governor's office. The Governor was human, and he had the curiosity to ask his secretary later in the day if Alban Torel had really gone to the club.

"Yes, sir. He had tiffin there."

"It must have wanted some nerve."

Alban entered the club jauntily and joined the group of men standing at the bar. He talked to them in the breezy, cordial tone he always used with them. It was designed to put them at their ease. They had been discussing him ever since Stratton had come back to Port Wallace with his story, sneering at him and laughing at him, and all who had resented his superciliousness, and they were the majority, were triumphant because his pride had had a fall. But they were so taken aback at seeing him now, so confused to find him as confident as ever, that it was they who were embarrassed.

One man, though he knew perfectly, asked him what he was doing in Port Wallace.

"Oh, I came about the riot on the Alud Estate. H.E. wanted

to see me. He does not see eye to eye with me about it. The silly old ass has fired me. I'm going home as soon as he appoints a D.O. to take over."

There was a moment of awkwardness. One, more kindly disposed than the others, said:

"I'm awfully sorry."

Alban shrugged his shoulders.

"My dear fellow, what can you do with a perfect damned fool? The only thing is to let him stew in his own juice."

When the Governor's secretary had told his chief as much of this as he thought discreet, the Governor smiled.

"Courage is a queer thing. I would rather have shot myself than go to the club just then and face all those fellows."

A fortnight later, having sold to the incoming D.O. all the decorations that Anne had taken so much trouble about, with the rest of their things in packing-cases and trunks, they arrived at Port Wallace to await the local steamer that was to take them to Singapore. The padre's wife invited them to stay with her, but Anne refused; she insisted that they should go to the hotel. An hour after their arrival she received a very kind little letter from the Governor's wife asking her to go and have tea with her. She went. She found Mrs. Hannay alone, but in a minute the Governor joined them. He expressed his regret that she was leaving and told her how sorry he was for the cause.

"It's very kind of you to say that," said Anne, smiling gaily, "but you mustn't think I take it to heart. I'm entirely on Alban's side. I think what he did was absolutely right and if you don't mind my saying so I think you've treated him most unjustly."

"Believe me, I hated having to take the step I took."

"Don't let's talk about it," said Anne.

"What are your plans when you get home?" asked Mrs. Hannay.

Anne began to chat brightly. You would have thought she had not a care in the world. She seemed in great spirits at going home. She was jolly and amusing and made little jokes. When she took leave of the Governor and his wife she thanked them for all their kindness. The Governor escorted her to the door.

The next day but one, after dinner, they went on board the clean and comfortable little ship. The padre and his wife saw them off. When they went into their cabin they found a large parcel on Anne's bunk. It was addressed to Alban. He opened it and saw that it was an immense powder-puff.

"Hullo, I wonder who sent us this," he said, with a laugh. "It must be for you, darling."

Anne gave him a quick look. She went pale. The brutes! How could they be so cruel? She forced herself to smile.

"It's enormous, isn't it? I've never seen such a large powder-puff in my life."

But when he had left the cabin and they were out at sea, she threw it passionately overboard.

And now, now that they were back in London and Sondurah was nine thousand miles away, she clenched her hands as she thought of it. Somehow, it seemed the worst thing of all. It was so wantonly unkind to send that absurd object to Alban, Powder-Puff Percy; it showed such a petty spite. Was that their idea of humour? Nothing had hurt her more and even now she felt that it was only by holding on to herself that she could prevent herself from crying. Suddenly she started, for the door opened and Alban came in. She was still sitting in the chair in which he had left her.

"Hullo, why haven't you dressed?" He looked about the room. "You haven't unpacked."

"No."

"Why on earth not?"

"I'm not going to unpack. I'm not going to stay here. I'm leaving you."

"What are you talking about?"

"I've stuck it out till now. I made up my mind I would till we got home. I set my teeth, I've borne more than I thought it possible to bear, but now it's finished. I've done all that could be expected of me. We're back in London now and I can go."

He looked at her in utter bewilderment.

"Are you mad, Anne?"

"Oh, my God, what I've endured! The journey to Singapore, with all the officers knowing, and even the Chinese stewards. And at Singapore, the way people looked at us at the hotel, and the sympathy I had to put up with, the bricks they dropped and their embarrassment when they realised what they'd done. My God, I could have killed them. That interminable journey home. There wasn't a single passenger on the ship who didn't know. The contempt they had for you and the kindness they went out of their way to show me. And you so self-complacent and so pleased with yourself, seeing nothing, feeling nothing. You must have the hide of a rhinoceros. The misery of seeing you so chatty and agreeable. Pariahs, that's what we were. You seemed to ask them to snub you. How can anyone be so shameless?"

She was flaming with passion. Now that at last she need not wear the mask of indifference and pride that she had forced herself to assume she cast aside all reserve and all self-control. The words poured from her trembling lips in a virulent stream.

"My dear, how can you be so absurd?" he said good-naturedly, smiling. "You must be very nervous and high-strung to have got such ideas in your head. Why didn't you tell me? You're like a country bumpkin who comes to London and thinks everyone is staring at him. Nobody bothered about us, and if they did what on earth did it matter? You ought to have more sense than to bother about what a lot of fools say. And what do you imagine they were saying?"

"They were saying you'd been fired."

"Well, that was true," he laughed.

"They said you were a coward."

"What of it?"

"Well, you see, that was true too."

He looked at her for a moment reflectively. His lips tightened a little.

"And what makes you think so?" he asked acidly.

"I saw it in your eyes, that day the news came, when you refused to go to the estate and I followed you into the hall when you went to fetch your topee. I begged you to go, I felt that whatever the danger you must take it, and suddenly I saw the fear in your eyes. I nearly fainted with the horror."

"I should have been a fool to risk my life to no purpose. Why should I? Nothing that concerned me was at stake. Courage is the obvious virtue of the stupid. I don't attach any particular importance to it."

"How do you mean that nothing that concerned you was at stake? If that's true then your whole life is a sham. You've given away everything you stood for, everything we both stand for. You've let all of us down. We did set ourselves up on a pinnacle, we did think ourselves better than the rest of them because we loved literature and art and music, we weren't content to live a life of ignoble jealousies and vulgar tittle-tattle, we did cherish the things of the spirit, and we loved beauty. It was our food and drink. They laughed at us and sneered at us. That was inevitable. The ignorant and the common naturally hate and fear those who are interested in things they don't understand. We didn't care. We called them Philistines. We despised them and we had a right to despise them. Our justification was that we were better and nobler and wiser and braver than they were. And you weren't better, and you weren't nobler, you weren't braver. When the crisis came you slunk away like a whipped cur with his tail between his legs. You of all people hadn't the right to be a coward. They despise *us* now and they have the right to despise us. Us and all we stood for. Now they can say that art and beauty are all rot; when it comes to a pinch people like us always let you down. They never stopped looking for a chance to turn and rend us and you gave it to them. They can say that they always expected it. It's a triumph for them. I used to be furious because they called you Powder-Puff Percy. Did you know they did?"

"Of course. I thought it very vulgar, but it left me entirely indifferent."

"It's funny that their instinct should have been so right."

"Do you mean to say you've been harbouring this against me all these weeks? I should never have thought you capable of it."

"I couldn't let you down when everyone was against you. I was too proud for that. Whatever happened I swore to myself that I'd stick to you till we got home. It's been torture."

"Don't you love me any more?"

"Love you? I loathe the very sight of you."

"Anne!"

"God knows I loved you. For eight years I worshipped the ground you trod on. You were everything to me. I believed in you as some people believe in God. When I saw the fear in your eyes that day, when you told me that you weren't going to risk your life for a kept woman and her half-caste brats, I was shattered. It was as though someone had wrenched my heart out of my body and trampled on it. You killed my love there and then, Alban. You killed it stone-dead. Since then when you've kissed me I've had to clench my hands so as not to turn my face away. The mere thought of anything else makes me feel physically sick. I loathe your complacence and your frightful insensitiveness. Perhaps I could have forgiven it if it had been just a moment's weakness and if afterwards you'd been ashamed. I should have been miserable, but I think my love was so great that I should only have felt pity for you. But you're incapable of shame. And now I believe in nothing. You're only a silly, pretentious vulgar poseur. I would rather be the wife of a second-rate planter so long as he had the common human virtues of a man than the wife of a fake like you."

He did not answer. Gradually his face began to discompose. Those handsome, regular features of his horribly distorted and suddenly he broke out into loud sobs. She gave a little cry.

"Don't, Alban, don't."

"Oh, darling, how can you be so cruel to me? I adore you. I'd give my whole life to please you. I can't live without you."

She put out her arms as though to ward off a blow.

"No, no, Alban, don't try to move me. I can't. I must go. I can't live with you any more. It would be frightful. I can never forget. I must tell you the truth, I have only contempt for you and repulsion."

He sank down at her feet and tried to cling to her knees. With a gasp she sprang up and he buried his head in the empty chair. He cried painfully with sobs that tore his chest. The sound was horrible. The tears streamed from Anne's eyes and, putting her hands to her ears to shut out that dreadful, hysterical sobbing, blindly stumbling she rushed to the door and ran out.

The Book-Bag

SOME people read for instruction, which is praiseworthy, and some for pleasure, which is innocent, but not a few read from habit, and I suppose that this is neither innocent nor praiseworthy. Of that lamentable company am I. Conversation after a time bores me, games tire me, and my own thoughts, which we are told are the unfailing resource of a sensible man, have a tendency to run dry. Then I fly to my book as the opium-smoker to his pipe. I would sooner read the catalogue of the Army and Navy Stores or Bradshaw's Guide than nothing at all, and indeed I have spent many delightful hours over both these works. At one time I never went out without a second-hand bookseller's list in my pocket. I know no reading more fruity. Of course to read in this way is as reprehensible as doping, and I never cease to wonder at the impertinence of great readers who, because they are such, look down on the illiterate. From the standpoint of what eternity is it better to have read a thousand books than to have ploughed a million furrows? Let us admit that reading with us is just a drug that we cannot do without—who of this band does not know the restlessness that attacks him when he has been severed from reading too long, the apprehension and irritability, and the sigh of relief which the sight of a printed page extracts from him?—and so let us be no more vainglorious than the poor slaves of the hypodermic needle or the pint-pot.

And like the dope-fiend who cannot move from place to place without taking with him a plentiful supply of his deadly balm I never venture far without a sufficiency of reading matter. Books are so necessary to me that when in a railway train I have become aware that fellow-travellers have come away without a single one I have been seized with a veritable dismay. But when I am starting on a long journey the problem is formidable. I have learnt my lesson. Once, imprisoned by illness for three months in a hill-town in Java, I came to the end of all the books I had brought with me, and knowing no Dutch was obliged to buy the school-books from which intelligent Javanese, I suppose, acquired knowledge of French and German. So I read again after five-and-twenty years the frigid plays of Goethe, the fables of La Fontaine and the tragedies of the tender and exact Racine. I have the greatest admiration for Racine, but I admit that to read his plays one after the other requires a certain effort in a person who is suffering from colitis. Since then I have made a point of travelling with the largest sack made for carrying soiled linen and filling it to the brim with books to suit every possible occasion and every mood. It weighs a ton and strong porters reel under its weight. Custom-house officials look at it askance, but recoil from it with consternation when I give them my word that it contains nothing but books. Its inconvenience is that the particular work I suddenly hanker to read is always at the bottom and it is impossible for me to get it without emptying the book-bag's entire contents upon the floor. Except for this, however, I should perhaps never have heard the singular history of Olive Hardy.

I was wandering about Malaya, staying here and there, a week or two if there was a rest-house or a hotel, and a day or so if I was obliged to inflict myself on a planter or a District Officer whose hospitality I had no wish to abuse; and at the moment I happened to be at Penang. It is a pleasant little town, with a hotel that has always seemed to me very agreeable, but the stranger finds little to do there and time hung a trifle heavily on my hands. One morning I received a letter from a man I knew only by name. This was Mark Featherstone. He was Acting Resident, in the absence on leave of the Resident, at a place called Tenggarah. There was a sultan there and it appeared that a water festival of some sort was to take place which Featherstone thought would interest me. He said that he would be glad if I would come and stay with him for a few days. I wired to tell him that I should be delighted and next day took the train to Tenggarah. Featherstone met me at the station. He was a man of about thirty-five, I should think, tall and handsome, with fine eyes and a strong, stern face. He had a wiry black moustache and bushy eyebrows. He looked more like a soldier than a government official. He was very smart in white ducks, with a white topee, and he wore his clothes with elegance. He was a little shy, which seemed odd in a strapping fellow of resolute mien, but I surmised that this was only because he was unused to the society of that strange fish, a writer, and I hoped in a little to put him at his ease.

"My boys 'll look after your barang," he said. "We'll go down to the club. Give them your keys and they'll unpack before we get back."

I told him that I had a good deal of luggage and thought it better to leave everything at the station but what I particularly wanted. He would not hear of it.

"It doesn't matter a bit. It'll be safer at my house. It's always better to have one's barang with one."

"All right."

I gave my keys and the ticket for my trunk and my book-bag to a Chinese boy who stood at my host's elbow. Outside the station a car was waiting for us and we stepped in.

"Do you play bridge?" asked Featherstone.

"I do."

"I thought most writers didn't."

"They don't," I said. "It's generally considered among authors a sign of deficient intelligence to play cards."

The club was a bungalow, pleasing but unpretentious; it had a large reading-room, a billiard-room with one table, and a small card-room. When we arrived it was empty but for one or two persons reading the English weeklies, and we walked through to the tennis courts, where a couple of sets were being played. A number of people were sitting on the verandah, looking on, smoking and sipping long drinks. I was introduced to one or two of them. But the light was failing and soon the players could hardly see the ball. Featherstone asked one of the men I had been introduced to if he would like a rubber. He said he would. Featherstone looked about for a fourth. He caught sight of a man sitting a little by himself, paused for a second, and went up to him. The two exchanged a few words and then came towards us. We strolled in to the card-room. We had a nice game. I did not pay much attention to the two men who made up the four. They stood me drinks and I, a temporary member of the club, returned the compliment. The drinks were very small, quarter whiskies, and in the two hours we played each of us was able to show his open-handedness without an excessive consumption of alcohol. When the advancing hour suggested that the next rubber must be the last we changed from whisky to gin pahits. The rubber came to an end. Featherstone called for the book and the winnings and losings of each one of us were set down. One of the men got up.

"Well, I must be going," he said.

"Going back to the estate?" asked Featherstone.

"Yes," he nodded. He turned to me. "Shall you be here to-morrow?"

"I hope so."

He went out of the room.

"I'll collect my mem and get along home to dinner," said the other.

"We might be going too," said Featherstone.

"I'm ready whenever you are," I replied.

We got into the car and drove to his house. It was a longish drive. In the darkness I could see nothing much, but presently I realised that we were going up a rather steep hill. We reached the Residency.

It had been an evening like any other, pleasant, but not at all exciting, and I had spent I don't know how many just like it. I did not expect it to leave any sort of impression on me.

Featherstone led me into his sitting-room. It looked comfortable, but it was a trifle ordinary. It had large basket arm-chairs covered with cretonne and on the walls were a great many framed photographs; the tables were littered with papers, magazines and official reports, with pipes, yellow tins of straight-cut cigarettes and pink tins of tobacco. In a row of shelves were untidily stacked a good many books, their bindings stained with damp and the ravages of white ants. Featherstone showed me my room and left me with the words:

"Shall you be ready for a gin pahit in ten minutes?"

"Easily," I said.

I had a bath and changed and went downstairs. Featherstone, ready before me, mixed our drinks as he heard me clatter down the wooden staircase. We dined. We talked. The festival which I had been invited to see was the next day but one, but Featherstone told me he had arranged for me before that to be received by the Sultan.

"He's a jolly old boy," he said. "And the palace is a sight for sore eyes."

After dinner we talked a little more, Featherstone put on the gramophone, and we looked at the latest illustrated papers that had arrived from England. Then we went to bed. Featherstone came to my room to see that I had everything I wanted.

"I suppose you haven't any books with you," he said. "I haven't got a thing to read."

"Books?" I cried.

I pointed to my book-bag. It stood upright, bulging oddly, so that it looked like a humpbacked gnome somewhat the worse for liquor.

"Have you got books in there? I thought that was your dirty linen or a camp-bed or something. Is there anything you can lend me?"

"Look for yourself."

Featherstone's boys had unlocked the bag, but quailing before the sight that then discovered itself had done no more. I knew from long experience how to unpack it. I threw it over on its side, seized its leather bottom and, walking backwards, dragged the sack away from its contents. A river of books poured on to the floor. A look of stupefaction came upon Featherstone's face.

"You don't mean to say you travel with as many books as that? By George, what a snip!"

He bent down and turning them over rapidly looked at the titles. There were books of all kinds. Volumes of verse, novels, philosophical works, critical studies (they say books about books are profitless, but they certainly make very pleasant reading), biographies, history; there were books to read when you were ill and books to read when your brain, all alert, craved for something to grapple with; there were books that you had always wanted to read, but in the hurry of life at home had never found time to; there were books to read at sea when you were meandering through narrow waters on a tramp steamer, and there were books for bad weather when your whole cabin creaked and you had to wedge yourself in your bunk in order not to fall out; there were books chosen solely for their length, which you took with you when on some expedition you had to travel light, and there were the books you could read when you could read nothing else. Finally Featherstone picked out a life of Byron that had recently appeared.

"Hullo, what's this?" he said. "I read a review of it some time ago."

"I believe it's very good," I replied. "I haven't read it yet."

"May I take it? It'll do for me to-night at all events."

"Of course. Take anything you like."

"No, that's enough. Well, good-night. Breakfast at eight-thirty."

When I came down next morning the head boy told me that Featherstone, who had been at work since six, would be in shortly. While I waited for him I glanced at his shelves.

"I see you've got a grand library of books on bridge," I remarked as we sat down to breakfast.

"Yes, I get every one that comes out. I'm very keen on it."

"That fellow we were playing with yesterday plays a good game."

"Which? Hardy?"

"I don't know. Not the one who said he was going to collect his wife. The other."

"Yes, that was Hardy. That was why I asked him to play. He doesn't come to the club very often."

"I hope he will to-night."

"I wouldn't bank on it. He has an estate about thirty miles away. It's a longish ride to come just for a rubber of bridge."

"Is he married?"

L

"No. Well, yes. But his wife is in England."

"It must be awfully lonely for those men who live by themselves on those estates," I said.

"Oh, he's not so badly off as some. I don't think he much cares about seeing people. I think he'd be just as lonely in London."

There was something in the way that Featherstone spoke that struck me as a little strange. His voice had what I can only describe as a shuttered tone. He seemed suddenly to have moved away from me. It was as though one were passing along a street at night and paused for a second to look in at a lighted window that showed a comfortable room and suddenly an invisible hand pulled down a blind. His eyes, which habitually met those of the person he was talking to with frankness, now avoided mine and I had a notion that it was not only my fancy that read in his face an expression of pain. It was drawn for a moment as it might be by a twinge of neuralgia. I could not think of anything to say and Featherstone did not speak. I was conscious that his thoughts, withdrawn from me and what we were about, were turned upon a subject unknown to me. Presently he gave a little sigh, very slight, but unmistakable, and seemed with a deliberate effort to pull himself together.

"I'm going down to the office immediately after breakfast," he said. "What are you going to do with yourself?"

"Oh, don't bother about me. I shall slack around. I'll stroll down and look at the town."

"There's not much to see."

"All the better. I'm fed up with sights."

I found that Featherstone's verandah gave me sufficient entertainment for the morning. It had one of the most enchanting views I had seen in the F.M.S. The Residency was built on the top of a hill and the garden was large and well cared for. Great trees gave it almost the look of an English park. It had vast lawns and there Tamils, black and emaciated, were scything with deliberate and beautiful gestures. Beyond and below the jungle grew thickly to the bank of a broad, winding and swiftly flowing river, and on the other side of this, as far as the eye could reach, stretched the wooded hills of Tenggarah. The contrast between the trim lawns, so strangely English, and the savage growth of the jungle beyond pleasantly titillated the fancy. I sat and read and smoked. It is my business to be curious about people and I asked myself how the peace of this scene, charged nevertheless with a tremulous and dark significance, affected Featherstone who lived with it. He knew it under every aspect: at dawn when the mist rising from the river shrouded it with a ghostly pall; in the splendour of noon; and at last when the shadowy gloaming crept softly out of the jungle, like an army making its way with caution in unknown country, and presently enveloped the green lawns and the great flowering trees and the flaunting cassias in the silent night. I wondered whether, unbeknownst to him, the tender and yet strangely sinister aspect of the scene, acting on his nerves and his loneliness, imbued him with some mystical quality so that the life he led, the life of the capable administrator, the sportsman and the good fellow, on occasion seemed to him not quite real. I smiled at my own fancies, for certainly the conversation we had had the night before had not indicated in him any stirrings of the soul. I had thought him quite nice. He had been at Oxford and was a member of a good London club. He seemed to attach a good deal of importance to social things. He was a gentleman and slightly conscious of the fact that he belonged to a better class than most of the Englishmen his life brought him in contact with. I gathered from the various silver pots that adorned his dining-room that he excelled in games. He played tennis and billiards. When he went on leave he hunted and, anxious to keep his weight down, he dieted carefully. He talked a good deal of what he would do when he retired. He hankered after the life of a country gentleman. A little house in Leicestershire, a couple of hunters and neighbours to play bridge with. He would have his pension and he had a little money of his own. But meanwhile he worked hard and did his work, if not brilliantly, certainly with competence. I have no doubt that he was looked upon by his superiors as a reliable officer. He was cut upon a pattern that I knew too well to find very interesting. He was like a novel that is careful, honest and efficient, yet a little ordinary, so that you seem to have read it all before, and you turn the pages listlessly, knowing that it will never afford you a surprise or move you to excitement.

But human beings are incalculable and he is a fool who tells himself that he knows what a man is capable of.

In the afternoon Featherstone took me to see the Sultan. We were received by one of his sons, a shy, smiling youth who acted as his A.D.C. He was dressed in a neat blue suit, but round his waist he wore a sarong, white flowers on a yellow ground, on his head a red fez, and on his feet knobby American shoes. The palace, built in the Moorish style, was like a very big doll's house and it was painted bright yellow, which is the royal colour. We were led into a spacious room, furnished with the sort of furniture you would find in an English lodging-house at the seaside, but the chairs were covered with yellow silk. On the floor was a Brussels carpet and on the walls photographs in very grand gilt frames of the Sultan at various state functions. In a cabinet was a large collection of all kinds of fruit done entirely in crochet work. The Sultan came in with several attendants. He was a man of fifty, perhaps, short and stout, dressed in trousers and tunic of a large white-and-yellow check; round his middle he wore a very beautiful yellow sarong and on his head a white fez. He had large handsome friendly eyes. He gave us coffee to drink, sweet cakes to eat and cheroots to smoke. Conversation was not difficult, for he was affable, and he told me that he had never been to a theatre or played cards, for he was very religious, and he had four wives and twenty-four children. The only bar to the happiness of his life seemed to be that common decency obliged him to divide his time equally between his four wives. He said that an hour with one was a month and with another five minutes. I remarked that Professor Einstein—or was it Bergson?—had made similar observations upon time and indeed on this question had given the world much to ponder over. Presently we took our leave and the Sultan presented me with some beautiful white Malaccas.

In the evening we went to the club. One of the men we had played with the day before got up from his chair as we entered.

"Ready for a rubber?" he said.

"Where's our fourth?" I asked.

"Oh, there are several fellows here who'll be glad to play."

"What about the man we played with yesterday?" I had forgotten his name.

"Hardy? He's not here."

"It's not worth while waiting for him," said Featherstone.

"He very seldom comes to the club. I was surprised to see him last night."

I did not know why I had the impression that behind the very ordinary words of these two men there was an odd sense of embarrassment. Hardy had made no impression on me and I did not even remember what he looked like. He was just a fourth at the bridge table. I had a feeling that they had something against him. It was no business of mine and I was quite content to play with a man who at that moment joined us. We certainly had a more cheerful game than before. A good deal of chaff passed from one side of the table to the other. We played less serious bridge. We laughed. I wondered if it was only that they were less shy of the stranger who had happened in upon them or if the presence of Hardy had caused in the other two a certain constraint. At half-past eight we broke up and Featherstone and I went back to dine at his house.

After dinner we lounged in arm-chairs and smoked cheroots. For some reason our conversation did not flow easily. I tried topic after topic, but could not get Featherstone to interest himself in any of them. I began to think that in the last twenty-four hours he had said all he had to say. I fell somewhat discouraged into silence. It prolonged itself and again, I did not know why, I had a faint sensation that it was charged with a significance that escaped me. I felt slightly uncomfortable. I had that queer feeling that one sometimes has when sitting in an empty room that one is not by oneself. Presently I was conscious that Featherstone was steadily looking at me. I was sitting by a lamp, but he was in shadow so that the play of his features was hidden from me. But he had very large brilliant eyes and in the half darkness they seemed to shine dimly. They were like new boot-buttons that caught a reflected light. I wondered why he looked at me like that. I gave him a glance and catching his eyes insistently fixed upon me faintly smiled.

"Interesting book that one you lent me last night," he said suddenly, and I could not help thinking his voice did not sound quite natural. The words issued from his lips as though they were pushed from behind.

"Oh, the *Life of Byron*?" I said breezily. "Have you read it already?"

"A good deal of it. I read till three."

"I've heard it's very well done. I'm not sure that Byron interests me so much as all that. There was so much in him that was so frightfully second-rate. It makes one rather uncomfortable."

"What do you think is the real truth of that story about him and his sister?"

"Augusta Leigh? I don't know very much about it. I've never read *Astarte*."

"Do you really think they were in love with one another?"

"I suppose so. Isn't it generally believed that she was the only woman he ever genuinely loved?"

"Can you understand it?"

"I can't really. It doesn't particularly shock me. It just seems to me very unnatural. Perhaps 'unnatural' isn't the right word. It's incomprehensible to me. I can't throw myself into the state of feeling in which such a thing seems possible. You know, that's how a writer gets to know the people he writes about, by standing himself in their shoes and feeling with their hearts."

I knew I did not make myself very clear, but I was trying to describe a sensation, an action of the subconscious, which from experience was perfectly familiar to me, but which no words I knew could precisely indicate. I went on:

"Of course she was only his half-sister, but just as habit kills love I should have thought habit would prevent its arising. When two persons have known one another all their lives and lived together in close contact I can't imagine how or why that sudden spark should flash that results in love. The probabilities are that they would be joined by mutual affection and I don't know anything that is more contrary to love than affection."

I could just see in the dimness the outline of a smile flicker for a moment on my host's heavy, and it seemed to me then, somewhat saturnine face.

"You only believe in love at first sight?"

"Well, I suppose I do, but with the proviso that people may have met twenty times before seeing one another. 'Seeing' has an active side and a passive one. Most people we run across mean so little to us that we never bestir ourselves to look at them. We just suffer the impression they make on us."

"Oh, but one's often heard of couples who've known one another for years and it's never occurred to one they cared two straws for each other and suddenly they go and get married. How do you explain that?"

"Well, if you're going to bully me into being logical and consistent, I should suggest that their love is of a different kind. After all, passion isn't the only reason for marriage. It may not even be the best one. Two people may marry because they're lonely or because they're good friends or for convenience's sake. Though I said that affection was the greatest enemy of love, I would never deny that it's a very good substitute. I'm not sure that a marriage founded on it isn't the happiest."

"What did you think of Tim Hardy?"

I was a little surprised at the sudden question, which seemed to have nothing to do with the subject of our conversation.

"I didn't think of him very much. He seemed quite nice. Why?"

"Did he seem to you just like everybody else?"

"Yes. Is there anything peculiar about him? If you'd told me that, I'd have paid more attention to him."

"He's very quiet, isn't he? I suppose no one who knew nothing about him would give him a second thought."

I tried to remember what he looked like. The only thing that had struck me when we were playing cards was that he had fine hands. It passed idly through my mind that they were not the sort of hands I should have expected a planter to have. But why a planter should have different hands from anybody else I did not trouble to ask myself. His were somewhat large, but very well formed with peculiarly long fingers, and the nails were of an admirable shape. They were virile and yet oddly sensitive hands. I noticed this and thought no more about it. But if you are a writer instinct and the habit of years enable you to store up impressions that you are not aware of. Sometimes of course they do not correspond with the facts and a woman for example may remain in your subconsciousness as a dark, massive and ox-eyed creature when she is indeed rather small and of a nondescript colouring. But that is of no consequence. The impression may very well be more exact than the sober truth. And now, seeking to call up from the depths of me a picture of this man I had a feeling of some ambiguity. He was clean-shaven and his face, oval but not thin, seemed strangely pale under the tan of long exposure to the tropical sun. His features were vague. I did not know whether I remembered it or only imagined now that his rounded chin gave one the impression of a certain weakness. He had thick brown hair, just turning grey, and a long wisp fell down constantly over his forehead. He pushed it back with a gesture that had become habitual. His brown eyes were rather large and gentle, but perhaps a little sad; they had a melting softness which, I could imagine, might be very appealing.

After a pause Featherstone continued:

"It's rather strange that I should run across Tim Hardy here after all these years. But that's the way of the F.M.S. People move about and you find yourself in the same place as a man you'd known years before in another part of the country. I first knew Tim when he had an estate near Sibuku. Have you ever been there?"

"No. Where is it?"

"Oh, it's up north. Towards Siam. It wouldn't be worth your while to go. It's just like every other place in the F.M.S. But it was rather nice. It had a jolly little club and there were some quite decent people. There was the schoolmaster and the head of the police, the doctor, the padre and the government engineer. The usual lot, you know. A few planters. Three or four women. I was A.D.O. It was one of my first jobs. Tim Hardy had an estate about twenty-five miles away. He lived there with his sister. They had a bit of money of their own and he'd bought the place. Rubber was pretty good then and he wasn't doing at all badly. We rather cottoned on to one another. Of course it's a toss-up with planters. Some of them are very good fellows, but they're not exactly . . ." he sought for a word or a phrase that did not sound snobbish. "Well, they're not the sort of people you'd be likely to meet at home. Tim and Olive were of one's own class, if you understand what I mean."

"Olive was the sister?"

"Yes. They'd had a rather unfortunate past. Their parents had separated when they were quite small, seven or eight, and the mother had taken Olive and the father had kept Tim. Tim went to Clifton, they were West Country people, and only came home for the holidays. His father was a retired naval man who lived at Fowey. But Olive went with her mother to Italy. She was educated in Florence; she spoke Italian perfectly and French too. For all those years Tim and Olive never saw one another once, but they used to write to one another regularly. They'd been very much attached when they were children. As far as I could understand, life when their people were living together had been rather stormy with all sorts of scenes and upsets, you know the sort of thing that happens when two people who are married don't get on together, and that had thrown them on their own resources. They were left a good deal to themselves. Then Mrs. Hardy died and Olive came home to England and went back to her father. She was eighteen then and Tim was seventeen. A year later the war broke out. Tim joined up and his father, who was over fifty, got some job at Portsmouth. I take it he had been a hard liver and a heavy drinker. He broke down before the end of the war and died after a lingering illness. They don't seem to have had any relations. They were the last of a rather old family; they had a fine old house in Dorsetshire that had belonged to them for a good many generations, but they had never been able to afford to live in it and it was always let. I remember seeing photographs of it. It was very much a gentleman's house, of grey stone and rather stately, with a coat of arms carved over the front door and mullioned windows. Their great ambition was to make enough money to be able to live in it. They used to talk about it a lot. They never spoke as though either of them would marry, but always as though it were a settled thing that they would remain together. It was rather funny considering how young they were."

"How old were they then?" I asked.

"Well, I suppose he was twenty-five or twenty-six and she was a year older. They were awfully kind to me when I first went up to Sibuku. They took a fancy to me at once. You see, we had more in common than most of the people there. I think they were glad of my company. They weren't particularly popular."

"Why not?" I asked.

"They were rather reserved and you couldn't help seeing that they liked their own society better than other people's. I don't know if you've noticed it, but that always seems to put people's backs up. They resent it somehow if they have a feeling that you can get along very well without them."

"It's tiresome, isn't it?" I said.

"It was rather a grievance to the other planters that Tim was his own master and had private means. They had to put up with an old Ford to get about in, but Tim had a real car. Tim and Olive were very nice when they came to the club and they played in the tennis tournaments and all that sort of thing, but you had an impression that they were always glad to get away again. They'd dine out with people and make themselves very pleasant, but it was pretty obvious that they'd just as soon have stayed at home. If you had any sense you couldn't blame them. I don't know if you've been much to planters' houses. They're a bit dreary. A lot of gimcrack furniture and silver ornaments and tiger skins. And the food's uneatable. But the Hardys had made their bungalow rather nice. There was nothing very grand in it; it was just easy and homelike and comfortable. Their living-room was like a drawing-room in an English country house. You felt that their things meant something to them and that they had had them a long time. It was a very jolly house to stay at. The bungalow was in the middle of the estate, but it was on the brow of a little hill and you looked right over the rubber trees to the sea in the distance. Olive took a lot of trouble with her garden and it was really topping. I never saw such a show of cannas. I used to go there for week-ends. It was only about half an hour's drive to the sea and we'd take our lunch with us and bathe and sail. Tim kept a small boat there. Those days were grand. I never knew one could enjoy oneself so much. It's a beautiful bit of coast and it was really extraordinarily romantic. Then in the evenings we'd play patience and chess or turn on the gramophone. The cooking was damned good too. It was a change from what one generally got. Olive had taught their cook to make all sorts of Italian dishes and we used to have great wallops of macaroni and risotto and gnocchi and things like that. I couldn't help envying them their life, it was so jolly and peaceful, and when they talked of what they'd do when they went back to England for good I used to tell them they'd always regret what they'd left.

" 'We've been very happy here,' said Olive.

"She had a way of looking at Tim, with a slow, sidelong glance from under her long eyelashes, that was rather engaging.

"In their own house they were quite different from what they were when they went out. They were so easy and cordial. Everybody admitted that and I'm bound to say that people enjoyed going there. They often asked people over. They had the gift of making you feel at home. It was a very happy house, if you know what I mean. Of course no one could help seeing how attached they were to one another. And whatever people said about their being stand-offish and self-centred, they were bound to be rather touched by the affection they had for one another. People said they couldn't have been more united if they were married, and when you saw how some couples got on you couldn't help thinking they made most marriages look rather like a wash-out. They seemed to think the same things at the same time. They had little private jokes that made them laugh like children. They were so charming with one another, so gay and happy, that really to stay with them was, well, a spiritual refreshment. I don't know what else you could call it. When you left them, after a couple of days at the bungalow, you felt that you'd absorbed some of their peace and their sober gaiety. It was as though your soul had been sluiced with cool clear water. You felt strangely purified."

It was singular to hear Featherstone talking in this exalted strain. He looked so spruce in his smart white coat, technically known as a bum-freezer, his moustache was so trim, his thick curly hair so carefully brushed, that his high-flown language made me a trifle uncomfortable. But I realised that he was trying to express in his clumsy way a very sincerely felt emotion.

"What was Olive Hardy like?" I asked.

"I'll show you. I've got quite a lot of snapshots."

He got up from his chair and going to a shelf brought me a large album. It was the usual thing, indifferent photographs of people in groups and unflattering likenesses of single figures. They were in bathing dress or in shorts or tennis things, generally with their faces screwed up because the sun blinded them, or puckered by the distortion of laughter. I recognised Hardy, not much changed after ten years, with his wisp of hair hanging across his forehead. I remembered him better now that I saw the snapshots. In them he looked nice and fresh and young. He had an alertness of expression that was attractive and that I certainly had not noticed when I saw him. In his eyes was a sort of eagerness for life that danced and sparkled through the fading print. I glanced at the photographs of his sister. Her bathing dress showed that she had a good figure, well-developed, but slender; and her legs were long and slim.

"They look rather alike," I said.

"Yes, although she was a year older they might have been twins, they were so much alike. They both had the same oval face and that pale skin without any colour in the cheeks, and they both had those soft brown eyes, very liquid and appealing, so that you felt whatever they did you could never be angry with them. And they both had a sort of careless elegance that made them look charming whatever they wore and however untidy they were. He's lost that now, I suppose, but he certainly had it when I first knew him. They always rather reminded me of the brother and sister in *Twelfth Night*. You know whom I mean."

"Viola and Sebastian."

"They never seemed to belong quite to the present. There was something Elizabethan about them. I don't think it was only because I was very young then that I couldn't help feeling they were strangely romantic somehow. I could see them living in Illyria."

I gave one of the snapshots another glance.

"The girl looks as though she had a good deal more character than her brother," I remarked.

"She had. I don't know if you'd have called Olive beautiful, but she was awfully attractive. There was something poetic in her, a sort of lyrical quality, as it were, that coloured her movements, her acts and everything about her. It seemed to exalt her above common cares. There was something so candid in her expression, so courageous and independent in her bearing, that—oh, I don't know, it made mere beauty just flat and dull."

"You speak as if you'd been in love with her," I interrupted.

"Of course I was. I should have thought you'd guessed that at once. I was frightfully in love with her."

"Was it love at first sight?" I smiled.

"Yes, I think it was, but I didn't know it for a month or so. When it suddenly struck me that what I felt for her—I don't know how to explain it, it was a sort of shattering turmoil that affected every bit of me—that that was love, I knew I'd felt it all along. It was not only her looks, though they were awfully alluring, the smoothness of her pale skin and the way her hair fell over her forehead and the grave sweetness of her brown eyes, it was more than that; you had a sensation of well-being when you were with her, as though you could relax and be quite natural and needn't pretend to be anything you weren't. You felt she was incapable of meanness. It was impossible to think of her as envious of other people or catty. She seemed to have a natural generosity of soul.

One could be silent with her for an hour at a time and yet feel that one had had a good time."

"A rare gift," I said.

"She was a wonderful companion. If you made a suggestion to do something she was always glad to fall in with it. She was the least exacting girl I ever knew. You could throw her over at the last minute and however disappointed she was it made no difference. Next time you saw her she was just as cordial and serene as ever."

"Why didn't you marry her?"

Featherstone's cheroot had gone out. He threw the stub away and deliberately lit another. He did not answer for a while. It may seem strange to persons who live in a highly civilised state that he should confide these intimate things to a stranger; it did not seem strange to me. I was used to it. People who live so desperately alone, in the remote places of the earth, find it a relief to tell someone whom in all probability they will never meet again the story that has burdened perhaps for years their waking thoughts and their dreams at night. And I have an inkling that the fact of your being a writer attracts their confidence. They feel that what they tell you will excite your interest in an impersonal way that makes it easier for them to discharge their souls. Besides, as we all know from our own experience, it is never unpleasant to talk about oneself.

"Why didn't you marry her?" I had asked him.

"I wanted to badly enough," Featherstone answered at length. "But I hesitated to ask her. Although she was always so nice to me and so easy to get on with, and we were such good friends, I always felt that there was something a little mysterious in her. Although she was so simple, so frank and natural, you never quite got over the feeling of an inner kernel of aloofness, as if deep in her heart she guarded, not a secret, but a sort of privacy of the soul that not a living person would ever be allowed to know. I don't know if I make myself clear."

"I think so."

"I put it down to her upbringing. They never talked of their mother, but somehow I got the impression that she was one of those neurotic, emotional women who wreck their own happiness and are a pest to everyone connected with them. I had a suspicion that she'd led rather a hectic life in Florence and it struck me that Olive owed her beautiful serenity to a disciplined effort of her own will and that her aloofness was a sort of citadel she'd built to protect herself from the knowledge of all sorts of shameful things. But of course that aloofness was awfully captivating. It was strangely exciting to think that if she loved you, and you were married to her, you would at last pierce right into the hidden heart of that mystery; and you felt that if you could share that with her it would be as it were a consummation of all you'd ever desired in your life. Heaven wouldn't be in it. You know, I felt about it just like Bluebeard's wife about the forbidden chamber in the castle. Every room was open to me, but I should never rest till I had gone into that last one that was locked against me."

My eye was caught by a chik-chak, a little brown house lizard with a large head, high up on the wall. It is a friendly little beast and it is good to see it in a house. It watched a fly. It was quite still. On a sudden it made a dart and then as the fly flew away fell back with a sort of jerk into a strange immobility.

"And there was another thing that made me hesitate. I couldn't bear the thought that if I proposed to her and she refused me she wouldn't let me come to the bungalow in the same old way. I should have hated that, I enjoyed going there so awfully. It made me so happy to be with her. But you know, sometimes one can't help oneself. I did ask her at last, but it was almost by accident. One evening, after dinner, when we were sitting on the verandah by ourselves, I took her hand. She withdrew it at once.

" 'Why did you do that?' I asked her.

" 'I don't very much like being touched,' she said. She turned her head a little and smiled. 'Are you hurt? You mustn't mind, it's just a funny feeling I have. I can't help it.'

" 'I wonder if it's ever occurred to you that I'm frightfully fond of you,' I said.

"I expect I was terribly awkward about it, but I'd never proposed to anyone before." Featherstone gave a little sound that was not quite a chuckle and not quite a sigh. "For the matter of that, I've never proposed to anyone since. She didn't say anything for a minute. Then she said:

" 'I'm very glad, but I don't think I want you to be anything more than that.'

" 'Why not?' I asked.

" 'I could never leave Tim.'

" 'But supposing he marries?'

" 'He never will.'

"I'd gone so far then that I thought I'd better go on. But my throat was so dry that I could hardly speak. I was shaking with nervousness.

" 'I'm frightfully in love with you, Olive. I want to marry you more than anything in the world.'

"She put her hand very gently on my arm. It was like a flower falling to the ground.

" 'No, dear, I can't,' she said.

"I was silent. It was difficult for me to say what I wanted to. I'm naturally rather shy. She was a girl. I couldn't very well tell her that it wasn't quite the same thing living with a husband and living with a brother. She was normal and healthy; she must want to have babies; it wasn't reasonable to starve her natural instincts. It was such waste of her youth. But it was she who spoke first.

" 'Don't let's talk about this any more,' she said. 'D'you mind? It did strike me once or twice that perhaps you cared for me. Tim noticed it. I was sorry because I was afraid it would break up our friendship. I don't want it to do that, Mark. We do get on so well together, the three of us, and we have such jolly times. I don't know what we should do without you now.'

" 'I thought of that too,' I said.

" 'D'you think it need?' she asked me.

" 'My dear, I don't want it to,' I said. 'You must know how much I love coming here. I've never been so happy anywhere before!'

" 'You're not angry with me?'

" 'Why should I be? It's not your fault. It only means that you're not in love with me. If you were you wouldn't care a hang about Tim.'

" 'You are rather sweet,' she said.

"She put her arm round my neck and kissed me lightly on the cheek. I had a notion that in her mind it settled our relation. She adopted me as a second brother.

"A few weeks later Tim went back to England. The tenant of their house in Dorset was leaving and though there was another in the offing, he thought he ought to be on the spot to conduct negotiations. And he wanted some new machinery for the estate. He thought he'd get it at the same time. He didn't expect to be gone more than three months and Olive made up her mind not to go. She knew hardly anyone in England, and it was practically a foreign country to her, she didn't mind being left alone, and she wanted to look after the estate. Of course they could have put a manager in charge, but that wasn't the same thing. Rubber was falling and in case of accidents it was just as well that one or other of them should be there. I promised Tim I'd look after her and if she wanted me she could always call me up. My proposal hadn't changed anything. We carried on as though nothing had happened.

I don't know whether she'd told Tim. He made no sign that he knew. Of course I loved her as much as ever, but I kept it to myself. I have a good deal of self-control, you know. I had a sort of feeling I hadn't a chance. I hoped eventually my love would change into something else and we could just be wonderful friends. It's funny, it never has, you know. I suppose I was hit too badly ever to get quite over it.

"She went down to Penang to see Tim off and when she came back I met her at the station and drove her home. I couldn't very well stay at the bungalow while Tim was away, but I went over every Sunday and had tiffin and we'd go down to the sea and have a bathe. People tried to be kind to her and asked her to stay with them, but she wouldn't. She seldom left the estate. She had plenty to do. She read a lot. She was never bored. She seemed quite happy in her own company, and when she had visitors it was only from a sense of duty. She didn't want them to think her ungracious. But it was an effort and she told me she heaved a sigh of relief when she saw the last of them and could again enjoy without disturbance the peaceful loneliness of the bungalow. She was a very curious girl. It was strange that at her age she should be so indifferent to parties and the other small gaieties the station afforded. Spiritually, if you know what I mean, she was entirely self-supporting. I don't know how people found out that I was in love with her; I thought I'd never given myself away in anything, but I had hints here and there that they knew. I gathered they thought Olive hadn't gone home with her brother on my account. One woman, a Mrs. Sergison, the policeman's wife, actually asked me when they were going to be able to congratulate me. Of course I pretended I didn't know what she was talking about, but it didn't go down very well. I couldn't help being amused. I meant so little to Olive in that way that I really believe she'd entirely forgotten that I'd asked her to marry me. I can't say she was unkind to me, I don't think she could have been unkind to anyone; but she treated me with just the casualness with which a sister might treat a younger brother. She was two or three years older than I was. She was always terribly glad to see me, but it never occurred to her to put herself out for me; she was almost amazingly intimate with me, but unconsciously, you know, as you might be with a person you'd known so well all your life that you never thought of putting on frills with him. I might not have been a man at all, but an old coat that she wore all the time because it was easy and comfortable and she didn't mind what she did with it. I should have been crazy not to see that she was a thousand miles away from loving me.

"Then one day, three or four weeks before Tim was due back, when I went to the bungalow I saw she'd been crying. I was startled. She was always so composed. I'd never seen her upset over anything.

" 'Hullo, what's the matter?' I said.

" 'Nothing.'

" 'Come off it, darling,' I said. 'What have you been crying about?'

"She tried to smile.

" 'I wish you hadn't got such sharp eyes,' she said. 'I think I'm being silly. I've just had a cable from Tim to say he's postponed his sailing.'

" 'Oh, my dear, I am sorry,' I said. 'You must be dreadfully disappointed.'

" 'I've been counting the days. I want him back so badly.'

" 'Does he say why he's postponing?' I asked.

" 'No, he says he's writing. I'll show you the cable.'

"I saw that she was very nervous. Her slow quiet eyes were filled with apprehension and there was a little frown of anxiety between her brows. She went into her bedroom and in a moment came back with the cable. I felt that she was watching me anxiously as I read. So far as I remember it ran: *Darling, I cannot sail on the seventh after all. Please forgive me. Am writing fully. Fondest love. Tim.*

" 'Well, perhaps the machinery he wanted isn't ready and he can't bring himself to sail without it,' I said.

" 'What could it matter if it came by a later ship? Anyhow, it'll be hung up at Penang.'

" 'It may be something about the house.'

" 'If it is why doesn't he say so? He must know how frightfully anxious I am.'

" 'It wouldn't occur to him,' I said. 'After all, when you're away you don't realise that the people you've left behind don't know something that you take as a matter of course.'

"She smiled again, but now more happily.

" 'I dare say you're right. In point of fact Tim is a little like that. He's always been rather slack and casual. I dare say I've been making a mountain out of a molehill. I must just wait patiently for his letter.'

"Olive was a girl with a lot of self-control and I saw her by an effort of will pull herself together. The little line between her eyebrows vanished and she was once more her serene, smiling and kindly self. She was always gentle: that day she had a mildness so heavenly that it was shattering. But for the rest of the time I could see that she kept her restlessness in check only by the deliberate exercise of her common sense. It was as though she had a foreboding of ill. I was with her the day before the mail was due. Her anxiety was all the more pitiful to see because she took such pains to hide it. I was always busy on mail day, but I promised to go up to the estate later on and hear the news. I was just thinking of starting when Hardy's seis came along in the car with a message from the amah asking me to go at once to her mistress. The amah was a decent, elderly woman to whom I had given a dollar or two and said that if anything went wrong on the estate she was to let me know at once. I jumped into my car. When I arrived I found the amah waiting for me on the steps.

" 'A letter came this morning,' she said.

"I interrupted her. I ran up the steps. The sitting-room was empty.

" 'Olive,' I called.

"I went into the passage and suddenly I heard a sound that froze my heart. The amah had followed me and now she opened the door of Olive's room. The sound I had heard was the sound of Olive crying. I went in. She was lying on her bed, on her face, and her sobs shook her from head to foot. I put my hand on her shoulder.

" 'Olive, what is it?' I asked.

" 'Who's that?' she cried. She sprang to her feet suddenly, as though she were scared out of her wits. And then: 'Oh, it's you,' she said. She stood in front of me, with her head thrown back and her eyes closed, and the tears streamed from them. It was dreadful. 'Tim's married,' she gasped, and her face screwed up in a sort of grimace of pain.

"I must admit that for one moment I had a thrill of exultation, it was like a little electric shock tingling through my heart; it struck me that now I had a chance, she might be willing to marry me; I knew it was terribly selfish of me; you see, the news had taken me by surprise; but it was only for a moment, after that I was melted by her awful distress and the only thing I felt was deep sorrow because she was unhappy. I put my arm round her waist.

" 'Oh, my dear, I'm so sorry,' I said. 'Don't stay here. Come into the sitting-room and sit down and we'll talk about it. Let me give you something to drink.'

"She let me lead her into the next room and we sat down on the sofa. I told the amah to fetch the whisky and syphon and I mixed her a good strong stengah and made her drink a little. I took her

in my arms and rested her head on my shoulder. She let me do
what I liked with her. The great tears streamed down her poor
face.

" 'How could he?' she moaned. 'How could he?'

" 'My darling,' I said, 'it was bound to happen sooner or later.
He's a young man. How could you expect him never to marry?
It's only natural.'

" 'No, no, no,' she gasped.

"Tight-clenched in her hand I saw that she had a letter and I
guessed that it was Tim's.

" 'What does he say?' I asked.

"She gave a frightened movement and clutched the letter to her
heart as though she thought I would take it from her.

" 'He says he couldn't help himself. He says he had to. What
does it mean?'

" 'Well, you know, in his way he's just as attractive as you are.
He has so much charm. I suppose he just fell madly in love with
some girl and she with him.'

" 'He's so weak,' she moaned.

" 'Are they coming out?' I asked.

" 'They sailed yesterday. He says it won't make any difference.
He's insane. How *can* I stay here?'

"She began to cry hysterically. It was torture to see that girl,
usually so calm, utterly shattered by her emotion. I had always
felt that her lovely serenity masked a capacity for deep feeling.
But the abandon of her distress simply broke me up. I held her in
my arms and kissed her, her eyes and her wet cheek and her hair.
I don't think she knew what I was doing. I was hardly conscious
of it myself. I was so deeply moved.

" 'What shall I do?' she wailed.

" 'Why don't you marry me?' I said.

"She tried to withdraw herself from me, but I wouldn't let her
go.

" 'After all, it would be a way out,' I said.

" 'How can I marry you?' she moaned. 'I'm years older than you
are.'

" 'Oh, what nonsense, two or three. What do I care?'

" 'No, no.'

" 'Why not?' I said.

" 'I don't love you,' she said.

" 'What does that matter? I love you.'

"I don't know what I said. I told her that I'd try to make her
happy. I said I'd never ask anything from her but what she was

prepared to give me. I talked and talked. I tried to make her see reason. I felt that she didn't want to stay there, in the same place as Tim, and I told her that I'd be moved soon to some other district. I thought that might tempt her. She couldn't deny that we'd always got on awfully well together. After a time she did seem to grow a little quieter. I had a feeling that she was listening to me. I had even a sort of feeling that she knew that she was lying in my arms and that it comforted her. I made her drink a drop more whisky. I gave her a cigarette. At last I thought I might be just mildly facetious.

" 'You know, I'm not a bad sort really,' I said. 'You might do worse.'

" 'You don't know me,' she said. 'You know nothing whatever about me.'

" 'I'm capable of learning,' I said.

"She smiled a little.

" 'You're awfully kind, Mark,' she said.

" 'Say yes, Olive,' I begged.

"She gave a deep sigh. For a long time she stared at the ground. But she did not move and I felt the softness of her body in my arms. I waited. I was frightfully nervous and the minutes seemed endless.

" 'All right,' she said at last, as though she were not conscious that any time had passed between my prayer and her answer.

"I was so moved that I had nothing to say. But when I wanted to kiss her lips, she turned her face away, and wouldn't let me. I wanted us to be married at once, but she was quite firm that she wouldn't. She insisted on waiting till Tim came back. You know how sometimes you see so clearly in people's thoughts that you're more certain of them than if they'd spoken them; I saw that she couldn't quite believe that what Tim had written was true and that she had a sort of miserable hope that it was all a mistake and he wasn't married after all. It gave me a pang, but I loved her so much, I just bore it. I was willing to bear anything. I adored her. She wouldn't even let me tell anyone that we were engaged. She made me promise not to say a word till Tim's return. She said she couldn't bear the thought of the congratulations and all that. She wouldn't even let me make any announcement of Tim's marriage. She was obstinate about it. I had a notion that she felt if the fact were spread about it gave it a certainty that she didn't want it to have.

"But the matter was taken out of her hands. News travels mysteriously in the East. I don't know what Olive had said in the amah's hearing when first she received the news of Tim's marriage; anyhow, the Hardys' seis told the Sergisons' and Mrs. Sergison attacked me the next time I went into the club.

" 'I hear Tim Hardy's married,' she said.

" 'Oh?' I answered, unwilling to commit myself.

"She smiled at my blank face, and told me that her amah having told her the rumour she had rung up Olive and asked her if it was true. Olive's answer had been rather odd. She had not exactly confirmed it, but said that she had received a letter from Tim telling her he was married.

" 'She's a strange girl,' said Mrs. Sergison. 'When I asked her for details she said she had none to give and when I said: "Aren't you thrilled?" she didn't answer.'

" 'Olive's devoted to Tim, Mrs. Sergison,' I said. 'His marriage has naturally been a shock to her. She knows nothing about Tim's wife. She's nervous about her.'

" 'And when are you two going to be married?' she asked me abruptly.

" 'What an embarrassing question!' I said, trying to laugh it off.

"She looked at me shrewdly.

" 'Will you give me your word of honour that you're not engaged to her?'

"I didn't like to tell her a deliberate lie, nor to ask her to mind her own business, and I'd promised Olive faithfully that I would say nothing till Tim got back. I hedged.

" 'Mrs. Sergison,' I said, 'when there's anything to tell I promise that you'll be the first person to hear it. All I can say to you now is that I do want to marry Olive more than anything in the world.'

" 'I'm very glad that Tim's married,' she answered. 'And I hope she'll marry you very soon. It was a morbid and unhealthy life that they led up there, those two, they kept far too much to themselves and they were far too much absorbed in one another.'

"I saw Olive practically every day. I felt that she didn't want me to make love to her, and I contented myself with kissing her when I came and when I went. She was very nice to me, kindly and thoughtful; I knew she was glad to see me and sorry when it was time for me to go. Ordinarily, she was apt to fall into silence, but during this time she talked more than I had ever heard her talk before. But never of the future and never of Tim and his wife. She told me a lot about her life in Florence with her mother. She had led a strange lonely life, mostly with servants and governesses, while her mother, I suspected, engaged in one affair after another with vague Italian counts and Russian princes. I guessed that by the time she was fourteen there wasn't much she didn't know. It was natural for her to be quite unconventional: in the only world she knew till she was eighteen conventions weren't mentioned because they didn't exist. Gradually, Olive seemed to regain her serenity and I should have thought that she was beginning to accustom herself to the thought of Tim's marriage if it hadn't been that I couldn't but notice how pale and tired she looked. I made up my mind that the moment he arrived I'd press her to marry me at once. I could get short leave whenever I asked for it, and by the time that was up I thought I could manage a transfer to some other post. What she wanted was change of air and fresh scenes.

"We knew, of course, within a day when Tim's ship would reach Penang, but it was a question whether she'd get in soon enough for him to catch the train and I wrote to the P. & O. agent asking him to telegraph as soon as he had definite news. When I got the wire and took it up to Olive I found that she'd just received one from Tim. The ship had docked early and he was arriving next day. The train was supposed to get in at eight o'clock in the morning, but it was liable to be anything from one to six hours late, and I bore with me an invitation from Mrs. Sergison asking Olive to come back with me to stay the night with her so that she would be on the spot and need not go to the station till the news came through that the train was coming.

"I was immensely relieved. I thought that when the blow at last fell Olive wouldn't feel it so much. She had worked herself up into such a state that I couldn't help thinking that she must have a reaction now. She might take a fancy to her sister-in-law. There was no reason why they shouldn't all three get on very well together. To my surprise Olive said she wasn't coming down to the station to meet them.

" 'They'll be awfully disappointed,' I said.

" 'I'd rather wait here,' she answered. She smiled a little. 'Don't argue with me, Mark, I've quite made up my mind.'

" 'I've ordered breakfast in my house,' I said.

" 'That's all right. You meet them and take them to your house and give them breakfast, and then they can come along here afterwards. Of course I'll send the car down.'

" 'I don't suppose they'll want to breakfast if you're not there,' I said.

" 'Oh, I'm sure they will. If the train gets in on time they wouldn't have thought of breakfasting before it arrived and they'll be hungry. They won't want to take this long drive without anything to eat.'

"I was puzzled. She had been looking forward so intensely to Tim's coming, it seemed strange that she should want to wait all by herself while the rest of us were having a jolly breakfast. I supposed she was nervous and wanted to delay as long as possible meeting the strange woman who had come to take her place. It seemed unreasonable, I couldn't see that an hour sooner or an hour later could make any difference, but I knew women were funny, and anyhow I felt Olive wasn't in the mood for me to press it.

" 'Telephone when you're starting so that I shall know when to expect you,' she said.

" 'All right,' I said, 'but you know I shan't be able to come with them. It's my day for going to Lahad.'

"This was a town that I had to go to once a week to take cases. It was a good way off and one had to ferry across a river, which took some time, so that I never got back till late. There were a few Europeans there and a club. I generally had to go on there for a bit to be sociable and see that things were getting along all right.

" 'Besides,' I added, 'with Tim bringing his wife home for the first time I don't suppose he'll want me about. But if you'd like to ask me to dinner I'll be glad to come to that.'

"Olive smiled.

" 'I don't think it'll be my place to issue any more invitations, will it?' she said. 'You must ask the bride.'

"She said this so lightly that my heart leaped. I had a feeling that at last she had made up her mind to accept the altered circumstances and, what was more, was accepting them with cheerfulness. She asked me to stay to dinner. Generally I left about eight and dined at home. She was very sweet, almost tender, and I was happier than I'd been for weeks. I had never been more desperately in love with her. I had a couple of gin pahits and I think I was in rather good form at dinner. I know I made her laugh. I felt that at last she was casting away the load of misery that had oppressed her. This was why I didn't let myself be very much disturbed by what happened at the end.

" 'Don't you think that it's about time you were leaving a presumably maiden lady?' she said.

"She spoke in a manner that was so quietly gay that I answered without hesitation:

" 'Oh, my dear, if you think you've got a shred of reputation left you deceive yourself. You're surely not under the impression that the ladies of Sibuku don't know that I've been coming to see you every day for a month. The general feeling is that if we're not married it's high time we were. Don't you think it would be just as well if I broke it to them that we're engaged?'

" 'Oh, Mark, you mustn't take our engagement very seriously,' she said.

"I laughed.

" 'How else do you expect me to take it? It is serious.'

"She shook her head a little.

" 'No. I was upset and hysterical that day. You were being very sweet to me. I said yes because I was too miserable to say no. But now I've had time to collect myself. Don't think me unkind. I made a mistake. I've been very much to blame. You must forgive me.'

" 'Oh, darling, you're talking nonsense. You've got nothing against me.'

"She looked at me steadily. She was quite calm. She had even a little smile at the back of her eyes.

" 'I can't marry you. I can't marry anyone. It was absurd of me ever to think I could.'

"I didn't answer at once. She was in a queer state and I thought it better not to insist.

" 'I suppose I can't drag you to the altar by main force,' I said.

"I held out my hand and she gave me hers. I put my arms round her, and she made no attempt to withdraw. She suffered me to kiss her as usual on her cheek.

"Next morning I met the train. For once in a way it was punctual. Tim waved to me as his carriage passed the place where I was standing, and by the time I had walked up he had already jumped out and was handing down his wife. He grasped my hand warmly.

" 'Where's Olive?' he said, with a glance along the platform. 'This is Sally.'

"I shook hands with her and at the same time explained why Olive was not there.

" 'It was frightfully early, wasn't it?' said Mrs. Hardy.

"I told them that the plan was for them to come and have a bit of breakfast at my house and then drive home.

" 'I'd love a bath,' said Mrs. Hardy.

" 'You shall have one,' I said.

"She was really an extremely pretty little thing, very fair, with enormous blue eyes and a lovely little straight nose. Her skin, all milk and roses, was exquisite. A little of the chorus girl type, of course, and you may happen to think that rather namby-pamby, but in that style she was enchanting. We drove to my house, they both had a bath and Tim a shave; I just had two minutes alone with him. He asked me how Olive had taken his marriage. I told him she'd been upset.

" 'I was afraid so,' he said, frowning a little. He gave a short sigh. 'I couldn't do anything else.'

"I didn't understand what he meant. At that moment Mrs. Hardy joined us and slipped her arm through her husband's. He took her hand in his and gently pressed it. He gave her a look that had in it something pleased and humorously affectionate, as though he didn't take her quite seriously, but enjoyed his sense of proprietorship and was proud of her beauty. She really was lovely. She was not at all shy, she asked me to call her Sally before we'd known one another ten minutes, and she was quick in the uptake. Of course, just then she was excited at arriving. She's never been East and everything thrilled her. It was quite obvious that she was head over heels in love with Tim. Her eyes never left him and she hung on his words. We had a jolly breakfast and then we parted. They got into their car to go home and I into mine to go to Lahad. I promised to go straight to the estate from there and in point of fact it was out of my way to pass by my house. I took a change with me. I didn't see why Olive shouldn't like Sally very much, she was frank and gay, and ingenuous; she was extremely young, she couldn't have been more than nineteen, and her wonderful prettiness couldn't fail to appeal to Olive. I was just as glad to have had a reasonable excuse to leave the three of them by themselves for the day, but as I started out from Lahad I had a notion that by the time I arrived they would all be pleased to see me. I drove up to the bungalow and blew my horn two or three times, expecting someone to appear. Not a soul. The place was in total darkness. I was surprised. It was absolutely silent. I couldn't make it out. They must be in. Very odd, I thought. I waited a moment, then got out of the car and walked up the steps. At the top of them I stumbled over something. I swore and bent down to see what it was; it had felt like a body. There was a cry and I saw it was the amah. She shrank back cowering as I touched her and broke into loud wails.

" 'What's the hell's the matter?' I cried, and then I felt a hand on my arm and heard a voice: Tuan, Tuan. I turned and in the darkness recognised Tim's head boy. He began to speak in little frightened gasps. I listened to him with horror. What he told me was unspeakable. I pushed him aside and rushed into the house. The sitting-room was dark. I turned on the light. The first thing I saw was Sally huddled up in an arm-chair. She was startled by my sudden appearance and cried out. I could hardly speak. I asked her if it was true. When she told me it was I felt the room suddenly going round and round me. I had to sit down. As the car that bore Tim and Sally drove up the road that led to the house and Tim sounded the claxon to announce their arrival and the boys and the amah ran out to greet them there was the sound of a shot. They ran to Olive's room and found her lying in front of the looking-glass in a pool of blood. She had shot herself with Tim's revolver.

" 'Is she dead?' I said.

" 'No, they sent for the doctor, and he took her to the hospital.'

"I hardly knew what I was doing. I didn't even trouble to tell Sally where I was going. I got up and staggered to the door. I got into the car and told my seis to drive like hell to the hospital. I rushed in. I asked where she was. They tried to bar my way, but I pushed them aside. I knew where the private rooms were. Someone clung to my arm, but I shook him off. I vaguely understood that the doctor had given instructions that no one was to go into the room. I didn't care about that. There was an orderly at the door; he put out his arm to prevent me from passing. I swore at him and told him to get out of my way. I suppose I made a row, I was beside myself; the door was opened and the doctor came out.

" 'Who's making all this noise?' he said. 'Oh, it's you. What do you want?'

" 'Is she dead?' I asked.

" 'No. But she's unconscious. She never regained consciousness. It's only a matter of an hour or two.'

" 'I want to see her.'

" 'You can't.'

" 'I'm engaged to her.'

" 'You?' he cried, and even at that moment I was aware that he looked at me strangely. 'That's all the more reason.'

"I didn't know what he meant. I was stupid with horror.

" 'Surely you can do something to save her,' I cried.

"He shook his head.

" 'If you saw her you wouldn't wish it,' he said.

"I stared at him aghast. In the silence I heard a man's convulsive sobbing.

" 'Who's that?' I asked.

" 'Her brother.'

"Then I felt a hand on my arm. I looked round and saw it was Mrs. Sergison.

" 'My poor boy,' she said, 'I'm so sorry for you.'

" 'What on earth made her do it?' I groaned.

" 'Come away, my dear,' said Mrs. Sergison. 'You can do no good here.'

" 'No, I must stay,' I said.

" 'Well, go and sit in my room,' said the doctor.

"I was so broken that I let Mrs. Sergison take me by the arm and lead me into the doctor's private room. She made me sit down. I couldn't bring myself to realise that it was true. I thought it was a horrible nightmare from which I must awake. I don't know how long we sat there. Three hours. Four hours. At last the doctor came in.

" 'It's all over,' he said.

"Then I couldn't help myself, I began to cry. I didn't care what they thought of me. I was so frightfully unhappy.

"We buried her next day.

"Mrs. Sergison came back to my house and sat with me for a while. She wanted me to go to the club with her. I hadn't the heart. She was very kind, but I was glad when she left me by myself. I tried to read, but the words meant nothing to me. I felt dead inside. My boy came in and turned on the lights. My head was aching like mad. Then he came back and said that a lady wished to see me. I asked who it was. He wasn't quite sure, but he thought it must be the new wife of the man at Putatan. I couldn't imagine what she wanted. I got up and went to the door. He was right. It was Sally. I asked her to come in. I noticed that she was deathly white. I felt sorry for her. It was a frightful experience for a girl of that age and for a bride a miserable home-coming. She sat down. She was very nervous. I tried to put her at her ease by saying conventional things. She made me very uncomfortable because she stared at me with those enormous blue eyes of hers, and they were simply ghastly with horror. She interrupted me suddenly.

" 'You're the only person here I know,' she said. 'I had to come to you. I want you to get me away from here.'

"I was dumbfounded.

" 'What *do* you mean?' I said.

" 'I don't want you to ask me any questions. I just want you to get me away. At once. I want to go back to England!'

" 'But you can't leave Tim like that just now,' I said. 'My dear, you must pull yourself together. I know it's been awful for you. But think of Tim. I mean, he'll be miserable. If you have any love for him the least you can do is to try and make him a little less unhappy.'

" 'Oh, you don't know,' she cried. 'I can't tell you. It's too horrible. I beseech you to help me. If there's a train to-night let me get on it. If I can only get to Penang I can get a ship. I can't stay in this place another night. I shall go mad.'

"I was absolutely bewildered.

" 'Does Tim know?' I asked her.

" 'I haven't seen Tim since last night. I'll never see him again I'd rather die.'

"I wanted to gain a little time.

" 'But how can you go without your things? Have you got any luggage?'

" 'What does that matter?' she cried impatiently. 'I've got what I want for the journey.'

" 'Have you any money?'

" 'Enough. Is there a train to-night?'

" 'Yes,' I said. 'It's due just after midnight.'

" 'Thank God. Will you arrange everything? Can I stay here till then?'

" 'You're putting me in a frightful position,' I said. 'I don't know what to do for the best. You know, it's an awfully serious step you're taking.'

" 'If you knew everything you'd know it was the only possible thing to do.'

" 'It'll create an awful scandal here. I don't know what people'll say. Have you thought of the effect on Tim?' I was worried and unhappy. 'God knows I don't want to interfere in what isn't my business. But if you want me to help you I ought to know enough to feel justified in doing so. You must tell me what's happened.'

" 'I can't. I can only tell you that I know everything.'

"She hid her face with her hands and shuddered. Then she gave herself a shake as though she were recoiling from some frightful sight.

" 'He had no right to marry me. It was monstrous.'

"And as she spoke her voice rose shrill and piercing. I was afraid she was going to have an attack of hysterics. Her pretty doll-like face was terrified and her eyes stared as though she could never close them again.

" 'Don't you love him any more?' I asked.

" 'After that?'

" 'What will you do if I refuse to help you?' I said.

" 'I suppose there's a clergyman here or a doctor. You can't refuse to take me to one of them.'

" 'How did you get here?'

" 'The head boy drove me. He got a car from somewhere.'

" 'Does Tim know you've gone?'

" 'I left a letter for him.'

" 'He'll know you're here.'

" 'He won't try to stop me. I promise you that. He daren't. For God's sake don't you try either. I tell you I shall go mad if I stay here another night.'

"I sighed. After all she was of an age to decide for herself."

I, the writer of this, hadn't spoken for a long time.

"Did you know what she meant?" I asked Featherstone.

He gave me a long, haggard look.

"There was only one thing she could mean. It was unspeakable. Yes, I knew all right. It explained everything. Poor Olive. Poor sweet. I suppose it was unreasonable of me, at that moment I only felt a horror of that little pretty fair-haired thing with her terrified eyes. I hated her. I didn't say anything for a while. Then I told her I'd do as she wished. She didn't even say thank you. I think she knew what I felt about her. When it was dinner-time I made her eat something and then she asked me if there was a room she could go and lie down in till it was time to go to the station. I showed her into my spare room and left her. I sat in the sitting-room and waited. My God, I don't think the time has ever passed so slowly for me. I thought twelve would never strike. I rang up the station and was told the train wouldn't be in till nearly two. At midnight she came back to the sitting-room and we sat there for an hour and a half. We had nothing to say to one another and we didn't speak. Then I took her to the station and put her on the train."

"Was there an awful scandal?"

Featherstone frowned.

"I don't know. I applied for short leave. After that I was moved to another post. I heard that Tim had sold his estate and bought another. But I didn't know where. It was a shock to me at first when I found him here."

Featherstone, getting up, went over to a table and mixed himself a whisky and soda. In the silence that fell now I heard the monotonous chorus of the croaking frogs. And suddenly the bird that is known as the fever-bird, perched in a tree close to the house, began to call. First, three notes in a descending, chromatic scale, then five, then four. The varying notes of the scale succeeded one another with maddening persistence. One was compelled to listen and to count them, and because one did not know how many there would be it tortured one's nerves.

"Blast that bird," said Featherstone. "That means no sleep for me to-night."

French Joe

IT was Captain Bartlett who told me of him. I do not think that many people have been to Thursday Island. It is in the Torres Straits and is so called because it was discovered on a Thursday by Captain Cook. I went there since they told me in Sydney that it was the last place God ever made. They said there was nothing to see and warned me that I should probably get my throat cut. I had come up from Sydney in a Japanese tramp and they put me ashore in a small boat. It was the middle of the night and there was not a soul on the jetty. One of the sailors who landed my kit told me that if I turned to the left I should presently come to a two-storey building and this was the hotel. The boat pushed off and I was left alone. I do not much like being separated from my luggage, but I like still less to pass the night on a jetty and sleep on hard stones; so I shouldered a bag and set out. It was pitch dark. I seemed to walk much more than a few hundred yards which they had spoken of and was afraid I had missed my way, but at last saw dimly a building which seemed to be important enough to suggest that it might be the hotel. No light showed, but my eyes by now were pretty well accustomed to the darkness and I found a door. I struck a match, but could see no bell. I knocked; there was no reply; I knocked again, with my stick, as loudly as I could, then a window above me was opened and a woman's voice asked me what I wanted.

"I've just got off the *Shika Maru*," I said. "Can I have a room?"

"I'll come down."

I waited a little longer, and the door was opened by a woman in a red flannel dressing-gown. Her hair was hanging over her shoulders in long black wisps. In her hand she held a paraffin lamp. She greeted me warmly, a little stoutish woman, with keen eyes and a nose suspiciously red, and bade me come in. She took me upstairs and showed me a room.

"Now you sit down," she said, "and I'll make up the bed before you can say Jack Robinson. What will you 'ave? A drop of whisky would do you good, I should think. You won't want to be washing at this time of night, I'll bring you a towel in the morning."

And while she made the bed she asked me who I was and what I had come to Thursday Island for. She could see I wasn't a sea-faring man—all the pilots came to this hotel and had done for twenty years—and she didn't know what business could have brought me. I wasn't that fellow as was coming to inspect the Customs, was I? She'd 'eard they were sending someone from Sydney. I asked her if there were any pilots staying there then. Yes, there was one, Captain Bartlett, did I know him? A queer fish he was and no mistake. Hadn't got a hair on his head, but the way he could put his liquor away, well, it was a caution. There, the bed was ready and she expected I'd sleep like a top and one thing she could say was, the sheets were clean. She lit the end of a candle and bade me good-night.

Captain Bartlett certainly was a queer fish, but he is of no moment to my present purpose; I made his acquaintance at dinner next day —before I left Thursday Island I had eaten turtle soup so often that I have ceased to look upon it as a luxury—and it was because in the course of conversation I mentioned that I spoke French that he asked me to go and see French Joe.

"It'll be a treat to the old fellow to talk his own lingo for a bit. He's ninety-three, you know."

For the last two years, not because he was ill but because he was old and destitute, he had lived in the hospital and it was here that I visited him. He was lying in bed, in flannel pyjamas much too large for him, a little shrivelled old man with vivacious eyes, a short white beard and bushy black eyebrows. He was glad to speak French with me, which he spoke with the marked accent of his native isle, for he was a Corsican, but he had dwelt so many years among English-speaking people that he no longer spoke his mother tongue with accuracy. He used English words as though they were French, making verbs of them with French terminations. He talked very quickly, with broad gestures, and his voice for the most part was clear and strong; but now and then it seemed suddenly to fade away so that it sounded as though he spoke from the grave. The hushed and hollow sound gave me an eerie feeling. Indeed I could not look upon him still as of this world. His real name was Joseph de Paoli. He was a nobleman and a gentleman. He was of the same family as the general we have all read of in Boswell's *Johnson*, but he showed no interest in his famous ancestor.

"We have had so many generals in our family," he said. "You know, of course, that Napoleon Bonaparte was a connection of mine. No, I have never read Boswell. I have not read books. I have lived."

He had entered the French army in 1851. Seventy-five years ago. It is terrifying. As a lieutenant of artillery ("like my cousin Bonaparte," he said) he had fought the Russians in the Crimea and as a captain the Prussians in 1870. He showed me a scar on his bald pate from an Uhlan's lance and then with a dramatic gesture told how he had thrust his sword in the Uhlan's body with such violence that he could not withdraw it. The Uhlan fell dead and the sword remained in the body. But the Empire perished and he joined the communists. For six weeks he fought against the government troops under Monsieur Thiers. To me Thiers is but a shadowy figure, and it was startling and even a trifle comic to hear French Joe speak with passionate hatred of a man who has been dead for half a century. His voice rose into a shrill scream as he repeated the insults, Oriental in their imagery, which in the council he had flung at the head of this mediocre statesman. French Joe was tried and sentenced to five years in New Caledonia.

"They should have shot me," he said, "but, dirty cowards, they dared not."

Then came the long journey in a sailing vessel, and the antipodes, and his wrath flamed out again when he spoke of the indignity thrust upon him, a political prisoner, when they herded him with vulgar criminals. The ship put in at Melbourne and one of the officers, a fellow-Corsican, enabled him to slip over the side. He swam ashore and, taking his friend's advice, went straight to the police-station. No one there could understand a word he said, but an interpreter was sent for, his dripping papers were examined and he was told that so long as he did not set foot on a French ship he was safe.

"Freedom," he cried to me. "Freedom."

Then came a long series of adventures. He cooked, taught French, swept streets, worked in the gold mines, tramped, starved, and at last found his way to New Guinea. Here he underwent the most astonishing of his experiences, for drifting into the savage interior, and they are cannibals there still, after a hundred desperate adventures and hair-breadth escapes he made himself king of some wild tribe.

"Look at me, my friend," he said, "I who lie here on a hospital bed, the object of charity, have been monarch of all I surveyed. Yes, it is something to say that I have been a king."

But eventually he came into collision with the British and his sovereignty passed from him. He fled the country and started life once more. It is clear that he was a fellow of resource for eventually he came to own a fleet of pearling luggers on Thursday Island. It looked as though at last he had reached a haven of peace and, an elderly man now, he looked forward to a prosperous and even respectable old age. A hurricane destroyed his boats and ruin fell upon him. He never recovered. He was too old to make a fresh start, and since then had earned as best he could a precarious livelihood till at last, beaten, he had accepted the hospital's kindly shelter.

"But why did you not go back to France or Corsica? An amnesty was granted to the communists a quarter of a century ago."

"What are France and Corsica to me after fifty years? A cousin of mine seized my land. We Corsicans never forget and never forgive. If I had gone back I should have had to kill him. He had his children."

"Funny old French Joe," smiled the hospital nurse who stood at the end of his bed.

"At all events you have had a fine life," I said.

"Never. Never. I have had a frightful life. Misfortune has followed me wherever I turned my steps and look at me now: I am rotten, fit for nothing but the grave. I thank God that I had no children to inherit the curse that is upon me."

"Why, Joe, I thought you didn't believe in God," said the nurse.

"It is true. I am a sceptic. I have never seen a sign that there is in the scheme of things an intelligent purpose. If the universe is the contrivance of some being, that being can only be a criminal imbecile." He shrugged his shoulders. "Anyhow, I have not got much longer in this filthy world and then I shall go and see for myself what is the real truth of the whole business."

The nurse told me it was time to leave the old man and I took his hand to bid him farewell. I asked him if there was anything I could do for him.

"I want nothing," he said. "I only want to die." His black shining eyes twinkled. "But meanwhile I should be grateful for a packet of cigarettes."

German Harry

I was in Thursday Island and I wanted very much to go to New Guinea. Now the only way in which I could do this was by getting a pearling lugger to take me across the Arafura Sea. The pearl fishery at that time was in a bad way and a flock of neat little craft lay anchored in the harbour. I found a skipper with nothing much to do (the journey to Merauke and back could hardly take him less than a month) and with him I made the necessary arrangements. He engaged four Torres Straits islanders as crew (the boat was but nineteen tons) and we ransacked the local store for canned goods. A day or two before I sailed a man who owned a number of pearlers came to me and asked whether on my way I would stop at the island of Trebucket and leave a sack of flour, another of rice, and some magazines for the hermit who lived there.

I pricked up my ears. It appeared that the hermit had lived by himself on this remote and tiny island for thirty years, and when opportunity occurred provisions were sent to him by kindly souls. He said that he was a Dane, but in the Torres Straits he was known as German Harry. His history went back a long way. Thirty years before, he had been an able seaman on a sailing vessel that was wrecked in those treacherous waters. Two boats managed to get away and eventually hit upon the desert island of Trebucket. This is well out of the line of traffic and it was three years before any ship sighted the castaways. Sixteen men had landed on the island, but when at last a schooner, driven from her course by stress of weather, put in for shelter, no more than five were left. When the storm abated the skipper took four of these on board and eventually landed them at Sydney. German Harry refused to go with them. He said that during those three years he had seen such terrible things that he had a horror of his fellow-men and wished never to live with them again. He would say no more. He was absolutely fixed in his determination to stay, entirely by himself, in that lonely place. Though now and then opportunity had been given him to leave he had never taken it.

A strange man and a strange story. I learned more about him as we sailed across the desolate sea. The Torres Straits are peppered with islands and at night we anchored on the lee of one or other of them. Of late new pearling grounds have been discovered near Trebucket and in the autumn pearlers, visiting it now and then, have given German Harry various necessities so that he has been able to make himself sufficiently comfortable. They bring him papers, bags of flour and rice, and canned meats. He has a whale boat and used to go fishing in it, but now he is no longer strong enough to manage its unwieldy bulk. There is abundant pearl shell on the reef that surrounds his island and this he used to collect and sell to the pearlers for tobacco, and sometimes he found a good pearl for which he got a considerable sum. It is believed that he has, hidden away somewhere, a collection of magnificent pearls. During the war no pearlers came out and for years he never saw a living soul. For all he knew, a terrible epidemic had killed off the entire human race and he was the only man alive. He was asked later what he thought.

"I thought something had happened," he said.

He ran out of matches and was afraid that his fire would go out, so he only slept in snatches, putting wood on his fire from time to time all day and all night. He came to the end of his provisions and lived on chickens, fish and coconuts. Sometimes he got a turtle.

During the last four months of the year there may be two or three pearlers about and not infrequently after the day's work they will row in and spend an evening with him. They try to make him drunk and then they ask him what happened during those three years after the two boat-loads came to the island. How was it that sixteen landed and at the end of that time only five were left? He never says a word. Drunk or sober he is equally silent on that subject and if they insist grows angry and leaves them.

I forget if it was four or five days before we sighted the hermit's little kingdom. We had been driven by bad weather to take shelter and had spent a couple of days at an island on the way. Trebucket is a low island, perhaps a mile round, covered with coconuts, just raised above the level of the sea and surrounded by a reef so that it can be approached only on one side. There is no opening in the reef and the lugger had to anchor a mile from the shore. We got into a dinghy with the provisions. It was a stiff pull and even within the reef the sea was choppy. I saw the little hut, sheltered by trees, in which German Harry lived, and as we approached he sauntered down slowly to the water's edge. We shouted a greeting, but he did not answer. He was a man of over seventy, very bald, hatchet-faced, with a grey beard, and he walked with a roll so that you could never have taken him for anything but a sea-faring man. His sun-burn made his blue eyes look very pale and they were surrounded by wrinkles as though for long years he had spent interminable hours scanning the vacant sea. He wore dungarees and a singlet, patched, but neat and clean. The house to which he presently led us consisted of a single room with a roof of corrugated iron. There was a bed in it, some rough stools which he himself had made, a table, and his various household utensils. Under a tree in front of it was a table and a bench. Behind was an enclosed run for his chickens.

I cannot say that he was pleased to see us. He accepted our gifts as a right, without thanks, and grumbled a little because something or other he needed had not been brought. He was silent and morose. He was not interested in the news we had to give him, for the outside world was no concern of his: the only thing he cared about was his island. He looked upon it with a jealous, proprietary right; he called it "my health resort" and he feared that the coconuts that covered it would tempt some enterprising trader. He looked at me with suspicion. He was sombrely curious to know what I was doing in these seas. He used words with difficulty, talking to himself rather than to us, and it was a little uncanny to hear him mumble away as though we were not there. But he was moved when my skipper told him that an old man of his own age whom he had known for a long time was dead.

"Old Charlie dead—that's too bad. Old Charlie dead."

He repeated it over and over again. I asked him if he read.

"Not much," he answered indifferently.

He seemed to be occupied with nothing but his food, his dogs and his chickens. If what they tell us in books were true his long communion with nature and the sea should have taught him many subtle secrets. It hadn't. He was a savage. He was nothing but a narrow, ignorant and cantankerous sea-faring man. As I looked at the wrinkled, mean old face I wondered what was the story of those three dreadful years that had made him welcome this long imprisonment. I sought to see behind those pale blue eyes of his what secrets they were that he would carry to his grave. And then I foresaw the end. One day a pearl fisher would land on the island and German Harry would not be waiting for him, silent and suspicious, at the water's edge. He would go up to the hut and there, lying on the bed, unrecognisable, he would see all that remained of what had once been a man. Perhaps then he would hunt high and low for the great mass of pearls that has haunted the fancy of so many adventurers. But I do not believe he would find it: German Harry would have seen to it that none should discover the treasure, and the pearls would rot in their hiding place. Then the pearl fisher would go back into his dinghy and the island once more be deserted of man.

The Four Dutchmen

THE Van Dorth Hotel at Singapore was far from grand. The bed-rooms were dingy and the mosquito nets patched and darned; the bath-houses, all in a row and detached from the bedrooms, were dank and smelly. But it had character. The people who stayed there, masters of tramps whose round ended at Singapore, mining engineers out of a job and planters taking a holiday, to my mind bore a more romantic air than the smart folk, globe-trotters, government officials and their wives, wealthy merchants, who gave luncheon-parties at the Europe and played golf and danced and were fashionable. The Van Dorth had a billiard-room, with a table with a threadbare cloth, where ships' engineers and clerks in insurance offices played snooker. The dining-room was large and bare and silent. Dutch families on the way to Sumatra ate solidly through their dinner without exchanging a word with one another, and single gentlemen on a business trip from Batavia devoured a copious meal while they intently read their paper. On two days a week there was rijstafel and then a few residents of Singapore who had a fancy for this dish came for tiffin. The Van Dorth Hotel should have been a depressing place, but somehow it wasn't; its quaintness saved it. It had a faint aroma of something strange and half-forgotten. There was a scrap of garden facing the street where you could sit in the shade of trees and drink cold beer. In that crowded and busy city, though motors whizzed past and rickshaws passed continuously, the coolies' feet pattering on the road and their bells ringing, it had the remote peacefulness of a corner of Holland. It was the third time I had stayed at the Van Dorth. I had been told about it first by the skipper of a Dutch tramp, the S.S. *Utrecht*, on which I had travelled from Merauke in New Guinea to Macassar. The journey took the best part of a month, since the ship stopped at a number of islands in the Malay Archipelago, the Aru and the Kei Islands, Banda-Neira, Amboina and others of which I have even forgotten the names, sometimes for an hour or two, sometimes for a day, to take on or discharge cargo. It was a charming, monotonous and diverting trip. When we dropped anchor the agent came out in his launch, and generally the Dutch Resident, and we gathered on deck under the awning and the captain ordered beer. The news of the island was exchanged for the news of the world. We brought papers and mail. If we were staying long enough the Resident asked us to dinner and, leaving the ship in charge of the second officer, we all (the captain, the chief officer, the engineer, the super-cargo and I) piled into the launch and went ashore. We spent a merry evening. These little islands, one so like another, allured my fancy just because I knew that I should never see them again. It made them strangely unreal, and as we sailed away and they vanished into the sea and sky it was only by an effort of the imagina-tion that I could persuade myself that they did not with my last glimpse of them cease to exist.

But there was nothing illusive, mysterious or fantastic about the captain, the chief officer, the chief engineer and the supercargo. Their solidity was amazing. They were the four fattest men I ever saw. At first I had great difficulty in telling them apart, for though one, the supercargo, was dark and the others were fair, they looked astonishingly alike. They were all big, with large round bare red faces, with large fat arms and large fat legs and large fat bellies. When they went ashore they buttoned up their stengah-shifters and then their great double chins bulged over the collars and they looked as though they would choke. But generally they wore them un-buttoned. They sweated freely and wiped their shiny faces with bandanas and vigorously fanned themselves with palm-leaf fans.

It was a treat to see them at tiffin. Their appetites were enormous. They had rijstafel every day, and each seemed to vie with the other how high he could pile his plate. They loved it hot and strong.

"In dis country you can't eat a ting onless it's tasty," said the skipper.

"De only way to keep yourself up in dis country is to eat hearty," said the chief.

They were the greatest friends, all four of them; they were like schoolboys together, playing absurd little pranks with one another. They knew each other's jokes by heart and no sooner did one of them start the familiar lines than he would splutter with laughter so violently, the heavy shaking laughter of the fat man, that he could not go on, and then the others began to laugh too. They rolled about in their chairs, and grew redder and redder, hotter and hotter, till the skipper shouted for beer, and each, gasping but happy, drank his bottle in one enchanted draught. They had been on this run together for five years and when, a little time before, the chief officer had been offered a ship of his own he refused it. He would not leave his companions. They had made up their minds that when the first of them retired they would all retire.

"All friends and a good ship. Good grub and good beer. Vot can a sensible man vant more?"

At first they were a little stand-offish with me. Although the ship had accommodation for half a dozen passengers, they did not often get any, and never one whom they did not know. I was a stranger and a foreigner. They liked their bit of fun and did not want anyone to interfere with it. But they were all of them very fond of bridge, and on occasion the chief and the engineer had duties that prevented one or the other from playing. They were willing to put up with me when they discovered that I was ready to make a fourth whenever I was wanted. Their bridge was as incredibly fantastic as they were. They played for infinitesimal stakes, five cents a hundred: they did not want to win one another's money, they said, it was the game they liked. But what a game! Each was wildly determined to play the hand and hardly one was dealt without at least a small slam being declared. The rule was that if you could get a peep at somebody else's cards you did and if you could get away with a revoke you told your partner when there was no danger it could be claimed and you both roared with laughter till the tears rolled down your fat cheeks. But if your partner had insisted on taking the bid away from you and had called a grand slam on five spades to the queen, whereas you were positive on your seven little diamonds you could have made it easily, you could always score him off by redoubling without a trick in your hand. He went down two or three thousand and the glasses on the table danced with the laughter that shook your opponents.

I could never remember their difficult Dutch names, but knowing them anonymously as it were, only by the duties they performed, as one knows the characters Pantaloon, Harlequin and Punchinello, of the old Italian comedy, added grotesquely to their drollery. The mere sight of them, all four together, set you laughing, and I think they got a good deal of amusement from the astonishment they caused in strangers. They boasted that they were the four most famous Dutchmen in the East Indies. To me not the least comic part of them was their serious side. Sometimes late at night, when they had given up all pretence of still wearing their uniforms, and one or the other of them lay by my side on a long chair in a pyjama jacket and a sarong, he would grow sentimental. The chief engineer, due to retire soon, was meditating marriage with a widow whom he had met when last he was home and spending the rest of his life in a little town with old red-brick houses on the shores of the Zuyder Zee. But the captain was very susceptible to the charms of the native girls and his thick English became almost unintelligible from emotion when he described to me the effect they had on him. One of these days he would buy himself a house on the hills in Java and marry a pretty little Javanese. They were so small and so gentle and they made no noise, and he would dress her in silk sarongs and give her gold chains to wear round her neck and gold bangles to put on her arms. But the chief mocked him.

"Silly all dat is. Silly. She goes mit all your friends and de house boys and everybody. By de time you retire, my dear, vot you'll vant vill be a nurse, not a vife."

"Me?" cried the skipper. "I shall want a vife ven I'm eighty!"

He had picked up a little thing last time the ship was at Macassar and as we approached that port he began to be all of a flutter. The chief officer shrugged fat and indulgent shoulders. The captain was always losing his head over one brazen hussy after another, but his passion never survived the interval between one stop at a port and the next, and then the chief was called in to smooth out the difficulties that ensued. And so it would be this time.

"De old man suffers from fatty degeneration of de heart. But so long as I'm dere to look after him not much harm comes of it. He vastes his money and dat's a pity, but as long as he's got it to vaste, why shouldn't he?"

The chief officer had a philosophic soul.

At Macassar then I disembarked, and bade farewell to my four fat friends.

"Make another journey with us," they said. "Come back next year or the year after. You'll find us all here just the same as ever."

A good many months had passed since then and I had wandered through more than one strange land. I had been to Bali and Java and Sumatra; I had been to Cambodia and Annam; and now, feeling as though I were home again, I sat in the garden of the Van Dorth Hotel. It was cool in the very early morning and having had breakfast I was looking at back numbers of the *Straits Times* to find out what had been happening in the world since last I had been within reach of papers. Nothing very much. Suddenly my eyes caught a headline: *The* Utrecht *Tragedy. Supercargo and Chief Engineer. Not Guilty.* I read the paragraph carelessly and then I sat up. The *Utrecht* was the ship of my four fat Dutchmen and apparently the supercargo and the chief engineer had been on trial for murder. It couldn't be my two fat friends. The names were given, but the names meant nothing to me. The trial had taken place in Batavia. No details were given in this paragraph; it was only a brief announcement that after the judges had considered the speeches of the prosecution and of the defence their verdict was as stated. I was astounded. It was incredible that the men I knew could have committed a murder. I could not find out who had been murdered. I looked through back numbers of the paper. Nothing.

I got up and went to the manager of the hotel, a genial Dutchman, who spoke admirable English, and showed him the paragraph. "That's the ship I sailed on. I was in her for nearly a month. Surely these fellows aren't the men I knew. The men I knew were enormously fat."

"Yes, that's right," he answered. "They were celebrated all through the Dutch East Indies, the four fattest men in the service. It's been a terrible thing. It made a great sensation. And they were friends. I knew them all. The best fellows in the world."

"But what happened?"

He told me the story and answered my horrified questions. But there were things I wanted to know that he couldn't tell me. It was all confused. It was unbelievable. What actually had happened was only conjecture. Then someone claimed the manager's attention and I went back to the garden. It was getting hot now and I went up to my room. I was strangely shattered.

It appeared that on one of the trips the captain took with him a Malay girl that he had been carrying on with and I wondered if it was the one he had been so eager to see when I was on board. The other three had been against her coming—what did they want with a woman in the ship? it would spoil everything—but the captain insisted and she came. I think they were all jealous of her. On that journey they didn't have the fun they generally had. When they wanted to play bridge the skipper was dallying with the girl in his cabin; when they touched at a port and went ashore the time seemed long to him till he could get back to her. He was crazy about her. It was the end of all their larks. The chief officer was more bitter against her than anybody: he was the captain's particular chum, they had been shipmates ever since they first came out from Holland; more than once high words passed between them on the subject of the captain's infatuation. Presently those old friends spoke to one another only when their duties demanded it. It was the end of the good fellowship that had so long obtained between the four fat men. Things went from bad to worse. There was a feeling among the junior officers that something untoward was pending. Uneasiness. Tension. Then one night the ship was aroused by the sound of a shot and the screams of the Malay girl. The supercargo and the chief engineer tumbled out of their bunks and they found the captain, a revolver in his hand, at the door of the chief officer's cabin. He pushed past them and went on deck. They entered and found the chief officer dead and the girl cowering behind the door. The captain had found them in bed together and had killed the chief. How he had discovered what was going on didn't seem to be known, nor what was the meaning of the intrigue. Had the chief induced the girl to come to his cabin in order to get back on the captain, or had she, knowing his ill-will and anxious to placate him, lured him to become her lover? It was a mystery that would never be solved. A dozen possible explanations flashed across my mind. While the engineer and the supercargo were in the cabin, horror-struck at the sight before them, another shot was heard. They knew at once what had happened. They rushed up the companion. The captain had gone to his cabin and blown his brains out. Then the story grew dark and enigmatic. Next morning the Malay girl was nowhere to be found and when the second officer, who had taken command of the ship, reported this to the supercargo, the supercargo said: "She's probably jumped overboard. It's the best thing she could have done. Good riddance to bad rubbish." But one of the sailors on the watch, just before dawn, had seen the supercargo and the chief engineer carry something up on deck, a bulky package, about the size of a native woman, look about them to see that they were unobserved, and drop it overboard; and it was said all over the ship that these two to avenge their friends had sought the girl out in her cabin and strangled her and flung her body into the sea. When the ship arrived at Macassar they were arrested and taken to Batavia to be tried for murder. The evidence was flimsy and they were acquitted. But all through the East Indies they knew that the supercargo and the chief engineer had executed justice on the trollop who had caused the death of the two men they loved.

And thus ended the comic and celebrated friendship of the four fat Dutchmen.

The Back of Beyond

GEORGE MOON was sitting in his office. His work was finished, and he lingered there because he hadn't the heart to go down to the club. It was getting on towards tiffin time, and there would be a good many fellows hanging about the bar. Two or three of them would offer him a drink. He could not face their heartiness. Some he had known for thirty years. They had bored him, and on the whole he disliked them, but now that he was seeing them for the last time it gave him a pang. To-night they were giving him a farewell dinner. Everyone would be there and they were presenting him with a silver tea-service that he did not in the least want. They would make speeches in which they would refer eulogistically to his work in the colony, express their regret at his departure and wish him long life to enjoy his well-earned leisure. He would reply suitably. He had prepared a speech in which he surveyed the changes that had taken place in the F.M.S. since first, a raw cadet, he had landed at Singapore. He would thank them for their loyal co-operation with him during the term which it had been his privilege to serve as Resident at Timbang Belud, and draw a glowing picture of the future that awaited the country as a whole and Timbang Belud in particular. He would remind them that he had known it as a poverty-stricken village with a few Chinese shops and left it now a prosperous town with paved streets down which ran trams, with stone houses, a rich Chinese settlement and a club-house second in splendour only to that of Singapore. They would sing "For he's a jolly good fellow" and "Auld Lang Syne". Then they would dance and a good many of the younger men would get drunk. The Malays had already given him a farewell party and the Chinese an interminable feast. To-morrow a vast concourse would see him off at the station and that would be the end of him. He wondered what they would say of him. The Malays and the Chinese would say that he had been stern, but acknowledge that he had been just. The planters had not liked him. They thought him hard because he would not let them ride roughshod over their labour. His subordinates had feared him. He drove them. He had no patience with slackness or inefficiency. He had never spared himself and saw no reason why he should spare others. They thought him inhuman. It was true that there was nothing come-hither in him. He could not throw off his official position when he went to the club and laugh at bawdy stories, chaff and be chaffed. He was conscious that his arrival cast a gloom, and to play bridge with him (he liked to play every day from six to eight) was looked upon as a privilege rather than an entertainment. When at some other table a young men's four as the evening wore on grew hilarious, he caught glances thrown in his direction and sometimes an older member would stroll up to the noisy ones and in an undertone advise them to be quiet. George Moon sighed a little. From an official standpoint his career had been a success, he had been the youngest Resident ever appointed in the F.M.S., and for exceptional services a C.M.G. had been conferred upon him; but from the human it had perhaps been otherwise. He had earned respect, respect for his ability, industry and trustworthiness, but he was too clear-sighted to think for a moment that he had inspired affection. No one would regret him. In a few months he would be forgotten.

He smiled grimly. He was not sentimental. He had enjoyed his authority, and it gave him an austere satisfaction to know that he had kept everyone up to the mark. It did not displease him to think that he had been feared rather than loved. He saw his life as a problem in higher mathematics, the working-out of which had required intense application of all his powers, but of which the result had not the least practical consequence. Its interest lay in its intricacy and its beauty in its solution. But like pure beauty it led nowhither. His future was blank. He was fifty-five, and full of energy, and to himself his mind seemed as alert as ever, his experience of men and affairs was wide: all that remained to him was to settle down in a country town in England or in a cheap part of the Riviera and play bridge with elderly ladies and golf with retired colonels. He had met, when on leave, old chiefs of his, and had observed with what difficulty they adapted themselves to the change in their circumstances. They had looked forward to the freedom that would be theirs when they retired and had pictured the charming uses to which they would put their leisure. Mirage. It was not very pleasant to be obscure after having dwelt in a spacious Residency, to make do with a couple of maids when you had been accustomed to the service of half a dozen Chinese boys and, above all, it was not pleasant to realise that you did not matter a row of beans to anyone when you had grown used to the delicate flattery of knowing that a word of praise could delight and a frown humiliate all sorts and conditions of men.

George Moon stretched out his hand and helped himself to a cigarette from the box on his desk. As he did so he noticed all the little lines on the back of his hand and the thinness of his shrivelled fingers. He frowned with distaste. It was the hand of an old man. There was in his office a Chinese mirror-picture that he had bought long ago and that he was leaving behind. He got up and looked at himself in it. He saw a thin yellow face, wrinkled and tight-lipped, thin grey hair and grey tired eyes. He was tallish, very spare, with narrow shoulders, and he held himself erect. He had always played polo and even now could beat most of the younger men at tennis. When you talked to him he kept his eyes fixed on your face, listening attentively, but his expression did not change, and you had no notion what effect your words had on him. Perhaps he did not realise how disconcerting this was. He seldom smiled.

An orderly came in with a name written on a chit. George Moon looked at it and told him to show the visitor in. He sat down once more in his chair and looked with his cold eyes at the door through which in a moment the visitor would come. It was Tom Saffary, and he wondered what he wanted. Presumably something to do with the festivity that night. It had amused him to hear that Tom Saffary was the head of the committee that had organised it, for their relations during the last year had been far from cordial. Saffary was a planter and one of his Tamil overseers had lodged a complaint against him for assault. The Tamil had been grossly insolent to him and Saffary had given him a thrashing. George Moon realised that the provocation was great, but he had always set his face against the planters taking the law in their own hands, and when the case was tried he sentenced Saffary to a fine. But when the court rose, to show that there was no ill-feeling he asked Saffary to luncheon: Saffary, resentful of what he thought an unmerited affront, curtly refused and since then had declined to have any social relations with the Resident. He answered when George Moon, casually, but resolved not to be affronted, spoke to him; but would neither play bridge nor tennis with him. He was manager of the largest rubber estate in the district, and George Moon asked himself sardonically whether he had arranged the dinner and collected subscriptions for the presentation because he thought his dignity required it or whether, now that his Resident was leaving, it appealed to his sentimentality to make a noble gesture. It tickled George Moon's frigid sense of humour to think that it would fall to Tom Saffary to make the principal speech of the evening, in which he would enlarge upon the departing Resident's admirable qualities and voice the community's regret at their irreparable loss.

Tom Saffary was ushered in. The Resident rose from his chair, shook hands with him and thinly smiled.

"How do you do? Sit down. Won't you have a cigarette?"

"How do you do?"

Saffary took the chair to which the Resident motioned him, and the Resident waited for him to state his business. He had a notion that his visitor was embarrassed. He was a big, burly, stout fellow, with a red face and a double chin, curly black hair and blue eyes. He was a fine figure of a man, strong as a horse, but it was plain that he did himself too well. He drank a good deal and ate too heartily. But he was a good business man and a hard worker. He ran his estate efficiently. He was popular in the community. He was generally known as a good chap. He was free with his money and ready to lend a helping hand to anyone in distress. It occurred to the Resident that Saffary had come in order before the dinner to compose the difference between them. The emotion that might have occasioned such a desire excited in the Resident's sensibility a very faint, good-humoured contempt. He had no enemies because individuals did not mean enough to him for him to hate any of them, but if he had, he thought, he would have hated them to the end.

"I dare say you're a bit surprised to see me here this morning, and I expect, as it's your last day and all that, you're pretty busy."

George Moon did not answer, and the other went on.

"I've come on rather an awkward business. The fact is that my wife and I won't be able to come to the dinner to-night, and after that unpleasantness we had together last year I thought it only right to come and tell you that it has nothing to do with that. I think you treated me very harshly; it's not the money I minded, it was the indignity, but bygones are bygones. Now that you're leaving I don't want you to think that I bear any more ill-feeling towards you."

"I realised that when I heard that you were chiefly responsible for the send-off you're giving me," answered the Resident civilly. "I'm sorry that you won't be able to come to-night."

"I'm sorry, too. It's on account of Knobby Clarke's death." Saffary hesitated for a moment. "My wife and I were very much upset by it."

"It was very sad. He was a great friend of yours, wasn't he?"

"He was the greatest friend I had in the colony."

Tears shone in Tom Saffary's eyes. Fat men are very emotional, thought George Moon.

"I quite understand that in that case you should have no heart for what looks like being a rather uproarious party," he said kindly. "Have you heard anything of the circumstances?"

"No, nothing but what appeared in the paper."

"He seemed all right when he left here."

"As far as I know he'd never had a day's illness in his life."

"Heart, I suppose. How old was he?"

"Same age as me. Thirty-eight."

"That's young to die."

Knobby Clarke was a planter and the estate he managed was next door to Saffary's. George Moon had liked him. He was a rather ugly man, sandy, with high cheek-bones and hollow temples, large pale eyes in deep sockets and a big mouth. But he had an attractive smile and an easy manner. He was amusing and could tell a good story. He had a careless good-humour that people found pleasing. He played games well. He was no fool. George Moon would have said he was somewhat colourless. In the course of his career he had known a good many men like him. They came and went. A fortnight before, he had left for England on leave and the Resident knew that the Saffarys had given a large dinner-party on his last night. He was married and his wife of course went with him.

"I'm sorry for her," said George Moon. "It must have been a terrible blow. He was buried at sea, wasn't he?"

"Yes. That's what it said in the paper."

The news had reached Timbang the night before. The Singapore papers arrived at six, just as people were getting to the club, and a good many men waited to play bridge or billiards till they had had a glance at them. Suddenly one fellow had called out:

"I say, do you see this? Knobby's dead."

"Knobby who? Not Knobby Clarke?"

There was a three-line paragraph in a column of general intelligence.

"*Messrs. Star, Mosley & Co. have received a cable informing them that Mr. Harold Clarke of Timbang Batu died suddenly on his way home and was buried at sea.*"

A man came up and took the paper from the speaker's hand, and incredulously read the note for himself. Another peered over his shoulder. Such as happened to be reading the paper turned to the page in question and read the three indifferent lines.

"By George," cried one.

"I say, what tough luck," said another.

"He was as fit as a fiddle when he left here."

A shiver of dismay pierced those hearty, jovial, careless men, and each one for a moment remembered that he too was mortal. Other members came in and as they entered, braced by the thought of the six o'clock drink, and eager to meet their friends, they were met by the grim tidings.

"I say, have you heard? Poor Knobby Clarke's dead."

"No? I say, how awful!"

"Rotten luck, isn't it?"

"Rotten."

"Damned good sort."

"One of the best."

"It gave me quite a turn when I saw it in the paper just by chance."

"I don't wonder."

One man with the paper in his hand went into the billiard-room to break the news. They were playing off the handicap for the Prince of Wales's Cup. That august personage had presented it to the club on the occasion of his visit to Timbang Belud. Tom Saffary was playing against a man called Douglas, and the Resident, who had been beaten in the previous round, was seated with about a dozen others watching the game. The marker was monotonously calling out the score. The newcomer waited for Saffary to finish his break and then called out to him.

"I say, Tom, Knobby's dead."

"Knobby? It's not true."

The other handed him the paper. Three or four gathered round to read with him.

"Good God!"

There was a moment's awed silence. The paper was passed from hand to hand. It was odd that none seemed willing to believe till he saw it for himself in black and white.

"Oh, I am sorry."

"I say, it's awful for his wife," said Tom Saffary. "She was going to have a baby. My poor missus'll be upset."

"Why, it's only a fortnight since he left here."

"He was all right then."

"In the pink."

Saffary, his fat red face sagging a little, went over to a table and, seizing his glass, drank deeply.

"Look here, Tom," said his opponent, "would you like to call the game off?"

"Can't very well do that." Saffary's eye sought the score board and he saw that he was ahead. "No, let's finish. Then I'll go home and break it to Violet."

Douglas had his shot and made fourteen. Tom Saffary missed an easy in-off, but left nothing. Douglas played again, but did not score and again Saffary missed a shot that ordinarily he could have been sure of. He frowned a little. He knew his friends had betted on him pretty heavily and he did not like the idea of failing them. Douglas made twenty-two. Saffary emptied his glass and by an effort of will that was quite patent to the sympathetic onlookers settled down to concentrate on the game. He made a break of eighteen and when he just failed to do a long Jenny they gave him a round of applause. He was sure of himself now and began to score quickly. Douglas was playing well too, and the match grew exciting to watch. The few minutes during which Saffary's attention wandered had allowed his opponent to catch up with him, and now it was anybody's game.

"Spot two hundred and thirty-five," called the Malay, in his queer clipped English. "Plain two hundred and twenty-eight. Spot to play."

Douglas made eight, and then Saffary, who was plain, drew up to two hundred and forty. He left his opponent a double balk. Douglas hit neither ball, and so gave Saffary another point.

"Spot two hundred and forty-three," called the marker. "Plain two hundred and forty-one. Plain to play."

Saffary played three beautiful shots off the red and finished the game.

"A popular victory," the bystanders cried.

"Congratulations, old man," said Douglas.

"Boy," called Saffary, "ask these gentlemen what they'll have. Poor old Knobby."

He sighed heavily. The drinks were brought and Saffary signed the chit. Then he said he'd be getting along. Two others had already begun to play.

"Sporting of him to go on like that," said someone when the door was closed on Saffary.

"Yes, it shows grit."

"For a while I thought his game had gone all to pieces."

"He pulled himself together in grand style. He knew there were a lot of bets on him. He didn't want to let his backers down."

"Of course it's a shock, a thing like that."

"They were great pals. I wonder what he died of."

"Good shot, sir."

George Moon, remembering this scene, thought it strange that Tom Saffary, who on hearing of his friend's death had shown such self-control, should now apparently take it so hard. It might be that just as in the war a man when hit often did not know it till some time afterwards, Saffary had not realised how great a blow to him Harold Clarke's death was till he had had time to think it over. It seemed to him, however, more probable that Saffary, left to himself, would have carried on as usual, seeking sympathy for his loss in the company of his fellows, but that his wife's conventional sense of propriety had insisted that it would be bad form to go to a party when the grief they were suffering from made it only decent for them to eschew for a little festive gatherings. Violet Saffary was a nice little woman, three or four years younger than her husband; not very pretty, but pleasant to look at and always becomingly dressed; amiable, ladylike and unassuming. In the days when he had been on friendly terms with the Saffarys the Resident had from time to time dined with them. He had found her agreeable, but not very amusing. They had never talked but of commonplace things. Of late he had seen little of her. When they chanced to meet she always gave him a friendly smile, and on occasion he said one or two civil words to her. But it was only by an effort of memory that he distinguished her from half a dozen of the other ladies in the community whom his official position brought him in contact with.

Saffary had presumably said what he had come to say and the Resident wondered why he did not get up and go. He sat heaped up in his chair oddly, so that it gave you the feeling that his skeleton had ceased to support him and his considerable mass of flesh was falling in on him. He looked dully at the desk that separated him from the Resident. He sighed deeply.

"You must try not to take it too hard, Saffary," said George Moon. "You know how uncertain life is in the East. One has to resign oneself to losing people one's fond of."

Saffary's eyes slowly moved from the desk, and he fixed them on George Moon's. They stared unwinking. George Moon liked people to look him in the eyes. Perhaps he felt that when he thus held their vision he held them in his power. Presently two tears formed themselves in Saffary's blue eyes and slowly ran down his cheeks. He had a strangely puzzled look. Something had frightened him. Was it death? No. Something that he thought worse. He looked cowed. His mien was cringing so that he made you think of a dog unjustly beaten.

"It's not that," he faltered. "I could have borne that."

George Moon did not answer. He held that big, powerful man with his cold level gaze and waited. He was pleasantly conscious of his absolute indifference. Saffary gave a harassed glance at the papers on the desk.

"I'm afraid I'm taking up too much of your time."

"No, I have nothing to do at the moment."

Saffary looked out of the window. A little shudder passed between his shoulders. He seemed to hesitate.

"I wonder if I might ask your advice," he said at last.

"Of course," said the Resident, with the shadow of a smile, "that's one of the things I'm here for."

"It's a purely private matter."

"You may be quite sure that I shan't betray any confidence you place in me."

"No, I know you wouldn't do that, but it's rather an awkward thing to speak about, and I shouldn't feel very comfortable meeting you afterwards. But you're going away to-morrow, and that makes it easier, if you understand what I mean."

"Quite."

Saffary began to speak, in a low voice, sulkily, as though he were ashamed, and he spoke with the awkwardness of a man unused to words. He went back and said the same thing over again. He got mixed up. He started a long, elaborate sentence and then broke off abruptly because he did not know how to finish it. George Moon listened in silence, his face a mask, smoking, and he only took his eyes off Saffary's face to reach for another cigarette from the box in front of him and light it from the stub of that which he was just finishing. And while he listened he saw, as it were a background, the monotonous round of the planter's life. It was like an accompaniment of muted strings that threw into sharper relief the calculated dissonances of an unexpected melody.

With rubber at so low a price every economy had to be exercised and Tom Saffary, notwithstanding the size of the estate, had to do work which in better times he had had an assistant for. He rose before dawn and went down to the lines where the coolies were assembled. When there was just enough light to see he read out the names, ticking them off according to the answers, and assigned the various squads to their work. Some tapped, some weeded, and others tended the ditches. Saffary went back to his solid breakfast, lit his pipe and sallied forth again to inspect the coolies' quarters. Children were playing and babies sprawling here and there. On the sidewalks Tamil women cooked their rice. Their black skins shone with oil. They were draped about in dull red cotton and wore gold ornaments in their hair. There were handsome creatures among them, upright of carriage, with delicate features and small, exquisite hands; but Saffary looked upon them only with distaste. He set out on his rounds. On his well-grown estate the trees planted in rows gave one a charming feeling of the prim forest of a German fairy-tale. The ground was thick with dead leaves. He was accompanied by a Tamil overseer, his long black hair done in a chignon, bare-footed, in sarong and baju, with a showy ring on his finger. Saffary walked hard, jumping the ditches when he came to them, and soon he dripped with sweat. He examined the trees to see that they were properly tapped, and when he came across a coolie at work looking at the shavings and if they were too thick swore at him and docked him half a day's pay. When a tree was not to be tapped any more he told the overseer to take away the cup and the wire that held it to the trunk. The weeders worked in gangs.

At noon Saffary returned to the bungalow and had a drink of beer which, because there was no ice, was luke-warm. He stripped the khaki shorts, the flannel shirt, the heavy boots and stockings in which he had been walking, and shaved and bathed. He lunched in a sarong and baju. He lay off for half an hour, and then went down to his office and worked till five; he had tea and went to the club. About eight he started back for the bungalow, dined, and half an hour after went to bed.

But last night he went home immediately he had finished his match. Violet had not accompanied him that day. When the Clarkes were there they had met at the club every afternoon, but now they had gone home she came less often. She said there was no one there who much amused her and she had heard everything everyone had to say till she was fed to the teeth. She did not play bridge and it was dull for her to wait about while he played. She told Tom he need not mind leaving her alone. She had plenty of things to do in the house.

As soon as she saw him back so early she guessed that he had come to tell her that he had won his match. He was like a child in his self-satisfaction over one of these small triumphs. He was a kindly, simple creature and she knew that his pleasure at winning was not only on his own account, but because he thought it must give her pleasure too. It was rather sweet of him to hurry home in order to tell her all about it without delay.

"Well, how did your match go?" she said as soon as he came lumbering into the sitting-room.

"I won."

"Easily?"

"Well, not as easily as I should have. I was a bit ahead, and then I stuck, I couldn't do a thing, and you know what Douglas is, not at all showy, but steady, and he pulled up with me. Then I said to myself, well, if I don't buck up I shall get a licking, I had a bit of luck here and there, and then, to cut a long story short, I beat him by seven."

"Isn't that splendid? You ought to win the cup now, oughtn't you?"

"Well, I've got three matches more. If I can get into the semi-finals I ought to have a chance."

Violet smiled. She was anxious to show him that she was as much interested as he expected her to be.

"What made you go to pieces when you did?"

His face sagged.

"That's why I came back at once. I'd have scratched only I thought it wasn't fair on the fellows who'd backed me. I don't know how to tell you, Violet."

She gave him a questioning look.

"Why, what's the matter? Not bad news?"

"Rotten. Knobby's dead."

For a full minute she stared at him, and her face, her neat friendly little face, grew haggard with horror. At first it seemed as though she could not understand.

"What *do* you mean?" she cried.

"It was in the paper. He died on board. They buried him at sea."

Suddenly she gave a piercing cry and fell headlong to the floor. She had fainted dead away.

"Violet," he cried, and threw himself down on his knees and took her head in his arms. "Boy, boy."

A boy, startled by the terror in his master's voice, rushed in and Saffary shouted to him to bring brandy. He forced a little between Violet's lips. She opened her eyes, and as she remembered they grew dark with anguish. Her face was screwed up like a little child's when it is just going to burst into tears. He lifted her up in his arms and laid her on the sofa. She turned her head away.

"Oh, Tom, it isn't true. It can't be true."

"I'm afraid it is."

"No, no, no."

She burst into tears. She wept convulsively. It was dreadful to hear her. Saffary did not know what to do. He knelt beside her and tried to soothe her. He sought to take her in his arms, but with a sudden gesture she repelled him.

"Don't touch me," she cried, and she said it so sharply that he was startled.

He rose to his feet.

"Try not to take it too hard, sweetie," he said. "I know it's been an awful shock. He was one of the best."

She buried her face in the cushions and wept despairingly. It tortured him to see her body shaken by those uncontrollable sobs. She was beside herself. He put his hand gently on her shoulder.

"Darling, don't give way like that. It's so bad for you."

She shook herself free from his hand.

"For God's sake leave me alone," she cried. "Oh, Hal, Hal." He had never heard her call the dead man that before. Of course his name was Harold, but everyone called him Knobby. "What shall I do?" she wailed. "I can't bear it. I can't bear it."

Saffary began to grow a trifle impatient. So much grief did seem to him exaggerated. Violet was not normally so emotional. He supposed it was the damned climate. It made women nervous and high-strung. Violet hadn't been home for four years. She was not hiding her face now. She lay, almost falling off the sofa, her mouth open in the extremity of her pain, and the tears streamed from her staring eyes. She was distraught.

"Have a little more brandy," he said. "Try and pull yourself together, darling. You can't do Knobby any good by getting in such a state."

With a sudden gesture she sprang to her feet and pushed him aside. She gave him a look of hatred.

"Go away, Tom. I don't want your sympathy. I want to be left alone."

She walked swiftly over to an arm-chair and threw herself down in it. She flung back her head and her poor white face was wrenched into a grimace of agony.

"Oh, it's not fair," she moaned. "What's to become of me now? Oh, God, I wish I were dead."

"Violet."

His voice quavered with pain. He was very nearly crying too. She stamped her foot impatiently.

"Go away, I tell you. Go away."

He started. He stared at her and suddenly gasped. A shudder passed through his great bulk. He took a step towards her and stopped, but his eyes never left her white, tortured face; he stared as though he saw in it something that appalled him. Then he dropped his head and without a word walked out of the room. He went into a little sitting-room they had at the back, but seldom used, and sank heavily into a chair. He thought. Presently the gong sounded for dinner. He had not had his bath. He gave his hands a glance. He could not be bothered to wash them. He walked slowly into the dining-room. He told the boy to go and tell Violet that dinner was ready. The boy came back and said she did not want any.

"All right. Let me have mine then," said Saffary.

He sent Violet in a plate of soup and a piece of toast, and when the fish was served put some on a plate for her and gave it to the boy. But the boy came back with it at once.

"Mem, she say no wantchee," he said.

Saffary ate his dinner alone. He ate from habit, solidly, through the familiar courses. He drank a bottle of beer. When he had finished the boy brought him a cup of coffee and he lit a cheroot. Saffary sat still till he had finished it. He thought. At last he got up and went back into the large verandah which was where they always sat. Violet was still huddled in the chair in which he had left her. Her eyes were closed, but she opened them when she heard him come. He took a light chair and sat down in front of her.

"What *was* Knobby to you, Violet?" he said.

She gave a slight start. She turned away her eyes, but did not speak.

"I can't quite make out why you should have been so frightfully upset by the news of his death."

"It was an awful shock."

"Of course. But it seems very strange that anyone should go simply all to pieces over the death of a friend."

"I don't understand what you mean," she said.

She could hardly speak the words and he saw that her lips were trembling.

"I've never heard you call him Hal. Even his wife called him Knobby."

She did not say anything. Her eyes, heavy with grief, were fixed on vacancy.

"Look at me, Violet."

She turned her head slightly and listlessly gazed at him.

"Was he your lover?"

She closed her eyes and tears flowed from them. Her mouth was strangely twisted.

"Haven't you got anything to say at all?"

She shook her head.

"You must answer me, Violet."

"I'm not fit to talk to you now," she moaned. "How can you be so heartless?"

"I'm afraid I don't feel very sympathetic at the moment. We must get this straight now. Would you like a drink of water?"

"I don't want anything."

"Then answer my question."

"You have no right to ask it. It's insulting."

"Do you ask me to believe that a woman like you who hears of the death of someone she knew is going to faint dead away and then, when she comes to, is going to cry like that? Why, one wouldn't be so upset over the death of one's only child. When we heard of your mother's death you cried of course, anyone would, and I know you were utterly miserable, but you came to me for comfort and you said you didn't know what you'd have done without me."

"This was so frightfully sudden."

"Your mother's death was sudden, too."

"Naturally I was very fond of Knobby."

"How fond? So fond that when you heard he was dead you didn't know and you didn't care what you said? Why did you say it wasn't fair? Why did you say, 'What's going to become of me now?'"

She sighed deeply. She turned her head this way and that like a sheep trying to avoid the hands of the butcher.

"You mustn't take me for an utter fool, Violet. I tell you it's impossible that you should be so shattered by the blow if there hadn't been something between you."

"Well, if you think that, why do you torture me with questions?"

"My dear, it's no good shilly-shallying. We can't go on like this. What d'you think I'm feeling?"

She looked at him when he said this. She hadn't thought of him at all. She had been too much absorbed in her own misery to be concerned with his.

"I'm so tired," she sighed.

He leaned forward and roughly seized her wrist.

"Speak," he cried.

"You're hurting me."

"And what about me? D'you think you're not hurting me? How can you have the heart to let me suffer like this?"

He let go of her arm and sprang to his feet. He walked to the end of the room and back again. It looked as though the movement had suddenly roused him to fury. He caught her by the shoulders and dragged her to her feet. He shook her.

"If you don't tell me the truth I'll kill you," he cried.

"I wish you would," she said.

"He was your lover?"

"Yes."

"You swine."

With one hand still on her shoulder so that she could not move he swung back his other arm and with a flat palm struck her repeatedly, with all his strength, on the side of her face. She quivered under the blows, but did not flinch or cry out. He struck her again and again. All at once he felt her strangely inert, he let go of her and she sank unconscious to the floor. Fear seized him. He bent down and touched her, calling her name. She did not move. He lifted her up and put her back into the chair from which a little while before he had pulled her. The brandy that had been brought when first she fainted was still in the room and he fetched it and tried to force it down her throat. She choked and it spilt over her chin and neck. One side of her pale face was livid from the blows of his heavy hand. She sighed a little and opened her eyes. He held the glass again to her lips, supporting her head, and she sipped a little of the neat spirit. He looked at her with penitent, anxious eyes.

"I'm sorry, Violet. I didn't mean to do that. I'm dreadfully ashamed of myself. I never thought I could sink so low as to hit a woman."

Though she was feeling very weak and her face was hurting, the flicker of a smile crossed her lips. Poor Tom. He did say things like that. He felt like that. And how scandalised he would be if you asked him why a man shouldn't hit a woman. But Saffary, seeing the wan smile, put it down to her indomitable courage. By God, she's a plucky little woman, he thought. Game isn't the word.

"Give me a cigarette," she said.

He took one out of his case and put it in her mouth. He made two or three ineffectual attempts to strike his lighter. It would not work.

"Hadn't you better get a match?" she said.

For the moment she had forgotten her heart-rending grief and was faintly amused at the situation. He took a box from the table and held the lighted match to her cigarette. She inhaled the first puff with a sense of infinite relief.

"I can't tell you how ashamed I am, Violet," he said. "I'm disgusted with myself. I don't know what came over me."

"Oh, that's all right. It was very natural. Why don't you have a drink? It'll do you good."

Without a word, his shoulders all hunched up as though the burden that oppressed him were material, he helped himself to a brandy and soda. Then, still silent, he sat down. She watched the blue smoke curl into the air.

"What are you going to do?" she said at last.

He gave a weary gesture of despair.

"We'll talk about that to-morrow. You're not in a fit state to-night. As soon as you've finished your cigarette you'd better go to bed."

"You know so much, you'd better know everything."

"Not now, Violet."

"Yes, now."

She began to speak. He heard her words, but could hardly make sense of them. He felt like a man who has built himself a house with loving care and thought to live in it all his life, and then, he does not understand why, sees the housebreakers come and with their picks and heavy hammers destroy it room by room, till what was a fair dwelling-place is only a heap of rubble. What made it so awful was that it was Knobby Clarke who had done this thing. They had come out to the F.M.S. on the same ship and had worked at first on the same estate. They call the young planter a creeper and you can tell him in the streets of Singapore by his double felt hat and his khaki coat turned up at the wrists. Callow youths who saunter about staring and are inveigled by wily Chinese into buying worthless truck from Birmingham which they send home as Eastern curios, sit in the lounges of cheap hotels drinking innumerable stengahs, and after an evening at the pictures get into rickshaws and finish the night in the Chinese quarter. Tom and Knobby were inseparable. Tom, a big, powerful fellow, simple, very honest, hard-working; and Knobby, ungainly, but curiously attractive, with his deep-set eyes, hollow cheeks and large humorous mouth. It was Knobby who made the jokes and Tom who laughed at them. Tom married first. He met Violet when he went on leave. The daughter of a doctor killed in the war, she was governess in the house of some people who lived in the same place as his father. He fell in love with her because she was alone in the world, and his tender heart was touched by the thought of the drab life that lay before her. But Knobby married because Tom had and he felt lost without him, a girl who had come East to spend the winter with relations. Enid Clarke had been very pretty then in her blonde way, and full-face she was pretty still, though her skin, once so clear and fresh, was already faded; but she had a very weak, small, insignificant chin and in profile reminded you of a sheep. She had pretty flaxen hair, straight, because in the heat it would not keep its wave, and china-blue eyes. Though but twenty-six, she had already a tired look. A year after marriage she had a baby, but it died when only two years old. It was after this that Tom Saffary managed to get Knobby the post of manager of the estate next his own. The two men pleasantly resumed their old familiarity, and their wives, who till then had not known one another very well, soon made friends. They copied one another's frocks and lent one another servants and crockery when they gave a party. The four of them met every day. They went everywhere together. Tom Saffary thought it grand.

The strange thing was that Violet and Knobby Clarke lived on

these terms of close intimacy for three years before they fell in love
with one another. Neither saw love approaching. Neither suspected
that in the pleasure each took in the other's company there was
anything more than the casual friendship of two persons thrown
together by the circumstances of life. To be together gave them no
particular happiness, but merely a quiet sense of comfort. If by
chance a day passed without their meeting they felt unaccountably
bored. That seemed very natural. They played games together.
They danced together. They chaffed one another. The revelation
came to them by what looked like pure accident. They had all been
to a dance at the club and were driving home in Saffary's car. The
Clarkes' estate was on the way and he was dropping them at their
bungalow. Violet and Knobby sat in the back. He had had a good
deal to drink, but was not drunk; their hands touched by chance,
and he took hers and held it. They did not speak. They were all
tired. But suddenly the exhilaration of the champagne left him and
he was cold sober. They knew in a flash that they were madly in
love with one another and at the same moment they realised that
they had never been in love before. When they reached the Clarkes's
Tom said:

"You'd better hop in beside me, Violet."

"I'm too exhausted to move," she said.

Her legs seemed so weak that she thought she would never be
able to stand.

When they met next day neither referred to what had happened,
but each knew that something inevitable had passed. They behaved
to one another as they had always done, they continued to behave
so for weeks, but they felt that everything was different. At last
flesh and blood could stand it no longer and they became lovers.
But the physical tie seemed to them the least important element
in their relation, and indeed their way of living made it impossible
for them, except very seldom, to enjoy any intimate connection.
It was enough that they saw one another, though in the company
of others, every day; a glance, a touch of the hand, assured them
of their love, and that was all that mattered. The sexual act was
no more than an affirmation of the union of their souls.

They very seldom talked of Tom or Enid. If sometimes they
laughed together at their foibles it was not unkindly. It might
have seemed odd to them to realise how completely these two
people whom they saw so constantly had ceased to matter to them
if they had given them enough thought to consider the matter.
Their relations with them fell into the routine of life that nobody
notices, like shaving oneself, dressing and eating three meals a

day. They felt tenderly towards them. They even took pains to please them, as you would with a bed-ridden invalid, because their own happiness was so great that in charity they must do what they could for others less fortunate. They had no scruples. They were too much absorbed in one another to be touched even for a moment by remorse. Beauty now excitingly kindled the pleasant humdrum life they had led so long.

But then an event took place that filled them with consternation. The company for which Tom worked entered into negotiations to buy extensive rubber plantations in British North Borneo and invited Tom to manage them. It was a better job than his present one, with a higher salary, and since he would have assistants under him he would not have to work so hard. Saffary welcomed the offer. Both Clarke and Saffary were due for leave and the two couples had arranged to travel home together. They had already booked their passages. This changed everything. Tom would not be able to get away for at least a year. By the time the Clarkes came back the Saffarys would be settled in Borneo. It did not take Violet and Knobby long to decide that there was only one thing to do. They had been willing enough to go on as they were, notwithstanding the hindrances to the enjoyment of their love, when they were certain of seeing one another continually; they felt that they had endless time before them and the future was coloured with a happiness that seemed to have no limit; but neither could suffer for an instant the thought of separation. They made up their minds to run away together, and then it seemed to them on a sudden that every day that passed before they could be together always and all the time was a day lost. Their love took another guise. It flamed into a devouring passion that left them no emotion to waste on others. They cared little for the pain they must cause Tom and Enid. It was unfortunate, but inevitable. They made their plans deliberately. Knobby on the pretence of business would go to Singapore and Violet, telling Tom that she was going to spend a week with friends on an estate down the line, would join him there. They would go over to Java and thence take ship to Sydney. In Sydney Knobby would look for a job. When Violet told Tom that the Mackenzies had asked her to spend a few days with them, he was pleased.

"That's grand. I think you want a change, darling," he said. "I've fancied you've been looking a bit peaked lately."

He stroked her cheek affectionately. The gesture stabbed her heart.

"You've always been awfully good to me, Tom," she said, her eyes suddenly filled with tears.

"Well, that's the least I could be. You're the best little woman in the world."

"Have you been happy with me these eight years?"

"Frightfully."

"Well, that's something, isn't it? No one can ever take that away from you."

She had told herself that he was the kind of man who would soon console himself. He liked women for themselves and it would not be long after he had regained his freedom before he found someone that he would wish to marry. And he would be just as happy with his new wife as he had been with her. Perhaps he would marry Enid. Enid was one of those dependent little things that somewhat exasperated her and she did not think her capable of deep feeling. Her vanity would be hurt; her heart would not be broken. But now that the die was cast, everything settled and the day fixed, she had a qualm. Remorse beset her. She wished that it had been possible not to cause those two people such fearful distress. She faltered.

"We've had a very good time here, Tom," she said. "I wonder if it's wise to leave it all. We're giving up a certainty for we don't know what."

"My dear child, it's a chance in a million and much better money."

"Money isn't everything. There's happiness."

"I know that, but there's no reason why we shouldn't be just as happy in B.N.B. And besides, there was no alternative. I'm not my own master. The directors want me to go and I must, and that's all there is to it."

She sighed. There was no alternative for her either. She shrugged her shoulders. It was hateful to cause others pain; sometimes you couldn't help yourself. Tom meant no more to her than the casual man on the voyage out who was civil to you: it was absurd that she should be asked to sacrifice her life for him.

The Clarkes were due to sail for England in a fortnight and this determined the date of their elopement. The days passed. Violet was restless and excited. She looked forward with a joy that was almost painful to the peace that she anticipated when they were once on board the ship and could begin the life which she was sure would give her at last perfect happiness.

She began to pack. The friends she was supposed to be going to stay with entertained a good deal and this gave her an excuse to take quite a lot of luggage. She was starting next day. It was eleven o'clock in the morning and Tom was making his round of the estate. One of the boys came to her room and told her that Mrs. Clarke was there and at the same moment she heard Enid calling her. Quickly closing the lid of her trunk, she went out on to the verandah. To her astonishment Enid came up to her, flung her arms round her neck and kissed her eagerly. She looked at Enid and saw that her cheeks, usually pale, were flushed and that her eyes were shining. Enid burst into tears.

"What on earth's the matter, darling?" she cried.

For one moment she was afraid that Enid knew everything. But Enid was flushed with delight and not with jealousy or anger.

"I've just seen Dr. Harrow," she said. "I didn't want to say anything about it. I've had two or three false alarms, but this time he says it's all right."

A sudden coldness pierced Violet's heart.

"What do you mean? You're not going to . . ."

She looked at Enid and Enid nodded.

"Yes, he says there's no doubt about it at all. He thinks I'm at least three months gone. Oh, my dear, I'm so wildly happy."

She flung herself again into Violet's arms and clung to her, weeping.

"Oh, darling, don't."

Violet felt herself grow pale as death and knew that if she didn't keep a tight hold of herself she would faint.

"Does Knobby know?"

"No, I didn't say a word. He was so disappointed before. He was so frightfully cut up when baby died. He's wanted me to have another so badly."

Violet forced herself to say the things that were expected of her, but Enid was not listening. She wanted to tell the whole story of her hopes and fears, of her symptoms, and then of her interview with the doctor. She went on and on.

"When are you going to tell Knobby?" Violet asked at last. "Now, when he gets in?"

"Oh, no, he's tired and hungry when he gets back from his round. I shall wait till to-night after dinner."

Violet repressed a movement of exasperation; Enid was going to make a scene of it and was choosing her moment; but after all, it was only natural. It was lucky, for it would give her the chance to see Knobby first. As soon as she was rid of her she rang him up. She knew that he always looked in at his office on his way home, and she left a message asking him to call her. She was only afraid that he would not do so till Tom was back, but she had to take her chance of that. The bell rang and Tom had not yet come in.

"Hal?"

"Yes."

"Will you be at the hut at three?"

"Yes. Has anything happened?"

"I'll tell you when I see you. Don't worry."

She rang off. The hut was a little shelter on Knobby's estate which she could get to without difficulty and where they occasionally met. The coolies passed it while they worked and it had no privacy; but it was a convenient place for them without exciting comment to exchange a few minutes' conversation. At three Enid would be resting and Tom at work in his office.

When Violet walked up Knobby was already there. He gave a gasp.

"Violet, how white you are."

She gave him her hand. They did not know what eyes might be watching them and their behaviour here was always such as anyone could observe.

"Enid came to see me this morning. She's going to tell you to-night. I thought you ought to be warned. She's going to have a baby."

"Violet!"

He looked at her aghast. She began to cry. They had never talked of the relations they had, he with his wife and she with her husband. They ignored the subject because it was to each horribly painful. Violet knew what her own life was; she satisfied her husband's appetite, but, with a woman's strange nonchalance, because to do so gave her no pleasure, attached no importance to it; but somehow she had persuaded herself that with Hal it was different. He felt now instinctively how bitterly what she had learned wounded her. He tried to excuse himself.

"Darling, I couldn't help myself."

She cried silently and he watched her with miserable eyes.

"I know it seems beastly," he said, "but what could I do? It wasn't as if I had any reason to . . ."

She interrupted him.

"I don't blame you. It was inevitable. It's only because I'm stupid that it gives me such a frightful pain in my heart."

"Darling!"

"We ought to have gone away together two years ago. It was madness to think we could go on like this."

"Are you sure Enid's right? She thought she was in the family way three or four years ago."

"Oh, yes, she's right. She's frightfully happy. She says you wanted a child so badly."

"It's come as such an awful surprise. I don't seem able to realise it yet."

She looked at him. He was staring at the leaf-strewn earth with harassed eyes. She smiled a little.

"Poor Hal." She sighed deeply. "There's nothing to be done about it. It's the end of us."

"What do you mean?" he cried.

"Oh, my dear, you can't very well leave her now, can you? It was all right before. She would have been unhappy, but she would have got over it. But now it's different. It's not a very nice time for a woman anyhow. For months she feels more or less ill. She wants affection. She wants to be taken care of. It would be frightful to leave her to bear it all alone. We couldn't be such beasts."

"Do you mean to say you want me to go back to England with her?"

She nodded gravely.

"It's lucky you're going. It'll be easier when you get away and we don't see one another every day."

"But I can't live without you now."

"Oh, yes, you can. You must. I can. And it'll be worse for me, because I stay behind and I shall have nothing."

"Oh, Violet, it's impossible."

"My dear, it's no good arguing. The moment she told me I saw it meant that. That's why I wanted to see you first. I thought the shock might lead you to blurt out the whole truth. You know I love you more than anything in the world. She's never done me any harm. I couldn't take you away from her now. It's bad luck on both of us, but there it is, I simply wouldn't dare to do a filthy thing like that."

"I wish I were dead," he moaned.

"That wouldn't do her any good, or me either," she smiled.

"What about the future? Have we got to sacrifice our whole lives?"

"I'm afraid so. It sounds rather grim, darling, but I suppose sooner or later we shall get over it. One gets over everything."

She looked at her wrist-watch.

"I ought to be getting back. Tom will be in soon. We're all meeting at the club at five."

"Tom and I are supposed to be playing tennis." He gave her a pitiful look. "Oh, Violet, I'm so frightfully unhappy."

"I know. So am I. But we shan't do any good by talking about it."

She gave him her hand, but he took her in his arms and kissed her, and when she released herself her cheeks were wet with his tears. But she was so desperate she could not cry.

Ten days later the Clarkes sailed.

While George Moon was listening to as much of this story as Tom Saffary was able to tell him, he reflected in his cool, detached way how odd it was that these commonplace people, leading lives so monotonous, should have been convulsed by such a tragedy. Who would have thought that Violet Saffary, so neat and demure, sitting in the club reading the illustrated papers or chatting with her friends over a lemon squash, should have been eating her heart out for love of that ordinary man? George Moon remembered seeing Knobby at the club that evening before he sailed. He seemed in great spirits. Fellows envied him because he was going home. Those who had recently come back told him by no means to miss the show at the Pavilion. Drink flowed freely. The Resident had not been asked to the farewell party the Saffarys gave for the Clarkes, but he knew very well what it had been like, the good cheer, the cordiality, the chaff, and then after dinner the gramophone turned on and everyone dancing. He wondered what Violet and Clarke had felt as they danced together. It gave him an odd sensation of dismay to think of the despair that must have filled their hearts while they pretended to be so gay.

And with another part of his mind George Moon thought of his own past. Very few knew that story. After all, it had happened twenty-five years ago.

"What are you going to do now, Saffary?" he asked.

"Well, that's what I wanted you to advise me about. Now that Knobby's dead I don't know what's going to happen to Violet if I divorce her. I was wondering if I oughtn't to let her divorce me."

"Oh, you want to divorce?"

"Well, I must."

George Moon lit another cigarette and watched for a moment the smoke that curled away into the air.

"Did you ever know that I'd been married?"

"Yes, I think I'd heard. You're a widower, aren't you?"

"No, I divorced my wife. I have a son of twenty-seven. He's farming in New Zealand. I saw my wife the last time I was home on leave. We met at a play. At first we didn't recognise one another. She spoke to me. I asked her to lunch at the Berkeley."

George Moon chuckled to himself. He was alone. It was a musical comedy. He found himself sitting next to a large fat dark woman whom he vaguely thought he had seen before, but the play was just starting and he did not give her a second look. When the curtain fell after the first act she looked at him with bright eyes and spoke.

"How are you, George?"

It was his wife. She had a bold, friendly manner and was very much at her ease.

"It's a long time since we met," she said.

"It is."

"How has life been treating you?"

"Oh, all right."

"I suppose you're a Resident now. You're still in the Service, aren't you?"

"Yes. I'm retiring soon, worse luck."

"Why? You look very fit."

"I'm reaching the age limit. I'm supposed to be an old buffer and no good any more."

"You're lucky to have kept so thin. I'm terrible, aren't I?"

"You don't look as though you were wasting away."

"I know. I'm stout and I'm growing stouter all the time. I can't help it and I love food. I can't resist cream and bread and potatoes."

George Moon laughed, but not at what she said; at his own thoughts. In years gone by it had sometimes occurred to him that he might meet her, but he had never thought that the meeting would take this turn. When the play was ended and with a smile she bade him good-night, he said:

"I suppose you wouldn't lunch with me one day?"

"Any day you like."

They arranged a date and duly met. He knew that she had married the man on whose account he had divorced her, and he judged by her clothes that she was in comfortable circumstances. They drank a cocktail. She ate the *hors-d'œuvres* with gusto. She was fifty if she was a day, but she carried her years with spirit. There was something jolly and careless about her, she was quick on the uptake, chatty, and she had the hearty, infectious laugh of the fat woman who has let herself go. If he had not known that her family had for a century been in the Indian Civil Service he would have thought that she had been a chorus girl. She was not flashy, but she had a sort of flamboyance of nature that suggested the stage. She was not in the least embarrassed.

"You never married again, did you?" she asked him.

"No."

"Pity. Because it wasn't a success the first time there's no reason why it shouldn't have been the second."

"There's no need for me to ask if you've been happy."

N

"I've got nothing to complain of. I think I've got a happy nature. Jim's always been very good to me; he's retired now, you know, and we live in the country, and I adore Betty."

"Who's Betty?"

"Oh, she's my daughter. She got married two years ago. I'm expecting to be a grandmother almost any day."

"That ages us a bit."

She gave a laugh.

"Betty's twenty-two. It was nice of you to ask me to lunch, George. After all, it would be silly to have any feelings about something that happened so long ago as all that."

"Idiotic."

"We weren't fitted to one another and it's lucky we found it out before it was too late. Of course I was foolish, but then I was very young. Have you been happy too?"

"I think I can say I've been a success."

"Oh, well, that's probably all the happiness you were capable of."

He smiled in appreciation of her shrewdness. And then, putting the whole matter aside easily, she began to talk of other things. Though the courts had given him custody of their son, he, unable to look after him, had allowed his mother to have him. The boy had emigrated at eighteen and was now married. He was a stranger to George Moon, and he was aware that if he met him in the street he would not recognise him. He was too sincere to pretend that he took much interest in him. They talked of him, however, for a while, and then they talked of actors and plays.

"Well," she said at last, "I must be running away. I've had a lovely lunch. It's been fun meeting you, George. Thanks so much."

He put her into a taxi and taking off his hat walked down Piccadilly by himself. He thought her quite a pleasant, amusing woman: he laughed to think that he had ever been madly in love with her. There was a smile on his lips when he spoke again to Tom Saffary.

"She was a damned good-looking girl when I married her. That was the trouble. Though, of course, if she hadn't been I'd never have married her. They were all after her like flies round a honey-pot. We used to have awful rows. And at last I caught her out. Of course I divorced her."

"Of course."

"Yes, but I know I was a damned fool to do it." He leaned forward. "My dear Saffary, I know now that if I'd had any sense I'd have shut my eyes. She'd have settled down and made me an excellent wife."

He wished he were able to explain to his visitor how grotesque it had seemed to him when he sat and talked with that jolly, comfortable and good-humoured woman that he should have made so much fuss about what now seemed to him to matter so little.

"But one has one's honour to think of," said Saffary.

"Honour be damned. One has one's happiness to think of. Is one's honour really concerned because one's wife hops into bed with another man? We're not crusaders, you and I, or Spanish grandees. I *liked* my wife. I don't say I haven't had other women. I have. But she had just that something that none of the others could give me. What a fool I was to throw away what I wanted more than anything in the world because I couldn't enjoy exclusive possession of it!"

"You're the last man I should ever have expected to hear speak like that."

George Moon smiled thinly at the embarrassment that was so clearly expressed on Saffary's fat troubled face.

"I'm probably the first man you've heard speak the naked truth," he retorted.

"Do you mean to say that if it were all to do over again you would act differently?"

"If I were twenty-seven again I suppose I should be as big a fool as I was then. But if I had the sense I have now I'll tell you what I'd do if I found my wife had been unfaithful to me. I'd do just what you did last night: I'd give her a damned good hiding and let it go at that."

"Are you asking me to forgive Violet?"

The Resident shook his head slowly and smiled.

"No. You've forgiven her already. I'm merely advising you not to cut off your nose to spite your face."

Saffary gave him a worried look. It disconcerted him to know that this cold precise man should see in his heart emotions which seemed so unnatural to himself that he thrust them out of his consciousness.

"You don't know the circumstances," he said. "Knobby and I were almost like brothers. I got him this job. He owed everything to me. And except for me Violet might have gone on being a governess for the rest of her life. It seemed such a waste; I couldn't help feeling sorry for her. If you know what I mean, it was pity that first made me take any notice of her. Don't you think it's a bit thick that when you've been thoroughly decent with people they should go out of their way to do the dirty on you? It's such awful ingratitude."

"Oh, my dear boy, one mustn't expect gratitude. It's a thing that no one has a right to. After all, you do good because it gives you pleasure. It's the purest form of happiness there is. To expect thanks for it is really asking too much. If you get it, well, it's like a bonus on shares on which you've already received a dividend; it's grand, but you mustn't look upon it as your due."

Saffary frowned. He was perplexed. He could not quite make it out that George Moon should think so oddly about things that it had always seemed to him there were no two ways of thinking about. After all there were limits. I mean, if you had any sense of decency you had to behave like a tuan. There was your own self-respect to think of. It was funny that George Moon should give reasons that looked so damned plausible for doing something that, well, damn it, you had to admit you'd be only too glad to do if you could see your way to do it. Of course George Moon was queer. No one ever quite understood him.

"Knobby Clarke is dead, Saffary. You can't be jealous of him any more. No one knows a thing except you and me and your wife, and to-morrow I'm going away for ever. Why don't you let bygones be bygones?"

"Violet would only despise me."

George Moon smiled and, unexpectedly on that prim, fastidious face, his smile had a singular sweetness.

"I know her very little. I always thought her a very nice woman. Is she as detestable as that?"

Saffary gave a start and reddened to his ears.

"No, she's an angel of goodness. It's me who's detestable for saying that of her." His voice broke and he gave a little sob. "God knows I only want to do the right thing."

"The right thing is the kind thing."

Saffary covered his face with his hands. He could not curb the emotion that shook him.

"I seem to be giving, giving all the time, and no one does a God-damned thing for me. It doesn't matter if my heart is broken, I must just go on." He drew the back of his hand across his eyes and sighed deeply. "I'll forgive her."

George Moon looked at him reflectively for a little.

"I wouldn't make too much of a song and dance about it, if I were you," he said. "You'll have to walk warily. She'll have a lot to forgive too."

"Because I hit her, you mean? I know, that was awful of me."

"Not a bit. It did her a power of good. I didn't mean that. You're behaving very generously, old boy, and, you know, one needs a devil of a lot of tact to get people to forgive one one's generosity.

Fortunately women are frivolous and they very quickly forget the benefits conferred upon them. Otherwise, of course, there'd be no living with them."

Saffary looked at him open-mouthed.

"Upon my word you're a rum 'un, Moon," he said. "Sometimes you seem as hard as nails and then you talk so that one thinks you're almost human, and then, just as one thinks one's misjudged you and you have a heart after all, you come out with something that just shocks one. I suppose that's what they call a cynic."

"I haven't deeply considered the matter," smiled George Moon, "but if to look truth in the face and not resent it when it's unpalatable, and take human nature as you find it, smiling when it's absurd and grieved without exaggeration when it's pitiful, is to be cynical, then I suppose I'm a cynic. Mostly human nature is both absurd and pitiful, but if life has taught you tolerance you find in it more to smile at than to weep."

When Tom Saffary left the room the Resident lit himself with deliberation the last cigarette he meant to smoke before tiffin. It was a new rôle for him to reconcile an angry husband with an erring wife and it caused him a discreet amusement. He continued to reflect upon human nature. A wintry smile hovered upon his thin and pallid lips. He recalled with what interest in the dry creeks of certain places along the coast he had often stood and watched the Jumping Johnnies. There were hundreds of them sometimes, from little things of a couple of inches long to great fat fellows as long as your foot. They were the colour of the mud they lived in. They sat and looked at you with large round eyes and then with a sudden dash buried themselves in their holes. It was extraordinary to see them scudding on their flappers over the surface of the mud. It teemed with them. They gave you a fearful feeling that the mud itself was mysteriously become alive and an atavistic terror froze your heart when you remembered that such creatures, but gigantic and terrible, were once the only inhabitants of the earth. There was something uncanny about them, but something amusing too. They reminded you very much of human beings. It was quite entertaining to stand there for half an hour and observe their gambols.

George Moon took his topee off the peg and not displeased with life stepped out into the sunshine.

P. & O.

Mrs. Hamlyn lay on her long chair and lazily watched the passengers come along the gangway. The ship had reached Singapore in the night, and since dawn had been taking on cargo; the winches had been grinding away all day, but by now her ears were accustomed to their insistent clamour. She had lunched at the Europe, and for lack of anything better to do had driven in a rickshaw through the gay, multitudinous streets of the city. Singapore is the meeting-place of many races. The Malays, though natives of the soil, dwell uneasily in towns, and are few; and it is the Chinese, supple, alert and industrious, who throng the streets; the dark-skinned Tamils walk on their silent, naked feet, as though they were but brief sojourners in a strange land, but the Bengalis, sleek and prosperous, are easy in their surroundings, and self-assured; the sly and obsequious Japanese seem busy with pressing and secret affairs; and the English in their topees and white ducks, speeding past in motor-cars or at leisure in their rickshaws, wear a nonchalant and careless air. The rulers of these teeming peoples take their authority with a smiling unconcern. And now, tired and hot, Mrs. Hamlyn waited for the ship to set out again on her long journey across the Indian Ocean.

She waved a rather large hand, for she was a big woman, to the doctor and Mrs. Linsell as they came on board. She had been on the ship since she left Yokohama, and had watched with acid amusement the intimacy which had sprung up between the two. Linsell was a naval officer who had been attached to the British Embassy at Tokio, and she had wondered at the indifference with which he took the attentions that the doctor paid his wife. Two men came along the gangway, new passengers, and she amused herself by trying to discover from their demeanour whether they were single or married. Close by, a group of men were sitting together on rattan chairs, planters she judged by their khaki suits and wide-brimmed double felt hats, and they kept the deck-steward busy with their orders. They were talking loudly and laughing, for they had all drunk enough to make them somewhat foolishly hilarious, and they were evidently giving one of their number a send-off; but Mrs. Hamlyn could not tell which it was that was to be a fellow-passenger. The time was growing short. More passengers arrived, and then Mr. Jephson with dignity strolled up the gangway. He was a consul and was going home on leave. He had joined the ship at Shanghai and had immediately set about making himself agreeable to Mrs. Hamlyn. But just then she was disinclined for anything in the nature of a flirtation. She frowned as she thought of the reason which was taking her back to England. She would be spending Christmas at sea, far from anyone who cared two straws about her, and for a moment she felt a little twist at her heartstrings; it vexed her that a subject which she was so resolute to put away from her should so constantly intrude on her unwilling mind.

But a warning bell clanged loudly, and there was a general movement among the men who sat beside her.

"Well, if we don't want to be taken on we'd better be toddling," said one of them.

They rose and walked towards the gangway. Now that they were all shaking hands she saw who it was that they had come to see the last of. There was nothing very interesting about the man on whom Mrs. Hamlyn's eyes rested, but because she had nothing better to do she gave him more than a casual glance. He was a big fellow, well over six feet high, broad and stout; he was dressed in a bedraggled suit of khaki drill and his hat was battered and shabby. His friends left him, but they bandied chaff from the quay, and Mrs. Hamlyn noticed that he had a strong Irish brogue; his voice was full, loud and hearty.

Mrs. Linsell had gone below and the doctor came and sat down beside Mrs. Hamlyn. They told one another their small adventures of the day. The bell sounded again and presently the ship slid away from the wharf. The Irishman waved a last farewell to his friends, and then sauntered towards the chair on which he had left papers and magazines. He nodded to the doctor.

"Is that someone you know?" asked Mrs. Hamlyn.

"I was introduced to him at the club before tiffin. His name is Gallagher. He's a planter."

After the hubbub of the port and the noisy bustle of departure, the silence of the ship was marked and grateful. They steamed slowly past green-clad, rocky cliffs (the P. & O. anchorage was in a charming and secluded cove), and came out into the main harbour. Ships of all nations lay at anchor, a great multitude, passenger boats, tugs, lighters, tramps; and beyond, behind the breakwater, you saw the crowded masts, a bare straight forest, of the native junks. In the soft light of the evening the busy scene was strangely touched with mystery, and you felt that all those vessels, their activity for the moment suspended, waited for some event of a peculiar significance.

Mrs. Hamlyn was a bad sleeper and when the dawn broke she was in the habit of going on deck. It rested her troubled heart to watch the last faint stars fade before the encroaching day, and at that early hour the glassy sea had often an immobility which seemed to make all earthly sorrows of little consequence. The light was wan, and there was a pleasant shiver in the air. But next morning, when she went to the end of the promenade deck, she found that someone was up before her. It was Mr. Gallagher. He was watching the low coast of Sumatra which the sunrise like a magician seemed to call forth from the dark sea. She was startled and a little vexed, but before she could turn away he had seen her and nodded.

"Up early," he said. "Have a cigarette?"

He was in pyjamas and slippers. He took his case from his coat pocket and handed it to her. She hesitated. She had on nothing but a dressing-gown and a little lace cap which she had put over her tousled hair, and she knew that she must look a sight; but she had her reasons for scourging her soul.

"I suppose a woman of forty has no right to mind how she looks," she smiled, as though he must know what vain thoughts occupied her. She took the cigarette. "But you're up early too."

"I'm a planter. I've had to get up at five in the morning for so many years that I don't know how I'm going to get out of the habit."

"You'll not find it will make you very popular at home."

She saw his face better now that it was not shadowed by a hat. It was agreeable without being handsome. He was of course much too fat, and his features, which must have been good enough when he was a young man, were thickened. His skin was red and bloated. But his dark eyes were merry; and though he could not have been less than five and forty his hair was black and thick. He gave you an impression of great strength. He was a heavy, ungraceful, commonplace man, and Mrs. Hamlyn, except for the promiscuity of ship-board, would never have thought it worth while to talk to him.

"Are you going home on leave?" she hazarded.

"No, I'm going home for good."

His black eyes twinkled. He was of a communicative turn, and before it was time for Mrs. Hamlyn to go below in order to have her bath he had told her a good deal about himself. He had been in the Federated Malay States for twenty-five years, and for the last ten had managed an estate in Selantan. It was a hundred miles from anything that could be described as civilisation and the life had been lonely; but he had made money; during the rubber boom he had done very well, and with an astuteness which was unexpected in a man who looked so happy-go-lucky he had invested his savings in government stock. Now that the slump had come he was prepared to retire.

"What part of Ireland do you come from?" asked Mrs. Hamlyn.

"Galway."

Mrs. Hamlyn had once motored through Ireland and she had a vague recollection of a sad and moody town with great stone warehouses, deserted and crumbling, which faced the melancholy sea. She had a sensation of greenness and of soft rain, of silence and of resignation. Was it here that Mr. Gallagher meant to spend the rest of his life? He spoke of it with boyish eagerness. The thought of his vitality in that grey world of shadows was so incongruous that Mrs. Hamlyn was intrigued.

"Does your family live there?" she asked.

"I've got no family. My mother and father are dead. So far as I know I haven't a relation in the world."

He had made all his plans, he had been making them for twenty-five years, and he was pleased to have someone to talk to of all these things that he had been obliged for so long only to talk to himself about. He meant to buy a house and he would keep a motor-car. He was going to breed horses. He didn't much care about shooting; he had shot a lot of big game during his first years in the F.M.S.; but now he had lost his zest. He didn't see why the beasts of the jungle should be killed; he had lived in the jungle so long. But he could hunt.

"Do you think I'm too heavy?" he asked.

Mrs. Hamlyn, smiling, looked him up and down with appraising eyes.

"You must weigh a ton," she said.

He laughed. The Irish horses were the best in the world, and he'd always kept pretty fit. You had a devil of a lot of walking exercise on a rubber estate and he'd played a good deal of tennis. He'd soon get thin in Ireland. Then he'd marry. Mrs. Hamlyn looked silently at the sea coloured now with the tenderness of the sunrise. She sighed.

"Was it easy to drag up all your roots? Is there no one you regret leaving behind? I should have thought after so many years, however much you'd looked forward to going home, when the time came at last to go it must have given you a pang."

"I was glad to get out. I was fed up. I never want to see the country again or anyone in it."

One or two early passengers now began to walk round the deck and Mrs. Hamlyn, remembering that she was scantily clad, went below.

During the next day or two she saw little of Mr. Gallagher, who passed his time in the smoking-room. Owing to a strike the ship was not touching at Colombo and the passengers settled down to a pleasant voyage across the Indian Ocean. They played deck games, they gossiped about one another, they flirted. The approach of Christmas gave them an occupation, for someone had suggested that there should be a fancy-dress dance on Christmas Day, and the ladies set about making their dresses. A meeting was held of the first-class passengers to decide whether the second-class passengers should be invited, and notwithstanding the heat the discussion was animated. The ladies said that the second-class passengers would only feel ill-at-ease. On Christmas Day it was to be expected that they would drink more than was good for them and unpleasantness might ensue. Everyone who spoke insisted that there was in his (or her) mind no idea of class distinction, no one would be so snobbish as to think there was any difference between first- and second-class passengers as far as that went, but it would really be kinder to the second-class passengers not to put them in a false position. They would enjoy themselves much more if they had a party of their own in the second-class cabin. On the other hand, no one wanted to hurt their feelings, and of course one had to be more democratic nowadays (this was in reply to the wife of a missionary in China who said she had travelled on the P. & O. for thirty-five years and she had never heard of the second-class passengers being invited to a dance in the first-class saloon) and even though they wouldn't enjoy it, they might like to come. Mr. Gallagher, dragged unwillingly from the card-table, because it had been foreseen that the voting would be close, was asked his opinion by the consul. He was taking home in the second-class a man who had been employed on his estate. He raised his massive bulk from the couch on which he sat.

"As far as I'm concerned I've only got this to say: I've got the man who was looking after our engines with me. He's a rattling good fellow, and he's just as fit to come to your party as I am. But he won't come because I'm going to make him so drunk on Christmas Day that by six o'clock he'll be fit for nothing but to be put to bed."

Mr. Jephson, the consul, gave a distorted smile. On account of his official position, he had been chosen to preside at the meeting and he wished the matter to be taken seriously. He was a man who often said that if a thing was worth doing it was worth doing well.

"I gather from your observations," he said, not without acidity, "that the question before the meeting does not seem to you of great importance."

"I don't think it matters a tinker's curse," said Gallagher, with twinkling eyes.

Mrs. Hamlyn laughed. The scheme was at last devised to invite the second-class passengers, but to go to the captain privily and point out to him the advisability of withholding his consent to their coming into the first-class saloon. It was on the evening of the day on which this happened that Mrs. Hamlyn, having dressed for dinner, came on deck at the same time as Mr. Gallagher.

"Just in time for a cocktail, Mrs. Hamlyn," he said jovially.

"I'd like one. To tell you the truth I need cheering up."

"Why?" he smiled.

Mrs. Hamlyn thought his smile attractive, but she did not want to answer his question.

"I told you the other morning," she answered cheerfully. "I'm forty."

"I never met a woman who insisted on the fact so much."

They went into the lounge and the Irishman ordered a dry Martini for her and a gin pahit for himself. He had lived too long in the East to drink anything else.

"You've got hiccups," said Mrs. Hamlyn.

"Yes, I've had them all the afternoon," he answered carelessly. "It's rather funny, they came on just as we got out of sight of land."

"I daresay they'll pass off after dinner."

They drank, the second bell rang, and they went into the dining-saloon.

"You don't play bridge?" he said, as they parted.

"No."

Mrs. Hamlyn did not notice that she saw nothing of Gallagher for two or three days. She was occupied with her own thoughts. They crowded upon her when she was sewing; they came between her and the novel with which she sought to cheat their insistence. She had hoped that as the ship took her further away from the scene of her unhappiness, the torment of her mind would be eased; but contrariwise, each day that brought her nearer England increased her distress. She looked forward with dismay to the bleak emptiness of the life that awaited her; and then, turning her exhausted wits from a prospect that made her flinch, she considered, as she had done she knew not how many times before, the situation from which she had fled.

She had been married for twenty years. It was a long time and of course she could not expect her husband to be still madly in love with her; she was not madly in love with him; but they were good friends and they understood one another. Their marriage, as marriages go, might very well have been looked upon as a success. Suddenly she discovered that he had fallen in love. She would not have objected to a flirtation, he had had those before, and she had chaffed him about them; he had not minded that, it somewhat flattered him, and they had laughed together at an inclination which was neither deep nor serious. But this was different. He was in love as passionately as a boy of eighteen. He was fifty-two. It was ridiculous. It was indecent. And he loved without sense or prudence: by the time the hideous fact was forced upon her all the foreigners in Yokohama knew it. After the first shock of astonished anger, for he was the last man from whom such a folly might have been expected, she tried to persuade herself that she could have understood, and so have forgiven, if he had fallen in love with a girl. Middle-aged men often make fools of themselves with flappers, and after twenty years in the Far East she knew that the fifties were the dangerous age for men. But he had no excuse. He was in love with a woman eight years older than herself. It was grotesque, and it made her, his wife, perfectly absurd. Dorothy Lacom was hard on fifty. He had known her for eighteen years, for Lacom, like her own husband, was a silk merchant in Yokohama. Year in, year out, they had seen one another three or four times a week, and once, when they happened to be in England together, had shared a house at the seaside. But nothing! Not till a year ago had there been anything between them but a chaffing friendship. It was incredible. Of course Dorothy was a handsome woman; she had a good figure, over-developed, perhaps, but still comely; with bold black eyes and a red mouth and lovely hair; but all that she had had years before. She was forty-eight. Forty-eight!

Mrs. Hamlyn tackled her husband at once. At first he swore that there was not a word of truth in what she accused him of, but she had her proofs; he grew sulky; and at last he admitted what he could no longer deny. Then he said an astonishing thing.

"Why should you care?" he asked.

It maddened her. She answered him with angry scorn. She was voluble, finding in the bitterness of her heart wounding things to say. He listened to her quietly.

"I've not been such a bad husband to you for the twenty years we've been married. For a long time now we've only been friends. I have a great affection for you, and this hasn't altered it in the very smallest degree. I'm giving Dorothy nothing that I take away from you."

"But what have you to complain of in me?"

"Nothing. No man could want a better wife."

"How can you say that when you have the heart to treat me so cruelly?"

"I don't want to be cruel to you. I can't help myself."

"But what on earth made you fall in love with her?"

"How can I tell? You don't think I wanted to, do you?"

"Couldn't you have resisted?"

"I tried. I think we both tried."

"You talk as though you were twenty. Why, you're both middle-aged people. She's eight years older than I am. It makes me look such a perfect fool."

He did not answer. She did not know what emotions seethed in her heart. Was it jealousy that seemed to clutch at her throat, anger, or was it merely wounded pride?

"I'm not going to let it go on. If only you and she were concerned I would divorce you, but there's her husband, and then there are the children. Good heavens, does it occur to you that if they were girls instead of boys she might be a grandmother by now?"

"Easily."

"What a mercy that we have no children!"

He put out an affectionate hand as though to caress her, but she drew back with horror.

"You've made me the laughing-stock of all my friends. For all our sakes I'm willing to hold my tongue, but only on the condition that everything stops now, at once, and for ever."

He looked down and played reflectively with a Japanese knick-knack that was on the table.

"I'll tell Dorothy what you say," he replied at last.

She gave him a little bow, silently, and walked past him out of the room. She was too angry to observe that she was somewhat melodramatic.

She waited for him to tell her the result of his interview with Dorothy Lacom, but he made no further reference to the scene. He was quiet, polite and silent; and at last she was obliged to ask him.

"Have you forgotten what I said to you the other day?" she inquired, frigidly.

"No. I talked to Dorothy. She wished me to tell you that she is desperately sorry that she has caused you so much pain. She would like to come and see you, but she is afraid you wouldn't like it."

"What decision have you come to?"

He hesitated. He was very grave, but his voice trembled a little.

"I'm afraid there's no use in our making a promise we shouldn't be able to keep."

"That settles it then," she answered.

"I think I should tell you that if you brought an action for divorce we should have to contest it. You would find it impossible to get the necessary evidence and you would lose your case."

"I wasn't thinking of doing that. I shall go back to England and consult a lawyer. Nowadays these things can be managed fairly easily, and I shall throw myself on your generosity. I dare say you will enable me to get my freedom without bringing Dorothy Lacom into the matter."

He sighed.

"It's an awful muddle, isn't it? I don't want you to divorce me, but of course I'll do anything I can to meet your wishes."

"What on earth do you expect me to do?" she cried, her anger rising again. "Do you expect me to sit still and be made a damned fool of?"

"I'm awfully sorry to put you in a humiliating position." He looked at her with harassed eyes. "I'm quite sure we didn't want to fall in love with one another. We're both of us very conscious of our age. Dorothy, as you say, is old enough to be a grandmother and I'm a baldish, stoutish gentleman of fifty-two. When you fall in love at twenty you think your love will last for ever, but at fifty you know so much, about life and about love, and you know that it will last so short a time." His voice was low and rueful. It was as though before his mind's eye he saw the sadness of autumn and the leaves falling from the trees. He looked at her gravely. "And at that age you feel that you can't afford to throw away the chance of happiness which a freakish destiny has given you. In five years it will certainly be over, and perhaps in six months. Life is rather drab and grey, and happiness is so rare. We shall be dead so long."

It gave Mrs. Hamlyn a bitter sensation of pain to hear her husband, a matter-of-fact and practical man, speak in a strain which was quite new to her. He had gained on a sudden a wistful and tragic personality of which she knew nothing. The twenty years during which they had lived together had no power over him and she was helpless in face of his determination. She could do nothing but go, and now, resentfully determined to get the divorce with which she had threatened him, she was on her way to England.

The smooth sea, upon which the sun beat down so that it shone like a sheet of glass, was as empty and hostile as life in which there was no place for her. For three days no other craft had broken in upon the solitariness of that expanse. Now and again its even surface was scattered for the twinkling of an eye by the scurry of flying fish. The heat was so great that even the most energetic of passengers had given up deck games, and now (it was after luncheon) such as were not resting in their cabins lay about on chairs. Linsell strolled towards her and sat down.

"Where's Mrs. Linsell?" asked Mrs. Hamlyn.

"Oh, I don't know. She's about somewhere."

His indifference exasperated her. Was it possible that he did not see that his wife and the surgeon were falling in love with one another? Yet, not so very long ago, he must have cared. Their marriage had been romantic. They had become engaged when Mrs. Linsell was still at school and he little more than a boy. They must have been a charming, handsome pair, and their youth and their mutual love must have been touching. And now, after so short a time, they were tired of one another. It was heartbreaking. What had her husband said?

"I suppose you're going to live in London when you get home?" asked Linsell lazily, for something to say.

"I suppose so," said Mrs. Hamlyn.

It was hard to reconcile herself to the fact that she had nowhere to go, and where she lived mattered not in the least to anyone alive. Some association of ideas made her think of Gallagher. She envied the eagerness with which he was returning to his native land, and she was touched, and at the same time amused, when she remembered the exuberant imagination he showed in describing the house he meant to live in and the wife he meant to marry. Her friends in Yokohama, apprised in confidence of her determination to divorce her husband, had assured her that she would marry again. She did not much want to enter a second time upon a state which had once so disappointed her, and besides, most men would think twice before they suggested marriage to a woman of forty. Mr. Gallagher wanted a buxom young person.

"Where is Mr. Gallagher?" she asked the submissive Linsell. "I haven't seen him for the last day or two."

"Didn't you know? He's ill."

"Poor thing. What's the matter with him?"

"He's got hiccups."

Mrs. Hamlyn laughed.

"Hiccups don't make one ill, do they?"

"The surgeon is rather worried. He's tried all sorts of things, but he can't stop them."

"How very odd."

She thought no more about it, but next morning, chancing upon the surgeon, she asked him how Mr. Gallagher was. She was surprised to see his boyish, cheerful face darken and grow perplexed.

"I'm afraid he's very bad, poor chap."

"With hiccups?" she cried in amazement.

It was a disorder that really it was impossible to take seriously.

"You see, he can't keep any food down. He can't sleep. He's fearfully exhausted. I've tried everything I can think of." He hesitated. "Unless I can stop them soon—I don't quite know what'll happen."

Mrs. Hamlyn was startled.

"But he's so strong. He seemed so full of vitality."

"I wish you could see him now."

"Would he like me to go and see him?"

"Come along."

Gallagher had been moved from his cabin into the ship's hospital, and as they approached it they heard a loud hiccup. The sound, perhaps owing to its connection with insobriety, had in it something ludicrous. But Gallagher's appearance gave Mrs. Hamlyn a shock. He had lost flesh and the skin hung about his neck in loose folds; under the sunburn his face was pale. His eyes, before, full of fun and laughter, were haggard and tormented. His great body was shaken incessantly by the hiccups and now there was nothing ludicrous in the sound; to Mrs. Hamlyn, for no reason that she knew, it seemed strangely terrifying. He smiled when she came in.

"I'm sorry to see you like this," she said.

"I shan't die of it, you know," he gasped. "I shall reach the green shores of Erin all right."

There was a man sitting beside him and he rose as they entered.

"This is Mr. Pryce," said the surgeon. "He was in charge of the machinery on Mr. Gallagher's estate."

Mrs. Hamlyn nodded. This was the second-class passenger to whom Gallagher had referred when they had discussed the party which was to be given on Christmas Day. He was a very small man, but sturdy, with a pleasantly impudent countenance and an air of self-assurance.

"Are you glad to be going home?" asked Mrs. Hamlyn.

"You bet I am, lady," he answered.

The intonation of the few words told Mrs. Hamlyn that he was a cockney and, recognising the cheerful, sensible, good-humoured and careless type, her heart warmed to him.

"You're not Irish?" she smiled.

"Not me, miss. London's my 'ome and I shan't be sorry to see it again, I can tell you."

Mrs. Hamlyn never thought it offensive to be called miss.

"Well, sir, I'll be getting along," he said to Gallagher, with the beginning of a gesture as though he were going to touch a cap which he hadn't got on.

Mrs. Hamlyn asked the sick man whether she could do anything for him and in a minute or two left him with the doctor. The little cockney was waiting outside the door.

"Can I speak to you a minute or two, miss?" he asked.

"Of course."

The hospital cabin was aft and they stood, leaning against the rail, and looked down on the well-deck where lascars and stewards off duty were lounging about on the covered hatches.

"I don't know exactly 'ow to begin," said Pryce, uncertainly, a serious look strangely changing his lively, puckered face. "I've been with Mr. Gallagher for four years now and a better gentleman you wouldn't find in a week of Sundays."

He hesitated again.

"I don't like it and that's the truth."

"What don't you like?"

"Well, if you ask me 'e's for it, and the doctor don't know it. I told 'im, but 'e won't listen to a word I say."

"You mustn't be too depressed, Mr. Pryce. Of course the doctor's young, but I think he's quite clever, and people don't die of hiccups, you know. I'm sure Mr. Gallagher will be all right in a day or two."

"You know when it come on? Just as we was out of sight of land. She said 'e'd never see 'is 'ome."

Mrs. Hamlyn turned and faced him. She stood a good three inches taller than he.

"What do you mean?"

"My belief is, it's a spell been put on 'im, if you understand what I mean. Medicine's going to do 'im no good. You don't know them Malay women like what I do."

For a moment Mrs. Hamlyn was startled, and because she was startled she shrugged her shoulders and laughed.

"Oh, Mr. Pryce, that's nonsense."

"That's what the doctor said when I told 'im. But you mark my words, 'e'll die before we see land again."

The man was so serious that Mrs. Hamlyn, vaguely uneasy, was against her will impressed.

"Why should anyone cast a spell on Mr. Gallagher?" she asked.

"Well, it's a bit awkward speakin' of it to a lady."

"Please tell me."

Pryce was so embarrassed that at another time Mrs. Hamlyn would have had difficulty in concealing her amusement.

"Mr. Gallagher's lived a long time up-country, if you understand what I mean, and of course it's lonely, and you know what men are, miss."

"I've been married for twenty years," she replied, smiling.

"I beg your pardon, ma'am. The fact is he had a Malay girl living with him. I don't know 'ow long, ten or twelve years, I think. Well, when 'e made up 'is mind to come 'ome for good she didn't say nothing. She just sat there. He thought she'd carry on no end, but she didn't. Of course 'e provided for 'er all right, 'e gave 'er a little 'ouse for herself, an' 'e fixed it up so as so much should be paid 'er every month. 'E wasn't mean, I will say that for 'im, an' she knew all along as 'e'd be going some time. She didn't cry or anything. When 'e packed up all 'is things and sent them off, she just sat there an' watched 'em go. And when 'e sold 'is furniture to the Chinks she never said a word. He'd give 'er all she wanted. And when it was time for 'im to go so as to catch the boat she just kep' on sitting on the steps of the bungalow, you know, and she just looked an' said nothing. He wanted to say good-bye to 'er, same as anyone would, an', would you believe it? she never even moved. 'Aren't you going to say good-bye to me,' he says. A rare funny look come over 'er face. And do you know what she says? 'You go,' she says; they 'ave a funny way of talking, them natives, not like we 'ave, 'you go,' she says, 'but I tell you that you will never come to your own country. When the land sinks into the sea, death will come upon you, an' before them as goes with you sees the land again, death will have took you.' It gave me quite a turn."

"What did Mr. Gallagher say?" asked Mrs. Hamlyn.

"Oh, well, you know what 'e is. He just laughed. 'Always merry and bright,' 'e says and 'e jumps into the motor, an' off we go."

Mrs. Hamlyn saw the bright and sunny road that ran through the rubber estates, with their trim green trees, carefully spaced, and their silence, and then wound its way up hill and down through the tangled jungle. The car raced on, driven by a reckless Malay, with its white passengers, past Malay houses that stood away from the road among the coconut trees, sequestered and taciturn, and through busy villages where the market-place was crowded with dark-skinned little people in gay sarongs. Then towards evening it reached the trim, modern town, with its clubs and its golf links, its well-ordered rest-house, its white people, and its railway-station, from which the two men could take the train to Singapore. And the woman sat on the steps of the bungalow, empty till the new manager moved in, and watched the road down which the car had panted, watched the car as it sped on, and watched till at last it was lost in the shadow of the night.

"What was she like?" Mrs. Hamlyn asked.

"Oh, well, to my way of thinking them Malay women are all very much alike, you know," Pryce answered. "Of course she wasn't so young any more, and you know what they are, them natives, they run to fat something terrible."

"Fat?"

The thought, absurdly enough, filled Mrs. Hamlyn with dismay.

"Mr. Gallagher was always one to do himself well, if you understand what I mean."

The idea of corpulence at once brought Mrs. Hamlyn back to common sense. She was impatient with herself because for an instant she had seemed to accept the little cockney's suggestion.

"It's perfectly absurd, Mr. Pryce. Fat women can't throw spells on people at a distance of a thousand miles. In fact life is very difficult for a fat woman anyway."

"You can laugh, miss, but unless something's done, you mark my words, the governor's for it. And medicine ain't goin' to save him, not white man's medicine."

"Pull yourself together, Mr. Pryce. This fat lady had no particular grievance against Mr. Gallagher. As these things are done in the East he seems to have treated her very well. Why should she wish him any harm?"

"We don't know 'ow they look at things. Why, a man can live there for twenty years with one of them natives, and d'you think 'e knows what's goin' on in that black heart of hers? Not 'im!"

She could not smile at his melodramatic language, for his intensity was impressive. And she knew, if anyone did, that the hearts of men, whether their skins are yellow or white or brown, are incalculable.

"But even if she felt angry with him, even if she hated him and wanted to kill him, what could she do?" It was strange that Mrs. Hamlyn with her questions was trying now, unconsciously, to reassure herself. "There's no poison that could start working after six or seven days."

"I never said it was poison."

"I'm sorry, Mr. Pryce," she smiled, "but I'm not going to believe in a magic spell, you know."

"You've lived in the East?"

"Off and on for twenty years."

"Well, if you can say what they can do and what they can't, it's more than I can." He clenched his fist and beat it on the rail with sudden, angry violence. "I'm fed up with the bloody country. It's got on my nerves, that's what it is. We're no match for them, us white men, and that's a fact. If you'll excuse me I think I'll go an' 'ave a tiddley. I've got the jumps."

He nodded abruptly and left her. Mrs. Hamlyn watched him, a sturdy, shuffling little man in shabby khaki, slither down the companion into the waist of the ship, walk across it with bent head, and disappear into the second-class saloon. She did not know why he left with her a vague uneasiness. She could not get out of her mind that picture of a stout woman, no longer young, in a sarong, a coloured jacket and gold ornaments, who sat on the steps of a bungalow looking at an empty road. Her heavy face was painted, but in her large, tearless eyes there was no expression. The men who drove in the car were like schoolboys going home for the holidays. Gallagher gave a sigh of relief. In the early morning, under the bright sky, his spirits bubbled. The future was like a sunny road that wandered through a wide-flung, wooded plain.

Later in the day Mrs. Hamlyn asked the doctor how his patient did. The doctor shook his head.

"I'm done. I'm at the end of my tether." He frowned unhappily. "It's rotten luck, striking a case like this. It would be bad enough at home, but on board ship . . ."

He was an Edinburgh man, but recently qualified, and he was taking this voyage as a holiday before settling down to practice. He felt himself aggrieved. He wanted to have a good time and, faced with this mysterious illness, he was worried to death. Of course he was inexperienced, but he was doing everything that could be done and it exasperated him to suspect that the passengers thought him an ignorant fool.

"Have you heard what Mr. Pryce thinks?" asked Mrs. Hamlyn.

"I never heard such rot. I told the captain and he's right up in the air. He doesn't want it talked about. He thinks it'll upset the passengers."

"I'll be as silent as the grave."

The surgeon looked at her sharply.

"Of course you don't believe that there can be any truth in nonsense of that sort?" he asked.

"Of course not." She looked out at the sea, which shone, blue and oily and still, all round them. "I've lived in the East a long time," she added. "Strange things happen there."

"This is getting on my nerves," said the doctor.

Near them two little Japanese gentlemen were playing deck quoits. They were trim and neat in their tennis shirts, white trousers and buckram shoes. They looked very European, they even called the score to one another in English, and yet somehow to look at them filled Mrs. Hamlyn at that moment with a vague disquiet. Because they seemed to wear so easily a disguise there was about them something sinister. Her nerves too were on edge.

And presently, no one quite knew how, the notion spread through the ship that Gallagher was bewitched. While the ladies sat about on their deck-chairs, stitching away at the costumes they were making for the fancy-dress party on Christmas Day, they gossiped about it in undertones, and the men in the smoking-room talked of it over their cocktails. A good many of the passengers had lived long in the East and from the recesses of their memory they produced strange and inexplicable stories. Of course it was absurd to think seriously that Gallagher was suffering from a malignant spell, such things were impossible, and yet this and that was a fact and no one had been able to explain it. The doctor had to confess that he could suggest no cause for Gallagher's condition, he was able to give a physiological explanation, but why these terrible spasms should have suddenly assailed him he did not say. Feeling vaguely to blame, he tried to defend himself.

"Why, it's the sort of case you might never come across in the whole of your practice," he said. "It's rotten luck."

He was in wireless communication with passing ships, and suggestions for treatment came from here and there.

"I've tried everything they tell me," he said irritably. "The doctor of the Japanese boat advised adrenalin. How the devil does he expect me to have adrenalin in the middle of the Indian Ocean?"

There was something impressive in the thought of this ship speeding through a deserted sea, while to her from all parts came unseen messages. She seemed at that moment strangely alone and yet the centre of the world. In the lazaret the sick man, shaken by the cruel spasms, gasped for life. Then the passengers became conscious that the ship's course was altered, and they heard that the captain had made up his mind to put in at Aden. Gallagher was to be landed there and taken to the hospital, where he could have attention which on board was impossible. The chief engineer received orders to force his engines. The ship was an old one and she throbbed with the greater effort. The passengers had grown used to the sound and feel of her engines, and now the greater vibration shook their nerves with a new sensation. It would not pass into each one's unconsciousness, but beat on their sensibilities so that each felt a personal concern. And still the wide sea was empty of traffic, so that they seemed to traverse an empty world. And now the uneasiness which had descended upon the ship, but which no one had been willing to acknowledge, became a definite malaise. The passengers grew irritable, and people quarrelled over trifles which at another time would have seemed insignificant. Mr. Jephson made his hackneyed jokes, but no one any longer repaid him with a smile. The Linsells had an altercation, and Mrs. Linsell was heard late at night walking round the deck with her husband and uttering in a low, tense voice a stream of vehement reproaches. There was a violent scene in the smoking-room one night over a game of bridge, and the reconciliation which followed it was attended with general intoxication. People talked little of Gallagher, but he was seldom absent from their thoughts. They examined the route map. The doctor said now that Gallagher could not live more than three or four days, and they discussed acrimoniously what was the shortest time in which Aden could be reached. What happened to him after he was landed was no affair of theirs; they did not want him to die on board.

Mrs. Hamlyn saw Gallagher every day. With the suddenness with which after tropical rain in the spring you seem to see the herbage grow before your very eyes, she saw him go to pieces. Already his skin hung loosely on his bones, and his double chin was like the wrinkled wattle of a turkey-cock. His cheeks were sunken. You saw now how large his frame was, and through the sheet under which he lay his bony structure was like the skeleton of a prehistoric giant. For the most part he lay with his eyes closed, torpid with morphia, but shaken still with terrible spasms, and when now and again he opened his eyes they were preternaturally large; they looked at you vaguely, perplexed and troubled, from the depths of their bony sockets. But when, emerging from his stupor, he recognised Mrs. Hamlyn, he forced a gallant smile to his lips.

"How are you, Mr. Gallagher?" she said.

"Getting along, getting along. I shall be all right when we get out of this confounded heat. Lord, how I look forward to a dip in the Atlantic. I'd give anything for a good long swim. I want to feel the cold grey sea of Galway beating against my chest."

Then the hiccup shook him from the crown of his head to the sole of his foot. Mr. Pryce and the stewardess shared the care of him. The little cockney's face wore no longer its look of impudent gaiety, but instead was sullen.

"The captain sent for me yesterday," he told Mrs. Hamlyn when they were alone. "He gave me a rare talking to."

"What about?"

"He said 'e wouldn't 'ave all this hoodoo stuff. He said it was frightening the passengers and I'd better keep a watch on me tongue or I'd 'ave 'im to reckon with. It's not my doing. I never said a word except to you and the doctor."

"It's all over the ship."

"I know it is. D'you think it's only me that's saying it? All them Lascars and the Chinese, they all know what's the matter with him. You don't think you can teach them much, do you? They know it ain't a natural illness."

Mrs. Hamlyn was silent. She knew through the amahs of some of the passengers that there was no one on the ship, except the whites, who doubted that the woman whom Gallagher had left in distant Selantan was killing him with her magic. All were convinced that as they sighted the barren rocks of Arabia his soul would be parted from his body.

"The captain says if he hears of me trying any hanky-panky he'll confine me to my cabin for the rest of the voyage," said Pryce, suddenly, a surly frown on his puckered face.

"What do you mean by hanky-panky?"

He looked at her for a moment fiercely as though she too were an object of the anger he felt against the captain.

"The doctor's tried every damned thing he knows, and he's wire-lessed all over the place, and what good 'as 'e done? Tell me that. Can't 'e see the man's dying? There's only one way to save him now."

"What do you mean?"

"It's magic what's killing 'im, and it's only magic what'll save him. Oh, don't you say it can't be done. I've seen it with me own eyes." His voice rose, irritable and shrill. "I've seen a man dragged from the jaws of death, as you might say, when they got in a *pawang*, what we call a witch-doctor, an' 'e did 'is little tricks. I seen it with me own eyes, I tell you."

Mrs. Hamlyn did not speak. Pryce gave her a searching look.

"One of them Lascars on board, he's a witch-doctor, same as the *pawang* that we 'ave in the F.M.S. An' 'e says he'll do it. Only he must 'ave a live animal. A cock would do."

"What do you want a live animal for?" Mrs. Hamlyn asked, frowning a little.

The cockney looked at her with quick suspicion.

"If you take my advice you won't know anything about it. But I tell you what, I'm going to leave no stone unturned to save my governor. An' if the captain 'ears of it and shuts me up in me cabin, well, let 'im."

At that moment Mrs. Linsell came up and Pryce with his quaint gesture of salute left them. Mrs. Linsell wanted Mrs. Hamlyn to fit the dress she had been making herself for the fancy-dress ball, and on the way down to the cabin she spoke to her anxiously of the possibility that Mr. Gallagher might die on Christmas Day. They could not possibly have the dance if he did. She had told the doctor that she would never speak to him again if this happened, and the doctor had promised her faithfully that he would keep the man alive over Christmas Day somehow.

"It would be nice for him, too," said Mrs. Linsell.

"For whom?" asked Mrs. Hamlyn.

"For poor Mr. Gallagher. Naturally no one likes to die on Christmas Day. Do they?"

"I don't really know," said Mrs. Hamlyn.

That night, after she had been asleep a little while, she awoke weeping. It dismayed her that she should cry in her sleep. It was as though then the weakness of the flesh mastered her, and, her will broken, she were defenceless against a natural sorrow. She turned over in her mind, as so often before, the details of the disaster which had so profoundly affected her; she repeated the conversations with her husband, wishing she had said this and blaming herself because she had said the other. She wished with all her heart that she had remained in comfortable ignorance of her husband's infatuation, and asked herself whether she would not have been wiser to pocket her pride and shut her eyes to the unwelcome truth. She was a woman of the world, and she knew too well how much more she lost in separating herself from her husband than his love; she lost the settled establishment and the assured position, the ample means and the support of a recognised background. She had known of many separated wives, living equivocally on smallish incomes, and knew how quickly their friends found them tiresome. And she was lonely. She was as lonely as the ship that throbbed her hasting way through an unpeopled sea, and lonely as the friendless man who lay dying in the ship's lazaret. Mrs. Hamlyn knew that her thoughts had got the better of her now and that she would not easily sleep again. It was very hot in her cabin. She looked at the time; it was between four and half-past; she must pass two mortal hours before broke the reassuring day.

She slipped into a kimono and went on deck. The night was sombre and although the sky was unclouded no stars were visible. Panting and shaking, the old ship under full steam lumbered through the darkness. The silence was uncanny. Mrs. Hamlyn with bare feet groped her way slowly along the deserted deck.

It was so black that she could see nothing. She came to the end of the promenade deck and leaned against the rail. Suddenly she started and her attention was fixed, for on the lower deck she caught a fitful glow. She leaned forward cautiously. It was a little fire, and she saw only the glow because the naked backs of men, crouched round, hid the flame. At the edge of the circle she divined, rather than saw, a stocky figure in pyjamas. The rest were natives, but this was a European. It must be Pryce and she guessed immediately that some dark ceremony of exorcism was in progress. Straining her ears she heard a low voice muttering a string of secret words. She began to tremble. She was aware that they were too intent upon their business to think that anyone was watching them, but she dared not move. Suddenly, rending the sultry silence of the night like a piece of silk violently torn in two, came the crowing of a cock. Mrs. Hamlyn almost shrieked. Mr. Pryce was trying to save the life of his friend and master by a sacrifice to the strange gods of the East. The voice went on, low and insistent. Then in the dark circle there was a movement, something was happening, she knew not what; there was a cluck-cluck from the cock, angry and frightened, and then a strange, indescribable sound; the magician was cutting the cock's throat; then silence; there were vague doings that she could not follow, and in a little while it looked as though someone were stamping out the fire. The figures she had dimly seen were dissolved in the night and all once more was still. She heard again the regular throbbing of the engines.

Mrs. Hamlyn stood still for a little while, strangely shaken, and then walked slowly along the deck. She found a chair and lay down in it. She was trembling still. She could only guess what had happened. She did not know how long she lay there, but at last she felt that the dawn was approaching. It was not yet day, and it was no longer night. Against the darkness of the sky she could now see the ship's rail. Then she saw a figure come towards her. It was a man in pyjamas.

"Who's that?" she cried nervously.

"Only the doctor," came a friendly voice.

"Oh! What are you doing here at this time of night?"

"I've been with Gallagher." He sat down beside her and lit a cigarette. "I've given him a good strong hypodermic and he's quiet now."

"Has he been very ill?"

"I thought he was going to pass out. I was watching him, and suddenly he started up on his bed and began to talk Malay. Of course I couldn't understand a thing. He kept on saying one word over and over again."

"Perhaps it was a name, a woman's name."

"He wanted to get out of bed. He's a damned powerful man even now. By George, I had a struggle with him. I was afraid he'd throw himself overboard. He seemed to think someone was calling him."

"When was that?" asked Mrs. Hamlyn, slowly.

"Between four and half-past. Why?"

"Nothing."

She shuddered.

Later in the morning when the ship's life was set upon its daily round, Mrs. Hamlyn passed Pryce on the deck, but he gave her a brief greeting and walked on with quickly averted gaze. He looked tired and overwrought. Mrs. Hamlyn thought again of that fat woman, with golden ornaments in her thick, black hair, who sat on the steps of the deserted bungalow and looked at the road which ran through the trim lines of the rubber trees.

It was fearfully hot. She knew now why the night had been so dark. The sky was no longer blue, but a dead, level white; its surface was too even to give the effect of cloud; it was as though in the upper air the heat hung like a pall. There was no breeze and the sea, as colourless as the sky, was smooth and shining like the dye in a dyer's vat. The passengers were listless; when they walked round the deck they panted, and beads of sweat broke out on their foreheads. They spoke in undertones. Something uncanny and disquieting brooded over the ship, and they could not bring themselves to laugh. A feeling of resentment arose in their hearts; they were alive and well, and it exasperated them that, so near, a man should be dying and by the fact (which was after all no concern of theirs) so mysteriously affect them. A planter in the smoking-room over a gin sling said brutally what most of them felt, though none had confessed.

"Well, if he's going to peg out," he said, "I wish he'd hurry up and get it over. It gives me the creeps."

The day was interminable. Mrs. Hamlyn was thankful when the dinner hour arrived. So much time, at all events, was passed. She sat at the doctor's table.

"When do we reach Aden?" she asked.

"Some time to-morrow. The captain says we shall sight land between five and six in the morning."

She gave him a sharp look. He stared at her for a moment, then dropped his eyes and reddened. He remembered that the woman, the fat woman sitting on the bungalow steps, had said that Gallagher would never see the land. Mrs. Hamlyn wondered whether he, the sceptical, matter-of-fact young doctor, was wavering at last. He frowned a little and then, as though he sought to pull himself together, looked at her once more.

"I shan't be sorry to hand over my patient to the hospital people at Aden, I can tell you," he said.

Next day was Christmas Eve. When Mrs. Hamlyn awoke from a troubled sleep the dawn was breaking. She looked out of her port-hole and saw that the sky was clear and silvery; during the night the haze had melted, and the morning was brilliant. With a lighter heart she went on deck. She walked as far forward as she could go. A late star twinkled palely close to the horizon. There was a shimmer on the sea as though a loitering breeze passed playful fingers over its surface. The light was wonderfully soft, tenuous like a budding wood in spring, and crystalline so that it reminded you of the bubbling of water in a mountain brook. She turned to look at the sun rising rosy in the east, and saw coming towards her the doctor. He wore his uniform; he had not been to bed all night; he was dishevelled and he walked, with bowed shoulders, as though he were dog-tired. She knew at once that Gallagher was dead. When he came up to her she saw that he was crying. He looked so young then that her heart went out to him. She took his hand.

"You poor dear," she said. "You're tired out."

"I did all I could," he said. "I wanted so awfully to save him."

His voice shook and she saw that he was almost hysterical.

"When did he die?" she asked.

He closed his eyes, trying to control himself, and his lips trembled.

"A few minutes ago."

Mrs. Hamlyn sighed. She found nothing to say. Her gaze wandered across the calm, dispassionate and ageless sea. It stretched on all sides of them as infinite as human sorrow. But on a sudden her eyes were held, for there, ahead of them, on the horizon was something which looked like a precipitous and massy cloud. But its outline was too sharp to be a cloud's. She touched the doctor on the arm.

"What's that?"

He looked at it for a moment and under his sunburn she saw him grow white.

"Land."

Once more Mrs. Hamlyn thought of the fat Malay woman who sat silent on the steps of Gallagher's bungalow. Did she know?

They buried him when the sun was high in the heavens. They stood on the lower deck and on the hatches, the first- and second-class passengers, the white stewards and the European officers. The missionary read the burial service.

"Man that is born of a woman hath but a short time to live, and is full of misery. He cometh up, and is cut down, like a flower; he fleeth as it were a shadow, and never continueth in one stay."

Pryce looked down at the deck with knit brows. His teeth were tight clenched. He did not grieve, for his heart was hot with anger. The doctor and the consul stood side by side. The consul bore to a nicety the expression of an official regret, but the doctor, clean-shaven now, in his neat fresh uniform and his gold braid, was pale and harassed. From him Mrs. Hamlyn's eyes wandered to Mrs. Linsell. She was pressed against her husband, weeping, and he was holding her hand tenderly. Mrs. Hamlyn did not know why this sight singularly affected her. At that moment of grief, her nerves distraught, the little woman went by instinct to the protection and support of her husband. But then Mrs. Hamlyn felt a little shudder pass through her and she fixed her eyes on the seams in the deck, for she did not want to see what was toward. There was a pause in the reading. There were various movements. One of the officers gave an order. The missionary's voice continued.

"Forasmuch as it has pleased Almighty God of his great mercy to take unto himself the soul of our dear brother here departed: we therefore commend his body to the deep, to be turned into corruption, looking for the resurrection of the body when the sea shall give up its dead."

Mrs. Hamlyn felt the hot tears flow down her cheeks. There was a dull splash. The missionary's voice went on.

When the service was finished the passengers scattered; the second-class passengers returned to their quarters and a bell rang to summon them to luncheon. But the first-class passengers sauntered aimlessly about the promenade deck. Most of the men made for the smoking-room and sought to cheer themselves with whiskies and sodas and with gin slings. But the consul put up a notice on the board outside the dining-saloon summoning the passengers to a meeting. Most of them had an idea for what purpose it was called, and at the appointed hour they assembled. They were more cheerful than they had been for a week and they chattered with a gaiety which was only subdued by a mannerly reserve. The consul, an eyeglass in his eye, said that he had gathered them together to discuss the question of the fancy-dress dance on the following day. He knew they all had the deepest sympathy for Mr. Gallagher and he would have proposed that they should combine to send an appropriate message to the deceased's relatives; but his papers had been examined by the purser and no trace could be found of any relative or friend with whom it was possible to communicate. The late Mr. Gallagher appeared to be quite alone in the world. Meanwhile he (the consul) ventured to offer his sincere sympathy to the doctor, who, he was quite sure, had done everything that was possible in the circumstances.

"Hear, hear," said the passengers.

They had all passed through a very trying time, proceeded the consul, and to some it might seem that it would be more respectful to the deceased's memory if the fancy-dress ball were postponed till New Year's Eve. This, however, he told them frankly was not his view, and he was convinced that Mr. Gallagher himself would not have wished it. Of course it was a question for the majority to decide. The doctor got up and thanked the consul and the passengers for the kind things that had been said of him, it had of course been a very trying time, but he was authorised by the captain to say that the captain expressly wished all the festivities to be carried out on Christmas Day as though nothing had happened. He (the doctor) told them in confidence that the captain felt the passengers had got into a rather morbid state, and thought it would do them all good if they had a jolly good time on Christmas Day. Then the missionary's wife rose and said they mustn't think only of themselves; it had been arranged by the Entertainment Committee that there should be a Christmas Tree for the children, immediately after the first-class passengers' dinner, and the children had been looking forward to seeing everyone in fancy-dress; it would be too bad to disappoint them; she yielded to no one in her respect for the dead, and she sympathised with anyone who felt too sad to think of dancing just then, her own heart was very heavy, but she did feel it would be merely selfish to give way to a feeling which could do no good to anyone. Let them think of the little ones. This very much impressed the passengers. They wanted to forget the brooding terror which had hung over the boat for so many days, they were alive and they wanted to enjoy themselves; but they had an uneasy notion that it would be decent to exhibit a certain grief. It was quite another matter if they could do as they wished from altruistic motives. When the consul called for a show of hands everyone, but

Mrs. Hamlyn and one old lady who was rheumatic, held up an eager arm.

"The ayes have it," said the consul. "And I venture to congratulate the meeting on a very sensible decision."

It was just going to break up when one of the planters got on his feet and said he wished to offer a suggestion. Under the circumstances didn't they all think it would be as well to invite the second-class passengers? They had all come to the funeral that morning. The missionary jumped up and seconded the motion. The events of the last few days had drawn them all together, he said, and in the presence of death all men were equal. The consul again addressed them. This matter had been discussed at a previous meeting, and the conclusion had been reached that it would be pleasanter for the second-class passengers to have their own party, but circumstances alter cases, and he was distinctly of opinion that their previous decision should be reversed.

"Hear, hear," said the passengers.

A wave of democratic feeling swept over them and the motion was carried by acclamation. They separated light-heartedly, they felt charitable and kindly. Everyone stood everyone else drinks in the smoking-room.

And so, on the following evening, Mrs. Hamlyn put on her fancy-dress. She had no heart for the gaiety before her, and for a moment had thought of feigning illness, but she knew no one would believe her, and was afraid to be thought affected. She was dressed as Carmen and she could not resist the vanity of making herself as attractive as possible. She darkened her eyelashes and rouged her cheeks. The costume suited her. When the bugle sounded and she went into the saloon she was received with flattering surprise. The consul (always a humorist) was dressed as a ballet-girl and was greeted with shouts of delighted laughter. The missionary and his wife, self-conscious but pleased with themselves, were very grand as Manchus. Mrs. Linsell, as Columbine, showed all that was possible of her very pretty legs. Her husband was an Arab sheik and the doctor was a Malay sultan.

A subscription had been collected to provide champagne at dinner and the meal was hilarious. The company had provided crackers in which were paper hats of various shapes and these the passengers put on. There were paper streamers too which they threw at one another and little balloons which they beat from one to the other across the room. They laughed and shouted. They were very gay. No one could say that they were not having a good time. As soon as dinner was finished they went into the saloon, where the Christmas

Tree, with candles lit, was ready, and the children were brought in, shrieking with delight, and given presents. Then the dance began. The second-class passengers stood about shyly round the part of the deck reserved for dancing and occasionally danced with one another.

"I'm glad we had them," said the consul, dancing with Mrs. Hamlyn. "I'm all for democracy, and I think they're very sensible to keep themselves to themselves."

But she noticed that Pryce was not to be seen, and when an opportunity presented asked one of the second-class passengers where he was.

"Blind to the world," was the answer. "We put him to bed in the afternoon and locked him up in his cabin."

The consul claimed her for another dance. He was very facetious. Suddenly Mrs. Hamlyn felt that she could not bear it any more, the noise of the amateur band, the consul's jokes, the gaiety of the dancers. She knew not why, but the merriment of those people passing on their ship through the night and the solitary sea affected her on a sudden with horror. When the consul released her she slipped away and, with a look to see that no one had noticed her, ascended the companion to the boat deck. Here everything was in darkness. She walked softly to a spot where she knew she would be safe from all intrusion. But she heard a faint laugh and she caught sight in a hidden corner of a Columbine and a Malay sultan. Mrs. Linsell and the doctor had resumed already the flirtation which the death of Gallagher had interrupted.

Already all those people had put out of their minds with a kind of ferocity the thought of that poor lonely man who had so strangely died in their midst. They felt no compassion for him, but resentment rather, because on his account they had been ill-at-ease. They seized upon life avidly. They made their jokes, they flirted, they gossiped. Mrs. Hamlyn remembered what the consul had said, that among Mr. Gallagher's papers no letters could be found, not the name of a single friend to whom the news of his death might be sent, and she knew not why this seemed to her unbearably tragic. There was something mysterious in a man who could pass through the world in such solitariness. When she remembered how he had come on deck in Singapore, so short a while since, in such rude health, full of vitality, and his arrogant plans for the future, she was seized with dismay. Those words of the burial service filled her with a solemn awe: *Man that is born of a woman hath but a short time to live, and is full of misery. He cometh up, and is cut down, like a flower* . . . Year in, year out, he had made his plans for the future, he wanted to live so much and he had so much to live for, and then just when he stretched out his hand—oh, it was pitiful; it made all the other distresses of the world of small account. Death with its mystery was the only thing that really mattered. Mrs. Hamlyn leaned over the rail and looked at the starry sky. Why did people make themselves unhappy? Let them weep for the death of those they loved, death was terrible always, but for the rest, was it worth while to be wretched, to harbour malice, to be vain and uncharitable? She thought again of herself and her husband and the woman he so strangely loved. He too had said that we live to be happy so short a time and we are so long dead. She pondered long and intently, and suddenly, as summer lightning flashes across the darkness of the night, she made a discovery which filled her with tremulous surprise; for she found that in her heart was no longer anger with her husband nor jealousy of her rival. A notion dawned on some remote horizon of her consciousness and like the morning sun suffused her soul with a tender, blissful glow. Out of the tragedy of that unknown Irishman's death she gathered elatedly the courage for a desperate resolution. Her heart beat quickly, she was impatient to carry it into effect. A passion for self-sacrifice seized her.

The music had stopped, the ball was over; most of the passengers would have gone to bed and the rest would be in the smoking-room. She went down to her cabin and met no one on the way. She took her writing pad and wrote a letter to her husband:

My dear. It is Christmas Day and I want to tell you that my heart is filled with kindly thoughts towards both of you. I have been foolish and unreasonable. I think we should allow those we care for to be happy in their own way, and we should care for them enough not to let it make us unhappy. I want you to know that I grudge you none of the joy that has so strangely come into your life. I am no longer jealous, nor hurt, nor vindictive. Do not think I shall be unhappy or lonely. If ever you feel that you need me, come to me, and I will welcome you with a cheerful spirit and without reproach or ill-will. I am most grateful for all the years of happiness and of tenderness that you gave me, and in return I wish to offer you an affection which makes no claim on you and is, I hope, utterly disinterested. Think kindly of me and be happy, happy, happy.

She signed her name and put the letter into an envelope. Though it would not go till they reached Port Said she wanted to place it at once in the letter-box. When she had done this, beginning to undress, she looked at herself in the glass. Her eyes were shining and under her rouge her colour was bright. The future was no longer desolate, but bright with a fair hope. She slipped into bed and fell at once into a sound and dreamless sleep.

Episode

IT was quite a small party, because our hostess liked general conversation; we never sat down to dinner more than eight, and
generally only six, and after dinner when we went up to the drawing-
room the chairs were so arranged that it was impossible for two persons to go into a huddle in a corner and so break things up. I was
glad on arriving to find that I knew everyone. There were two nice
clever women besides our hostess and two men besides myself.
One was my friend Ned Preston. Our hostess made it a point never
to ask wives with their husbands, because she said each cramped the
other's style and if they didn't like to come separately they needn't
come at all. But since her food and her wine were good and the talk
almost always entertaining they generally came. People sometimes
accused her of asking husbands more often than wives, but she
defended herself by saying that she couldn't possibly help it because
more men were husbands than women were wives.

Ned Preston was a Scot, a good-humoured, merry soul, with a
gift for telling a story, sometimes too lengthily, for he was un-
commonly loquacious, but with dramatic intensity. He was a
bachelor with a small income which sufficed for his modest needs,
and in this he was lucky since he suffered from that form of chronic
tuberculosis which may last for years without killing you, but which
prevents you from working for your living. Now and then he would
be ill enough to stay in bed for two or three weeks, but then he would
get better and be as gay, cheerful and talkative as ever. I doubt
whether he had enough money to live in an expensive sanatorium
and he certainly hadn't the temperament to suit himself to its life.
He was worldly. When he was well he liked to go out, out to lunch,
out to dinner, and he liked to sit up late into the night smoking his
pipe and drinking a good deal of whisky. If he had been content to
live the life of an invalid he might have been alive now, but he
wasn't; and who can blame him? He died at the age of fifty-five of a
hæmorrhage which he had one night after coming home from some
house where, he may well have flattered himself, he was the success
of the party.

He had that febrile vitality that some consumptives have, and
was always looking for an occupation to satisfy his desire for activity.
I don't know how he heard that at Wormwood Scrubs they were in
want of prison visitors, but the idea took his fancy so he went to the

O   1141

Home Office and saw the official in charge of prisons to offer his services. The job is unpaid, and though a number of persons are willing to undertake it, either from compassion or curiosity, they are apt to grow tired of it, or find it takes up too much time, and the prisoners whose problems, interests and future they have been concerned with are left somewhat in the lurch. The Home Office people consequently are wary of taking on anyone who does not look as if he would persevere, and they make careful enquiries into the applicant's antecedents, character and general suitability. Then he is given a trial, is discreetly watched, and if the impression is unfavourable is politely thanked and told that his services are no longer required. But Ned Preston satisfied the dour and shrewd official who interviewed him that he was in every way reliable, and from the beginning he got on well with the governor, the warders and the prisoners. He was entirely lacking in class-consciousness, so prisoners, whatever their station in life, felt at ease with him. He neither preached nor moralised. He had never done a criminal, or even a mean, thing in his life, but he treated the crime of the prisoners he had to deal with as though it were an illness like his own tuberculosis which was a nuisance you had to put up with, but which it did no good to talk about.

Wormwood Scrubs is a first offenders' prison and it is a building, grim and cold, of forbidding appearance. Ned took me over it once and I had goose-flesh as the gates were unlocked for us and we went in. We passed through the halls in which the men were working.

"If you see any pals of yours take no notice of them," Ned said to me. "They don't like it."

"Am I likely to see any pals of mine?" I asked dryly.

"You never can tell. I shouldn't be surprised if you had had friends who'd passed bad cheques once too often or were caught in a compromising situation in one of the parks. You'd be surprised how often I run across chaps I've met out at dinner."

One of Ned's duties was to see prisoners through the first difficult days of their confinement. They were often badly shaken by their trial and sentence; and when, after the preliminary proceedings they had to go through on entering the goal, the stripping, the bath, the medical examination and the questioning, the getting into prison clothes, they were led into a cell and locked up, they were apt to break down. Sometimes they cried hysterically; sometimes they could neither eat nor sleep. Ned's business then was to cheer them, and his breezy manner, his natural kindliness, often worked wonders. If they were anxious about their wives and children he would go to see them and if they were destitute provide them with money. He brought them news so that they might get over the awful feeling that they were shut away from the common interests of their fellow-men. He read the sporting papers to be able to tell them what horse had won an important race or whether the champion had won his fight. He would advise them about their future, and when the time approached for their release see what jobs they were fitted for and then persuade employers to give them a chance to make good.

Since everyone is interested in crime it was inevitable that sooner or later, with Ned there, the conversation should turn upon it. It was after dinner and we were sitting comfortably in the drawing-room with drinks in our hands.

"Had any interesting cases at the Scrubs lately, Ned?" I asked him.

"No, nothing much."

He had a high, rasping voice and his laugh was a raucous cackle. He broke into it now.

"I went to see an old girl to-day who was a packet of fun. Her husband's a burglar. The police have known about him for years, but they've never been able to get him till just now. Before he did a job he and his wife concocted an alibi, and though he's been arrested three or four times and sent up for trial, the police have never been able to break it and he's always got off. Well, he was arrested again a little while ago, but he wasn't upset, the alibi he and his wife had made up was perfect and he expected to be acquitted as he'd been before. His wife went into the witness-box and to his utter amazement she didn't give the alibi and he was convicted. I went to see him. He wasn't so much worried at being in gaol as puzzled by his wife not having spoken up, and he asked me to go and see her and ask what the game was. Well, I went, and d'you know what she said to me? She said: 'Well, sir, it's like this; it was such a beautiful alibi I just couldn't bear to waste it.'"

Of course we all laughed. The story-teller likes an appreciative audience, and Ned Preston was never disinclined to hold the floor. He narrated two or three more anecdotes. They tended to prove a point he was fond of making, that in what till we all got democratic in England were called the lower orders there was more passion, more romance, more disregard of consequences than could ever be found in the well-to-do and presumably educated classes, whom prudence has made timid and convention inhibited.

"Because the working man doesn't read much," he said, "because he has no great gift for expressing himself, you think he has no imagination. You're wrong. He's extravagantly imaginative.

Because he's a great husky brute you think he has no nerves. You're wrong again. He's a bundle of nerves."

Then he told us a story which I shall tell as best I can in my own words.

Fred Manson was a good-looking fellow, tall, well-made, with blue eyes, good features and a friendly, agreeable smile, but what made him remarkable so that people turned round in the streets to stare at him was that he had a thick head of hair, with a great wave in it, of a deep rich red. It was really a great beauty. Perhaps it was this that gave him so sensual a look. His maleness was like a heady perfume. His eyebrows were thick, only a little lighter than his hair, and he was lucky enough not to have the ugly skin that so often disfigures red-heads. His was a smooth olive. His eyes were bold, and when he smiled or laughed, which in the healthy vitality of his youth he did constantly, his expression was wonderfully alluring. He was twenty-two and he gave you the rather pleasant impression of just loving to be alive. It was inevitable that with such looks and above all with that troubling sexuality he should have success with women. He was charming, tender and passionate, but immensely promiscuous. He was not exactly callous or brazen, he had a kindly nature, but somehow or other he made it quite clear to the objects of his passing fancy that all he wanted was a little bit of fun and that it was impossible for him to remain faithful to anyone.

Fred was a postman. He worked in Brixton. It is a densely populated part of London, and has the curious reputation of harbouring more criminals than any other suburb because trams run to it from across the river all night long, so that when a man has done a job of housebreaking in the West End he can be sure of getting home without difficulty. Fred liked his job. Brixton is a district of innumerable streets lined with little houses inhabited by the people who work in the neighbourhood and also by clerks, shop-assistants, skilled workers of one sort or another whose jobs take them every day across the river. He was strong and healthy and it was a pleasure to him to walk from street to street delivering the letters. Sometimes there would be a postal packet to hand in or a registered letter that had to be signed for, and then he would have the opportunity of seeing people. He was a sociable creature. It was never long before he was well known on whatever round he was assigned to. After a time his job was changed. His duty then was to go to the red pillar-boxes into which the letters were put, empty them, and take the contents to the main post-office of the district. His bag would be pretty heavy sometimes by the time he was through, but he was proud of his strength and the weight only made him laugh.

One day he was emptying a box in one of the better streets, a street of semi-detached houses, and had just closed his bag when a girl came running along.

"Postman," she cried, "take this letter, will you. I want it to go by this post most particularly."

He gave her his good-natured smile.

"I never mind obliging a lady," he said, putting down his bag and opening it.

"I wouldn't trouble you, only it's urgent," she said as she handed him the letter she had in her hand.

"Who is it to—a feller?" he grinned.

"None of your business."

"All right, be haughty. But I tell you this, he's no good. Don't you trust him."

"You've got a nerve," she said.

"So they tell me."

He took off his cap and ran his hand through his mop of curling red hair. The sight of it made her gasp.

"Where d'you get your perm?" she asked with a giggle.

"I'll show you one of these days if you like."

He was looking down at her with his amused eyes, and there was something about him that gave her a funny little feeling in the pit of her stomach.

"Well, I must be on my way," he said. "If I don't get on with the job pretty damn quick I don't know what'll happen to the country."

"I'm not detaining you," she said coolly.

"That's where you make a mistake," he answered.

He gave her a look that made her heart beat nineteen to the dozen and she felt herself blushing all over. She turned away and ran back to the house. Fred noticed it was four doors away from the pillar-box. He had to pass it and as he did so he looked up. He saw the net curtains twitch and knew she was watching. He felt pleased with himself. During the next few days he looked at the house whenever he passed it, but never caught a glimpse of the girl. One afternoon he ran across her by chance just as he was entering the street in which she lived.

"Hulloa," he said, stopping.

"Hulloa."

She blushed scarlet.

"Haven't seen you about lately."

"You haven't missed much."

"That's what you think."

1146 THE WORLD OVER

She was prettier than he remembered, dark-haired, dark-eyed, rather tall, slight, with a good figure, a pale skin and very white teeth.

"What about coming to the pictures with me one evening?"

"Taking a lot for granted, aren't you?"

"It pays," he said with his impudent, charming grin.

She couldn't help laughing.

"Not with me, it doesn't."

"Oh, come on. One's only young once."

There was something so attractive in him that she couldn't bring herself to give him a saucy answer.

"I couldn't really. My people wouldn't like me going out with a fellow I don't know. You see, I'm the only one they have and they think a rare lot of me. Why, I don't even know your name."

"Well, I can tell you, can't I? Fred. Fred Manson. Can't you say you're going to the pictures with a girl friend?"

She had never felt before what she was feeling then. She didn't know if it was pain or pleasure. She was strangely breathless.

"I suppose I could do that."

They fixed the night, the time and the place. Fred was waiting for her and they went in, but when the picture started and he put his arm round her waist, without a word, her eyes fixed on the screen, she quietly took it away. He took hold of her hand, but she withdrew it. He was surprised. That wasn't the way girls usually behaved. He didn't know what one went to the pictures for if it wasn't to have a bit of a cuddle. He walked home with her after the show. She told him her name. Grace Carter. Her father had a shop of his own in the Brixton Road, he was a draper and he had four assistants.

"He must be doing well," said Fred.

"He doesn't complain."

Gracie was a student at London University. When she got her degree she was going to be a school teacher.

"What d'you want to do that for when there's a good business waiting for you?"

"Pa doesn't want me to have anything to do with the shop—not after the education he's given me. He wants me to better myself, if you know what I mean."

Her father had started life as an errand boy, then become a draper's assistant and because he was hard-working, honest and intelligent was now owner of a prosperous little business. Success had given him grand ideas for his only child. He didn't want her to have anything to do with trade. He hoped she'd marry a professional man perhaps, or at least someone in the City. Then he'd sell the business and retire, and Gracie would be quite the lady.

When they reached the corner of her street Gracie held out her hand.

"You'd better not come to the door," she said.

"Aren't you going to kiss me good-night?"

"I am not."

"Why?"

"Because I don't want to."

"You'll come to the pictures again, won't you?"

"I think I'd better not."

"Oh, come on."

There was such a warm urgency in his voice that she felt as though her knees would give way.

"Will you behave if I do?" He nodded. "Promise?"

"Swop me bob."

He scratched his head when he left her. Funny girl. He'd never met anyone quite like her. Superior, there was no doubt about that. There was something in her voice that got you. It was warm and soft. He tried to think what it was like. It was like as if the words kissed you. Sounded silly, that did, but that's just what it was like.

From then on they went to the pictures once or twice a week. After a while she allowed him to put his arm round her waist and to hold her hand, but she never let him go farther than that.

"Have you ever been kissed by a fellow?" he asked her once.

"No, I haven't," she said simply. "My ma's funny, she says you've got to keep a man's respect."

"I'd give anything in the world just to kiss you, Gracie."

"Don't be so silly."

"Won't you let me just once?" She shook her head. "Why not?"

"Because I like you too much," she said hoarsely, and then walked quickly away from him.

It gave him quite a turn. He wanted her as he'd never wanted a woman before. What she'd said finished him. He'd been thinking of her a lot, and he'd looked forward to the evenings they spent together as he'd never looked forward to anything in his life. For the first time he was uncertain of himself. She was above him in every way, what with her father making money hand over fist and her education and everything, and him only a postman. They had made a date for the following Friday night and he was in a fever of anxiety lest she shouldn't come. He repeated to himself over and over again what she'd said: perhaps it meant that she'd made up her mind to drop him. When at last he saw her walking along the street he almost sobbed with relief. That evening he neither put his arm round her nor took her hand and when he walked her home he never said a word.

"You're very quiet to-night, Fred," she said at last. "What's the matter with you?"

He walked a few steps before he answered.

"I don't like to tell you."

She stopped suddenly and looked up at him. There was terror on her face.

"Tell me whatever it is," she said unsteadily.

"I'm gone, I can't help myself, I'm so stuck on you I can't see straight. I didn't know what it was to love like I love you."

"Oh, is that all? You gave me such a fright. I thought you were going to say you were going to be married."

"Me? Who d'you take me for? It's you I want to marry."

"Well, what's to prevent you, silly?"

"Gracie! D'you mean it?"

He flung his arms round her and kissed her full on the mouth. She didn't resist. She returned his kiss and he felt in her a passion as eager as his own.

They arranged that Gracie should tell her parents that she was engaged to him and that on the Sunday he should come and be introduced to them. Since the shop stayed open late on Saturday and by the time Mr. Carter got home he was tired out, it was not till after dinner on Sunday that Gracie broke her news. George Carter was a brisk, not very tall man, but sturdy, with a high colour, who with increasing prosperity had put on weight. He was more than rather bald and he had a bristle of grey moustache. Like many another employer who has risen from the working class he was a slave-driver and he got as much work out of his assistants for as little money as was possible. He had an eye for everything and he wouldn't put up with any nonsense, but he was reasonable and even kindly, so that they did not dislike him. Mrs. Carter was a quiet, nice woman, with a pleasant face and the remains of good looks. They were both in the early fifties, for they had married late after "walking out" for nearly ten years.

They were very much surprised when Gracie told them what she had to tell, but not displeased.

"You are a sly one," said her father. "Why, I never suspected for a minute you'd taken up with anyone. Well, I suppose it had to come sooner or later. What's his name?"

"Fred Manson."

"A fellow you met at college?"

"No. You must have seen him about. He clears our pillar-box. He's a postman."

"Oh, Gracie," cried Mrs. Carter, "you can't mean it. You can't marry a common postman, not after all the education we've given you."

For an instant Mr. Carter was speechless. He got redder in the face than ever.

"Your ma's right, my girl," he burst out now. "You can't throw yourself away like that. Why, it's ridiculous."

"I'm not throwing myself away. You wait till you see him."

Mrs. Carter began to cry.

"It's such a come-down. It's such a humiliation. I shall never be able to hold up my head again."

"Oh, Ma, don't talk like that. He's a nice fellow and he's got a good job."

"You don't understand," she moaned.

"How d'you get to know him?" Mr. Carter interrupted. "What sort of a family's he got?"

"His pa drives one of the post-office vans," Gracie answered defiantly.

"Working-class people."

"Well, what of it? His pa's worked twenty-four years for the post-office and they think a lot of him."

Mrs. Carter was biting the corner of her handkerchief.

"Gracie, I want to tell you something. Before your pa and me got married I was in domestic service. He wouldn't ever let me tell you because he didn't want you to be ashamed of me. That's why we was engaged all those years. The lady I was with said she'd leave me something in her will if I stayed with her till she passed away."

"It was that money that gave me my start," Mr. Carter broke in. "Except for that I'd never have been where I am to-day. And I don't mind telling you your ma's the best wife a man ever had."

"I never had a proper education," Mrs. Carter went on, "but I always was ambitious. The proudest moment of my life was when your pa said we could afford a girl to help me and he said then: 'The time'll come when you have a cook *and* a house-maid,' and he's been as good as his word, and now you're going back to what I come from. I'd set my heart on your marrying a gentleman."

She began crying again. Gracie loved her parents and couldn't bear to see them so distressed.

"I'm sorry, Ma, I knew it would be a disappointment to you, but I can't help it, I can't really. I love him so, I love him so terribly. I'm sure you'll like him when you see him. We're going for a walk on the Common this afternoon. Can't I bring him back to supper?"

Mrs. Carter gave her husband a harassed look. He sighed.

"I don't like it and it's no good pretending I do, but I suppose we'd better have a look at him."

Supper passed off better than might have been expected. Fred wasn't shy, and he talked to Gracie's parents as though he had known them all his life. If to be waited on by a maid, if to sup in a dining-room furnished in solid mahogany and afterwards to sit in a drawing-room that had a grand piano in it was new to him, he showed no embarrassment. After he had gone and they were alone in their bedroom Mr. and Mrs. Carter talked him over.

"He is handsome, you can't deny that," she said.

"Handsome is as handsome does. D'you think he's after her money?"

"Well, he must know that you've got a tidy little bit tucked away somewhere, but he's in love with her all right."

"Oh, what makes you think that?"

"Why, you've only got to see the way he looks at her."

"Well, that's something at all events."

In the end the Carters withdrew their opposition on the condition that the young things shouldn't marry until Gracie had taken her degree. That would give them a year, and at the back of their minds was the hope that by then she would have changed her mind. They saw a good deal of Fred after that. He spent every Sunday with them. Little by little they began quite to like him. He was so easy, so gay, so full of high spirits, and above all so obviously head over ears in love with Gracie, that Mrs. Carter soon succumbed to his charm, and after a while even Mr. Carter was prepared to admit that he didn't seem a bad fellow. Fred and Gracie were happy. She went to London every day to attend lectures and worked hard. They spent blissful evenings together. He gave her a very nice engagement ring and often took her out to dinner in the West End and to a play. On fine Sundays he drove her out into the country in a car that he said a friend had lent him. When she asked him if he could afford all the money he spent on her he laughed, and said a chap had given him a tip on an outsider and he'd made a packet. They talked interminably of the little flat they would have when they were married and the fun it would be to furnish it. They were more in love with one another than ever.

Then the blow fell. Fred was arrested for stealing money from the letters he collected. Many people, to save themselves the trouble of buying postal orders, put notes in their envelopes, and it wasn't difficult to tell that they were there. Fred went up for trial, pleaded guilty, and was sentenced to two years' hard labour. Gracie went to the trial. Up to the last moment she had hoped that he would be able to prove his innocence. It was a dreadful shock to her when he pleaded guilty. She was not allowed to see him. He went straight from the dock to the prison van. She went home and, locking herself up in her bedroom, threw herself on the bed and wept. When Mr. Carter came back from the shop Gracie's mother went up to her room.

"Gracie, you're to come downstairs," she said. "Your father wants to speak to you."

Gracie got up and went down. She did not trouble to dry her eyes.

"Seen the paper?" he said, holding out to her the *Evening News*. She didn't answer.

"Well, that's the end of that young man," he went on harshly.

They too, Gracie's parents, had been shocked when Fred was arrested, but she was so distressed, she was so convinced that everything could be explained, that they hadn't had the heart to tell her that she must have nothing more to do with him. But now they felt it time to have things out with her.

"So that's where the money came from for those dinners and theatres. And the car. I thought it funny he should have a friend who'd lend him a car on Sundays when he'd be wanting it himself. He hired it, didn't he?"

"I suppose so," she answered miserably. "I just believed what he told me."

"You've had a lucky escape, my girl, that's all I can say."

"He only did it because he wanted to give me a good time. He didn't want me to think I couldn't have everything as nice when I was with him as what I've been used to at home."

"You're not going to make excuses for him, I hope. He's a thief, that's what he is."

"I don't care," she said sullenly.

"You don't care? What d'you mean by that?"

"Exactly what I say. I'm going to wait for him and the moment he comes out I'm going to marry him."

Mrs. Carter gave a gasp of horror.

"Gracie, you can't do a thing like that," she cried. "Think of the disgrace. And what about us? We've always held our heads high. He's a thief, and once a thief always a thief."

"Don't go on calling him a thief," Gracie shrieked, stamping her

foot with rage. "What he did he did just because he loved me. I
don't care if he is a thief. I love him more than ever I loved him.
You don't know what love is. You waited ten years to marry Pa just
so as an old woman should leave you some money. D'you call that
love?"

"You leave your ma out of this," Mr. Carter shouted. Then
an idea occurred to him and he gave her a piercing glance. "Have
you *got* to marry the feller?"

Gracie blushed furiously.

"No. There's never been anything of that sort. And not through
any fault of mine either. He loved me too much. He didn't want to
do anything perhaps he'd regret afterwards."

Often on summer evenings in the country when they'd been lying
in a field in one another's arms, mouth to mouth, her desire had
been as intense as his. She knew how much he wanted her and she
was ready to give him what he asked. But when things got too
desperate he'd suddenly jump up and say:

"Come on, let's walk."

He'd drag her to her feet. She knew what was in his mind. He
wanted to wait till they were married. His love had given him a
delicacy of sentiment that he'd never known before. He couldn't
make it out himself, but he had a funny sort of feeling about her,
he felt that if he had her before marriage it would spoil things.
Because she guessed what was in his heart she loved him all the
more.

"I don't know what's come over you," moaned Mrs. Carter.
"You was always such a good girl. You've never given us a day's
uneasiness."

"Stop it, Ma," said Mr. Carter violently. "We've got to get this
straight once and for all. You've got to give up this man, see? I've
got me own position to think of and if you think I'm going to have a
gaol-bird for a son-in-law you'd better think again. I've had enough
of this nonsense. You've got to promise me that you'll have nothing
more to do with the feller ever."

"D'you think I'm going to give him up now? How often d'you
want me to tell you I'm going to marry him the moment he gets
out?"

"All right, then you can get out of my house and get out pretty
damn quick. And stay out."

"Pa!" cried Mrs. Carter.

"Shut up."

"I'll be glad to go," said Gracie.

"Oh, will you? And how d'you think you're going to live?"

"I can work, can't I? I can get a job at Payne & Perkins. They'll be glad to have me."

"Oh, Gracie, you couldn't go and work in a shop. You can't demean yourself like that," said Mrs. Carter.

"Will you shut up, Ma," shouted Mr. Carter, beside himself now with rage. "Work, will you? You that's never done a stroke of work in your life except that tomfoolery at the college. Bright idea it was of your ma's to give you an education. Fat lot of good it'll be to you when you've got to stand on your feet for hours and got to be civil and pleasant to a lot of old trouts who just try and give you all the trouble they can just to show how superior they are. I bet you'll like it when you're bawled out by the manageress because you're not bright and snappy. All right, marry your gaol-bird. I suppose you know you'll have to keep him too. You don't think anyone's going to give him a job, do you, not with his record. Get out, get out, get out."

He had worked himself up to such a pitch of fury that he sank panting into a chair. Mrs. Carter, frightened, poured out a glass of water and gave him some to drink. Gracie slipped out of the room.

Next day, when her father had gone to work and her mother was out shopping, she left the house with such effects as she could get into a suit-case. Payne & Perkins was a large department store in the Brixton Road, and with her good appearance and pleasant manner she found no difficulty in getting taken on. She was put in the ladies' lingerie. For a few days she stayed at the Y.W.C.A. and then arranged to share a room with one of the girls who worked with her.

Ned Preston saw Fred in the evening of the day he went to gaol. He found him shattered, but only because of Gracie. He took his thieving very lightly.

"I had to do the right thing by her, didn't I? Her people, they didn't think I was good enough for her; I wanted to show them I was just as good as they were. When we went up to the West End I couldn't give her a sandwich and half of bitter in a pub, why, she's never been in a pub in her life, I *had* to take her to a restaurant. If people are such fools as to put money in letters, well, they're just asking for it."

But he was frightened. He wasn't sure that Gracie would see it like that.

"I've got to know what she's going to do. If she chucks me now—well, it's the end of everything for me, see? I'll find some way of doing meself in, I swear to God I will."

He told Ned the whole story of his love for Gracie.

"I could have had her over and over again if I'd wanted to. And I did want to and so did she. I knew that. But I respected her, see? She's not like other girls. She's one in a thousand, I tell you."

He talked and talked. He stormed, he wept. From that confused torrent of words emerged one thing very clearly. A passionate, a frenzied love. Ned promised that he would see the girl.

"Tell her I love her, tell her that what I did I just did because I wanted her to have the best of everything, and tell her I just can't live without her."

As soon as he could find time Ned Preston went to the Carters' house, but when he asked for Gracie the maid who opened the door told him that she didn't live there any more. Then he asked to see her mother.

"I'll go and see if she's in."

He gave the maid his card, thinking the name of his club engraved in the corner would impress Mrs. Carter enough to make her willing to see him. The maid left him at the door, but in a minute or two asked him to come in. He was shown into the stiff and little-used sitting-room. Mrs. Carter kept him waiting for some time and when she came in, holding his card in the tips of her fingers, he guessed it was because she had thought fit to change her dress. The black silk she wore was evidently a dress for occasions. He told her his connection with Wormwood Scrubs and said that he had to do with a man named Frederick Manson. The moment he mentioned the name Mrs. Carter assumed a hostile attitude.

"Don't speak to me of that man," she cried. "A thief, that's what he is. The trouble he's caused us. They ought to have given him five years, they ought."

"I'm sorry he's caused you trouble," said Ned mildly. "Perhaps if you'd give me a few facts I might help to straighten things out."

Ned Preston certainly had a way with him. Perhaps Mrs. Carter was impressed because he was a gentleman. "Class he is," she probably said to herself. Anyhow it was not long before she was telling him the whole story. She grew upset as she told it and began to cry.

"And now she's gone and left us. Run away. I don't know how she could bring herself to do a thing like that. God knows, we love her. She's all we've got and we done everything in the world for her. Her pa never meant it when he told her to get out of the house. Only she was so obstinate. He got in a temper, he always was a quick-tempered man, he was just as upset as I was when we found she'd gone. And d'you know what's she's been and gone and done? Got herself a job at Payne & Perkins. Mr. Carter can't abide them. Cutting prices all the time they are. Unfair competition, he calls it. And to think of our Gracie working with a lot of shop-girls—oh, it's so humiliating."

Ned made a mental note of the store's name. He hadn't been at all sure of getting Gracie's address out of Mrs. Carter.

"Have you seen her since she left you?" he asked.

"Of course I have. I knew they'd jump at her at Payne & Perkins, a superior girl like that, and I went there, and there she was, sure enough—in the ladies' lingerie. I waited outside till closing time and then I spoke to her. I asked her to come home. I said her pa was willing to let bygones be bygones. And d'you know what she said? She said she'd come home if we never said a word against Fred and if we was prepared to have her marry him as soon as ever he got out. Of course I had to tell her pa. I never saw him in such a state, I thought he was going to have a fit, he said he'd rather see her dead at his feet than married to that gaol-bird."

Mrs. Carter again burst into tears and as soon as he could Ned Preston left her. He went to the department store, up to the ladies' lingerie, and asked for Grace Carter. She was pointed out to him and he went up to her.

"Can I speak to you for a minute? I've come from Fred Manson."

She went deathly white. For a moment it seemed that she could not utter a word.

"Follow me, please."

She took him into a passage smelling of disinfectants which seemed to lead to the lavatories. They were alone. She stared at him anxiously.

"He sends you his love. He's worried about you. He's afraid you're awfully unhappy. What he wants to know really is if you're going to chuck him."

"Me?" Her eyes filled with tears, but on her face was a look of ecstasy. "Tell him that nothing matters to me as long as he loves me. Tell him I'd wait twenty years for him if I had to. Tell him I'm counting the days till he gets out so as we can get married."

For fear of the manageress she couldn't stay away from her work for more than a minute or two. She gave Ned all the loving messages she could get into the time to give Fred Manson. Ned didn't get to the Scrubs till nearly six. The prisoners are allowed to put down their tools at five-thirty and Fred had just put his down. When Ned entered the cell he turned pale and sank on to the bed as though his anxiety was such that he didn't trust his legs. But when Ned told him his news he gave a gasp of relief. For a while he couldn't trust himself to speak.

"I knew you'd seen her the moment you came in. I smelt her."

He sniffed as though the smell of her body were strong in his nostrils, and his face was as it were a mask of desire. His features on a sudden seemed strangely blurred.

"You know, it made me feel quite uncomfortable so that I had to look the other way," said Ned Preston when he told us this, with a cackle of his shrill laughter. "It was sex in its nakedness all right."

Fred was an exemplary prisoner. He worked well, he gave no trouble. Ned suggested books for him to read and he took them out of the library, but that was about as far as he got.

"I can't get on well with them somehow," he said. "I start reading and then I begin thinking of Gracie. You know, when she kisses you ordinary-like—oh, it's so sweet, but when she kisses you really, my God, it's lovely."

Fred was allowed to see Gracie once a month, but their meetings, with a glass screen between, under the eyes of a warder, were so painful that after several visits they agreed it would be better if she didn't come any more. A year passed. Owing to his good behaviour he could count on a remittance of his sentence and so would be free in another six months. Gracie had saved every penny she could out of her wages and now as the time approached for Fred's release she set about getting a home ready for him. She took two rooms in a house and furnished them on the hire purchase system. One room of course was to be their bedroom and the other the living-room and kitchen. There was an old-fashioned range in it and this she had taken out and replaced by a gas-stove. She wanted everything to be nice and new and clean and comfortable. She took pains to make the two little rooms bright and pretty. To do all this she had to go without all but the barest necessities of existence and she grew thin and pale. Ned suspected that she was starving herself and when he went to see her took a box of chocolates or a cake so that she should have at least something to eat. He brought the prisoner news of what Gracie was doing and she made him promise to give him accurate accounts of every article she bought. He took fond, more than fond, passionate messages from one to the other. He was convinced that Fred would go straight in future and he got him a job as commissionaire from a firm that had a chain of restaurants in London. The wages were good and by calling taxis or fetching cars he would be able to make money on the side. He was to start work as soon as he came out of gaol. Gracie took the necessary steps so that they could get married at once. The eighteen months of

Fred's imprisonment were drawing to an end. Gracie was in a fever of excitement.

It happened then that Ned Preston had one of his periodical bouts of illness and was unable to go to the prison for three weeks. It bothered him, for he didn't like to abandon his prisoners, so as soon as he could get out of bed he went to the Scrubs. The chief warder told him that Manson had been asking for him.

"I think you'd better go and see him. I don't know what's the matter with him. He's been acting rather funny since you've been away."

It was just a fortnight before Fred was due to be released. Ned Preston went to his cell.

"Well, Fred, how are you?" he asked. "Sorry I haven't been able to come and see you. I've been ill, and I haven't been able to see Gracie either. She must be all of a dither by now."

"Well, I want you to go and see her."

His manner was so surly that Ned was taken aback. It was unlike him to be anything but pleasant and civil.

"Of course I will."

"I want you to tell her that I'm not going to marry her."

Ned was so astounded that for a minute he could only stare blankly at Fred Manson.

"What on earth d'you mean?"

"Exactly what I say."

"You can't let her down now. Her people have thrown her out. She's been working all this time to get a home ready for you. She's got the licence and everything."

"I don't care. I'm not going to marry her."

"But why, why, why?"

Ned was flabbergasted. Fred Manson was silent for a bit. His face was dark and sullen.

"I'll tell you. I've thought about her night and day for eighteen months and now I'm sick to death of her."

When Ned Preston reached this point of his story our hostess and our fellow guests broke into loud laughter. He was plainly taken aback. There was some little talk after that and the party broke up. Ned and I, having to go in the same direction, walked along Piccadilly together. For a time we walked in silence.

"I noticed you didn't laugh with the others," he said abruptly.

"I didn't think it funny."

"What d'you make of it?"

"Well, I can see his point, you know. Imagination's an odd thing, it dries up; I suppose, thinking of her incessantly all that time he'd exhausted every emotion she could give him, and I think it was quite literally true, he'd just got sick to death of her. He'd squeezed the lemon dry and there was nothing to do but throw away the rind."

"I didn't think it funny either. That's why I didn't tell them the rest of the story. I wouldn't accept it at first. I thought it was just hysteria or something. I went to see him two or three days running. I argued with him. I really did my damnedest. I thought if he'd only see her it would be all right, but he wouldn't even do that. He said he hated the sight of her. I couldn't move him. At last I had to go and tell her."

We walked on a little longer in silence.

"I saw her in that beastly, stinking corridor. She saw at once there was something the matter and she went awfully white. She wasn't a girl to show much emotion. There was something gracious and rather noble about her face. Tranquil. Her lips quivered a bit when I told her and she didn't say anything for a minute. When she spoke it was quite calmly, as though—well, as though she'd just missed a bus and would have to wait for another. As though it was a nuisance, you know, but nothing to make a song and dance about. 'There's nothing for me to do now but put my head in the gas-oven,' she said.

"And she did."

The Kite

I KNOW this is an odd story. I don't understand it myself and if I set it down in black and white it is only with a faint hope that when I have written it I may get a clearer view of it, or rather with the hope that some reader, better acquainted with the complications of human nature than I am, may offer me an explanation that will make it comprehensible to me. Of course the first thing that occurs to me is that there is something Freudian about it. Now, I have read a good deal of Freud, and some books by his followers, and intending to write this story I have recently flipped through again the volume published by the Modern Library which contains his basic writings. It was something of a task, for he is a dull and verbose writer, and the acrimony with which he claims to have originated such and such a theory shows a vanity and a jealousy of others working in the same field which somewhat ill become the man of science. I believe, however, that he was a kindly and benign old party. As we know, there is often a great difference between the man and the writer. The writer may be bitter, harsh and brutal, while the man may be so meek and mild that he wouldn't say boo to a goose. But that is neither here nor there. I found nothing in my re-reading of Freud's works that cast any light on the subject I had in mind. I can only relate the facts and leave it at that.

First of all I must make it plain that it is not my story and that I knew none of the persons with whom it is concerned. It was told me one evening by my friend Ned Preston, and he told it me because he didn't know how to deal with the circumstances and he thought, quite wrongly as it happened, that I might be able to give him some advice that would help him. In a previous story I have related what I thought the reader should know about Ned Preston, and so now I need only remind him that my friend was a prison visitor at Wormwood Scrubs. He took his duties very seriously and made the prisoners' troubles his own. We had been dining together at the Café Royal in that long, low room with its absurd and charming decoration which is all that remains of the old Café Royal that painters have loved to paint; and we were sitting over our coffee and liqueurs and, so far as Ned was concerned against his doctor's orders, smoking very long and very good Havanas.

"I've got a funny chap to deal with at the Scrubs just now," he said, after a pause, "and I'm blowed if I know how to deal with him."

"What's he in for?" I asked.

"He left his wife and the court ordered him to pay so much a week in alimony and he's absolutely refused to pay it. I've argued with him till I was blue in the face. I've told him he's only cutting off his nose to spite his face. He says he'll stay in goal all his life rather than pay her a penny. I tell him he can't let her starve, and all he says is: 'Why not?' He's perfectly well behaved, he's no trouble, he works well, he seems quite happy, he's just getting a lot of fun out of thinking what a devil of a time his wife is having."

"What's he got against her?"

"She smashed his kite."

"She did what?" I cried.

"Exactly that. She smashed his kite. He says he'll never forgive her for that till his dying day."

"He must be crazy."

"No, he isn't, he's a perfectly reasonable, quite intelligent, decent fellow."

Herbert Sunbury was his name, and his mother, who was very refined, never allowed him to be called Herb or Bertie, but always Herbert, just as she never called her husband Sam but only Samuel. Mrs. Sunbury's first name was Beatrice, and when she got engaged to Mr. Sunbury and he ventured to call her Bea she put her foot down firmly.

"Beatrice I was christened," she said, "and Beatrice I always have been and always shall be, to you and to my nearest and dearest."

She was a little woman, but strong, active and wiry, with a sallow skin, sharp, regular features and small, beady eyes. Her hair, suspiciously black for her age, was always very neat, and she wore it in the style of Queen Victoria's daughters, which she had adopted as soon as she was old enough to put it up and had never thought fit to change. The possibility that she did something to keep her hair its original colour was, if such was the case, her only concession to frivolity, for, far from using rouge or lipstick, she had never in her life so much as passed a powder-puff over her nose. She never wore anything but black dresses of good material, but made (by a little woman round the corner) regardless of fashion after a pattern that was both serviceable and decorous. Her only ornament was a thin gold chain from which hung a small gold cross.

Samuel Sunbury was a little man too. He was as thin and spare as his wife, but he had sandy hair, gone very thin now so that he had to wear it very long on one side and brush it carefully over the large bald patch. He had pale blue eyes and his complexion was pasty. He was a clerk in a lawyer's office and had worked his way up from office boy to a respectable position. His employer called him Mr. Sunbury and sometimes asked him to see an unimportant client. Every morning for twenty-four years Samuel Sunbury had taken the same train to the City, except of course on Sundays and during his fortnight's holiday at the seaside, and every evening he had taken the same train back to the suburb in which he lived. He was neat in his dress; he went to work in quiet grey trousers, a black coat and a bowler hat, and when he came home he put on his slippers and a black coat which was too old and shiny to wear at the office; but on Sundays when he went to the chapel he and Mrs. Sunbury attended he wore a morning coat with his bowler. Thus he showed his respect for the day of rest and at the same time registered a protest against the ungodly who went bicycling or lounged about the streets until the pubs opened. On principle the Sunburys were total abstainers, but on Sundays, when to make up for the frugal lunch, consisting of a scone and butter with a glass of milk, which Samuel had during the week, Beatrice gave him a good dinner of roast beef and Yorkshire pudding, for his health's sake she liked him to have a glass of beer. Since she wouldn't for the world have kept liquor in the house, he sneaked out with a jug after morning service and got a quart from the pub round the corner; but nothing would induce him to drink alone, so, just to be sociable-like, she had a glass too.

Herbert was the only child the Lord had vouchsafed to them, and this certainly through no precaution on their part. It just happened that way. They doted on him. He was a pretty baby and then a good-looking child. Mrs. Sunbury brought him up carefully. She taught him to sit up at table and not put his elbows on it, and she taught him how to use his knife and fork like a little gentleman. She taught him to stretch out his little finger when he took his teacup to drink out of it and when he asked why, she said:

"Never you mind. That's how it's done. It shows you know what's what."

In due course Herbert grew old enough to go to school. Mrs. Sunbury was anxious because she had never let him play with the children in the street.

"Evil communications corrupt good manners," she said. "I always have kept myself to myself and I always shall keep myself to myself."

Although they had lived in the same house ever since they were married she had taken care to keep her neighbours at a distance.

"You never know who people are in London," she said. "One thing leads to another, and before you know where you are you're mixed up with a lot of riff-raff and you can't get rid of them."

She didn't like the idea of Herbert being thrown into contact with a lot of rough boys at the County Council school and she said to him:

"Now, Herbert, do what I do; keep yourself to yourself and don't have anything more to do with them than you can help."

But Herbert got on very well at school. He was a good worker and far from stupid. His reports were excellent. It turned out that he had a good head for figures.

"If that's a fact," said Samuel Sunbury, "he'd better be an accountant. There's always a good job waiting for a good accountant."

So it was settled there and then that this was what Herbert was to be. He grew tall.

"Why, Herbert," said his mother, "soon you'll be as tall as your dad."

By the time he left school he was two inches taller, and by the time he stopped growing he was five feet ten.

"Just the right height," said his mother. "Not too tall and not too short."

He was a nice-looking boy, with his mother's regular features and dark hair, but he had inherited his father's blue eyes, and though he was rather pale his skin was smooth and clear. Samuel Sunbury had got him into the office of the accountants who came twice a year to do the accounts of his own firm and by the time he was twenty-one he was able to bring back to his mother every week quite a nice little sum. She gave him back three half-crowns for his lunches and ten shillings for pocket money, and the rest she put in the Savings Bank for him against a rainy day.

When Mr. and Mrs. Sunbury went to bed on the night of Herbert's twenty-first birthday, and in passing I may say that Mrs. Sunbury never went to bed, she retired, but Mr. Sunbury, who was not quite so refined as his wife, always said: "Me for Bedford,"—when then Mr. and Mrs. Sunbury went to bed, Mrs. Sunbury said:

"Some people don't know how lucky they are; thank the Lord, I do. No one's ever had a better son than our Herbert. Hardly a day's illness in his life and he's never given me a moment's worry. It just shows if you bring up somebody right they'll be a credit to you. Fancy him being twenty-one, I can hardly believe it."

"Yes, I suppose before we know where we are he'll be marrying and leaving us."

"What should he want to do that for?" asked Mrs. Sunbury with asperity. "He's got a good home here, hasn't he? Don't you go putting silly ideas into his head, Samuel, or you and me'll have words and you know that's the last thing I want. Marry indeed! He's got more sense than that. He knows when he's well off. He's got sense, Herbert has."

Mr. Sunbury was silent. He had long ago learnt that it didn't get him anywhere with Beatrice to answer back.

"I don't hold with a man marrying till he knows his own mind," she went on. "And a man doesn't know his own mind till he's thirty or thirty-five."

"He was pleased with his presents," said Mr. Sunbury to change the conversation.

"And so he ought to be," said Mrs. Sunbury still upset.

They had in fact been handsome. Mr. Sunbury had given him a silver wrist-watch, with hands that you could see in the dark, and Mrs. Sunbury had given him a kite. It wasn't by any means the first one she had given him. That was when he was seven years old, and it happened this way. There was a large common near where they lived and on Saturday afternoons when it was fine Mrs. Sunbury took her husband and son for a walk there. She said it was good for Samuel to get a breath of fresh air after being cooped up in a stuffy office all the week. There were always a lot of people on the common, but Mrs. Sunbury who liked to keep herself to herself kept out of their way as much as possible.

"Look at them kites, Mum," said Herbert suddenly one day.

There was a fresh breeze blowing and a number of kites, small and large, were sailing through the air.

"*Those*, Herbert, not them," said Mrs. Sunbury.

"Would you like to go and see where they start, Herbert?" asked his father.

"Oh, yes, Dad."

There was a slight elevation in the middle of the common and as they approached it they saw boys and girls and some men racing down it to give their kites a start and catch the wind. Sometimes they didn't and fell to the ground, but when they did they would rise and as the owner unravelled his string go higher and higher. Herbert looked with ravishment.

"Mum, can I have a kite?" he cried.

He had already learnt that when he wanted anything it was better to ask his mother first.

"Whatever for?" she said.

"To fly it, Mum."

"If you're so sharp you'll cut yourself," she said.

Mr. and Mrs. Sunbury exchanged a smile over the little boy's head. Fancy him wanting a kite. Growing quite a little man he was.

"If you're a good boy and wash your teeth regular every morning without me telling you I shouldn't be surprised if Santa Claus didn't bring you a kite on Christmas Day."

Christmas wasn't far off and Santa Claus brought Herbert his first kite. At the beginning he wasn't very clever at managing it, and Mr. Sunbury had to run down the hill himself and start it for him. It was a very small kite, but when Herbert saw it swim through the air and felt the little tug it gave his hand he was thrilled; and then every Saturday afternoon, when his father got back from the City, he would pester his parents to hurry over to the common. He quickly learnt how to fly it, and Mr. and Mrs. Sunbury, their hearts swelling with pride, would watch him from the top of the knoll while he ran down and as the kite caught the breeze lengthened the cord in his hand.

It became a passion with Herbert, and as he grew older and bigger his mother bought him larger and larger kites. He grew very clever at gauging the winds and could do things with his kite you wouldn't have thought possible. There were other kite-flyers on the common, not only children, but men, and since nothing brings people together so naturally as a hobby they share it was not long before Mrs. Sunbury, notwithstanding her exclusiveness, found that she, her Samuel and her son were on speaking terms with all and sundry. They would compare their respective kites and boast of their accomplishments. Sometimes Herbert, a big boy of sixteen now, would challenge another kite-flyer. Then he would manœuvre his kite to windward of the other fellow's, allow his cord to drift against his, and by a sudden jerk bring the enemy kite down. But long before this Mr. Sunbury had succumbed to his son's enthusiasm and he would often ask to have a go himself. It must have been a funny sight to see him running down the hill in his striped trousers, black coat and bowler hat. Mrs. Sunbury would trot sedately behind him and when the kite was sailing free would take the cord from him and watch it as it soared. Saturday afternoon became the great day of the week for them, and when Mr. Sunbury and Herbert left the house in the morning to catch their train to the City the first thing they did was to look up at the sky to see if it was flying weather. They liked best of all a gusty day, with uncertain winds, for that gave them the best chance to exercise their skill. All through the week, in the evenings, they talked about it. They were contemptuous of smaller kites than theirs and envious of bigger ones. They discussed the performances of other flyers as hotly, and as scornfully, as boxers or football-players discuss their rivals. Their ambition was to have a bigger kite than anyone else and a kite that would go higher. They had long given up a cord, for the kite they gave Herbert on his twenty-first birthday was seven feet high, and they used piano wire wound round a drum. But that did not satisfy Herbert. Somehow or other he had heard of a box-kite which had been invented by somebody, and the idea appealed to him at once. He thought he could devise something of the sort himself and since he could draw a little he set about making designs of it. He got a small model made and tried it out one afternoon, but it wasn't a success. He was a stubborn boy and he wasn't going to be beaten. Something was wrong, and it was up to him to put it right.

Then an unfortunate thing happened. Herbert began to go out after supper. Mrs. Sunbury didn't like it much, but Mr. Sunbury reasoned with her. After all, the boy was twenty-two, and it must be dull for him to stay home all the time. If he wanted to go for a walk or see a movie there was no great harm. Herbert had fallen in love. One Saturday evening, after they'd had a wonderful time on the common, while they were at supper, out of a clear sky he said suddenly:

"Mum, I've asked a young lady to come in to tea to-morrow. Is that all right?"

"You done what?" said Mrs. Sunbury, for a moment forgetting her grammar.

"You heard, Mum."

"And may I ask who she is and how you got to know her?"

"Her name's Bevan, Betty Bevan, and I met her first at the pictures one Saturday afternoon when it was raining. It was an accident like. She was sitting next me and she dropped her bag and I picked it up and she said thank you and so naturally we got talking."

"And d'you mean to tell me you fell for an old trick like that? Dropped her bag indeed!"

"You're making a mistake, Mum, she's a nice girl, she is really and well educated too."

"And when did all this happen?"

"About three months ago."

"Oh, you met her three months ago and you've asked her to come to tea to-morrow?"

"Well, I've seen her since of course. That first day, after the show, I asked her if she'd come to the pictures with me on the

1166 THE WORLD OVER

Tuesday evening, and she said she didn't know, perhaps she would and perhaps she wouldn't. But she came all right."

"She would. I could have told you that."

"And we've been going to the pictures about twice a week ever since."

"So that's why you've taken to going out so often?"

"That's right. But, look, I don't want to force her on you, if you don't want her to come to tea I'll say you've got a headache and take her out."

"Your mum will have her to tea all right," said Mr. Sunbury. "Won't you, dear? It's only that your mum can't abide strangers. She never has liked them."

"I keep myself to myself," said Mrs. Sunbury gloomily. "What does she do?"

"She works in a typewriting office in the City and she lives at home, if you call it home; you see, her mum died and her dad married again, and they've got three kids and she doesn't get on with her step-ma. Nag, nag, nag all the time, she says."

Mrs. Sunbury arranged the tea very stylishly. She took the knick-knacks off a little table in the sitting-room, which they never used, and put a tea-cloth on it. She got out the tea-service and the plated tea-kettle which they never used either, and she made scones, baked a cake, and cut thin bread-and-butter.

"I want her to see that we're not just nobody," she told her Samuel.

Herbert went to fetch Miss Bevan, and Mr. Sunbury intercepted them at the door in case Herbert should take her into the dining-room where normally they ate and sat. Herbert gave the tea-table a glance of surprise as he ushered the young woman into the sitting-room.

"This is Betty, Mum," he said.

"Miss Bevan, I presume," said Mrs. Sunbury.

"That's right, but call me Betty, won't you?"

"Perhaps the acquaintance is a bit short for that," said Mrs. Sunbury with a gracious smile. "Won't you sit down, Miss Bevan?"

Strangely enough, or perhaps not strangely at all, Betty Bevan looked very much as Mrs. Sunbury must have looked at her age. She had the same sharp features and the same rather small beady eyes, but her lips were scarlet with paint, her cheeks lightly rouged and her short black hair permanently waved. Mrs. Sunbury took in all this at a glance, and she reckoned to a penny how much her smart rayon dress had cost, her extravagantly high-heeled shoes and the saucy hat on her head. Her frock was very short and she showed

a good deal of flesh-coloured stocking. Mrs. Sunbury, disapproving
of her make-up and of her apparel, took an instant dislike to her,
but she had made up her mind to behave like a lady, and if she didn't
know how to behave like a lady nobody did, so that at first things
went well. She poured out tea and asked Herbert to give a cup to his
lady friend.

"Ask Miss Bevan if she'll have some bread-and-butter or a scone,
Samuel, my dear."

"Have both," said Samuel, handing round the two plates, in his
coarse way. "I like to see people eat hearty."

Betty insecurely perched a piece of bread-and-butter and a scone
on her saucer and Mrs. Sunbury talked affably about the weather.
She had the satisfaction of seeing that Betty was getting more and
more ill-at-ease. Then she cut the cake and pressed a large piece on
her guest. Betty took a bite at it and when she put it in her saucer it
fell to the ground.

"Oh, I am sorry," said the girl, as she picked it up.

"It doesn't matter at all, I'll cut you another piece," said Mrs.
Sunbury.

"Oh, don't bother, I'm not particular. The floor's clean."

"I hope so," said Mrs. Sunbury with an acid smile, "but I
wouldn't dream of letting you eat a piece of cake that's been on the
floor. Bring it here, Herbert, and I'll give Miss Bevan some more."

"I don't want any more, Mrs. Sunbury, I don't really."

"I'm sorry you don't like my cake. I made it specially for you."
She took a bit. "It tastes all right to me."

"It's not that, Mrs. Sunbury, it's a beautiful cake, it's only that
I'm not hungry."

She refused to have more tea and Mrs. Sunbury saw she was
glad to get rid of the cup. "I expect they have their meals in the
kitchen," she said to herself. Then Herbert lit a cigarette.

"Give us a fag, Herb," said Betty. "I'm simply dying for a
smoke."

Mrs. Sunbury didn't approve of women smoking, but she only
raised her eyebrows slightly.

"We prefer to call him Herbert, Miss Bevan," she said.

Betty wasn't such a fool as not to see that Mrs. Sunbury had been
doing all she could to make her uncomfortable, and now she saw a
chance to get back on her.

"I know," she said. "When he told me his name was Herbert I
nearly burst out laughing. Fancy calling anyone Herbert. A
scream, I call it."

"I'm sorry you don't like the name my son was given at his

baptism. I think it's a very nice name. But I suppose it all depends on what sort of class of people one is."

Herbert stepped in to the rescue.

"At the office they call me Bertie, Mum."

"Then all I can say is, they're a lot of very common men."

Mrs. Sunbury lapsed into a dignified silence and the conversation, such as it was, was maintained by Mr. Sunbury and Herbert. It was not without satisfaction that Mrs. Sunbury perceived that Betty was offended. She also perceived that the girl wanted to go, but didn't quite know how to manage it. She was determined not to help her. Finally Herbert took the matter into his own hands.

"Well, Betty, I think it's about time we were getting along," he said. "I'll walk back with you."

"Must you go already?" said Mrs. Sunbury, rising to her feet. "It's been a pleasure, I'm sure."

"Pretty little thing," said Mr. Sunbury tentatively after the young things had left.

"Pretty my foot. All that paint and powder. You take my word for it, she'd look very different with her face washed and without a perm. Common, that's what she is, common as dirt."

An hour later Herbert came back. He was angry.

"Look here, Mum, what d'you mean by treating the poor girl like that? I was simply ashamed of you."

"Don't talk to your mother like that, Herbert," she flared up. "You didn't ought to have brought a woman like that into my house. Common, she is, common as dirt."

When Mrs. Sunbury got angry not only did her grammar grow shaky, but she wasn't quite safe on her aitches. Herbert took no notice of what she said.

"She said she'd never been so insulted in her life. I had a rare job pacifying her."

"Well, she's never coming here again, I tell you that straight."

"That's what you think. I'm engaged to her, so put that in your pipe and smoke it."

Mrs. Sunbury gasped.

"You're not?"

"Yes, I am. I've been thinking about it for a long time, and then she was so upset to-night I felt sorry for her, so I popped the question and I had a rare job persuading her, I can tell you."

"You fool," screamed Mrs. Sunbury. "You fool."

There was quite a scene then. Mrs. Sunbury and her son went at it hammer and tongs, and when poor Samuel tried to intervene they both told him roughly to shut up. At last Herbert flung out of the room and out of the house and Mrs. Sunbury burst into angry tears.

No reference was made next day to what had passed. Mrs. Sunbury was frigidly polite to Herbert and he was sullen and silent. After supper he went out. On Saturday he told his father and mother that he was engaged that afternoon and wouldn't be able to come to the common with them.

"I dare say we shall be able to do without you," said Mrs. Sunbury grimly.

It was getting on to the time for their usual fortnight at the seaside. They always went to Herne Bay, because Mrs. Sunbury said you had a nice class of people there, and for years they had taken the same lodgings. One evening, in as casual a way as he could, Herbert said:

"By the way, Mum, you'd better write and tell them I shan't be wanting my room this year. Betty and me are getting married and we're going to Southend for the honeymoon."

For a moment there was dead silence in the room.

"Bit sudden-like, isn't it, Herbert?" said Mr. Sunbury uneasily.

"Well, they're cutting down at Betty's office and she's out of a job, so we thought we'd better get married at once. We've taken two rooms in Dabney Street and we're furnishing out of my Savings Bank money."

Mrs. Sunbury didn't say a word. She went deathly pale and tears rolled down her thin cheeks.

"Oh, come on, Mum, don't take it so hard," said Herbert. "A fellow has to marry sometime. If Dad hadn't married you, I shouldn't be here now, should I?"

Mrs. Sunbury brushed her tears away with an impatient hand.

"Your dad didn't marry me; I married 'im. I knew he was steady and respectable. I knew he'd make a good 'usband and father. I've never 'ad cause to regret it and no more 'as your dad. That's right, Samuel, isn't it?"

"Right as rain, Beatrice," he said quickly.

"You know, you'll like Betty when you get to know her. She's a nice girl, she is really. I believe you'd find you had a lot in common. You must give her a chance, Mum."

"She's never going to set foot in this house only over my dead body."

"That's absurd, Mum. Why, everything'll be just the same if you'll only be reasonable. I mean, we can go flying on Saturday afternoons same as we always did. Just this time I've been engaged it's been difficult. You see, she can't see what there is in kite-flying, but she'll come round to it, and after I'm married it'll be different, I mean I can come and fly with you and Dad; that stands to reason."

"That's what you think. Well, let me tell you that if you marry that woman you're not going to fly my kite. I never gave it you, I bought it out of the housekeeping money, and it's mine, see."

"All right then, have it your own way. Betty says it's a kid's game anyway and I ought to be ashamed of myself, flying a kite at my age."

He got up and once more stalked angrily out of the house. A fortnight later he was married. Mrs. Sunbury refused to go to the wedding and wouldn't let Samuel go either. They went for their holiday and came back. They resumed their usual round. On Saturday afternoons they went to the common by themselves and flew their enormous kite. Mrs. Sunbury never mentioned her son. She was determined not to forgive him. But Mr. Sunbury used to meet him on the morning train they both took and they chatted a little when they managed to get into the same carriage. One morning Mr. Sunbury looked up at the sky.

"Good flying weather to-day," he said.

"D'you and Mum still fly?"

"What do you think? She's getting as clever as I am. You should see her with her skirts pinned up running down the hill. I give you my word, I never knew she had it in her. Run? Why, she can run better than what I can."

"Don't make me laugh, Dad!"

"I wonder you don't buy a kite of your own, Herbert. You've been always so keen on it."

"I know I was. I did suggest it once, but you know what women are. Betty said: 'Be your age,' and oh, I don't know what all. I don't want a kid's kite, of course, and them big kites cost money. When we started to furnish Betty said it was cheaper in the long run to buy the best and so we went to one of them hire purchase places and what with paying them every month and the rent, well, I haven't got any more money than just what we can manage on. They say it doesn't cost any more to keep two than one, well, that's not my experience so far."

"Isn't she working?"

"Well, no, she says after working for donkeys' years as you might say, now she's married she's going to take it easy, and of course someone's got to keep the place clean and do the cooking."

So it went on for six months, and then one Saturday afternoon when the Sunburys were as usual on the common Mrs. Sunbury said to her husband:

"Did you see what I saw, Samuel?"

"I saw Herbert, if that's what you mean. I didn't mention it because I thought it would only upset you."

"Don't speak to him. Pretend you haven't seen him."

Herbert was standing among the idle lookers-on. He made no attempt to speak to his parents, but it did not escape Mrs. Sunbury that he followed with all his eyes the flight of the big kite he had flown so often. It began to grow chilly and the Sunburys went home. Mrs. Sunbury's face was brisk with malice.

"I wonder if he'll come next Saturday," said Samuel.

"If I didn't think betting wrong I'd bet you sixpence he will, Samuel. I've been waiting for this all along."

"You have?"

"I knew from the beginning he wouldn't be able to keep away from it."

She was right. On the following Saturday and on every Saturday after that when the weather was fine Herbert turned up on the common. No intercourse passed. He just stood there for a while looking on and then strolled away. But after things had been going on like this for several weeks, the Sunburys had a surprise for him. They weren't flying the big kite which he was used to, but a new one, a box-kite, a small one, on the model for which he had made the designs himself. He saw it was creating a lot of interest among the other kite-flyers; they were standing round it and Mrs. Sunbury was talking volubly. The first time Samuel ran down the hill with it the thing didn't rise, but flopped miserably on the ground, and Herbert clenched his hands and ground his teeth. He couldn't bear to see it fail. Mr. Sunbury climbed up the little hill again, and the second time the box-kite took the air. There was a cheer among the bystanders. After a while Mr. Sunbury pulled it down and walked back with it to the hill. Mrs. Sunbury went up to her son.

"Like to have a try, Herbert?"

He caught his breath.

"Yes, Mum, I should."

"It's just a small one because they say you have to get the knack of it. It's not like the old-fashioned sort. But we've got specifications for a big one, and they say when you get to know about it and the wind's right you can go up to two miles with it."

Mr. Sunbury joined them.

"Samuel, Herbert wants to try the kite."

Mr. Sunbury handed it to him, a pleased smile on his face, and Herbert gave his mother his hat to hold. Then he raced down the hill, the kite took the air beautifully, and as he watched it rise his heart was filled with exultation. It was grand to see that little black thing soaring so sweetly, but even as he watched it he thought of the great big one they were having made. They'd never be able to manage that. Two miles in the air, Mum had said. Whew!

"Why don't you come back and have a cup of tea, Herbert," said Mrs. Sunbury, "and we'll show you the designs for the new one they want to build for us. Perhaps you could make some suggestions."

He hesitated. He'd told Betty he was just going for a walk to stretch his legs, she didn't know he'd been coming to the common every week, and she'd be waiting for him. But the temptation was irresistible.

"I don't mind if I do," he said.

After tea they looked at the specifications. The kite was huge, with gadgets he had never seen before, and it would cost a lot of money.

"You'll never be able to fly it by yourselves," he said.

"We can try."

"I suppose you wouldn't like me to help you just at first?" he asked uncertainly.

"Mightn't be a bad idea," said Mrs. Sunbury.

It was late when he got home, much later than he thought, and Betty was vexed.

"Wherever have you been, Herb? I thought you were dead. Supper's waiting and everything."

"I met some fellows and got talking."

She gave him a sharp look, but didn't answer. She sulked.

After supper he suggested they should go to a movie, but she refused.

"You go if you want to," she said. "I don't care to."

On the following Saturday he went again to the common and again his mother let him fly the kite. They had ordered the new one and expected to get it in three weeks. Presently his mother said to him:

"Elizabeth is here."

"Betty?"

"Spying on you."

It gave him a nasty turn, but he put on a bold front.

"Let her spy. I don't care."

But he was nervous and wouldn't go back to tea with his parents. He went straight home. Betty was waiting for him.

"So that's the fellows you got talking to. I've been suspicious for some time, you going for a walk on Saturday afternoons, and all of a sudden I tumbled to it. Flying a kite, you, a grown man. Contemptible I call it."

"I don't care what you call it. I like it, and if you don't like it you can lump it."

"I won't have it and I tell you that straight. I'm not going to have you make a fool of yourself."

"I've flown a kite every Saturday afternoon ever since I was a kid, and I'm going to fly a kite as long as ever I want to."

"It's that old bitch, she's just trying to get you away from me. I know her. If you were a man you'd never speak to her again, not after the way she's treated me."

"I won't have you call her that. She's my mother and I've got the right to see her as often as ever I want to."

The quarrel went on hour after hour. Betty screamed at him and Herbert shouted at her. They had had trifling disagreements before, because they were both obstinate, but this was the first serious row they had had. They didn't speak to one another on the Sunday, and during the rest of the week, though outwardly there was peace between them, their ill-feeling rankled. It happened that the next two Saturdays it poured with rain. Betty smiled to herself when she saw the downpour, but if Herbert was disappointed he gave no sign of it. The recollection of their quarrel grew dim. Living in two rooms as they did, sleeping in the same bed, it was inevitable that they should agree to forget their differences. Betty went out of her way to be nice to her Herb, and she thought that now she had given him a taste of her tongue and he knew she wasn't going to be put upon by anyone, he'd be reasonable. He was a good husband in his way, generous with his money and steady. Give her time and she'd manage him all right.

But after a fortnight of bad weather it cleared.

"Looks as if we're going to have good flying weather to-morrow," said Mr. Sunbury as they met on the platform to await their morning train. "The new kite's come."

"It has?"

"Your mum says of course we'd like you to come and help us with it, but no one's got the right to come between a man and his wife, and if you're afraid of Betty, her kicking up a rumpus, I mean, you'd better not come. There's a young fellow we've got to know on the common who's just mad about it, and he says he'll get it to fly if anybody can."

Herbert was seized with a pang of jealousy.

P

"Don't you let any strangers touch our kite. I'll be there all right."

"Well, you think it over, Herbert, and if you don't come we shall quite understand."

"I'll come," said Herbert.

So next day when he got back from the City he changed from his business clothes into slacks and an old coat. Betty came into the bedroom.

"What are you doing?"

"Changing," he answered gaily. He was so excited, he couldn't keep the secret to himself. "Their new kite's come and I'm going to fly it."

"Oh no, you're not," she said. "I won't have it."

"Don't be a fool, Betty. I'm going, I tell you, and if you don't like it you can do the other thing."

"I'm not going to let you, so that's that."

She shut the door and stood in front of it. Her eyes flashed and her jaw was set. She was a little thing and he was a tall strong man. He took hold of her two arms to push her out of the way, but she kicked him violently on the shin.

"D'you want me to give you a sock on the jaw?"

"If you go you don't come back," she shouted.

He caught her up, though she struggled and kicked, threw her on to the bed and went out.

If the small box-kite had caused an excitement on the common it was nothing to what the new one caused. But it was difficult to manage, and though they ran and panted and other enthusiastic flyers helped them Herbert couldn't get it up.

"Never mind," he said, "we'll get the knack of it presently. The wind's not right to-day, that's all."

He went back to tea with his father and mother and they talked it over just as they had talked in the old days. He delayed going because he didn't fancy the scene Betty would make him, but when Mrs. Sunbury went into the kitchen to get supper ready he had to go home. Betty was reading the paper. She looked up.

"Your bag's packed," she said.

"My what?"

"You heard what I said. I said if you went you needn't come back. I forgot about your things. Everything's packed. It's in the bedroom."

He looked at her for a moment with surprise. She pretended to be reading again. He would have liked to give her a good hiding.

"All right, have it your own way," he said.

He went into the bedroom. His clothes were packed in a suit-case, and there was a brown-paper parcel in which Betty had put whatever was left over. He took the bag in one hand, the parcel in the other, walked through the sitting-room without a word and out of the house. He walked to his mother's and rang the bell. She opened the door.

"I've come home, Mum," he said.

"Have you, Herbert? Your room's ready for you. Put your things down and come in. We were just sitting down to supper." They went into the dining-room. "Samuel, Herbert's come home. Run out and get a quart of beer."

Over supper and during the rest of the evening he told them the trouble he had had with Betty.

"Well, you're well out of it, Herbert," said Mrs. Sunbury when he had finished. "I told you she was no wife for you. Common she is, common as dirt, and you who's always been brought up so nice."

He found it good to sleep in his own bed, the bed he'd been used to all his life, and to come down to breakfast on the Sunday morning, unshaved and unwashed, and read the *News of the World*.

"We won't go to chapel this morning," said Mrs. Sunbury. "It's been an upset to you, Herbert; we'll all take it easy to-day."

During the week they talked a lot about the kite, but they also talked a lot about Betty. They discussed what she would do next.

"She'll try and get you back," said Mrs. Sunbury.

"A fat chance she's got of doing that," said Herbert.

"You'll have to provide for her," said his father.

"Why should he do that?" cried Mrs. Sunbury. "She trapped him into marrying her and now she's turned him out of the home he made for her."

"I'll give her what's right as long as she leaves me alone."

He was feeling more comfortable every day, in fact he was beginning to feel as if he'd never been away, he settled in like a dog in its own particular basket; it was nice having his mother to brush his clothes and mend his socks; she gave him the sort of things he'd always eaten and liked best; Betty was a scrappy sort of cook, it had been fun just at first, like picnicking, but it wasn't the sort of eating a man could get his teeth into, and he could never get over his mother's idea that fresh food was better than the stuff you bought in tins. He got sick of the sight of tinned salmon. Then it was nice to have space to move about in rather than be cooped up in two small rooms, one of which had to serve as a kitchen as well.

"I never made a bigger mistake in my life than when I left home, Mum," he said to her once.

"I know that, Herbert, but you're back now and you've got no cause ever to leave it again."

His salary was paid on Friday and in the evening when they had just finished supper the bell rang.

"That's her," they said with one voice.

Herbert went pale. His mother gave him a glance.

"You leave it to me," she said. "I'll see her."

She opened the door. Betty was standing on the threshold. She tried to push her way in, but Mrs. Sunbury prevented her.

"I want to see Herb."

"You can't. He's out."

"No, he isn't. I watched him go in with his dad and he hasn't come out again."

"Well, he doesn't want to see you, and if you start making a disturbance I'll call the police."

"I want my week's money."

"That's all you've ever wanted of him." She took out her purse. "There's thirty-five shillings for you."

"Thirty-five shillings? The rent's twelve shillings a week."

"That's all you're going to get. He's got to pay his board here, hasn't he?"

"And then there's the instalments on the furniture."

"We'll see about that when the time comes. D'you want the money or don't you?"

Confused, unhappy, browbeaten, Betty stood irresolutely. Mrs. Sunbury thrust the money in her hand and slammed the door in her face. She went back to the dining-room.

"I've settled her hash all right," she said.

The bell rang again, it rang repeatedly, but they did not answer it, and presently it stopped. They guessed that Betty had gone away.

It was fine next day, with just the right velocity in the wind, and Herbert, after failing two or three times, found he had got the knack of flying the big box-kite. It soared into the air and up and up as he unreeled the wire.

"Why, it's a mile up if it's a yard," he told his mother excitedly.

He had never had such a thrill in his life.

Several weeks passed by. They concocted a letter for Herbert to write in which he told Betty that so long as she didn't molest him or members of his family she would receive a postal order for thirty-five shillings every Saturday morning and he would pay the instalments on the furniture as they came due. Mrs. Sunbury had been much against this, but Mr. Sunbury, for once at variance with her, and Herbert agreed that it was the right thing to do. Herbert by then had learnt the ways of the new kite and was able to do great things with it. He no longer bothered to have contests with the other kite-flyers. He was out of their class. Saturday afternoons were his moments of glory. He revelled in the admiration he aroused in the bystanders and enjoyed the envy he knew he excited in the less fortunate flyers. Then one evening when he was walking back from the station with his father Betty waylaid him.

"Hulloa, Herb," she said.

"Hulloa."

"I want to talk to my husband alone, Mr. Sunbury."

"There's nothing you've got to say to me that my dad can't hear," said Herbert sullenly.

She hesitated. Mr. Sunbury fidgeted. He didn't know whether to stay or go.

"All right, then," she said. "I want you to come back home, Herb. I didn't mean it that night when I packed your bag. I only did it to frighten you. I was in a temper. I'm sorry for what I did. It's all so silly, quarrelling about a kite."

"Well, I'm not coming back, see. When you turned me out you did me the best turn you ever did me."

Tears began to trickle down Betty's cheeks.

"But I love you, Herb. If you want to fly your silly old kite, you fly it, I don't care so long as you come back."

"Thank you very much, but it's not good enough. I know when I'm well off and I've had enough of married life to last me a life-time. Come on, Dad."

They walked on quickly and Betty made no attempt to follow them. On the following Sunday they went to chapel and after dinner Herbert went to the coal-shed where they kept the kite to have a look at it. He just couldn't keep away from it. He doted on it. In a minute he rushed back, his face white, with a hatchet in his hand.

"She's smashed it up. She did it with this."

The Sunburys gave a cry of consternation and hurried to the coal-shed. What Herbert had said was true. The kite, the new, expensive kite, was in fragments. It had been savagely attacked with the hatchet, the woodwork was all in pieces, the reel was hacked to bits.

"She must have done it while we were at chapel. Watched us go out, that's what she did."

"But how did she get in?" asked Mr. Sunbury.

"I had two keys. When I came home I noticed one was missing, but I didn't think anything about it."

"You can't be sure she did it, some of them fellows on the common have been very snooty, I wouldn't put it past them to have done this."

"Well, we'll soon find out," said Herbert. "I'll go and ask her, and if she did it I'll kill her."

His rage was so terrible that Mrs. Sunbury was frightened.

"And get yourself hung for murder? No, Herbert, I won't let you go. Let your dad go, and when he comes back we'll decide what to do."

"That's right, Herbert, let me go."

They had a job to persuade him, but in the end Mr. Sunbury went. In half an hour he came back.

"She did it all right. She told me straight out. She's proud of it. I won't repeat her language, it fair startled me, but the long and short of it was she was jealous of the kite. She said Herbert loved the kite more than he loved her and so she smashed it up and if she had to do it again she'd do it again."

"Lucky she didn't tell me that. I'd have wrung her neck even if I'd had to swing for it. Well, she never gets another penny out of me, that's all."

"She'll sue you," said his father.

"Let her."

"The instalment on the furniture is due next week, Herbert," said Mrs. Sunbury quietly. "In your place I wouldn't pay it."

"Then they'll just take it away," said Samuel, "and all the money he's paid on it so far will be wasted."

"Well, what of it?" she answered. "He can afford it. He's rid of her for good and all and we've got him back and that's the chief thing."

"I don't care twopence about the money," said Herbert. "I can see her face when they come and take the furniture away. It meant a lot to her, it did, and the piano, she set a rare store on that piano."

So on the following Friday he did not send Betty her weekly money, and when she sent him on a letter from the furniture people to say that if he didn't pay the instalment due by such and such a date they would remove it, he wrote back and said he wasn't in a position to continue the payments and they could remove the furniture at their convenience. Betty took to waiting for him at the station, and when he wouldn't speak to her followed him down the street screaming curses at him. In the evenings she would come to the house and ring the bell till they thought they would go mad, and Mr. and Mrs. Sunbury had the greatest difficulty in preventing Herbert from going out and giving her a sound thrashing. Once she threw a stone and broke the sitting-room window. She wrote obscene and abusive postcards to him at his office. At last she went to the magistrate's court and complained that her husband had left her and wasn't providing for her support. Herbert received a summons. They both told their story and if the magistrate thought it a strange one he didn't say so. He tried to effect a reconciliation between them, but Herbert resolutely refused to go back to his wife. The magistrate ordered him to pay Betty twenty-five shillings a week. He said he wouldn't pay it.

"Then you'll go to prison," said the magistrate. "Next case."

But Herbert meant what he said. On Betty's complaint he was brought once more before the magistrate, who asked him what reason he had for not obeying the order.

"I said I wouldn't pay her and I won't, not after she smashed my kite. And if you send me to prison I'll go to prison."

The magistrate was stern with him this time.

"You're a very foolish young man," he said. "I'll give you a week to pay the arrears, and if I have any more nonsense from you you'll go to prison till you come to your senses."

Herbert didn't pay, and that is how my friend Ned Preston came to know him and I heard the story.

"What d'you make of it?" asked Ned as he finished. "You know, Betty isn't a bad girl. I've seen her several times, there's nothing wrong with her except her insane jealousy of Herbert's kite; and he isn't a fool by any means. In fact he's smarter than the average. What d'you suppose there is in kite-flying that makes the damned fool so mad about it?"

"I don't know," I answered. I took my time to think. "You see, I don't know a thing about flying a kite. Perhaps it gives him a sense of power as he watches it soaring towards the clouds and of mastery over the elements as he seems to bend the winds of heaven to his will. It may be that in some queer way he identifies himself with the kite flying so free and so high above him, and it's as it were an escape from the monotony of life. It may be that in some dim, confused way it represents an ideal of freedom and adventure. And you know, when a man once gets bitten with the virus of the ideal not all the King's doctors and not all the King's surgeons can rid him of it. But all this is very fanciful and I dare say it's just stuff and nonsense. I think you'd better put your problem before someone who knows a lot more about the psychology of the human animal than I do."

A Woman of Fifty

My friend Wyman Holt is a professor of English Literature in one of the smaller universities of the Middle West, and hearing that I was speaking in a near-by city—near-by as distances go in the vastness of America—he wrote to ask if I would come and give a talk to his class. He suggested that I should stay with him for a few days so that he could show me something of the surrounding country. I accepted the invitation, but told him that my engagements would prevent me from spending more than a couple of nights with him. He met me at the station, drove me to his house and after we had had a drink we walked over to the campus. I was somewhat taken aback to find so many people in the hall in which I was to speak, for I had not expected more than twenty at the outside and I was not prepared to give a solemn lecture, but only an informal chat. I was more than a little intimidated to see a number of middle-aged and elderly persons, some of whom I suspected were members of the faculty, and I was afraid they would find what I had to say very superficial. However, there was nothing to do but to start and, after Wyman had introduced me to the audience in a manner that I very well knew I couldn't live up to, that is what I did. I said my say, I answered as best I could a number of questions, and then I retired with Wyman into a little room at the back of the stage from which I had spoken.

Several people came in. They said the usual kindly things to me that are said on these occasions, and I made the usual polite replies. I was thirsting for a drink. Then a woman came in and held out her hand to me.

"How very nice it is to see you again," she said. "It's years since we last met."

To the best of my belief I'd never set eyes on her before. I forced a cordial smile to my tired, stiff lips, shook her proffered hand effusively and wondered who the devil she was. My professor must have seen from my face that I was trying to place her, for he said:

"Mrs. Greene is married to a member of our faculty and she gives a course on the Renaissance and Italian literature."

"Really," I said. "Interesting."

I was no wiser than before.

"Has Wyman told you that you're dining with us to-morrow night?"

"I'm very glad," I said.

"It's not a party. Only my husband, his brother and my sister-in-law. I suppose Florence has changed a lot since then."

"Florence?" I said to myself. "Florence?"

That was evidently where I'd known her. She was a woman of about fifty with grey hair simply done and marcelled without exaggeration. She was a trifle too stout and she was dressed neatly enough, but without distinction, in a dress that I guessed had been bought ready-made at the local branch of a big store. She had rather large eyes of a pale blue and a poor complexion; she wore no rouge and had used a lipstick but sparingly. She seemed a nice creature. There was something maternal in her demeanour, something placid and fulfilled, which I found appealing. I supposed that I had run across her on one of my frequent visits to Florence and because it was perhaps the only time she had been there our meeting made more of an impression on her than on me. I must confess that my acquaintance with the wives of members of a faculty is very limited, but she was just the sort of person I should have expected the wife of a professor to be, and picturing her life, useful but uneventful, on scanty means, with its little social gatherings, its bickerings, its gossip, its busy dullness, I could easily imagine that her trip to Florence must linger with her as a thrilling and unforgettable experience.

On the way back to his house Wyman said to me:

"You'll like Jasper Greene. He's clever."

"What's he a professor of?"

"He's not a professor; he's an instructor. A fine scholar. He's her second husband. She was married to an Italian before."

"Oh?" That didn't chime in with my ideas at all. "What was her name?"

"I haven't a notion. I don't believe it was a great success." Wyman chuckled. "That's only a deduction I draw from the fact that she hasn't a single thing in the house to suggest that she ever spent any time in Italy. I should have expected her to have at least a refectory table, an old chest or two and an embroidered cope hanging on the wall."

I laughed. I knew those rather dreary pieces that people buy when they're in Italy, the gilt wooden candlesticks, the Venetian glass mirrors and the high-backed, comfortless chairs. They look well enough when you see them in the crowded shops of the dealers in antiques, but when you bring them to another country they're too often a sad disappointment. Even if they're genuine, which they seldom are, they look ill-at-ease and out of place.

"Laura has money," Wyman went on. "When they married she furnished the house from cellar to attic in Chicago. It's quite a show place; it's a little masterpiece of hideousness and vulgarity. I never go into the living-room without marvelling at the unerring taste with which she picked out exactly what you'd expect to find in the bridal suite of a second-class hotel in Atlantic City."

To explain this irony I should state that Wyman's living-room was all chromium and glass, rough modern fabrics, with a boldly Cubist rug on the floor, and on the walls Picasso prints and drawings by Tchelicheff. However, he gave me a very good dinner. We spent the evening chatting pleasantly about things that mutually interest us and finished it with a couple of bottles of beer. I went to bed in a room of somewhat aggressive modernity. I read for a while and then putting out the light composed myself to sleep.

"Laura?" I said to myself. "Laura what?"

I tried to think back. I thought of all the people I knew in Florence, hoping that by association I might recall when and where I had come in contact with Mrs. Greene. Since I was going to dine with her I wanted to recall something that would prove that I had not forgotten her. People look upon it as a slight if you don't remember them. I suppose we all attach a sort of importance to ourselves, and it is humiliating to realise that we have left no impression at all upon the persons we have associated with. I dozed off, but before I fell into the blessedness of deep sleep, my subconscious, released from the effort of striving at recollection, I suppose, grew active and I was suddenly wide awake, for I remembered who Laura Greene was. It was no wonder that I had forgotten her, for it was twenty-five years since I had seen her, and then only haphazardly during a month I spent in Florence.

It was just after the First World War. She had been engaged to a man who was killed in it and she and her mother had managed to get over to France to see his grave. They were San Francisco people. After doing their sad errand they had come down to Italy and were spending the winter in Florence. At that time there was quite a large colony of English and Americans. I had some American friends, a Colonel Harding and his wife, colonel because he had occupied an important position in the Red Cross, who had a handsome villa in the Via Bolognese, and they asked me to stay with them. I spent most of my mornings sightseeing and met my friends at Doney's in the Via Tornabuoni round about noon to drink a cocktail. Doney's was the gathering-place of everybody one knew, Americans, English and such of the Italians as frequented their society. There you heard all the gossip of the town. There was generally a lunch-party either at a restaurant or at one or other of the villas with their fine old gardens a mile or two from the centre of the city. I had been given a card to the Florence Club, and in the afternoon Charley Harding and I used to go there to play bridge or a dangerous game of poker with a pack of thirty-two cards. In the evening there would be a dinner-party with more bridge perhaps and often dancing. One met the same people all the time, but the group was large enough, the people sufficiently various, to prevent it from being tedious. Every-one was more or less interested in the arts, as was only right and proper in Florence, so that, idle as life seemed, it was not entirely frivolous.

Laura and her mother, Mrs. Clayton, a widow, lived in one of the better boarding-houses. They appeared to be comfortably off. They had come to Florence with letters of introduction and soon made many friends. Laura's story appealed to the sympathies, and people were glad on that account to do what they could for the two women, but they were in themselves nice and quickly became liked for themselves. They were hospitable and gave frequent lunches at one or other of the restaurants where one ate macaroni and the inevitable scaloppini, and drank Chianti. Mrs. Clayton was perhaps a little lost in this cosmopolitan society, where matters that were strange to her were seriously or gaily talked about, but Laura took to it as though it were her native element. She engaged an Italian woman to teach her the language and soon was reading the *Inferno* with her; she devoured books on the art of the Renaissance and on Florentine history, and I some-times came across her, Baedeker in hand, at the Uffizzi or in some church studiously examining works of art.

She was twenty-four or twenty-five then and I was well over forty, so that though we often met we became cordially acquainted rather than intimate. She was by no means beautiful, but she was comely in rather an unusual way; she had an oval face with bright blue eyes and very dark hair which she wore very simply, parted in the middle, drawn over her ears and tied in a chignon low on the nape of her neck. She had a good skin and a naturally high colour; her features were good without being remarkable and her teeth were even, small and white; but her chief asset was her easy grace of movement, and I was not surprised when they told me that she danced "divinely". Her figure was very good, somewhat fuller than was the fashion of the moment; and I think what made her attractive was the odd mingling in her appearance of the Madonna in an altar-piece by one of the later Italian painters and a suggestion of sensuality. It certainly made her very alluring to the Italians who gathered at Doney's in the morning or were occasionally invited to lunch or dinner in the American or English villas. She was evidently accustomed to dealing with amorous young men, for though she was charming, gracious and friendly with them she kept them at their distance. She quickly discovered that they were all looking for an American heiress who would restore the family fortunes, and with a demure amusement which I found admirable made them delicately understand that she was far from rich. They sighed a little and turned their attentions at Doney's, which was their happy hunting-ground, to more likely objects. They continued to dance with her, and to keep their hand in flirted with her, but their aspirations ceased to be matrimonial.

But there was one young man who persisted. I knew him slightly because he was one of the regular poker-players at the club. I played occasionally. It was impossible to win and the disgruntled foreigners used sometimes to say that the Italians ganged up on us, but it may be only that they knew the particular game they played better than we did. Laura's admirer, Tito di San Pietro, was a bold and even reckless player and would often lose sums he could ill afford. (That was not his real name, but I call him that since his own is famous in Florentine history.) He was a good-looking youth, neither short nor tall, with fine black eyes, thick black hair brushed back from his forehead and shining with oil, an olive skin, and features of classical regularity. He was poor and he had some vague occupation, which did not seem to interfere with his amusements, but he was always beautifully dressed. No one quite knew where he lived, in a furnished room perhaps or in the attic of some relation; and all that remained of his ancestors' great possessions was a cinquecento villa about thirty miles from the city. I never saw it, but I was told that it was of amazing beauty, with a great neglected garden of cypresses and live oaks, overgrown borders of box, terraces, artificial grottoes and crumbling statues. His widowed father, the count, lived there alone and subsisted on the wine he made from the vines of the small property he still owned and the oil from his olive trees. He seldom came to Florence, so I never met him, but Charley Harding knew him fairly well.

"He's a perfect specimen of the Tuscan nobleman of the old school," he said. "He was in the diplomatic service in his youth and he knows the world. He has beautiful manners and such an air, you almost feel he's doing you a favour when he says how d'you do to you. He's a brilliant talker. Of course he hasn't a penny, he squandered the little he inherited on gambling and women, but he bears his poverty with great dignity. He acts as though money were something beneath his notice."

"What sort of age is he?" I asked.

"Fifty, I should say, but he's still the handsomest man I've ever seen in my life."

"Oh?"

"You describe him, Bessie. When he first came here he made a pass at Bessie. I've never been quite sure how far it went."

"Don't be a fool, Charley," Mrs. Harding laughed.

She gave him the sort of look a woman gives her husband when she has been married to him many years and is quite satisfied with him.

"He's very attractive to women and he knows it," she said. "When he talks to you he gives you the impression that you're the only woman in the world and of course it's flattering. But it's only a game and a woman would have to be a perfect fool to take him seriously. He *is* very handsome. Tall and spare and he holds himself well. He has great dark liquid eyes, like the boy's; his hair is snow-white, but very thick still, and the contrast with his bronzed, young face is really breath-taking. He has a ravaged, rather battered look, but at the same time a look of such distinction, it's really quite incredibly romantic."

"He also has his great dark liquid eyes on the main chance," said Charley Harding dryly. "And he'll never let Tito marry a girl who has no more money than Laura."

"She has about five thousand dollars a year of her own," said Bessie. "And she'll get that much more when her mother dies."

"Her mother can live for another thirty years, and five thousand a year won't go far to keep a husband, a father and two or three children, and restore a ruined villa with practically not a stick of furniture in it."

"I think the boy's desperately in love with her."

"How old is he?" I asked.

"Twenty-six."

A few days after this Charley, on coming back to lunch, since for once we were lunching by ourselves, told me that he had run across Mrs. Clayton in the Via Tornabuoni and she had said that she and Laura were driving out that afternoon with Tito to meet his father and see the villa.

"What d'you suppose that means?" asked Bessie.

"My guess is that Tito is taking Laura to be inspected by his old man, and if he approves he's going to ask her to marry him."

"And will he approve?"

"Not on your life."

But Charley was wrong. After the two women had been shown over the house they were taken for a walk round the garden. Without exactly knowing how it had happened Mrs. Clayton found herself alone in an alley with the old count. She spoke no Italian, but he had been an attaché in London and his English was tolerable.

"Your daughter is charming, Mrs. Clayton," he said. "I am not surprised that my Tito has fallen in love with her."

Mrs. Clayton was no fool and it may be that she too had guessed why the young man had asked them to go and see the ancestral villa.

"Young Italians are very impressionable. Laura is sensible enough not to take their attentions too seriously."

"I was hoping she was not quite indifferent to the boy."

"I have no reason to believe that she likes him any more than any other of the young men who dance with her," Mrs. Clayton answered somewhat coldly. "I think I should tell you at once that my daughter has a very moderate income and she will have no more till I die."

"I will be frank with you. I have nothing in the world but this house and the few acres that surround it. My son could not afford to marry a penniless girl, but he is not a fortune-hunter and he loves your daughter."

The count had not only the grand manner but a great deal of charm and Mrs. Clayton was not insensible to it. She softened a little.

"All that is neither here nor there. We don't arrange our children's marriage in America. If Tito wants to marry her, let him ask her, and if she's prepared to marry him she'll presumably say so."

"Unless I am greatly mistaken that is just what he is doing now. I hope with all my heart that he will be successful."

They strolled on and presently saw walking towards them the two young people hand in hand. It was not difficult to guess what had passed. Tito kissed Mrs. Clayton's hand and his father on both cheeks.

"Mrs. Clayton, Papa, Laura has consented to be my wife."

The engagement made something of a stir in Florentine society and a number of parties were given for the young couple. It was quite evident that Tito was very much in love, but less so that Laura was. He was good-looking, adoring, high-spirited and gay;

it was likely enough that she loved him; but she was a girl who did not display emotion and she remained what she had always been, somewhat placid, amiable, serious but friendly, and easy to talk to. I wondered to what extent she had been influenced to accept Tito's offer by his great name, with its historical associations, and the sight of that beautiful house with its lovely view and the romantic garden.

"Anyhow there's no doubt about its being a love match on his side," said Bessie Harding, when we were talking it over. "Mrs. Clayton tells me that neither Tito nor his father has shown any desire to know how much Laura has."

"I'd bet a million dollars that they know to the last cent what she's got and they've calculated exactly how much it comes to in *lire*," said Harding with a grunt.

"You're a beastly old man, darling," she answered.

He gave another grunt.

Shortly after that I left Florence. The marriage took place from the Hardings' house and a vast crowd came to it, ate their food and drank their champagne. Tito and his wife took an apartment on the Lungarno and the old count returned to his lonely villa in the hills. I did not go to Florence again for three years and then only for a week. I was staying once more with the Hardings. I asked about my old friends and then remembered Laura and her mother.

"Mrs. Clayton went back to San Francisco," said Bessie, "and Laura and Tito live at the villa with the count. They're very happy."

"Any babies?"

"No."

"Go on," said Harding.

Bessie gave her husband a look.

"I cannot imagine why I've lived thirty years with a man I dislike so much," she said. "They gave up the apartment on the Lungarno. Laura spent a good deal of money doing things to the villa, there wasn't a bathroom in it, she put in central heating, and she had to buy a lot of furniture to make it habitable, and then Tito lost a small fortune playing poker and poor Laura had to pay up."

"Hadn't he got a job?"

"It didn't amount to anything and it came to an end."

"What Bessie means by that is that he was fired," Harding put in.

"Well, to cut a long story short, they thought it would be more economical to live at the villa and Laura had the idea that it would keep Tito out of mischief. She loves the garden and she's made it lovely. Tito simply worships her and the old count's taken quite a fancy to her. So really it's all turned out very well."

"It may interest you to know that Tito was in last Thursday," said Harding. "He played like a madman and I don't know how much he lost."

"Oh, Charley. He promised Laura he'd never play again."

"As if a gambler ever kept a promise like that. It'll be like last time. He'll burst into tears and say he loves her and it's a debt of honour and unless he can get the money he'll blow his brains out. And Laura will pay as she paid before."

"He's weak, poor dear, but that's his only fault. Unlike most Italian husbands he's absolutely faithful to her and he's kindness itself." She looked at Harding with a sort of humorous grimness. "I've yet to find a husband who was perfect."

"You'd better start looking around pretty soon, dear, or it'll be too late," he retorted with a grin.

I left the Hardings and returned to London. Charley Harding and I corresponded in a desultory sort of way, and about a year later I got a letter from him. He told me as usual what he had been doing in the interval, and mentioned that he had been to Montecatini for the baths and had gone with Bessie to visit friends in Rome; he spoke of the various people I knew in Florence, So and So had just bought a Bellini and Mrs. Such and Such had gone to America to divorce her husband. Then he went on: "I suppose you've heard about the San Pietros. It's shaken us all and we can talk of nothing else. Laura's terribly upset, poor thing, and she's going to have a baby. The police keep on questioning her and that doesn't make it any easier for her. Of course we brought her to stay here. Tito comes up for trial in another month."

I hadn't the faintest notion what all this was about. So I wrote at once to Harding asking him what it meant. He answered with a long letter. What he had to tell me was terrible. I will relate the bare and brutal facts as shortly as I can. I learned them partly from Harding's letter and partly from what he and Bessie told me when two years later I was with them once more.

The count and Laura took to one another at once and Tito was pleased to see how quickly they had formed an affectionate friendship, for he was as devoted to his father as he was in love with his wife. He was glad that the count began to come more often to Florence than he had been used to. They had a spare room in the apartment and on occasion he spent two or three nights with them. He and Laura would go bargain-hunting in the antique shops and buy old pieces to put in the villa. He had tact and knowledge and little by little the house, with its spacious rooms and marble floors, lost its forlorn air and became a friendly place to live in. Laura had a passion for gardening and she and the count spent long hours together planning and then supervising the workmen who were restoring the gardens to their ancient, rather stately, beauty.

Laura made light of it when Tito's financial difficulties forced them to give up the apartment in Florence; she had had enough of Florentine society by then and was not displeased to live altogether in the grand house that had belonged to his ancestors. Tito liked city life and the prospect dismayed him, but he could not complain since it was his own folly that had made it necessary for them to cut down expenses. They still had the car and he amused himself by taking long drives while his father and Laura were busy, and if they knew that now and then he went into Florence to have a flutter at the club they shut their eyes to it. So a year passed. Then, he hardly knew why, he was seized with a vague misgiving. He couldn't put his finger on anything; he had an uneasy feeling that perhaps Laura didn't care for him so much as she had at first; sometimes it seemed to him that his father was inclined to be impatient with him; they appeared to have a great deal to say to one another, but he got the impression that he was being edged out of their conversation, as though he were a child who was expected to sit still and not interrupt while his elders talked of things over his head; he had a notion that often his presence was unwelcome to them and that they were more at their ease when he was not there. He knew his father, and his reputation, but the suspicion that arose in him was so horrible that he refused to entertain it. And yet sometimes he caught a look passing between them that disconcerted him, there was a tender possessiveness in his father's eyes, a sensual complacency in Laura's, which, if he had seen it in others, would have convinced him that they were lovers. But he couldn't, he wouldn't, believe that there was anything between them. The count couldn't help making love to a woman and it was likely enough that Laura felt his extraordinary fascination, but it was shameful to suppose for a moment that they, these two people he loved, had formed a criminal, almost an incestuous, connection. He was sure that Laura had no idea that there was anything more in her feeling than the natural affection of a young, happily-married woman for her father-in-law. Notwithstanding he thought it better that she should not remain in everyday contact with his father, and one day he suggested that they should go back to live in Florence. Laura and the count were astonished that he should propose such a thing and would not hear of it. Laura said that, having spent so much money on the villa, she couldn't afford to set up another establishment, and the count that it was absurd to leave it, now that Laura had made it so comfortable, to live in a wretched apartment in the city. An argument started and Tito got rather excited. He took some remark of Laura's to mean that if she lived at the villa it was to keep him out of temptation. This reference to his losses at the poker-table angered him.

"You always throw your money in my face," he said passionately. "If I'd wanted to marry money I'd have had the sense to marry someone who had a great deal more than you."

Laura went very pale and glanced at the count.

"You have no right to speak to Laura like that," he said. "You are an ill-mannered oaf."

"I shall speak to my wife exactly as I choose."

"You are mistaken. So long as you are in my house you will treat her with the respect which is her right and your duty."

"When I want lessons in behaviour from you, Father, I will let you know."

"You are very impertinent, Tito. You will kindly leave the room."

He looked very stern and dignified and Tito, furious and yet slightly intimidated, leapt to his feet and stalked out slamming the door behind him. He took the car and drove into Florence. He won quite a lot of money that day (lucky at cards, unlucky in love) and to celebrate his winnings got more than a little drunk. He did not go back to the villa till the following morning. Laura was as friendly and placid as ever, but his father was somewhat cool. No reference was made to the scene. But from then on things went from bad to worse. Tito was sullen and moody, the count critical, and on occasion sharp words passed between them. Laura did not interfere, but Tito gained the impression that after a dispute that had been more than acrimonious Laura interceded with his father, for the count thenceforward, refusing to be annoyed, began to treat him with the tolerant patience with which you would treat a wayward child. He convinced himself that they were acting in concert and his suspicions grew formidable. They even increased when Laura in her good-natured way, saying that it must be very dull for him to remain so much in the country, encouraged him to go more often to Florence to see his friends. He jumped to the conclusion that she said this only to be rid of him. He began to watch them. He would enter suddenly a room in which he knew they were, expecting to catch them in a compromising position, or silently follow them to a secluded part of the garden. They were chatting unconcernedly of trivial things. Laura greeted him with a pleasant smile. He could put his finger on nothing to confirm his torturing suspicions. He started to drink. He grew nervous and irritable. He had no proof, no proof whatever, that there was anything between them, and yet in his bones he was certain that they were grossly, shockingly deceiving him. He brooded till he felt he was going mad. A dark aching fire within him consumed his being. On one of his visits to Florence he bought a pistol. He made up his mind that if he could have proof of what in his heart he was certain of, he would kill them both.

I don't know what brought on the final catastrophe. All that came out at the trial was that, driven beyond endurance, Tito had gone one night to his father's room to have it out with him. His father mocked and laughed at him. They had a furious quarrel and Tito took out his pistol and shot the count dead. Then he collapsed and fell, weeping hysterically, on his father's body; the repeated shots brought Laura and the servants rushing in. He jumped up and grabbed the pistol, to shoot himself he said afterwards, but he hesitated or they were too quick for him, and they snatched it out of his hand. The police were sent for. He spent most of his time in prison weeping; he would not eat and had to be forcibly fed; he told the examining magistrate that he had killed his father because he was his wife's lover. Laura, examined and examined again, swore that there had never been anything between the count and herself but a natural affection. The murder filled the Florentine public with horror. The Italians were convinced of her guilt, but her friends, English and American, felt that she was incapable of the crime of which she was accused. They went about saying that Tito was neurotic and insanely jealous and in his stupid way had mistaken her American freedom of behaviour for a criminal passion. On the face of it Tito's charge was absurd. Carlo di San Pietro was nearly thirty years older than she, an elderly man with white hair; who could suppose that there would have been anything between her and her father-in-law, when her husband was young, handsome and in love with her?

It was in Harding's presence that she saw the examining magistrate and the lawyers who had been engaged to defend Tito. They had decided to plead insanity. Experts for the defence examined him and decided that he was insane, experts for the prosecution examined him and decided that he was sane. The fact that he had bought a pistol three months before he committed the dreadful crime went to prove that it was premeditated. It was discovered that he was deeply in debt and his creditors were pressing him; the only means he had of settling with them was by selling the villa, and his father's death put him in possession of it. There is no capital punishment in Italy, but murder with premeditation is punished by solitary confinement for life. On the approach of the trial the lawyers came to Laura and told her that the only way in which Tito could be saved from this was for her to admit in court that the count had been her lover. Laura went very pale. Harding protested violently. He said they had no right to ask her to perjure herself and ruin her reputation to save that shiftless, drunken gambler whom she had been so unfortunate as to marry. Laura remained silent for a while.

"Very well," she said at last, "if that's the only way to save him I'll do it."

Harding tried to dissuade her, but she was decided.

"I should never have a moment's peace if I knew that Tito had to spend the rest of his life alone in a prison cell."

And that is what happened. The trial opened. She was called and under oath stated that for more than a year her father-in-law had been her lover. Tito was declared insane and sent to an asylum. Laura wanted to leave Florence at once, but in Italy the preliminaries to a trial are endless and by then she was near her time. The Hardings insisted on her remaining with them till she was confined. She had a child, a boy, but it only lived twenty-four hours. Her plan was to go back to San Francisco and live with her mother till she could find a job, for Tito's extravagance, the money she had spent on the villa, and then the cost of the trial had seriously impoverished her.

It was Harding who told me most of this; but one day when he was at the club and I was having a cup of tea with Bessie and we were again talking over these tragic happenings she said to me:

"You know, Charley hasn't told you the whole story because he doesn't know it. I never told him. Men are funny in some ways; they're much more easily shocked than women."

I raised my eyebrows, but said nothing.

"Just before Laura went away we had a talk. She was very low and I thought she was grieving over the loss of her baby. I wanted to say something to help her. 'You mustn't take the baby's death too hardly,' I said. 'As things are, perhaps it's better it died.' 'Why?' she said. 'Think what the poor little thing's future would have been with a murderer for his father.' She looked at me for a moment in that strange quiet way of hers. And then what d'you think she said?"

"I haven't a notion," said I.

"She said: 'What makes you think his father was a murderer?'" I felt myself grow as red as a turkey-cock. I could hardly believe my ears. 'Laura, what *do* you mean?' I said. 'You were in court,' she said. 'You heard me say Carlo was my lover.'"

Bessie Harding stared at me as she must have stared at Laura.

"What did you say then?" I asked.

"What was there for me to say? I said nothing. I wasn't so much horrified, I was bewildered. Laura looked at me and, believe it or not, I'm convinced there was a twinkle in her eyes. I felt a perfect fool."

"Poor Bessie," I smiled.

Poor Bessie, I repeated to myself now as I thought of this strange story. She and Charley were long since dead and by their death I had lost good friends. I went to sleep then, and next day Wyman Holt took me for a long drive.

We were to dine with the Greenes at seven and we reached their house on the dot. Now that I had remembered who Laura was I was filled with an immense curiosity to see her again. Wyman had exaggerated nothing. The living-room into which we went was the quintessence of commonplace. It was comfortable enough, but there was not a trace of personality in it. It might have been furnished *en bloc* by a mail-order house. It had the bleakness of a government office. I was introduced first to my host Jasper Greene and then to his brother Emery and to his brother's wife Fanny. Jasper Greene was a large, plump man with a moon face and a shock of black, coarse, unkempt hair. He wore large cellulose-rimmed spectacles. I was staggered by his youth. He could not have been much over thirty and was therefore nearly twenty years younger than Laura. His brother, Emery, a composer and teacher in a New York school of music, might have been seven or eight and twenty. His wife, a pretty little thing, was an actress for the moment out of a job. Jasper Greene mixed us some very adequate cocktails but for a trifle too much vermouth, and we sat down to dinner. The conversation was gay and even boisterous. Jasper and his brother were loud-voiced and all three of them, Jasper, Emery and Emery's wife, were loquacious talkers. They chaffed one another, they joked and laughed; they discussed art, literature, music and the theatre. Wyman and I joined in when we had a chance, which was not often; Laura did not try to. She sat at the head of the table, serene, with an amused, indulgent smile on her lips as she listened to their scatter-brained nonsense; it was not stupid nonsense, mind you, it was intelligent and modern, but it was nonsense all the same. There was something maternal in her attitude, and I was reminded oddly of a sleek dachshund lying quietly in the sun while she looks lazily, and yet watchfully, at her litter of puppies romping round her. I wondered whether it crossed her mind that all this chatter about art didn't amount to much when compared with those incidents of blood and passion that she remembered. But did she remember? It had all happened a long time ago and perhaps it seemed no more than a bad dream. Perhaps these commonplace surroundings were part of her deliberate effort to forget, and to be among these young people was restful to her spirit. Perhaps Jasper's clever stupidity was a comfort. After that searing tragedy it might be that she wanted nothing but the security of the humdrum.

Possibly because Wyman was an authority on the Elizabethan drama the conversation at one moment touched on that. I had already discovered that Jasper Greene was prepared to lay down the law on subjects all and sundry, and now he delivered himself as follows:

"Our theatre has gone all to pot because the dramatists of our day are afraid to deal with the violent emotions which are the proper subject matter of tragedy," he boomed. "In the sixteenth century they had a wealth of melodramatic and bloody themes to suit their purpose and so they produced great plays. But where can our playwrights look for themes? Our Anglo-Saxon blood is too phlegmatic, too supine, to provide them with material they can make anything of, and so they are condemned to occupy themselves with the trivialities of social intercourse."

I wondered what Laura thought of this, but I took care not to catch her eye. She could have told them a story of illicit love, jealousy and parricide which would have been meat to one of Shakespeare's successors, but had he treated it, I suppose he would have felt bound to finish it with at least one more corpse strewn about the stage. The end of her story, as I knew it now, was unexpected certainly, but sadly prosaic and a trifle grotesque. Real life more often ends things with a whimper than with a bang. I wondered too why she had gone out of her way to renew our old acquaintance. Of course she had no reason to suppose that I knew as much as I did; perhaps with a true instinct she was confident that I would not give her away; perhaps she didn't care if I did. I stole a glance at her now and then while she was quietly listening to the excited babbling of the three young people, but her friendly, pleasant face told me nothing. If I hadn't known otherwise I would have sworn that no untoward circumstance had ever troubled the course of her uneventful life.

The evening came to an end and this is the end of my story, but for the fun of it I am going to relate a small incident that happened when Wyman and I got back to his house. We decided to have a bottle of beer before going to bed and went into the kitchen to fetch it. The clock in the hall struck eleven and at that moment the phone rang. Wyman went to answer it and when he came back was quietly chortling to himself.

"What's the joke?" I asked.

"It was one of my students. They're not supposed to call members of the faculty after ten-thirty, but he was all hot and bothered. He asked me how evil had come into the world."

"And did you tell him?"

"I told him that St. Thomas Aquinas had got hot and bothered too about that very question and he'd better worry it out for himself. I said that when he found the solution he was to call me, no matter what time it was. Two o'clock in the morning if he liked."

"I think you're pretty safe not to be disturbed for many a long night," I said.

"I won't conceal from you that I have formed pretty much the same impression myself," he grinned.

Mayhew

THE lives of most men are determined by their environment. They accept the circumstances amid which fate has thrown them not only with resignation but even with good will. They are like street-cars running contentedly on their rails and they despise the sprightly flivver that dashes in and out of the traffic and speeds so jauntily across the open country. I respect them; they are good citizens, good husbands, and good fathers, and of course somebody has to pay the taxes; but I do not find them exciting. I am fascinated by the men, few enough in all conscience, who take life in their own hands and seem to mould it to their own liking. It may be that we have no such thing as free will, but at all events we have the illusion of it. At a cross-road it does seem to us that we might go either to the right or to the left and, the choice once made, it is difficult to see that the whole course of the world's history obliged us to take the turning we did.

I never met a more interesting man than Mayhew. He was a lawyer in Detroit. He was an able and a successful one. By the time he was thirty-five he had a large and a lucrative practice, he had amassed a competence, and he stood on the threshold of a distinguished career. He had an acute brain, an attractive personality, and uprightness. There was no reason why he should not become, financially or politically, a power in the land. One evening he was sitting in his club with a group of friends and they were perhaps a little the worse (or the better) for liquor. One of them had recently come from Italy and he told them of a house he had seen at Capri, a house on the hill, overlooking the Bay of Naples, with a large and shady garden. He described to them the beauty of the most beautiful island in the Mediterranean.

"It sounds fine," said Mayhew. "Is that house for sale?"

"Everything is for sale in Italy."

"Let's send 'em a cable and make an offer for it."

"What in heaven's name would you do with a house in Capri?"

"Live in it," said Mayhew.

He sent for a cable form, wrote it out, and despatched it. In a few hours the reply came back. The offer was accepted.

Mayhew was no hypocrite and he made no secret of the fact that he would never have done so wild a thing if he had been sober, but when he was he did not regret it. He was neither an impulsive nor an emotional man, but a very honest and sincere one. He would never have continued from bravado in a course that he had come to the conclusion was unwise. He made up his mind to do exactly as he had said. He did not care for wealth and he had enough money on which to live in Italy. He thought he could do more with life than spend it on composing the trivial quarrels of unimportant people. He had no definite plan. He merely wanted to get away from a life that had given him all it had to offer. I suppose his friends thought him crazy; some must have done all they could to dissuade him. He arranged his affairs, packed up his furniture and started.

Capri is a gaunt rock of austere outline, bathed in a deep blue sea; but its vineyards, green and smiling, give it a soft and easy grace. It is friendly, remote and debonair. I find it strange that Mayhew should have settled on this lovely island, for I never knew a man more insensible to beauty. I do not know what he sought there: happiness, freedom, or merely leisure; I know what he found. In this place which appeals so extravagantly to the senses he lived a life entirely of the spirit. For the island is rich with historic associations and over it broods always the enigmatic memory of Tiberius the Emperor. From his windows which over-looked the Bay of Naples, with the noble shape of Vesuvius changing colour with the changing light, Mayhew saw a hundred places that recalled the Romans and the Greeks. The past began to haunt him. All that he saw for the first time, for he had never been abroad before, excited his fancy; and in his soul stirred the creative imagina-tion. He was a man of energy. Presently he made up his mind to write a history. For some time he looked about for a subject, and at last decided on the second century of the Roman Empire. It was little known and it seemed to him to offer problems analogous with those of our own day.

He began to collect books and soon he had an immense library. His legal training had taught him to read quickly. He settled down to work. At first he had been accustomed to foregather in the evening with the painters, writers and suchlike who met in the little tavern near the Piazza, but presently he withdrew himself, for his absorption in his studies became more pressing. He had been accustomed to bathe in that bland sea and to take long walks among the pleasant vineyards, but little by little, grudging the time, he ceased to do so. He worked harder than he had ever worked in Detroit. He would start at noon and work all through the night till the whistle of the steamer that goes every morning from Capri to Naples told him that it was five o'clock and time to go to bed.

His subject opened out before him, vaster and more significant, and he imagined a work that would put him for ever beside the great historians of the past. As the years went by he was to be found seldom in the ways of men. He could be tempted to come out of his house only by a game of chess or the chance of an argument. He loved to set his brain against another's. He was widely read now, not only in history, but in philosophy and science; and he was a skilful controversialist, quick, logical and incisive. But he had good-humour and kindliness; though he took a very human pleasure in victory, he did not exult in it to your mortification.

When first he came to the island he was a big, brawny fellow, with thick black hair and a black beard, of a powerful physique; but gradually his skin became pale and waxy; he grew thin and frail. It was an odd contradiction in the most logical of men that, though a convinced and impetuous materialist, he despised the body; he looked upon it as a vile instrument which he could force to do the spirit's bidding. Neither illness nor lassitude prevented him from going on with his work. For fourteen years he toiled unremittingly. He made thousands and thousands of notes. He sorted and classified them. He had his subject at his finger ends, and at last was ready to begin. He sat down to write. He died.

The body that he, the materialist, had treated so contumeliously took its revenge on him.

That vast accumulation of knowledge is lost for ever. Vain was that ambition, surely not an ignoble one, to set his name beside those of Gibbon and Mommsen. His memory is treasured in the hearts of a few friends, fewer, alas! as the years pass on, and to the world he is unknown in death as he was in life.

And yet to me his life was a success. The pattern is good and complete. He did what he wanted, and he died when his goal was in sight and never knew the bitterness of an end achieved.

The Lotus Eater

Most people, the vast majority in fact, lead the lives that circumstances have thrust upon them, and though some repine, looking upon themselves as round pegs in square holes, and think that if things had been different they might have made a much better showing, the greater part accept their lot, if not with serenity, at all events with resignation. They are like tram-cars travelling for ever on the selfsame rails. They go backwards and forwards, backwards and forwards, inevitably, till they can go no longer and then are sold as scrap-iron. It is not often that you find a man who has boldly taken the course of his life into his own hands. When you do, it is worth while having a good look at him.

That was why I was curious to meet Thomas Wilson. It was an interesting and a bold thing he had done. Of course the end was not yet and until the experiment was concluded it was impossible to call it successful. But from what I had heard it seemed he must be an odd sort of fellow and I thought I should like to know him. I had been told he was reserved, but I had a notion that with patience and tact I could persuade him to confide in me. I wanted to hear the facts from his own lips. People exaggerate, they love to romanticise, and I was quite prepared to discover that his story was not nearly so singular as I had been led to believe.

And this impression was confirmed when at last I made his acquaintance. It was on the Piazza in Capri, where I was spending the month of August at a friend's villa, and a little before sunset, when most of the inhabitants, native and foreign, gather together to chat with their friends in the cool of the evening. There is a terrace that overlooks the Bay of Naples, and when the sun sinks slowly into the sea the island of Ischia is silhouetted against a blaze of splendour. It is one of the most lovely sights in the world. I was standing there with my friend and host watching it, when suddenly he said:

"Look, there's Wilson."

"Where?"

"The man sitting on the parapet, with his back to us. He's got a blue shirt on."

I saw an undistinguished back and a small head of grey hair short and rather thin.

"I wish he'd turn round," I said.

"He will presently."

"Ask him to come and have a drink with us at Morgano's."

"All right."

The instant of overwhelming beauty had passed and the sun, like the top of an orange, was dipping into a wine-red sea. We turned round and leaning our backs against the parapet looked at the people who were sauntering to and fro. They were all talking their heads off and the cheerful noise was exhilarating. Then the church bell, rather cracked, but with a fine resonant note, began to ring. The Piazza at Capri, with its clock tower over the footpath that leads up from the harbour, with the church up a flight of steps, is a perfect setting for an opera by Donizetti, and you felt that the voluble crowd might at any moment break out into a rattling chorus. It was charming and unreal.

I was so intent on the scene that I had not noticed Wilson get off the parapet and come towards us. As he passed us my friend stopped him.

"Hulloa, Wilson, I haven't seen you bathing the last few days."

"I've been bathing on the other side for a change."

My friend then introduced me. Wilson shook hands with me politely, but with indifference; a great many strangers come to Capri for a few days, or a few weeks, and I had no doubt he was constantly meeting people who came and went; and then my friend asked him to come along and have a drink with us.

"I was just going back to supper," he said.

"Can't it wait?" I asked.

"I suppose it can," he smiled.

Though his teeth were not very good his smile was attractive. It was gentle and kindly. He was dressed in a blue cotton shirt and a pair of grey trousers, much creased and none too clean, of a thin canvas, and on his feet he wore a pair of very old espadrilles. The get-up was picturesque, and very suitable to the place and the weather, but it did not at all go with his face. It was a lined, long face, deeply sunburned, thin-lipped, with small grey eyes rather close together and tight, neat features. The grey hair was carefully brushed. It was not a plain face, indeed in his youth Wilson might have been good-looking, but a prim one. He wore the blue shirt, open at the neck, and the grey canvas trousers, not as though they belonged to him, but as though, shipwrecked in his pyjamas, he had been fitted out with odd garments by compassionate strangers. Notwithstanding this careless attire he looked like the manager of a branch office in an insurance company, who should by rights be wearing a black coat with pepper-and-salt trousers, a white collar and an unobjectionable tie. I could very well see myself going to him to claim the insurance money when I had lost a watch, and being rather disconcerted while I answered the questions he put to me by his obvious impression, for all his politeness, that people who made such claims were either fools or knaves.

Moving off, we strolled across the Piazza and down the street till we came to Morgano's. We sat in the garden. Around us people were talking in Russian, German, Italian and English. We ordered drinks. Donna Lucia, the host's wife, waddled up and in her low, sweet voice passed the time of day with us. Though middle-aged now and portly, she had still traces of the wonderful beauty that thirty years before had driven artists to paint so many bad portraits of her. Her eyes, large and liquid, were the eyes of Hera and her smile was affectionate and gracious. We three gossiped for a while, for there is always a scandal of one sort or another in Capri to make a topic of conversation, but nothing was said of particular interest and in a little while Wilson got up and left us. Soon afterwards we strolled up to my friend's villa to dine. On the way he asked me what I had thought of Wilson.

"Nothing," I said. "I don't believe there's a word of truth in your story."

"Why not?"

"He isn't the sort of man to do that sort of thing."

"How does anyone know what anyone is capable of?"

"I should put him down as an absolutely normal man of business who's retired on a comfortable income from gilt-edged securities. I think your story's just the ordinary Capri tittle-tattle."

"Have it your own way," said my friend.

We were in the habit of bathing at a beach called the Baths of Tiberius. We took a fly down the road to a certain point and then wandered through lemon groves and vineyards, noisy with cicadas and heavy with the hot smell of the sun, till we came to the top of the cliff down which a steep winding path led to the sea. A day or two later, just before we got down my friend said:

"Oh, there's Wilson back again."

We scrunched over the beach, the only drawback to the bathing-place being that it was shingle and not sand, and as we came along Wilson saw us and waved. He was standing up, a pipe in his mouth, and he wore nothing but a pair of trunks. His body was dark brown, thin but not emaciated, and, considering his wrinkled face and grey hair, youthful. Hot from our walk, we undressed quickly and plunged at once into the water. Six feet from the shore it was thirty feet deep, but so clear that you could see the bottom. It was warm, yet invigorating.

When I got out Wilson was lying on his belly, with a towel under him, reading a book. I lit a cigarette and went and sat down beside him.

"Had a nice swim?" he asked.

He put his pipe inside his book to mark the place and closing it put it down on the pebbles beside him. He was evidently willing to talk.

"Lovely," I said. "It's the best bathing in the world."

"Of course people think those were the Baths of Tiberius." He waved his hand towards a shapeless mass of masonry that stood half in the water and half out. "But that's all rot. It was just one of his villas, you know."

I did. But it is just as well to let people tell you things when they want to. It disposes them kindly towards you if you suffer them to impart information. Wilson gave a chuckle.

"Funny old fellow, Tiberius. Pity they're saying now there's not a word of truth in all those stories about him."

He began to tell me all about Tiberius. Well, I had read my Suetonius too and I had read histories of the Early Roman Empire, so there was nothing very new to me in what he said. But I observed that he was not ill-read. I remarked on it.

"Oh, well, when I settled down here I was naturally interested, and I have plenty of time for reading. When you live in a place like this, with all its associations, it seems to make history so actual. You might almost be living in historical times yourself."

I should remark here that this was in 1913. The world was an easy, comfortable place and no one could have imagined that anything might happen seriously to disturb the serenity of existence.

"How long have you been here?" I asked.

"Fifteen years." He gave the blue and placid sea a glance, and a strangely tender smile hovered on his thin lips. "I fell in love with the place at first sight. You've heard, I daresay, of the mythical German who came here on the Naples boat just for lunch and a look at the Blue Grotto and stayed forty years; well, I can't say I exactly did that, but it's come to the same thing in the end. Only it won't be forty years in my case. Twenty-five. Still, that's better than a poke in the eye with a sharp stick."

I waited for him to go on. For what he had just said looked indeed as though there might be something after all in the singular story I had heard. But at that moment my friend came dripping out of the water very proud of himself because he had swum a mile, and the conversation turned to other things.

After that I met Wilson several times, either in the Piazza or on the beach. He was amiable and polite. He was always pleased to have a talk and I found out that he not only knew every inch of the island but also the adjacent mainland. He had read a great deal on all sorts of subjects, but his speciality was the history of Rome and on this he was very well informed. He seemed to have little imagination and to be of no more than average intelligence. He laughed a good deal, but with restraint, and his sense of humour was tickled by simple jokes. A commonplace man. I did not forget the odd remark he had made during the first short chat we had had by ourselves, but he never so much as approached the topic again. One day on our return from the beach, dismissing the cab at the Piazza, my friend and I told the driver to be ready to take us up to Anacapri at five. We were going to climb Monte Solaro, dine at a tavern we favoured, and walk down in the moonlight. For it was full moon and the views by night were lovely. Wilson was standing by while we gave the cabman instructions, for we had given him a lift to save him the hot dusty walk, and more from politeness than for any other reason I asked him if he would care to join us.

"It's my party," I said.

"I'll come with pleasure," he answered.

But when the time came to set out my friend was not feeling well, he thought he had stayed too long in the water, and would not face the long and tiring walk. So I went alone with Wilson. We climbed the mountain, admired the spacious view, and got back to the inn as night was falling, hot, hungry and thirsty. We had ordered our dinner beforehand. The food was good, for Antonio was an excellent cook, and the wine came from his own vineyard. It was so light that you felt you could drink it like water and we finished the first bottle with our macaroni. By the time we had finished the second we felt that there was nothing much wrong with life. We sat in a little garden under a great vine laden with grapes. The air was exquisitely soft. The night was still and we were alone. The maid brought us *bel paese* cheese and a plate of figs. I ordered coffee and strega, which is the best liqueur they make in Italy. Wilson would not have a cigar, but lit his pipe.

"We've got plenty of time before we need start," he said, "the moon won't be over the hill for another hour."

"Moon or no moon," I said briskly, "of course we've got plenty of time. That's one of the delights of Capri, that there's never any hurry."

"Leisure," he said. "If people only knew! It's the most priceless thing a man can have and they're such fools they don't even know it's something to aim at. Work? They work for work's sake. They haven't got the brains to realise that the only object of work is to obtain leisure."

Wine has the effect on some people of making them indulge in general reflections. These remarks were true, but no one could have claimed that they were original. I did not say anything, but struck a match to light my cigar.

"It was full moon the first time I came to Capri," he went on reflectively. "It might be the same moon as to-night."

"It was, you know," I smiled.

He grinned. The only light in the garden was what came from an oil lamp that hung over our heads. It had been scanty to eat by, but it was good now for confidences.

"I didn't mean that. I mean, it might be yesterday. Fifteen years it is, and when I look back it seems like a month. I'd never been to Italy before. I came for my summer holiday. I went to Naples by boat from Marseilles and I had a look round, Pompeii, you know, and Paestum and one or two places like that; then I came here for a week. I liked the look of the place right away, from the sea, I mean, as I watched it come closer and closer; and then when we got into the little boats from the steamer and landed at the quay, with all that crowd of jabbering people who wanted to take your luggage, and the hotel touts, and the tumbledown houses on the Marina and the walk up to the hotel, and dining on the terrace —well, it just got me. That's the truth. I didn't know if I was standing on my head or my heels. I'd never drunk Capri wine before, but I'd heard of it; I think I must have got a bit tight. I sat on that terrace after they'd all gone to bed and watched the moon over the sea, and there was Vesuvius with a great red plume of smoke rising up from it. Of course I know now that wine I drank was ink, Capri wine my eye, but I thought it all right then. But it wasn't the wine that made me drunk, it was the shape of the island and those jabbering people, the moon and the sea and the oleander in the hotel garden. I'd never seen an oleander before."

It was a long speech and it had made him thirsty. He took up his glass, but it was empty. I asked him if he would have another stregna.

"It's sickly stuff. Let's have a bottle of wine. That's sound, that is, pure juice of the grape and can't hurt anyone."

I ordered more wine, and when it came filled the glasses. He took a long drink and after a sigh of pleasure went on.

"Next day I found my way to the bathing-place we go to. Not bad bathing, I thought. Then I wandered about the island. As luck would have it, there was a *festa* up at the Punta di Timberio and I ran straight into the middle of it. An image of the Virgin and priests, acolytes swinging censers, and a whole crowd of jolly, laughing, excited people, a lot of them all dressed up. I ran across an Englishman there and asked him what it was all about. 'Oh, it's the feast of the Assumption,' he said, 'at least that's what the Catholic Church says it is, but that's just their hanky-panky. It's the festival of Venus. Pagan, you know. Aphrodite rising from the sea and all that.' It gave me quite a funny feeling to hear him. It seemed to take one a long way back, if you know what I mean. After that I went down one night to have a look at the Faraglioni by moonlight. If the fates had wanted me to go on being a bank manager they oughtn't to have let me take that walk."

"You were a bank manager, were you?" I asked.

I had been wrong about him, but not far wrong.

"Yes. I was manager of the Crawford Street branch of the York and City. It was convenient for me because I lived up Hendon way. I could get from door to door in thirty-seven minutes."

He puffed at his pipe and relit it.

"That was my last night, that was. I'd got to be back at the bank on Monday morning. When I looked at those two great rocks sticking out of the water, with the moon above them, and all the little lights of the fishermen in their boats catching cuttle-fish, all so peaceful and beautiful, I said to myself, well, after all, why should I go back? It wasn't as if I had anyone dependent on me. My wife had died of bronchial pneumonia four years before and the kid went to live with her grandmother, my wife's mother. She was an old fool, she didn't look after the kid properly and she got blood-poisoning, they amputated her leg, but they couldn't save her and she died, poor little thing."

"How terrible," I said.

"Yes, I was cut up at the time, though of course not so much as if the kid had been living with me, but I dare say it was a mercy. Not much chance for a girl with only one leg. I was sorry about my wife too. We got on very well together. Though I don't know if it would have continued. She was the sort of woman who was always bothering about what other people'd think. She didn't like travelling. Eastbourne was her idea of a holiday. D'you know, I'd never crossed the Channel till after her death."

"But I suppose you've got other relations, haven't you?"

"None. I was an only child. My father had a brother, but he

Q

went to Australia before I was born. I don't think anyone could easily be more alone in the world than I am. There wasn't any reason I could see why I shouldn't do exactly what I wanted. I was thirty-four at that time."

He had told me he had been on the island for fifteen years. That would make him forty-nine. Just about the age I should have given him.

"I'd been working since I was seventeen. All I had to look forward to was doing the same old thing day after day till I retired on my pension. I said to myself, is it worth it? What's wrong with chucking it all up and spending the rest of my life down here? It was the most beautiful place I'd ever seen. But I'd had a business training, I was cautious by nature. 'No,' I said, 'I won't be carried away like this, I'll go to-morrow like I said I would and think it over. Perhaps when I get back to London I'll think quite differently.' Damned fool, wasn't I? I lost a whole year that way."

"You didn't change your mind, then?"

"You bet I didn't. All the time I was working I kept thinking of the bathing here and the vineyards and the walks over the hills and the moon and the sea, and the Piazza in the evening when everyone walks about for a bit of a chat after the day's work is over. There was only one thing that bothered me: I wasn't sure if I was justified in not working like everybody else did. Then I read a sort of history book, by a man called Marion Crawford it was, and there was a story about Sybaris and Crotona. There were two cities; and in Sybaris they just enjoyed life and had a good time, and in Crotona they were hardy and industrious and all that. And one day the men of Crotona came over and wiped Sybaris out, and then after a while a lot of other fellows came over from somewhere else and wiped Crotona out. Nothing remains of Sybaris, not a stone, and all that's left of Crotona is just one column. That settled the matter for me."

"Oh?"

"It came to the same in the end, didn't it? And when you look back now, who were the mugs?"

I did not reply and he went on.

"The money was rather a bother. The bank didn't pension one off till after thirty years' service, but if you retired before that they gave you a gratuity. With that and what I'd got for the sale of my house and the little I'd managed to save, I just hadn't enough to buy an annuity to last the rest of my life. It would have been silly to sacrifice everything so as to lead a pleasant life and not have a sufficient income to make it pleasant. I wanted to have a little place of my own, a servant to look after me, enough to buy tobacco, decent food, books now and then, and something over for emergencies. I knew pretty well how much I needed. I found I had just enough to buy an annuity for twenty-five years."

"You were thirty-five at the time?"

"Yes. It would carry me on till I was sixty. After all, no one can be certain of living longer than that, a lot of men die in their fifties, and by the time a man's sixty he's had the best of life."

"On the other hand no one can be sure of dying at sixty," I said.

"Well, I don't know. It depends on himself, doesn't it?"

"In your place I should have stayed on at the bank till I was entitled to my pension."

"I should have been forty-seven then. I shouldn't have been too old to enjoy my life here, I'm older than that now and I enjoy it as much as I ever did, but I should have been too old to experience the particular pleasure of a young man. You know, you can have just as good a time at fifty as you can at thirty, but it's not the same sort of good time. I wanted to live the perfect life while I still had the energy and the spirit to make the most of it. Twenty-five years seemed a long time to me, and twenty-five years of happiness seemed worth paying something pretty substantial for. I'd made up my mind to wait a year and I waited a year. Then I sent in my resignation and as soon as they paid me my gratuity I bought the annuity and came on here."

"An annuity for twenty-five years?"

"That's right."

"Have you never regretted?"

"Never. I've had my money's worth already. And I've got ten years more. Don't you think after twenty-five years of perfect happiness one ought to be satisfied to call it a day?"

"Perhaps."

He did not say in so many words what he would do then, but his intention was clear. It was pretty much the story my friend had told me, but it sounded different when I heard it from his own lips. I stole a glance at him. There was nothing about him that was not ordinary. No one, looking at that neat, prim face, could have thought him capable of an unconventional action. I did not blame him. It was his own life that he had arranged in this strange manner, and I did not see why he should not do what he liked with it. Still, I could not prevent the little shiver that ran down my spine.

"Getting chilly?" he smiled. "We might as well start walking down. The moon'll be up by now."

Before we parted Wilson asked me if I would like to go and see his house one day; and two or three days later, finding out where he lived, I strolled up to see him. It was a peasant's cottage, well away from the town, in a vineyard, with a view of the sea. By the side of the door grew a great oleander in full flower. There were only two small rooms, a tiny kitchen and a lean-to in which fire-wood could be kept. The bedroom was furnished like a monk's cell, but the sitting-room, smelling agreeably of tobacco, was comfortable enough, with two large arm-chairs that he had brought from England, a large roll-top desk, a cottage piano and crowded bookshelves. On the walls were framed engravings of pictures by G. F. Watts and Lord Leighton. Wilson told me that the house belonged to the owner of the vineyard who lived in another cottage higher up the hill, and his wife came in every day to do the rooms and the cooking. He had found the place on his first visit to Capri, and taking it on his return for good had been there ever since. Seeing the piano and music open on it, I asked him if he would play.

"I'm no good, you know, but I've always been fond of music and I get a lot of fun out of strumming."

He sat down at the piano and played one of the movements from a Beethoven sonata. He did not play very well. I looked at his music, Schumann and Schubert, Beethoven, Bach and Chopin. On the table on which he had his meals was a greasy pack of cards. I asked him if he played patience.

"A lot."

From what I saw of him then and from what I heard from other people I made for myself what I think must have been a fairly accurate picture of the life he had led for the last fifteen years. It was certainly a very harmless one. He bathed; he walked a great deal, and he seemed never to lose his sense of the beauty of the island which he knew so intimately; he played the piano and he played patience; he read. When he was asked to a party he went and, though a trifle dull, was agreeable. He was not affronted if he was neglected. He liked people, but with an aloofness that prevented intimacy. He lived thriftily, but with sufficient comfort. He never owed a penny. I imagine he had never been a man whom sex had greatly troubled, and if in his younger days he had now and then a passing affair with a visitor to the island whose head was turned by the atmosphere, his emotion, while it lasted, remained, I am pretty sure, well under his control. I think he was determined that nothing should interfere with his independence of spirit. His only passion was for the beauty of nature, and he sought felicity in the simple and natural things that life offers to everyone. You may say that it was a grossly selfish existence. It was. He was of no use to anybody, but on the other hand he did nobody any harm. His only object was his own happiness, and it looked as though he had attained it. Very few people know where to look for happiness; fewer still find it. I don't know whether he was a fool or a wise man. He was certainly a man who knew his own mind. The odd thing about him to me was that he was so immensely commonplace. I should never have given him a second thought but for what I knew, that on a certain day, ten years from then, unless a chance illness cut the thread before, he must deliberately take leave of the world he loved so well. I wondered whether it was the thought of this, never quite absent from his mind, that gave him the peculiar zest with which he enjoyed every moment of the day.

I should do him an injustice if I omitted to state that he was not at all in the habit of talking about himself. I think the friend I was staying with was the only person in whom he had confided. I believe he only told me the story because he suspected I already knew it, and on the evening on which he told it me he had drunk a good deal of wine.

My visit drew to a close and I left the island. The year after, war broke out. A number of things happened to me, so that the course of my life was greatly altered, and it was thirteen years before I went to Capri again. My friend had been back some time, but he was no longer so well off, and had moved into a house that had no room for me; so I was putting up at the hotel. He came to meet me at the boat and we dined together. During dinner I asked him where exactly his house was.

"You know it," he answered. "It's the little place Wilson had. I've built on a room and made it quite nice."

With so many other things to occupy my mind I had not given Wilson a thought for years; but now, with a little shock, I remembered. The ten years he had before him when I made his acquaintance must have elapsed long ago.

"Did he commit suicide as he said he would?"

"It's a rather grim story."

Wilson's plan was all right. There was only one flaw in it and this, I suppose, he could not have foreseen. It had never occurred to him that after twenty-five years of complete happiness, in this quiet backwater, with nothing in the world to disturb his serenity, his character would gradually lose its strength. The will needs obstacles in order to exercise its power; when it is never thwarted, when no effort is needed to achieve one's desires, because one has placed one's desires only in the things that can be obtained by stretching out one's hand, the will grows impotent. If you walk on a level all the time the muscles you need to climb a mountain will atrophy. These observations are trite, but there they are. When Wilson's annuity expired he had no longer the resolution to make the end which was the price he had agreed to pay for that long period of happy tranquillity. I do not think, as far as I could gather, both from what my friend told me and afterwards from others, that he wanted courage. It was just that he couldn't make up his mind. He put it off from day to day.

He had lived on the island for so long and had always settled his accounts so punctually that it was easy for him to get credit; never having borrowed money before, he found a number of people who were willing to lend him small sums when now he asked for them. He had paid his rent regularly for so many years that his landlord, whose wife Assunta still acted as his servant, was content to let things slide for several months. Everyone believed him when he said that a relative had died and that he was temporarily embarrassed because owing to legal formalities he could not for some time get the money that was due to him. He managed to hang on after this fashion for something over a year. Then he could get no more credit from the local tradesmen, and there was no one to lend him any more money. His landlord gave him notice to leave the house unless he paid up the arrears of rent before a certain date.

The day before this he went into his tiny bedroom, closed the door and the window, drew the curtain and lit a brazier of charcoal. Next morning when Assunta came to make his breakfast she found him insensible but still alive. The room was draughty, and though he had done this and that to keep out the fresh air he had not done it very thoroughly. It almost looked as though at the last moment, and desperate though his situation was, he had suffered from a certain infirmity of purpose. Wilson was taken to the hospital, and though very ill for some time he at last recovered. But as a result either of the charcoal poisoning or of the shock he was no longer in complete possession of his faculties. He was not insane, at all events not insane enough to be put in an asylum, but he was quite obviously no longer in his right mind.

"I went to see him," said my friend. "I tried to get him to talk, but he kept looking at me in a funny sort of way, as though he couldn't quite make out where he'd seen me before. He looked rather awful lying there in bed, with a week's growth of grey beard on his chin; but except for that funny look in his eyes he seemed quite normal."

"What funny look in his eyes?"

"I don't know exactly how to describe it. Puzzled. It's an absurd comparison, but suppose you threw a stone up into the air and it didn't come down but just stayed there . . ."

"It would be rather bewildering," I smiled.

"Well, that's the sort of look he had."

It was difficult to know what to do with him. He had no money and no means of getting any. His effects were sold, but for too little to pay what he owed. He was English, and the Italian authorities did not wish to make themselves responsible for him. The British Consul in Naples had no funds to deal with the case. He could of course be sent back to England, but no one seemed to know what could be done with him when he got there. Then Assunta, the servant, said that he had been a good master and a good tenant, and as long as he had the money had paid his way; he could sleep in the woodshed in the cottage in which she and her husband lived, and he could share their meals. This was suggested to him. It was difficult to know whether he understood or not. When Assunta came to take him from the hospital he went with her without remark. He seemed to have no longer a will of his own. She had been keeping him now for two years.

"It's not very comfortable, you know," said my friend. "They've rigged him up a ramshackle bed and given him a couple of blankets, but there's no window, and it's icy cold in winter and like an oven in summer. And the food's pretty rough. You know how these peasants eat: macaroni on Sundays and meat once in a blue moon."

"What does he do with himself all the time?"

"He wanders about the hills. I've tried to see him two or three times, but it's no good; when he sees you coming he runs like a hare. Assunta comes down to have a chat with me now and then and I give her a bit of money so that she can buy him tobacco, but God knows if he ever gets it."

"Do they treat him all right?" I asked.

"I'm sure Assunta's kind enough. She treats him like a child. I'm afraid her husband's not very nice to him. He grudges the cost of his keep. I don't believe he's cruel or anything like that, but I think he's a bit sharp with him. He makes him fetch water and clean the cow-shed and that sort of thing."

"It sounds pretty rotten," I said.

"He brought it on himself. After all, he's only got what he deserved."

"I think on the whole we all get what we deserve," I said. "But that doesn't prevent its being rather horrible."

Two or three days later my friend and I were taking a walk. We were strolling along a narrow path through an olive grove.

"There's Wilson," said my friend suddenly. "Don't look, you'll only frighten him. Go straight on."

I walked with my eyes on the path, but out of the corners of them I saw a man hiding behind an olive tree. He did not move as we approached, but I felt that he was watching us. As soon as we had passed I heard a scamper. Wilson, like a hunted animal, had made for safety. That was the last I ever saw of him.

He died last year. He had endured that life for six years. He was found one morning on the mountainside lying quite peacefully as though he had died in his sleep. From where he lay he had been able to see those two great rocks called the Faraglioni which stand out of the sea. It was full moon and he must have gone to see them by moonlight. Perhaps he died of the beauty of that sight.

Salvatore

I WONDER if I can do it.

I knew Salvatore first when he was a boy of fifteen with a pleasant, ugly face, a laughing mouth and care-free eyes. He used to spend the morning lying about the beach with next to nothing on and his brown body was as thin as a rail. He was full of grace. He was in and out of the sea all the time, swimming with the clumsy, effortless stroke common to the fisher boys. Scrambling up the jagged rocks on his hard feet, for except on Sundays he never wore shoes, he would throw himself into the deep water with a cry of delight. His father was a fisherman who owned his own little vine-yard and Salvatore acted as nursemaid to his two younger brothers. He shouted to them to come inshore when they ventured out too far and made them dress when it was time to climb the hot, vine-clad hill for the frugal midday meal.

But boys in those Southern parts grow apace and in a little while he was madly in love with a pretty girl who lived on the Grande Marina. She had eyes like forest pools and held herself like a daughter of the Cæsars. They were affianced, but they could not marry till Salvatore had done his military service, and when he left the island which he had never left in his life before, to become a sailor in the navy of King Victor Emmanuel, he wept like a child. It was hard for one who had never been less free than the birds to be at the beck and call of others; it was harder still to live in a battleship with strangers instead of in a little white cottage among the vines; and when he was ashore, to walk in noisy, friendless cities with streets so crowded that he was frightened to cross them, when he had been used to silent paths and the mountains and the sea. I suppose it had never struck him that Ischia, which he looked at every evening (it was like a fairy island in the sunset) to see what the weather would be like next day, or Vesuvius, pearly in the dawn, had anything to do with him at all; but when he ceased to have them before his eyes he realised in some dim fashion that they were as much part of him as his hands and his feet. He was dreadfully homesick. But it was hardest of all to be parted from the girl he loved with all his passionate young heart. He wrote to her (in his childlike handwriting) long, ill-spelt letters in which he told her how constantly he thought of her and how much he longed to be back. He was sent here and there, to Spezzia, to Venice, to Bari and finally to China. Here he fell ill of some mysterious ailment that kept him in hospital for months. He bore it with the mute and uncomprehending patience of a dog. When he learnt that it was a form of rheumatism that made him unfit for further service his heart exulted, for he could go home; and he did not bother, in fact he scarcely listened, when the doctors told him that he would never again be quite well. What did he care when he was going back to the little island he loved so well and the girl who was waiting for him?

When he got into the rowing-boat that met the steamer from Naples and was rowed ashore he saw his father and mother standing on the jetty and his two brothers, big boys now, and he waved to them. His eyes searched among the crowd that waited there, for the girl. He could not see her. There was a great deal of kissing when he jumped up the steps and they all, emotional creatures, cried a little as they exchanged their greetings. He asked where the girl was. His mother told him that she did not know; they had not seen her for two or three weeks; so in the evening when the moon was shining over the placid sea and the lights of Naples twinkled in the distance he walked down to the Grande Marina to her house. She was sitting on the doorstep with her mother. He was a little shy because he had not seen her for so long. He asked her if she had not received the letter that he had written to her to say that he was coming home. Yes, they had received a letter, and they had been told by another of the island boys that he was ill. Yes, that was why he was back; was it not a piece of luck? Oh, but they had heard that he would never be quite well again. The doctors talked a lot of nonsense, but he knew very well that now he was home again he would recover. They were silent for a little, and then the mother nudged the girl. She did not try to soften the blow. She told him straight out, with the blunt directness of her race, that she could not marry a man who would never be strong enough to work like a man. They had made up their minds, her mother and father and she, and her father would never give his consent.

When Salvatore went home he found that they all knew. The girl's father had been to tell them what they had decided, but they had lacked the courage to tell him themselves. He wept on his mother's bosom. He was terribly unhappy, but he did not blame the girl. A fisherman's life is hard and it needs strength and endurance. He knew very well that a girl could not afford to marry a man who might not be able to support her. His smile was very sad and his eyes had the look of a dog that has been beaten, but he did not complain, and he never said a hard word of the girl he had loved so well. Then, a few months later, when he had settled down to the common round, working in his father's vineyard and fishing, his mother told him that there was a young woman in the village who was willing to marry him. Her name was Assunta.

"She's as ugly as the devil," he said.

She was older than he, twenty-four or twenty-five, and she had been engaged to a man who, while doing his military service, had been killed in Africa. She had a little money of her own and if Salvatore married her she could buy him a boat of his own and they could take a vineyard that by a happy chance happened at that moment to be without a tenant. His mother told him that Assunta had seen him at the *festa* and had fallen in love with him. Salvatore smiled his sweet smile and said he would think about it. On the following Sunday, dressed in the stiff black clothes in which he looked so much less well than in the ragged shirt and trousers of every day, he went up to High Mass at the parish church and placed himself so that he could have a good look at the young woman. When he came down again he told his mother that he was willing.

Well, they were married and they settled down in a tiny white-washed house in the middle of a handsome vineyard. Salvatore was now a great big husky fellow, tall and broad, but still with that ingenuous smile and those trusting, kindly eyes that he had had as a boy. He had the most beautiful manners I have ever seen in my life. Assunta was a grim-visaged female, with decided features, and she looked old for her years. But she had a good heart and she was no fool. I used to be amused by the little smile of devotion that she gave her husband when he was being very masculine and masterful; she never ceased to be touched by his gentle sweetness. But she could not bear the girl who had thrown him over, and notwithstanding Salvatore's smiling expostulations she had nothing but harsh words for her. Presently children were born to them.

It was a hard enough life. All through the fishing season towards evening he set out in his boat with one of his brothers for the fishing grounds. It was a long pull of six or seven miles, and he spent the night catching the profitable cuttlefish. Then there was the long row back again in order to sell the catch in time for it to go on the early boat to Naples. At other times he was working in his vineyard from dawn till the heat drove him to rest and then again, when it was a trifle cooler, till dusk. Often his rheumatism prevented him from doing anything at all and then he would lie about the beach, smoking cigarettes, with a pleasant word for everyone notwithstanding the pain that racked his limbs. The foreigners who came down to bathe and saw him there said that these Italian fishermen were lazy devils.

Sometimes he used to bring his children down to give them a bath. They were both boys and at this time the elder was three and the younger less than two. They sprawled about at the water's edge stark naked and Salvatore standing on a rock would dip them in the water. The elder one bore it with stoicism, but the baby screamed lustily. Salvatore had enormous hands, like legs of mutton, coarse and hard from constant toil, but when he bathed his children, holding them so tenderly, drying them with delicate care, upon my word they were like flowers. He would seat the naked baby on the palm of his hand and hold him up, laughing a little at his smallness, and his laugh was like the laughter of an angel. His eyes then were as candid as his child's.

I started by saying that I wondered if I could do it and now I must tell you what it is that I have tried to do. I wanted to see whether I could hold your attention for a few pages while I drew for you the portrait of a man, just an ordinary fisherman who possessed nothing in the world except a quality which is the rarest, the most precious and the loveliest that anyone can have. Heaven only knows why he should so strangely and unexpectedly have possessed it. All I know is that it shone in him with a radiance that, if it had not been so unconscious and so humble, would have been to the common run of men hardly bearable. And in case you have not guessed what the quality was, I will tell you. Goodness, just goodness.

The Wash-Tub

POSITANO stands on the side of a steep hill, a disarray of huddled white houses, their tiled roofs washed pale by the suns of a hundred years; but unlike many of these Italian towns perched out of harm's way on a rocky eminence it does not offer you at one delightful glance all it has to give. It has quaint streets that zigzag up the hill and battered, painted houses in the baroque style, but very late, in which Neapolitan noblemen led for a season lives of penurious grandeur. It is indeed almost excessively picturesque and in winter its two or three modest hotels are crowded with painters, male and female, who in their different ways acknowledge by their daily labours the emotion it has excited in them. Some take infinite pains to place on canvas every window and every tile their peering eyes can discover and doubtless achieve the satisfaction that rewards honest industry. "At all events it's sincere," they say modestly when they show you their work. Some, rugged and dashing, in a fine frenzy attack their canvas with a pallet knife charged with a wad of paint, and they say: "You see, what I was trying to bring out was my personality." They slightly close their eyes and tentatively murmur: "I think it's rather me, don't you?" And there are some who give you highly entertaining arrangements of spheres and cubes and utter sombrely: "That's how I see it!" These for the most part are strong silent men who waste no words.

But Positano looks full south and the chances are that in summer you will have it to yourself. The hotel is clean and cool and there is a terrace, overhung with vines, where you can sit at night and look at the sea bespangled with dim stars. Down at the Marina, on the quay, is a little tavern where you can dine under an archway off anchovies and ham, macaroni and fresh-caught mullet, and drink cold wine. Once a day the steamer from Naples comes in, bringing the mail, and for a quarter of an hour gives the beach (there is no port and the passengers are landed in small boats) an air of animation.

One August, tiring of Capri where I had been staying, I made up my mind to spend a few days at Positano, so I hired a fishing-boat and rowed over. I stopped on the way in a shady cove to bathe and lunch and sleep, and did not arrive till evening. I strolled up the hill, my two bags following me on the heads of two sturdy women, to the hotel, and was surprised to learn that I was not its only guest.

The waiter, whose name was Giuseppe, was an old friend of mine, and at that season he was boots, porter, chambermaid and cook as well. He told me that an American signore had been staying there for three months.

"Is he a painter or a writer or something?" I asked.

"No, *Signore*, he's a gentleman."

Odd, I thought. No foreigners came to Positano at that time of year but German *Wandervögel*, looking hot and dusty, with satchels on their backs, and they only stayed overnight. I could not imagine anyone wishing to spend three months there; unless of course he were hiding. And since all London had been excited by the flight earlier in the year of an eminent, but dishonest, financier, the amusing thought occurred to me that this mysterious stranger was perhaps he. I knew him slightly and trusted that my sudden arrival would not disconcert him.

"You'll see the *Signore* at the Marina," said Giuseppe, as I was setting out to go down again. "He always dines there."

He was certainly not there when I arrived. I asked what there was for dinner and drank an americano, which is by no means a bad substitute for a cocktail. In a few minutes, however, a man walked in who could be no other than my fellow-guest at the hotel and I had a moment's disappointment when I saw that it was not the absconding financier. A tall, elderly man, bronzed after his summer on the Mediterranean, with a handsome, thin face. He wore a very neat, even smart, suit of cream-coloured silk and no hat. His grey hair was cut very short, but was still thick. There was ease in his bearing, and elegance. He looked round the half-dozen tables under the archway at which the natives of the place were playing cards or dominoes and his eyes rested on me. They smiled pleasantly. He came up.

"I hear you have just arrived at the hotel. Giuseppe suggested that as he couldn't come down here to effect an introduction you wouldn't mind if I introduced myself. Would it bore you to dine with a total stranger?"

"Of course not. Sit down."

He turned to the maid who was laying a cover for me and in beautiful Italian told her that I would eat with him. He looked at my americano.

"I have got them to stock a little gin and French vermouth for me. Would you allow me to mix you a very dry Martini?"

"Without hesitation."

"It gives an exotic note to the surroundings which brings out the local colour."

He certainly made a very good cocktail and with added appetite we ate the ham and anchovies with which our dinner began. My host had a pleasant humour and his fluent conversation was agreeable.

"You must forgive me if I talk too much," he said presently. "This is the first chance I've had to speak English for three months. I don't suppose you will stay here long and I mean to make the most of it."

"Three months is a long time to stay at Positano."

"I've hired a boat and I bathe and fish. I read a great deal. I have a good many books here and if there's anything I can lend you I shall be very glad."

"I think I have enough reading matter. But I should love to look at what you have. It's always fun looking at other people's books."

He gave me a sharp look and his eyes twinkled.

"It also tells you a good deal about them," he murmured.

When we finished dinner we went on talking. The stranger was well-read and interested in a diversity of topics. He spoke with so much knowledge of painting that I wondered if he was an art critic or a dealer. But then it appeared that he had been reading Suetonius and I came to the conclusion that he was a college professor. I asked him his name.

"Barnaby," he answered.

"That's a name that has recently acquired an amazing celebrity."

"Oh, how so?"

"Have you never heard of the celebrated Mrs. Barnaby? She's a compatriot of yours."

"I admit that I've seen her name in the papers rather frequently of late. Do you know her?"

"Yes, quite well. She gave the grandest parties all last season and I went to them whenever she asked me. Everyone did. She's an astounding woman. She came to London to do the season, and, by George, she did it. She just swept everything before her."

"I understand she's very rich?"

"Fabulously, I believe, but it's not that that has made her success. Plenty of American women have money. Mrs. Barnaby has got where she has by sheer force of character. She never pretends to be anything but what she is. She's natural. She's priceless. You know her history, of course?"

My friend smiled.

"Mrs. Barnaby may be a great celebrity in London, but to the best of my belief in America she is almost inconceivably unknown."

I smiled also, but within me; I could well imagine how shocked this distinguished and cultured man would be by the rollicking humour, the frankness, with its tang of the soil, and the rich and vital experience of the amazing Mrs. Barnaby.

"Well, I'll tell you about her. Her husband appears to be a very rough diamond; he's a great hulking fellow, she says, who could fell a steer with his fist. He's known in Arizona as One-Bullet Mike."

"Good gracious! Why?"

"Well, years ago in the old days he killed two men with a single shot. She says he's handier with his gun even now than any man West of the Rockies. He's a miner, but he's been a cowpuncher, a gun-runner and God knows what in his day."

"A thoroughly Western type," said my professor a trifle acidly, I thought.

"Something of a desperado, I imagine. Mrs. Barnaby's stories about him are a real treat. Of course everyone's been begging her to let him come over, but she says he'd never leave the wide open spaces. He struck oil a year or two ago and now he's got all the money in the world. He must be a great character. I've heard her keep the whole dinner-table spellbound when she's talked of the old days when they roughed it together. It gives you quite a thrill when you see this grey-haired woman, not at all pretty, but exquisitely dressed, with the most wonderful pearls, and hear her tell how she washed the miners' clothes and cooked for the camp. Your American women have an adaptability that's really stupendous. When you see Mrs. Barnaby sitting at the head of her table, perfectly at home with princes of the blood, ambassadors, cabinet ministers and the duke of this and the duke of that, it seems almost incredible that only a few years ago she was cooking the food of seventy miners."

"Can she read or write?"

"I suppose her invitations are written by her secretary, but she's by no means an ignorant woman. She told me she used to make a point of reading for an hour every night after the fellows in camp had gone to bed."

"Remarkable!"

"On the other hand One-Bullet Mike only learnt to write his name when he suddenly found himself under the necessity of signing cheques."

We walked up the hill to our hotel and before separating for the night arranged to take our luncheon with us next day and row over to a cove that my friend had discovered. We spent a charming day bathing, reading, eating, sleeping and talking, and we dined together in the evening. The following morning, after breakfast on the terrace, I reminded Barnaby of his promise to show me his books.

"Come right along."

I accompanied him to his bedroom, where Giuseppe, the waiter, was making his bed. The first thing I caught sight of was a photograph in a gorgeous frame of the celebrated Mrs. Barnaby. My friend caught sight of it too and suddenly turned pale with anger.

"You fool, Giuseppe. Why have you taken that photograph out of my wardrobe? Why the devil did you think I put it away?"

"I didn't know, Signore. That's why I put it back on the *Signore's* table. I thought he liked to see the portrait of his *signora*."

I was staggered.

"Is my Mrs. Barnaby your wife?" I cried.

"She is."

"Good Lord, are you One-Bullet Mike?"

"Do I look it?"

I began to laugh.

"I'm bound to say you don't."

I glanced at his hands. He smiled grimly and held them out.

"No, sir, I have never felled a steer with my naked fist."

For a moment we stared at one another in silence.

"She'll never forgive me," he moaned. "She wanted me to take a false name, and when I wouldn't she was quite vexed with me. She said it wasn't safe. I said it was bad enough to hide myself in Positano for three months, but I'd be damned if I'd use any other name than my own." He hesitated. "I throw myself on your mercy. I can do nothing but trust to your generosity not to disclose a secret that you have discovered by the most unlikely chance."

"I will be as silent as the grave, but honestly I don't understand. What does it all mean?"

"I am a doctor by profession and for the last thirty years my wife and I have lived in Pennsylvania. I don't know if I have struck you as a roughneck, but I venture to say that Mrs. Barnaby is one of the most cultivated women I have ever known. Then a cousin of hers died and left her a very large fortune. There's no mistake about that. My wife is a very, very rich woman. She has always read a great deal of English fiction and her one desire was to have a London season and entertain and do all the grand things she had read about in books. It was her money and although the prospect did not particularly tempt me, I was very glad that she should gratify her wish. We sailed last April. The young Duke and Duchess of Hereford happened to be on board."

"I know. It was they who first launched Mrs. Barnaby. They

were crazy about her. They've boomed her like an army of press-agents."

"I was ill when we sailed, I had a carbuncle which confined me to my stateroom, and Mrs. Barnaby was left to look after herself. Her deck-chair happened to be next the duchess's, and from a remark she overheard it occurred to her that the English aristocracy were not so wrapped up in our social leaders as one might have expected. My wife is a quick little woman and she remarked to me that if you had an ancestor who signed Magna Charta perhaps you were not excessively impressed because the grandfather of one of your acquaintances sold skunks and the grandfather of another ran ferryboats. My wife has a very keen sense of humour. Getting into conversation with the duchess, she told her a little Western anecdote, and to make it more interesting told it as having happened to herself. Its success was immediate. The duchess begged for another and my wife ventured a little further. Twenty-four hours later she had the duke and duchess eating out of her hand. She used to come down to my stateroom at intervals and tell me of her progress. In the innocence of my heart I was tickled to death and since I had nothing else to do, I sent to the library for the works of Bret Harte and primed her with effective touches."

I slapped my forehead.

"We said she was as good as Bret Harte," I cried.

"I had a grand time thinking of the consternation of my wife's friends when at the end of the voyage I appeared and we told them the truth. But I reckoned without my wife. The day before we reached Southampton Mrs. Barnaby told me that the Herefords were arranging parties for her. The duchess was crazy to introduce her to all sorts of wonderful people. It was a chance in a thousand; but of course I should spoil everything, she admitted that she had been forced by the course of events to represent me as very different from what I was. I did not know that she had already transformed me into One-Bullet Mike, but I had a shrewd suspicion that she had forgotten to mention that I was on board. Well, to make a long story short, she asked me to go to Paris for a week or two till she had consolidated her position. I didn't mind that. I was much more inclined to do a little work at the Sorbonne than to go to parties in Mayfair, and so leaving her to go on to Southampton, I got off at Cherbourg. But when I had been in Paris ten days she flew over to see me. She told me that her success had exceeded her wildest dreams: it was ten times more wonderful than any of the novels; but my appearance would ruin it all. Very well, I said, I would stay in Paris. She didn't like the idea of that; she said she'd never have a moment's peace so long as I was so near and I might run across someone who knew me. I suggested Vienna or Rome. They wouldn't do either, and at last I came here and here have I been hiding like a criminal for three interminable months."

"Do you mean to say you never killed the two gamblers, shooting one with your right hand and the other with your left?"

"Sir, I have never fired a pistol in my life."

"And what about the attack on your log-cabin by the Mexican bandits when your wife loaded your guns for you and you stood the siege for three days till the Federal troops rescued you?"

Mr. Barnaby smiled grimly.

"I never heard that one. Isn't it a trifle crude?"

"Crude! It was as good as any Wild West picture."

"If I may venture a guess, that is where my wife in all probability got the idea."

"But the wash-tub. Washing the miners' clothes and all that. You don't know how she made us roar with that story. Why, she swam into London Society in her wash-tub."

I began to laugh.

"She's made the most gorgeous fools of us all," I said.

"She's made a pretty considerable fool of me, I would have you observe," remarked Mr. Barnaby.

"She's a marvellous woman and you're right to be proud of her. I always said she was priceless. She realised the passion for romance that beats in every British heart and she's given us exactly what we wanted. I wouldn't betray her for worlds."

"It's all very fine for you, sir. London may have gained a wonderful hostess, but I'm beginning to think that I have lost a perfectly good wife."

"The only place for One-Bullet Mike is the great open West. My dear Mr. Barnaby, there is only one course open to you now. You must continue to disappear."

"I'm very much obliged to you."

I thought he replied with a good deal of acidity.

A Man with a Conscience

St. Laurent de Maroni is a pretty little place. It is neat and clean. It has an Hôtel de Ville and a Palais de Justice of which many a town in France would be proud. The streets are wide, and the fine trees that border them give a grateful shade. The houses look as though they had just had a coat of paint. Many of them nestle in little gardens, and in the gardens are palm trees and flame of the forest; cannas flaunt their bright colours and crotons their variety; the bougainvillæas, purple or red, riot profusely, and the elegant hibiscus offers its gorgeous flowers with a negligence that seems almost affected. St. Laurent de Maroni is the centre of the French penal settlements of Guiana, and a hundred yards from the quay at which you land is the great gateway of the prison camp. These pretty little houses in their tropical gardens are the residence of the prison officials, and if the streets are neat and clean it is because there is no lack of convicts to keep them so. One day, walking with a casual acquaintance, I came upon a young man, in the round straw hat and the pink and white stripes of the convict's uniform, who was standing by the road-side with a pick. He was doing nothing.

"Why are you idling?" my companion asked him.

The man gave his shoulders a scornful shrug.

"Look at the blade of grass there," he answered. "I've got twenty years to scratch it away."

St. Laurent de Maroni exists for the group of prison camps of which it is the centre. Such trade as it has depends on them; its shops, kept by Chinese, are there to satisfy the wants of the warders, the doctors and the numerous officials who are connected with the penal settlements. The streets are silent and deserted. You pass a convict with a dispatch-case under his arm; he has some job in the administration; or another with a basket; he is a servant in somebody's house. Sometimes you come upon a little group in the charge of a warder; often you see them strolling to or from the prison unguarded. The prison gates are open all day long and the prisoners freely saunter in and out. If you see a man not in the prison uniform he is probably a freed man who is condemned to spend a number of years in the colony and who, unable to get work, living on the edge of starvation, is drinking himself to death on the cheap strong rum which is called tafia.

There is an hotel at St. Laurent de Maroni and here I had my meals. I soon got to know by sight the habitual frequenters. They came in and sat each at his little table, ate their meals in silence and went out again. The hotel was kept by a coloured woman, and the man she lived with, an ex-convict, was the only waiter. But the Governor of the colony, who lives at Cayenne, had put at my disposal his own bungalow and it was there I slept. An old Arab looked after it; he was a devout Mohammedan, and at intervals during the day I heard him say his prayers. To make my bed, keep my rooms tidy and run errands for me, the commandant of the prison had assigned me another convict. Both were serving life sentences for murder; the commandant told me that I could place entire confidence in them; they were as honest as the day, and I could leave anything about without the slightest risk. But I will not conceal from the reader that when I went to bed at night I took the precaution to lock my door and to bolt my shutters. It was foolish no doubt, but I slept more comfortably.

I had come with letters of introduction, and both the governor of the prison settlements and the commandant of the camp at St. Laurent did everything they could to make my visit agreeable and instructive. I will not here narrate all I heard and saw. I am not a reporter. It is not my business to attack or to defend the system which the French have thought fit to adopt in regard to their criminals. Besides, the system is now condemned; prisoners will soon cease to be sent out to French Guiana, to suffer the illnesses incidental to the climate and the work in malarial jungles to which so many are relegated, to endure nameless degradations, to lose hope, to rot, to die. I will only say that I saw no physical cruelty. On the other hand I saw no attempt to make the criminal on the expiration of his sentence a useful citizen. I saw nothing done for his spiritual welfare. I heard nothing of classes that he could attend in order to improve his education or organised games that might distract his mind. I saw no library where he could get books to read when his day's work was done. I saw a condition of affairs that only the strongest character could hope to surmount. I saw a brutishness that must reduce all but a very few to apathy and despair.

All this has nothing to do with me. It is vain to torment oneself over sufferings that one cannot alleviate. My object here is to tell a story. As I am well aware, one can never know everything there is to be known about human nature. One can be sure only of one thing, and that is that it will never cease to have a surprise in store for you. When I had got over the impression of bewilderment, surprise and horror to which my first visit to the prison camp gave rise, I bethought myself that there were certain matters that I was interested to enquire into. I should inform the reader that three-quarters of the convicts at St. Laurent de Maroni are there for murder. This is not official information and it may be that I exaggerate; every prisoner has a little book in which are set down his crime, his sentence, his punishments, and whatever else the authorities think necessary to keep note of; and it was from an examination of a considerable number of these that I formed my estimate. It gave me something of a shock to realise that in England far, far the greater number of these men whom I saw working in shops, lounging about the verandahs of their dormitories or sauntering through the streets would have suffered capital punishment. I found them not at all disinclined to speak of the crime for which they had been convicted, and in pursuance of my purpose I spent the better part of one day enquiring into crimes of passion. I wanted to know exactly what was the motive that had made a man kill his wife or his girl. I had a notion that jealousy and wounded honour might not perhaps tell the whole story. I got some curious replies, and among them one that was not to my mind lacking in humour. This was from a man working in the carpenter's shop who had cut his wife's throat; when I asked him why he had done it, he answered with a shrug of the shoulders: *Manque d'entente*. His casual tone made the best translation of this: We didn't get on very well. I could not help observing that if men in general looked upon this as an adequate reason for murdering their wives, the mortality in the female sex would be alarming. But after putting a good many questions to a good many men I arrived at the conclusion that at the bottom of nearly all these crimes was an economic motive; they had killed their wives or mistresses not only from jealousy, because they were unfaithful to them, but also because somehow it affected their pockets. A woman's infidelity was sometimes an occasion of financial loss, and it was this in the end that drove a man to his desperate act; or, himself in need of money to gratify other passions, he murdered because his victim was an obstacle to his exclusive possession of it. I do not conclude that a man never kills his woman because his love is spurned or his honour tarnished, I only offer my observation on these particular cases as a curious sidelight on human nature. I should not venture to deduce from it a general rule.

I spent another day enquiring into the matter of conscience. Moralists have sought to persuade us that it is one of the most powerful agents in human behaviour. Now that reason and pity have agreed to regard hell-fire as a hateful myth, many good men

have seen in conscience the chief safeguard that shall induce the
human race to walk in the way of righteousness. Shakespeare has
told us that it makes cowards of us all. Novelists and playwrights
have described for us the pangs that assail the wicked; they have
vividly pictured the anguish of a stricken conscience and the sleepless nights it occasions; they have shown it poisoning every pleasure
till life is so intolerable that discovery and punishment come as a
welcome relief. I had often wondered how much of all this was true.
Moralists have an axe to grind; they must draw a moral. They think
that if they say a thing often enough people will believe it. They are
apt to state that a thing is so when they consider it desirable that it
should be. They tell us that the wages of sin is death; we know very
well that it is not always. And so far as the authors of fiction are
concerned, the playwrights and the novelists, when they get hold
of an effective theme they are disposed to make use of it without
bothering very much whether it agrees with the facts of life. Certain
statements about human nature become, as it were, common
property and so are accepted as self-evident. In the same way
painters for ages painted shadows black, and it was not till the
impressionists looked at them with unprejudiced eyes and painted
what they saw that we discovered that shadows were coloured. It
had sometimes struck me that perhaps conscience was the expression
of a high moral development, so that its influence was strong only in
those whose virtue was so shining that they were unlikely to commit
any action for which they could seriously reproach themselves. It is
generally accepted that murder is a shocking crime, and it is the
murderer above all other criminals who is supposed to suffer remorse.
His victim, we have been led to believe, haunts his dreams in horrify-
ing nightmares, and the recollection of his dreadful deed tortures his
waking hours. I could not miss the opportunity to enquire into
the truth of this. I had no intention of insisting if I encountered
reticence or distress, but I found in none of those with whom I talked
any such thing. Some said that in the same circumstances they
would do as they had done before. Determinists without knowing it,
they seemed to look upon their action as ordained by a fate over
which they had no control. Some appeared to think that their
crime was committed by someone with whom they had no connection.

"When one's young, one's foolish," they said, with a careless
gesture or a deprecating smile.

Others told me that if they had known what the punishment was
they would suffer, they would certainly have held their hands. I
found in none any regret for the human being they had violently

bereft of life. It seemed to me that they had no more feeling for the creature they had killed than if it had been a pig whose throat they had cut in the way of business. Far from feeling pity for their victim, they were more inclined to feel anger because he had been the occasion of their imprisonment in that distant land. In only one man did I discern anything that might appropriately be called a conscience, and his story was so remarkable that I think it well worth narrating. For in this case it was, so far as I can understand, remorse that was the motive of the crime. I noticed the man's number, which was printed on the chest of the pink and white pyjamas of his prison uniform, but I have forgotten it. Anyhow it is of no consequence. I never knew his name. He did not offer to tell me and I did not like to ask it. I will call him Jean Charvin.

I met him on my first visit to the camp with the commandant. We were walking through a courtyard round which were cells, not punishment cells, but individual cells which are given to well-behaved prisoners who ask for them. They are sought after by those to whom the promiscuity of the dormitories is odious. Most of them were empty, for their occupants were engaged in their various employments. Jean Charvin was at work in his cell, writing at a small table, and the door was open. The commandant called him and he came out. I looked into the cell. It contained a fixed hammock, with a dingy mosquito-net; by the side of this was a small table on which were his bits and pieces, a shaving-mop and a razor, a hairbrush and two or three battered books. On the walls were photographs of persons of respectable appearance and illustrations from picture papers. He had been sitting on his bed to write and the table on which he had been writing was covered with papers. They looked like accounts. He was a handsome man, tall, erect and lean, with flashing dark eyes and clean-cut, strong features. The first thing I noticed about him was that he had a fine head of long, naturally-waving dark brown hair. This at once made him look different from the rest of the prisoners, whose hair is close-cropped, but cropped so badly, in ridges, that it gives them a sinister look. The commandant spoke to him of some official business, and then as we were leaving added in a friendly way:

"I see your hair is growing well."

Jean Charvin reddened and smiled. His smile was boyish and engaging.

"It'll be some time yet before I get it right again."

The commandant dismissed him and we went on.

"He's a very decent fellow," he said. "He's in the accountant's department, and he's had leave to let his hair grow. He's delighted."

"What is he here for?" I asked.

"He killed his wife. But he's only got six years. He's clever and a good worker. He'll do well. He comes from a very decent family and he's had an excellent education."

I thought no more of Jean Charvin, but by chance I met him next day on the road. He was coming towards me. He carried a black dispatch-case under his arm, and except for the pink and white stripes of his uniform and the ugly round straw hat that concealed his handsome head of hair, you might have taken him for a young lawyer on his way to court. He walked with a long, leisurely stride, and he had an easy, you might almost say a gallant, bearing. He recognised me, and taking off his hat bade me good-morning. I stopped, and for something to say asked him where he was going. He told me he was taking some papers from the governor's office to the bank. There was a pleasing frankness in his face, and his eyes, his really beautiful eyes, shone with good will. I supposed that the vigour of his youth was such that it made life, notwithstanding his position and his surroundings, more than tolerable, even pleasant. You would have said that here was a young man without a care in the world.

"I hear you're going to St. Jean to-morrow," he said.

"Yes. It appears I must start at dawn."

St. Jean is a camp seventeen kilometres from St. Laurent, and it is here that are interned the habitual criminals who have been sentenced to transportation after repeated terms of imprisonment. They are petty thieves, confidence men, forgers, tricksters and suchlike; the prisoners of St. Laurent, condemned for more serious offences, look upon them with contempt.

"You should find it an interesting experience," Jean Charvin said, with his frank and engaging smile. "But keep your pocket-book buttoned up, they'd steal the shirt off your back if they had half a chance. They're a dirty lot of scoundrels!"

That afternoon, waiting till the heat of the day was less, I sat on the verandah outside my bedroom and read: I had drawn the jalousies and it was tolerably cool. My old Arab came up the stairs on his bare feet, and in his halting French told me that there was a man from the commandant who wanted to see me.

"Send him up," I said.

In a moment the man came, and it was Jean Charvin. He told me that the commandant had sent him to give me a message about my excursion next day to St. Jean. When he had delivered it I asked him if he would not sit down and have a cigarette with me. He wore a cheap wrist-watch and he looked at it.

"I have a few minutes to spare. I should be glad to." He sat down and lit the cigarette I offered him. He gave me a smiling look of his soft eyes. "Do you know, this is the first time I've ever been asked to sit down since I was sentenced." He inhaled a long whiff of his cigarette. "Egyptian. I haven't smoked an Egyptian cigarette for three years."

The convicts make their own cigarettes out of a coarse, strong tobacco that is sold in square blue packets. Since one is not allowed to pay them for the services they may render you, but may give them tobacco, I had bought a good many packets of this.

"How does it taste?"

"One gets accustomed to everything and, to tell you the truth, my palate is so vitiated, I prefer the stuff we get here."

"I'll give you a couple of packets."

I went into my room and fetched them. When I returned he was looking at some books that were lying on the table.

"Are you fond of reading?" I asked.

"Very. I think the want of books is what I most suffer from now. The few I can get hold of I'm forced to read over and over again."

To so great a reader as myself no deprivation seems more insupportable than the lack of books.

"I have several French ones in my bag. I'll look them out and if you care to have them I'll give them to you if you can come along again."

My offer was due only in part to kindness; I wanted to have another chance of a talk with him.

"I should have to show them to the commandant. He would only let me keep them if there was no doubt they couldn't possibly corrupt my morals. But he's a good-natured man, I don't think he'll make any difficulties."

There was a hint of slyness in the smile with which he said this, and I suspected that he had taken the measure of the well-meaning, conscientious chief of the camp and knew pretty well how to get on the right side of him. It would have been unjust to blame him if he exercised tact, and even cunning, to render his lot as tolerable as might be.

"The commandant has a very good opinion of you."

"He's a fine man. I'm very grateful to him, he's done a great deal for me. I'm an accountant by profession and he's put me in the accountant's department. I love figures, it gives me an intense satisfaction to deal with them, they're living things to me, and now that I can handle them all day long I feel myself again."

"And are you glad to have a cell of your own?"

"It's made all the difference. To be herded with fifty men, the scum of the earth, and never to be alone for a minute—it was awful. That was the worst of all. At home, at Le Havre, that is where I lived, I had an apartment, modest of course, but my own, and we had a maid who came in by the day. We lived decently. It made it ten times harder for me than for the rest, most of them, who have never known anything but squalor, filth and promiscuity."

I had asked him about the cell in the hope that I could get him to talk about the life that is led in those vast dormitories in which the men are locked from five in the evening till five next morning. During these twelve hours they are their own masters. A warder can enter, they told me, only at the risk of his life. They have no light after eight o'clock, but from sardine-tins, a little oil, and a rag they make lamps by the light of which they can see enough to play cards. They gamble furiously, not for love, but for the money they keep secreted on their bodies; they are unscrupulous ruthless men, and naturally enough bitter quarrels often arise. They are settled with knives. Often in the morning, when the dormitory is opened, a man is found dead, but no threats, no promises, will induce anyone to betray the slayer. Other things Jean Charvin told me which I cannot narrate. He told me of one young fellow who had come out from France on the same ship with himself and with whom he had made friends. He was a good-looking boy. One day he went to the commandant and asked him if he could have a cell to himself. The commandant asked him why he wanted one. He explained. The commandant looked through his list and told him that at the moment all were occupied, but that as soon as there was a vacancy he should have one. Next morning when the dormitory was opened, he was found dead on his hammock with his belly ripped open to the breast-bone.

"They're savage brutes, and if one isn't a brute by the time one arrives only a miracle can save one from becoming as brutal as the rest."

Jean Charvin looked at his watch and got up. He walked away from me and then, with his charming smile, turned and faced me.

"I must go now. If the commandant gives me permission I will come and get the books you were kind enough to offer me."

In Guiana you do not shake hands with a convict, and a tactful man, taking leave of you, puts himself in such a position that there can be no question of your offering him your hand or of refusing his should he, forgetting for a moment, instinctively tender it. Heaven knows, it would have meant nothing to me to shake hands with Jean

Charvin; it gave me a pang to see the care he had taken to spare me embarrassment.

I saw him twice more during my stay at St. Laurent. He told me his story, but I will tell it now in my words rather than in his, for I had to piece it together from what he said at one time and another, and what he left out I have had to supply out of my own imagination. I do not believe it has led me astray. It was as though he had given me three letters out of a number of five-letter words; the chances are that I have guessed most of the words correctly.

Jean Charvin was born and bred in the great seaport of Le Havre. His father had a good post in the Customs. Having finished his education, he did his military service, and then looked about for a job. Like a great many other young Frenchmen he was prepared to sacrifice the hazardous chance of wealth for a respectable security. His natural gift for figures made it easy for him to get a place in the accountant's department of a large exporting house. His future was assured. He could look forward to earning a sufficient income to live in the modest comfort of the class to which he belonged. He was industrious and well-behaved. Like most young Frenchmen of his generation he was athletic. He swam and played tennis in summer, and in winter he bicycled. On two evenings a week to keep himself fit he spent a couple of hours in a gymnasium. Through his childhood, his adolescence and his young manhood, he lived in the constant companionship of a boy called, shall we say for the purposes of this narrative, Henri Renard, whose father was also an official in the Customs. Jean and Riri went to school together, played together, worked for their examinations together, spent their holidays together, for the two families were intimate, had their first affairs with girls together, partnered one another in the local tennis tournaments, and did their military service together. They never quarrelled. They were never so happy as in one another's society. They were inseparable. When the time came for them to start working they decided that they would go into the same firm; but that was not so easy; Jean tried to get Riri a job in the exporting house that had engaged him, but could not manage it, and it was not till a year later that Riri got something to do. But by then trade was as bad at Le Havre as everywhere else, and in a few months he found himself once more without employment.

Riri was a light-hearted youth, and he enjoyed his leisure. He danced, bathed and played tennis. It was thus that he made the acquaintance of a girl who had recently come to live at Le Havre. Her father had been a captain in the colonial army and on his death her mother had returned to Le Havre, which was her native place.

Marie-Louise was then eighteen. She had spent almost all her life in Tonkin. This gave her an exotic attraction for the young men who had never been out of France in their lives, and first Riri, then Jean, fell in love with her. Perhaps that was inevitable; it was certainly unfortunate. She was a well-brought-up girl, an only child, and her mother, besides her pension, had a little money of her own. It was evident that she could be pursued only with a view to marriage. Of course Riri, dependent for the while entirely on his father, could not make an offer that there was the least chance of Madame Meurice, Marie-Louise's mother, accepting; but having the whole day to himself he was able to see a great deal more of Marie-Louise than Jean could. Madame Meurice was something of an invalid, so that Marie-Louise had more liberty than most French girls of her age and station. She knew that both Riri and Jean were in love with her, she liked them both and was pleased by their attentions, but she gave no sign that she was in love with either. It was impossible to tell which she preferred. She was well aware that Riri was not in a position to marry her.

"What did she look like?" I asked Jean Charvin.

"She was small, with a pretty little figure, with large grey eyes, a pale skin and soft, mouse-coloured hair. She was rather like a little mouse. She was not beautiful, but pretty, in a quaint demure way; there was something very appealing about her. She was easy to get on with. She was simple and unaffected. You couldn't help feeling that she was reliable and would make anyone a good wife."

Jean and Riri hid nothing from one another and Jean made no secret of the fact that he was in love with Marie-Louise, but Riri had met her first and it was an understood thing between them that Jean should not stand in his way. At length she made her choice. One day Riri waited for Jean to come away from his office and told him that Marie-Louise had consented to marry him. They had arranged that as soon as he got a job his father should go to her mother and make the formal offer. Jean was hard hit. It was not easy to listen with eager sympathy to the plans that the excitable and enchanted Riri made for the future. But he was too much attached to Riri to feel sore with him; he knew how lovable he was and he could not blame Marie-Louise. He tried with all his might to accept honestly the sacrifice he made on the altar of friendship.

"Why did she choose him rather than you?" I asked.

"He had immense vitality. He was the gayest, most amusing lad you ever met. His high spirits were infectious. You couldn't be dull in his company."

"He had pep," I smiled.

"And an incredible charm."

"Was he good-looking?"

"No, not very. He was shorter than me, slight and wiry; but he had a nice, good-humoured face." Jean Charvin smiled rather pleasantly. "I think without any vanity I can say that I was better-looking than Riri."

But Riri did not get a job. His father, tired of keeping him in idleness, wrote to everyone he could think of, the members of his family and his friends in various parts of France, asking them if they could not find something, however modest, for Riri to do; and at last he got a letter from a cousin in Lyons who was in the silk business to say that his firm were looking for a young man to go out to Phnom-Penh, in Cambodia, where they had a branch, to buy native silk for them. If Riri was willing to take the job he could get it for him.

Though like all French parents Riri's hated him to emigrate, there seemed no help for it, and it was determined, although the salary was small, that he must go. He was not disinclined. Cambodia was not so far from Tonkin, and Marie-Louise must be familiar with the life. She had so often talked of it that he had come to the conclusion that she would be glad to go back to the East. To his dismay she told him that nothing would induce her to. In the first place she could not desert her mother, whose health was obviously declining; and then, after having at last settled down in France, she was determined never again to leave it. She was sympathetic to Riri, but resolute. With nothing else in prospect his father would not hear of his refusing the offer; there was no help for it, he had to go. Jean hated losing him, but from the moment Riri told him his bad news, he had realised with an exulting heart that fate was playing into his hands. With Riri out of his way for five years at least, and unless he were incompetent with the probability that he would settle in the East for good, Jean could not doubt that after a while Marie-Louise would marry him. His circumstances, his settled, respectable position in Le Havre, where she could be near her mother, would make her think it very sensible; and when she was no longer under the spell of Riri's charm there was no reason why her great liking for him should not turn to love. Life changed for him. After months of misery he was happy again, and though he kept them to himself he too now made great plans for the future. There was no need any longer to try not to love Marie-Louise.

Suddenly his hopes were shattered. One of the shipping firms at Le Havre had a vacancy, and it looked as though the application that Riri had quickly made would be favourably considered. A friend in the office told him that it was a certainty. It would settle everything. It was an old and conservative house, and it was well known that when you once got into it you were there for life. Jean Charvin was in despair, and the worst of it was that he had to keep his anguish to himself. One day the director of his own firm sent for him.

When he reached this point Jean stopped. A harassed look came into his eyes.

"I'm going to tell you something now that I've never told to anyone before. I'm an honest man, a man of principle; I'm going to tell you of the only discreditable action I've ever done in my life."

I must remind the reader here that Jean Charvin was wearing the pink and white stripes of the convict's uniform, with his number stencilled on his chest, and that he was serving a term of imprisonment for the murder of his wife.

"I couldn't imagine what the director wanted with me. He was sitting at his desk when I went into his office, and he gave me a searching look.

" 'I want to ask you a question of great importance,' he said. 'I wish you to treat it as confidential. I shall of course treat your answer as equally so.'

"I waited. He went on:

" 'You've been with us for a considerable time. I am very well satisfied with you, there is no reason why you shouldn't reach a very good position in the firm. I put implicit confidence in you.'

" 'Thank you, sir,' I said. 'I will always try to merit your good opinion.'

" 'The question at issue is this. Monsieur Untel is proposing to engage Henri Renard. He is very particular about the character of his employees, and in this case it is essential that he shouldn't make a mistake. Part of Henri Renard's duties would be to pay the crews of the firm's ships, and many hundreds of thousand francs will pass through his hands. I know that Henri Renard is your great friend and that your families have always been very intimate. I put you on your honour to tell me whether Monsieur Untel would be justified in engaging this young man.'

"I saw at once what the question meant. If Riri got the job he would stay and marry Marie-Louise, if he didn't he would go out to Cambodia and I should marry her. I swear to you it was not I who answered, it was someone who stood in my shoes and spoke with my voice, I had nothing to do with the words that came from my mouth.

" '*Monsieur le directeur*,' I said, 'Henri and I have been friends all our lives. We have never been separated for a week. We went to school together; we shared our pocket-money and our mistresses when we were old enough to have them; we did our military service together.'

" 'I know. You know him better than anyone in the world. That is why I ask you these questions.'

" 'It is not fair, *Monsieur le directeur*. You are asking me to betray my friend. I cannot, and I will not answer your questions.'

"The director gave me a shrewd smile. He thought himself much cleverer than he really was.

" 'Your answer does you credit, but it has told me all I wished to know.' Then he smiled kindly. I suppose I was pale, I dare say I was trembling a little. 'Pull yourself together, my dear boy; you're upset and I can understand it. Sometimes in life one is faced by a situation where honesty stands on the one side and loyalty on the other. Of course one mustn't hesitate, but the choice is bitter. I shall not forget your behaviour in this case and on behalf of Monsieur Untel I thank you.'

"I withdrew. Next morning Riri received a letter informing him that his services were not required, and a month later he sailed for the Far East."

Six months after this Jean Charvin and Marie-Louise were married. The marriage was hastened by the increasing gravity of Madame Meurice's illness. Knowing that she could not live long, she was anxious to see her daughter settled before she died. Jean wrote to Riri telling him the facts and Riri wrote back warmly congratulating him. He assured him that he need have no compunctions on his behalf; when he had left France he realised that *he* could never marry Marie-Louise, and he was glad that Jean was going to. He was finding consolation at Phnom-Penh. His letter was very cheerful. From the beginning Jean had told himself that Riri, with his mercurial temperament, would soon forget Marie-Louise, and his letter looked as if he had already done so. He had done him no irreparable injury. It was a justification. For if *he* had lost Marie-Louise he would have died; with him it was a matter of life and death.

For a year Jean and Marie-Louise were extremely happy. Madame Meurice died, and Marie-Louise inherited a couple of hundred thousand francs; but with the depression and the unstable currency they decided not to have a child till the economic situation was less uncertain. Marie-Louise was a good and frugal housekeeper. She was an affectionate, amiable and satisfactory wife. She was placid.

This before he married her had seemed to Jean a rather charming trait, but as time wore on it was borne in upon him that her placidity came from a certain lack of emotional ardour. It concealed no depth. He had always thought she was like a little mouse; there was something mouse-like in her furtive reticences; she was oddly serious about trivial matters and could busy herself indefinitely with things that were of no consequence. She had her own tiny little set of interests and they left no room in her pretty sleek head for any others. She sometimes began a novel, but seldom cared to finish it. Jean was obliged to admit to himself that she was rather dull. The uneasy thought came to him that perhaps it had not been worth while to do a dirty trick for her sake. It began to worry him. He missed Riri. He tried to persuade himself that what was done was done and that he had really not been a free agent, but he could not quite still the prickings of his conscience. He wished now that when the director of his firm spoke to him he had answered differently.

Then a terrible thing happened. Riri contracted typhoid fever and died. It was a frightful shock for Jean. It was a shock to Marie-Louise too; she paid Riri's parents the proper visit of condolence, but she neither ate less heartily nor slept less soundly. Jean was exasperated by her composure.

"Poor chap, he was always so gay," she said, "he must have hated dying. But why did he go out there? I told him the climate was bad; it killed my father and I knew what I was talking about."

Jean felt that he had killed him. If he had told the director all the good he knew of Riri, knew as no one else in the world did, he would have got the post and would now be alive and well.

"I shall never forgive myself," he thought. "I shall never be happy again. Oh, what a fool I was, and what a cad!"

He wept for Riri. Marie-Louise sought to comfort him. She was a kind little thing and she loved him.

"You mustn't take it too hardly. After all, you wouldn't have seen him for five years, and you'd have found him so changed that there wouldn't have been anything between you any more. He would have been a stranger to you. I've seen that sort of thing happen so often. You'd have been delighted to see him, and in half an hour you'd have discovered that you had nothing to say to one another."

"I dare say you're right," he sighed.

"He was too scatter-brained ever to have amounted to anything very much. He never had your firmness of character and your clear, solid intellect."

He knew what she was thinking. What would have been her

R

position now if she had followed Riri to Indo-China and found herself at twenty-one a widow with nothing but her own two hundred thousand francs to live on? It was a lucky escape and she congratulated herself on her good sense. Jean was a husband of whom she could be proud. He was earning good money. Jean was tortured by remorse. What he had suffered before was nothing to what he suffered now. The anguish that the recollection of his treachery caused him was worse than a physical pain gnawing at his vitals. It would assail him suddenly when he was in the middle of his work and twist his heartstrings with a violent pang. His agony was such that he craved for relief, and it was only by an effort of all his will that he prevented himself from making a full confession to Marie-Louise. But he knew how she would take it; she would not be shocked, she would think it rather a clever trick and be even subtly flattered that for her sake he had been guilty of a despicable act. She could not help him. He began to dislike her. For it was for her that he had done the shameful thing, and what was she? An ordinary, commonplace, rather calculating little woman.

"What a fool I've been," he repeated.

He did not even find her pretty any more. He knew now that she was terribly stupid. But of course she was not to blame for that, she was not to blame because he had been false to his friend; and he forced himself to be as sweet and tender to her as he had always been. He did whatever she wanted. She had only to express a wish for him to fulfil it if it was in his power. He tried to pity her, he tried to be tolerant; he told himself that from her own petty standpoint she was a good wife, methodical, saving, and in her manner, dress and appearance a credit to a respectable young man. All that was true; but it was on her account that Riri had died, and he loathed her. She bored him to distraction. Though he said nothing, though he was kind, amiable and indulgent, he could often have killed her. When he did, however, it was almost without meaning to. It was ten months after Riri's death, and Riri's parents, Monsieur and Madame Renard, gave a party to celebrate the engagement of their daughter. Jean had seen little of them since Riri's death and he did not want to go. But Marie-Louise said they must; he had been Riri's greatest friend and it would be a grave lack of politeness on Jean's part not to attend an important celebration in the family. She had a keen sense of social obligation.

"Besides, it'll be a distraction for you. You've been in poor spirits for so long, a little amusement will do you good. There'll be champagne, won't there? Madame Renard doesn't like spending money, but on an occasion like this she'll have to sacrifice herself."

Marie-Louise chuckled slyly when she thought what a wrench it would be to Madame Renard to unloose her purse-strings.

The party had been very gay. It gave Jean a nasty turn when he found that they were using Riri's old room for the women to put their wraps in and the men their coats. There was plenty of champagne. Jean drank a great deal to drown the bitter remorse that tormented him. He wanted to deaden the sound in his ears of Riri's laugh and to shut his eyes to the good-humour of his shining glance. It was three o'clock when they got home. Next day was Sunday, so Jean had no work to go to. They slept late. The rest I can tell in Jean Charvin's own words.

"I had a headache when I woke. Marie-Louise was not in bed. She was sitting at the dressing-table brushing her hair. I've always been very keen on physical culture, and I was in the habit of doing exercises every morning. I didn't feel very much inclined to do them that morning, but after all that champagne I thought I'd better. I got out of bed and took up my Indian clubs. Our bedroom was fairly large and there was plenty of room to swing them between the bed and the dressing-table where Marie-Louise was sitting. I did my usual exercises. Marie-Louise had started a little while before having her hair cut differently, quite short, and I thought it repulsive. From the back she looked like a boy, and the stubble of cropped hair on her neck made me feel rather sick. She put down her brushes and began to powder her face. She gave a nasty little laugh.

" 'What are you laughing at?' I asked.

" 'Madame Renard. That was the same dress she wore at our wedding, she'd had it dyed and done over; but it didn't deceive me. I'd have known it anywhere.'

"It was such a stupid remark, it infuriated me. I was seized with rage, and with all my might I hit her over the head with my Indian club. I broke her skull, apparently, and she died two days later in hospital without recovering consciousness."

He paused for a moment. I handed him a cigarette and lit another myself.

"I was glad she did. We could never have lived together again, and it would have been very hard to explain my action."

"Very."

"I was arrested and tried for murder. Of course I swore it was an accident, I said the club had slipped out of my hand, but the medical evidence was against me. The prosecution proved that such an injury as Marie-Louise had suffered could only have been caused by a violent and deliberate blow. Fortunately for me they could find no motive. The public prosecutor tried to make out that I had been jealous of the attentions some man had paid her at the party and that we had quarrelled on that account, but the man he mentioned swore that he had done nothing to arouse my suspicions and others at the party testified that we had left the best of friends. They found on the dressing-table an unpaid dressmaker's bill and the prosecutor suggested that we had quarrelled about that, but I was able to prove that Marie-Louise paid for her clothes out of her own money, so that the bill could not possibly have been the cause of a dispute. Witnesses came forward and said that I had always been kind to Marie-Louise. We were generally looked upon as a devoted couple. My character was excellent and my employer spoke in the highest terms of me. I was never in danger of losing my head, and at one moment I thought I had a chance of getting off altogether. In the end I was sentenced to six years. I don't regret what I did, for from that day, all the time I was in prison awaiting my trial, and since, while I've been here, I've ceased to worry about Riri. If I believed in ghosts I'd be inclined to say that Marie-Louise's death has laid Riri's. Anyhow, my conscience is at rest, and after all the torture I suffered I can assure you that everything I've gone through since is worth it; I feel I can now look the world in the face again."

I know that this is a fantastic story; I am by way of being a realist, and in the stories I write I seek verisimilitude. I eschew the bizarre as scrupulously as I avoid the whimsical. If this had been a tale that I was inventing I would certainly have made it more probable. As it is, unless I had heard it with my own ears I am not sure that I should believe it. I do not know whether Jean Charvin told me the truth, and yet the words with which he closed his final visit to me had a convincing ring. I had asked him what were his plans for the future.

"I have friends working for me in France," he answered. "A great many people thought at the time that I was the victim of a grave miscarriage of justice; the director of my firm is convinced that I was unjustly condemned; and I may get a reduction of my sentence. Even if I don't, I think I can count upon getting back to France at the end of my six years. You see, I'm making myself very useful here. The accounts were very badly kept when I took them over, and I've got them in apple-pie order. There have been leakages, and I am convinced that if they'll give me a free hand, I can stop them. The commandant likes me and I'm certain that he'll do everything he can for me. At the worst I shan't be much over thirty when I get back."

"But won't you find it rather difficult to get work?"

"A clever accountant like me, and a man who's honest and industrious, can always get work. Of course I shan't be able to live in Le Havre, but the director of my firm has business connections at Lille and Lyons and Marseilles. He's promised to do something for me. No, I look forward to the years to come with a good deal of confidence. I shall settle down somewhere, and as soon as I'm comfortably fixed up I shall marry. After what I've been through I want a home."

We were sitting in one of the corners of the verandah that surrounded my house in order to get any draught there might be, and on the north side I had left a jalousie undrawn. The strip of sky you saw with a single coconut tree on one side, its green foliage harsh against the blue, looked like an advertisement for a tropical cruise. Jean Charvin's eyes searched the distance as though he sought to see the future.

"But next time I marry," he said thoughtfully, "I shan't marry for love, I shall marry for money."

An Official Position

HE was a sturdy broad-shouldered fellow, of the middle height; though his bones were well covered as became his age, which was fifty, he was not fat; he had a ruddy complexion which neither the heat of the sun nor the unwholesomeness of the climate had affected. It was good rich blood that ran through his veins. His hair was brown and thick, and only at the temples touched with grey; he was very proud of his fair, handsome moustache and he kept it carefully brushed. There was a pleasant twinkle in his blue eyes. You would have said that this was a man whom life had treated well. There was in his appearance an air of good nature and in his vigour a glow of health that gave you confidence. He reminded you of one of those well-fed, rubicund burghers in an old Dutch picture, with their pink-cheeked wives, who made money and enjoyed the good things with which their industry provided them. He was, however, a widower. His name was Louis Remire, and his number 68763. He was serving a twelve-year sentence at St. Laurent de Maroni, the great penal settlement of French Guiana, for killing his wife, but partly because he had served in the police force at Lyons, his native town, and partly on account of his good character, he had been given an official position. He had been chosen among nearly two hundred applicants to be the public executioner.

That was why he was allowed to sport the handsome moustache of which he took so much care. He was the only convict who wore one. It was in a manner of speaking his badge of office. That also was why he was allowed to wear his own clothes. The convicts wear pyjamas in pink and white stripes, round straw hats and clumsy boots with wooden soles and leather tops. Louis Remire wore espadrilles on his bare feet, blue cotton trousers, and a khaki shirt the open neck of which exposed to view his hairy and virile chest. When you saw him strolling about the public garden, with a kindly eye looking at the children, black or half-caste, who played there, you would have taken him for a respectable shopkeeper who was enjoying an hour's leisure. He had his own house. That was not only one of the perquisites of his office, but it was a necessity, since if he had lodged in the prison camp the convicts would have made short work of him. One morning he would have been found with his belly ripped open. It was true that the house was small, it was just a wooden shack of one room, with a lean-to that served as a kitchen; but it was surrounded by a tiny garden, within a palisade, and in the garden grew bananas, papaias and such vegetables as the climate allowed him to raise. The garden faced the sea and was surrounded by a coconut grove. The situation was charming. It was only a quarter of a mile from the prison, which was convenient for his rations. They were fetched by his assistant, who lived with him. The assistant, a tall, gawky, ungainly fellow, with deep-set, staring eyes and cavernous jaws, was serving a life sentence for rape and murder; he was not very intelligent, but in civil life he had been a cook and it was wonderful what, with the help of the vegetables they grew and such condiments as Louis Remire could afford to buy at the Chinese grocer's, he managed to do with the soup, potatoes and cabbage, and eternal beef, beef for three hundred and sixty-five days of the year, which the prison kitchens provided. It was on this account that Louis Remire had pressed his claim on the commandant when it had been found necessary to get a new assistant. The last one's nerves had given way and, absurdly enough, thought Louis Remire with a good-natured laugh, he had developed scruples about capital punishment; now, suffering from neurasthenia, he was on the Ile St. Joseph, where the insane were confined.

His present assistant happened to be ill. He had high fever, and looked very much as if he were going to die. It had been necessary to send him to hospital. Louis Remire was sorry; he would not easily find so good a cook again. It was bad luck that this should have happened just now, for next day there was a job of work to be done. Six men were to be executed. Two were Algerians, one was a Pole, another a Spaniard from the mainland, and only two were French. They had escaped from prison in a band and gone up the river. For nearly twelve months, stealing, raping and killing they had spread terror through the colony. People scarcely dared move from their homesteads. Recaptured at last, they had all been sentenced to death, but the sentence had to be confirmed by the Minister of the Colonies, and the confirmation had only just arrived. Louis Remire could not manage without help, and besides there was a lot to arrange beforehand; it was particularly unfortunate that on this occasion of all others he should have to depend on an inexperienced man. The commandant had assigned to him one of the turnkeys. The turnkeys are convicts like the others, but they have been given their places for good behaviour and they live in separate quarters. They are on the side of the authorities and so are disliked by the other prisoners. Louis Remire was a conscientious fellow, and he was anxious that everything next day should go without a hitch. He arranged that his temporary assistant should come that afternoon to the place where the guillotine was kept so that he might explain to him thoroughly how it worked and show him exactly what he would have to do.

The guillotine, when not in use, stood in a small room which was part of the prison building, but which was entered by a separate door from the outside. When he sauntered along there at the appointed hour he found the man already waiting. He was a large-limbed, coarse-faced fellow. He was dressed in the pink and white stripes of the prison garb, but as turnkey he wore a felt hat instead of the straw of common convicts.

"What are you here for?"

The man shrugged his shoulders.

"I killed a farmer and his wife."

"H'm. How long have you got?"

"Life."

He looked a brute, but you could never be sure of people. He had himself seen a warder, a big, powerful man, faint dead away at an execution. He did not want his assistant to have an attack of nerves at the wrong moment. He gave him a friendly smile, and with his thumb pointed to the closed door behind which stood the guillotine.

"This is another sort of job," he said. "There are six of them, you know. They're a bad lot. The sooner they're out of the way the better."

"Oh, that's all right. After what I've seen in this place I'm scared of nothing. It means no more to me than cutting the head off a chicken."

Louis Remire unlocked the door and walked in. His assistant followed him. The guillotine in that small room, hardly larger than a cell, seemed to take up a great deal of space. It stood grim and sinister. Louis Remire heard a slight gasp and turning round saw that the turnkey was staring at the instrument with terrified eyes. His face was sallow and drawn from the fever and the hookworm from which all the convicts intermittently suffered, but now its pallor was ghastly. The executioner smiled good-naturedly.

"Gives you a turn, does it? Have you never seen it before?"

"Never."

Louis Remire gave a little throaty chuckle.

"If you had, I suppose you wouldn't have survived to tell the tale. How did you escape it?"

"I was starving when I did my job. I'd asked for something to eat and they set the dogs on me. I was condemned to death. My lawyer went to Paris and he got the President to reprieve me."

"It's better to be alive than dead, there's no denying that," said Louis Remire, with that agreeable twinkle in his eyes.

He always kept his guillotine in perfect order. The wood, a dark hard native wood somewhat like mahogany, was highly polished; but there was a certain amount of brass, and it was Louis Remire's pride that this should be as bright and clean as the brass-work on a yacht. The knife shone as though it had just come out of the workshop. It was necessary not only to see that everything functioned properly, but to show his assistant how it functioned. It was part of the assistant's duty to refix the rope when the knife had dropped, and to do this he had to climb a short ladder.

It was with the satisfaction of a competent workman who knows his job from A to Z that Remire entered upon the necessary explanations. It gave him a certain quiet pleasure to point out the ingenuity of the apparatus. The condemned man was strapped to the bascule, a sort of shelf, and this by a simple mechanism was precipitated down and forwards so that the man's neck was conveniently under the knife. The conscientious fellow had brought with him a banana stem, about five feet long, and the turnkey had wondered why. He was now to learn. The stem was of about the same circumference and consistency as the human neck, so that it afforded a very good way, not only of showing a novice how the apparatus worked, but of making sure beforehand that it was in perfect order. Louis Remire placed the banana stem in position. He released the knife. It fell with incredible speed and with a great bang. From the time the man was attached to the bascule to the time his head was off only thirty seconds elapsed. The head fell in the basket. The executioner took it up by the ears and exhibited it to those whose duty it was to watch the execution. He uttered the solemn words:

"*Au nom du peuple français justice est faite.* In the name of the French people justice is done."

Then he dropped the head back into the basket. To-morrow, with six to be despatched, the trunk would have to be unstrapped from the bascule and placed with the head on a stretcher, and the next man brought forward. They were taken in the order of their guilt. The least guilty, executed first, were spared the horror of seeing the death of their mates.

"We shall have to be careful that the right head goes with the right body," said Louis Remire, in that rather jovial manner of his, "or there may be no end of confusion at the Resurrection."

He let down the knife two or three times in order to make quite sure that the assistant understood how to fix it, and then getting his cleaning-materials from the shelf on which he kept them set him to work on the brass. Though it was spotless he thought that a final polish would do no harm. He leaned against the wall and idly smoked cigarettes.

Finally everything was in order and Louis Remire dismissed the assistant till midnight. At midnight they were moving the guillotine from the room in which it stood to the prison yard. It was always a bit of a job to set it up again, but it had to be in place an hour before dawn, at which time the execution took place. Louis Remire strolled slowly home to his shack. The afternoon was drawing to its close, and as he walked along he passed a working party who were returning to the prison. They spoke to one another in undertones and he guessed that they spoke of him; some looked down, two or three threw him a glance of hatred and one spat on the ground. Louis Remire, the end of a cigarette sticking to his lip, looked at them with irony. He was indifferent to the loathing, mingled with fear, with which they regarded him. It did not matter to him that not one of them would speak to him, and it only amused him to think that there was hardly one who would not gladly have thrust a knife into his guts. He had a supreme contempt for them all. He could take care of himself. He could use a knife as well as any of them, and he had confidence in his strength. The convicts knew that men were to be executed next day, and as always before an execution they were depressed and nervous. They went about their work in sullen silence, and the warders had to be more than usually on the alert.

"They'll settle down when it's all over," said Louis Remire as he let himself into his little compound.

The dogs barked as he came along, and brave though he was, he listened to their uproar with satisfaction. With his own assistant ill, so that he was alone in the house, he was not sorry that he had the protection of those two savage mongrels. They prowled about the coconut grove outside his compound all night and they would give him good warning if anyone lurked there. They could be relied on to spring at the throat of any stranger who ventured too near. If his predecessor had had these dogs he wouldn't have come to his end.

The man who had been executioner before Louis Remire had only held the job a couple of years when one day he disappeared. The authorities thought he had run away; he was known to have a bit of money, and it was very probable that he had managed to make arrangements with the captain of a schooner to take him to Brazil. His nerves had given way. He had gone two or three times to the governor of the prison and told him that he feared for his life. He was convinced that the convicts were out to kill him. The governor felt pretty sure that his fears were groundless and paid no attention, but when the man was nowhere to be found he concluded that his terror had got the better of him and he had preferred to run the danger of escape, and the danger of being recaptured and put back into prison, rather than face the risk of an avenging convict's knife. About three weeks later the warder in charge of a working party in the jungle noticed a great flock of vultures clustered round a tree. These vultures, called urubus, are large black birds, of a horrible aspect, and they fly about the market-place of St. Laurent, picking up the offal that is left there by the starving liberated convicts, and flit heavily from tree to tree in the neat, well-kept streets of the town. They fly in the prison yard to remind the convicts that if they attempt an escape into the jungle their end, ten to one, will be to have their bones picked clean by these loathsome creatures. They were fighting and screaming in such a mass round the tree that the warder thought there was something strange there. He reported it and the commandant sent a party to see. They found a man hanging by the neck from one of the branches, and when they cut him down discovered that he was the executioner. It was given out that he had committed suicide, but there was a knife-thrust in his back, and the convicts knew that he had been stabbed and then, still alive, taken to the jungle and hanged.

Louis Remire had no fear that anything of that sort would happen to him. He knew how his predecessor had been caught. The job had not been done by the convicts. By the French law when a man is sentenced to hard labour for a certain number of years he has at the expiration of his sentence to remain in the colony for the same number of years. He is free, but he may not stir from the spot that is assigned to him as a residence. In certain circumstances he can get a concession and if he works hard he manages to scrape a bare living from it, but after a long term of penal servitude, during which he has lost all power of initiative, what with the debilitating effect of fever, hookworm and so on, he is unfit for heavy and continuous labour, and so most of the liberated men subsist on begging, larceny, smuggling tobacco or money to the prisoners, and loading and unloading cargoes when two or three times a month a steamer comes into the harbour. It was the wife of one of these freed men that had been the means of the undoing of Louis Remire's predecessor. She was a coloured woman, young and pretty, with a neat little figure and mischievous eyes. The plot was well-considered. The executioner was a burly, sanguine man, of ardent passions. She had thrown herself in his way, and when she caught his approving glance, had cast him a saucy look. He saw her a day or two later in the public garden. He did not venture to speak to her (no one, man, woman or child, would be seen speaking to him), but when he winked at her she smiled. One evening he met her walking through the coconut grove that surrounded his compound. No one was about. He got into conversation with her. They only exchanged a few words, for she was evidently terrified of being seen with him. But she came again to the coconut grove. She played him carefully till his suspicions were allayed; she teased his desires; she made him give her little presents, and at last on the promise of what was for both of them quite a sum of money she agreed to come one dark night to the compound. A ship had just come in and her husband would be working till dawn. It was when he opened the door for her and she hesitated to come in as though at the last moment she could not make up her mind, that he stepped outside to draw her in, and fell to the ground with the violence of the knife-thrust in his back.

"The fool," muttered Louis Remire. "He only got what he deserved. He should have smelt a rat. The eternal vanity of man."

For his part he was through with women. It was on account of women that he found himself in the situation he was in now, at least on account of one woman; and besides, at his time of life, his passions were assuaged. There were other things in life and after a certain age a man, if he was sensible, turned his attention to them. He had always been a great fisherman. In the old days, at home in France before he had had his misfortune, as soon as he came off duty, he took his rod and line and went down to the Rhône. He got a lot of fishing now. Every morning, till the sun grew hot, he sat on his favourite rock and generally managed to get enough for the prison governor's table. The governor's wife knew the value of things and beat him down on the price he asked, but he did not blame her for that; she knew that he had to take what she was prepared to give and it would have been stupid of her to pay a penny more than she had to. In any case it brought in a little money useful for tobacco and rum and other odds and ends. But this evening he was going to fish for himself. He got his bait from the lean-to, and his rod, and settled down on his rock. No fish was so good as the fish you caught yourself, and by now he knew which were those that were good to eat and which were so tough and flavourless that you could only throw them back into the sea. There was one sort that, fried in real olive oil, was as good as mullet. He had not been sitting there five minutes when his float gave a sudden jerk, and when he pulled up his line, there, like an answer to prayer, was one of those very fish wriggling on the hook. He took it off, banged its head on the rock, and putting it down, replaced his bait. Four of them would make a good supper, the best a man could have, and with a night's hard work before him he needed a hearty meal. He would not have time to fish to-morrow morning. First of all the scaffold would have to be taken down and the pieces brought back to the room in which it was kept, and there would be a lot of cleaning to do. It was a bloody business; last time he had had his pants so soaked that he had been able to do nothing with them and had had to throw them away. The brass would have to be polished, the knife would have to be honed. He was not a man to leave a job half finished, and by the time it was through he would be pretty peckish. It would be worth while to catch a few more fish and put them in a cool place so that he could have a substantial breakfast. A cup of coffee, a couple of eggs and a bit of fried fish; he could do with that. Then he would have a good sleep; after a night on his feet, the anxiety of an inexperienced assistant, and the clearing away of all the mess, God knew he would deserve it.

In front of him was spread the bay in a noble sweep, and in the distance was a little island green with trees. The afternoon was exquisitely still. Peace descended on the fisherman's soul. He watched his float idly. When you came to think of it, he reflected, he might be a great deal worse off; some of them, the convicts he meant, the convicts who swarmed in the prison a few hundred yards away from him, some of them had such a nostalgia for France that they went mad with melancholy; but he was a bit of a philosopher, so long as he could fish he was content; and did it really matter if he watched his float on the southern sea or in the Rhône? His thoughts wandered back to the past. His wife was an intolerable woman and he did not regret that he had killed her. He had never meant to marry her. She was a dressmaker, and he had taken a fancy to her because she was always neatly and smartly dressed. She seemed respectable and ladylike. He would not have been surprised if she had looked upon herself as a cut above a policeman. But he had a way with him. She soon gave him to understand that she was no snob, and when he made the customary advances he discovered to his relief, for he was not a man who considered that resistance added a flavour to conquest, that she was no prude. He liked to be seen with her when he took her out to dinner. She talked intelligently, and she was economical. She knew where they could dine well at the cheapest price. His situation was enviable. It added to his satisfaction that he could gratify the sexual desires natural to his healthy temperament at so moderate an expense. When she came to him and said she was going to have a baby it seemed natural enough that they should get married. He was earning good wages, and it was time that he should settle down. He often grew tired of eating, *en pension*, at a restaurant, and he looked forward to having his own home and home cooking. Well, it turned out that it had been a mistake about the baby, but Louis Remire was a good-natured fellow, and he didn't hold it up against Adèle. But he found, as many men have found before, that the wife was a very different woman from the mistress. She was jealous and possessive. She seemed to think that on a Sunday afternoon he ought to take her for a walk instead of going out fishing, and she made it a grievance that, on coming off duty, he would go to the café. There was one café he frequented where other fishermen went and where he met men with whom he had a lot in common. He found it much pleasanter to spend his free evenings there over a glass or two of beer, whiling away the time with a game of cards, than to sit at home with his wife. She began to make scenes. Though sociable and jovial by nature he had a quick temper. There was a rough crowd at Lyons, and sometimes you could not manage them unless you were prepared to show a certain amount of firmness. When his wife began to make a nuisance of herself it never occurred to him that there was any other way of dealing with her than that he adopted. He let her know the strength of his hand. If she had been a sensible woman she would have learnt her lesson, but she was not a sensible woman. He found occasion more and more often to apply a necessary correction; she revenged herself by screaming the place down and by telling the neighbours—they lived in a two-roomed apartment on the fifth floor of a big house—what a brute he was. She told them that she was sure he would kill her one day. And yet never was there a more good-natured man than Louis Remire; she blamed him for the money he spent at the café, she accused him of wasting it on other women; well, in his position he had opportunities now and then, and as any man would he took them, and he was easy with his money, he never minded paying a round of drinks for his friends, and when a girl who had been nice to him wanted a new hat or a pair of silk stockings he wasn't the man to say no. His wife looked upon money that he did not spend on her as money stolen from her; she tried to make him account for every penny he spent, and when in his jovial way he told her he had thrown it out of the window, she was infuriated. Her tongue grew bitter and her voice was rasping. She was in a sullen rage with him all the time. She could not speak without saying something disagreeable. They led a cat-and-dog life. Louis Remire used to tell his friends what a harridan she was, he used to tell them that he wished ten times a day that he had never married her, and sometimes he would add that if an epidemic of influenza did not carry her off he would really have to kill her.

It was these remarks, made merely in jest, and the fact that she had so often told the neighbours that she knew he would murder her, that had sent him to St. Laurent de Maroni with a twelve-year sentence. Otherwise he might very well have got off with three or four years in a French prison. The end had come one hot summer's day. He was, which was rare for him, in a bad temper. There was a strike in progress and the strikers had been violent. The police had had to make a good many arrests and the men had not submitted to this peaceably. Louis Remire had got a nasty blow on the jaw and he had had to make free use of his truncheon. To get the arrested men to the station had been a hot and tiring job. On coming off duty he had gone home to get out of his uniform and was intending to go to the café and have a glass of beer and a pleasant game of cards. His jaw was hurting him. His wife chose that moment to ask him for money and when he told her that he had none to give her she made a scene. He had plenty of money to go to the café, but none for her to buy a scrap of food with, she could starve for all he cared. He told her to shut up, and then the row began. She got in front of the door and swore that he should not pass till he gave her money. He told her to get out of the way and took a step towards her. She whipped out his service revolver which he had taken off when he removed his uniform and threatened that she would shoot him if he moved a step. He was used to dealing with dangerous criminals, and the words were hardly out of her mouth before he had sprung upon her and snatched the revolver out of her hand. She screamed and hit him in the face. She hit him exactly where his jaw most hurt him. Blind with rage and mad with pain, he fired, he fired twice and she fell to the floor. For a moment he stood and stared at her. He was dazed. She looked as if she were dead. His first feeling was one of indescribable relief. He listened. No one seemed to have heard the sound of the shot. The neighbours must be out. That was a bit of luck, for it gave him time to do what he had to do in his own way. He changed back into his uniform, went out, locking the door behind him and putting the key in his pocket; he stopped for five minutes at his familiar café to have a glass of beer and then returned to the police-station he had lately left. On account of the day's disturbances the chief inspector was still there. Louis Remire went to his room and told him what had happened. He spent the night in a cell adjoining those of the strikers he had so recently himself arrested. Even at that tragic moment he was struck by the irony of the situation.

Louis Remire had on frequent occasions appeared as a police witness in criminal cases and he knew how eager are a man's companions to give any information that may damage him when he gets into trouble. It had caused him a certain grim amusement to realise how often it happened that a conviction was obtained only by the testimony of a prisoner's best friends. But notwithstanding his experience he was amazed, when his own case came up for trial, to listen to the evidence given by the proprietor of the little café he had so much frequented, and to that of the men who for years had fished with him, played cards with him and drunk with him. They seemed to have treasured every careless word he had ever uttered, the complaints he had made about his wife and the joking threats he had from time to time made that he would get even with her. He knew that at the time they had taken them no more seriously than he meant them. If he was able to do them a small service, and a man in the force often has it in his power to do one, he never hesitated. He had never been ungenerous with his money. You would have thought as you listened to them in the witness-box that it gave them the most intense satisfaction to disclose every trivial detail that could damage him.

From what appeared at the trial you would have thought that he was a bad man, dissolute, of violent temper, extravagant, idle and corrupt. He knew that he was nothing of the kind. He was just an ordinary, good-natured, easy-going fellow, who was willing to let you go your way if you would let him go his. It was true that he liked his game of cards and his glass of beer, it was true that he liked a pretty girl, but what of it? When he looked at the jury he wondered how many of them would come out of it any better than he if all their errors, all their rash words, all their follies were thus laid bare. He did not resent the long term of penal servitude to which he was sentenced. He was an officer of the law; he had committed a crime and it was right that he should be punished. But he was not a criminal; he was the victim of an unfortunate accident.

At St. Laurent de Maroni, in the prison camp, wearing the pink and white stripe of the prison garb and the ugly straw hat, he remembered still that he had been a policeman and that the convicts with whom he must now consort had always been his natural enemies. He despised and disliked them. He had as little to do with them as he could. And he was not frightened of them. He knew them too well. Like all the rest he had a knife and he showed that he was prepared to use it. He did not want to interfere with anybody, but he was not going to allow anyone to interfere with him.

The chief of the Lyons police had liked him, his character while in the force had been exemplary, and the *fiche* which accompanied every prisoner spoke well of him. He knew that what officials like is a prisoner who gives no trouble, who accepts his position with cheerfulness and who is willing. He got a soft job; very soon he got a cell of his own and so escaped the horrible promiscuity of the dormitories; he got on well with the warders, they were decent chaps, most of them, and knowing that he had formerly been in the police they treated him more as a comrade than as a convict. The commandant of the prison trusted him. Presently he got the job of servant to one of the prison officials. He slept in the prison, but otherwise enjoyed complete freedom. He took the children of his master to school every day and fetched them at the end of their school hours. He made toys for them. He accompanied his mistress to market and carried back the provisions she bought. He spent long hours gossiping with her. The family liked him. They liked his chaffing manner and his good-natured smile. He was industrious and trustworthy. Life once more was tolerable.

But after three years his master was transferred to Cayenne. It was a blow. But it happened just then that the post of executioner fell free and he obtained it. Now once more he was in the service of the state. He was an official. However humble his residence it was his own. He need no longer wear the prison uniform. He could grow his hair and his moustache. He cared little if the convicts looked upon him with horror and contempt. That was how he looked upon them. Scum. When he took the bleeding head of an executed man from the basket and holding it by the ears pronounced those solemn words: *Au nom du peuple français justice est faite,* he felt that he did represent the Republic. He stood for law and order. He was the protector of society against that vast horde of ruthless criminals.

He got a hundred francs for each execution. That and what the governor's wife paid him for his fish provided him with many a pleasant comfort and not a few luxuries. And now as he sat on his rock in the peace of eventide he considered what he would do with the money he would earn next day. Occasionally he got a bite, now and then a fish; he drew it out of the water, took it off the hook and put on fresh bait; but he did this mechanically, and it did not disturb the current of his thoughts. Six hundred francs. It was a respectable sum. He scarcely knew what to do with it. He had everything he wanted in his little house, he had a good store of groceries, and plenty of rum for one who was as little of a drinker as he was; he needed no fishing tackle; his clothes were good enough. The only thing was to put it aside. He already had a tidy little sum hidden in the ground at the root of a papaia tree. He chuckled when he thought how Adèle would have stared had she known that he was actually saving. It would have been balm to her avaricious soul. He was saving up gradually for when he was released. That was the difficult moment for the convicts. So long as they were in prison they had a roof over their heads and food to eat, but when they were released, with the obligation of staying for so many years more in the colony, they had to shift for themselves. They all said the same thing: it was at the expiration of their term that their real punishment began. They could not get work. Employers mistrusted them. Contractors would not engage them because the prison authorities hired out convict labour at a price that defied competition. They slept in the open, in the market-place, and for food were often glad to go to the Salvation Army. But the Salvation Army made them work hard for what they gave and besides forced them to listen to their services. Sometimes they committed a violent crime merely to get back to the safety of prison. Louis Remire was not going to take any risks. He meant to amass a sufficient capital to start in business. He ought to be able to get permission to settle in Cayenne, and there he might open a bar. People might hesitate to come at first because he had been the executioner, but if he provided good liquor they would get over their prejudice, and with his jovial manner, with his experience in keeping order, he ought to be able to make a go of it. Visitors came to Cayenne now and then and they would come out of curiosity. It would be something interesting to tell their friends when they got home that the best rum punch they had had in Cayenne was at the executioner's. But he had a good many years to go yet, and if there really was something he needed there was no reason why he shouldn't get it. He racked his brains. No, there wasn't a thing in the world he wanted. He was surprised. He allowed his eyes to wander from his float. The sea was wonderfully calm and now it was rich with all the colour of the setting sun. In the sky already a solitary star twinkled. A thought came to him that filled him with an extraordinary sensation.

"But if there's nothing in the world you want, surely that's happiness." He stroked his handsome moustache and his blue eyes shone softly. "There are no two ways about it, I'm a happy man and till this moment I never knew it."

The notion was so unexpected that he did not know what to make of it. It was certainly a very odd one. But there it was, as obvious to anyone with a logical mind as a proposition of Euclid.

"Happy, that's what I am. How many men can say the same? In St. Laurent de Maroni of all places, and for the first time in my life."

The sun was setting. He had caught enough fish for his supper and enough for his breakfast. He drew in his line, gathered up his fish, and went back to his house. It stood but a few yards from the sea. It did not take him long to light his fire and in a little while he had four little fish cheerfully frizzling in a pan. He was always very particular about the oil he used. The best olive oil was expensive, but it was worth the money. The prison bread was good, and after he had fried his fish, he fried a couple of pieces of bread in the rest of the oil. He sniffed the savoury smell with satisfaction. He lit a lamp, washed a lettuce grown in his own garden, and mixed himself a salad. He had a notion that no one in the world could mix a salad better than he. He drank a glass of rum and ate his supper with appetite. He gave a few odds and ends to the two mongrel dogs who were lying at his feet, and then, having washed up, for he was by nature a tidy man and when he came in to breakfast next morning did not want to find things in a mess, let the dogs out of the compound to wander about the coconut grove. He took the lamp into the house, made himself comfortable in his deck-chair, and smoking a cigar smuggled in from the neighbouring Dutch Colony settled down to read one of the French papers that had arrived by the last mail. Replete, his mind at ease, he could not but feel that life, with all its disadvantages, was good to live. He was still affected by the amused surprise that had overcome him when it suddenly occurred to him that he was a happy man. When you considered that men spent their lives seeking for happiness, it seemed hardly believable that he had found it. Yet the fact stared him in the face. A man who has everything he wants is happy, he had everything he wanted; therefore he was happy. He chuckled as a new thought crossed his mind.

"There's no denying it, I owe it to Adèle."

Old Adèle. What a foul woman!

Presently he decided that he had better have a nap; he set his alarm clock for a quarter to twelve and lying down on his bed in a few minutes was fast asleep. He slept soundly and no dreams troubled him. He woke with a start when the alarm sounded, but in a moment remembered why he had set it. He yawned and stretched himself lazily.

"Ah, well, I suppose I must get to work. Every job has its inconveniences."

He slipped from under his mosquito-net and relit his lamp. To freshen himself he washed his hands and face, and then as a protection against the night air drank a glass of rum. He thought for a moment of his inexperienced assistant and wondered whether it would be wise to take some rum in a flask with him.

"It would be a pretty business if his nerves went back on him."

It was unfortunate that so many as six men had to be executed. If there had been only one, it wouldn't have mattered so much his assistant being new to the game; but with five others waiting there, it would be awkward if there were a hitch. He shrugged his shoulders. They would just have to do the best they could. He passed a comb through his tousled hair and carefully brushed his handsome moustache. He lit a cigarette. He walked through his compound, unlocked the door in the stout palisade that surrounded it, and locked it again behind him. There was no moon. He whistled for his dogs. He was surprised that they did not come. He whistled again. The brutes. They'd probably caught a rat and were fighting over it. He'd give them a good hiding for that; he'd teach them not to come when he whistled. He set out to walk in the direction of the prison. It was dark under the coconut trees and he would just as soon have had the dogs with him. Still there were only fifty yards to go and then he would be out in the open. There were lights in the governor's house, and it gave him confidence to see them. He smiled, for he guessed what those lights at that late hour meant; the governor, with the execution before him at dawn, was finding it hard to sleep. The anxiety, the malaise, that affected convicts and ex-convicts alike on the eve of an execution, had got on his nerves. It was true that there was always the chance of an outbreak then, and the warders went around with their eyes skinned and their hands ready to draw their guns at a suspicious movement.

Louis Remire whistled for his dogs once more, but they did not come. He could not understand it. It was a trifle disquieting. He was a man who habitually walked slowly, strolling along with a sort of roll, but now he hastened his pace. He spat the cigarette out of his mouth. It had struck him that it was prudent not to betray his whereabouts by the light it gave. Suddenly he stumbled against something. He stopped dead. He was a brave man, with nerves of steel, but on a sudden he felt sick with terror. It was something soft and rather large that he had stumbled against, and he was pretty sure what it was. He wore espadrilles, and with one foot he cautiously felt the object on the ground before him. Yes, he was right. It was one of his dogs. It was dead. He took a step backwards and drew his knife. He knew it was no good to shout.

The only house in the neighbourhood was the prison governor's, it faced the clearing just beyond the coconut grove; but they would not hear him, or if they did would not stir. St. Laurent de Maroni was not a place where you went out in the dead of night when you heard a man calling for help. If next day one of the freed convicts was found lying dead, well, it was no great loss. Louis Remire saw in a flash what had happened.

He thought rapidly. They had killed his dogs while he was sleeping. They must have got them when he had put them out of his compound after supper. They must have thrown them some poisoned meat and the brutes had snatched at it. If the one he had stumbled over was near his house it was because it tried to crawl home to die. Louis Remire strained his eyes. He could see nothing. The night was pitch black. He could hardly see the trunks of the coconut trees a yard away from him. His first thought was to make a rush for his shack. If he got back to the safety of that he could wait till the prison people, wondering why he did not come, sent to fetch him. But he knew he could never get back. He knew they were there in the darkness, the men who had killed his dogs; he would have to fumble with the key to find the lock and before he found it he would have a knife plunged in his back. He listened intently. There was not a sound. And yet he felt that there were men there, lurking behind the trees, and they were there to kill him. They would kill him as they had killed his dogs. And he would die like a dog. There was more than one certainly. He knew them, there were three or four of them at least, there might be more, convicts in service in private houses who were not obliged to get back to the camp till a late hour, or desperate and starving freed men who had nothing to lose. For a moment he hesitated what to do. He dared not make a run for it, they might easily have put a rope across the pathway that led from his house to the open, and if he tripped he was done for. The coconut trees were loosely planted and among them his enemies would see him as little as he saw them. He stepped over the dead dog and plunged into the grove. He stood with his back to a tree to decide how he should proceed. The silence was terrifying. Suddenly he heard a whisper and the horror of it was frightful. Again a dead silence. He felt he must move on, but his feet seemed rooted to the ground. He felt that they were peering at him out of the darkness and it seemed to him that he was as visible to them as though he stood in the broad light of day. Then from the other side was a little cough. It came as such a shock that Louis Remire nearly screamed. He was conscious now that they were all round him. He could expect no mercy from those robbers and murderers. He remembered the other executioner, his predecessor, whom they had carried still alive into the jungle, whose eyes they had gouged out, and whom they had left hanging for the vultures to devour. His knees began to tremble. What a fool he had been to take on the job! There were soft jobs he could have found in which you ran no risk. It was too late to think of that. He pulled himself together. He had no chance of getting out of the coconut grove alive, he knew that; he wanted to be sure that he would be dead. He tightened his grip on his knife. The awful part was that he could hear no one, he could see no one, and yet he knew that they were lurking there waiting to strike. For one moment he had a mad idea, he would throw his knife away and shout out to them that he was unarmed and they could come and kill him in safety. But he knew them; they would never be satisfied merely to kill him. Rage seized him. He was not the man to surrender tamely to a pack of criminals. He was an honest man and an official of the state; it was his duty to defend himself. He could not stay there all night. It was better to get it over quickly. Yet that tree at his back seemed to offer a sort of security, he could not bring himself to move. He stared at the trunk of a tree in front of him and suddenly it moved and he realised with horror that it was a man. That made up his mind for him and with a huge effort he stepped forwards. He advanced slowly and cautiously. He could hear nothing, he could see nothing. But he knew that as he advanced they advanced too. It was as though he were accompanied by an invisible bodyguard. He thought he could hear the sound of their naked feet on the ground. His fear had left him. He walked on, keeping as close to the trees as he could, so that they should have less chance of attacking him from behind; a wild hope sprang up in his breast that they would be afraid to strike, they knew him, they all knew him, and whoever struck the first blow would be lucky if he escaped a knife in his own guts; he had only another thirty yards to go, and once in the open, able to see, he could make a fight for it. A few yards more and then he would run for his life. Suddenly something happened that made him start out of his skin, and he stopped dead. A light was flashed and in that heavy darkness the sudden glare was terrifying. It was an electric torch. Instinctively he sprang to a tree and stood with his back to it. He could not see who held the light. He was blinded by it. He did not speak. He held his knife low, he knew that when they struck it was in the belly, and if someone flung himself at him he was prepared to strike back. He was going to sell his life dearly. For half a minute perhaps the light shone on his face, but it seemed to him an eternity. He thought now that he discerned dimly the faces of men. Then a word broke the horrible silence.

"Throw."

At the same instant a knife came flying through the air and struck him on the breast-bone. He threw up his hands and as he did so someone sprang at him and with a great sweep of the knife ripped up his belly. The light was switched off. Louis Remire sank to the ground with a groan, a terrible groan of pain. Five, six men gathered out of the gloom and stood over him. With his fall the knife that had stuck in his breast-bone was dislodged. It lay on the ground. A quick flash of the torch showed where it was. One of the men took it and with a single, swift motion cut Remire's throat from ear to ear.

"*Au nom du peuple français justice est faite,*" he said.

They vanished into the darkness and in the coconut grove was the immense silence of death.

Winter Cruise

CAPTAIN ERDMANN knew Miss Reid very little till the *Friedrich Weber* reached Haiti. She came on board at Plymouth, but by then he had taken on a number of passengers, French, Belgian and Haitian, many of whom had travelled with him before, and she was placed at the chief engineer's table. The *Friedrich Weber* was a freighter sailing regularly from Hamburg to Cartagena on the Colombian coast and on the way touching at a number of islands in the West Indies. She carried phosphates and cement from Germany and took back coffee and timber; but her owners, the Brothers Weber, were always willing to send her out of her route if a cargo of any sort made it worth their while. The *Friedrich Weber* was prepared to take cattle, mules, potatoes or anything else that offered the chance of earning an honest penny. She carried passengers. There were six cabins on the upper deck and six below. The accommodation was not luxurious, but the food was good, plain and abundant, and the fares were cheap. The round trip took nine weeks and was not costing Miss Reid more than forty-five pounds. She looked forward not only to seeing many interesting places, with historical associations, but also to acquiring a great deal of information that would enrich her mind.

The agent had warned her that till the ship reached Port au Prince in Haiti she would have to share a cabin with another woman. Miss Reid did not mind that, she liked company, and when the steward told her that her companion was Madame Bollin she thought at once that it would be a very good opportunity to rub up her French. She was only very slightly disconcerted when she found that Madame Bollin was coal-black. She told herself that one had to accept the rough with the smooth and that it takes all sorts to make a world. Miss Reid was a good sailor, as indeed was only to be expected since her grandfather had been a naval officer, but after a couple of roughish days the weather was fine and in a very short while she knew all her fellow-passengers. She was a good mixer. That was one of the reasons why she had made a success of her business; she owned a tea-room at a celebrated beauty spot in the west of England and she always had a smile and a pleasant word for every customer who came in; she closed down in the winter and for the last four years had taken a cruise. You met such interesting people, she said, and you always learnt something. It was true that the passengers on the *Friedrich Weber* weren't of quite so good a class as those she had met the year before on her Mediterranean cruise, but Miss Reid was not a snob, and though the table manners of some of them shocked her somewhat, determined to look upon the bright side of things she decided to make the best of them. She was a great reader and she was glad, on looking at the ship's library, to find that there were a lot of books by Phillips Oppenheim, Edgar Wallace and Agatha Christie; but with so many people to talk to she had no time for reading and she made up her mind to leave them till the ship emptied herself at Haiti.

"After all," she said, "human nature is more important than literature."

Miss Reid had always had the reputation of being a good talker and she flattered herself that not once during the many days they were at sea had she allowed the conversation at table to languish. She knew how to draw people out, and whenever a topic seemed to be exhausted she had a remark ready to revive it or another topic waiting on the tip of her tongue to set the conversation off again. Her friend Miss Price, daughter of the late Vicar of Campden, who had come to see her off at Plymouth, for she lived there, had often said to her:

"You know, Venetia, you have a mind like a man. You're never at a loss for something to say."

"Well, I think if you're interested in everyone, everyone will be interested in you," Miss Reid answered modestly. "Practice makes perfect, and I have the infinite capacity for taking pains which Dickens said was genius."

Miss Reid was not really called Venetia, her name was Alice, but disliking it she had, when still a girl, adopted the poetic name which she felt so much better suited to her personality.

Miss Reid had a great many interesting talks with her fellow-passengers and she was really sorry when the ship at length reached Port au Prince and the last of them disembarked. The *Friedrich Weber* stopped two days there, during which she visited the town and the neighbourhood. When they sailed she was the only passenger. The ship was skirting the coast of the island stopping off at a variety of ports to discharge or to take on cargo.

"I hope you will not feel embarrassed alone with so many men, Miss Reid," said the captain heartily as they sat down to midday dinner.

She was placed on his right hand and at table besides sat the first mate, the chief engineer and the doctor.

"I'm a woman of the world, Captain. I always think if a lady is a lady gentlemen will be gentlemen."

"We're only rough sailor men, madam, you mustn't expect too much."

"Kind hearts are more than coronets and simple faith than Norman blood, Captain," answered Miss Reid.

He was a short, thick-set man, with a clean-shaven head and a red, clean-shaven face. He wore a white stengah-shifter, but except at meal-times unbuttoned at the neck and showing his hairy chest. He was a jovial fellow. He could not speak without bellowing. Miss Reid thought him quite an eccentric, but she had a keen sense of humour and was prepared to make allowances for that. She took the conversation in hand. She had learnt a great deal about Haiti on the voyage out and more during the two days she had spent there, but she knew that men liked to talk rather than to listen, so she put them a number of questions to which she already knew the answers; oddly enough they didn't. In the end she found herself obliged to give quite a little lecture, and before dinner was over, *Mittag Essen* they called it in their funny way, she had imparted to them a great deal of interesting information about the history and economic situation of the Republic, the problems that confronted it and its prospects for the future. She talked rather slowly, in a refined voice, and her vocabulary was extensive.

At nightfall they put in at a small port where they were to load three hundred bags of coffee, and the agent came on board. The captain asked him to stay to supper and ordered cocktails. As the steward brought them Miss Reid swam into the saloon. Her movements were deliberate, elegant and self-assured. She always said that you could tell at once by the way she walked if a woman was a lady. The captain introduced the agent to her and she sat down.

"What is that you men are drinking?" she asked.

"A cocktail. Will you have one, Miss Reid?"

"I don't mind if I do."

She drank it and the captain somewhat doubtfully asked her if she would have another.

"Another? Well, just to be matey."

The agent, much whiter than some, but a good deal darker than many, was the son of a former minister of Haiti to the German court, and having lived for many years in Berlin spoke good German. It was indeed on this account that he had got a job with a German shipping firm. On the strength of this Miss Reid, during supper, told them all about a trip down the Rhine that she had once taken. Afterwards she and the agent, the skipper, the doctor and the mate sat round a table and drank beer. Miss Reid made it her business to draw the agent out. The fact that they were loading coffee suggested to her that he would be interested in learning how they grew tea in Ceylon, yes, she had been to Ceylon on a cruise, and the fact that his father was a diplomat made it certain that he would be interested in the royal family of England. She had a very pleasant evening. When she at last retired to rest, for she would never have thought of saying she was going to bed, she said to herself:

"There's no doubt that travel is a great education."

It was really an experience to find herself along with all those men. How they would laugh when she told them all about it when she got home! They would say that things like that only happened to Venetia. She smiled when she heard the captain on deck singing with that great booming voice of his. Germans were so musical. He had a funny way of strutting up and down on his short legs singing Wagner tunes to words of his own invention. It was *Tannhaüser* he was singing now (that lovely thing about the evening star) but knowing no German Miss Reid could only wonder what absurd words he was putting to it. It was as well.

"Oh, what a bore that woman is, I shall certainly kill her if she goes on much longer." Then he broke into Siegfried's martial strain. "She's a bore, she's a bore, she's a bore. I shall throw her into the sea."

And that of course is what Miss Reid was. She was a crashing, she was a stupendous, she was an excruciating bore. She talked in a steady monotone, and it was no use to interrupt her because then she started again from the beginning. She had an insatiable thirst for information and no casual remark could be thrown across the table without her asking innumerable questions about it. She was a great dreamer and she narrated her dreams at intolerable length. There was no subject upon which she had not something prosy to say. She had a truism for every occasion. She hit on the commonplace like a hammer driving a nail into the wall. She plunged into the obvious like a clown in a circus jumping through a hoop. Silence did not abash her. Those poor men far away from their homes and the patter of little feet, and with Christmas coming on, no wonder they felt low; she redoubled her efforts to interest and amuse them. She was determined to bring a little gaiety into their dull lives. For that was the awful part of it: Miss Reid meant well. She was not only having a good time herself, but she was trying to give all of them a good time. She was convinced that they liked her as much as she liked them. She felt that she was doing her bit to make the party a success and she was naïvely happy to think that she was succeeding. She told them all about her friend Miss Price and how often she had said to her: Venetia, no one ever has a dull moment in your company. It was the captain's duty to be polite to a passenger and however much he would have liked to tell her to hold her silly tongue he could not, but even if he had been free to say what he liked, he knew that he could not have brought himself to hurt her feelings. Nothing stemmed the torrent of her loquacity. It was as irresistible as a force of nature. Once in desperation they began talking German, but Miss Reid stopped this at once.

"Now I won't have you saying things I don't understand. You ought all to make the most of your good luck in having me all to yourselves and practise your English."

"We were talking of technical matters that would only bore you, Miss Reid," said the captain.

"I'm never bored. That's why, if you won't think me a wee bit conceited to say so, I'm never boring. You see, I like to know things. Everything interests me and you never know when a bit of information won't come in useful."

The doctor smiled dryly.

"The captain was only saying that because he was embarrassed. In point of fact he was telling a story that was not fit for the ears of a maiden lady."

"I may be a maiden lady but I'm also a woman of the world, I don't expect sailors to be saints. You need never be afraid of what you say before me, Captain, I shan't be shocked. I should love to hear your story."

The doctor was a man of sixty with thin grey hair, a grey moustache and small bright blue eyes. He was a silent, bitter man, and however hard Miss Reid tried to bring him into the conversation it was almost impossible to get a word out of him. But she wasn't a woman who would give in without a struggle, and one morning when they were at sea and she saw him sitting on deck with a book, she brought her chair next to his and sat down beside him.

"Are you fond of reading, Doctor?" she said brightly.

"Yes."

"So am I. And I suppose like all Germans you're musical."

"I'm fond of music."

"So am I. The moment I saw you I thought you looked clever."

He gave her a brief look and pursing his lips went on reading. Miss Reid was not disconcerted.

"But of course one can always read. I always prefer a good talk to a good book. Don't you?"

"No."

"How very interesting. Now do tell me why?"

"I can't give you a reason."

"That's very strange, isn't it? But then I always think human nature is strange. I'm terribly interested in people, you know. I always like doctors, they know so much about human nature, but I could tell you some things that would surprise even you. You learn a great deal about people if you run a tea-shop like I do, that's to say if you keep your eyes open."

The doctor got up.

"I must ask you to excuse me, Miss Reid. I have to go and see a patient."

"Anyhow I've broken the ice now," she thought, as he walked away. "I think he was only shy."

But a day or two later the doctor was not feeling at all well. He had an internal malady that troubled him now and then, but he was used to it and disinclined to talk about it. When he had one of his attacks he only wanted to be left alone. His cabin was small and stuffy, so he settled himself on a long chair on deck and lay with his eyes closed. Miss Reid was walking up and down to get the half-hour's exercise she took morning and evening. He thought that if he pretended to be asleep she would not disturb him. But when she had passed him half a dozen times she stopped in front of him and stood quite still. Though he kept his eyes closed he knew that she was looking at him.

"Is there anything I can do, Doctor?" she said.

He started.

"Why, what should there be?"

He gave her a glance and saw that her eyes were deeply troubled.

"You look dreadfully ill," she said.

"I'm in great pain."

"I know. I can see that. Can't something be done?"

"No, it'll pass off presently."

She hesitated for a moment then went away. Presently she returned.

"You look so uncomfortable with no cushions or anything. I've brought you my own pillow that I always travel with. Do let me put it behind your head."

He felt at that moment too ill to remonstrate. She lifted his head gently and put the soft pillow behind it. It really did make him feel more comfortable. She passed her hand across his forehead and it was cool and soft.

"Poor dear," she said. "I know what doctors are. They haven't the first idea how to take care of themselves."

She left him, but in a minute or two returned with a chair and a bag. The doctor when he saw her gave a twitch of anguish.

"Now I'm not going to let you talk, I'm just going to sit beside you and knit. I always think it's a comfort when one isn't feeling very well to have someone near."

She sat down and taking an unfinished muffler out of her bag began busily to ply her needles. She never said a word. And strangely enough the doctor found her company a solace. No one else on board had even noticed that he was ill, he had felt lonely, and the sympathy of that crashing bore was grateful to him. It soothed him to see her silently working and presently he fell asleep. When he awoke she was still working. She gave him a little smile, but did not speak. His pain had left him and he felt much better.

He did not go into the saloon till late in the afternoon. He found the captain and Hans Krause, the mate, having a glass of beer together.

"Sit down, Doctor," said the captain. "We're holding a council of war. You know that the day after to-morrow is Sylvester Abend."

"Of course."

Sylvester Abend, New Year's Eve, is an occasion that means a great deal to a German and they had all been looking forward to it. They had brought a Christmas tree all the way from Germany with them.

"At dinner to-day Miss Reid was more talkative than ever. Hans and I have decided that something must be done about it."

"She sat with me for two hours this morning in silence. I suppose she was making up for lost time."

"It's bad enough to be away from one's home and family just now anyway and all we can do is to make the best of a bad job. We want to enjoy our Sylvester Abend, and unless something is done about Miss Reid we haven't a chance."

"We can't have a good time if she's with us," said the mate. "She'll spoil it as sure as eggs is eggs."

"How do you propose to get rid of her, short of throwing her overboard?" smiled the doctor. "She's not a bad old soul; all she wants is a lover."

"At her age?" cried Hans Krause.

"Especially at her age. That inordinate loquacity, that passion for information, the innumerable questions she asks, her prosiness, the way she goes on and on—it is all a sign of her clamouring virginity. A lover would bring her peace. Those jangled nerves of hers would relax. At least for an hour she would have lived. The deep satisfaction which her being demands would travel through those exacerbated centres of speech, and we should have quiet."

It was always a little difficult to know how much the doctor meant what he said and when he was having a joke at your expense. The captain's blue eyes, however, twinkled mischievously.

"Well, Doctor, I have great confidence in your powers of diagnosis. The remedy you suggest is evidently worth trying, and since you are a bachelor it is clear that it is up to you to apply it."

"Pardon me, Captain, it is my professional duty to prescribe remedies for the patients under my charge in this ship, but not to administer them personally. Besides, I am sixty."

"I am a married man with grown-up children," said the captain. "I am old and fat and asthmatic, it is obvious that I cannot be expected to undertake a task of this kind. Nature cut me out for the rôle of a husband and father, not for that of a lover."

"Youth in these matters is essential and good looks are advantageous," said the doctor gravely.

The captain gave a great bang on the table with his fist.

"You are thinking of Hans. You're quite right. Hans must do it."

The mate sprang to his feet.

"Me? Never."

"Hans, you are tall, handsome, strong as a lion, brave and young. We have twenty-three days more at sea before we reach Hamburg, you wouldn't desert your trusted old captain in an emergency or let down your good friend the doctor?"

"No, Captain, it's asking too much of me. I have been married less than a year and I love my wife. I can hardly wait to get back to Hamburg. She is yearning for me as I am yearning for her. I will not be unfaithful to her, especially with Miss Reid."

"Miss Reid's not so bad," said the doctor.

"Some people might call her even nice-looking," said the captain.

And indeed when you took Miss Reid feature by feature she was not in fact a plain woman. True, she had a long, stupid face, but her brown eyes were large and she had very thick lashes; her brown hair was cut short and curled rather prettily over her neck; she hadn't a bad skin, and she was neither too fat nor too thin. She was not old as people go nowadays, and if she had told you that she was forty you would have been quite willing to believe it. The only thing against her was that she was drab and dull.

"Must I then for twenty-three mortal days endure the prolixity of that tedious woman? Must I for twenty-three mortal days answer her inane questions and listen to her fatuous remarks? Must I, an old man, have my Sylvester Abend, the jolly evening I was looking forward to, ruined by the unwelcome company of that intolerable virgin? And all because no one can be found to show a little gallantry, a little human kindness, a spark of charity to a lonely woman. I shall wreck the ship."

"There's always the radio-operator," said Hans.

The captain gave a loud shout.

"Hans, let the ten thousand virgins of Cologne arise and call you blessed. Steward," he bellowed, "tell the radio-operator that I want him."

The radio-operator came into the saloon and smartly clicked his heels together. The three men looked at him in silence. He wondered uneasily whether he had done something for which he was to be hauled over the coals. He was above the middle height, with square shoulders and narrow hips, erect and slender, his tanned, smooth skin looked as though a razor had never touched it, he had large eyes of a startling blue and a mane of curling golden hair. He was a perfect specimen of young Teutonic manhood. He was so healthy, so vigorous, so much alive that even when he stood some way from you, you felt the glow of his vitality.

"Aryan, all right," said the captain. "No doubt about that. How old are you, my boy?"

"Twenty-one, sir."

"Married?"

"No, sir."

"Engaged?"

The radio-operator chuckled. There was an engaging boyishness in his laugh.

"No, sir."

"You know that we have a female passenger on board?"

"Yes, sir."

"Do you know her?"

"I've said good-morning to her when I've seen her on deck."

The captain assumed his most official manner. His eyes, which generally twinkled with fun, were stern and he got a sort of bark into his rich, fruity voice.

"Although this is a cargo-boat and we carry valuable freight, we also take such passengers as we can get, and this is a branch of our business that the company is anxious to encourage. My instructions are to do everything possible to promote the happiness and comfort of the passengers. Miss Reid needs a lover. The doctor and I have come to the conclusion that you are well suited to satisfy Miss Reid's requirements."

"Me, sir?"

The radio-operator blushed scarlet and then began to giggle, but quickly composed himself when he saw the set faces of the three men who confronted him.

"But she's old enough to be my mother."

"That at your age is a matter of no consequence. She is a woman of the highest distinction and allied to all the great families of England. If she were German she would be at least a countess. That you should have been chosen for this responsible position is an honour that you should greatly appreciate. Furthermore, your English is halting and this will give you an excellent opportunity to improve it."

"That of course is something to be thought of," said the radio-operator. "I know that I want practice."

"It is not often in this life that it is possible to combine pleasure with intellectual improvement, and you must congratulate yourself on your good fortune."

"But if I may be allowed to put the question, sir, why does Miss Reid want a lover?"

"It appears to be an old English custom for unmarried women of exalted rank to submit themselves to the embraces of a lover at this time of year. The company is anxious that Miss Reid should be treated exactly as she would be on an English ship, and we trust that if she is satisfied, with her aristocratic connections she will be able to persuade many of her friends to take cruises in the line's ships."

"Sir, I must ask to be excused."

"It is not a request that I am making, it is an order. You will present yourself to Miss Reid, in her cabin, at eleven o'clock to-night."

"What shall I do when I get there?"

"Do?" thundered the captain. "Do? Act naturally."

With a wave of the hand he dismissed him. The radio-operator clicked his heels, saluted and went out.

"Now let us have another glass of beer," said the captain.

At supper that evening Miss Reid was at her best. She was

s

verbose. She was playful. She was refined. There was not a
truism that she failed to utter. There was not a commonplace
that she forbore to express. She bombarded them with foolish
questions. The captain's face grew redder and redder as he sought
to contain his fury; he felt that he could not go on being polite
to her any longer and if the doctor's remedy did not help, one day
he would forget himself and give her, not a piece, but the whole of
his mind.

"I shall lose my job," he thought, "but I'm not sure that it
wouldn't be worth it."

Next day they were already sitting at table when she came in to
dinner.

"Sylvester Abend to-morrow," she said, brightly. That was the
sort of thing she would say. She went on: "Well, what have you
all been up to this morning?"

Since they did exactly the same thing every day, and she knew
very well what that was, the question was enraging. The captain's
heart sank. He briefly told the doctor what he thought of him.

"Now, no German, please," said Miss Reid archly. "You know
I don't allow that, and why, Captain, did you give the poor doctor
that sour look? It's Christmas time, you know; peace and goodwill to all men. I'm so excited about to-morrow evening, and will
there be candles on the Christmas tree?"

"Naturally."

"How thrilling! I always think a Christmas tree without candles
isn't a Christmas tree. Oh, d'you know, I had such a funny experience last night. I can't understand it at all."

A startled pause. They all looked intently at Miss Reid. For
once they hung on her lips.

"Yes," she went on in that monotonous, rather finicking way
of hers, "I was just getting into bed last night when there was a
knock at my door. 'Who is it?' I said. 'It's the radio-operator,'
was the answer. 'What is it?' I said. 'Can I speak to you?' he said."

They listened with rapt attention.

" 'Well, I'll just pop on a dressing-gown,' I said, 'and open the
door.' So I popped on a dressing-gown and opened the door.
The radio-operator said: 'Excuse me, miss, but do you want to
send a radio?' Well, I did think it was funny his coming at that
hour to ask me if I wanted to send a radio, I just laughed in his
face, it appealed to my sense of humour if you understand what I
mean, but I didn't want to hurt his feelings so I said: 'Thank you
so much, but I don't think I want to send a radio.' He stood there,
looking so funny, as if he was quite embarrassed, so I said: 'Thank

you all the same for asking me,' and then I said 'Good-night, pleasant dreams' and shut the door."

"The damned fool," cried the captain.

"He's young, Miss Reid," the doctor put in. "It was excess of zeal. I suppose he thought you would want to send a New Year's greeting to your friends and he wished you to get the advantage of the special rate."

"Oh, I didn't mind at all. I like these queer little things that happen to one when one's travelling. I just get a good laugh out of them."

As soon as dinner was over and Miss Reid had left them the captain sent for the radio-operator.

"You idiot, what in heaven's name made you ask Miss Reid last night whether she wanted to send a radio?"

"Sir, you told me to act naturally. I am a radio-operator. I thought it natural to ask her if she wanted to send a radio. I didn't know what else to say."

"God in heaven," shouted the captain, "when Siegfried saw Brunhilde lying on her rock and cried: *Das ist kein Mann*" (the captain sang the words, and being pleased with the sound of his voice, repeated the phrase two or three times before he continued), "did Siegfried when she awoke ask her if she wished to send a radio, to announce to her papa, I suppose, that she was sitting up after her long sleep and taking notice?"

"I beg most respectfully to draw your attention to the fact that Brunhilde was Siegfried's aunt. Miss Reid is a total stranger to me."

"He did not reflect that she was his aunt. He knew only that she was a beautiful and defenceless woman of obviously good family and he acted as any gentleman would have done. You are young, handsome, Aryan to the tips of your fingers, the honour of Germany is in your hands."

"Very good, sir. I will do my best."

That night there was another knock on Miss Reid's door.

"Who is it?"

"The radio-operator. I have a radio for you, Miss Reid."

"For me?" She was surprised, but it at once occurred to her that one of her fellow-passengers who had got off at Haiti had sent her New Year's greetings. "How very kind people are," she thought. "I'm in bed. Leave it outside the door."

"It needs an answer. Ten words prepaid."

Then it couldn't be a New Year's greeting. Her heart stopped beating. It could only mean one thing; her shop had been burned to the ground. She jumped out of bed.

"Slip it under the door and I'll write the answer and slip it back to you."

The envelope was pushed under the door and as it appeared on the carpet it had really a sinister look. Miss Reid snatched it up and tore the envelope open. The words swam before her eyes and she couldn't for a moment find her spectacles. This is what she read:

"Happy New Year. Stop. Peace and goodwill to all men. Stop. You are very beautiful. Stop. I love you. Stop. I must speak to you. Stop. Signed: Radio Operator."

Miss Reid read this through twice. Then she slowly took off her spectacles and hid them under a scarf. She opened the door.

"Come in," she said.

Next day was New Year's Eve. The officers were cheerful and a little sentimental when they sat down to dinner. The stewards had decorated the saloon with tropical creepers to make up for holly and mistletoe, and the Christmas tree stood on a table with the candles ready to be lit at supper time. Miss Reid did not come in till the officers were seated, and when they bade her good-morning she did not speak but merely bowed. They looked at her curiously. She ate a good dinner, but uttered never a word. Her silence was uncanny. At last the captain could stand it no longer, and he said:

"You're very quiet to-day, Miss Reid."

"I'm thinking," she remarked.

"And will you not tell us your thoughts, Miss Reid?" the doctor asked playfully.

She gave him a cool, you might almost have called it a super-cilious, look.

"I prefer to keep them to myself, Doctor. I will have a little more of that hash, I've got a very good appetite."

They finished the meal in a blessed silence. The captain heaved a sigh of relief. That was what meal-time was for, to eat, not to chatter. When they had finished he went up to the doctor and wrung his hand.

"Something has happened, Doctor."

"It has happened. She's a changed woman."

"But will it last?"

"One can only hope for the best."

Miss Reid put on an evening dress for the evening's celebration, a very quiet black dress, with artificial roses at her bosom and a long string of imitation jade round her neck. The lights were dimmed and the candles on the Christmas tree were lit. It felt a little like being in church. The junior officers were supping in the saloon that evening and they looked very smart in their white uniforms. Champagne was served at the company's expense and after supper they had a *Maibowle*. They pulled crackers. They sang songs to the gramophone, *Deutschland, Deutschland über Alles, Alt Heidelberg* and *Auld Lang Syne*. They shouted out the tunes lustily, the captain's voice rising loud above the others, and Miss Reid joining in with a pleasing contralto. The doctor noticed that Miss Reid's eyes from time to time rested on the radio-operator, and in them he read an expression of some bewilderment.

"He's a good-looking fellow, isn't he?" said the doctor.

Miss Reid turned round and looked at the doctor coolly.

"Who?"

"The radio-operator. I thought you were looking at him."

"Which is he?"

"The duplicity of women," the doctor muttered, but with a smile he answered: "He's sitting next to the chief engineer."

"Oh, of course, I recognise him now. You know, I never think it matters what a man looks like. I'm so much more interested in a man's brains than in his looks."

"Ah," said the doctor.

They all got a little tight, including Miss Reid, but she did not lose her dignity and when she bade them good-night it was in her best manner.

"I've had a very delightful evening. I shall never forget my New Year's Eve on a German boat. It's been very interesting. Quite an experience."

She walked steadily to the door, and this was something of a triumph, for she had drunk drink for drink with the rest of them through the evening.

They were all somewhat jaded next day. When the captain, the mate, the doctor and the chief engineer came down to dinner they found Miss Reid already seated. Before each place was a small parcel tied up in pink ribbon. On each was written: Happy New Year. They gave Miss Reid a questioning glance.

"You've all been so very kind to me I thought I'd like to give each of you a little present. There wasn't much choice at Port au Prince, so you mustn't expect too much."

There was a pair of briar pipes for the captain, half a dozen silk handkerchiefs for the doctor, a cigar-case for the mate and a couple of ties for the chief engineer. They had dinner and Miss Reid retired to her cabin to rest. The officers looked at one another uncomfortably. The mate fiddled with the cigar-case she had given him.

"I'm a little ashamed of myself," he said at last.

The captain was pensive and it was plain that he too was a trifle uneasy.

"I wonder if we ought to have played that trick on Miss Reid," he said. "She's a good old soul and she's not rich; she's a woman who earns her own living. She must have spent the best part of a hundred marks on these presents. I almost wish we'd left her alone."

The doctor shrugged his shoulders.

"You wanted her silenced and I've silenced her."

"When all's said and done, it wouldn't have hurt us to listen to her chatter for three weeks more," said the mate.

"I'm not happy about her," added the captain. "I feel there's something ominous in her quietness."

She had spoken hardly a word during the meal they had just shared with her. She seemed hardly to listen to what they said.

"Don't you think you ought to ask her if she's feeling quite well, doctor?" suggested the captain.

"Of course she's feeling quite well. She's eating like a wolf. If you want enquiries made you'd much better make them of the radio-operator."

"You may not be aware of it, Doctor, but I am a man of great delicacy."

"I am a man of heart myself," said the doctor.

For the rest of the journey those men spoilt Miss Reid outrageously. They treated her with the consideration they would have shown to someone who was convalescent after a long and dangerous illness. Though her appetite was excellent they sought to tempt her with new dishes. The doctor ordered wine and insisted on her sharing his bottle with him. They played dominoes with her. They played chess with her. They played bridge with her. They engaged her in conversation. But there was no doubt about it, though she responded to their advances with politeness, she kept herself to herself. She seemed to regard them with something very like disdain; you might almost have thought that she looked upon those men and their efforts to be amiable as pleasantly ridiculous. She seldom spoke unless spoken to. She read detective stories and at night sat on deck looking at the stars. She lived a life of her own.

At last the journey drew to its close. They sailed up the English Channel on a still grey day; they sighted land. Miss Reid packed her trunk. At two o'clock in the afternoon they docked at Plymouth. The captain, the mate and the doctor came along to say good-bye to her.

"Well, Miss Reid," said the captain in his jovial way, "we're sorry to lose you, but I suppose you're glad to be getting home."

"You've been very kind to me, you've all been very kind to me, I don't know what I've done to deserve it. I've been very happy with you. I shall never forget you."

She spoke rather shakily, she tried to smile, but her lips quivered, and tears ran down her cheeks. The captain got very red. He smiled awkwardly.

"May I kiss you, Miss Reid?"

She was taller than he by half a head. She bent down and he planted a fat kiss on one wet cheek and a fat kiss on the other. She turned to the mate and the doctor. They both kissed her.

"What an old fool I am," she said. "Everybody's so good."

She dried her eyes and slowly, in her graceful, rather absurd way, walked down the companion. The captain's eyes were wet. When she reached the quay she looked up and waved to someone on the boat deck.

"Who's she waving to?" asked the captain.

"The radio-operator."

Miss Price was waiting on the quay to welcome her. When they had passed the Customs and got rid of Miss Reid's heavy luggage they went to Miss Price's house and had an early cup of tea. Miss Reid's train did not start till five. Miss Price had much to tell Miss Reid.

"But it's too bad of me to go on like this when you've just come home. I've been looking forward to hearing all about your journey."

"I'm afraid there's not very much to tell."

"I can't believe that. Your trip was a success, wasn't it?"

"A distinct success. It was very nice."

"And you didn't mind being with all those Germans?"

"Of course they're not like English people. One had to get used to their ways. They sometimes do things that—well, that English people wouldn't do, you know. But I always think that one has to take things as they come."

"What sort of things do you mean?"

Miss Reid looked at her friend calmly. Her long, stupid face had a placid look, and Miss Price never noticed that in the eyes was a strangely mischievous twinkle.

"Things of no importance really. Just funny, unexpected, rather nice things. There's no doubt that travel is a wonderful education."

Mabel

I WAS at Pagan, in Burma, and from there I took the steamer to Mandalay, but a couple of days before I got there, when the boat tied up for the night at a riverside village, I made up my mind to go ashore. The skipper told me that there was there a pleasant iittle club in which I had only to make myself at home; they were quite used to having strangers drop off like that from the steamer, and the secretary was a very decent chap; I might even get a game of bridge. I had nothing in the world to do, so I got into one of the bullock-carts that were waiting at the landing-stage and was driven to the club. There was a man sitting on the verandah and as I walked up he nodded to me and asked whether I would have a whisky and soda or a gin and bitters. The possibility that I would have nothing at all did not even occur to him. I chose the longer drink and sat down. He was a tall, thin, bronzed man, with a big moustache, and he wore khaki shorts and a khaki shirt. I never knew his name, but when we had been chatting a little while another man came in who told me he was the secretary, and he addressed my friend as George.

"Have you heard from your wife yet?" he asked him.

The other's eyes brightened.

"Yes, I had letters by this mail. She's having no end of a time."

"Did she tell you not to fret?"

George gave a little chuckle, but was I mistaken in thinking that there was in it the shadow of a sob?

"In point of fact she did. But that's easier said than done. Of course I know she wants a holiday, and I'm glad she should have it, but it's devilish hard on a chap." He turned to me. "You see, this is the first time I've ever been separated from my missus, and I'm like a lost dog without her."

"How long have you been married?"

"Five minutes."

The secretary of the club laughed.

"Don't be a fool, George. You've been married eight years."

After we had talked for a little, George, looking at his watch, said he must go and change his clothes for dinner and left us. The secretary watched him disappear into the night with a smile of not unkindly irony.

"We all ask him as much as we can now that he's alone," he told me. "He mopes so terribly since his wife went home."

"It must be very pleasant for her to know that her husband is as devoted to her as all that."

"Mabel is a remarkable woman."

He called the boy and ordered more drinks. In this hospitable place they did not ask you if you would have anything; they took it for granted. Then he settled himself in his long chair and lit a cheroot. He told me the story of George and Mabel.

They became engaged when he was home on leave, and when he returned to Burma it was arranged that she should join him in six months. But one difficulty cropped up after another; Mabel's father died, the war came, George was sent to a district unsuitable for a white woman; so that in the end it was seven years before she was able to start. He made all arrangements for the marriage, which was to take place on the day of her arrival, and went down to Rangoon to meet her. On the morning on which the ship was due he borrowed a motor-car and drove along to the dock. He paced the quay.

Then, suddenly, without warning, his nerve failed him. He had not seen Mabel for seven years. He had forgotten what she was like. She was a total stranger. He felt a terrible sinking in the pit of his stomach and his knees began to wobble. He couldn't go through with it. He must tell Mabel that he was very sorry, but he couldn't, he really couldn't marry her. But how could a man tell a girl a thing like that when she had been engaged to him for seven years and had come six thousand miles to marry him? He hadn't the nerve for that either. George was seized with the courage of despair. There was a boat at the quay on the very point of starting for Singapore; he wrote a hurried letter to Mabel, and without a stick of luggage, just in the clothes he stood up in, leaped on board.

The letter Mabel received ran somewhat as follows:

Dearest Mabel, I have been suddenly called away on business and do not know when I shall be back. I think it would be much wiser if you returned to England. My plans are very uncertain. Your loving George.

But when he arrived at Singapore he found a cable waiting for him.

Quite understand. Don't worry. Love. Mabel.

Terror made him quick-witted.

"By Jove, I believe she's following me," he said.

He telegraphed to the shipping-office at Rangoon and sure enough her name was on the passenger list of the ship that was now on its way to Singapore. There was not a moment to lose. He jumped on the train to Bangkok. But he was uneasy; she would have no difficulty in finding out that he had gone to Bangkok and it was just as simple for her to take the train as it had been for him. Fortunately there was a French tramp sailing next day for Saigon. He took it. At Saigon he would be safe; it would never occur to her that he had gone there; and if it did, surely by now she would have taken the hint. It is five days' journey from Bangkok to Saigon and the boat is dirty, cramped and uncomfortable. He was glad to arrive and took a rickshaw to the hotel. He signed his name in the visitors' book and a telegram was immediately handed to him. It contained but two words: *Love. Mabel*. They were enough to make him break into a cold sweat.

"When is the next boat for Hong-Kong?" he asked.

Now his flight grew serious. He sailed to Hong-Kong, but dared not stay there; he went to Manila; Manila was ominous; he went on to Shanghai: Shanghai was nerve-racking; every time he went out of the hotel he expected to run straight into Mabel's arms; no, Shanghai would never do. The only thing was to go to Yokohama. At the Grand Hotel at Yokohama a cable awaited him.

Sorry to have missed you at Manila. Love. Mabel.

He scanned the shipping intelligence with a fevered brow. Where was she now? He doubled back to Shanghai. This time he went straight to the club and asked for a telegram. It was handed to him.

Arriving shortly. Love. Mabel.

No, no, he was not so easy to catch as all that. He had already made his plans. The Yangtse is a long river and the Yangtse was falling. He could just about catch the last steamer that could get up to Chungking and then no one could travel till the following spring except by junk. Such a journey was out of the question for a woman alone. He went to Hankow and from Hankow to Ichang, he changed boats here and from Ichang through the rapids went to Chungking. But he was desperate now, he was not going to take any risks: there was a place called Cheng-tu, the capital of Szechuan, and it was four hundred miles away. It could only be reached by road, and the road was infested with brigands. A man would be safe there.

George collected chair-bearers and coolies and set out. It was with a sigh of relief that he saw at last the crenellated walls of the lonely Chinese city. From those walls at sunset you could see the snowy mountains of Tibet.

He could rest at last: Mabel would never find him there. The consul happened to be a friend of his and he stayed with him. He enjoyed the comfort of a luxurious house, he enjoyed his idleness after that strenuous escape across Asia, and above all he enjoyed his divine security. The weeks passed lazily one after the other.

One morning George and the consul were in the courtyard looking at some curios that a Chinese had brought for their inspection when there was a loud knocking at the great door of the Consulate. The door-man flung it open. A chair borne by four coolies entered, advanced, and was set down. Mabel stepped out. She was neat and cool and fresh. There was nothing in her appearance to suggest that she had just come in after a fortnight on the road. George was petrified. He was as pale as death. She went up to him.

"Hulloa, George, I was so afraid I'd missed you again."

"Hulloa, Mabel," he faltered.

He did not know what to say. He looked this way and that: she stood between him and the doorway. She looked at him with a smile in her blue eyes.

"You haven't altered at all," she said. "Men can go off so dreadfully in seven years and I was afraid you'd got fat and bald. I've been so nervous. It would have been terrible if after all these years I simply hadn't been able to bring myself to marry you after all."

She turned to George's host.

"Are you the consul?" she asked.

"I am."

"That's all right. I'm ready to marry him as soon as I've had a bath."

And she did.

Masterson

WHEN I left Colombo I had no notion of going to Keng Tung, but on the ship I met a man who told me he had spent five years there. He said it had an important market, held every five days, whither came natives of half a dozen countries and members of half a hundred tribes. It had pagodas darkly splendid and a remoteness that liberated the questing spirit from its anxiety. He said he would sooner live there than anywhere in the world. I asked him what it had offered him and he said, contentment. He was a tall, dark fellow with the aloofness of manner you often find in those who have lived much alone in unfrequented places. Men like this are a little restless in the company of others and though in the smoking-room of a ship or at the club bar they may be talkative and convivial, telling their story with the rest, joking and glad sometimes to narrate their unusual experiences, they seem always to hold something back. They have a life in themselves that they keep apart, and there is a look in their eyes, as it were turned inwards, that informs you that this hidden life is the only one that signifies to them. And now and then their eyes betray their weariness with the social round into which hazard or the fear of seeming odd has for a moment forced them. They seem often to long for the monotonous solitude of some place of their predilection where they can be once more alone with the reality they have found.

It was as much the manner of this chance acquaintance as what he told me that persuaded me to make the journey across the Shan States on which I now set out. From the rail-head in Upper Burma to the rail-head in Siam, whence I could get down to Bangkok, it was between six and seven hundred miles. Kind people had done everything possible to render the excursion easy for me and the President at Taunggyi had wired to me that he had made arrangements for mules and ponies to be ready for me on my arrival. I had bought in Rangoon such stores as seemed necessary, folding chairs and a table, a filter, lamps and I know not what. I took the train from Mandalay to Thazi, intending there to hire a car for Taunggyi, and a man I had met at the club at Mandalay and who lived at Thazi asked me to have brunch (the pleasant meal of Burma that combines breakfast and lunch) with him before I started. His name was Masterson. He was a man in the early thirties, with a pleasant friendly face, curling dark hair speckled with grey, and handsome dark eyes. He spoke with a singularly musical voice, very slowly, and this, I hardly know why, inspired you with confidence. You felt that a man who took such a long time to say what he had to say and had found the world with sufficient leisure to listen to him must have qualities that made him sympathetic to his fellows. He took the amiability of mankind for granted and I suppose he could only have done this because he was himself amiable. He had a nice sense of humour, without of course a quick thrust and parry, but agreeably sarcastic; it was of that agreeable type that applies common sense to the accidents of life and so sees them in a faintly ridiculous aspect. He was engaged in a business that kept him travelling up and down Burma most of the year and in his journeyings he had acquired the collector's habit. He told me that he spent all his spare money on buying Burmese curiosities and it was especially to see them that he asked me to have a meal with him.

The train got in early in the morning. He had warned me that, having to be at his office, he could not meet me; but brunch was at ten and he told me to go to his house as soon as I was finished with the one or two things I had to do in the town.

"Make yourself at home," he said, "and if you want a drink ask the boy for it. I'll get back as soon as I've got through with my business."

I found out where there was a garage and made a bargain with the owner of a very dilapidated Ford to take me and my baggage to Taunggyi. I left my Madrassi servant to see that everything was stowed in it that was possible and the rest tied on to the footboards, and strolled along to Masterson's house. It was a neat little bungalow in a road shaded by tall trees, and in the early light of a sunny day looked pretty and homelike. I walked up the steps and was hailed by Masterson.

"I got done more quickly than I expected. I shall have time to show you my things before brunch is ready. What will you have? I'm afraid I can only offer you a whisky and soda."

"Isn't it rather early for that?"

"Rather. But it's one of the rules of the house that nobody crosses the threshold without having a drink."

"What can I do but submit to the rule?"

He called the boy and in a moment a trim Burmese brought in a decanter, a syphon and glasses. I sat down and looked about the room. Though it was still so early the sun was hot outside and the jalousies were drawn. The light was pleasant and cool after the glare of the road. The room was comfortably furnished with rattan chairs and on the walls were water-colour paintings of English scenes. They were a little prim and old-fashioned and I guessed that they had been painted in her youth by the maiden and elderly aunt of my host. There were two of a cathedral I did not know, two or three of a rose garden and one of a Georgian house. When he saw my eyes for an instant rest upon this, he said:

"That was our house at Cheltenham."

"Oh, is that where you come from?"

Then there was his collection. The room was crowded with Buddhas and with figures, in bronze or wood, of the Buddha's disciples; there were boxes of all shapes, utensils of one kind and another, curiosities of every sort, and although there were far too many they were arranged with a certain taste so that the effect was pleasing. He had some lovely things. He showed them to me with pride, telling me how he had got this object and that, and how he had heard of another and hunted it down and the incredible astuteness he had employed to induce an unwilling owner to part with it. His kindly eyes shone when he described a great bargain and they flashed darkly when he inveighed against the unreasonableness of a vendor who rather than accept a fair price for a bronze dish had taken it away. There were flowers in the room, and it had not the forlorn look that so many bachelors' houses have in the East.

"You've made the place very comfortable," I said.

He gave the room a sweeping glance.

"It *was* all right. It's not much now."

I did not quite know what he meant. Then he showed me a long wooden gilt box, decorated with the glass mosaic that I had admired in the palace at Mandalay, but the workmanship was more delicate than anything I had seen there, and this with its gem-like richness had really something of the ornate exquisiteness of the Italian Renaissance.

"They tell me it's about a couple of hundred years old," he said. "They've not been able to turn out anything like this for a long time."

It was a piece made obviously for a king's palace and you wondered to what uses it had been put and what hands it had passed through. It was a jewel.

"What is the inside like?" I asked.

"Oh, nothing much. It's just lacquered."

He opened it and I saw that it contained three or four framed photographs.

"Oh, I'd forgotten those were there," he said.

His soft, musical voice had a queer sound in it, and I gave him a sidelong look. He was bronzed by the sun, but his face notwithstanding flushed a deeper red. He was about to close the box, and then he changed his mind. He took out one of the photographs and showed it to me.

"Some of these Burmese girls are rather sweet when they're young, aren't they?" he said.

The photograph showed a young girl standing somewhat self-consciously against the conventional background of a photographer's studio, a pagoda and a group of palm-trees. She was wearing her best clothes and she had a flower in her hair. But the embarrassment you saw she felt at having her picture taken did not prevent a shy smile from trembling on her lips and her large solemn eyes had nevertheless a roguish twinkle. She was very small and very slender.

"What a ravishing little thing," I said.

Then Masterson took out another photograph in which she sat with a child standing by her side, his hand timidly on her knee and a baby in her arms. The child stared straight in front of him with a look of terror on his face; he could not understand what that machine and the man behind it, his head under a black cloth, were up to.

"Are those her children?" I asked.

"And mine," said Masterson.

At that moment the boy came in to say that brunch was ready. We went into the dining-room and sat down.

"I don't know what you'll get to eat. Since my girl went away everything in the house has gone to blazes."

A sulky look came into his red honest face and I did not know what to reply.

"I'm so hungry that whatever I get will seem good," I hazarded.

He did not say anything and a plate of thin porridge was put before us. I helped myself to milk and sugar. Masterson ate a spoonful or two and pushed his plate aside.

"I wish I hadn't looked at those damned photographs," he said. "I put them away on purpose."

I did not want to be inquisitive or to force a confidence my host had no wish to give, but neither did I desire to seem so unconcerned as to prevent him from telling me something he had in his heart. Often in some lonely post in the jungle or in a stiff grand house, solitary in the midst of a teeming Chinese city, a man has told me stories about himself that I was sure he had never told to a living soul. I was a stray acquaintance whom he had never seen before and would never see again, a wanderer for a moment through his monotonous life, and some starved impulse led him to lay bare his soul. I have in this way learned more about men in a night (sitting over a syphon or two and a bottle of whisky, the hostile, inexplicable world outside the radius of an acetylene lamp) than I could have if I had known them for ten years. If you are interested in human nature it is one of the great pleasures of travel. And when you separate (for you have to be up betimes) sometimes they will say to you:

"I'm afraid I've bored you to death with all this nonsense. I haven't talked so much for six months. But it's done me good to get it off my chest."

The boy removed the porridge plates and gave each of us a piece of pale fried fish. It was rather cold.

"The fish is beastly, isn't it?" said Masterson. "I hate river fish, except trout; the only thing is to smother it with Worcester sauce."

He helped himself freely and passed me the bottle.

"She was a damned good housekeeper, my girl; I used to feed like a fighting-cock when she was here. She'd have had the cook out of the house in a quarter of an hour if he'd sent in muck like this."

He gave me a smile, and I noticed that his smile was very sweet. It gave him a peculiarly gentle look.

"It was rather a wrench parting with her, you know."

It was quite evident now that he wished to talk and I had no hesitation in giving him a lead.

"Did you have a row?"

"No. You could hardly call it a row. She lived with me five years and we never had a tiff even. She was the best-tempered little thing that ever was. Nothing seemed to put her out. She was always as merry as a cricket. You couldn't look at her without her lips breaking into a smile. She was always happy. And there was no reason why she shouldn't be. I was very good to her."

"I'm sure you were," I answered.

"She was mistress here. I gave her everything she wanted. Perhaps if I'd been more of a brute she wouldn't have gone away."

"Don't make me say anything so obvious as that women are incalculable."

He gave me a deprecating glance and there was a trace of shyness in the smile that just flickered in his eyes.

"Would it bore you awfully if I told you about it?"

"Of course not."

"Well, I saw her one day in the street and she rather took my fancy. I showed you her photograph, but the photograph doesn't begin to do her justice. It sounds silly to say about a Burmese girl, but she was like a rose-bud, not an English rose, you know, she was as little like that as the glass flowers on that box I showed you are like real flowers, but a rose grown in an Eastern garden that had something strange and exotic about it. I don't know how to make myself plain."

"I think I understand what you mean all the same," I smiled.

"I saw her two or three times and found out where she lived. I sent my boy to make enquiries about her, and he told me that her parents were quite willing that I should have her if we could come to an arrangement. I wasn't inclined to haggle and everything was settled in no time. Her family gave a party to celebrate the occasion and she came to live here. Of course I treated her in every way as my wife and put her in charge of the house. I told the boys that they'd got to take their orders from her and if she complained of any of them out they went. You know, some fellows keep their girls in the servants' quarters and when they go away on tour the girls have a rotten time. Well, I think that's a filthy thing to do. If you are going to have a girl to live with you the least you can do is to see that she has a good time.

"She was a great success and I was as pleased as Punch. She kept the house spotless. She saved me money. She wouldn't let the boys rob me. I taught her to play bridge and, believe me, she learned to play a damned good game."

"Did she like it?"

"Loved it. When people came here she couldn't have received them better if she'd been a duchess. You know, these Burmese have beautiful manners. Sometimes it would make me laugh to see the assurance with which she would receive my guests, government officials, you know, and soldiers who were passing through. If some young subaltern was rather shy she'd put him at his ease at once. She was never pushing or obtrusive, but just there when she was wanted and doing her best to see that everything went well and everyone had a good time. And I'll tell you what, she could mix the best cocktail you'd get anywhere between Rangoon and Bhamo. People used to say I was lucky."

"I'm bound to say I think you were," I said.

The curry was served and I piled my plate with rice and helped myself to chicken and then chose from a dozen little dishes the condiments I fancied. It was a good curry.

"Then she had her babies, three in three years, but one died

when it was six weeks old. I showed you a photograph of the two
that are living. Funny-looking little things, aren't they? Are you
fond of children?"

"Yes. I have a strange and almost unnatural passion for new-born
babies."

"I don't think I am, you know. I couldn't even feel very much
about my own. I've often wondered if it showed that I was rather a
rotter."

"I don't think so. I think the passion many people affect for
children is merely a fashionable pose. I have a notion that children
are all the better for not being burdened with too much parental
love."

"Then my girl asked me to marry her, legally I mean, in the
English way. I treated it as a joke. I didn't know how she'd got
such an idea in her head. I thought it was only a whim and I gave
her a gold bracelet to keep her quiet. But it wasn't a whim. She
was quite serious about it. I told her there was nothing doing.
But you know what women are, when they once set their mind
on getting something they never give you a moment's peace. She
wheedled and sulked, she cried, she appealed to my compassion,
she tried to extract a promise out of me when I was rather tight,
she was on the watch for me when I was feeling amorous, she nearly
tripped me when she was ill. She watched me more carefully,
I should think, than a stockbroker ever watched the market,
and I knew that, however natural she seemed, however occupied
with something else, she was always warily alert for the unguarded
moment when she could pounce on me and gain her point."

Masterson gave me once more his slow, ingenuous smile.

"I suppose women are pretty much the same all the world over,"
he said.

"I expect so," I answered.

"A thing I've never been able to understand is why a woman
thinks it worth while to make you do something you don't want
to. She'd rather you did a thing against the grain than not do it at
all. I don't see what satisfaction it can be to them."

"The satisfaction of triumph. A man convinced against his
will may be of the same opinion still, but a woman doesn't mind
that. She has conquered. She has proved her power."

Masterson shrugged his shoulders. He drank a cup of tea.

"You see, she said that sooner or later I was bound to marry an
English girl and turn her out. I said I wasn't thinking of marrying.
She said she knew all about that. And even if I didn't I should
retire some day and go back to England. And where would she

be then? It went on for a year. I held out. Then she said that if I wouldn't marry her she'd go and take the kids with her. I told her not to be a silly little fool. She said that if she left me now she could marry a Burman, but in a few years nobody would want her. She began to pack her things. I thought it was only a bluff and I called it: I said: 'Well, go if you want to, but if you do you won't come back.' I didn't think she'd give up a house like this, and the presents I made her, and all the pickings, to go back to her own family. They were as poor as church mice. Well, she went on packing her things. She was just as nice as ever to me, she was gay and smiling; when some fellows came to spend the night here she was just as cordial as usual, and she played bridge with us till two in the morning. I couldn't believe she meant to go and yet I was rather scared. I was very fond of her. She was a damned good sort."

"But if you were fond of her why on earth didn't you marry her? It had been a great success."

"I'll tell you. If I married her I'd have to stay in Burma for the rest of my life. Sooner or later I shall retire and then I want to go back to my old home and live there. I don't want to be buried out here, I want to be buried in an English churchyard. I'm happy enough here, but I don't want to live here always. I couldn't. I want England. Sometimes I get sick of this hot sunshine and these garish colours. I want grey skies and a soft rain falling and the smell of the country. I shall be a funny fat elderly man when I go back, too old to hunt even if I could afford it, but I can fish. I don't want to shoot tigers, I want to shoot rabbits. And I can play golf on a proper course. I know I shall be out of it, we fellows who've spent our lives out here always are, but I can potter about the local club and talk to retired Anglo-Indians. I want to feel under my feet the grey pavement of an English country town, I want to be able to go and have a row with the butcher because the steak he sent me in yesterday was tough, and I want to browse about second-hand bookshops. I want to be said how d'you do to in the street by people who knew me when I was a boy. And I want to have a walled garden at the back of my house and grow roses. I dare say it all sounds very humdrum and provincial and dull to you, but that's the sort of life my people have always lived and that's the sort of life I want to live myself. It's a dream if you like, but it's all I have, it means everything in the world to me, and I can't give it up."

He paused for a moment and looked into my eyes.

"Do you think me an awful fool?"

"No."

"Then one morning she came to me and said that she was off. She had her things put on a cart and even then I didn't think she meant it. Then she put the two children in a rickshaw and came to say good-bye to me. She began to cry. By George, that pretty well broke me up. I asked her if she really meant to go and she said yes, unless I married her. I shook my head. I very nearly yielded. I'm afraid I was crying too. Then she gave a great sob and ran out of the house. I had to drink about half a tumbler of whisky to steady my nerves."

"How long ago did this happen?"

"Four months. At first I thought she'd come back and then because I thought she was ashamed to make the first step I sent my boy to tell her that if she wanted to come I'd take her. But she refused. The house seemed awfully empty without her. At first I thought I'd get used to it, but somehow it doesn't seem to get any less empty. I didn't know how much she meant to me. She'd twined herself round my heart."

"I suppose she'll come back if you agree to marry her."

"Oh, yes, she told the boy that. Sometimes I ask myself if it's worth while to sacrifice my happiness for a dream. It is only a dream, isn't it? It's funny, one of the things that holds me back is the thought of a muddy lane I know, with great clay banks on both sides of it, and above, beech trees bending over. It's got a sort of cold, earthy smell that I can never quite get out of my nostrils. I don't blame her, you know. I rather admire her. I had no idea she had so much character. Sometimes I'm awfully inclined to give way." He hesitated for a little while. "I think, perhaps, if I thought she loved me I would. But of course, she doesn't; they never do, these girls who go and live with white men, I think she liked me, but that's all. What would you do in my place?"

"Oh, my dear fellow, how can I tell? Would you ever forget that dream?"

"Never."

At that moment the boy came in to say that my Madrassi servant with the Ford car had just come up. Masterson looked at his watch.

"You'll want to be getting off, won't you? And I must get back to my office. I'm afraid I've rather bored you with my domestic affairs."

"Not at all," I said.

We shook hands, I put on my topee, and he waved to me as the car drove off.

Princess September

FIRST the King of Siam had two daughters and he called them Night and Day. Then he had two more, so he changed the names of the first ones and called the four of them after the seasons, Spring and Autumn, Winter and Summer. But in course of time he had three others and he changed their names again and called all seven by the days of the week. But when his eighth daughter was born he did not know what to do till he suddenly thought of the months of the year. The Queen said there were only twelve and it confused her to have to remember so many new names, but the King had a methodical mind and when he made it up he never could change it if he tried. He changed the names of all his daughters and called them January, February, March (though of course in Siamese) till he came to the youngest, who was called August, and the next one was called September.

"That only leaves October, November, and December," said the Queen. "And after that we shall have to begin all over again."

"No, we shan't," said the King, "because I think twelve daughters are enough for any man and after the birth of dear little December I shall be reluctantly compelled to cut off your head."

He cried bitterly when he said this, for he was extremely fond of the Queen. Of course it made the Queen very uneasy because she knew that it would distress the King very much if he had to cut off her head. And it would not be very nice for her. But it so happened that there was no need for either of them to worry because September was the last daughter they ever had. The Queen only had sons after that and they were called by the letters of the alphabet, so there was no cause for anxiety there for a long time, since she had only reached the letter J.

Now the King of Siam's daughters had had their characters permanently embittered by having to change their names in this way, and the older ones, whose names of course had been changed oftener than the others, had their characters more permanently embittered. But September, who had never known what it was to be called anything but September (except of course by her sisters, who because their characters were embittered called her all sorts of names), had a very sweet and charming nature.

The King of Siam had a habit which I think might be usefully imitated in Europe. Instead of receiving presents on his birthday he gave them and it looks as though he liked it, for he used often to say he was sorry he had only been born on one day and so only had one birthday in the year. But in this way he managed in course of time to give away all his wedding presents and the loyal addresses which the mayors of the cities in Siam presented him with and all his own crowns which had gone out of fashion. One year on his birthday, not having anything else handy, he gave each of his daughters a beautiful green parrot in a beautiful golden cage. There were nine of them and on each cage was written the name of the month which was the name of the princess it belonged to. The nine princesses were very proud of their parrots and they spent an hour every day (for like their father they were of a methodical turn of mind) in teaching them to talk. Presently all the parrots could say God Save the King (in Siamese, which is very difficult) and some of them could say Pretty Polly in no less than seven oriental languages. But one day when the Princess September went to say good-morning to her parrot she found it lying dead at the bottom of its golden cage. She burst into a flood of tears, and nothing that her Maids of Honour could say comforted her. She cried so much that the Maids of Honour, not knowing what to do, told the Queen, and the Queen said it was stuff and nonsense and the child had better go to bed without any supper. The Maids of Honour wanted to go to a party, so they put the Princess September to bed as quickly as they could and left her by herself. And while she lay in her bed, crying still even though she felt rather hungry, she saw a little bird hop into her room. She took her thumb out of her mouth and sat up. Then the little bird began to sing and he sang a beautiful song all about the lake in the King's garden and the willow trees that looked at themselves in the still water and the goldfish that glided in and out of the branches that were reflected in it. When he had finished, the Princess was not crying any more and she quite forgot that she had had no supper.

"That was a very nice song," she said.

The little bird gave her a bow, for artists have naturally good manners, and they like to be appreciated.

"Would you care to have me instead of your parrot?" said the little bird. "It's true that I'm not so pretty to look at, but on the other hand I have a much better voice."

The Princess September clapped her hands with delight and then the little bird hopped on to the end of her bed and sang her to sleep.

When she awoke next day the little bird was still sitting there, and as she opened her eyes he said good-morning. The Maids of

Honour brought in her breakfast, and he ate rice out of her hand and he had his bath in her saucer. He drank out of it too. The Maids of Honour said they didn't think it was very polite to drink one's bath water, but the Princess September said that was the artistic temperament. When he had finished his breakfast he began to sing again so beautifully that the Maids of Honour were quite surprised, for they had never heard anything like it, and the Princess September was very proud and happy.

"Now I want to show you to my eight sisters," said the Princess.

She stretched out the first finger of her right hand so that it served as a perch and the little bird flew down and sat on it. Then, followed by her Maids of Honour, she went through the palace and called on each of the Princesses in turn, starting with January, for she was mindful of etiquette, and going all the way down to August. And for each of the Princesses the little bird sang a different song. But the parrots could only say God Save the King and Pretty Polly. At last she showed the little bird to the King and Queen. They were surprised and delighted.

"I knew I was right to send you to bed without any supper," said the Queen.

"This bird sings much better than the parrots," said the King.

"I should have thought you got quite tired of hearing people say God Save the King," said the Queen. "I can't think why those girls wanted to teach their parrots to say it too."

"The sentiment is admirable," said the King, "and I never mind how often I hear it. But I do get tired of hearing those parrots say Pretty Polly."

"They say it in seven different languages," said the Princesses.

"I dare say they do," said the King, "but it reminds me too much of my councillors. They say the same thing in seven different ways and it never means anything in any way they say it."

The Princesses, their characters as I have already said being naturally embittered, were vexed at this, and the parrots looked very glum indeed. But the Princess September ran through all the rooms of the palace, singing like a lark, while the little bird flew round and round her, singing like a nightingale, which indeed it was.

Things went on like this for several days and then the eight Princesses put their heads together. They went to September and sat down in a circle round her, hiding their feet as is proper for Siamese princesses to do.

"My poor September," they said. "We are sorry for the death of your beautiful parrot. It must be dreadful for you not to have a pet bird as we have. So we have all put our pocket-money together and we are going to buy you a lovely green and yellow parrot."

"Thank you for nothing," said September. (This was not very civil of her, but Siamese princesses are sometimes a little short with one another.) "I have a pet bird which sings the most charming songs to me and I don't know what on earth I should do with a green and yellow parrot."

January sniffed, then February sniffed, then March sniffed; in fact all the Princesses sniffed, but in their proper order of precedence. When they had finished September asked them:

"Why do you sniff? Have you all got colds in the head?"

"Well, my dear," they said, "it's absurd to talk of *your* bird when the little fellow flies in and out just as he likes." They looked round the room and raised their eyebrows so high that their foreheads entirely disappeared.

"You'll get dreadful wrinkles," said September.

"Do you mind our asking where your bird is now?" they said.

"He's gone to pay a visit to his father-in-law," said the Princess September.

"And what makes you think he'll come back?" asked the Princesses.

"He always does come back," said September.

"Well, my dear," said the eight Princesses, "if you'll take our advice you won't run any risks like that. If he comes back, and mind you, if he does you'll be lucky, pop him into the cage and keep him there. That's the only way you can be sure of him."

"But I like to have him fly about the room," said the Princess September.

"Safety first," said her sisters ominously.

They got up and walked out of the room, shaking their heads, and they left September very uneasy. It seemed to her that her little bird was away a long time and she could not think what he was doing. Something might have happened to him. What with hawks and men with snares you never knew what trouble he might get into. Besides, he might forget her, or he might take a fancy to somebody else; that would be dreadful; oh, she wished he were safely back again, and in the golden cage that stood there empty and ready. For when the Maids of Honour had buried the dead parrot they had left the cage in its old place.

Suddenly September heard a tweet-tweet just behind her ear and she saw the little bird sitting on her shoulder. He had come in so quietly and alighted so softly that she had not heard him.

"I wondered what on earth had become of you," said the Princess.

"I thought you'd wonder that," said the little bird. "The fact is I very nearly didn't come back to-night at all. My father-in-law was giving a party and they all wanted me to stay, but I thought you'd be anxious."

Under the circumstances this was a very unfortunate remark for the little bird to make.

September felt her heart go thump, thump against her chest, and she made up her mind to take no more risks. She put up her hand and took hold of the bird. This he was quite used to, she liked feeling his heart go pit-a-pat, so fast, in the hollow of her hand, and I think he liked the soft warmth of her little hand. So the bird suspected nothing and he was so surprised when she carried him over to the cage, popped him in, and shut the door on him for a moment he could think of nothing to say. But in a moment or two he hopped up on the ivory perch and said:

"What is the joke?"

"There's no joke," said September, "but some of mamma's cats are prowling about to-night, and I think you're much safer in there."

"I can't think why the Queen wants to have all those cats," said the little bird, rather crossly.

"Well, you see, they're very special cats," said the Princess, "they have blue eyes and a kink in their tails, and they're a speciality of the royal family, if you understand what I mean."

"Perfectly," said the little bird, "but why did you put me in this cage without saying anything about it? I don't think it's the sort of place I like."

"I shouldn't have slept a wink all night if I hadn't known you were safe."

"Well, just for this once I don't mind," said the little bird, "so long as you let me out in the morning."

He ate a very good supper and then began to sing. But in the middle of his song he stopped.

"I don't know what is the matter with me," he said, "but I don't feel like singing to-night."

"Very well," said September, "go to sleep instead."

So he put his head under his wing and in a minute was fast asleep. September went to sleep too. But when the dawn broke she was awakened by the little bird calling her at the top of his voice:

"Wake up, wake up," he said. "Open the door of this cage

and let me out. I want to have a good fly while the dew is still on the ground."

"You're much better off where you are," said September. "You have a beautiful golden cage. It was made by the best workman in my papa's kingdom, and my papa was so pleased with it that he cut off his head so that he should never make another."

"Let me out, let me out," said the little bird.

"You'll have three meals a day served by my Maids of Honour; you'll have nothing to worry you from morning till night, and you can sing to your heart's content."

"Let me out, let me out," said the little bird. And he tried to slip through the bars of the cage, but of course he couldn't, and he beat against the door but of course he couldn't open it. Then the eight Princesses came in and looked at him. They told September she was very wise to take their advice. They said he would soon get used to the cage and in a few days would quite forget that he had ever been free. The little bird said nothing at all while they were there, but as soon as they were gone he began to cry again: "Let me out, let me out."

"Don't be such an old silly," said September. "I've only put you in the cage because I'm so fond of you. I know what's good for you much better than you do yourself. Sing me a little song and I'll give you a piece of brown sugar."

But the little bird stood in the corner of his cage, looking out at the blue sky, and never sang a note. He never sang all day.

"What's the good of sulking?" said September. "Why don't you sing and forget your troubles?"

"How can I sing?" answered the bird. "I want to see the trees and the lake and the green rice growing in the fields."

"If that's all you want I'll take you for a walk," said September.

She picked up the cage and went out and she walked down to the lake round which grew the willow trees, and she stood at the edge of the rice-fields that stretched as far as the eye could see.

"I'll take you out every day," she said. "I love you and I only want to make you happy."

"It's not the same thing," said the little bird. "The rice-fields and the lake and the willow trees look quite different when you see them through the bars of a cage."

So she brought him home again and gave him his supper. But he wouldn't eat a thing. The Princess was a little anxious at this, and asked her sisters what they thought about it.

"You must be firm," they said.

"But if he won't eat, he'll die," she answered.

"That would be very ungrateful of him," they said. "He must know that you're only thinking of his own good. If he's obstinate and dies it'll serve him right and you'll be well rid of him."

September didn't see how that was going to do *her* very much good, but they were eight to one and all older than she, so she said nothing.

"Perhaps he'll have got used to his cage by to-morrow," she said.

And next day when she awoke she cried out good-morning in a cheerful voice. She got no answer. She jumped out of bed and ran to the cage. She gave a startled cry, for there the little bird lay, at the bottom, on his side, with his eyes closed, and he looked as if he were dead. She opened the door and putting her hand in lifted him out. She gave a sob of relief, for she felt that his little heart was beating still.

"Wake up, wake up, little bird," she said.

She began to cry and her tears fell on the little bird. He opened his eyes and felt that the bars of the cage were no longer round him.

"I cannot sing unless I'm free and if I cannot sing, I die," he said.

The Princess gave a great sob.

"Then take your freedom," she said, "I shut you in a golden cage because I loved you and wanted to have you all to myself. But I never knew it would kill you. Go. Fly away among the trees that are round the lake and fly over the green rice-fields. I love you enough to let you be happy in your own way."

She threw open the window and gently placed the little bird on the sill. He shook himself a little.

"Come and go as you will, little bird," she said. "I will never put you in a cage any more."

"I will come because I love you, little Princess," said the bird. "And I will sing you the loveliest songs I know. I shall go far away, but I shall always come back, and I shall never forget you." He gave himself another shake. "Good gracious me, how stiff I am," he said.

Then he opened his wings and flew right away into the blue. But the little Princess burst into tears, for it is very difficult to put the happiness of someone you love before your own, and with her little bird far out of sight she felt on a sudden very lonely. When her sisters knew what had happened they mocked her and said that the little bird would never return. But he did at last. And he sat on September's shoulder and ate out of her hand and sang her the beautiful songs he had learned while he was flying up and down the fair places of the world. September kept her window open day and night so that the little bird might come into her room whenever he felt inclined, and this was very good for her; so she grew extremely beautiful. And when she was old enough she married the King of Cambodia and was carried all the way to the city in which he lived on a white elephant. But her sisters never slept with their windows open, so they grew extremely ugly as well as disagreeable, and when the time came to marry them off they were given away to the King's councillors with a pound of tea and a Siamese cat.

A Marriage of Convenience

I LEFT Bangkok on a shabby little ship of four or five hundred tons. The dingy saloon, which served also as dining-room, had two narrow tables down its length with swivel chairs on both sides of them. The cabins were in the bowels of the ship and they were extremely dirty. Cockroaches walked about on the floor and however placid your temperament it is difficult not to be startled when you go to the wash-basin to wash your hands and a huge cockroach stalks leisurely out.

We dropped down the river, broad and lazy and smiling, and its green banks were dotted with little huts on piles standing at the water's edge. We crossed the bar; and the open sea, blue and still, spread before me. The look of it and the smell of it filled me with elation.

I had gone on board early in the morning and soon discovered that I was thrown amid the oddest collection of persons I had ever encountered. There were two French traders and a Belgian colonel, an Italian tenor, the American proprietor of a circus with his wife, and a retired French official with his. The circus proprietor was what is termed a good mixer, a type which according to your mood you fly from or welcome, but I happened to be feeling much pleased with life and before I had been on board an hour we had shaken for drinks, and he had shown me his animals. He was a very short fat man and his stengah-shifter, white but none too clean, outlined the noble proportions of his abdomen, but the collar was so tight that you wondered he did not choke. He had a red, clean-shaven face, a merry blue eye and short, untidy sandy hair. He wore a battered topee well on the back of his head. His name was Wilkins and he was born in Portland, Oregon. It appears that the Oriental has a passion for the circus and Mr. Wilkins for twenty years had been travelling up and down the East from Port Said to Yokohama (Aden, Bombay, Madras, Calcutta, Rangoon, Singapore, Penang, Bangkok, Saigon, Huë, Hanoi, Hong-Kong, Shanghai, their names roll on the tongue savourily, crowding the imagination with sunshine and strange sounds and a multicoloured activity) with his menagerie and his merry-go-rounds. It was a strange life he led, unusual and one that, one would have thought, must offer the occasion for all sorts of curious experiences, but the odd thing about him was that he was a perfectly commonplace little man and you would have been prepared to find him running a garage or keeping a third-rate hotel in a second-rate town in California. The fact is, and I have noticed it so often that I do not know why it should always surprise me, that the extraordinariness of a man's life does not make him extraordinary, but contrariwise if a man is extraordinary he will make extraordinariness out of a life as humdrum as that of a country curate. I wish I could feel it reasonable to tell here the story of the hermit I went to see on an island in the Torres Straits, a shipwrecked mariner who had lived there alone for thirty years, but when you are writing a book you are imprisoned by the four walls of your subject and though for the entertainment of my own digressing mind I set it down now I should be forced in the end, by my sense of what is fit to go between two covers and what is not, to cut it out. Anyhow, the long and short of it is that notwithstanding his long and intimate communion with nature and his thoughts the man was as dull, insensitive and vulgar an oaf at the end of this experience as he must have been at the beginning.

The Italian singer passed us and Mr. Wilkins told me that he was a Neapolitan who was on his way to Hong-Kong to rejoin his company, which he had been forced to leave owing to an attack of malaria in Bangkok. He was an enormous fellow, and very fat, and when he flung himself into a chair it creaked with dismay. He took off his topee, displayed a great head of long, curly, greasy hair, and ran podgy and beringed fingers through it.

"He ain't very sociable," said Mr. Wilkins. "He took the cigar I gave him, but he wouldn't have a drink. I shouldn't wonder if there wasn't somethin' rather queer about him. Nasty-lookin' guy, ain't he?"

Then a little fat woman in white came on deck holding by the hand a Wa-Wa monkey. It walked solemnly by her side.

"This is Mrs. Wilkins," said the circus proprietor, "and our youngest son. Draw up a chair, Mrs. Wilkins, and meet this gentleman. I don't know his name, but he's already paid for two drinks for me and if he can't shake any better than he has yet he'll pay for one for you too."

Mrs. Wilkins sat down with an abstracted, serious look, and with her eyes on the blue sea suggested that she did not see why she shouldn't have a lemonade.

"My, it's hot," she murmured, fanning herself with the topee which she took off.

"Mrs. Wilkins feels the heat," said her husband. "She's had twenty years of it now."

"Twenty-two and a half," said Mrs. Wilkins, still looking at the sea.

"And she's never got used to it yet."

"Nor never shall and you know it," said Mrs. Wilkins.

She was just the same size as her husband and just as fat, and she had a round red face like his and the same sandy, untidy hair. I wondered if they had married because they were so exactly alike, or if in the course of years they had acquired this astonishing resemblance. She did not turn her head but continued to look absently at the sea.

"Have you shown him the animals?" she asked.

"You bet your life I have."

"What did he think of Percy?"

"Thought him fine."

I could not but feel that I was being unduly left out of a conversation of which I was at all events partly the subject, so I asked:

"Who's Percy?"

"Percy's our eldest son. There's a flyin'-fish, Elmer. He's the oran-utan. Did he eat his food well this morning?"

"Fine. He's the biggest oran-utan in captivity. I wouldn't take a thousand dollars for him."

"And what relation is the elephant?" I asked.

Mrs. Wilkins did not look at me, but with her blue eyes still gazed indifferently at the sea.

"He's no relation," she answered. "Only a friend."

The boy brought lemonade for Mrs. Wilkins, a whisky and soda for her husband and a gin and tonic for me. We shook dice and I signed the chit.

"It must come expensive if he always loses when he shakes," Mrs. Wilkins murmured to the coast-line.

"I guess Egbert would like a sip of your lemonade, my dear," said Mr. Wilkins.

Mrs. Wilkins slightly turned her head and looked at the monkey sitting on her lap.

"Would you like a sip of mother's lemonade, Egbert?"

The monkey gave a little squeak and putting her arm round him she handed him a straw. The monkey sucked up a little lemonade and having drunk enough sank back against Mrs. Wilkins' ample bosom.

"Mrs. Wilkins thinks the world of Egbert," said her husband. "You can't wonder at it, he's her youngest."

Mrs. Wilkins took another straw and thoughtfully drank her lemonade.

"Egbert's all right," she remarked. "There's nothin' wrong with Egbert."

Just then the French official, who had been sitting down, got up and began walking up and down. He had been accompanied on board by the French minister at Bangkok, one or two secretaries and a prince of the royal family. There had been a great deal of bowing and shaking of hands and as the ship slipped away from the quay much waving of hats and handkerchiefs. He was evidently a person of consequence. I had heard the captain address him as Monsieur le Gouverneur.

"That's the big noise on this boat," said Mr. Wilkins. "He was Governor of one of the French colonies and now he's makin' a tour of the world. He came to see my circus at Bangkok. I guess I'll ask him what he'll have. What shall I call him, my dear?"

Mrs. Wilkins slowly turned her head and looked at the Frenchman, with the rosette of the Legion of Honour in his buttonhole, pacing up and down.

"Don't call him anythin'," she said. "Show him a hoop and he'll jump right through it."

I could not but laugh. Monsieur le Gouverneur was a little man, well below the average height, and smally made, with a very ugly little face and thick, almost negroid features; and he had a bushy grey head, bushy grey eyebrows and a bushy grey moustache. He did look a little like a poodle and he had the poodle's soft, intelligent and shining eyes. Next time he passed us Mr. Wilkins called out:

"*Monsoo. Qu'est ce que vous prenez?*" I cannot reproduce the eccentricities of his accent. "*Une petite verre de porto.*" He turned to me. "Foreigners, they all drink porto. You're always safe with that."

"Not the Dutch," said Mrs. Wilkins, with a look at the sea. "They won't touch nothin' but Schnapps."

The distinguished Frenchman stopped and looked at Mr. Wilkins with some bewilderment. Whereupon Mr. Wilkins tapped his breast and said:

"*Moa, proprietarre Cirque. Vous avez visité.*"

Then, for a reason that escaped me, Mr. Wilkins made his arms into a hoop and outlined the gestures that represented a poodle jumping through it. Then he pointed at the Wa-Wa that Mrs. Wilkins was still holding on her lap.

"*La petit fils de mon femme,*" he said.

Light broke upon the Governor and he burst into a peculiarly musical and infectious laugh. Mr. Wilkins began laughing too.

"*Oui, oui,*" he cried. "*Moa,* circus proprietor. *Une petite verre de porto. Oui. Oui. N'est ce pas?*"

"Mr. Wilkins talks French like a Frenchman," Mrs. Wilkins informed the passing sea.

"*Mais très volontiers,*" said the Governor, still smiling. I drew him up a chair and he sat down with a bow to Mrs. Wilkins.

"Tell poodle-face his name's Egbert," she said, looking at the sea.

I called the boy and we ordered a round of drinks.

"You sign the chit, Elmer," she said. "It's not a bit of good Mr. What's-his-name shakin' if he can't shake nothin' better than a pair of treys."

"*Vous comprenez le français, madame?*" asked the Governor politely.

"He wants to know if you speak French, my dear."

"Where does he think I was raised? Naples?"

Then the Governor, with exuberant gesticulation, burst into a torrent of English so fantastic that it required all my knowledge of French to understand what he was talking about.

Presently Mr. Wilkins took him down to look at his animals and a little later we assembled in the stuffy saloon for luncheon. The Governor's wife appeared and was put on the captain's right. The Governor explained to her who we all were and she gave us a gracious bow. She was a large woman, tall and of a robust build, of fifty-five perhaps, and she was dressed somewhat severely in black silk. On her head she wore a huge round topee. Her features were so large and regular, her form so statuesque, that you were reminded of the massive females who take part in processions. She would have admirably suited the rôle of Columbia or Britannia in a patriotic demonstration. She towered over her diminutive husband like a skyscraper over a shack. He talked incessantly, with vivacity and wit, and when he said anything amusing her heavy features relaxed into a large, fond smile.

"*Que tu es bête, mon ami,*" she said. She turned to the captain. "You must not pay any attention to him. He is always like that."

We had indeed a very amusing meal and when it was over we separated to our various cabins to sleep away the heat of the afternoon. In such a small ship having once made the acquaintance of my fellow passengers, it would have been impossible, even had I wished it, not to pass with them every moment of the day that I was not in my cabin. The only person who held himself aloof was the Italian tenor. He spoke to no one, but sat by himself as far forward as he could get, twanging a guitar in an undertone so that you had to strain your ears to catch the notes. We remained in sight of land and the sea was like a pail of milk. Talking of one thing and another we watched the day decline, we dined, and then

T

we sat out again on deck under the stars. The two traders played piquet in the hot saloon, but the Belgian colonel joined our little group. He was shy and fat and opened his mouth only to utter a civility. Soon, influenced perhaps by the night and encouraged by the darkness that gave him, up there in the bows, the sensation of being alone with the sea, the Italian tenor, accompanying himself on his guitar, began to sing, first in a low tone, and then a little louder, till presently, his music captivating him, he sang with all his might. He had the real Italian voice, all macaroni, olive oil and sunshine, and he sang the Neapolitan songs that I had heard in my youth in the Piazza San Ferdinando, and fragments from *La Bohème*, and *Traviata* and *Rigoletto*. He sang with emotion and false emphasis and his tremolo reminded you of every third-rate Italian tenor you had ever heard, but there in the openness of that lovely night his exaggerations only made you smile and you could not but feel in your heart a lazy sensual pleasure. He sang for an hour, perhaps, and we all fell silent; then he was still, but he did not move and we saw his huge bulk dimly outlined against the luminous sky.

I saw that the little French Governor had been holding the hand of his large wife and the sight was absurd and touching.

"Do you know that this is the anniversary of the day on which I first saw my wife?" he said, suddenly breaking the silence which had certainly weighed on him, for I had never met a more loquacious creature. "It is also the anniversary of the day on which she promised to be my wife. And, which will surprise you, they were one and the same."

"*Voyons, mon ami*," said the lady, "you are not going to bore our friends with that old story. You are really quite insupportable."

But she spoke with a smile on her large, firm face, and in a tone that suggested that she was quite willing to hear it again.

"But it will interest them, *mon petit chou*." It was in this way that he always addressed his wife and it was funny to hear this imposing and even majestic lady thus addressed by her small husband. "Will it not, *monsieur*?" he asked me. "It is a romance and who does not like romance, especially on such a night as this?"

I assured the Governor that we were all anxious and the Belgian colonel took the opportunity once more to be polite.

"You see, ours was a marriage of convenience pure and simple."

"*C'est vrai*," said the lady. "It would be stupid to deny it. But sometimes love comes after marriage and not before, and then it is better. It lasts longer."

I could not but notice that the Governor gave her hand an affectionate little squeeze.

"You see, I had been in the navy, and when I retired I was forty-nine. I was strong and active and I was very anxious to find an occupation. I looked about; I pulled all the strings I could. Fortunately I had a cousin who had some political importance. It is one of the advantages of democratic government that if you have sufficient influence, merit, which otherwise might pass unnoticed, generally receives its due reward."

"You are modesty itself, *mon pauvre ami*," said she.

"And presently I was sent for by the Minister to the Colonies and offered the post of Governor in a certain colony. It was a very distant spot that they wished to send me to and a lonely one, but I had spent my life wandering from port to port, and that was not a matter that troubled me. I accepted with joy. The minister told me that I must be ready to start in a month. I told him that would be easy for an old bachelor who had nothing much in the world but a few clothes and a few books.

" '*Comment, mon lieutenant*,' he cried. 'You are a bachelor?'

" 'Certainly,' I answered. 'And I have every intention of remaining one.'

" 'In that case I am afraid I must withdraw my offer. For this position it is essential that you should be married.'

"It is too long a story to tell you, but the gist of it was that owing to the scandal my predecessor, a bachelor, had caused by having native girls to live in the Residency and the consequent complaints of the white people, planters and the wives of functionaries, it had been decided that the next Governor must be a model of respectability. I expostulated. I argued. I recapitulated my services to the country and the services my cousin could render at the next elections. Nothing would serve. The minister was adamant.

" 'But what can I do?' I cried with dismay.

" 'You can marry,' said the minister.

" '*Mais voyons, monsieur le ministre*, I do not know any women. I am not a lady's man and I am forty-nine. How do you expect me to find a wife?'

" 'Nothing is more simple. Put an advertisement in the paper.'

"I was confounded. I did not know what to say.

" 'Well, think it over,' said the minister. 'If you can find a wife in a month you can go, but no wife no job. That is my last word.' He smiled a little, to him the situation was not without humour. 'And if you think of advertising I recommend the *Figaro*.'

"I walked away from the ministry with death in my heart. I knew the place to which they desired to appoint me and I knew it would suit me very well to live there; the climate was tolerable and the Residency was spacious and comfortable. The notion of being a Governor was far from displeasing me and, having nothing much but my pension as a naval officer, the salary was not to be despised. Suddenly I made up my mind. I walked to the offices of the *Figaro*, composed an advertisement and handed it in for insertion. But I can tell you, when I walked up the Champs Elysées afterwards my heart was beating much more furiously than it had ever done when my ship was stripped for action."

The Governor leaned forward and put his hand impressively on my knee.

"*Mon cher monsieur*, you will never believe it, but I had four thousand three hundred and seventy-two replies. It was an avalanche. I had expected half-a-dozen; I had to take a cab to take the letters to my hotel. My room was swamped with them. There were four thousand three hundred and seventy-two women who were willing to share my solitude and be a Governor's lady. It was staggering. They were of all ages from seventeen to seventy. There were maidens of irreproachable ancestry and the highest culture, there were unmarried ladies who had made a little slip at one period of their career and now desired to regularise their situation; there were widows whose husbands had died in the most harrowing circumstances; and there were widows whose children would be a solace to my old age. They were blonde and dark, tall and short, fat and thin; some could speak five languages and others could play the piano. Some offered me love and some craved for it; some could only give me a solid friendship but mingled with esteem; some had a fortune and others golden prospects. I was overwhelmed. I was bewildered. At last I lost my temper, for I am a passionate man, and I got up and I stamped on all those letters and all those photographs and I cried: I will marry none of them. It was hopeless, I had less than a month now and I could not see over four thousand aspirants to my hand in that time. I felt if I did not see them all, I should be tortured for the rest of my life by the thought that I had missed the one woman the fates had destined to make me happy. I gave it up as a bad job.

"I went out of my room hideous with all those photographs and littered papers and to drive care away went on to the boulevard and sat down at the Café de la Paix. After a time I saw a friend passing and he nodded to me and smiled. I tried to smile but my heart was sore. I realised that I must spend the years that remained to me in a cheap *pension* at Toulon or Brest as an *officier de marine en retraite*. *Zut!* My friend stopped and coming up to me sat down.

" 'What is making you look so glum, *mon cher*?' he asked me. 'You who are the gayest of mortals.'

"I was glad to have someone in whom I could confide my troubles and told him the whole story. He laughed consumedly. I have thought since that perhaps the incident had its comic side, but at the time, I assure you, I could see in it nothing to laugh at. I mentioned the fact to my friend not without asperity and then, controlling his mirth as best he could, he said to me: 'But, my dear fellow, do you really want to marry?' At this I entirely lost my temper.

" 'You are completely idiotic,' I said. 'If I did not want to marry, and what is more marry at once, within the next fortnight, do you imagine that I should have spent three days reading love letters from women I have never set eyes on?'

" 'Calm yourself and listen to me,' he replied. 'I have a cousin who lives in Geneva. She is Swiss, *du reste*, and she belongs to a family of the greatest respectability in the republic. Her morals are without reproach, she is of a suitable age, a spinster, for she has spent the last fifteen years nursing an invalid mother who has lately died, she is well educated, and *pardessus le marché* she is not ugly.'

" 'It sounds as though she were a paragon,' I said.

" 'I do not say that, but she has been well brought up and would become the position you have to offer her.'

" 'There is one thing you forget. What inducement would there be for her to give up her friends and her accustomed life to accompany in exile a man of forty-nine who is by no means a beauty?' "

Monsieur le Gouverneur broke off his narrative and shrugging his shoulders so emphatically that his head almost sank between them, turned to us.

"I am ugly. I admit it. I am of an ugliness that does not inspire terror or respect, but only ridicule, and that is the worst ugliness of all. When people see me for the first time they do not shrink with horror, there would evidently be something flattering in that, they burst out laughing. Listen, when the admirable Mr. Wilkins showed me his animals this morning, Percy, the oran-utan, held out his arms and but for the bars of the cage would have clasped me to his bosom as a long-lost brother. Once indeed when I was at the Jardin des Plantes in Paris and was told that one of the anthropoid apes had escaped I made my way to the exit as quickly as I could in fear that, mistaking me for the refugee, they would seize me and, notwithstanding my expostulations, shut me up in the monkey house."

"*Voyons, mon ami,*" said Madame his wife, in her deep slow voice, "you are talking even greater nonsense than usual. I do not say that you are an Apollo, in your position it is unnecessary that you should be, but you have dignity, you have poise, you are what any woman would call a fine man."

"I will resume my story. When I made this remark to my friend he replied: 'One can never tell with women. There is something about marriage that wonderfully attracts them. There would be no harm in asking her. After all it is regarded as a compliment by a woman to be asked in marriage. She can but refuse.'

" 'But I do not know your cousin and I do not see how I am to make her acquaintance. I cannot go to her house, ask to see her and when I am shown into the drawing-room say: *Voilà*, I have come to ask you to marry me. She would think I was a lunatic and scream for help. Besides, I am a man of extreme timidity, and I could never take such a step.'

" 'I will tell you what to do,' said my friend. 'Go to Geneva and take her a box of chocolates from me. She will be glad to have news of me and will receive you with pleasure. You can have a little talk and then if you do not like the look of her you take your leave and no harm is done. If on the other hand you do, we can go into the matter and you can make a formal demand for her hand.'

"I was desperate. It seemed the only thing to do. We went to a shop at once and bought an enormous box of chocolates and that night I took the train to Geneva. No sooner had I arrived than I sent her a letter to say that I was the bearer of a gift from her cousin and much wished to give myself the pleasure of delivering it in person. Within an hour I received her reply to the effect that she would be pleased to receive me at four o'clock in the afternoon. I spent the interval before my mirror and seventeen times I tied and retied my tie. As the clock struck four I presented myself at the door of her house and was immediately ushered into the drawing-room. She was waiting for me. Her cousin said she was not ugly. Imagine my surprise to see a young woman, *enfin* a woman still young, of a noble presence, with the dignity of Juno, the features of Venus, and in her expression the intelligence of Minerva."

"You are too absurd," said Madame. "But by now these gentlemen know that one cannot believe all you say."

"I swear to you that I do not exaggerate. I was so taken aback that I nearly dropped the box of chocolates. But I said to myself: *La garde meurt mais ne se rend pas.* I presented the box of chocolates. I gave her news of her cousin. I found her amiable. We talked for a quarter of an hour. And then I said to myself: *Allons-y.* I said to her:

" '*Mademoiselle*, I must tell you that I did not come here merely to give you a box of chocolates.'

"She smiled and remarked that evidently I must have had reasons to come to Geneva of more importance than that.

" 'I came to ask you to do me the honour of marrying me.' She gave a start.

" 'But, *monsieur*, you are mad,' she said.

" 'I beseech you not to answer till you have heard the facts,' I interrupted, and before she could say another word I told her the whole story. I told her about my advertisement in the *Figaro* and she laughed till the tears ran down her face. Then I repeated my offer.

" 'You are serious?' she asked.

" 'I have never been more serious in my life.'

" 'I will not deny that your offer has come as a surprise. I had not thought of marrying, I have passed the age; but evidently your offer is not one that a woman should refuse without consideration. I am flattered. Will you give me a few days to reflect?'

" '*Mademoiselle*, I am absolutely desolated,' I replied. 'But I have not time. If you will not marry me I must go back to Paris and resume my perusal of the fifteen or eighteen hundred letters that still await my attention.'

" 'It is quite evident that I cannot possibly give you an answer at once. I had not set eyes on you a quarter of an hour ago. I must consult my friends and my family.'

" 'What have they got to do with it? You are of full age. The matter is pressing. I cannot wait. I have told you everything. You are an intelligent woman. What can prolonged reflection add to the impulse of the moment?'

" 'You are not asking me to say yes or no this very minute? That is outrageous.'

" 'That is exactly what I am asking. My train goes back to Paris in a couple of hours.'

"She looked at me reflectively.

" 'You are quite evidently a lunatic. You ought to be shut up both for your own safety and that of the public.'

" 'Well, which is it to be?' I said. 'Yes or no?'

"She shrugged her shoulders.

" '*Mon Dieu*.' She waited a minute and I was on tenterhooks. 'Yes.'

The Governor waved his hand towards his wife.

"And there she is. We were married in a fortnight and I became Governor of a colony. I married a jewel, my dear sirs, a woman of the most charming character, one in a thousand, a woman of a masculine intelligence and a feminine sensibility, an admirable woman."

"But hold your tongue, *mon ami*," his wife said. "You are making me as ridiculous as yourself."

He turned to the Belgian colonel.

"Are you a bachelor, *mon colonel*? If so I strongly recommend you to go to Geneva. It is a nest" (*une pépinière* was the word he used) "of the most adorable young women. You will find a wife there as nowhere else. Geneva is besides a charming city. Do not waste a minute, but go there and I will give you a letter to my wife's nieces."

It was she who summed up the story.

"The fact is that in a marriage of convenience you expect less and so you are less likely to be disappointed. As you do not make senseless claims on one another there is no reason for exasperation. You do not look for perfection and so you are tolerant to one another's faults. Passion is all very well, but it is not a proper foundation for marriage. *Voyez-vous*, for two people to be happy in marriage they must be able to respect one another, they must be of the same condition and their interests must be alike; then if they are decent people and are willing to give and take, to live and let live, there is no reason why their union should not be as happy as ours." She paused. "But, of course, my husband is a very, very remarkable man."

Mirage

I HAD been wandering about the East for months and at last reached Haiphong. It is a commercial town and a dull one, but I knew that from there I could find a ship of sorts to take me to Hong-Kong. I had some days to wait and nothing to do. It is true that from Haiphong you can visit the Bay of Along, which is one of the *sehenswürdigkeiten* of Indo-China, but I was tired of sights. I contented myself with sitting in the cafés, for here it was none too warm and I was glad to get out of tropical clothes, and reading back numbers of *L'Illustration*, or for the sake of exercise taking a brisk walk along straight, wide streets. Haiphong is traversed by canals and sometimes I got a glimpse of a scene which in its varied life, with all the native craft on the water, was multicoloured and charming. There was one canal, with tall Chinese houses on each side of it, that had a pleasant curve. The houses were whitewashed, but the whitewash was discoloured and stained; with their grey roofs they made an agreeable composition against the pale sky. The picture had the faded elegance of an old water-colour. There was nowhere an emphatic note. It was soft and a little weary and inspired one with a faint melancholy. I was reminded I scarcely know why of an old maid I knew in my youth, a relic of the Victorian age, who wore black silk mittens and made crochet shawls for the poor, black for widows and white for married women. She had suffered in her youth, but whether from ill-health or unrequited love, no one exactly knew.

But there was a local paper at Haiphong, a small dingy sheet with stubby type the ink of which came off on your fingers, and it gave you a political article, the wireless news, advertisements and local intelligence. The editor, doubtless hard pressed for matter, printed the names of the persons, Europeans, natives of the country and Chinese, who had arrived at Haiphong or left it, and mine was put in with the rest. On the morning of the day before that on which the old tub I was taking was to sail for Hong-Kong I was sitting in the café of the hotel drinking a Dubonnet before luncheon when the boy came in and said that a gentleman wished to see me. I did not know a soul in Haiphong and asked who it was. The boy said he was an Englishman and lived there, but he could not tell me his name. The boy spoke very little French and it was hard for me to understand what he said. I was mystified, but told him to show the visitor in. A moment later he came back followed by a white man and pointed me out to him. The man gave me a look and walked towards me. He was a very tall fellow, well over six feet high, rather fat and bloated, with a red, clean-shaven face and extremely pale blue eyes. He wore very shabby khaki shorts and a stengah-shifter unbuttoned at the neck, and a battered helmet. I concluded at once that he was a stranded beachcomber who was going to touch me for a loan and wondered how little I could hope to get off for.

He came up to me and held out a large red hand with broken dirty nails.

"I don't suppose you remember me," he said. "My name's Grosely. I was at St. Thomas's Hospital with you. I recognised your name as soon as I saw it in the paper and I thought I'd look you up."

I had not the smallest recollection of him, but I asked him to sit down and offered him a drink. By his appearance I had first thought he would ask me for ten piastres and I might have given him five, but now it looked more likely that he would ask for a hundred and I should have to think myself lucky if I could content him with fifty. The habitual borrower always asks twice what he expects to get and it only dissatisfies him to give him what he has asked since then he is vexed with himself for not having asked more. He feels you have cheated him.

"Are you a doctor?" I asked.

"No, I was only at the bloody place a year."

He took off his sun-helmet and showed me a mop of grey hair, which much needed a brush. His face was curiously mottled and he did not look healthy. His teeth were badly decayed and at the corners of his mouth were empty spaces. When the boy came to take the orders he asked for brandy.

"Bring the bottle," he said. "*La bouteille.* Savvy?" He turned to me. "I've been living here for the last five years, but I can't get along with French somehow. I talk Tonkinese." He leaned his chair back and looked at me. "I remember you, you know. You used to go about with those twins. What was their name? I expect I've changed more than you have. I've spent the best part of my life in China. Rotten climate, you know. It plays hell with a man."

I still had not the smallest recollection of him. I thought it best to say so.

"Were you the same year as I was?" I asked.

"Yes. '92."

"It's a devil of a long time ago."

About sixty boys and young men entered the hospital every year; they were most of them shy and confused by the new life they were entering upon; many had never been in London before; and to me at least they were shadows that passed without any particular rhyme or reason across a white sheet. During the first year a certain number for one reason or another dropped out, and in the second year those that remained gained by degrees the beginnings of a personality. They were not only themselves, but the lectures one had attended with them, the scone and coffee one had eaten at the same table for luncheon, the dissection one had done at the same board in the same dissecting room, and *The Belle of New York* one had seen together from the pit of the Shaftesbury Theatre.

The boy brought the bottle of brandy and Grosely, if that was really his name, pouring himself out a generous helping drank it down at a gulp without water or soda.

"I couldn't stand doctoring," he said, "I chucked it. My people got fed up with me and I went out to China. They gave me a hundred pounds and told me to shift for myself. I was damned glad to get out, I can tell you. I guess I was just about as much fed up with them as they were with me. I haven't troubled them much since."

Then from somewhere in the depths of my memory a faint hint crept into the rim, as it were, of consciousness, as on a rising tide the water slides up the sand and then withdraws to advance with the next wave in a fuller volume. I had first an inkling of some shabby little scandal that had got into the papers. Then I saw a boy's face, and so gradually the facts recurred to me; I remembered him now. I didn't believe he was called Grosely then, I think he had a one-syllabled name, but that I was uncertain of. He was a very tall lad (I began to see him quite well), thin, with a slight stoop, he was only eighteen and had grown too fast for his strength, he had curly, shining brown hair, rather large features (they did not look so large now, perhaps because his face was fat and puffy) and a peculiarly fresh complexion, very pink and white, like a girl's. I imagine people, women especially, would have thought him a very handsome boy, but to us he was only a clumsy, shuffling lout. Then I remembered that he did not often come to lectures, no, it wasn't that I remembered, there were too many students in the theatre to recollect who was there and who wasn't. I remembered the dissecting room. He had a leg at the next table to the one I was working at and he hardly ever touched it; I forget why the men who had other parts of the body complained of his neglecting the work, I suppose somehow it interfered with them.

In those days a good deal of gossip went on over the dissection of a "part" and out of the distance of thirty years some of it came back to me. Someone started the story that Grosely was a very gay dog. He drank like a fish and was an awful womaniser. Most of those boys were very simple, and they had brought to the hospital the notions they had acquired at home and at school. Some were prudish and they were shocked; others, those who worked hard, sneered at him and asked how he could hope to pass his exams; but a good many were excited and impressed, he was doing what they would have liked to do if they had had the courage. Grosely had his admirers and you could often see him surrounded by a little band listening open-mouthed to stories of his adventures. Recollections now were crowding upon me. In a very little while he lost his shyness and assumed the airs of a man of the world. They must have looked absurd on this smooth-cheeked boy with his pink and white skin. Men (so they called themselves) used to tell one another of his escapades. He became quite a hero. He would make caustic remarks as he passed the museum and saw a pair of earnest students going over their anatomy together. He was at home in the public-houses of the neighbourhood and was on familiar terms with the barmaids. Looking back, I imagine that, newly arrived from the country and the tutelage of parents and schoolmasters, he was captivated by his freedom and the thrill of London. His dissipations were harmless enough. They were due only to the urge of youth. He lost his head.

But we were all very poor and we did not know how Grosely managed to pay for his garish amusements. We knew his father was a country doctor and I think we knew exactly how much he gave his son a month. It was not enough to pay for the harlots he picked up on the promenade at the Pavilion and for the drinks he stood his friends in the Criterion Bar. We told one another in awe-struck tones that he must be getting fearfully into debt. Of course he could pawn things, but we knew by experience that you could not get more than three pounds for a microscope and thirty shillings for a skeleton. We said he must be spending at least ten pounds a week. Our ideas were not very grand and this seemed to us the wildest pitch of extravagance. At last one of his friends disclosed the mystery: Grosely had discovered a wonderful system for making money. It amused and impressed us. None of us would have thought of anything so ingenious or have had the nerve to attempt it if he had. Grosely went to auctions, not Christie's, of course, but auctions in the Strand and Oxford Street, and in private houses, and bought anything portable that was going cheap. Then he took his purchase to a pawnbroker's and pawned it for ten shillings or a pound more than he had paid. He was making money, four or five pounds a week, and he said he was going to give up medicine and make a regular business of it. Not one of us had ever made a penny in his life and we regarded Grosely with admiration.

"By Jove, he's clever," we said.

"He's just about as sharp as they make them."

"That's the sort that ends up as a millionaire."

We were all very worldly-wise and what we didn't know about life at eighteen we were pretty sure wasn't worth knowing. It was a pity that when an examiner asked us a question we were so nervous that the answer often flew straight out of our head and when a nurse asked us to post a letter we blushed scarlet. It became known that the Dean had sent for Grosely and hauled him over the coals. He had threatened him with sundry penalties if he continued systematically to neglect his work. Grosely was indignant. He'd had enough of that sort of thing at school, he said, he wasn't going to let a horse-faced eunuch treat him like a boy. Damn it all, he was getting on for nineteen and there wasn't much you could teach him. The Dean had said he heard he was drinking more than was good for him. Damned cheek. He could carry his liquor as well as any man of his age, he'd been blind last Saturday and he meant to get blind next Saturday, and if anyone didn't like it he could do the other thing. Grosely's friends quite agreed with him that a man couldn't let himself be insulted like that.

But the blow fell at last and now I remembered quite well the shock it gave us all. I suppose we had not seen Grosely for two or three days, but he had been in the habit of coming to the hospital more and more irregularly, so if we thought anything about it, I imagine we merely said that he was off on one of his bats. He would turn up again in a day or so, rather pale, but with a wonderful story of some girl he had picked up and the time he had had with her. The anatomy lecture was at nine in the morning and it was a rush to get there in time. On this particular day little attention was paid to the lecturer, who, with a visible pleasure in his limpid English and admirable elocution, was describing I know not what part of the human skeleton, for there was much excited whispering along the benches and a newspaper was surreptitiously passed from hand to hand. Suddenly the lecturer stopped. He had a pedagogic sarcasm. He affected not to know the names of his students.

"I am afraid I am disturbing the gentleman who is reading the paper. Anatomy is a very tedious science and I regret that the regulations of the Royal College of Surgeons oblige me to ask you to give it enough of your attention to pass an examination in it. Any gentleman, however, who finds this impossible is at liberty to continue his perusal of the paper outside."

The wretched boy to whom this reproof was addressed reddened to the roots of his hair and in his embarrassment tried to stuff the newspaper in his pocket. The professor of anatomy observed him coldly.

"I am afraid, sir, that the paper is a little too large to go into your pocket," he remarked. "Perhaps you would be good enough to hand it down to me?"

The newspaper was passed from row to row to the well of the theatre, and, not content with the confusion to which he had put the poor lad, the eminent surgeon, taking it, asked:

"May I enquire what it is in the paper that the gentleman in question found of such absorbing interest?"

The student who gave it to him without a word pointed out the paragraph that we had all been reading. The professor read it and we watched him in silence. He put the paper down and went on with his lecture. The headline ran *Arrest of a Medical Student*. Grosely had been brought before the police-court magistrate for getting goods on credit and pawning them. It appears that this is an indictable offence and the magistrate had remanded him for a week. Bail was refused. It looked as though his method of making money by buying things at auctions and pawning them had not in the long run proved as steady a source of income as he expected and he had found it more profitable to pawn things that he was not at the expense of paying for. We talked the matter over excitedly as soon as the lecture was over and I am bound to say that, having no property ourselves, so deficient was our sense of its sanctity we could none of us look upon his crime as a very serious one; but with the natural love of the young for the terrible there were few who did not think he would get anything from two years' hard labour to seven years' penal servitude.

I do not know why, but I did not seem to have any recollection of what happened to Grosely. I think he may have been arrested towards the end of a session and his case may have come on again when we had all separated for holidays. I did not know if it was disposed of by the police-court magistrate or whether it went up for trial. I had a sort of feeling that he was sentenced to a short term of imprisonment, six weeks perhaps, for his operations had been pretty extensive; but I knew that he had vanished from our midst and in a little while was thought of no more. It was strange to me that after all these years I should recollect so much of the incident so clearly. It was as though, turning over an album of old snapshots, I saw all at once the photograph of a scene I had quite forgotten.

But of course in that gross elderly man with grey hair and mottled red face I should never have recognised the lanky pink-cheeked boy. He looked sixty, but I knew he must be much less than that. I wondered what he had done with himself in the intervening time. It did not look as though he had excessively prospered.

"What were you doing in China?" I asked him.

"I was a tide-waiter."

"Oh, were you?"

It is not a position of great importance and I took care to keep out of my tone any note of surprise. The tide-waiters are employees of the Chinese Customs whose duty it is to board the ships and junks at the various treaty ports and I think their chief business is to prevent opium-smuggling. They are mostly retired A.B.s from the Royal Navy and non-commissioned officers who have finished their time. I have seen them come on board at various places up the Yangtse. They hobnob with the pilot and the engineer, but the skipper is a trifle curt with them. They learn to speak Chinese more fluently than most Europeans and often marry Chinese women.

"When I left England I swore I wouldn't go back till I'd made my pile. And I never did. They were glad enough to get anyone to be a tide-waiter in those days, any white man I mean, and they didn't ask questions. They didn't care who you were. I was damned glad to get the job, I can tell you, I was about broke to the wide when they took me on. I only took it till I could get something better, but I stayed on, it suited me, I wanted to make money and I found out that a tide-waiter could make a packet if he knew the right way to go about it. I was with the Chinese Customs for the best part of twenty-five years and when I came away I wouldn't mind betting that lots of commissioners would have been glad to have the money I had."

He gave me a sly, mean look. I had an inkling of what he meant. But there was a point on which I was willing to be reassured; if he was going to ask me for a hundred piastres (I was resigned to that sum now) I thought I might just as well take the blow at once.

"I hope you kept it," I said.

"You bet I did. I invested all my money in Shanghai and when I left China I put it all in American railway bonds. Safety first is my motto. I know too much about crooks to take any risks myself."

I liked that remark, so I asked him if he wouldn't stay and have luncheon with me.

"No, I don't think I will. I don't eat much tiffin and anyway my chow's waiting for me at home. I think I'll be getting along." He got up and he towered over me. "But look here, why don't you come along this evening and see my place? I've married a Haiphong girl. Got a baby too. It's not often I get a chance of talking to anyone about London. You'd better not come to dinner. We only eat native food and I don't suppose you'd care for that. Come along about nine, will you?"

"All right," I said.

I had already told him that I was leaving Haiphong next day. He asked the boy to bring him a piece of paper so that he might write down his address. He wrote laboriously in the hand of a boy of fourteen.

"Tell the porter to explain to your rickshaw boy where it is. I'm on the second floor. There's no bell. Just knock. Well, see you later."

He walked out and I went in to luncheon.

After dinner I called a rickshaw and with the porter's help made the boy understand where I wanted to go. I found presently that he was taking me along the curved canal the houses of which had looked to me so like a faded Victorian water-colour; he stopped at one of them and pointed to the door. It looked so shabby and the neighbourhood was so squalid that I hesitated, thinking he had made a mistake. It seemed unlikely that Grosely could live so far in the native quarter and in a house so bedraggled. I told the rickshaw boy to wait and pushing open the door saw a dark staircase in front of me. There was no one about and the street was empty. It might have been the small hours of the morning. I struck a match and fumbled my way upstairs; on the second floor I struck another match and saw a large brown door in front of me. I knocked and in a moment it was opened by a little Tonkinese woman holding a candle. She was dressed in the earth-brown of the poorer classes, with a tight little black turban on her head; her lips and the skin round them were stained red with betel and when she opened her mouth to speak I saw that she had the black teeth and black gums that so disfigure these people. She said something in her native language and then I heard Grosely's voice:

"Come along in. I was beginning to think you weren't going to turn up."

I passed through a little dark ante-chamber and entered a large room that evidently looked on the canal. Grosely was lying on a long chair and he raised his length from it as I came in. He was reading the Hong-Kong papers by the light of a paraffin-lamp that stood on a table by his side.

"Sit down," he said, "and put your feet up."

"There's no reason I should take your chair."

"Go on. I'll sit on this."

He took a kitchen chair and sitting on it put his feet on the end of mine.

"That's my wife," he said pointing with his thumb at the Tonkinese woman who had followed me into the room. "And over there in the corner's the kid."

I followed his eyes and against the wall, lying on bamboo mats and covered with a blanket, I saw a child sleeping.

"Lively little beggar when he's awake. I wish you could have seen him. She's going to have another soon."

I glanced at her and the truth of what he said was apparent. She was very small, with tiny hands and feet, but her face was flat and the skin muddy. She looked sullen, but may only have been shy. She went out of the room and presently came back with a bottle of whisky, two glasses and a syphon. I looked round. There was a partition at the back of dark unpainted wood, which I suppose shut off another room, and pinned against the middle of this was a portrait cut out of an illustrated paper of John Galsworthy. He looked austere, mild and gentlemanly, and I wondered what he did there. The other walls were whitewashed, but the whitewash was dingy and stained. Pinned on to them were pages of pictures from the *Graphic* or the *Illustrated London News*.

"I put them up," said Grosely, "I thought they made the place look homelike."

"What made you put up Galsworthy? Do you read his books?"

"No, I didn't know he wrote books. I liked his face."

There were one or two torn and shabby rattan mats on the floor and in a corner a great pile of the *Hong-Kong Times*. The only furniture consisted of a wash-hand stand, two or three kitchen chairs, a table or two and a large teak native bed. It was cheerless and sordid.

"Not a bad little place, is it?" said Grosely. "Suits me all right. Sometimes I've thought of moving, but I don't suppose I ever shall now." He gave a little chuckle. "I came to Haiphong for forty-eight hours and I've been here five years. I was on my way to Shanghai really."

He was silent. Having nothing to say I said nothing. Then the little Tonkinese woman made a remark to him, which I could not of course understand, and he answered her. He was silent again for a minute or two, but I thought he looked at me as though he wanted to ask me something. I did not know why he hesitated.

"Have you ever tried smoking opium on your travels in the East?" he enquired at last, casually.

"Yes, I did once, at Singapore. I thought I'd like to see what it was like."

"What happened?"

"Nothing very thrilling, to tell you the truth. I thought I was going to have the most exquisite emotions. I expected visions, like de Quincey's, you know. The only thing I felt was a kind of physical well-being, the same sort of feeling that you get when you've had a Turkish bath and are lying in the cooling room, and then a peculiar activity of mind so that everything I thought of seemed extremely clear."

"I know."

"I really felt that two and two are four and there could not be the smallest doubt about it. But next morning—oh God! My head reeled. I was as sick as a dog, I was sick all day, I vomited my soul out, and as I vomited I said to myself miserably: And there are people who call this fun."

Grosely leaned back in his chair and gave a low mirthless laugh.

"I expect it was bad stuff. Or you went at it too hard. They saw you were a mug and gave you dregs that had been smoked already. They're enough to turn anybody up. Would you like to have another try now? I've got some stuff here that I know's good."

"No, I think once was enough for me."

"D'you mind if I have a pipe or two? You want it in a climate like this. It keeps you from getting dysentery. And I generally have a bit of a smoke about this time."

"Go ahead," I said.

He spoke again to the woman and she, raising her voice, called out something in a raucous tone. An answer came from the room behind the wooden partition and after a minute or two an old woman came out carrying a little round tray. She was shrivelled and old and when she entered gave me an ingratiating smile of her stained mouth. Grosely got up and crossed over to the bed and lay on it. The old woman set the tray down on the bed; on it was a spirit-lamp, a pipe, a long needle and a little round box of opium. She squatted on the bed and Grosely's wife got on it too and sat, her feet tucked up under her, with her back against the wall. Grosely watched the old woman while she put a little pellet of the drug on the needle, held it over the flame till it sizzled and then plugged it into the pipe. She handed it to him and with a great breath he inhaled it, he held the smoke for a little while and then blew it out in a thick grey cloud. He handed her back the pipe and she started to make another. Nobody spoke. He smoked three pipes in succession and then sank back.

"By George, I feel better now. I was feeling all in. She makes a wonderful pipe, this old hag. Are you sure you won't have one?"

"Quite."

"Please yourself. Have some tea then."

He spoke to his wife, who scrambled off the bed and went out of the room. Presently she came back with a little china pot of tea and a couple of Chinese bowls.

"A lot of people smoke here, you know. It does you no harm if you don't do it to excess. I never smoke more than twenty to twenty-five pipes a day. You can go on for years if you limit yourself to that. Some of the Frenchmen smoke as many as forty or fifty a day. That's too much. I never do that, except now and then when I feel I want a binge. I'm bound to say it's never done me any harm."

We drank our tea, pale and vaguely scented and clean on the palate. Then the old woman made him another pipe and then another. His wife had got back on to the bed and soon curling herself up at his feet went to sleep. Grosely smoked two or three pipes at a time, and while he was smoking seemed intent upon nothing else, but in the intervals he was loquacious. Several times I suggested going, but he would not let me. The hours wore on. Once or twice while he smoked I dozed. He told me all about himself. He went on and on. I spoke only to give him a cue. I cannot relate what he told me in his own words. He repeated himself. He was very long-winded and he told me his story confusedly, first a late bit, then an early bit, so that I had to arrange the sequence for myself; sometimes I saw that, afraid he had said too much, he held something back; sometimes he lied and I had to make a guess at the truth from the smile he gave me or the look in his eyes. He had not the words to describe what he had felt, and I had to conjecture his meaning from slangy metaphors and hackneyed, vulgar phrases. I kept on asking myself what his real name was, it was on the tip of my tongue and it irritated me not to be able to recall it, though why it should in the least matter to me I did not know. He was somewhat suspicious of me at first and I saw that this escapade of his in London and his imprisonment had been all these years a tormenting secret. He had always been haunted by the fear that sooner or later someone would find out.

"It's funny that even now you shouldn't remember me at the hospital," he said, looking at me shrewdly. "You must have a rotten memory."

"Hang it all, it's nearly thirty years ago. Think of the thousands of people I've met since then. There's no reason why I should remember you any more than you remember me."

"That's right. I don't suppose there is."

It seemed to reassure him. At last he had smoked enough and the old woman made herself a pipe and smoked it. Then she went over to the mat on which the child was lying and huddled down beside it. She lay so still that I supposed she had fallen directly asleep. When at last I went I found my boy curled up on the footboard of the rickshaw in so deep a slumber that I had to shake him. I knew where I was and I wanted air and exercise, so I gave him a couple of piastres and told him I would walk.

It was a strange story I carried away with me.

It was with a sort of horror that I had listened to Grosely, telling me of those twenty years he had spent in China. He had made money, I do not know how much, but from the way he talked I should think something between fifteen and twenty thousand pounds, and for a tide-waiter it was a fortune. He could not have come by it honestly, and little as I knew of the details of his trade, by his sudden reticences, by his leers and hints I guessed that there was no base transaction that, if it was made worth his while, he jibbed at. I suppose that nothing paid him better than smuggling opium, and his position gave him the opportunity to do this with safety and profit. I understood that his superior officers had often had their suspicions of him, but had never been able to get such proof of his malpractices as to justify them in taking any steps. They contented themselves with moving him from one port to another, but that did not disturb him; they watched him, but he was too clever for them. I saw that he was divided between the fear of telling me too much to his discredit and the desire to boast of his own astuteness. He prided himself on the confidence the Chinese had placed in him.

"They knew they could trust me," he said, "and it gave me a pull. I never double-crossed a Chinaman once."

The thought filled him with the complacency of the honest man. The Chinese discovered that he was keen on curios and they got in the habit of giving him bits or bringing him things to buy; he never made enquiries how they had come by them and he bought them cheap. When he had got a good lot he sent them to Peking and sold them at a handsome profit. I remembered how he had started his commercial career by buying things at auctions and pawning them. For twenty years by shabby shift and petty dishonesty he added pound to pound, and everything he made he invested in Shanghai. He lived penuriously, saving half his pay; he never went on leave because he did not want to waste his money, he would not have anything to do with the Chinese women, he wanted to keep himself free from any entanglement; he did not drink. He was consumed by one ambition, to save enough to be able to go back to England and live the life from which he had been snatched as a boy. That was the only thing he wanted. He lived in China as though in a dream; he paid no attention to the life around him; its colour and strangeness, its possibilities of pleasure, meant nothing to him. There was always before him the mirage of London, the Criterion Bar, himself standing with his foot on the rail, the promenade at the Empire and the Pavilion, the picked-up harlot, the serio-comic at the music-hall and the musical comedy at the Gaiety. This was life and love and adventure. This was romance. This was what he yearned for with all his heart. There was surely something impressive in the way in which during all those years he had lived like an anchorite with that one end in view of leading again a life that was so vulgar. It showed character.

"You see," he said to me, "even if I'd been able to get back to England on leave I wouldn't have gone. I didn't want to go till I could go for good. And then I wanted to do the thing in style."

He saw himself putting on evening clothes every night and going out with a gardenia in his buttonhole, and he saw himself going to the Derby in a long coat and a brown hat and a pair of opera glasses slung over his shoulder. He saw himself giving the girls a look over and picking out the one he fancied. He made up his mind that on the night he arrived in London he would get blind, he hadn't been drunk for twenty years; he couldn't afford to in his job, you had to keep your wits about you. He'd take care not to get drunk on the ship on the way home. He'd wait till he got to London. What a night he'd have! He thought of it for twenty years.

I do not know why Grosely left the Chinese Customs, whether the place was getting too hot for him, whether he had reached the end of his service or whether he had amassed the sum he had fixed. But at last he sailed. He went second class; he did not intend to start spending money till he reached London. He took rooms in Jermyn Street, he had always wanted to live there, and he went straight to a tailor's and ordered himself an outfit. Slap up. Then he

had a look round the town. It was different from how he remembered
it, there was much more traffic and he felt confused and a little at
sea. He went to the Criterion and found there was no longer a bar
where he had been used to lounge and drink. There was a restaurant
in Leicester Square where he had been in the habit of dining when
he was in funds, but he could not find it; he supposed it had been
torn down. He went to the Pavilion, but there were no women
there; he was rather disgusted and went on to the Empire, he found
they had done away with the promenade. It was rather a blow.
He could not quite make it out. Well, anyhow, he must be prepared
for changes in twenty years, and if he couldn't do anything else he
could get drunk. He had had fever several times in China and the
change of climate had brought it on again, he wasn't feeling any too
well, and after four or five drinks he was glad to go to bed.

That first day was only a sample of many that followed it. Everything went wrong. Grosely's voice grew peevish and bitter as he
told me how one thing and another had failed him. The old places
were gone, the people were different, he found it hard to make
friends, he was strangely lonely; he had never expected that in a
great city like London. That's what was wrong with it, London
had become too big, it wasn't the jolly, intimate place it had been
in the early nineties. It had gone to pieces. He picked up a few
girls, but they weren't as nice as the girls he had known before, they
weren't the fun they used to be, and he grew dimly conscious that
they thought him a rum sort of cove. He was only just over forty
and they looked upon him as an old man. When he tried to cotton
on to a lot of young fellows standing round a bar they gave him the
cold shoulder. Anyway, these young fellows didn't know how to
drink. He'd show them. He got soused every night, it was the only
thing to do in that damned place, but, by Jove, it made him feel
rotten next day. He supposed it was the climate of China. When he
was a medical student he could drink a bottle of whisky every night
and be as fresh as a daisy in the morning. He began to think more
about China. All sorts of things that he never knew he had noticed
came back to him. It wasn't a bad life he'd led there. Perhaps
he'd been a fool to keep away from those Chinese girls, they were
pretty little things some of them, and they didn't put on the airs
these English girls did. One could have a damned good time in
China if one had the money he had. One could keep a Chinese girl
and get into the club, and there'd be a lot of nice fellows to drink
with and play bridge with and billiards. He remembered the Chinese
shops and all the row in the streets and the coolies carrying loads and
the ports with the junks in them and the rivers with pagodas on

the banks. It was funny, he never thought much of China while he was there and now—well, he couldn't get it out of his mind. It obsessed him. He began to think that London was no place for a white man. It had just gone to the dogs, that was the long and short of it, and one day the thought came to him that perhaps it would be a good thing if he went back to China. Of course it was silly, he'd worked like a slave for twenty years to be able to have a good time in London, and it was absurd to go and live in China. With his money he ought to be able to have a good time anywhere. But somehow he couldn't think of anything else but China. One day he went to the pictures and saw a scene at Shanghai. That settled it. He was fed up with London. He hated it. He was going to get out and this time he'd get out for good. He had been home a year and a half, and it seemed longer to him than all his twenty years in the East. He took a passage on a French boat sailing from Marseilles, and when he saw the coast of Europe sink into the sea he heaved a great sigh of relief. When they got to Suez and he felt the first touch of the East he knew he had done the right thing. Europe was finished. The East was the only place.

He went ashore at Djibouti and again at Colombo and Singapore, but though the ship stopped for two days at Saigon he remained on board there. He'd been drinking a good deal and he was feeling a bit under the weather. But when they reached Haiphong, where they were staying for forty-eight hours, he thought he might just as well have a look at it. That was the last stopping-place before they got to China. He was bound for Shanghai. When he got there he meant to go to a hotel and look around a bit and then get hold of a girl and a place of his own. He would buy a pony or two and race. He'd soon make friends. In the East they weren't so stiff and stand-offish as they were in London. Going ashore, he dined at the hotel and after dinner got into a rickshaw and told the boy he wanted a woman. The boy took him to the shabby tenement in which I had sat for so many hours and there were the old woman and the girl who was now the mother of his child. After a while the old woman asked him if he wouldn't like to smoke. He had never tried opium, he had always been frightened of it, but now he didn't see why he shouldn't have a go. He was feeling good that night and the girl was a jolly cuddlesome little thing; she was rather like a Chinese girl, small and pretty, like an idol. Well, he had a pipe or two, and he began to feel very happy and comfortable. He stayed all night. He didn't sleep. He just lay, feeling very restful, and thought about things.

"I stopped there till my ship went on to Hong-Kong," he said. "And when she left I just stopped on."

"How about your luggage?" I asked.

For I am perhaps unworthily interested in the manner people combine practical details with the ideal aspects of life. When in a novel penniless lovers drive in a long, swift racing car over the distant hills I have always a desire to know how they managed to pay for it; and I have often asked myself how the characters of Henry James in the intervals of subtly examining their situation coped with the physiological necessities of their bodies.

"I only had a trunk full of clothes, I was never one to want much more than I stood up in, and I went down with the girl in a rickshaw to fetch it. I only meant to stay on till the next boat came through. You see, I was so near China here I thought I'd wait a bit and get used to things, if you understand what I mean, before I went on."

I did. Those last words of his revealed him to me. I knew that on the threshold of China his courage had failed him. England had been such a terrible disappointment that now he was afraid to put China to the test too. If that failed him he had nothing. For years England had been like a mirage in the desert. But when he had yielded to the attraction, those shining pools and the palm trees and the green grass were nothing but the rolling sandy dunes. He had China, and so long as he never saw it again he kept it.

"Somehow I stayed on. You know, you'd be surprised how quickly the days pass. I don't seem to have time to do half the things I want to. After all I'm comfortable here. The old woman makes a damned good pipe, and she's a jolly little girl, my girl, and then there's the kid. A lively young beggar. If you're happy somewhere what's the good of going somewhere else?"

"And are you happy here?" I asked him.

I looked round that large bare sordid room. There was no comfort in it and not one of the little personal things that one would have thought might have given him the feeling of home. Grosely had taken on this equivocal little apartment, which served as a house of assignation and as a place for Europeans to smoke opium in, with the old woman who kept it, just as it was, and he camped, rather than lived, there still as though next day he would pack his traps and go. After a little while he answered my question.

"I've never been so happy in my life. I often think I'll go on to Shanghai some day, but I don't suppose I ever shall. And God knows, I never want to see England again."

"Aren't you awfully lonely sometimes for people to talk to?"

"No. Sometimes a Chinese tramp comes in with an English skipper or a Scotch engineer, and then I go on board and we have a talk about old times. There's an old fellow here, a Frenchman who was in the Customs, and he speaks English; I go and see him sometimes. But the fact is I don't want anybody very much. I think a lot. It gets on my nerves when people come between me and my thoughts. I'm not a big smoker, you know, I just have a pipe or two in the morning to settle my stomach, but I don't really smoke till night. Then I think."

"What d'you think about?"

"Oh, all sorts of things. Sometimes about London and what it was like when I was a boy. But mostly about China. I think of the good times I had and the way I made my money, and I remember the fellows I used to know, and the Chinese. I had some narrow squeaks now and then, but I always came through all right. And I wonder what the girls would have been like that I might have had. Pretty little things. I'm sorry now I didn't keep one or two. It's a great country, China; I love those shops, with an old fellow sitting on his heels smoking a water-pipe, and all the shop-signs. And the temples. By George, that's the place for a man to live in. There's life."

The mirage shone before his eyes. The illusion held him. He was happy. I wondered what would be his end. Well, that was not yet. For the first time in his life perhaps he held the present in his hand.

The Letter

OUTSIDE on the quay the sun beat fiercely. A stream of motors, lorries and buses, private cars and hirelings, sped up and down the crowded thoroughfare, and every chauffeur blew his horn; rickshaws threaded their nimble path amid the throng, and the panting coolies found breath to yell at one another; coolies, carrying heavy bales, sidled along with their quick jog-trot and shouted to the passer-by to make way; itinerant vendors proclaimed their wares. Singapore is the meeting-place of a hundred peoples; and men of all colours, black Tamils, yellow Chinks, brown Malays, Armenians, Jews and Bengalis, called to one another in raucous tones. But inside the office of Messrs. Ripley, Joyce and Naylor it was pleasantly cool; it was dark after the dusty glitter of the street and agreeably quiet after its unceasing din. Mr. Joyce sat in his private room, at the table, with an electric fan turned full on him. He was leaning back, his elbows on the arms of the chair, with the tips of the outstretched fingers of one hand resting neatly against the tips of the outstretched fingers of the other. His gaze rested on the battered volumes of the Law Reports which stood on a long shelf in front of him. On the top of a cupboard were square boxes of japanned tin, on which were painted the names of various clients.

There was a knock at the door.

"Come in."

A Chinese clerk, very neat in his white ducks, opened it.

"Mr. Crosbie is here, sir."

He spoke beautiful English, accenting each word with precision, and Mr. Joyce had often wondered at the extent of his vocabulary. Ong Chi Seng was a Cantonese, and he had studied law at Gray's Inn. He was spending a year or two with Messrs. Ripley, Joyce and Naylor in order to prepare himself for practice on his own account. He was industrious, obliging, and of exemplary character.

"Show him in," said Mr. Joyce.

He rose to shake hands with his visitor and asked him to sit down. The light fell on him as he did so. The face of Mr. Joyce remained in shadow. He was by nature a silent man, and now he looked at Robert Crosbie for quite a minute without speaking. Crosbie was a big fellow, well over six feet high, with broad shoulders, and muscular. He was a rubber-planter, hard with the constant exercise of walking over the estate, and with the tennis which was his relaxation when the day's work was over. He was deeply sunburned. His hairy hands, his feet in clumsy boots were enormous, and Mr. Joyce found himself thinking that a blow of that great fist would easily kill the fragile Tamil. But there was no fierceness in his blue eyes; they were confiding and gentle; and his face, with its big, undistinguished features, was open, frank and honest. But at this moment it bore a look of deep distress. It was drawn and haggard.

"You look as though you hadn't had much sleep the last night or two," said Mr. Joyce.

"I haven't."

Mr. Joyce noticed now the old felt hat, with its broad double brim, which Crosbie had placed on the table; and then his eyes travelled to the khaki shorts he wore, showing his red hairy thighs, the tennis shirt open at the neck, without a tie, and the dirty khaki jacket with the ends of the sleeves turned up. He looked as though he had just come in from a long tramp among the rubber trees. Mr. Joyce gave a slight frown.

"You must pull yourself together, you know. You must keep your head."

"Oh, I'm all right."

"Have you seen your wife to-day?"

"No, I'm to see her this afternoon. You know, it is a damned shame that they should have arrested her."

"I think they had to do that," Mr. Joyce answered in his level, soft tone.

"I should have thought they'd have let her out on bail."

"It's a very serious charge."

"It is damnable. She did what any decent woman would do in her place. Only, nine women out of ten wouldn't have the pluck. Leslie's the best woman in the world. She wouldn't hurt a fly. Why, hang it all, man, I've been married to her for twelve years, do you think I don't know her? God, if I'd got hold of the man I'd have wrung his neck, I'd have killed him without a moment's hesitation. So would you."

"My dear fellow, everybody's on your side. No one has a good word to say for Hammond. We're going to get her off. I don't suppose either the assessors or the judge will go into court without having already made up their minds to bring in a verdict of not guilty."

"The whole thing's a farce," said Crosbie violently. "She ought never to have been arrested in the first place, and then it's terrible, after all the poor girl's gone through, to subject her to the ordeal of a trial. There's not a soul I've met since I've been in Singapore, man or woman, who hasn't told me that Leslie was absolutely justified. I think it's awful to keep her in prison all these weeks."

"The law is the law. After all, she confesses that she killed the man. It is terrible, and I'm dreadfully sorry for both you and for her."

"I don't matter a hang," interrupted Crosbie.

"But the fact remains that murder has been committed, and in a civilised community a trial is inevitable."

"Is it murder to exterminate noxious vermin? She shot him as she would have shot a mad dog."

Mr. Joyce leaned back again in his chair and once more placed the tips of his ten fingers together. The little construction he formed looked like the skeleton of a roof. He was silent for a moment.

"I should be wanting in my duty as your legal adviser," he said at last, in an even voice, looking at his client with his cool, brown eyes, "if I did not tell you that there is one point which causes me just a little anxiety. If your wife had only shot Hammond once, the whole thing would be absolutely plain sailing. Unfortunately she fired six times."

"Her explanation is perfectly simple. In the circumstances anyone would have done the same."

"I dare say," said Mr. Joyce, "and of course I think the explanation is very reasonable. But it's no good closing our eyes to the facts. It's always a good plan to put yourself in another man's place, and I can't deny that if I were prosecuting for the Crown that is the point on which I should centre my enquiry."

"My dear fellow, that's perfectly idiotic."

Mr. Joyce shot a sharp glance at Robert Crosbie. The shadow of a smile hovered over his shapely lips. Crosbie was a good fellow, but he could hardly be described as intelligent.

"I dare say it's of no importance," answered the lawyer, "I just thought it was a point worth mentioning. You haven't got very long to wait now, and when it's all over I recommend you to go off somewhere with your wife on a trip, and forget all about it. Even though we are almost dead certain to get an acquittal, a trial of that sort is anxious work, and you'll both want a rest."

For the first time Crosbie smiled, and his smile strangely changed his face. You forgot the uncouthness and saw only the goodness of his soul.

"I think I shall want it more than Leslie. She's borne up wonderfully. By God, there's a plucky little woman for you."

"Yes, I've been very much struck by her self-control," said the lawyer. "I should never have guessed that she was capable of such determination."

His duties as her counsel had made it necessary for him to have a good many interviews with Mrs. Crosbie since her arrest. Though things had been made as easy as could be for her, the fact remained that she was in gaol, awaiting her trial for murder, and it would not have been surprising if her nerves had failed her. She appeared to bear her ordeal with composure. She read a great deal, took such exercise as was possible, and by favour of the authorities worked at the pillow lace which had always formed the entertainment of her long hours of leisure. When Mr. Joyce saw her, she was neatly dressed in cool, fresh, simple frocks, her hair was carefully arranged, and her nails were manicured. Her manner was collected. She was able even to jest upon the little inconveniences of her position. There was something casual about the way in which she spoke of the tragedy, which suggested to Mr. Joyce that only her good breeding prevented her from finding something a trifle ludicrous in a situation which was eminently serious. It surprised him, for he had never thought that she had a sense of humour.

He had known her off and on for a good many years. When she paid visits to Singapore she generally came to dine with his wife and himself, and once or twice she had passed a week-end with them at their bungalow by the sea. His wife had spent a fortnight with her on the estate, and had met Geoffrey Hammond several times. The two couples had been on friendly, if not on intimate, terms, and it was on this account that Robert Crosbie had rushed over to Singapore immediately after the catastrophe and begged Mr. Joyce to take charge personally of his unhappy wife's defence.

The story she told him the first time he saw her she had never varied in the smallest detail. She told it as coolly then, a few hours after the tragedy, as she told it now. She told it connectedly, in a level, even voice, and her only sign of confusion was when a slight colour came into her cheeks as she described one or two of its incidents. She was the last woman to whom one would have expected such a thing to happen. She was in the early thirties, a fragile creature, neither short nor tall, and graceful rather than pretty. Her wrists and ankles were very delicate, but she was extremely thin, and you could see the bones of her hands through the white skin, and the veins were large and blue. Her face was colourless, slightly sallow, and her lips were pale. You did not notice the colour of her eyes. She had a great deal of light brown hair, and it had a slight natural wave; it was the sort of hair that with a little touching-up would have been very pretty, but you could not imagine that

Mrs. Crosbie would think of resorting to any such device. She was a quiet, pleasant, unassuming woman. Her manner was engaging, and if she was not very popular it was because she suffered from a certain shyness. This was comprehensible enough, for the planter's life is lonely, and in her own house, with people she knew, she was in her quiet way charming. Mrs. Joyce, after her fortnight's stay, had told her husband that Leslie was a very agreeable hostess. There was more in her, she said, than people thought; and when you came to know her you were surprised how much she had read and how entertaining she could be.

She was the last woman in the world to commit murder.

Mr. Joyce dismissed Robert Crosbie with such reassuring words as he could find and, once more alone in his office, turned over the pages of the brief. But it was a mechanical action, for all its details were familiar to him. The case was the sensation of the day, and it was discussed in all the clubs, at all the dinner tables, up and down the Peninsula, from Singapore to Penang. The facts that Mrs. Crosbie gave were simple. Her husband had gone to Singapore on business, and she was alone for the night. She dined by herself, late, at a quarter to nine, and after dinner sat in the sitting-room working at her lace. It opened on the verandah. There was no one in the bungalow, for the servants had retired to their own quarters at the back of the compound. She was surprised to hear a step on the gravel path in the garden, a booted step, which suggested a white man rather than a native, for she had not heard a motor drive up, and she could not imagine who could be coming to see her at that time of night. Someone ascended the few stairs that led up to the bungalow, walked across the verandah, and appeared at the door of the room in which she sat. At the first moment she did not recognise the visitor. She sat with a shaded lamp, and he stood with his back to the darkness.

"May I come in?" he said.

She did not even recognise the voice.

"Who is it?" she asked.

She worked with spectacles, and she took them off as she spoke.

"Geoff. Hammond."

"Of course. Come in and have a drink."

She rose and shook hands with him cordially. She was a little surprised to see him, for though he was a neighbour neither she nor Robert had been lately on very intimate terms with him, and she had not seen him for some weeks. He was the manager of a rubber estate nearly eight miles from theirs, and she wondered why he had chosen this late hour to come and see them.

"Robert's away," she said. "He had to go to Singapore for the night."

Perhaps he thought his visit called for some explanation, for he said:

"I'm sorry. I felt rather lonely to-night, so I thought I'd just come along and see how you were getting on."

"How on earth did you come? I never heard a car."

"I left it down the road. I thought you might both be in bed and asleep."

This was natural enough. The planter gets up at dawn in order to take the roll-call of the workers, and soon after dinner he is glad to go to bed. Hammond's car was in point of fact found next day a quarter of a mile from the bungalow.

Since Robert was away there was no whisky and soda in the room. Leslie did not call the boy, who was probably asleep, but fetched it herself. Her guest mixed himself a drink and filled his pipe.

Geoff. Hammond had a host of friends in the colony. He was at this time in the late thirties, but he had come out as a lad. He had been one of the first to volunteer on the outbreak of war, and had done very well. A wound in the knee caused him to be invalided out of the army after two years, but he returned to the Federated Malay States with a D.S.O. and an M.C. He was one of the best billiard-players in the colony. He had been a beautiful dancer and a fine tennis-player, but though able no longer to dance, and his tennis, with a stiff knee, was not so good as it had been, he had the gift of popularity and was universally liked. He was a tall, good-looking fellow, with attractive blue eyes and a fine head of black, curling hair. Old stagers said his only fault was that he was too fond of the girls, and after the catastrophe they shook their heads and vowed that they had always known this would get him into trouble.

He began now to talk to Leslie about the local affairs, the forthcoming races in Singapore, the price of rubber, and his chances of killing a tiger which had been lately seen in the neighbourhood. She was anxious to finish by a certain date the piece of lace on which she was working, for she wanted to send it home for her mother's birthday, and so put on her spectacles again, and drew towards her chair the little table on which stood the pillow.

"I wish you wouldn't wear those great horn-spectacles," he said. "I don't know why a pretty woman should do her best to look plain."

She was a trifle taken aback at this remark. He had never used that tone with her before. She thought the best thing was to make light of it.

"I have no pretensions to being a raving beauty, you know, and if you ask me point-blank, I'm bound to tell you that I don't care two pins if you think me plain or not."

"I don't think you're plain. I think you're awfully pretty."

"Sweet of you," she answered, ironically. "But in that case I can only think you half-witted."

He chuckled. But he rose from his chair and sat down in another by her side.

"You're not going to have the face to deny that you have the prettiest hands in the world," he said.

He made a gesture as though to take one of them. She gave him a little tap.

"Don't be an idiot. Sit down where you were before and talk sensibly, or else I shall send you home."

He did not move.

"Don't you know that I'm awfully in love with you?" he said.

She remained quite cool.

"I don't. I don't believe it for a minute, and even if it were true I don't want you to say it."

She was the more surprised at what he was saying, since during the seven years she had known him he had never paid her any particular attention. When he came back from the war they had seen a good deal of one another, and once when he was ill Robert had gone over and brought him back to their bungalow in his car. He had stayed with them for a fortnight. But their interests were dissimilar, and the acquaintance had never ripened into friendship. For the last two or three years they had seen little of him. Now and then he came over to play tennis, now and then they met him at some planter's who was giving a party, but it often happened that they did not set eyes on him for a month at a time.

Now he took another whisky and soda. Leslie wondered if he had been drinking before. There was something odd about him, and it made her a trifle uneasy. She watched him help himself with disapproval.

"I wouldn't drink any more if I were you," she said, good-humouredly still.

He emptied his glass and put it down.

"Do you think I'm talking to you like this because I'm drunk?" he asked abruptly.

"That is the most obvious explanation, isn't it?"

"Well, it's a lie. I've loved you ever since I first knew you. I've held my tongue as long as I could, and now it's got to come out. I love you, I love you, I love you."

She rose and carefully put aside the pillow.

"Good-night," she said.

"I'm not going now."

At last she began to lose her temper.

"But, you poor fool, don't you know that I've never loved anyone but Robert, and even if I didn't love Robert you're the last man I should care for."

"What do I care? Robert's away."

"If you don't go away this minute I shall call the boys, and have you thrown out."

"They're out of earshot."

She was very angry now. She made a movement as though to go on to the verandah, from which the house-boy would certainly hear her, but he seized her arm.

"Let me go," she cried furiously.

"Not much. I've got you now."

She opened her mouth and called "Boy, boy," but with a quick gesture he put his hand over it. Then before she knew what he was about he had taken her in his arms and was kissing her passionately. She struggled, turning her lips away from his burning mouth.

"No, no, no," she cried. "Leave me alone. I won't."

She grew confused about what happened then. All that had been said before she remembered accurately, but now his words assailed her ears through a mist of horror and fear. He seemed to plead for her love. He broke into violent protestations of passion. And all the time he held her in his tempestuous embrace. She was helpless, for he was a strong, powerful man, and her arms were pinioned to her sides; her struggles were unavailing, and she felt herself grow weaker; she was afraid she would faint, and his hot breath on her face made her feel desperately sick. He kissed her mouth, her eyes, her cheeks, her hair. The pressure of his arms was killing her. He lifted her off her feet. She tried to kick him, but he only held her more closely. He was carrying her now. He wasn't speaking any more, but she knew that his face was pale and his eyes hot with desire. He was taking her into the bedroom. He was no longer a civilised man, but a savage. And as he ran he stumbled against a table which was in the way. His stiff knee made him a little awkward on his feet, and with the burden of the woman in his arms he fell. In a moment she had snatched herself away from him. She ran round the sofa. He was up in a flash, and flung himself towards her. There was a revolver on the desk. She was not a nervous

U

woman, but Robert was to be away for the night, and she had meant to take it into her room when she went to bed. That was why it happened to be there. She was frantic with terror now. She did not know what she was doing. She heard a report. She saw Hammond stagger. He gave a cry. He said something, she didn't know what. He lurched out of the room on to the verandah. She was in a frenzy now, she was beside herself, she followed him out, yes, that was it, she must have followed him out, though she remembered nothing of it, she followed firing automatically, shot after shot, till the six chambers were empty. Hammond fell down on the floor of the verandah. He crumpled up into a bloody heap.

When the boys, startled by the reports, rushed up, they found her standing over Hammond with the revolver still in her hand and Hammond lifeless. She looked at them for a moment without speaking. They stood in a frightened, huddled bunch. She let the revolver fall from her hand, and without a word turned and went into the sitting-room. They watched her go into her bedroom and turn the key in the lock. They dared not touch the dead body, but looked at it with terrified eyes, talking excitedly to one another in undertones. Then the head-boy collected himself; he had been with them for many years, he was Chinese and a level-headed fellow. Robert had gone into Singapore on his motor-cycle, and the car stood in the garage. He told the seis to get it out; they must go at once to the Assistant District Officer and tell him what had happened. He picked up the revolver and put it in his pocket. The A.D.O., a man called Withers, lived on the outskirts of the nearest town, which was about thirty-five miles away. It took them an hour and a half to reach him. Everyone was asleep, and they had to rouse the boys. Presently Withers came out and they told him their errand. The head-boy showed him the revolver in proof of what he said. The A.D.O. went into his room to dress, sent for his car, and in a little while was following them back along the deserted road. The dawn was just breaking as he reached the Crosbies' bungalow. He ran up the steps of the verandah, and stopped short as he saw Hammond's body lying where he fell. He touched the face. It was quite cold.

"Where's mem?" he asked the house-boy.

The Chinese pointed to the bedroom. Withers went to the door and knocked. There was no answer. He knocked again.

"Mrs. Crosbie," he called.

"Who is it?"

"Withers."

There was another pause. Then the door was unlocked and

slowly opened. Leslie stood before him. She had not been to bed, and wore the tea-gown in which she had dined. She stood and looked silently at the A.D.O.

"Your house-boy fetched me," he said. "Hammond. What have you done?"

"He tried to rape me, and I shot him."

"My God. I say, you'd better come out here. You must tell me exactly what happened."

"Not now. I can't. You must give me time. Send for my husband."

Withers was a young man, and he did not know exactly what to do in an emergency which was so out of the run of his duties. Leslie refused to say anything till at last Robert arrived. Then she told the two men the story, from which since then, though she had repeated it over and over again, she had never in the slightest degree diverged.

The point to which Mr. Joyce recurred was the shooting. As a lawyer he was bothered that Leslie had fired not once, but six times, and the examination of the dead man showed that four of the shots had been fired close to the body. One might almost have thought that when the man fell she stood over him and emptied the contents of the revolver into him. She confessed that her memory, so accurate for all that had preceded, failed her here. Her mind was blank. It pointed to an uncontrollable fury; but uncontrollable fury was the last thing you would have expected from this quiet and demure woman. Mr. Joyce had known her a good many years, and had always thought her an unemotional person; during the weeks that had passed since the tragedy her composure had been amazing.

Mr. Joyce shrugged his shoulders.

"The fact is, I suppose," he reflected, "that you can never tell what hidden possibilities of savagery there are in the most respectable of women."

There was a knock at the door.

"Come in."

The Chinese clerk entered and closed the door behind him. He closed it gently, with deliberation, but decidedly, and advanced to the table at which Mr. Joyce was sitting.

"May I trouble you, sir, for a few words private conversation?" he said.

The elaborate accuracy with which the clerk expressed himself always faintly amused Mr. Joyce, and now he smiled.

"It's no trouble, Chi Seng," he replied.

"The matter on which I desire to speak to you, sir, is delicate and confidential."

"Fire away."

Mr. Joyce met his clerk's shrewd eyes. As usual Ong Chi Seng was dressed in the height of local fashion. He wore very shiny patent-leather shoes and gay silk socks. In his black tie was a pearl and ruby pin, and on the fourth finger of his left hand a diamond ring. From the pocket of his neat white coat protruded a gold fountain pen and a gold pencil. He wore a gold wrist-watch, and on the bridge of his nose invisible pince-nez. He gave a little cough.

"The matter has to do with the case R. *v.* Crosbie, sir."

"Yes?"

"A circumstance has come to my knowledge, sir, which seems to me to put a different complexion on it."

"What circumstance?"

"It has come to my knowledge, sir, that there is a letter in existence from the defendant to the unfortunate victim of the tragedy."

"I shouldn't be at all surprised. In the course of the last seven years I have no doubt that Mrs. Crosbie often had occasion to write to Mr. Hammond."

Mr. Joyce had a high opinion of his clerk's intelligence and his words were designed to conceal his thoughts.

"That is very probable, sir. Mrs. Crosbie must have communicated with the deceased frequently, to invite him to dine with her for example, or to propose a tennis game. That was my first thought when the matter was brought to my notice. This letter, however, was written on the day of the late Mr. Hammond's death."

Mr. Joyce did not flicker an eyelash. He continued to look at Ong Chi Seng with the smile of faint amusement with which he generally talked to him.

"Who has told you this?"

"The circumstances were brought to my knowledge, sir, by a friend of mine."

Mr. Joyce knew better than to insist.

"You will no doubt recall, sir, that Mrs. Crosbie has stated that until the fatal night she had had no communication with the deceased for several weeks."

"Have you got the letter?"

"No, sir."

"What are its contents?"

"My friend gave me a copy. Would you like to peruse it, sir?"

"I should."

Ong Chi Seng took from an inside pocket a bulky wallet. It was filled with papers, Singapore dollar notes and cigarette cards. From the confusion he presently extracted a half-sheet of thin notepaper and placed it before Mr. Joyce. The letter read as follows:

R. will be away for the night. I absolutely must see you. I shall expect you at eleven. I am desperate, and if you don't come I won't answer for the consequences. Don't drive up.—L.

It was written in the flowing hand which the Chinese were taught at the foreign schools. The writing, so lacking in character, was oddly incongruous with the ominous words.

"What makes you think that this note was written by Mrs. Crosbie?"

"I have every confidence in the veracity of my informant, sir," replied Ong Chi Seng. "And the matter can very easily be put to the proof. Mrs. Crosbie will, no doubt, be able to tell you at once whether she wrote such a letter or not."

Since the beginning of the conversation Mr. Joyce had not taken his eyes off the respectable countenance of his clerk. He wondered now if he discerned in it a faint expression of mockery.

"It is inconceivable that Mrs. Crosbie should have written such a letter," said Mr. Joyce.

"If that is your opinion, sir, the matter is of course ended. My friend spoke to me on the subject only because he thought, as I was in your office, you might like to know of the existence of this letter before a communication was made to the Deputy Public Prosecutor."

"Who has the original?" asked Mr. Joyce sharply.

Ong Chi Seng made no sign that he perceived in this question and its manner a change of attitude.

"You will remember, sir, no doubt, that after the death of Mr. Hammond it was discovered that he had had relations with a Chinese woman. The letter is at present in her possession."

That was one of the things which had turned public opinion most vehemently against Hammond. It came to be known that for several months he had had a Chinese woman living in his house.

For a moment neither of them spoke. Indeed everything had been said and each understood the other perfectly.

"I'm obliged to you, Chi Seng. I will give the matter my consideration."

"Very good, sir. Do you wish me to make a communication to that effect to my friend?"

"I dare say it would be as well if you kept in touch with him," Mr. Joyce answered with gravity.

"Yes, sir."

The clerk noiselessly left the room, shutting the door again with deliberation, and left Mr. Joyce to his reflections. He stared at the copy, in its neat, impersonal writing, of Leslie's letter. Vague suspicions troubled him. They were so disconcerting that he made an effort to put them out of his mind. There must be a simple explanation of the letter, and Leslie without doubt could give it at once, but, by heaven, an explanation was needed. He rose from his chair, put the letter in his pocket, and took his topee. When he went out Ong Chi Seng was busily writing at his desk.

"I'm going out for a few minutes, Chi Seng," he said.

"Mr. George Reed is coming by appointment at twelve o'clock, sir. Where shall I say you've gone?"

Mr. Joyce gave him a thin smile.

"You can say that you haven't the least idea."

But he knew perfectly well that Ong Chi Seng was aware that he was going to the gaol. Though the crime had been committed in Belanda and the trial was to take place at Belanda Bharu, since there was in the gaol no convenience for the detention of a white woman Mrs. Crosbie had been brought to Singapore.

When she was led into the room in which he waited she held out her thin, distinguished hand, and gave him a pleasant smile. She was as ever neatly and simply dressed, and her abundant, pale hair was arranged with care.

"I wasn't expecting to see you this morning," she said, graciously.

She might have been in her own house, and Mr. Joyce almost expected to hear her call the boy and tell him to bring the visitor a gin pahit.

"How are you?" he asked.

"I'm in the best of health, thank you." A flicker of amusement flashed across her eyes. "This is a wonderful place for a rest cure."

The attendant withdrew and they were left alone.

"Do sit down," said Leslie.

He took a chair. He did not quite know how to begin. She was so cool that it seemed almost impossible to say to her the thing he had come to say. Though she was not pretty there was something agreeable in her appearance. She had elegance, but it was the elegance of good breeding in which there was nothing of the artifice of society. You had only to look at her to know what sort of people she had and what kind of surroundings she had lived in. Her fragility gave her a singular refinement. It was impossible to associate her with the vaguest idea of grossness.

"I'm looking forward to seeing Robert this afternoon," she said, in her good-humoured, easy voice. (It was a pleasure to hear her

speak, her voice and her accent were so distinctive of her class.)
"Poor dear, it's been a great trial to his nerves. I'm thankful it'll all
be over in a few days."

"It's only five days now."

"I know. Each morning when I awake I say to myself, 'one less'."
She smiled then. "Just as I used to do at school and the holidays
were coming."

"By the way, am I right in thinking that you had no communication whatever with Hammond for several weeks before the catastrophe?"

"I'm quite positive of that. The last time we met was at a tennis-
party at the MacFarrens. I don't think I said more than two words
to him. They have two courts, you know, and we didn't happen to
be in the same sets."

"And you haven't written to him?"

"Oh, no."

"Are you quite sure of that?"

"Oh, quite," she answered, with a little smile. "There was
nothing I should write to him for except to ask him to dine or to
play tennis, and I hadn't done either for months."

"At one time you'd been on fairly intimate terms with him. How
did it happen that you had stopped asking him to anything?"

Mrs. Crosbie shrugged her thin shoulders.

"One gets tired of people. We hadn't anything very much in
common. Of course, when he was ill Robert and I did everything
we could for him, but the last year or two he'd been quite well, and
he was very popular. He had a good many calls on his time, and
there didn't seem to be any need to shower invitations upon him."

"Are you quite certain that was all?"

Mrs. Crosbie hesitated for a moment.

"Well, I may just as well tell you. It had come to our ears that
he was living with a Chinese woman, and Robert said he wouldn't
have him in the house, I had seen her myself."

Mr. Joyce was sitting in a straight-backed arm-chair, resting his
chin on his hand, and his eyes were fixed on Leslie. Was it his fancy
that, as she made this remark, her black pupils were filled on a
sudden, for the fraction of a second, with a dull red light? The effect
was startling. Mr. Joyce shifted in his chair. He placed the tips of
his ten fingers together. He spoke very slowly, choosing his words.

"I think I should tell you that there is in existence a letter in your
handwriting to Geoff. Hammond."

He watched her closely. She made no movement, nor did her face
change colour, but she took a noticeable time to reply.

"In the past I've often sent him little notes to ask him to something or other, or to get me something when I knew he was going to Singapore."

"This letter asks him to come and see you because Robert was going to Singapore."

"That's impossible. I never did anything of the kind."

"You'd better read it for yourself."

He took it out of his pocket and handed it to her. She gave it a glance and with a smile of scorn handed it back to him.

"That's not my handwriting."

"I know, it's said to be an exact copy of the original."

She read the words now, and as she read a horrible change came over her. Her colourless face grew dreadful to look at. It turned green. The flesh seemed on a sudden to fall away and her skin was tightly stretched over the bones. Her lips receded, showing her teeth, so that she had the appearance of making a grimace. She stared at Mr. Joyce with eyes that started from their sockets. He was looking now at a gibbering death's head.

"What does it mean?" she whispered.

Her mouth was so dry that she could utter no more than a hoarse sound. It was no longer a human voice.

"That is for you to say," he answered.

"I didn't write it. I swear I didn't write it."

"Be very careful what you say. If the original is in your handwriting it would be useless to deny it."

"It would be a forgery."

"It would be difficult to prove that. It would be easy to prove that it was genuine."

A shiver passed through her lean body. But great beads of sweat stood on her forehead. She took a handkerchief from her bag and wiped the palms of her hands. She glanced at the letter again and gave Mr. Joyce a sidelong look.

"It's not dated. If I had written it and forgotten all about it, it might have been written years ago. If you'll give me time, I'll try and remember the circumstances."

"I noticed there was no date. If this letter were in the hands of the prosecution they would cross-examine the boys. They would soon find out whether someone took a letter to Hammond on the day of his death."

Mrs. Crosbie clasped her hands violently and swayed in her chair so that he thought she would faint.

"I swear to you that I didn't write that letter."

Mr. Joyce was silent for a little while. He took his eyes from her distraught face, and looked down on the floor. He was reflecting.

"In these circumstances we need not go into the matter further," he said slowly, at last breaking the silence. "If the possessor of this letter sees fit to place it in the hands of the prosecution you will be prepared."

His words suggested that he had nothing more to say to her, but he made no movement of departure. He waited. To himself he seemed to wait a very long time. He did not look at Leslie, but he was conscious that she sat very still. She made no sound. At last it was he who spoke.

"If you have nothing more to say to me I think I'll be getting back to my office."

"What would anyone who read the letter be inclined to think that it meant?" she asked then.

"He'd know that you had told a deliberate lie," answered Mr. Joyce sharply.

"When?"

"You have stated definitely that you had had no communication with Hammond for at least three months."

"The whole thing has been a terrible shock to me. The events of that dreadful night have been a nightmare. It's not very strange if one detail has escaped my memory."

"It would be unfortunate, when your memory has reproduced so exactly every particular of your interview with Hammond, that you should have forgotten so important a point as that he came to see you in the bungalow on the night of his death at your express desire."

"I hadn't forgotten. After what happened I was afraid to mention it. I thought you'd none of you believe my story if I admitted that he'd come at my invitation. I dare say it was stupid of me; but I lost my head, and after I'd said that I'd had no communication with Hammond I was obliged to stick to it."

By now Leslie had recovered her admirable composure, and she met Mr. Joyce's appraising glance with candour. Her gentleness was very disarming.

"You will be required to explain, then, *why* you asked Hammond to come and see you when Robert was away for the night."

She turned her eyes full on the lawyer. He had been mistaken in thinking them insignificant, they were rather fine eyes, and unless he was mistaken they were bright now with tears. Her voice had a little break in it.

"It was a surprise I was preparing for Robert. His birthday is next month. I knew he wanted a new gun and you know I'm dreadfully stupid about sporting things. I wanted to talk to Geoff. about it. I thought I'd get him to order it for me."

"Perhaps the terms of the letter are not very clear to your recollection. Will you have another look at it?"

"No, I don't want to," she said quickly.

"Does it seem to you the sort of letter a woman would write to a somewhat distant acquaintance because she wanted to consult him about buying a gun?"

"I dare say it's rather extravagant and emotional. I do express myself like that, you know. I'm quite prepared to admit it's very silly." She smiled. "And after all, Geoff. Hammond wasn't quite a distant acquaintance. When he was ill I'd nursed him like a mother. I asked him to come when Robert was away, because Robert wouldn't have him in the house."

Mr. Joyce was tired of sitting so long in the same position. He rose and walked once or twice up and down the room, choosing the words he proposed to say; then he leaned over the back of the chair in which he had been sitting. He spoke slowly in a tone of deep gravity.

"Mrs. Crosbie, I want to talk to you very, very seriously. This case was comparatively plain sailing. There was only one point which seemed to me to require explanation: as far as I could judge, you had fired no less than four shots into Hammond when he was lying on the ground. It was hard to accept the possibility that a delicate, frightened, and habitually self-controlled woman, of gentle nature and refined instincts, should have surrendered to an absolutely uncontrolled frenzy. But of course it was admissible. Although Geoffrey Hammond was much liked and on the whole thought highly of, I was prepared to prove that he was the sort of man who might be guilty of the crime which in justification of your act you accused him of. The fact, which was discovered after his death, that he had been living with a Chinese woman gave us something very definite to go upon. That robbed him of any sympathy which might have been felt for him. We made up our minds to make use of the odium which such a connection cast upon him in the minds of all respectable people. I told your husband this morning that I was certain of an acquittal, and I wasn't just telling him that to give him heart. I do not believe the assessors would have left the court."

They looked into one another's eyes. Mrs. Crosbie was strangely still. She was like a little bird paralysed by the fascination of a snake. He went on in the same quiet tones.

"But this letter has thrown an entirely different complexion on

the case. I am your legal adviser, I shall represent you in court.
I take your story as you tell it me, and I shall conduct your defence
according to its terms. It may be that I believe your statements, and
it may be that I doubt them. The duty of counsel is to persuade the
court that the evidence placed before it is not such as to justify it in
bringing in a verdict of guilty, and any private opinion he may have
of the guilt or innocence of his client is entirely beside the point."

He was astonished to see in Leslie's eyes the flicker of a smile.
Piqued, he went on somewhat dryly:

"You're not going to deny that Hammond came to your house at
your urgent, and I may even say, hysterical invitation?"

Mrs. Crosbie, hesitating for an instant, seemed to consider.

"They can prove that the letter was taken to his bungalow by one
of the house-boys. He rode over on his bicycle."

"You mustn't expect other people to be stupider than you. The
letter will put them on the track of suspicions which have entered
nobody's head. I will not tell you what I personally thought when I
saw the copy. I do not wish you to tell me anything but what is
needed to save your neck."

Mrs. Crosbie gave a shrill cry. She sprang to her feet, white with
terror.

"You don't think they'd hang me?"

"If they came to the conclusion that you hadn't killed Hammond
in self-defence, it would be the duty of the assessors to bring in a
verdict of guilty. The charge is murder. It would be the duty of the
judge to sentence you to death."

"But what can they prove?" she gasped.

"I don't know what they can prove. You know. I don't want
to know. But if their suspicions are aroused, if they begin to make
enquiries, if the natives are questioned—what is it that can be
discovered?"

She crumpled up suddenly. She fell on the floor before he could
catch her. She had fainted. He looked round the room for water,
but there was none there, and he did not want to be disturbed. He
stretched her out on the floor, and kneeling beside her waited for her
to recover. When she opened her eyes he was disconcerted by the
ghastly fear that he saw in them.

"Keep quite still," he said. "You'll be better in a moment."

"You won't let them hang me," she whispered.

She began to cry, hysterically, while in undertones he sought to
quieten her.

"For goodness sake pull yourself together," he said.

"Give me a minute."

Her courage was amazing. He could see the effort she made to regain her self-control, and soon she was once more calm.

"Let me get up now."

He gave her his hand and helped her to her feet. Taking her arm, he led her to the chair. She sat down wearily.

"Don't talk to me for a minute or two," she said.

"Very well."

When at last she spoke it was to say something which he did not expect. She gave a little sigh.

"I'm afraid I've made rather a mess of things," she said.

He did not answer, and once more there was a silence.

"Isn't it possible to get hold of the letter?" she said at last.

"I do not think anything would have been said to me about it if the person in whose possession it is was not prepared to sell it."

"Who's got it?"

"The Chinese woman who was living in Hammond's house."

A spot of colour flickered for an instant on Leslie's cheek-bones.

"Does she want an awful lot for it?"

"I imagine that she has a very shrewd idea of its value. I doubt if it would be possible to get hold of it except for a very large sum."

"Are you going to let me be hanged?"

"Do you think it's so simple as all that to secure possession of an unwelcome piece of evidence? It's no different from suborning a witness. You have no right to make any such suggestion to me."

"Then what is going to happen to me?"

"Justice must take its course."

She grew very pale. A little shudder passed through her body.

"I put myself in your hands. Of course I have no right to ask you to do anything that isn't proper."

Mr. Joyce had not bargained for the little break in her voice which her habitual self-restraint made quite intolerably moving. She looked at him with humble eyes, and he thought that if he rejected their appeal they would haunt them for the rest of his life. After all, nothing could bring poor Hammond back to life again. He wondered what really was the explanation of that letter. It was not fair to conclude from it that she had killed Hammond without provocation. He had lived in the East a long time and his sense of professional honour was not perhaps so acute as it had been twenty years before. He stared at the floor. He made up his mind to do something which he knew was unjustifiable, but it stuck in his throat and he felt dully resentful towards Leslie. It embarrassed him a little to speak.

"I don't know exactly what your husband's circumstances are?"

Flushing a rosy red, she shot a swift glance at him.

"He has a good many tin shares and a small share in two or three rubber estates. I suppose he could raise money."

"He would have to be told what it was for."

She was silent for a moment. She seemed to think.

"He's in love with me still. He would make any sacrifice to save me. Is there any need for him to see the letter?"

Mr. Joyce frowned a little, and, quick to notice, she went on.

"Robert is an old friend of yours. I'm not asking you to do anything for me, I'm asking you to save a rather simple, kind man who never did you any harm from all the pain that's possible."

Mr. Joyce did not reply. He rose to go and Mrs. Crosbie, with the grace that was natural to her, held out her hand. She was shaken by the scene, and her look was haggard, but she made a brave attempt to speed him with courtesy.

"It's so good of you to take all this trouble for me. I can't begin to tell you how grateful I am."

Mr. Joyce returned to his office. He sat in his own room, quite still, attempting to do no work, and pondered. His imagination brought him many strange ideas. He shuddered a little. At last there was the discreet knock on the door which he was expecting. Ong Chi Seng came in.

"I was just going out to have my tiffin, sir," he said.

"All right."

"I didn't know if there was anything you wanted before I went, sir."

"I don't think so. Did you make another appointment for Mr. Reed?"

"Yes, sir. He will come at three o'clock."

"Good."

Ong Chi Seng turned away, walked to the door, and put his long slim fingers on the handle. Then, as though on an afterthought, he turned back.

"Is there anything you wish me to say to my friend, sir?"

Although Ong Chi Seng spoke English so admirably he had still a difficulty with the letter R, and he pronounced it "fliend."

"What friend?"

"About the letter Mrs. Crosbie wrote to Hammond deceased, sir."

"Oh! I'd forgotten about that. I mentioned it to Mrs. Crosbie and she denies having written anything of the sort. It's evidently a forgery."

Mr. Joyce took the copy from his pocket and handed it to Ong Chi Seng. Ong Chi Seng ignored the gesture.

"In that case, sir, I suppose there would be no objection if my fliend delivered the letter to the Deputy Public Prosecutor."

"None. But I don't quite see what good that would do your friend."

"My fliend, sir, thought it was his duty in the interests of justice."

"I am the last man in the world to interfere with anyone who wishes to do his duty, Chi Seng."

The eyes of the lawyer and of the Chinese clerk met. Not the shadow of a smile hovered on the lips of either, but they understood each other perfectly.

"I quite understand, sir," said Ong Chi Seng, "but from my study of the case R. *v.* Crosbie I am of opinion that the production of such a letter would be damaging to our client."

"I have always had a very high opinion of your legal acumen, Chi Seng."

"It has occurred to me, sir, that if I could persuade my fliend to induce the Chinese woman who has the letter to deliver it into our hands it would save a great deal of trouble."

Mr. Joyce idly drew faces on his blotting-paper.

"I suppose your friend is a business man. In what circumstances do you think he would be induced to part with the letter?"

"He has not got the letter. The Chinese woman has the letter. He is only a relation of the Chinese woman. She is an ignorant woman; she did not know the value of that letter till my fliend told her."

"What value did he put on it?"

"Ten thousand dollars, sir."

"Good God! Where on earth do you suppose Mrs. Crosbie can get ten thousand dollars! I tell you the letter's a forgery."

He looked up at Ong Chi Seng as he spoke. The clerk was unmoved by the outburst. He stood at the side of the desk, civil, cool and observant.

"Mr. Crosbie owns an eighth share of the Betong Rubber Estate and a sixth share of the Selantan River Rubber Estate. I have a fliend who will lend him the money on the security of his property."

"You have a large circle of acquaintance, Chi Seng."

"Yes, sir."

"Well, you can tell them all to go to hell. I would never advise Mr. Crosbie to give a penny more than five thousand for a letter that can be very easily explained."

"The Chinese woman does not want to sell the letter, sir. My fliend took a long time to persuade her. It is useless to offer her less than the sum mentioned."

Mr. Joyce looked at Ong Chi Seng for at least three minutes. The clerk bore the searching scrutiny without embarrassment. He stood in a respectful attitude with downcast eyes. Mr. Joyce knew his man. Clever fellow, Chi Seng, he thought, I wonder how much he's going to get out of it.

"Ten thousand dollars is a very large sum."

"Mr. Crosbie will certainly pay it rather than see his wife hanged, sir."

Again Mr. Joyce paused. What more did Chi Seng know than he had said? He must be pretty sure of his ground if he was obviously so unwilling to bargain. That sum had been fixed because whoever it was that was managing the affair knew it was the largest amount that Robert Crosbie could raise.

"Where is the Chinese woman now?" asked Mr. Joyce.

"She is staying at the house of my fliend, sir."

"Will she come here?"

"I think it more better if you go to her, sir. I can take you to the house to-night and she will give you the letter. She is a very ignorant woman, sir, and she does not understand cheques."

"I wasn't thinking of giving her a cheque. I will bring bank-notes with me."

"It would only be waste of valuable time to bring less than ten thousand dollars, sir."

"I quite understand."

"I will go and tell my fliend after I have had my tiffin, sir."

"Very good. You'd better meet me outside the club at ten o'clock to-night."

"With pleasure, sir," said Ong Chi Seng.

He gave Mr. Joyce a little bow and left the room. Mr. Joyce went out to have luncheon, too. He went to the club and here, as he had expected, he saw Robert Crosbie. He was sitting at a crowded table, and as he passed him, looking for a place, Mr. Joyce touched him on the shoulder.

"I'd like a word or two with you before you go," he said.

"Right you are. Let me know when you're ready."

Mr. Joyce had made up his mind how to tackle him. He played a rubber of bridge after luncheon in order to allow time for the club to empty itself. He did not want on this particular matter to see Crosbie in his office. Presently Crosbie came into the card-room and looked on till the game was finished. The other players went on their various affairs, and the two were left alone.

"A rather unfortunate thing has happened, old man," said Mr. Joyce, in a tone which he sought to render as casual as possible.

"It appears that your wife sent a letter to Hammond asking him to come to the bungalow on the night he was killed."

"But that's impossible," cried Crosbie. "She's always stated that she had had no communication with Hammond. I know from my own knowledge that she hadn't set eyes on him for a couple of months."

"The fact remains that the letter exists. It's in the possession of the Chinese woman Hammond was living with. Your wife meant to give you a present on your birthday, and she wanted Hammond to help her to get it. In the emotional excitement that she suffered from after the tragedy, she forgot all about it, and having once denied having any communication with Hammond she was afraid to say that she had made a mistake. It was, of course, very unfortunate, but I dare say it was not unnatural."

Crosbie did not speak. His large, red face bore an expression of complete bewilderment, and Mr. Joyce was at once relieved and exasperated by his lack of comprehension. He was a stupid man, and Mr. Joyce had no patience with stupidity. But his distress since the catastrophe had touched a soft spot in the lawyer's heart; and Mrs. Crosbie had struck the right note when she asked him to help her, not for her sake, but for her husband's.

"I need not tell you that it would be very awkward if this letter found its way into the hands of the prosecution. Your wife has lied, and she would be asked to explain the lie. It alters things a little if Hammond did not intrude, an unwanted guest, but came to your house by invitation. It would be easy to arouse in the assessors a certain indecision of mind."

Mr. Joyce hesitated. He was face to face now with his decision. If it had been a time for humour, he could have smiled at the reflection that he was taking so grave a step, and that the man for whom he was taking it had not the smallest conception of its gravity. If he gave the matter a thought, he probably imagined that what Mr. Joyce was doing was what any lawyer did in the ordinary run of business.

"My dear Robert, you are not only my client, but my friend. I think we must get hold of that letter. It'll cost a good deal of money. Except for that I should have preferred to say nothing to you about it."

"How much?"

"Ten thousand dollars."

"That's a devil of a lot. With the slump and one thing and another it'll take just about all I've got."

"Can you get it at once?"

"I suppose so. Old Charlie Meadows will let me have it on my tin shares and on those two estates I'm interested in."

"Then will you?"

"Is it absolutely necessary?"

"If you want your wife to be acquitted."

Crosbie grew very red. His mouth sagged strangely.

"But . . ." he could not find words, his face now was purple. " But I don't understand. She can explain. You don't mean to say they'd find her guilty? They couldn't hang her for putting a noxious vermin out of the way."

"Of course they wouldn't hang her. They might only find her guilty of manslaughter. She'd probably get off with two or three years."

Crosbie started to his feet and his red face was distraught with horror.

"Three years."

Then something seemed to dawn in that slow intelligence of his. His mind was darkness across which shot suddenly a flash of lightning, and though the succeeding darkness was as profound, there remained the memory of something not seen but perhaps just descried. Mr. Joyce saw that Crosbie's big red hands, coarse and hard with all the odd jobs he had set them to, trembled.

"What was the present she wanted to make me?"

"She says she wanted to give you a new gun."

Once more that great red face flushed a deeper red.

"When have you got to have the money ready?"

There was something odd in his voice now. It sounded as though he spoke with invisible hands clutching at his throat.

"At ten o'clock to-night. I thought you could bring it to my office at about six."

"Is the woman coming to you?"

"No, I'm going to her."

"I'll bring the money. I'll come with you."

Mr. Joyce looked at him sharply.

"Do you think there's any need for you to do that? I think it would be better if you left me to deal with this matter by myself."

"It's my money, isn't it? I'm going to come."

Mr. Joyce shrugged his shoulders. They rose and shook hands. Mr. Joyce looked at him curiously.

At ten o'clock they met in the empty club.

"Everything all right?" asked Mr. Joyce.

"Yes. I've got the money in my pocket."

"Let's go then."

They walked down the steps. Mr. Joyce's car was waiting for them in the square, silent at that hour, and as they came to it Ong Chi Seng stepped out of the shadow of a house. He took his seat beside the driver and gave him a direction. They drove past the Hôtel de l'Europe and turned up by the Sailors' Home to get into Victoria Street. Here the Chinese shops were still open, idlers lounged about, and in the roadway rickshaws and motor-cars and gharries gave a busy air to the scene. Suddenly their car stopped and Chi Seng turned round.

"I think it more better if we walk here, sir," he said.

They got out and he went on. They followed a step or two behind. Then he asked them to stop.

"You wait here, sir. I go in and speak to my fliend."

He went into a shop, open to the street, where three or four Chinese were standing behind the counter. It was one of those strange shops where nothing was on view, and you wondered what it was they sold there. They saw him address a stout man in a duck suit with a large gold chain across his breast, and the man shot a quick glance out into the night. He gave Chi Seng a key and Chi Seng came out. He beckoned to the two men waiting and slid into a doorway at the side of the shop. They followed him and found themselves at the foot of a flight of stairs.

"If you wait a minute I will light a match," he said, always resourceful. "You come upstairs, please."

He held a Japanese match in front of them, but it scarcely dispelled the darkness and they groped their way up behind him. On the first floor he unlocked a door and going in lit a gas-jet.

"Come in, please," he said.

It was a small square room, with one window, and the only furniture consisted of two low Chinese beds covered with matting. In one corner was a large chest, with an elaborate lock, and on this stood a shabby tray with an opium pipe on it and a lamp. There was in the room the faint, acrid scent of the drug. They sat down and Ong Chi Seng offered them cigarettes. In a moment the door was opened by the fat Chinaman whom they had seen behind the counter. He bade them good-evening in very good English, and sat down by the side of his fellow-countryman.

"The Chinese woman is just coming," said Chi Seng.

A boy from the shop brought in a tray with a teapot and cups and the Chinaman offered them a cup of tea. Crosbie refused. The Chinese talked to one another in undertones, but Crosbie and Mr. Joyce were silent. At last there was the sound of a voice outside; someone was calling in a low tone; and the Chinaman went to the door. He opened it, spoke a few words, and ushered a woman in. Mr. Joyce looked at her. He had heard much about her since Hammond's death, but he had never seen her. She was a stoutish person, not very young, with a broad, phlegmatic face, she was powdered and rouged and her eyebrows were a thin black line, but she gave you the impression of a woman of character. She wore a pale blue jacket and a white skirt, her costume was not quite European nor quite Chinese, but on her feet were little Chinese silk slippers. She wore heavy gold chains round her neck, gold bangles on her wrists, gold ear-rings and elaborate gold pins in her black hair. She walked in slowly, with the air of a woman sure of herself, but with a certain heaviness of tread, and sat down on the bed beside Ong Chi Seng. He said something to her and nodding she gave an incurious glance at the two white men.

"Has she got the letter?" asked Mr. Joyce.

"Yes, sir."

Crosbie said nothing, but produced a roll of five-hundred-dollar notes. He counted out twenty and handed them to Chi Seng.

"Will you see if that is correct?"

The clerk counted them and gave them to the fat Chinaman.

"Quite correct, sir."

The Chinaman counted them once more and put them in his pocket. He spoke again to the woman and she drew from her bosom a letter. She gave it to Chi Seng who cast his eyes over it.

"This is the right document, sir," he said, and was about to give it to Mr. Joyce when Crosbie took it from him.

"Let me look at it," he said.

Mr. Joyce watched him read and then held out his hand for it.

"You'd better let me have it."

Crosbie folded it up deliberately and put it in his pocket.

"No, I'm going to keep it myself. It's cost me enough money."

Mr. Joyce made no rejoinder. The three Chinese watched the little passage, but what they thought about it, or whether they thought, it was impossible to tell from their impassive countenances. Mr. Joyce rose to his feet.

"Do you want me any more to-night, sir?" said Ong Chi Seng.

"No." He knew that the clerk wished to stay behind in order to get his agreed share of the money, and he turned to Crosbie. "Are you ready?"

Crosbie did not answer, but stood up. The Chinaman went to the door and opened it for them. Chi Seng found a bit of candle and lit it in order to light them down, and the two Chinese accompanied them to the street. They left the woman sitting quietly on the bed smoking a cigarette. When they reached the street the Chinese left them and went once more upstairs.

"What are you going to do with that letter?" asked Mr. Joyce.

"Keep it."

They walked to where the car was waiting for them and here Mr. Joyce offered his friend a lift. Crosbie shook his head.

"I'm going to walk." He hesitated a little and shuffled his feet. "I went to Singapore on the night of Hammond's death partly to buy a new gun that a man I knew wanted to dispose of. Goodnight."

He disappeared quickly into the darkness.

Mr. Joyce was quite right about the trial. The assessors went into court fully determined to acquit Mrs. Crosbie. She gave evidence on her own behalf. She told her story simply and with straightforwardness. The D.P.P. was a kindly man and it was plain that he took no great pleasure in his task. He asked the necessary questions in a deprecating manner. His speech for the prosecution might really have been a speech for the defence, and the assessors took less than five minutes to consider their popular verdict. It was impossible to prevent the great outburst of applause with which it was received by the crowd that packed the court-house. The judge congratulated Mrs. Crosbie and she was a free woman.

No one had expressed a more violent disapprobation of Hammond's behaviour than Mrs. Joyce; she was a woman loyal to her friends and she had insisted on the Crosbies staying with her after the trial, for she in common with everyone else had no doubt of the result, till they could make arrangements to go away. It was out of the question for poor, dear, brave Leslie to return to the bungalow at which the horrible catastrophe had taken place. The trial was over by half-past twelve and when they reached the Joyces' house a grand luncheon was awaiting them. Cocktails were ready, Mrs. Joyce's million-dollar cocktail was celebrated through all the Malay States, and Mrs. Joyce drank Leslie's health. She was a talkative, vivacious woman, and now she was in the highest spirits. It was fortunate, for the rest of them were silent. She did not wonder; her husband never had much to say, and the other two were naturally exhausted from the long strain to which they had been subjected. During luncheon she carried on a bright and spirited monologue. Then coffee was served.

"Now, children," she said in her gay, bustling fashion, "you must have a rest and after tea I shall take you both for a drive to the sea."

Mr. Joyce, who lunched at home only by exception, had of course to go back to his office.

"I'm afraid I can't do that, Mrs. Joyce," said Crosbie. "I've got to get back to the estate at once."

"Not to-day?" she cried.

"Yes, now. I've neglected it for too long and I have urgent business. But I shall be very grateful if you will keep Leslie until we have decided what to do."

Mrs. Joyce was about to expostulate, but her husband prevented her.

"If he must go, he must, and there's an end of it."

There was something in the lawyer's tone which made her look at him quickly. She held her tongue and there was a moment's silence. Then Crosbie spoke again.

"If you'll forgive me, I'll start at once so that I can get there before dark." He rose from the table. "Will you come and see me off, Leslie?"

"Of course."

They went out of the dining-room together.

"I think that's rather inconsiderate of him," said Mrs. Joyce. "He must know that Leslie wants to be with him just now."

"I'm sure he wouldn't go if it wasn't absolutely necessary."

"Well, I'll just see that Leslie's room is ready for her. She wants a complete rest, of course, and then amusement."

Mrs. Joyce left the room and Joyce sat down again. In a short time he heard Crosbie start the engine of his motor-cycle and then noisily scrunch over the gravel of the garden path. He got up and went into the drawing-room. Mrs. Crosbie was standing in the middle of it, looking into space, and in her hand was an open letter. He recognised it. She gave him a glance as he came in and he saw that she was deathly pale.

"He knows," she whispered.

Mr. Joyce went up to her and took the letter from her hand. He lit a match and set the paper afire. She watched it burn. When he could hold it no longer he dropped it on the tiled floor and they both looked at the paper curl and blacken. Then he trod it into ashes with his foot.

"What does he know?"

She gave him a long, long stare and into her eyes came a strange look. Was it contempt or despair? Mr. Joyce could not tell.

"He knows that Geoff. was my lover."

Mr. Joyce made no movement and uttered no sound.

"He'd been my lover for years. He became my lover almost immediately after he came back from the war. We knew how careful we must be. When we became lovers I pretended I was tired of him, and he seldom came to the house when Robert was there. I used to drive out to a place we knew and he met me, two or three times a week, and when Robert went to Singapore he used to come to the bungalow late, when the boys had gone for the night. We saw one another constantly, all the time, and not a soul had the smallest suspicion of it. And then lately, a year ago, he began to change. I didn't know what was the matter. I couldn't believe that he didn't care for me any more. He always denied it. I was frantic. I made him scenes. Sometimes I thought he hated me. Oh, if you knew what agonies I endured. I passed through hell. I knew he didn't want me any more and I wouldn't let him go. Misery! Misery! I loved him. I'd given him everything. He was my life. And then I heard he was living with a Chinese woman. I couldn't believe it. I wouldn't believe it. At last I saw her, I saw her with my own eyes, walking in the village, with her gold bracelets and her necklaces, an old, fat, Chinese woman. She was older than I was. Horrible! They all knew in the kampong that she was his mistress. And when I passed her, she looked at me and I knew that she knew I was his mistress too. I sent for him. I told him I must see him. You've read the letter. I was mad to write it. I didn't know what I was doing. I didn't care. I hadn't seen him for ten days. It was a lifetime. And when last we'd parted he took me in his arms and kissed me, and told me not to worry. And he went straight from my arms to hers."

She had been speaking in a low voice, vehemently, and now she stopped and wrung her hands.

"That damned letter. We'd always been so careful. He always tore up any word I wrote to him the moment he'd read it. How was I to know he'd leave that one? He came, and I told him I knew about the Chinawoman. He denied it. He said it was only scandal. I was beside myself. I don't know what I said to him. Oh, I hated him then. I tore him limb from limb. I said everything I could to wound him. I insulted him. I could have spat in his face. And at last he turned on me. He told me he was sick and tired of me and never wanted to see me again. He said I bored him to death. And then he acknowledged that it was true about the Chinawoman. He said he'd known her for years, before the war, and she was the only woman who really meant anything to him, and the rest was just pastime. And he said he was glad I knew and now at last I'd leave him alone. And then I don't know what happened, I was beside myself, I saw red. I seized the revolver and I fired. He gave a cry and I saw I'd hit him. He staggered and rushed for the verandah. I ran after him and fired again. He fell and then I stood over him and I fired and fired till the revolver went click, click, and I knew there were no more cartridges."

At last she stopped, panting. Her face was no longer human, it was distorted with cruelty, and rage and pain. You would never have thought that this quiet, refined woman was capable of such fiendish passion. Mr. Joyce took a step backwards. He was absolutely aghast at the sight of her. It was not a face, it was a gibbering, hideous mask. Then they heard a voice calling from another room, a loud, friendly, cheerful voice. It was Mrs. Joyce.

"Come along, Leslie darling, your room's ready. You must be dropping with sleep."

Mrs. Crosbie's features gradually composed themselves. Those passions, so clearly delineated, were smoothed away as with your hand you would smooth a crumpled paper, and in a minute the face was cool and calm and unlined. She was a trifle pale, but her lips broke into a pleasant, affable smile. She was once more the well-bred and even distinguished woman.

"I'm coming, Dorothy dear. I'm sorry to give you so much trouble."

The Outstation

THE new assistant arrived in the afternoon. When the Resident, Mr. Warburton, was told that the prahu was in sight he put on his solar topee and went down to the landing-stage. The guard, eight little Dyak soldiers, stood to attention as he passed. He noted with satisfaction that their bearing was martial, their uniforms neat and clean, and their guns shining. They were a credit to him. From the landing-stage he watched the bend of the river round which in a moment the boat would sweep. He looked very smart in his spotless ducks and white shoes. He held under his arm a gold-headed Malacca cane which had been given him by the Sultan of Perak. He awaited the newcomer with mingled feelings. There was more work in the district than one man could properly do, and during his periodical tours of the country under his charge it had been inconvenient to leave the station in the hands of a native clerk, but he had been so long the only white man there that he could not face the arrival of another without misgiving. He was accustomed to loneliness. During the war he had not seen an English face for three years; and once when he was instructed to put up an afforestation officer he was seized with panic, so that when the stranger was due to arrive, having arranged everything for his reception, he wrote a note telling him he was obliged to go up-river, and fled; he remained away till he was informed by a messenger that his guest had left.

Now the prahu appeared in the broad reach. It was manned by prisoners, Dyaks under various sentences, and a couple of warders were waiting on the landing-stage to take them back to gaol. They were sturdy fellows, used to the river, and they rowed with a powerful stroke. As the boat reached the side a man got out from under the attap awning and stepped on shore. The guard presented arms.

"Here we are at last. By God, I'm as cramped as the devil. I've brought you your mail."

He spoke with exuberant joviality. Mr. Warburton politely held out his hand.

"Mr. Cooper, I presume?"

"That's right. Were you expecting anyone else?"

The question had a facetious intent, but the Resident did not smile.

"My name is Warburton. I'll show you your quarters. They'll bring your kit along."

He preceded Cooper along the narrow pathway and they entered a compound in which stood a small bungalow.

"I've had it made as habitable as I could, but of course no one has lived in it for a good many years."

It was built on piles. It consisted of a long living-room which opened on to a broad verandah, and behind, on each side of a passage, were two bedrooms.

"This'll do me all right," said Cooper.

"I dare say you want to have a bath and a change. I shall be very much pleased if you'll dine with me to-night. Will eight o'clock suit you?"

"Any old time will do for me."

The Resident gave a polite, but slightly disconcerted smile, and withdrew. He returned to the Fort where his own residence was. The impression which Allen Cooper had given him was not very favourable, but he was a fair man, and he knew that it was unjust to form an opinion on so brief a glimpse. Cooper seemed to be about thirty. He was a tall, thin fellow, with a sallow face in which there was not a spot of colour. It was a face all in one tone. He had a large, hooked nose and blue eyes. When, entering the bungalow, he had taken off his topee and flung it to a waiting boy, Mr. Warburton noticed that his large skull, covered with short, brown hair, contrasted somewhat oddly with a weak, small chin. He was dressed in khaki shorts and a khaki shirt, but they were shabby and soiled; and his battered topee had not been cleaned for days. Mr. Warburton reflected that the young man had spent a week on a coasting steamer and had passed the last forty-eight hours lying in the bottom of a prahu.

"We'll see what he looks like when he comes in to dinner."

He went into his room, where his things were as neatly laid out as if he had an English valet, undressed, and, walking down the stairs to the bath-house, sluiced himself with cool water. The only concession he made to the climate was to wear a white dinner jacket; but otherwise, in a boiled shirt and a high collar, silk socks and patent-leather shoes, he dressed as formally as though he were dining at his club in Pall Mall. A careful host, he went into the dining-room to see that the table was properly laid. It was gay with orchids, and the silver shone brightly. The napkins were folded into elaborate shapes. Shaded candles in silver candlesticks shed a soft light. Mr. Warburton smiled his approval and returned to the sitting-room to await his guest. Presently he appeared. Cooper was wearing the khaki shorts, the khaki shirt, and the ragged jacket in which he had landed. Mr. Warburton's smile of greeting froze on his face.

"Hulloa, you're all dressed up," said Cooper. "I didn't know you were going to do that. I very nearly put on a sarong."

"It doesn't matter at all. I dare say your boys were busy."

"You needn't have bothered to dress on my account, you know."

"I didn't. I always dress for dinner."

"Even when you're alone?"

"Especially when I'm alone," replied Mr. Warburton, with a frigid stare.

He saw a twinkle of amusement in Cooper's eyes, and he flushed an angry red. Mr. Warburton was a hot-tempered man; you might have guessed that from his red face with its pugnacious features and from his red hair now growing white; his blue eyes, cold as a rule and observing, could flash with sudden wrath; but he was a man of the world and he hoped a just one. He must do his best to get on with this fellow.

"When I lived in London I moved in circles in which it would have been just as eccentric not to dress for dinner every night as not to have a bath every morning. When I came to Borneo I saw no reason to discontinue so good a habit. For three years during the war I never saw a white man. I never omitted to dress on a single occasion on which I was well enough to come into dinner. You have not been very long in this country; believe me, there is no better way to maintain the proper pride which you should have in yourself. When a white man surrenders in the slightest degree to the influences that surround him he very soon loses his self-respect, and when he loses his self-respect you may be quite sure that the natives will soon cease to respect him."

"Well, if you expect me to put on a boiled shirt and a stiff collar in this heat I'm afraid you'll be disappointed."

"When you are dining in your own bungalow you will, of course, dress as you think fit, but when you do me the pleasure of dining with me, perhaps you will come to the conclusion that it is only polite to wear the costume usual in civilised society."

Two Malay boys, in sarongs and songkoks, with smart white coats and brass buttons, came in, one bearing gin pahits, and the other a tray on which were olives and anchovies. Then they went in to dinner. Mr. Warburton flattered himself that he had the best cook, a Chinese, in Borneo, and he took great trouble to have as good food as in the difficult circumstances was possible. He exercised much ingenuity in making the best of his materials.

"Would you care to look at the menu?" he said, handing it to Cooper.

It was written in French and the dishes had resounding names.

They were waited on by the two boys. In opposite corners of the room two more waved immense fans, and so gave movement to the sultry air. The fare was sumptuous and the champagne excellent.

"Do you do yourself like this every day?" said Cooper.

Mr. Warburton gave the menu a careless glance.

"I have not noticed that the dinner is any different from usual," he said. "I eat very little myself, but I make a point of having a proper dinner served to me every night. It keeps the cook in practice and it's good discipline for the boys."

The conversation proceeded with effort. Mr. Warburton was elaborately courteous and, it may be, found a slightly malicious amusement in the embarrassment which he thereby occasioned in his companion. Cooper had not been more than a few months in Sembulu, and Mr. Warburton's enquiries about friends of his in Kuala Solor were soon exhausted.

"By the way," he said presently, "did you meet a lad called Hennerley? He's come out recently, I believe."

"Oh yes, he's in the police. A rotten bounder."

"I should hardly have expected him to be that. His uncle is my friend Lord Barraclough. I had a letter from Lady Barraclough only the other day asking me to look out for him."

"I heard he was related to somebody or other. I suppose that's how he got the job. He's been to Eton and Oxford and he doesn't forget to let you know it."

"You surprise me," said Mr. Warburton. "All his family have been at Eton and Oxford for a couple of hundred years. I should have expected him to take it as a matter of course."

"I thought him a damned prig."

"To what school did you go?"

"I was born in Barbados. I was educated there."

"Oh, I see."

Mr. Warburton managed to put so much offensiveness into his brief reply that Cooper flushed. For a moment he was silent.

"I've had two or three letters from Kuala Solor," continued Mr. Warburton, "and my impression was that young Hennerley was a great success. They say he's a first-rate sportsman."

"Oh, yes, he's very popular. He's just the sort of fellow they would like in K.S. I haven't got much use for the first-rate sportsman myself. What does it amount to in the long run that a man can play golf and tennis better than other people? And who cares if he can make a break of seventy-five at billiards? They attach a damned sight too much importance to that sort of thing in England."

"Do you think so? I was under the impression that the first-rate sportsman had come out of the war certainly no worse than anyone else."

"Oh, if you're going to talk of the war then I do know what I'm talking about. I was in the same regiment as Hennerley and I can tell you that the men couldn't stick him at any price."

"How do you know?"

"Because I was one of the men."

"Oh, you hadn't got a commission."

"A fat chance I had of getting a commission. I was what was called a Colonial. I hadn't been to a public school and I had no influence. I was in the ranks the whole damned time."

Cooper frowned. He seemed to have difficulty in preventing himself from breaking out into violent invective. Mr. Warburton watched him, his little blue eyes narrowed, watched him and formed his opinion. Changing the conversation, he began to speak to Cooper about the work that would be required of him, and as the clock struck ten he rose.

"Well, I won't keep you any more. I dare say you're tired by your journey."

They shook hands.

"Oh, I say, look here," said Cooper, "I wonder if you can find me a boy. The boy I had before never turned up when I was starting from K.S. He took my kit on board and all that, and then disappeared. I didn't know he wasn't there till we were out of the river."

"I'll ask my head-boy. I have no doubt he can find you someone."

"All right. Just tell him to send the boy along and if I like the look of him I'll take him."

There was a moon, so that no lantern was needed. Cooper walked across from the Fort to his bungalow.

"I wonder why on earth they've sent me a fellow like that?" reflected Mr. Warburton. "If that's the kind of man they're going to get out now I don't think much of it."

He strolled down his garden. The Fort was built on the top of a little hill and the garden ran down to the river's edge; on the bank was an arbour, and hither it was his habit to come after dinner to smoke a cheroot. And often from the river that flowed below him a voice was heard, the voice of some Malay too timorous to venture into the light of day, and a complaint or an accusation was softly wafted to his ears, a piece of information was whispered to him or a useful hint, which otherwise would never have come into his official ken. He threw himself heavily into a long rattan chair. Cooper! An envious, ill-bred fellow, bumptious, self-assertive and vain. But Mr. Warburton's irritation could not withstand the silent beauty of the night. The air was scented with the sweet-smelling flowers of a tree that grew at the entrance to the arbour, and the fire-flies, sparkling dimly, flew with their slow and silvery flight. The moon made a pathway on the broad river for the light feet of Sila's bride, and on the further bank a row of palm trees was delicately silhouetted against the sky. Peace stole into the soul of Mr. Warburton.

He was a queer creature and he had had a singular career. At the age of twenty-one he had inherited a considerable fortune, a hundred thousand pounds, and when he left Oxford he threw himself into the gay life, which in those days (now Mr. Warburton was a man of four-and-fifty) offered itself to the young man of good family. He had his flat in Mount Street, his private hansom, and his hunting-box in Warwickshire. He went to all the places where the fashionable congregate. He was handsome, amusing, and generous. He was a figure in the society of London in the early nineties, and society then had not lost its exclusiveness nor its brilliance. The Boer War which shook it was unthought of; the Great War which destroyed it was prophesied only by the pessimists. It was no unpleasant thing to be a rich young man in those days, and Mr. Warburton's chimney-piece during the season was packed with cards for one great function after another. Mr. Warburton displayed them with complacency. For Mr. Warburton was a snob. He was not a timid snob, a little ashamed of being impressed by his betters, nor a snob who sought the intimacy of persons who had acquired celebrity in politics or notoriety in the arts, nor the snob who was dazzled by riches; he was the naked, unadulterated common snob who dearly loved a lord. He was touchy and quick-tempered, but he would much rather have been snubbed by a person of quality than flattered by a commoner. His name figured insignificantly in Burke's Peerage, and it was marvellous to watch the ingenuity he used to mention his distant relationship to the noble family he belonged to; but never a word did he say of the honest Liverpool manufacturer from whom, through his mother, a Miss Gubbins, he had come by his fortune. It was the terror of his fashionable life that at Cowes, maybe, or at Ascot, when he was with a duchess or even with a prince of the blood, one of these relatives would claim acquaintance with him.

His failing was too obvious not soon to become notorious, but its extravagance saved it from being merely despicable. The great whom he adored laughed at him, but in their hearts felt his adoration not unnatural. Poor Warburton was a dreadful snob, of course,

but after all he was a good fellow. He was always ready to back
a bill for an impecunious nobleman, and if you were in a tight
corner you could safely count on him for a hundred pounds. He
gave good dinners. He played whist badly, but never minded how
much he lost if the company was select. He happened to be a
gambler, an unlucky one, but he was a good loser, and it was impossible not to admire the coolness with which he lost five hundred
pounds at a sitting. His passion for cards, almost as strong as his
passion for titles, was the cause of his undoing. The life he led was
expensive and his gambling losses were formidable. He began to
plunge more heavily, first on horses, and then on the Stock Exchange. He had a certain simplicity of character, and the unscrupulous found him an ingenuous prey. I do not know if he ever
realised that his smart friends laughed at him behind his back, but I
think he had an obscure instinct that he could not afford to appear
other than careless of his money. He got into the hands of money-
lenders. At the age of thirty-four he was ruined.

He was too much imbued with the spirit of his class to hesitate
in the choice of his next step. When a man in his set had run
through his money, he went out to the colonies. No one heard
Mr. Warburton repine. He made no complaint because a noble
friend had advised a disastrous speculation, he pressed nobody to
whom he had lent money to repay it, he paid his debts (if he had
only known it, the despised blood of the Liverpool manufacturer
came out in him there), sought help from no one, and, never having
done a stroke of work in his life, looked for a means of livelihood. He
remained cheerful, unconcerned and full of humour. He had no
wish to make anyone with whom he happened to be uncomfortable
by the recital of his misfortune. Mr. Warburton was a snob, but he
was also a gentleman.

The only favour he asked of any of the great friends in whose
daily company he had lived for years was a recommendation. The
able man who was at that time Sultan of Sembulu took him into his
service. The night before he sailed he dined for the last time at his
club.

"I hear you're going away, Warburton," the old Duke of Hereford
said to him.

"Yes, I'm going to Borneo."

"Good God, what are you going there for?"

"Oh, I'm broke."

"Are you? I'm sorry. Well, let us know when you come back. I
hope you have a good time."

"Oh yes. Lots of shooting, you know."

The Duke nodded and passed on. A few hours later Mr. Warburton watched the coast of England recede into the mist, and he left behind everything which to him made life worth living.

Twenty years had passed since then. He kept up a busy correspondence with various great ladies and his letters were amusing and chatty. He never lost his love for titled persons and paid careful attention to the announcements in *The Times* (which reached him six weeks after publication) of their comings and goings. He perused the column which records births, deaths, and marriages, and he was always ready with his letter of congratulation or condolence. The illustrated papers told him how people looked and on his periodical visits to England, able to take up the threads as though they had never been broken, he knew all about any new person who might have appeared on the social surface. His interest in the world of fashion was as vivid as when himself had been a figure in it. It still seemed to him the only thing that mattered.

But insensibly another interest had entered into his life. The position he found himself in flattered his vanity; he was no longer the sycophant craving the smiles of the great, he was the master whose word was law. He was gratified by the guard of Dyak soldiers who presented arms as he passed. He liked to sit in judgement on his fellow men. It pleased him to compose quarrels between rival chiefs. When the head-hunters were troublesome in the old days he set out to chastise them with a thrill of pride in his own behaviour. He was too vain not to be of dauntless courage, and a pretty story was told of his coolness in adventuring single-handed into a stockaded village and demanding the surrender of a bloodthirsty pirate. He became a skilful administrator. He was strict, just and honest.

And little by little he conceived a deep love for the Malays. He interested himself in their habits and customs. He was never tired of listening to their talk. He admired their virtues, and with a smile and a shrug of the shoulders condoned their vices.

"In my day," he would say, "I have been on intimate terms with some of the greatest gentlemen in England, but I have never known finer gentlemen than some well-born Malays whom I am proud to call my friends."

He liked their courtesy and their distinguished manners, their gentleness and their sudden passions. He knew by instinct exactly how to treat them. He had a genuine tenderness for them. But he never forgot that he was an English gentleman, and he had no patience with the white men who yielded to native customs. He made no surrenders. And he did not imitate so many of the white men in taking a native woman to wife, for an intrigue of this nature, however sanctified by custom, seemed to him not only shocking but undignified. A man who had been called George by Albert Edward, Prince of Wales, could hardly be expected to have any connection with a native. And when he returned to Borneo from his visits to England it was now with something like relief. His friends, like himself, were no longer young, and there was a new generation which looked upon him as a tiresome old man. It seemed to him that the England of to-day had lost a good deal of what he had loved in the England of his youth. But Borneo remained the same. It was home to him now. He meant to remain in service as long as was possible, and the hope in his heart was that he would die before at last he was forced to retire. He had stated in his will that wherever he died he wished his body to be brought back to Sembulu, and buried among the people he loved within the sound of the softly flowing river.

But these emotions he kept hidden from the eyes of men; and no one, seeing this spruce, stout, well-set-up man, with his clean-shaven strong face and his whitening hair, would have dreamed that he cherished so profound a sentiment.

He knew how the work of the station should be done, and during the next few days he kept a suspicious eye on his assistant. He saw very soon that he was painstaking and competent. The only fault he had to find with him was that he was brusque with the natives.

"The Malays are shy and very sensitive," he said to him. "I think you will find that you will get much better results if you take care always to be polite, patient and kindly."

Cooper gave a short, grating laugh.

"I was born in Barbados and I was in Africa in the war. I don't think there's much about niggers that I don't know."

"I know nothing," said Mr. Warburton acidly. "But we were not talking of them. We were talking of Malays."

"Aren't they niggers?"

"You are very ignorant," replied Mr. Warburton.

He said no more.

On the first Sunday after Cooper's arrival he asked him to dinner. He did everything ceremoniously, and though they had met on the previous day in the office and later, on the Fort verandah where they drank a gin and bitters together at six o'clock, he sent a polite note across to the bungalow by a boy. Cooper, however unwillingly, came in evening dress and Mr. Warburton, though gratified that his wish was respected, noticed with disdain that the young man's clothes were badly cut and his shirt ill-fitting. But Mr. Warburton was in a good temper that evening.

"By the way," he said to him, as he shook hands, "I've talked to my head-boy about finding you someone and he recommends his nephew. I've seen him and he seems a bright and willing lad. Would you like to see him?"

"I don't mind."

"He's waiting now."

Mr. Warburton called his boy and told him to send for his nephew. In a moment a tall, slender youth of twenty appeared. He had large dark eyes and a good profile. He was very neat in his sarong, a little white coat, and a fez, without a tassel, of plum-covered velvet. He answered to the name of Abas. Mr. Warburton looked on him with approval, and his manner insensibly softened as he spoke to him in fluent and idiomatic Malay. He was inclined to be sarcastic with white people, but with the Malays he had a happy mixture of condescension and kindliness. He stood in the place of the Sultan. He knew perfectly how to preserve his own dignity and at the same time put a native at his ease.

"Will he do?" said Mr. Warburton, turning to Cooper.

"Yes, I dare say he's no more of a scoundrel than any of the rest of them."

Mr. Warburton informed the boy that he was engaged, and dismissed him.

"You're very lucky to get a boy like that," he told Cooper. "He belongs to a very good family. They came over from Malacca nearly a hundred years ago."

"I don't much mind if the boy who cleans my shoes and brings me a drink when I want it has blue blood in his veins or not. All I ask is that he should do what I tell him and look sharp about it."

Mr. Warburton pursed his lips, but made no reply.

They went in to dinner. It was excellent, and the wine was good. Its influence presently had its effect on them, and they talked not only without acrimony, but even with friendliness. Mr. Warburton liked to do himself well, and on Sunday night he made it a habit to do himself even a little better than usual. He began to think he was unfair to Cooper. Of course he was not a gentleman, but that was not his fault, and when you got to know him it might be that he would turn out a very good fellow. His faults, perhaps, were faults of manner. And he was certainly good at his work, quick, conscientious and thorough. When they reached the dessert Mr. Warburton was feeling kindly disposed towards all mankind.

"This is your first Sunday, and I'm going to give you a very special

x

glass of port. I've only got about two dozen of it left and I keep it for special occasions."

He gave his boy instructions and presently the bottle was brought. Mr. Warburton watched the boy open it.

"I got this port from my old friend Charles Hollington. He'd had it for forty years, and I've had it for a good many. He was well-known to have the best cellar in England."

"Is he a wine merchant?"

"Not exactly," smiled Mr. Warburton. "I was speaking of Lord Hollington of Castle Reagh. He's one of the richest peers in England. A very old friend of mine. I was at Eton with his brother."

This was an opportunity that Mr. Warburton could never resist, and he told a little anecdote of which the only point seemed to be that he knew an Earl. The port was certainly very good; he drank a glass and then a second. He lost all caution. He had not talked to a white man for months. He began to tell stories. He showed himself in the company of the great. Hearing him, you would have thought that at one time ministries were formed and policies decided on his suggestion whispered into the ear of a duchess or thrown over the dinner-table to be gratefully acted on by the confidential adviser of the Sovereign. The old days at Ascot, Goodwood and Cowes lived again for him. Another glass of port. There were the great house-parties in Yorkshire and in Scotland to which he went every year.

"I had a man called Foreman then, the best valet I ever had, and why do you think he gave me notice? You know in the House-keeper's Room the ladies' maids and the gentlemen's gentlemen sit according to the precedence of their masters. He told me he was sick of going to party after party at which I was the only commoner. It meant that he always had to sit at the bottom of the table, and all the best bits were taken before a dish reached him. I told the story to the old Duke of Hereford, and he roared. 'By God, sir,' he said, 'if I were King of England, I'd make you a viscount just to give your man a chance.' 'Take him yourself, Duke,' I said. 'He's the best valet I've ever had.' 'Well, Warburton,' he said, 'if he's good enough for you he's good enough for me. Send him along.'"

Then there was Monte Carlo, where Mr. Warburton and the Grand Duke Fyodor, playing in partnership, had broken the bank one evening; and there was Marienbad. At Marienbad Mr. Warburton had played baccarat with Edward VII.

"He was only Prince of Wales then, of course. I remember him saying to me, 'George, if you draw on a five you'll lose your shirt.' He was right; I don't think he ever said a truer word in his life. He was a wonderful man. I always said he was the greatest diplomatist in Europe. But I was a young fool in those days, I hadn't the sense to take his advice. If I had, if I'd never drawn on a five, I dare say I shouldn't be here to-day."

Cooper was watching him. His brown eyes, deep in their sockets, were hard and supercilious, and on his lips was a mocking smile. He had heard a good deal about Mr. Warburton in Kuala Solor, not a bad sort, and he ran his district like clockwork, they said, but by heaven, what a snob! They laughed at him good-naturedly, for it was impossible to dislike a man who was so generous and so kindly, and Cooper had already heard the story of the Prince of Wales and the game of baccarat. But Cooper listened without indulgence. From the beginning he had resented the Resident's manner. He was very sensitive, and he writhed under Mr. Warburton's polite sarcasms. Mr. Warburton had a knack of receiving a remark of which he disapproved with a devastating silence. Cooper had lived little in England and he had a peculiar dislike of the English. He resented especially the public-school boy since he always feared that he was going to patronise him. He was so much afraid of others putting on airs with him that, in order as it were to get in first, he put on such airs as to make everyone think him insufferably conceited.

"Well, at all events the war has done one good thing for us," he said at last. "It's smashed up the power of the aristocracy. The Boer War started it, and 1914 put the lid on."

"The great families of England are doomed," said Mr. Warburton with the complacent melancholy of an *émigré* who remembered the court of Louis XV. "They cannot afford any longer to live in their splendid palaces and their princely hospitality will soon be nothing but a memory."

"And a damned good job too in my opinion."

"My poor Cooper, what can you know of the glory that was Greece and the grandeur that was Rome?"

Mr. Warburton made an ample gesture. His eyes for an instant grew dreamy with a vision of the past.

"Well, believe me, we're fed up with all that rot. What we want is a business government by business men. I was born in a Crown Colony, and I've lived practically all my life in the colonies. I don't give a row of pins for a lord. What's wrong with England is snobbishness. And if there's anything that gets my goat it's a snob."

A snob! Mr. Warburton's face grew purple and his eyes blazed with anger. That was a word that had pursued him all his life. The great ladies whose society he had enjoyed in his youth were not inclined to look upon his appreciation of themselves as unworthy, but even great ladies are sometimes out of temper and more than once Mr. Warburton had had the dreadful word flung in his teeth. He knew, he could not help knowing, that there were odious people who called him a snob. How unfair it was! Why, there was no vice he found so detestable as snobbishness. After all, he liked to mix with people of his own class, he was only at home in their company, and how in heaven's name could anyone say that was snobbish? Birds of a feather.

"I quite agree with you," he answered. "A snob is a man who admires or despises another because he is of a higher social rank than his own. It is the most vulgar failing of our English middle-class."

He saw a flicker of amusement in Cooper's eyes. Cooper put up his hand to hide the broad smile that rose to his lips, and so made it more noticeable. Mr. Warburton's hands trembled a little.

Probably Cooper never knew how greatly he had offended his chief. A sensitive man himself he was strangely insensitive to the feelings of others.

Their work forced them to see one another for a few minutes now and then during the day, and they met at six to have a drink on Mr. Warburton's verandah. This was an old-established custom of the country which Mr. Warburton would not for the world have broken. But they ate their meals separately, Cooper in his bungalow and Mr. Warburton at the Fort. After the office work was over they walked till dusk fell, but they walked apart. There were but few paths in this country where the jungle pressed close upon the plantations of the village, and when Mr. Warburton caught sight of his assistant passing along with his loose stride, he would make a circuit in order to avoid him. Cooper with his bad manners, his conceit in his own judgment and his intolerance had already got on his nerves; but it was not till Cooper had been on the station for a couple of months that an incident happened which turned the Resident's dislike into bitter hatred.

Mr. Warburton was obliged to go up-country on a tour of inspection, and he left the station in Cooper's charge with more confidence, since he had definitely come to the conclusion that he was a capable fellow. The only thing he did not like was that he had no indulgence. He was honest, just and painstaking, but he had no sympathy for the natives. It bitterly amused Mr. Warburton to observe that this man who looked upon himself as every man's equal should look upon so many men as his own inferiors. He was hard, he had no patience with the native mind, and he was a bully. Mr.

Warburton very quickly realised that the Malays disliked and feared him. He was not altogether displeased. He would not have liked it very much if his assistant had enjoyed a popularity which might rival his own. Mr. Warburton made his elaborate preparations, set out on his expedition, and in three weeks returned. Meanwhile the mail had arrived. The first thing that struck his eyes when he entered his sitting-room was a great pile of open newspapers. Cooper had met him, and they went into the room together. Mr. Warburton turned to one of the servants who had been left behind, and sternly asked him what was the meaning of those open papers. Cooper hastened to explain.

"I wanted to read all about the Wolverhampton murder, and so I borrowed your *Times*. I brought them back again. I knew you wouldn't mind."

Mr. Warburton turned on him, white with anger.

"But I do mind. I mind very much."

"I'm sorry," said Cooper, with composure. "The fact is, I simply couldn't wait till you came back."

"I wonder you didn't open my letters as well."

Cooper, unmoved, smiled at his chief's exasperation.

"Oh, that's not quite the same thing. After all, I couldn't imagine you'd mind my looking at your newspapers. There's nothing private in them."

"I very much object to anyone reading my paper before me." He went up to the pile. There were nearly thirty numbers there. "I think it extremely impertinent of you. They're all mixed up."

"We can easily put them in order," said Cooper, joining him at the table.

"Don't touch them," cried Mr. Warburton.

"I say, it's childish to make a scene about a little thing like that."

"How dare you speak to me like that?"

"Oh, go to hell," said Cooper, and he flung out of the room.

Mr. Warburton, trembling with passion, was left contemplating his papers. His greatest pleasure in life had been destroyed by those callous, brutal hands. Most people living in out-of-the-way places when the mail comes tear open impatiently their papers and taking the last ones first glance at the latest news from home. Not so Mr. Warburton. His newsagent had instructions to write on the outside of the wrapper the date of each paper he despatched, and when the great bundle arrived Mr. Warburton looked at these dates and with his blue pencil numbered them. His head-boy's orders were to place one on the table every morning in the verandah with the early cup of tea and it was Mr. Warburton's especial delight to break the wrapper as he sipped his tea, and read the morning paper. It gave him the illusion of living at home. Every Monday morning he read the Monday *Times* of six weeks back, and so went through the week. On Sunday he read the *Observer*. Like his habit of dressing for dinner it was a tie to civilisation. And it was his pride that no matter how exciting the news was he had never yielded to the temptation of opening a paper before its allotted time. During the war the suspense sometimes had been intolerable, and when he read one day that a push was begun he had undergone agonies of suspense which he might have saved himself by the simple expedient of opening a later paper which lay waiting for him on a shelf. It had been the severest trial to which he had ever exposed himself, but he victoriously surmounted it. And that clumsy fool had broken open those neat tight packages because he wanted to know whether some horrid woman had murdered her odious husband.

Mr. Warburton sent for his boy and told him to bring wrappers. He folded up the papers as neatly as he could, placed a wrapper round each and numbered it. But it was a melancholy task.

"I shall never forgive him," he said. "Never."

Of course his boy had been with him on his expedition; he never travelled without him, for his boy knew exactly how he liked things, and Mr. Warburton was not the kind of jungle traveller who was prepared to dispense with his comforts; but in the interval since their arrival he had been gossiping in the servants' quarters. He had learnt that Cooper had had trouble with his boys. All but the youth Abas had left him. Abas had desired to go too, but his uncle had placed him there on the instructions of the Resident, and he was afraid to leave without his uncle's permission.

"I told him he had done well, Tuan," said the boy. "But he is unhappy. He says it is not a good house, and he wishes to know if he may go as the others have gone."

"No, he must stay. The Tuan must have servants. Have those who went been replaced?"

"No, Tuan, no one will go."

Mr. Warburton frowned. Cooper was an insolent fool, but he had an official position and must be suitably provided with servants. It was not seemly that his house should be improperly conducted.

"Where are the boys who ran away?"

"They are in the kampong, Tuan."

"Go and see them to-night, and tell them that I expect them to be back in Tuan Cooper's house at dawn to-morrow."

"They say they will not go, Tuan."

"On my order?"

The boy had been with Mr. Warburton for fifteen years, and he knew every intonation of his master's voice. He was not afraid of him, they had gone through too much together, once in the jungle the Resident had saved his life, and once, upset in some rapids, but for him the Resident would have been drowned; but he knew when the Resident must be obeyed without question.

"I will go to the kampong," he said.

Mr. Warburton expected that his subordinate would take the first opportunity to apologise for his rudeness, but Cooper had the ill-bred man's inability to express regret; and when they met next morning in the office he ignored the incident. Since Mr. Warburton had been away for three weeks it was necessary for them to have a somewhat prolonged interview. At the end of it, Mr. Warburton dismissed him.

"I don't think there's anything else, thank you." Cooper turned to go, but Mr. Warburton stopped him. "I understand you've been having some trouble with your boys."

Cooper gave a harsh laugh.

"They tried to blackmail me. They had the damned cheek to run away, all except that incompetent fellow Abas—he knew when he was well off—but I just sat tight. They've all come to heel again."

"What do you mean by that?"

"This morning they were all back on their jobs, the Chinese cook and all. There they were, as cool as cucumbers; you would have thought they owned the place. I suppose they'd come to the conclusion that I wasn't such a fool as I looked."

"By no means. They came back on my express order."

Cooper flushed slightly.

"I should be obliged if you wouldn't interfere with my private concerns."

"They're not your private concerns. When your servants run away it makes you ridiculous. You are perfectly free to make a fool of yourself, but I cannot allow you to be made a fool of. It is unseemly that your house should not be properly staffed. As soon as I heard that your boys had left you, I had them told to be back in their places at dawn. That'll do."

Mr. Warburton nodded to signify that the interview was at an end. Cooper took no notice.

"Shall I tell you what I did? I called them and gave the whole bally lot the sack. I gave them ten minutes to get out of the compound."

Mr. Warburton shrugged his shoulders.

"What makes you think you can get others?"

"I've told my own clerk to see about it."

Mr. Warburton reflected for a moment.

"I think you behaved very foolishly. You will do well to remember in future that good masters make good servants."

"Is there anything else you want to teach me?"

"I should like to teach you manners, but it would be an arduous task, and I have not the time to waste. I will see that you get boys."

"Please don't put yourself to any trouble on my account. I'm quite capable of getting them for myself."

Mr. Warburton smiled acidly. He had an inkling that Cooper disliked him as much as he disliked Cooper, and he knew that nothing is more galling than to be forced to accept the favours of a man you detest.

"Allow me to tell you that you have no more chance of getting Malay or Chinese servants here now than you have of getting an English butler or a French chef. No one will come to you except on an order from me. Would you like me to give it?"

"No."

"As you please. Good-morning."

Mr. Warburton watched the development of the situation with acrid humour. Cooper's clerk was unable to persuade Malay, Dyak or Chinese to enter the house of such a master. Abas, the boy who remained faithful to him, knew how to cook only native food, and Cooper, a coarse feeder, found his gorge rise against the everlasting rice. There was no water-carrier, and in that great heat he needed several baths a day. He cursed Abas, but Abas opposed him with sullen resistance and would not do more than he chose. It was galling to know that the lad stayed with him only because the Resident insisted. This went on for a fortnight and then, one morning, he found in his house the very servants whom he had previously dismissed. He fell into a violent rage, but he had learnt a little sense, and this time, without a word, he let them stay. He swallowed his humiliation, but the impatient contempt he had felt for Mr. Warburton's idiosyncrasies changed into a sullen hatred: the Resident with this malicious stroke had made him the laughing-stock of all the natives.

The two men now held no communication with one another. They broke the time-honoured custom of sharing, notwithstanding personal dislike, a drink at six o'clock with any white man who happened to be at the station. Each lived in his own house as though the other did not exist. Now that Cooper had fallen into the work, it was necessary for them to have little to do with one another in the office. Mr. Warburton used his orderly to send any message he had to give his assistant, and his instructions he sent by formal letter. They saw one another constantly, that was inevitable, but did not exchange half a dozen words in a week. The fact that they could not avoid catching sight of one another got on their nerves. They brooded over their antagonism, and Mr. Warburton, taking his daily walk, could think of nothing but how much he detested his assistant.

And the dreadful thing was that in all probability they would remain thus, facing each other in deadly enmity, till Mr. Warburton went on leave. It might be three years. He had no reason to send in a complaint to headquarters: Cooper did his work very well, and at that time men were hard to get. True, vague complaints reached him and hints that the natives found Cooper harsh. There was certainly a feeling of dissatisfaction among them. But when Mr. Warburton looked into specific cases, all he could say was that Cooper had shown severity where mildness would not have been misplaced, and had been unfeeling when himself would have been sympathetic. He had done nothing for which he could be taken to task. But Mr. Warburton watched him. Hatred will often make a man clear-sighted, and he had a suspicion that Cooper was using the natives without consideration, yet keeping within the law, because he felt that thus he could exasperate his chief. One day perhaps he would go too far. None knew better than Mr. Warburton how irritable the incessant heat could make a man and how difficult it was to keep one's self-control after a sleepless night. He smiled softly to himself. Sooner or later Cooper would deliver himself into his hand.

When at last the opportunity came, Mr. Warburton laughed aloud. Cooper had charge of the prisoners; they made roads, built sheds, rowed when it was necessary to send the prahu up or down stream, kept the town clean and otherwise usefully employed themselves. If well-behaved they even on occasion served as houseboys. Cooper kept them hard at it. He liked to see them work. He took pleasure in devising tasks for them; and seeing quickly enough that they were being made to do useless things the prisoners worked badly. He punished them by lengthening their hours. This was contrary to the regulations, and as soon as it was brought to the attention of Mr. Warburton, without referring the matter back to his subordinate, he gave instructions that the old hours should be kept; Cooper, going out for his walk, was astounded to see the prisoners strolling back to the gaol; he had given instructions that they were not to knock off till dusk. When he asked the warder in charge why they had left off work he was told that it was the Resident's bidding.

White with rage he strode to the Fort. Mr. Warburton, in his spotless white ducks and his neat topee, with a walking-stick in his hand, followed by his dogs, was on the point of starting out on his afternoon stroll. He had watched Cooper go, and knew that he had taken the road by the river. Cooper jumped up the steps and went straight up to the Resident.

"I want to know what the hell you mean by countermanding my order that the prisoners were to work till six," he burst out, beside himself with fury.

Mr. Warburton opened his cold blue eyes very wide and assumed an expression of great surprise.

"Are you out of your mind? Are you so ignorant that you do not know that that is not the way to speak to your official superior?"

"Oh, go to hell. The prisoners are my pidgin, and you've got no right to interfere. You mind your business and I'll mind mine. I want to know what the devil you mean by making a damned fool of me. Everyone in the place will know that you've countermanded my order."

Mr. Warburton kept very cool.

"You had no power to give the order you did. I countermanded it because it was harsh and tyrannical. Believe me, I have not made half such a damned fool of you as you have made of yourself."

"You disliked me from the first moment I came here. You've done everything you could to make the place impossible for me because I wouldn't lick your boots for you. You got your knife into me because I wouldn't flatter you."

Cooper, spluttering with rage, was nearing dangerous ground, and Mr. Warburton's eyes grew on a sudden colder and more piercing.

"You are wrong. I thought you were a cad, but I was perfectly satisfied with the way you did your work."

"You snob. You damned snob. You thought me a cad because I hadn't been to Eton. Oh, they told me in K.S. what to expect. Why, don't you know that you're the laughing-stock of the whole country? I could hardly help bursting into a roar of laughter when you told your celebrated story about the Prince of Wales. My God, how they shouted at the club when they told it. By God, I'd rather be the cad I am than the snob you are."

He got Mr. Warburton on the raw.

"If you don't get out of my house this minute I shall knock you down," he cried.

The other came a little closer to him and put his face in his.

"Touch me, touch me," he said. "By God, I'd like to see you hit me. Do you want me to say it again? Snob. Snob."

Cooper was three inches taller than Mr. Warburton, a strong, muscular young man. Mr. Warburton was fat and fifty-four. His clenched fist shot out. Cooper caught him by the arm and pushed him back.

"Don't be a damned fool. Remember I'm not a gentleman. I know how to use my hands."

He gave a sort of hoot, and grinning all over his pale, sharp face jumped down the verandah steps. Mr. Warburton, his heart in his anger pounding against his ribs, sank exhausted into a chair. His body tingled as though he had prickly heat. For one horrible moment he thought he was going to cry. But suddenly he was conscious that his head-boy was on the verandah and instinctively regained control of himself. The boy came forward and filled him a glass of whisky and soda. Without a word Mr. Warburton took it and drank it to the dregs.

"What do you want to say to me?" asked Mr. Warburton, trying to force a smile on to his strained lips.

"Tuan, the assistant Tuan is a bad man. Abas wishes again to leave him."

"Let him wait a little. I shall write to Kuala Solor and ask that Tuan Cooper should go elsewhere."

"Tuan Cooper is not good with the Malays."

"Leave me."

The boy silently withdrew. Mr. Warburton was left alone with his thoughts. He saw the club at Kuala Solor, the men sitting round the table in the window in their flannels, when the night had driven them in from golf and tennis, drinking whiskies and gin pahits, and laughing when they told the celebrated story of the Prince of Wales and himself at Marienbad. He was hot with shame and misery. A snob! They all thought him a snob. And he had always thought them very good fellows, he had always been gentleman enough to let it make no difference to him that they were of very second-rate position. He hated them now. But his hatred for them was nothing compared with his hatred for Cooper. And if it had come to blows Cooper could have thrashed him. Tears of mortification ran down his red, fat face. He sat there for a couple of hours smoking cigarette after cigarette, and he wished he were dead.

At last the boy came back and asked him if he would dress for dinner. Of course! He always dressed for dinner. He rose wearily from his chair and put on his stiff shirt and the high collar. He sat down at the prettily decorated table, and was waited on as usual by the two boys while two others waved their great fans. Over there in the bungalow, two hundred yards away, Cooper was eating a filthy meal clad only in a sarong and a baju. His feet were bare and while he ate he probably read a detective story. After dinner Mr. Warburton sat down to write a letter. The Sultan was away, but he wrote, privately and confidentially, to his representative. Cooper did his work very well, he said, but the fact was that he couldn't get on with him. They were getting dreadfully on each other's nerves and he would look upon it as a very great favour if Cooper could be transferred to another post.

He despatched the letter next morning by special messenger. The answer came a fortnight later with the month's mail. It was a private note, and ran as follows:

My dear Warburton,

I do not want to answer your letter officially, and so I am writing you a few lines myself. Of course if you insist I will put the matter up to the Sultan, but I think you would be much wiser to drop it. I know Cooper is a rough diamond, but he is capable, and he had a pretty thin time in the war, and I think he should be given every chance. I think you are a little too much inclined to attach importance to a man's social position. You must remember that times have changed. Of course it's a very good thing for a man to be a gentleman, but it's better that he should be competent and hard-working. I think if you'll exercise a little tolerance you'll get on very well with Cooper.

Yours very sincerely,

Richard Temple.

The letter dropped from Mr. Warburton's hand. It was easy to read between the lines. Dick Temple, whom he had known for twenty years, Dick Temple who came from quite a good county family, thought him a snob, and for that reason had no patience with his request. Mr. Warburton felt on a sudden discouraged with life. The world of which he was a part had passed away and the future belonged to a meaner generation. Cooper represented it and Cooper he hated with all his heart. He stretched out his hand to fill his glass, and at the gesture his head-boy stepped forward.

"I didn't know you were there."

The boy picked up the official letter. Ah, that was why he was waiting.

"Does Tuan Cooper go, Tuan?"

"No."

"There will be a misfortune."

For a moment the words conveyed nothing to his lassitude. But only for a moment. He sat up in his chair and looked at the boy. He was all attention.

"What do you mean by that?"

"Tuan Cooper is not behaving rightly with Abas."

Mr. Warburton shrugged his shoulders. How should a man like Cooper know how to treat servants? Mr. Warburton knew the type: he would be grossly familiar with them at one moment and rude and inconsiderate the next.

"Let Abas go back to his family."

"Tuan Cooper holds back his wages so that he may not run away. He has paid him nothing for three months. I tell him to be patient. But he is angry, he will not listen to reason. If the Tuan continues to use him ill there will be a misfortune."

"You were right to tell me."

The fool! Did he know so little of the Malays as to think he could safely injure them? It would serve him damned well right if he got a kris in his back. A kris. Mr. Warburton's heart seemed on a sudden to miss a beat. He had only to let things take their course and one fine day he would be rid of Cooper. He smiled faintly as the phrase, a masterly inactivity, crossed his mind. And now his heart beat a little quicker, for he saw the man he hated lying on his face in a pathway of the jungle with a knife in his back. A fit end for the cad and the bully. Mr. Warburton sighed. It was his duty to warn him, and of course he must do it. He wrote a brief and formal note to Cooper asking him to come to the Fort at once.

In ten minutes Cooper stood before him. They had not spoken to one another since the day when Mr. Warburton had nearly struck him. He did not now ask him to sit down.

"Did you wish to see me?" asked Cooper.

He was untidy and none too clean. His face and hands were covered with little red blotches where mosquitoes had bitten him and he had scratched himself till the blood came. His long, thin face bore a sullen look.

"I understand that you are again having trouble with your servants. Abas, my head-boy's nephew, complains that you have held back his wages for three months. I consider it a most arbitrary proceeding. The lad wishes to leave you, and I certainly do not blame him. I must insist on your paying what is due to him."

"I don't choose that he should leave me. I am holding back his wages as a pledge of his good behaviour."

"You do not know the Malay character. The Malays are very sensitive to injury and ridicule. They are passionate and revengeful. It is my duty to warn you that if you drive this boy beyond a certain point you run a great risk."

Cooper gave a contemptuous chuckle.

"What do you think he'll do?"

"I think he'll kill you."

"Why should you mind?"

"Oh, I wouldn't," replied Mr. Warburton, with a faint laugh. "I should bear it with the utmost fortitude. But I feel the official obligation to give you a proper warning."

"Do you think I'm afraid of a damned nigger?"

"It's a matter of entire indifference to me."

"Well, let me tell you this, I know how to take care of myself; that boy Abas is a dirty, thieving rascal, and if he tries any monkey tricks on me, by God, I'll wring his bloody neck."

"That was all I wished to say to you," said Mr. Warburton. "Good-evening."

Mr. Warburton gave him a little nod of dismissal. Cooper flushed, did not for a moment know what to say or do, turned on his heel and stumbled out of the room. Mr. Warburton watched him go with an icy smile on his lips. He had done his duty. But what would he have thought had he known that when Cooper got back to his bungalow, so silent and cheerless, he threw himself down on his bed and in his bitter loneliness on a sudden lost all control of himself? Painful sobs tore his chest and heavy tears rolled down his thin cheeks.

After this Mr. Warburton seldom saw Cooper, and never spoke to him. He read his *Times* every morning, did his work at the office, took his exercise, dressed for dinner, dined and sat by the river smoking his cheroot. If by chance he ran across Cooper he cut him dead. Each, though never for a moment unconscious of the propinquity, acted as though the other did not exist. Time did nothing to assuage their animosity. They watched one another's actions and each knew what the other did. Though Mr. Warburton had been a keen shot in his youth, with age he had acquired a distaste for killing the wild things of the jungle, but on Sundays and holidays Cooper went out with his gun: if he got something it was a triumph over Mr. Warburton; if not, Mr. Warburton shrugged his shoulders and chuckled. These counter-jumpers trying to be sportsmen! Christmas was a bad time for both of them: they ate their dinners alone, each in his own quarters, and they got deliberately drunk. They were the only white men within two hundred miles and they lived within shouting distance of each other. At the beginning of the year Cooper went down with fever, and when Mr. Warburton caught sight of him again he was surprised to see how thin he had grown. He looked ill and worn. The solitude, so much more unnatural because it was due to no necessity, was getting on his nerves. It was getting on Mr. Warburton's too, and often he could not sleep at night. He lay awake brooding. Cooper was drinking heavily and surely the breaking point was near; but in his dealings with the natives he took care to do nothing that might expose him to his chief's rebuke. They fought a grim and silent battle with one another. It was a test of endurance. The months passed, and neither gave sign of weakening. They were like men dwelling in regions of eternal night, and their souls were oppressed with the knowledge that never would the day dawn for them. It looked as though their lives would continue for ever in this dull and hideous monotony of hatred.

And when at last the inevitable happened it came upon Mr. Warburton with all the shock of the unexpected. Cooper accused the boy Abas of stealing some of his clothes, and when the boy denied the theft took him by the scruff of the neck and kicked him down the steps of the bungalow. The boy demanded his wages and Cooper flung at his head every word of abuse he knew. If he saw him in the compound in an hour he would hand him over to the police. Next morning the boy waylaid him outside the Fort when he was walking over to his office, and again demanded his wages. Cooper struck him in the face with his clenched fist. The boy fell to the ground and got up with blood streaming from his nose.

Cooper walked on and set about his work. But he could not attend to it. The blow had calmed his irritation, and he knew that he had gone too far. He was worried. He felt ill, miserable and discouraged. In the adjoining office sat Mr. Warburton, and his impulse was to go and tell him what he had done; he made a movement in his chair, but he knew with what icy scorn he would listen to the story. He could see his patronising smile. For a moment he had an uneasy fear of what Abas might do. Warburton had warned him all right. He sighed. What a fool he had been! But he shrugged his shoulders impatiently. He did not care; a fat lot he had to live for. It was all Warburton's fault; if he hadn't put his back up nothing like this would have happened. Warburton had made life a hell for him from the start. The snob. But they were all like that: it was because he was a Colonial. It was a damned shame that he had never got his commission in the war; he was as good as anyone else. They were a lot of dirty snobs. He was damned if he was going to knuckle under now. Of course Warburton would hear of what had happened; the old devil knew everything. He wasn't afraid. He wasn't afraid of any Malay in Borneo, and Warburton could go to blazes.

He was right in thinking that Mr. Warburton would know what had happened. His head-boy told him when he went in to tiffin.

"Where is your nephew now?"

"I do not know, Tuan. He has gone."

Mr. Warburton remained silent. After luncheon as a rule he slept a little, but to-day he found himself very wide awake. His eyes involuntarily sought the bungalow where Cooper was now resting.

The idiot! Hesitation for a little was in Mr. Warburton's mind. Did the man know in what peril he was? He supposed he ought to send for him. But each time he had tried to reason with Cooper, Cooper had insulted him. Anger, furious anger welled up suddenly in Mr. Warburton's heart, so that the veins on his temples stood out and he clenched his fists. The cad had had his warning. Now let him take what was coming to him. It was no business of his, and if anything happened it was not his fault. But perhaps they would wish in Kuala Solor that they had taken his advice and transferred Cooper to another station.

He was strangely restless that night. After dinner he walked up and down the verandah. When the boy went away to his own quarters, Mr. Warburton asked him whether anything had been seen of Abas.

"No, Tuan, I think maybe he has gone to the village of his mother's brother."

Mr. Warburton gave him a sharp glance, but the boy was looking down, and their eyes did not meet. Mr. Warburton went down to the river and sat in his arbour. But peace was denied him. The river flowed ominously silent. It was like a great serpent gliding with sluggish movement towards the sea. And the trees of the jungle over the water were heavy with a breathless menace. No bird sang. No breeze ruffled the leaves of the cassias. All around him it seemed as though something waited.

He walked across the garden to the road. He had Cooper's bungalow in full view from there. There was a light in his sitting-room, and across the road floated the sound of rag-time. Cooper was playing his gramophone. Mr. Warburton shuddered; he had never got over his instinctive dislike of that instrument. But for that he would have gone over and spoken to Cooper. He turned and went back to his own house. He read late into the night, and at last he slept. But he did not sleep very long, he had terrible dreams, and he seemed to be awakened by a cry. Of course that was a dream too, for no cry—from the bungalow for instance—could be heard in his room. He lay awake till dawn. Then he heard hurried steps and the sound of voices, his head-boy burst suddenly into the room without his fez, and Mr. Warburton's heart stood still.

"Tuan, Tuan."

Mr. Warburton jumped out of bed.

"I'll come at once."

He put on his slippers, and in his sarong and pyjama-jacket walked across his compound and into Cooper's. Cooper was lying in bed, with his mouth open, and a kris sticking in his heart. He had been killed in his sleep. Mr. Warburton started, but not because he had not expected to see just such a sight, he started because he felt in himself a sudden glow of exultation. A great burden had been lifted from his shoulders.

Cooper was quite cold. Mr. Warburton took the kris out of the wound, it had been thrust in with such force that he had to use an effort to get it out, and looked at it. He recognised it. It was a kris that a dealer had offered him some weeks before, and which he knew Cooper had bought.

"Where is Abas?" he asked sternly.

"Abas is at the village of his mother's brother."

The sergeant of the native police was standing at the foot of the bed.

"Take two men and go to the village and arrest him."

Mr. Warburton did what was immediately necessary. With set face he gave orders. His words were short and peremptory. Then he went back to the Fort. He shaved and had his bath, dressed and went into the dining-room. By the side of his plate *The Times* in its wrapper lay waiting for him. He helped himself to some fruit. The head-boy poured out his tea while the second handed him a dish of eggs. Mr. Warburton ate with a good appetite. The head-boy waited.

"What is it?" asked Mr. Warburton.

"Tuan, Abas, my nephew, was in the house of his mother's brother all night. It can be proved. His uncle will swear that he did not leave the kampong."

Mr. Warburton turned upon him with a frown.

"Tuan Cooper was killed by Abas. You know it as well as I know it. Justice must be done."

"Tuan, you would not hang him?"

Mr. Warburton hesitated an instant, and though his voice remained set and stern a change came into his eyes. It was a flicker which the Malay was quick to notice and across his own eyes flashed an answering look of understanding.

"The provocation was very great. Abas will be sentenced to a term of imprisonment." There was a pause while Mr. Warburton helped himself to marmalade. "When he has served a part of his sentence in prison I will take him into this house as a boy. You can train him in his duties. I have no doubt that in the house of Tuan Cooper he got into bad habits."

"Shall Abas give himself up, Tuan?"

"It would be wise of him."

The boy withdrew. Mr. Warburton took his *Times* and neatly slit the wrapper. He loved to unfold the heavy, rustling pages. The morning, so fresh and cool, was delicious and for a moment his eyes wandered out over the garden with a friendly glance. A great weight had been lifted from his mind. He turned to the columns in which were announced the births, deaths, and marriages. That was what he always looked at first. A name he knew caught his attention. Lady Ormskirk had had a son at last. By George, how pleased the old dowager must be! He would write her a note of congratulation by the next mail.

Abas would make a very good house-boy.

That fool Cooper!

The Portrait of a Gentleman

I ARRIVED in Seoul towards evening and after dinner, tired by the
long railway journey from Peking, to stretch my cramped legs I
went for a walk. I wandered at random along a narrow and busy
street. The Koreans in their long white gowns and their little
white top-hats were amusing to look at and the open shops displayed wares that arrested my foreign eyes. Presently I came to a
second-hand bookseller's and catching sight of shelves filled with
English books went in to have a look at them. I glanced at the
titles and my heart sank. They were commentaries on the Old
Testament, treatises on the Epistles of St. Paul, sermons and lives
of divines doubtless eminent, but whose names were unfamiliar to
me; I am an ignorant person. I supposed that this was the library
of some missionary whom death had claimed in the midst of his
labours and whose books then had been purchased by a Japanese
bookseller. The Japanese are astute, but I could not imagine who
in Seoul would be found to buy a work in three volumes on the
Epistle to the Corinthians. But as I was turning away, between
volume two and volume three of this treatise I noticed a little book
bound in paper. I do not know what induced me to take it out.
It was called *The Complete Poker Player* and its cover was illustrated
with a hand holding four aces. I looked at the title-page. The
author was Mr. John Blackbridge, actuary and counsellor-at-law,
and the preface was dated 1879. I wondered how this work
happened to be among the books of a deceased missionary and
I looked in one or two of them to see if I could find his name.
Perhaps it was there only by accident. It may be that it was the
entire library of a stranded gambler and had found its way to those
shelves when his effects were sold to pay his hotel bill. But I
preferred to think that it was indeed the property of the missionary
and that when he was weary of reading divinity he rested his mind
by the perusal of these lively pages. Perhaps somewhere in Korea,
at night and alone in his mission-house, he dealt innumerable
poker hands in order to see for himself whether you could really
only get a straight flush once in sixty-five thousand hands. But the
owner of the shop was looking at me with disfavour so I turned to
him and asked the price of the book. He gave it a contemptuous
glance and told me I could have it for twenty sen. I put it in my
pocket.

I do not remember that for so small a sum I have ever purchased better entertainment. For Mr. John Blackbridge in these pages of his did a thing that no writer can do who deliberately tries to, but that, if done unconsciously, gives a book a rare and precious savour; he painted a complete portrait of himself. He stands before the reader so vividly that I was convinced that a wood-cut of him figured as a frontispiece and I was surprised to discover, on looking at the book again the other day, that there was nothing of the kind. I see him very distinctly as a man of middle-age, in a black frock-coat and a chimney-pot hat, wearing a black satin stock; he is clean-shaven and his jaw is square; his lips are thin and his eyes wary; his face is sallow and somewhat wrinkled. It is a countenance not without severity, but when he tells a story or makes one of his dry jokes his eyes light up and his smile is winning. He enjoyed his bottle of Burgundy, but I cannot believe that he ever drank enough to confuse his excellent faculties. He was just rather than merciful at the card-table and he was prepared to punish presumption with rigour. He had few illusions, for here are some of the things that life had taught him: "Men hate those whom they have injured; men love those whom they have benefited; men naturally avoid their benefactors; men are universally actuated by self-interest; gratitude is a lively sense of expected benefits; promises are never forgotten by those to whom they are made, usually by those who make them."

It may be presumed that he was a Southerner, for while speaking of Jack Pots, which he describes as a frivolous attempt to make the game more interesting, he remarks that they are not popular in the South. "This last fact," he says, "contains much promise, because the South is the conservative portion of the country, and may be relied on as the last resort of good sense in social matters. The revolutionary Kossuth made no progress below Richmond; neither Spiritualism, nor Free Love, nor Communism, has ever been received with the least favour by the Southern mind; and it is for this reason that we greatly respect the Southern verdict upon the Jack Pot." It was in his day an innovation and he condemned it. "The time has arrived when all additions to the present standard combinations in Draw Poker must be worthless; the game being complete. The Jack Pot," he says, " was invented (in Toledo, Ohio) by reckless players to compensate losses incurred by playing against cautious players; and the principle is the same as if a party should play whist for stakes, and all be obliged every few minutes to stop, and purchase tickets in a lottery; or raffle for a turkey; or share a deal in Keno."

Poker is a game for gentlemen (he does not hesitate to make frequent use of this abused word; he lived in a day when to be a gentleman had its obligations but also its privileges) and a straight flush is to be respected, not because you make money on it ("I have never seen anyone make much money upon a straight flush," he says) but "because it prevents any hand from being *absolutely* the winning hand, and thus relieves gentlemen from the necessity of betting on a certainty. Without the use of straights, and hence without the use of a straight flush, four aces would be a certainty and no gentleman could do more than *call* on them." This, I confess, catches me on the raw, for once in my life I had a straight flush, and bet on it till I was called.

Mr. John Blackbridge had personal dignity, rectitude, humour and common sense. "The amusements of mankind," he says, "have not as yet received proper recognition at the hands of the makers of the civil law, and of the unwritten social law," and he had no patience with the persons who condemn the most agreeable pastime that has been invented, namely gambling, because risk is attached to it. Every transaction in life is a risk, he truly observes, and involves the question of loss and gain. "To retire to rest at night is a practice that is fortified by countless precedents, and it is generally regarded as prudent and necessary. Yet it is surrounded by risks of every kind." He enumerates them and finally sums up his argument with these reasonable words: "If social circles welcome the banker and merchant who live by taking fair risks for the sake of profit, there is no apparent reason why they should not at least tolerate the man who at times employs himself in giving and taking fair risks for the sake of amusement." But here his good sense is obvious. "Twenty years of experience in the city of New York, both professionally (you must not forget that he is an actuary and counsellor-at-law) and as a student of social life, satisfy me that the average American gentleman in a large city has not over three thousand dollars a year to spend upon amusements. Will it be fair to devote more than one-third of this fund to cards? I do not think that anyone will say that one-third is not ample allowance for a single amusement. Given, therefore, a thousand dollars a year for the purpose of playing Draw Poker, what should be the limit of the stakes, in order that the average American gentleman may play the game with a contented mind, and with the certainty not only that he can pay his losses, but that his winnings will be paid to him?" Mr. Blackbridge has no doubt that the answer is two dollars and a half. "The game of Poker should be intellectual and not emotional; and it is impossible to exclude the emotions from it, if the stakes are so high that the question of loss and gain penetrates to the feelings." From this quotation it may be seen that Mr. Blackbridge looked upon poker as only on the side a game of chance. He considered that it needed as much force of character, mental ability, power of decision and insight into motive to play poker as to govern a country or to lead an army, and I have an idea that on the whole he would have thought it a more sensible use of a man's faculties.

I am tempted to quote interminably, for Mr. Blackbridge seldom writes a sentence that is other than characteristic, and his language is excellent; it is dignified as befits his subject and his condition (he does not forget that he is a gentleman), measured, clear and pointed. His phrase takes an ample sweep when he treats of mankind and its foibles, but he can be as direct and simple as you please. Could anything be better than this terse but adequate description of a card-sharper? "He was a very good-looking man of about forty years of age, having the appearance of one who had been leading a temperate and thoughtful life." But I will content myself with giving a few of his aphorisms and wise saws chosen almost at random from the wealth of his book.

"Let your chips talk for you. A silent player is so far forth, a mystery; and a mystery is always feared."

"In this game never do anything that you are not compelled to; while cheerfully responding to your obligations."

"At Draw Poker all statements not called for by the laws of the game, or supported by ocular demonstration, may be set down as fictitious; designed to enliven the path of truth throughout the game, as flowers in summer enliven the margins of the highway."

"Lost money is never recovered. After losing you may win, but the losing does not bring the winning."

"No gentleman will ever play any game of cards with the design of habitually winning and never losing."

"A gentleman is always willing to pay a fair price for recreation and amusement."

". . . that habit of mind which continually leads us to undervalue the mental force of other men, while we continually overvalue their good luck."

"The injury done to your capital by a loss is never compensated by the benefit done to your capital by a gain of the same amount."

"Players usually straddle when they are in bad luck, upon the principle that bad play and bad luck united will win. A slight degree of intoxication aids to perfect this intellectual deduction."

"Euchre is a contemptible game."

"The lower cards as well as the lower classes are only useful in combination or in excess, and cannot be depended upon under any other circumstances."

"It is a hard matter to hold four Aces as steadily as a pair, but the table will bear their weight with as much equanimity as a pair of deuces."

Of good luck and bad luck: "To feel emotions over such incidents is unworthy of a man; and it is much more unworthy to express them. But no words need be wasted over practices which all men despise in others; and, in their reflecting moments, lament in themselves."

"Endorsing for your friends is a bad habit, but it is nothing to playing Poker on credit. . . . Debit and credit ought never to interfere with the fine intellectual calculations of this game."

There is a grand ring in his remarks on the player who has trained his intellect to bring logic to bear upon the principles and phenomena of the game. "He will thus feel a constant sense of security amid all possible fluctuations that occur, and he will also abstain from pressing an ignorant or an intellectually weak opponent, beyond what may be necessary either for the purpose of playing the game correctly, or of punishing presumption."

I leave Mr. John Blackbridge with this last word and I can hear him saying it gently, but with a tolerant smile:

"For we must take human nature as it is."

Raw Material

I HAVE long had in mind a novel in which a card-sharper was the principal character; and, going up and down the world, I have kept my eyes open for members of this profession. Because the idea is prevalent that it is a slightly dishonourable one the persons who follow it do not openly acknowledge the fact. Their reticence is such that it is often not till you have become quite closely acquainted with them, or even have played cards with them two or three times, that you discover in what fashion they earn their living. But even then they have a disinclination to enlarge upon the mysteries of their craft. They have a weakness for passing themselves off for cavalrymen, commercial agents or landed proprietors. This snobbish attitude makes them the most difficult class in the world for the novelist to study. It has been my good fortune to meet a number of these gentlemen, and though I have found them affable, obliging and debonair, I have no sooner hinted, however discreetly, at my curiosity (after all purely professional) in the technique of their calling than they have grown shy and uncommunicative. An airy reference on my part to stacking the cards has made them assume immediately the appearance of a clam. I am not easily discouraged, and learning by experience that I could hope for no good results from a direct method, I have adopted the oblique. I have been childlike with them and bland. I have found that they gave me their attention and even their sympathy. Though they confessed honestly that they had never read a word I had written they were interested by the fact that I was a writer. I suppose they felt obscurely that I too followed a calling that the Philistine regarded without indulgence. But I have been forced to gather my facts by a bold surmise. It has needed patience and industry.

It may be imagined with what enthusiasm I made the acquaintance a little while ago of two gentlemen who seemed likely to add appreciably to my small store of information. I was travelling from Haiphong on a French liner going East, and they joined the ship at Hong-Kong. They had gone there for the races and were now on their way back to Shanghai. I was going there too, and thence to Peking. I soon learned that they had come from New York for a trip, were bound for Peking also, and by a happy coincidence meant to return to America in the ship in which I had myself booked a passage. I was naturally attracted to them, for they were pleasant fellows, but it was not till a fellow-passenger warned me that they were professional gamblers that I settled down to complete enjoyment of their acquaintance. I had no hope that they would ever discuss with frankness their interesting occupation, but I expected from a hint here, from a casual remark there, to learn some very useful things.

One—Campbell was his name—was a man in the late thirties, small, but so well built as not to look short, slender, with large, melancholy eyes and beautiful hands. But for a premature baldness he would have been more than commonly good-looking. He was neatly dressed. He spoke slowly, in a low voice, and his movements were deliberate. The other was made on another pattern. He was a big, burly man with a red face and crisp black hair, of powerful appearance, strong in the arm and pugnacious. His name was Peterson.

The merits of the combination were obvious. The elegant, exquisite Campbell had the subtle brain, the knowledge of character, and the deft hands; but the hazards of the card-sharper's life are many, and when it came to a scrap Peterson's ready fist must often have proved invaluable. I do not know how it spread through the ship so quickly that a blow of Peterson's would stretch any man out. But during the short voyage from Hong-Kong to Shanghai they never even suggested a game of cards. Perhaps they had done well during the race-week and felt entitled to a holiday. They were certainly enjoying the advantages of not living for the time in a dry country and I do not think I do them an injustice if I say that for the most part they were far from sober. Each one talked little of himself but willingly of the other. Campbell informed me that Peterson was one of the most distinguished mining engineers in New York and Peterson assured me that Campbell was an eminent banker. He said that his wealth was fabulous. And who was I not to accept ingenuously all that was told me? But I thought it negligent of Campbell not to wear jewellery of a more expensive character. It seemed to me that to use a silver cigarette-case was rather careless.

I stayed but a day in Shanghai, and though I met the pair again in Peking I was then so much engaged that I saw little of them. I thought it a little odd that Campbell should spend his entire time in the hotel. I do not think he even went to see the Temple of Heaven. But I could quite understand that from his point of view Peking was unsatisfactory and I was not surprised when the pair returned to Shanghai, where I knew the wealthy merchants played for big money. I met them again in the ship that was to take us across the Pacific and I could not but sympathise with my friends when I saw that the passengers were little inclined to gamble. There were no rich people among them. It was a dull crowd. Campbell indeed suggested a game of poker, but no one would play more than twenty-dollar table stakes, and Peterson, evidently not thinking it worth his while, would not join. Although we played afternoon and evening through the journey he sat down with us only on the last day. I suppose he thought he might just as well make his bar chits, and this he did very satisfactorily in a single sitting. But Campbell evidently loved the game for itself. Of course it is only if you have a passion for the business by which you earn your living that you can make a success of it. The stakes were nothing to him and he played all day and every day. It fascinated me to see the way in which he dealt the cards, very slowly, with his delicate hands. His eyes seemed to bore through the back of each one. He drank heavily, but remained quiet and self-controlled. His face was expressionless. I judged him to be a perfect card-player and I wished that I could see him at work. It increased my esteem for him to see that he could take what was only a relaxation so seriously.

I parted with the pair at Victoria and concluded that I should never see them again. I set about sorting my impressions and made notes of the various points that I thought would prove useful.

When I arrived in New York I found an invitation to luncheon at the Ritz with an old friend of mine. When I went she said to me:

"It's quite a small party. A man is coming whom I think you'll like. He's a prominent banker; he's bringing a friend with him."

The words were hardly out of her mouth when I saw coming up to us Campbell and Peterson. The truth flashed across me: Campbell really was an opulent banker; Peterson really was a distinguished engineer; they were not card-sharpers at all. I flattered myself I kept my face, but as I blandly shook hands with them I muttered under my breath furiously:

"Impostors!"

Straight Flush

I AM not a bad sailor and when under stress of weather the game broke up I did not go below. We were in the habit of playing poker into the small hours, a mild game that could hurt nobody, but it had been blowing all day and with nightfall the wind strengthened to half a gale. One or two of our bunch admitted that they felt none too comfortable and one or two others played with unwonted detachment. But even if you are not sick dirty weather at sea is an unpleasant thing. I hate the fool who tells you he loves a storm and tramping the deck lustily vows that it can never be too rough for him. When the woodwork groans and creaks, glasses crash to the floor and you lurch in your chair as the ship heels over, when the wind howls and the waves thunder against the side, I very much prefer dry land. I think no one was sorry when one of the players said he had had enough, and the last round of jack pots was agreed to without demur. I remained alone in the smoking-room, for I knew I should not easily get to sleep in that racket and I could not read in bed with any comfort when the North Pacific kept dashing itself against my port-holes. I shuffled together the two packs we had been playing with and set out a complicated patience.

I had been playing about ten minutes when the door was opened with a blast of wind that sent my cards flying, and two passengers, rather breathless, slipped into the smoking-room. We were not a full ship and we were ten days out from Hong-Kong, so that I had had time to become acquainted with pretty well everyone on board. I had spoken on several occasions to the pair who now entered, and seeing me by myself they came over to my table.

They were very old men, both of them. That perhaps was what had brought them together, for they had first met when they got on board at Hong-Kong, and now you saw them sitting together in the smoking-room most of the day, not talking very much, but just comfortable to be side by side, with a bottle of Vichy water between them. They were very rich old men too and that was a bond between them. The rich feel at ease in one another's company. They know that money means merit. Their experience of the poor is that they always want something. It is true that the poor admire the rich and it is pleasant to be admired, but they envy them as well and this prevents their admiration from being quite candid. Mr. Rosenbaum was a little hunched-up Jew, very frail in clothes that looked too big for him, and he gave you the impression of hanging on to mortality only by a hair. His ancient, emaciated body looked as though it were already attacked by the corruption of the grave. The only expression his face ever bore was one of cunning, but it was purely habitual, the result of ever so many years' astuteness; he was a kindly, friendly person, very free with his drinks and cigars, and his charity was world-famous. The other was called Donaldson. He was a Scot, but had gone to California as a little boy and made a great deal of money mining. He was short and stout, with a red, clean-shaven, shiny face and no hair but a sickle of silver above his neck, and very gentle eyes. Whatever force he had had to make his way in the world had been worn away by the years and he was now a picture of mild beneficence.

"I thought you'd turned in long ago," I remarked.

"I should have," returned the Scot, "only Mr. Rosenbaum kept me up talking of old times."

"What's the good of going to bed when you can't sleep?" said Mr. Rosenbaum.

"Walk ten times round the deck with me to-morrow morning and you'll sleep all right."

"I've never taken any exercise in my life and I'm not going to begin now."

"That's foolishness. You'd be twice the man you are now if you'd taken exercise. Look at me. You'd never think I was seventy-nine, would you?"

Mr. Rosenbaum looked critically at Mr. Donaldson.

"No, I wouldn't. You're very well preserved. You look younger than me and I'm only seventy-six. But then I never had a chance to take care of myself."

At that moment the steward came up.

"The bar's just going to close, gentlemen. Is there anything I can get you?"

"It's a stormy night," said Mr. Rosenbaum. "Let's have a bottle of champagne."

"Small Vichy for me," said Mr. Donaldson.

"Oh, very well, small Vichy for me too."

The steward went away.

"But mind you," continued Mr. Rosenbaum testily, "I wouldn't have done without the things you've done without, not for all the money in the world."

Mr. Donaldson gave me his gentle smile.

"Mr. Rosenbaum can't get over it because I've never touched a card nor a drop of alcohol for fifty-seven years."

"Now I ask you, what sort of a life is that?"

"I was a very heavy drinker when I was a young fellow and a desperate gambler, but I had a very terrible experience. It was a lesson to me and I took it."

"Tell him about it," said Mr. Rosenbaum. "He's an author. He'll write it up and perhaps he'll be able to make his passage money."

"It's not a story I like telling very much even now. I'll make it as short as I can. Me and three others had staked out a claim, friends all of us, and the oldest wasn't twenty-five; there was me and my partner and a couple of brothers, McDermott their name was, but they were more like friends than brothers. What was one's was the other's, and one wouldn't go into town without the other went too, and they were always laughing and joking together. A fine clean pair of boys, over six feet high both of them, and handsome. We were a wild bunch and we had pretty good luck on the whole and when we made money we didn't hesitate to spend it. Well, one night we'd all been drinking very heavily and we started a poker game. I guess we were a good deal drunker than we realised. Anyhow suddenly a row started between the McDermotts. One of them accused the other of cheating. 'You take that back,' cried Jamie. 'I'll see you in hell first,' says Eddie. And before me and my partner could do anything Jamie had pulled out his gun and shot his brother dead."

The ship gave a huge roll and we all clung to our seats. In the steward's pantry there was a great clatter as bottles and glasses slid along a shelf. It was strange to hear that grim little story told by that mild old man. It was a story of another age and you could hardly believe that this fat, red-faced little fellow, with his silver fringe of hair, in a dinner jacket, two large pearls in his shirt-front, had really taken part in it.

"What happened then?" I asked.

"We sobered up pretty quick. At first Jamie couldn't believe Eddie was dead. He took him in his arms and kept calling him. 'Eddie,' he says, 'wake up, old boy, wake up.' He cried all night and next day we rode in with him to town, forty miles it was, me on one side of him and my partner on the other, and handed him over to the sheriff. I was crying too when we shook hands with him and said good-bye. I told my partner I'd never touch a card again or drink as long as I lived, and I never have, and I never will."

Mr. Donaldson looked down, and his lips were trembling. He seemed to see again that scene of long ago. There was one thing I should have liked to ask him about, but he was evidently so much moved I did not like to. They seem not to have hesitated, his partner and himself, but delivered up this wretched boy to justice as though it were the most natural thing in the world. It suggested that even in those rough, wild men the respect for the law had somehow the force of an instinct. A little shiver ran through me. Mr. Donaldson emptied his glass of Vichy and with a curt good-night left us.

"The old fellow's getting a bit childish," said Mr. Rosenbaum. "I don't believe he was ever very bright."

"Well, apparently he was bright enough to make an awful lot of money."

"But how? In those days in California you didn't want brains to make money, you only wanted luck. I know what I'm talking about. Johannesburg was the place where you had to have your wits about you. Joburg in the 'eighties. It was grand. We were a tough lot of guys, I can tell you. It was each for himself and the devil take the hindmost."

He took a meditative sip of his Vichy.

"You talk of your cricket and baseball, your golf and tennis and football, you can have them, they're all very well for boys; is it a reasonable thing, I ask you, for a grown man to run about and hit a ball? Poker's the only game fit for a grown man. Then your hand is against every man and every man's hand is against yours. Team-work? Who ever made a fortune by team-work? There's only one way to make a fortune and that's to down the fellow who's up against you."

"I didn't know you were a poker player," I interrupted. "Why don't you take a hand one evening?"

"I don't play any more. I've given it up too, but for the only reason a man should. I can't see myself giving it up because a friend of mine was unlucky enough to get killed. Anyway a man who's damn fool enough to get killed isn't worth having as a friend. But in the old days! If you wanted to know what poker was you ought to have been in South Africa then. It was the biggest game I've ever seen. And they were fine players; there wasn't a crooked dodge they weren't up to. It was grand. Just to give you an example, one night I was playing with some of the biggest men in Johannesburg and I was called away. There was a couple of thousand pounds in the pot! 'Deal me a hand, I won't keep you waiting,' I said. 'All right,' they said, 'don't hurry.' Well, I wasn't gone more than a minute. When I came back I picked up my cards and saw I'd got a straight flush to the queen. I didn't say a word, I just threw in my hand. I knew my company. And do you know, I was wrong."

"What do you mean? I don't understand."

"It was a perfectly straight deal and the pot was won on three sevens. But how could I tell that? Naturally I thought someone else had a straight flush to the king. It looked to me just the sort of hand I might lose a hundred thousand pounds on."

"Too bad," I said.

"I very nearly had a stroke. And it was on account of another pat straight flush that I gave up playing poker. I've only had about five in my life."

"I believe the chances are nearly sixty-six thousand to one against."

"In San Francisco it was, the year before last. I'd been playing in poor luck all the evening. I hadn't lost much money because I never had a chance to play. I'd hardly had a pair and if I got a pair I couldn't improve. Then I got a hand just as bad as the others and I didn't come in. The man next me wasn't playing either and I showed him my hand. 'That's the kind of thing I've been getting all the evening,' I said. 'How can anyone be expected to play with cards like that?' 'Well, I don't know what more you want,' he said, as he looked at them. 'Most of us would be prepared to come in on a straight flush.' 'What's that,' I cried. I was trembling like a leaf. I looked at the cards again. I thought I had two or three little hearts and two or three little diamonds. It was a straight flush in hearts all right and I hadn't seen it. My eyes, it was. I knew what it meant. Old age. I don't cry much. I'm not that sort of man. But I couldn't help it then. I tried to control myself, but the tears just rolled down my cheeks. Then I got up. 'I'm through, gentlemen,' I said. 'When a man's eyes are so dim that he can't see a straight flush when it's dealt him he has no business to play poker. Nature's given me a hint and I'm taking it. I'll never play poker again as long as I live.' I cashed in my chips, all but one, and I left the house. I've never played since."

Mr. Rosenbaum took a chip out of his waistcoat pocket and showed it to me.

"I kept this as a souvenir. I always carry it about with me. I'm a sentimental old fool, I know that, but, you see, poker was the only thing I cared for. Now I've only got one thing left."

"What is that?" I asked.

A smile flickered across his cunning little face and behind his thick glasses his rheumy eyes twinkled with ironic glee. He looked incredibly astute and malicious. He gave the thin, high-pitched cackle of an old man amused and answered with a single word "Philanthropy."

The End of the Flight

I SHOOK hands with the skipper and he wished me luck. Then I went down to the lower deck crowded with passengers, Malays, Chinese and Dyaks, and made my way to the ladder. Looking over the ship's side I saw that my luggage was already in the boat. It was a large, clumsy-looking craft, with a great square sail of bamboo matting, and it was crammed full of gesticulating natives. I scrambled in and a place was made for me. We were about three miles from the shore and a stiff breeze was blowing. As we drew near I saw that the coconut trees in a green abundance grew to the water's edge, and among them I saw the brown roofs of the village. A Chinese who spoke English pointed out to me a white bungalow as the residence of the District Officer. Though he did not know it, it was with him that I was going to stay. I had a letter of introduction to him in my pocket.

I felt somewhat forlorn when I landed and my bags were set down beside me on the glistening beach. This was a remote spot to find myself in, this little town on the north coast of Borneo, and I felt a trifle shy at the thought of presenting myself to a total stranger with the announcement that I was going to sleep under his roof, eat his food and drink his whisky, till another boat came in to take me to the port for which I was bound.

But I might have spared myself these misgivings, for the moment I reached the bungalow and sent in my letter he came out, a sturdy, ruddy, jovial man, of thirty-five perhaps, and greeted me with heartiness. While he held my hand he shouted to a boy to bring drinks and to another to look after my luggage. He cut short my apologies.

"Good God, man, you have no idea how glad I am to see you. Don't think I'm doing anything for you in putting you up. The boot's on the other leg. And stay as long as you damned well like. Stay a year."

I laughed. He put away his day's work, assuring me that he had nothing to do that could not wait till the morrow, and threw himself into a long chair. We talked and drank and talked. When the heat of the day wore off we went for a long tramp in the jungle and came back wet to the skin. A bath and a change were very grateful, and then we dined. I was tired out and though my host was plainly willing to go on talking straight through the night I was obliged to beg him to allow me to go to bed.

"All right, I'll just come along to your room and see everything's all right."

It was a large room with verandahs on two sides of it, sparsely furnished, but with a huge bed protected by mosquito netting.

"The bed is rather hard. Do you mind?"

"Not a bit. I shall sleep without rocking to-night."

My host looked at the bed reflectively.

"It was a Dutchman who slept in it last. Do you want to hear a funny story?"

I wanted chiefly to go to bed, but he *was* my host, and being at times somewhat of a humorist myself I know that it is hard to have an amusing story to tell and find no listener.

"He came on the boat that brought you, on its last journey along the coast, he came into my office and asked where the dak bungalow was. I told him there wasn't one, but if he hadn't anywhere to go I didn't mind putting him up. He jumped at the invitation. I told him to have his kit sent along.

" 'This is all I've got,' he said.

"He held out a little shiny black grip. It seemed a bit scanty, but it was no business of mine, so I told him to go along to the bungalow and I'd come as soon as I was through with my work. While I was speaking the door of my office was opened and my clerk came in. The Dutchman had his back to the door and it may be that my clerk opened it a bit suddenly. Anyhow, the Dutchman gave a shout, he jumped about two feet into the air and whipped out a revolver.

" 'What the hell are you doing?' I said.

"When he saw it was the clerk he collapsed. He leaned against the desk, panting, and upon my word he was shaking as though he'd got fever.

" 'I beg your pardon,' he said. 'It's my nerves. My nerves are terrible.'

" 'It looks like it,' I said.

"I was rather short with him. To tell you the truth I wished I hadn't asked him to stop with me. He didn't look as though he'd been drinking a lot and I wondered if he was some fellow the police were after. If he were, I said to myself, he could hardly be such a fool as to walk right into the lion's den.

" 'You'd better go and lie down,' I said.

"He took himself off, and when I got back to my bungalow I found him sitting quite quietly, but bolt upright, on the verandah. He'd had a bath and shaved and put on clean things and he looked fairly presentable.

Y

" 'Why are you sitting in the middle of the place like that?'
I asked him. 'You'll be much more comfortable in one of the long
chairs.'

" 'I prefer to sit up,' he said.

"Queer, I thought. But if a man in this heat would rather sit
up than lie down it's his own lookout. He wasn't much to look at,
tallish and heavily built, with a square head and close-cropped
bristly hair. I should think he was about forty. The thing that
chiefly struck me about him was his expression. There was a look
in his eyes, blue eyes they were and rather small, that beat me altogether; and his face sagged as it were; it gave you the feeling he was
going to cry. He had a way of looking quickly over his left shoulder
as though he thought he heard something. By God, he was nervous.
But we had a couple of drinks and he began to talk. He spoke
English very well; except for a slight accent you'd never have known
that he was a foreigner, and I'm bound to admit he was a good
talker. He'd been everywhere and he'd read any amount. It was a
treat to listen to him.

"We had three or four whiskies in the afternoon and a lot of gin
pahits later on, so that when dinner came along we were by way of
being rather hilarious and I'd come to the conclusion that he was a
damned good fellow. Of course we had a lot of whisky at dinner and
I happened to have a bottle of Benedictine, so we had some liqueurs
afterwards. I can't help thinking we both got very tight.

"And at last he told me why he'd come. It was a rum story."

My host stopped and looked at me with his mouth slightly open
as though, remembering it now, he was struck again with its rum-
ness.

"He came from Sumatra, the Dutchman, and he'd done something to an Achinese and the Achinese had sworn to kill him. At
first he made light of it, but the fellow tried two or three times and
it began to be rather a nuisance, so he thought he'd better go away
for a bit. He went over to Batavia and made up his mind to have a
good time. But when he'd been there a week he saw the fellow
slinking along a wall. By God, he'd followed him. It looked as
though he meant business. The Dutchman began to think it was
getting beyond a joke and he thought the best thing he could do
would be to skip off to Soerabaya. Well, he was strolling about there
one day, you know how crowded the streets are, when he happened
to turn round and saw the Achinese walking quite quietly just behind him. It gave him a turn. It would give anyone a turn.

"The Dutchman went straight back to his hotel, packed his
things, and took the next boat to Singapore. Of course he put up

at the Van Wyck, all the Dutch stay there, and one day when he was having a drink in the courtyard in front of the hotel, the Achinese walked in as bold as brass, looked at him for a minute, and walked out again. The Dutchman told me he was just paralysed. The fellow could have stuck his kris into him there and then and he wouldn't have been able to move a hand to defend himself. The Dutchman knew he was just biding his time, that damned native was going to kill him, he saw it in his eyes; and he went all to pieces."

"But why didn't he go to the police?" I asked.

"I don't know. I expect it wasn't a thing he wanted the police to be mixed up in."

"But what had he done to the man?"

"I don't know that either. He wouldn't tell me. But by the look he gave when I asked him, I expect it was something pretty rotten. I have an idea he knew he deserved whatever the Achinese could do."

My host lit a cigarette.

"Go on," I said.

"The skipper of the boat that runs between Singapore and Kuching lives at the Van Wyck between trips and the boat was starting at dawn. The Dutchman thought it a grand chance to give the fellow the slip; he left his luggage at the hotel and walked down to the ship with the skipper, as if he were just going to see him off, and stayed on her when she sailed. His nerves were all anyhow by then. He didn't care about anything but getting rid of the Achinese. He felt pretty safe at Kuching. He got a room at the rest-house and bought himself a couple of suits and some shirts in the Chinese shops. But he told me he couldn't sleep. He dreamt of that man and half a dozen times he awakened just as he thought a kris was being drawn across his throat. By God, I felt quite sorry for him. He just shook as he talked to me and his voice was hoarse with terror. That was the meaning of the look I had noticed. You remember, I told you he had a funny look on his face and I couldn't tell what it meant. Well, it was fear.

"And one day when he was in the club at Kuching he looked out of the window and saw the Achinese sitting there. Their eyes met. The Dutchman just crumpled up and fainted. When he came to, his first idea was to get out. Well, you know, there's not a hell of a lot of traffic at Kuching and this boat that brought you was the only one that gave him a chance to get away quickly. He got on her. He was positive the man was not on board."

"But what made him come here?"

"Well, the old tramp stops at a dozen places on the coast and the

Achinese couldn't possibly guess he'd chosen this one because he only made up his mind to get off when he saw there was only one boat to take the passengers ashore, and there weren't more than a dozen people in it.

" 'I'm safe here for a bit at all events,' he said, 'and if I can only be quiet for a while I shall get my nerve back.'

" 'Stay as long as you like,' I said. 'You're all right here, at all events till the boat comes along next month, and if you like we'll watch the people who come off.'

"He was all over me. I could see what a relief it was to him.

"It was pretty late and I suggested to him that we should turn in. I took him to his room to see that it was all right. He locked the door of the bath-house and bolted the shutters, though I told him there was no risk, and when I left him I heard him lock the door I had just gone out of.

"Next morning when the boy brought me my tea I asked him if he'd called the Dutchman. He said he was just going to. I heard him knock and knock again. Funny, I thought. The boy hammered on the door, but there was no answer. I felt a little nervous, so I got up. I knocked too. We made enough noise to rouse the dead, but the Dutchman slept on. Then I broke down the door. The mosquito curtains were neatly tucked in round the bed. I pulled them apart. He was lying there on his back with his eyes wide open. He was as dead as mutton. A kris lay across his throat, and say I'm a liar if you like, but I swear to God it's true, there wasn't a wound about him anywhere. The room was empty.

"Funny, wasn't it?"

"Well, that all depends on your idea of humour," I replied.

My host looked at me quickly.

"You don't mind sleeping in that bed, do you?"

"N-no. But I'd just as soon you'd told me the story to-morrow morning."

A Casual Affair

I AM telling this story in the first person, though I am in no way connected with it, because I do not want to pretend to the reader that I know more about it than I really do. The facts are as I state them, but the reasons for them I can only guess, and it may be that when the reader has read them he will think me wrong. No one can know for certain. But if you are interested in human nature there are few things more diverting than to consider the motives that have resulted in certain actions. It was only by chance that I heard anything of the unhappy circumstances at all. I was spending two or three days on an island on the north coast of Borneo and the District Officer had very kindly offered to put me up. I had been roughing it for some time and I was glad enough to have a rest. The island had been at one time a place of some consequence, with a Governor of its own, but was so no longer; and now there was nothing much to be seen of its former importance except the imposing stone house in which the Governor had once lived and which now the District Officer, grumblingly because of its unnecessary size, inhabited. But it was a comfortable house to stay in, with an immense drawing-room, a dining-room large enough to seat forty people, and lofty, spacious bedrooms. It was shabby, because the government at Singapore very wisely spent as little money on it as possible; but I rather liked this, and the heavy official furniture gave it a sort of dull stateliness that was amusing. The garden was too large for the District Officer to keep up and it was a wild tangle of tropical vegetation. His name was Arthur Low; he was a quiet, smallish man in the later thirties, married, with two young children. The Lows had not tried to make themselves at home in this great place, but camped there, like refugees from a stricken area, and looked forward to the time when they would be moved to some other post where they could settle down in surroundings more familiar to them.

I took a fancy to them at once. The D.O. had an easy manner and a humorous way with him. I am sure he performed his various duties admirably, but he did everything he could to avoid the official demeanour. He was slangy of speech and pleasantly caustic. It was charming to see him play with the two children. It was quite obvious that he had found marriage a very satisfactory state. Mrs. Low was an extremely nice little woman, plump, with dark eyes under fine eyebrows, not very pretty, but certainly attractive. She looked healthy and she had high spirits. They chaffed one another continually and each one seemed to look upon the other as immensely comic. Their jokes were neither very good nor very new, but they thought them so killing that you were obliged to laugh with them.

I think they were glad to see me, especially Mrs. Low, for with nothing much to do but keep an eye on the house and the children, she was thrown very much on her own resources. There were so few white people on the island that the social life was soon exhausted; and before I had been there twenty-four hours she pressed me to stay a week, a month or a year. On the evening of my arrival they gave a dinner-party to which the official population, the government surveyor, the doctor, the schoolmaster, the chief of constabulary, were invited, but on the following evening the three of us dined by ourselves. At the dinner-party the guests had brought their house-boys to help, but that night we were waited on by the Lows' one boy and my travelling servant. They brought in the coffee and left us to ourselves. Low and I lit cheroots.

"You know that I've seen you before," said Mrs. Low.

"Where?" I asked.

"In London. At a party. I heard someone point you out to somebody else. In Carlton House Terrace at Lady Kastellan's."

"Oh? When was that?"

"Last time we were home on leave. There were Russian dancers."

"I remember. About two or three years ago. Fancy you being there!"

"That's exactly what we said to one another at the time," said Low, with his slow, engaging smile. "We'd never been at such a party in our lives."

"It made a great splash, you know," I said. "It was *the* party of the season. Did you enjoy it?"

"I hated every minute of it," said Mrs. Low.

"Don't let's overlook the fact that you insisted on going, Bee," said Low. "I knew we'd be out of it among all those swells. My dress clothes were the same I'd had at Cambridge and they'd never been much of a fit."

"I bought a frock specially at Peter Robinson's. It looked lovely in the shop. I wished I hadn't wasted so much money when I got there; I never felt so dowdy in my life."

"Well, it didn't much matter. We weren't introduced to anybody."

I remembered the party quite well. The magnificent rooms in

Carlton House Terrace had been decorated with great festoons of yellow roses and at one end of the vast drawing-room a stage had been erected. Special costumes of the Regency period had been designed for the dancers and a modern composer had written the music for the two charming ballets they danced. It was hard to look at it all and not allow the vulgar thought to cross one's mind that the affair must have cost an enormous amount of money. Lady Kastellan was a beautiful woman and a great hostess, but I do not think anyone would have ascribed to her any vast amount of kindliness, she knew too many people to care much for any one in particular, and I couldn't help wondering why she had asked to such a grand party two obscure and quite unimportant little persons from a distant colony.

"Had you known Lady Kastellan long?" I asked.

"We didn't know her at all. She sent us a card and we went because I wanted to see what she was like," said Mrs. Low.

"She's a very able woman," I said.

"I dare say she is. She hadn't an idea who we were when the butler man announced us, but she remembered at once. 'Oh, yes,' she said, 'you're poor Jack's friends. Do go and find yourselves seats where you can see. You'll adore Lifar, he's too marvellous.' And then she turned to say how d'you do to the next people. But she gave me a look. She wondered how much I knew and she saw at once that I knew everything."

"Don't talk such nonsense, darling," said Low. "How could she know all you think she did by just looking at you, and how could you tell what she was thinking?"

"It's true, I tell you. We said everything in that one look, and unless I'm very much mistaken I spoilt her party for her."

Low laughed and I smiled, for Mrs. Low spoke in a tone of triumphant vindictiveness.

"You are terribly indiscreet, Bee."

"Is she a great friend of yours?" Mrs. Low asked me.

"Hardly. I've met her here and there for fifteen years. I've been to a good many parties at her house. She gives very good parties and she always asks you to meet the people you want to see."

"What d'you think of her?"

"She's by way of being a considerable figure in London. She's amusing to talk to and she's nice to look at. She does a lot for art and music. What do *you* think of her?"

"I think she's a bitch," said Mrs. Low, with cheerful but decided frankness.

"That settles her," I said.

"Tell him, Arthur."

Low hesitated for a moment.

"I don't know that I ought to."

"If you don't, I shall."

"Bee's got her knife into her all right," he smiled. "It was rather a bad business really."

He made a perfect smoke-ring and watched it with absorption.

"Go on, Arthur," said Mrs. Low.

"Oh, well. It was before we went home last time. I was D.O. in Selangor and one day they came and told me that a white man was dead in a small town a couple of hours up the river. I didn't know there was a white man living there. I thought I'd better go and see about it, so I got in the launch and went up. I made enquiries when I got there. The police didn't know anything about him except that he'd been living there for a couple of years with a Chinese woman in the bazaar. It was rather a picturesque bazaar, tall houses on each side, with a board walk in between, built on piles on the river-bank, and there were awnings above to keep out the sun. I took a couple of policemen with me and they led me to the house. They sold brass-ware in the shop below and the rooms above were let out. The master of the shop took me up two flights of dark, rickety stairs, foul with every kind of Chinese stench, and called out when we got to the top. The door was opened by a middle-aged Chinese woman and I saw that her face was all bloated with weeping. She didn't say anything, but made way for us to pass. It wasn't much more than a cubby-hole under the roof; there was a small window that looked on the street, but the awning that stretched across it dimmed the light. There wasn't any furniture except a deal table and a kitchen chair with a broken back. On a mat against the wall a dead man was lying. The first thing I did was to have the window opened. The room was so frowsty that I retched, and the strongest smell was the smell of opium. There was a small oil-lamp on the table and a long needle, and of course I knew what they were there for. The pipe had been hidden. The dead man lay on his back with nothing on but a sarong and a dirty singlet. He had long brown hair, going grey, and a short beard. He was a white man all right. I examined him as best I could. I had to judge whether death was due to natural causes. There were no signs of violence. He was nothing but skin and bone. It looked to me as though he might very likely have died of starvation. I asked the man of the shop and the woman a number of questions. The policeman corroborated their statements. It appeared that the man coughed a great deal and brought up blood now and then, and his appearance suggested that he might very well have had T.B. The Chinaman said he'd been a confirmed opium smoker. It all seemed pretty obvious. Fortunately cases of that sort are rare, but they're not unheard-of—the white man who goes under and gradually sinks to the last stage of degradation. It appeared that the Chinese woman had been fond of him. She'd kept him on her own miserable earnings for the last two years. I gave the necessary instructions. Of course I wanted to know who he was. I supposed he'd been a clerk in some English firm or an assistant in an English store at Singapore or Kuala Lumpur. I asked the Chinese woman if he'd left any effects. Considering the destitution in which they'd lived it seemed a rather absurd question, but she went to a shabby suit-case that lay in a corner, opened it and showed me a square parcel about the size of two novels put together wrapped in an old newspaper. I had a look at the suit-case. It contained nothing of any value. I took the parcel."

Low's cheroot had gone out and he leaned over to relight it from one of the candles on the table.

"I opened it. Inside was another wrapping, and on this, in a neat well-educated writing: To the District Officer, me as it happened, and then the words: please deliver personally to the Viscountess Kastellan, 53 Carlton House Terrace, London, S.W. That was a bit of a surprise. Of course I had to examine the contents. I cut the string and the first thing I found was a gold and platinum cigar-ette case. As you can imagine I was mystified. From all I'd heard the pair of them, the dead man and the Chinese woman, had scarcely enough to eat, and the cigarette-case looked as if it had cost a packet. Besides the cigarette-case there was nothing but a bundle of letters. There were no envelopes. They were in the same neat writing as the directions and they were signed with the initial J. There were forty or fifty of them. I couldn't read them all there, but a rapid glance showed me that they were a man's love letters to a woman. I sent for the Chinese woman to ask her the name of the dead man. Either she didn't know or wouldn't tell me. I gave orders that he should be buried and got back into the launch to go home. I told Bee."

He gave her his sweet little smile.

"I had to be rather firm with Arthur," she said. "At first he wouldn't let me read the letters, but of course I wasn't going to put up with any nonsense like that."

"It was none of our business."

"You had to find out the name if you could."

"And where exactly did you come in?"

"Oh, don't be so silly," she laughed. "I should have gone mad if you hadn't let me read them."

"And did you find out his name?" I asked.

"No."

"Was there no address?"

"Yes, there was, and a very unexpected one. Most of the letters were written on Foreign Office paper."

"That was funny."

"I didn't quite know what to do. I had half a mind to write to the Viscountess Kastellan and explain the circumstances, but I didn't know what trouble I might be starting; the directions were to deliver the parcel to her personally, so I wrapped everything up again and put it in the safe. We were going home on leave in the spring and I thought the best thing was to leave everything over till then. The letters were by way of being rather compromising."

"To put it mildly," giggled Mrs. Low. "The truth is they gave the whole show away."

"I don't think we need go into that," said Low.

A slight altercation ensued; but I think on his part it was more for form's sake, since he must have known that his desire to preserve an official discretion stood small chance against his wife's determination to tell me everything. She had a down on Lady Kastellan and didn't care what she said about her. Her sympathies were with the man. Low did his best to tone down her rash assertions. He corrected her exaggerations. He told her that she'd let her imagination run away with her and had read into the letters more than was there. She would have done it. They'd evidently made a deep impression on her, and from her vivid account and Low's interruptions I gained a fairly coherent impression of them. It was plain for one thing that they were very moving.

"I can't tell you how it revolted me, the way Bee gloated over them," said Low.

"They were the most wonderful letters I've ever read. You never wrote letters like that to me."

"What a damned fool you would have thought me if I had," he grinned.

She gave him a charming, affectionate smile.

"I suppose I should, and yet, God knows I was crazy about you, and I'm damned if I know why."

The story emerged clearly enough. The writer, the mysterious J., presumably a clerk in the Foreign Office, had fallen in love with Lady Kastellan and she with him. They had become lovers and the early letters were passionately lyrical. They were happy. They expected their love to last for ever. He wrote to her immediately after he had left her and told her how much he adored her and how much she meant to him. She was never for a moment absent from his thoughts. It looked as though her infatuation was equal to his, for in one letter he justified himself because she had reproached him for not coming to some place where he knew she would be. He told her what agony it had been to him that a sudden job had prevented him from being with her when he'd so eagerly looked forward to it.

Then came the catastrophe. How it came or why one could only guess. Lord Kastellan learnt the truth. He not merely suspected his wife's infidelity, he had proofs of it. There was a fearful scene between them, she left him and went to her father's. Lord Kastellan announced his intention of divorcing her. The letters changed in character. J. wrote at once asking to see Lady Kastellan, but she begged him not to come. Her father insisted that they shouldn't meet. J. was distressed at her unhappiness and dismayed by the trouble he had brought upon her, and he was deeply sympathetic because of what she was enduring at home, for her father and mother were furious; but at the same time it was plain that he was relieved that the crisis had come. Nothing mattered except that they loved one another. He said he hated Kastellan. Let him bring his action. The sooner they could get married the better. The correspondence was one-sided, there were no letters from her, and one had to guess from his replies what she said in them. She was obviously frightened out of her wits and nothing that he could say helped. Of course he would have to leave the Foreign Office. He assured her that this meant nothing to him. He could get a job somewhere, in the colonies, where he would earn much more money. He was sure he could make her happy. Naturally there would be a scandal, but it would be forgotten, and away from England people would not bother. He besought her to have courage. Then it looked as though she had written somewhat peevishly. She hated being divorced, Kastellan refused to take the blame on himself and be made respondent, she did not want to leave London, it was her whole life, and bury herself in some God-forsaken place on the other side of nowhere. He answered unhappily. He said he would do anything she wanted. He implored her not to love him less and he was tortured by the thought that this disaster had changed her feelings for him. She reproached him for the mess they had got into; he did not try to defend himself; he was prepared to admit that he alone was to blame. Then it appeared that pressure was being brought to bear on Kastellan from some high quarter and there was even yet a chance that something might be arranged. Whatever she wrote

made J., the unknown J., desperate. His letter was almost in-
coherent. He begged her again to see him, he implored her to have
strength, he repeated that she meant everything in the world to him,
he was frightened that she would let people influence her, he asked
her to burn her boats behind her and bolt with him to Paris. He
was frantic. Then it seemed that for some days she did not write to
him. He could not understand. He did not know if she was receiving his letters. He was in an agony. The blow fell. She must
have written to say that if he would resign from the Foreign Office
and leave England her husband was prepared to take her back.
His answer was broken-hearted.

"He never saw through her for a moment," said Mrs. Low.

"What was there to see through?" I asked.

"Don't you know what she wrote to him? I do."

"Don't be such an ass, Bee. You can't possibly know."

"Ass yourself. Of course I do. She put it up to him. She threw
herself on his mercy. She dragged in her father and mother. She
brought in her children; I bet that was the first thought she'd given
them since they were born. She knew that he loved her so much
that he was willing to do everything in the world for her, even
lose her. She knew that he was prepared to accept the sacrifice
of his love, his life, his career, everything for her sake, and she let
him make it. She let the offer come from him. She let him persuade
her to accept it."

I listened to Mrs. Low with a smile, but with attention. She was
a woman and she felt instinctively how a woman in those circumstances would act. She thought it hateful, but she felt in her bones
that in just that way would she herself have acted. Of course it
was pure invention, with nothing but J.'s letter as a foundation, but I
had an impression that it was very likely.

That was the last letter in the bundle.

I was astonished. I had known Lady Kastellan for a good many
years, but only casually; and I knew her husband even less. He was
immersed in politics, he was Under-Secretary at the Home Office
at the time of the great do to which the Lows and I had been
invited; and I never saw him but in his own house. Lady Kastellan
had the reputation of being a beauty; she was tall and her figure
was good in a massive way. She had a lovely skin. Her blue eyes
were large, set rather wide apart and her face was broad. It gave
her a slightly cow-like look. She had pretty pale brown hair and she
held herself superbly. She was a woman of great self-possession,
and it amazed me to learn that she had ever surrendered to such
passion as the letters suggested. She was ambitious and there was

no doubt that she was very useful to Kastellan in his political life. I should have thought her incapable of indiscretion. Searching my memory I seemed to remember hearing years before that the Kastellans were not getting on very well, but I had never heard any details, and whenever I saw them it looked as though they were on very good terms with one another. Kastellan was a big, red-faced fellow with sleek black hair, jovial and loud-voiced, but with little shrewd eyes that watched and noted. He was industrious, an effective speaker, but a trifle pompous. He was a little too conscious of his own importance. He did not let you forget that he had rank and wealth. He was inclined to be patronising with people of less consequence than himself.

I could well believe that when he discovered that his wife was having an affair with a junior clerk in the Foreign Office there was a devil of a row. Lady Kastellan's father had been for many years permanent Under-Secretary for Foreign Affairs and it would have been more than usually embarrassing for his daughter to be divorced on account of one of his subordinates. For all I knew Kastellan was in love with his wife and he may have been teased by a very natural jealousy. But he was a proud man, deficient in humour. He feared ridicule. The rôle of the deceived husband is difficult to play with dignity. I do not suppose he wanted a scandal that might well jeopardise his political future. It may be that Lady Kastellan's advisers threatened to defend the case and the pros- pect of washing dirty linen in public horrified him. It is likely enough that pressure was brought to bear on him and the solution to forgive and take his wife back if her lover were definitely eliminated may have seemed the best to adopt. I have no doubt Lady Kastellan promised everything she was asked.

She must have had a bad fright. I didn't take such a severe view of her conduct as Mrs. Low. She was very young; she was not more than thirty-five now. Who could tell by what accident she had become J.'s mistress? I suspect that love had caught her unawares and that she was in the middle of an affair almost before she knew what she was about. She must always have been a cold, self-possessed woman, but it is just with people like that that nature at times plays strange tricks. I am prepared to believe that she lost her head completely. There is no means of knowing how Kastellan discovered what was going on, but the fact that she kept her lover's letters shows that she was too much in love to be prudent. Arthur Low had mentioned that it was strange to find in the dead man's possession his letters and not hers; but that seemed to me easily explainable. At the time of the catastrophe they were doubtless given back to him in exchange for hers. He very naturally kept them. Reading them again he could relive the love that meant everything in the world to him.

I didn't suppose that Lady Kastellan, devoured by passion, could ever have considered what would happen if she were found out. When the blow fell it is not strange that she was scared out of her wits. She may not have had more to do with her children than most women who live the sort of life she lived, but she may for all that not have wanted to lose them. I did not even know whether she had ever cared for her husband, but from what I knew of her I guessed that she was not indifferent to his name and wealth. The future must have looked pretty grim. She was losing everything, the grand house in Carlton House Terrace, the position, the security; her father could give her no money and her lover had still to find a job. It may not have been heroic that she should yield to the entreaties of her family, but it was comprehensible.

While I was thinking all this Arthur Low went on with his story.

"I didn't quite know how to set about getting in touch with Lady Kastellan," he said. "It was awkward not knowing the chap's name. However, when we got home I wrote to her. I explained who I was and said that I'd been asked to give her some letters and a gold and platinum cigarette-case by a man who'd recently died in my district. I said I'd been asked to deliver them to her in person. I thought perhaps she wouldn't answer at all or else communicate with me through a solicitor. But she answered all right. She made an appointment for me to come to Carlton House Terrace at twelve one morning. Of course it was stupid of me, but when finally I stood on the doorstep and rang the bell I was quite nervous. The door was opened by a butler. I said I had an appointment with Lady Kastellan. A footman took my hat and coat. I was led upstairs to an enormous drawing-room.

" 'I'll tell her ladyship you're here, sir,' the butler said.

"He left me and I sat on the edge of a chair and looked round. There were huge pictures on the walls, portraits you know, I don't know who they were by, Reynolds I should think and Romney, and there was a lot of Oriental china, and gilded consoles and mirrors. It was all terribly grand and it made me feel very shabby and insignificant. My suit smelt of camphor and it was baggy at the knees. My tie felt a bit loud. The butler came in again and asked me to go with him. He opened another door from the one I'd come in by and I found myself in a further room, not so large as the drawing-room, but large all the same and very grand too. A lady was standing by the fireplace. She looked at me as I came in and bowed slightly. I felt frightfully awkward as I walked along the whole length of the room and I was afraid of stumbling over the furniture. I can only hope I didn't look such a fool as I felt. She didn't ask me to sit down.

" 'I understand you have some things that you wish to deliver to me personally,' she said. 'It's very good of you to bother.'

"She didn't smile. She seemed perfectly self-possessed, but I had a notion that she was sizing me up. To tell you the truth it put my back up. I didn't much fancy being treated as if I were a chauffeur applying for a situation.

" 'Please don't mention it,' I said, rather stiffly. 'It's all in the day's work.'

" 'Have you got the things with you?' she asked.

"I didn't answer, but I opened the despatch-case I'd brought with me and took out the letters. I handed them to her. She accepted them without a word. She gave them a glance. She was very much made up, but I swear she went white underneath. The expression of her face didn't change. I looked at her hands. They were trembling a little. Then she seemed to pull herself together.

" 'Oh, I'm so sorry,' she said. 'Won't you sit down?'

"I took a chair. For a moment she didn't seem to know quite what to do. She held the letters in her hand. I, knowing what they were, wondered what she felt. She didn't give much away. There was a desk beside the chimney-piece and she opened a drawer and put them in. Then she sat down opposite me and asked me to have a cigarette. I handed her the cigarette-case. I'd had it in my breast pocket.

" 'I was asked to give you this too,' I said.

"She took it and looked at it. For a moment she didn't speak and I waited. I didn't quite know if I ought to get up and go.

" 'Did you know Jack well?' she asked suddenly.

" 'I didn't know him at all,' I answered. 'I never saw him until after his death.'

" 'I had no idea he was dead till I got your note,' she said. 'I'd lost sight of him for a long time. Of course he was a very old friend of mine.'

"I wondered if she thought I hadn't read the letters or if she'd forgotten what sort of letters they were. If the sight of them had given her a shock she had quite got over it by then. She spoke almost casually.

" 'What did he die of in point of fact?' she asked.

" 'Tuberculosis, opium and starvation,' I answered.

" 'How dreadful,' she said.

"But she said it quite conventionally. Whatever she felt she wasn't going to let me see. She was as cool as a cucumber, but I fancied, though it may have been only my fancy, that she was watching me, with all her wits about her, and wondering how much I knew. I think she'd have given a good deal to be certain of that.

" 'How did you happen to get hold of these things?' she asked me.

" 'I took possession of his effects after his death,' I explained. 'They were done up in a parcel and I was directed to give them to you.'

" 'Was there any need to undo the parcel?'

"I wish I could tell you what frigid insolence she managed to get into the question. It made me go white and I hadn't any make-up on to hide it. I answered that I thought it my duty to find out if I could who the dead man was. I should have liked to be able to communicate with his relations.

" 'I see,' she said.

"She looked at me as though that were the end of the interview and she expected me to get up and take myself off. But I didn't. I thought I'd like to get a bit of my own back. I told her how I'd been sent for and how I'd found him. I described the whole thing and I told her how, as far as I knew, there'd been no one at the end to take pity on him but a Chinese woman. Suddenly the door was opened and we both looked round. A big, middle-aged man came in and stopped when he saw me.

" 'I beg your pardon,' he said, 'I didn't know you were busy.'

" 'Come in,' she said, and when he had approached, 'This is Mr. Low. My husband.'

"Lord Kastellan gave me a nod.

" 'I just wanted to ask you,' he began, and then he stopped.

"His eyes had caught the cigarette-case that was still resting on Lady Kastellan's open hand. I don't know if she saw the look of enquiry in his eyes. She gave him a friendly little smile. She was quite amazingly mistress of herself.

" 'Mr. Low comes from the Federated Malay States. Poor Jack Almond's dead and he's left me his cigarette-case.'

" 'Really?' said Lord Kastellan. 'When did he die?'

" 'About six months ago,' I said.

"Lady Kastellan got up.

" 'Well, I won't keep you any longer. I dare say you're busy. Thank you so much for carrying out Jack's request.'

" 'Things are pretty bad just now in the F.M.S. if all I hear is true,' said Lord Kastellan.

"I shook hands with them both and Lady Kastellan rang a bell.
" 'Are you staying in London?' she asked, as I was going. 'I
wonder if you'd like to come to a little party I'm giving next week.'
" 'I have my wife with me,' I said.
" 'Oh, how very nice. I'll send you a card.'
"A couple of minutes later I found myself in the street. I was
glad to be alone. I'd had a bad shock. As soon as Lady Kastellan
mentioned the name I remembered. It was Jack Almond, the
wretched bum I'd found dead in the Chinese house, dead of starvation. I'd known him quite well. It never struck me for a moment
that it was he. Why, I'd dined and played cards with him, and
we'd played tennis together. It was awful to think of him dying
quite near me and me never knowing. He must have known he only
had to send me a message and I'd have done something. I made
my way into St. James's Park and sat down. I wanted to have a
good think."

I could understand that it was a shock to Arthur Low to discover
who the dead wastrel had been, for it was a shock to me too. Oddly
enough I also had known him. Not intimately, but as a man I met
at parties and now and then at a house in the country where we
were both passing the week-end. Except that it was years since I
had even thought of him it would have been stupid of me not to
put two and two together. With his name there flashed back into
my memory all my recollections of him. So that was why he had
suddenly thrown up a career he liked so much! At that time, it was
just after the war, I happened to know several people in the Foreign
Office; Jack Almond was thought the cleverest of all the young men
attached to it, and the highest posts the Diplomatic Service had to
offer were within his reach. Of course it meant waiting. But it did
seem absurd for him to fling away his chances in order to go into
business in the Far East. His friends did all they could to dissuade
him. He said he had had losses and found it impossible to live on his
salary. One would have thought he could scrape along till things
grew better. I remembered very well what he looked like. He was
tall and well-made, a trifle dressy, but he was young enough to carry
off his faultless clothes with a dash, with dark brown hair, very neat
and sleek, blue eyes with very long lashes, and a fresh brilliant
colour. He looked the picture of health. He was amusing, gay and
quick-witted. I never knew anyone who had more charm. It is a
dangerous quality and those who have it trade on it. Often they
think it enough to get them through life without any further effort.
It is well to be on one's guard against it. But with Jack Almond
it was the expression of a sweet and generous nature. He delighted

because he was delightful. He was entirely without conceit. He had a gift for languages, he spoke French and German without a trace of accent, and his manners were admirable. You felt that when the time came he would play the part of an ambassador to a foreign power in the grand style. No one could fail to like him. It was not strange that Lady Kastellan should have fallen madly in love with him. My fancy ran away with me. What is there more moving than young love? The walks together of that handsome pair in one of the parks in the warm evenings of early summer, the dances they went to where he held her in his arms, the enchantment of the secret they shared when they exchanged glances across a dinner-table, and the passionate encounters, hurried and dangerous, but worth a thousand risks, when at some clandestine meeting-place they could give themselves to the fulfilment of their desire. They drank the milk of Paradise.

How frightful that the end of it all should have been so tragic!

"How did you know him?" I now asked Low.

"He was with Dexter and Farmilow. You know, the shipping people. He had quite a good job. He'd brought letters to the Governor and people like that. I was in Singapore at the time. I think I met him first at the club. He was damned good at games and all that sort of thing. Played polo. He was a fine tennis-player. You couldn't help liking him."

"Did he drink, or what?"

"No." Arthur Low was quite emphatic. "He was one of the best. The women were crazy about him, and you couldn't blame them. He was one of the most decent fellows I've ever met."

I turned to Mrs. Low.

"Did you know him?"

"Only just. When Arthur and I were married we went to Perak. He was sweet, I remember that. He had the longest eyelashes I've ever seen on a man."

"He was out quite a long time without going home. Five years, I think. I don't want to use hackneyed phrases, but the fact is I can't say it in any other way, he'd won golden opinions. There were a certain number of fellows who'd been rather sick at his being shoved into a damned good job by influence, but they couldn't deny that he'd made good. We knew about his having been in the F.O. and all that, but he never put on any frills."

"I think what took me," Mrs. Low interrupted, "was that he was so tremendously alive. It bucked you up just to talk to him."

"He had a wonderful send-off when he sailed. I happened to

have run up to Singapore for a couple of days and I went to the dinner at the Europe the night before. We all got rather tight. It was a grand lark. There was quite a crowd to see him off. He was only going for six months. I think everybody looked forward to his coming back. It would have been better for him if he never had."

"Why, what happened then?"

"I don't know exactly. I'd been moved again, and I was right away north."

How exasperating! It is really much easier to invent a story out of your own head than to tell one about real people, of whom you not only must guess the motives, but whose behaviour even at crucial moments you are ignorant of.

"He was a very good chap, but he was never an intimate friend of ours, you know how cliquey Singapore is, and he moved in rather more exalted circles than we did; when we went north I forgot about him. But one day at the club I heard a couple of fellows talking. Walton and Kenning. Walton had just come up from Singapore. There'd been a big polo match.

" 'Did Almond play?' asked Kenning.

" 'You bet your life he didn't,' said Walton. 'They kicked him out of the team last season.'

"I interrupted.

" 'What *are* you talking about?' I said.

" 'Don't you know?' said Walton. 'He's gone all to pot, poor devil.'

" 'How?' I asked.

" 'Drink.'

" 'They say he dopes too,' said Kenning.

" 'Yes, I've heard that,' said Walton. 'He won't last long at that rate. Opium, isn't it?'

" 'If he doesn't look out he'll lose his job,' said Kenning.

"I couldn't make it out," Low went on. "He was the last man I should ever have expected to go that way. He was so typically English and he was a gentleman and all that. It appeared that Walton had travelled out with him on the same ship when Jack came back from leave. He joined the ship at Marseilles. He was rather low, but there was nothing funny about that; a lot of people don't feel any too good when they're leaving home and have to get back to the mill. He drank a good deal. Fellows do that sometimes too. But Walton said rather a curious thing about him. He said it looked as if the life had gone out of him. You couldn't help noticing it because he'd always had such high spirits.

There'd been a general sort of idea that he was engaged to some girl in England and on the ship they jumped to the conclusion that she'd thrown him over."

"That's what I said when Arthur told me," said Mrs. Low. "After all, five years is a long time to leave a girl."

"Anyhow they thought he'd get over it when he got back to work. But he didn't, unfortunately. He went from bad to worse. A lot of people liked him and they did all they could to persuade him to pull himself together. But there was nothing doing. He just told them to mind their own business. He was snappy and rude, which was funny because he'd always been so nice to everybody. Walton said you could hardly believe it was the same man. Government House dropped him and a lot of others followed suit. Lady Ormonde, the Governor's wife, was a snob, she knew he was well-connected and all that, and she wouldn't have given him the cold shoulder unless things had got pretty bad. He was a nice chap, Jack Almond, it seemed a pity that he should make such a mess of things. I was sorry, you know, but of course it didn't impair my appetite or disturb my night's sleep. A few months later I happened to be in Singapore myself, and when I went to the club I asked about him. He'd lost his job all right, it appeared that he often didn't go to the office for two or three days at a time; and I was told that someone had made him manager of a rubber estate in Sumatra in the hope that away from the temptations of Singapore he might pull himself together. You see, everyone had liked him so much, they couldn't bear the thought of his going under without some sort of a struggle. But it was no good. The opium had got him. He didn't keep the job in Sumatra long and he was back again in Singapore. I heard afterwards that you would hardly have recognised him. He'd always been so spruce and smart; he was shabby and unwashed and wild-eyed. A number of fellows at the club got together and arranged something. They felt they had to give him one more chance and they sent him out to Sarawak. But it wasn't any use. The fact is, I think, he didn't want to be helped. I think he just wanted to go to hell in his own way and be as quick as he could about it. Then he disappeared; someone said he'd gone home; anyhow he was forgotten. You know how people drop out in the F.M.S. I suppose that's why when I found a dead man in a sarong, with a beard, lying in a little smelly room in a Chinese house thirty miles from anywhere, it never occurred to me for a moment that it might be Jack Almond. I hadn't heard his name for years."

"Just think what he must have gone through in that time," said

Mrs. Low, and her eyes were bright with tears, for she had a good and tender heart.

"The whole thing's inexplicable," said Low.

"Why?" I asked.

"Well, if he was going to pieces, why didn't he do it when he first came out? His first five years he was all right. One of the best. If this affair of his had broken him you'd have expected him to break when it was all fresh. All that time he was as gay as a bird. You'd have said he hadn't a care in the world. From all I heard it was a different man who came back from leave."

"Something happened during those six months in London," said Mrs. Low. "That's obvious."

"We shall never know," sighed Low.

"But we can guess," I smiled. "That's where the novelist comes in. Shall I tell you what I think happened?"

"Fire away."

"Well, I think that during those first five years he was buoyed up by the sacrifice he'd made. He had a chivalrous soul. He had given up everything that made life worth living to him to save the woman he loved better than anything in the world. I think he had an exaltation of spirit that never left him. He loved her still, with all his heart; most of us fall in and out of love; some men can only love once, and I think he was one of them. And in a strange way he was happy because he'd been able to sacrifice his happiness for the sake of someone who was worthy of the sacrifice. I think she was always in his thoughts. Then he went home. I think he loved her as much as ever and I don't suppose he ever doubted that her love was as strong and enduring as his. I don't know what he expected. He may have thought she'd see it was no good fighting her inclination any more and would run away with him. It may have been that he'd have been satisfied to realise that she loved him still. It was inevitable that they should meet; they lived in the same world. He saw that she didn't care a row of pins for him any longer. He saw that the passionate girl had become a prudent, experienced woman of the world, he saw that she'd never loved him as he thought she loved him, and he may have suspected that she'd lured him coldly into making the sacrifice that was to save her. He saw her at parties, self-possessed and triumphant. He knew that the lovely qualities he'd ascribed to her were of his own imagining and she was just an ordinary woman who had been carried away by a momentary infatuation and having got over it had returned to her true life. A great name, wealth, social distinction, worldly success: those were the things that mattered to her. He'd sacrificed everything, his friends, his familiar surroundings, his profession, his usefulness in the world, all that gives value to existence—for nothing. He'd been cheated, and it broke him. Your friend Walton said the true thing, you noticed it yourself, he said it looked as if the life had gone out of him. It had. After that he didn't care any more, and perhaps the worst thing was that even with it all, though he knew Lady Kastellan for what she was, he loved her still. I know nothing more shattering than to love with all your heart, than not to be able however hard you try to break yourself of it, someone who you know is worthless. Perhaps that is why he took to opium. To forget and to remember."

It was a long speech I had made, and now I stopped.

"All that's only fancy," said Low.

"I know it is," I answered, "but it seems to fit the circumstances."

"There must have been a weak strain in him. Otherwise he could have fought and conquered."

"Perhaps. Perhaps there is always a certain weakness attached to such a great charm as he possessed. Perhaps few people love as wholeheartedly and as devotedly as he loved. Perhaps he didn't want to fight and conquer. I can't bring myself to blame him."

I didn't add, because I was afraid they would think it cynical, that maybe if only Jack Almond hadn't had those wonderfully long eyelashes he might now have been alive and well, minister to some foreign power and on the high road to the Embassy in Paris.

"Let's go into the drawing-room," said Mrs. Low. "The boy wants to clear the table."

And that was the end of Jack Almond.

Red

THE skipper thrust his hand into one of his trouser pockets and with difficulty, for they were not at the sides but in front and he was a portly man, pulled out a large silver watch. He looked at it and then looked again at the declining sun. The Kanaka at the wheel gave him a glance, but did not speak. The skipper's eyes rested on the island they were approaching. A white line of foam marked the reef. He knew there was an opening large enough to get his ship through, and when they came a little nearer he counted on seeing it. They had nearly an hour of daylight still before them. In the lagoon the water was deep and they could anchor comfortably. The chief of the village which he could already see among the coconut trees was a friend of the mate's, and it would be pleasant to go ashore for the night. The mate came forward at that minute and the skipper turned to him.

"We'll take a bottle of booze along with us and get some girls in to dance," he said.

"I don't see the opening," said the mate.

He was a Kanaka, a handsome, swarthy fellow, with somewhat the look of a later Roman emperor, inclined to stoutness; but his face was fine and clean-cut.

"I'm dead sure there's one right here," said the captain, looking through his glasses. "I can't understand why I can't pick it up. Send one of the boys up the mast to have a look."

The mate called one of the crew and gave him the order. The captain watched the Kanaka climb and waited for him to speak. But the Kanaka shouted down that he could see nothing but the unbroken line of foam. The captain spoke Samoan like a native, and he cursed him freely.

"Shall he stay up there?" asked the mate.

"What the hell good does that do?" answered the captain. "The blame fool can't see worth a cent. You bet your sweet life I'd find the opening if I was up there."

He looked at the slender mast with anger. It was all very well for a native who had been used to climbing up coconut trees all his life. He was fat and heavy.

"Come down," he shouted. "You're no more use than a dead dog. We'll just have to go along the reef till we find the opening."

It was a seventy-ton schooner with paraffin auxiliary, and it ran, when there was no head wind, between four and five knots an hour. It was a bedraggled object; it had been painted white a very long time ago, but it was now dirty, dingy, and mottled. It smelt strongly of paraffin and of the copra which was its usual cargo. They were within a hundred feet of the reef now and the captain told the steersman to run along it till they came to the opening. But when they had gone a couple of miles he realised that they had missed it. He went about and slowly worked back again. The white foam of the reef continued without interruption and now the sun was setting. With a curse at the stupidity of the crew the skipper resigned himself to waiting till next morning.

"Put her about," he said. "I can't anchor here."

They went out to sea a little and presently it was quite dark. They anchored. When the sail was furled the ship began to roll a good deal. They said in Apia that one day she would roll right over; and the owner, a German-American who managed one of the largest stores, said that no money was big enough to induce him to go out in her. The cook, a Chinese in white trousers, very dirty and ragged, and a thin white tunic, came to say that supper was ready, and when the skipper went into the cabin he found the engineer already seated at table. The engineer was a long, lean man with a scraggy neck. He was dressed in blue overalls and a sleeveless jersey which showed his thin arms tattooed from elbow to wrist.

"Hell, having to spend the night outside," said the skipper.

The engineer did not answer, and they ate their supper in silence. The cabin was lit by a dim oil-lamp. When they had eaten the canned apricots with which the meal finished the Chink brought them a cup of tea. The skipper lit a cigar and went on the upper deck. The island now was only a darker mass against the night. The stars were very bright. The only sound was the ceaseless breaking of the surf. The skipper sank into a deck-chair and smoked idly. Presently three or four members of the crew came up and sat down. One of them had a banjo and another a concertina. They began to play, and one of them sang. The native song sounded strange on these instruments. Then to the singing a couple began to dance. It was a barbaric dance, savage and primeval, rapid, with quick movements of the hands and feet and contortions of the body; it was sensual, sexual even, but sexual without passion. It was very animal, direct, weird without mystery, natural in short, and one might almost say childlike. At last they grew tired. They stretched themselves on the deck and slept, and all was silent. The skipper lifted himself heavily out of his chair and clambered down the companion. He went into his cabin and got out of his clothes. He climbed into his bunk and lay there. He panted a little in the heat of the night.

But next morning, when the dawn crept over the tranquil sea, the opening in the reef which had eluded them the night before was seen a little to the east of where they lay. The schooner entered the lagoon. There was not a ripple on the surface of the water. Deep down among the coral rocks you saw little coloured fish swim. When he had anchored his ship the skipper ate his breakfast and went on deck. The sun shone from an unclouded sky, but in the early morning the air was grateful and cool. It was Sunday, and there was a feeling of quietness, a silence as though nature were at rest, which gave him a peculiar sense of comfort. He sat, looking at the wooded coast, and felt lazy and well at ease. Presently a slow smile moved his lips and he threw the stump of his cigar into the water.

"I guess I'll go ashore," he said. "Get the boat out."

He climbed stiffly down the ladder and was rowed to a little cove. The coconut trees came down to the water's edge, not in rows, but spaced out with an ordered formality. They were like a ballet of spinsters, elderly but flippant, standing in affected attitudes with the simpering graces of a bygone age. He sauntered idly through them, along a path that could be just seen winding its tortuous way, and it led him presently to a broad creek. There was a bridge across it, but a bridge constructed of single trunks of coconut trees, a dozen of them, placed end to end and supported where they met by a forked branch driven into the bed of the creek. You walked on a smooth, round surface, narrow and slippery, and there was no support for the hand. To cross such a bridge required sure feet and a stout heart. The skipper hesitated. But he saw on the other side, nestling among the trees, a white man's house; he made up his mind and, rather gingerly, began to walk. He watched his feet carefully, and where one trunk joined on to the next and there was a difference of level, he tottered a little. It was with a gasp of relief that he reached the last tree and finally set his feet on the firm ground of the other side. He had been so intent on the difficult crossing that he never noticed anyone was watching him, and it was with surprise that he heard himself spoken to.

"It takes a bit of nerve to cross these bridges when you're not used to them."

He looked up and saw a man standing in front of him. He had evidently come out of the house which he had seen.

"I saw you hesitate," the man continued, with a smile on his lips, "and I was watching to see you fall in."

"Not on your life," said the captain, who had now recovered his confidence.

"I've fallen in myself before now. I remember, one evening I came back from shooting, and I fell in, gun and all. Now I get a boy to carry my gun for me."

He was a man no longer young, with a small beard, now somewhat grey, and a thin face. He was dressed in a singlet, without arms, and a pair of duck trousers. He wore neither shoes nor socks. He spoke English with a slight accent.

"Are you Neilson?" asked the skipper.

"I am."

"I've heard about you. I thought you lived somewheres round here."

The skipper followed his host into the little bungalow and sat down heavily in the chair which the other motioned him to take. While Neilson went out to fetch whisky and glasses he took a look round the room. It filled him with amazement. He had never seen so many books. The shelves reached from floor to ceiling on all four walls, and they were closely packed. There was a grand piano littered with music, and a large table on which books and magazines lay in disorder. The room made him feel embarrassed. He remembered that Neilson was a queer fellow. No one knew very much about him, although he had been in the islands for so many years, but those who knew him agreed that he was queer. He was a Swede.

"You've got one big heap of books here," he said, when Neilson returned.

"They do no harm," answered Neilson with a smile.

"Have you read them all?" asked the skipper.

"Most of them."

"I'm a bit of a reader myself. I have the *Saturday Evening Post* sent me regler."

Neilson poured his visitor a good stiff glass of whisky and gave him a cigar. The skipper volunteered a little information.

"I got in last night, but I couldn't find the opening, so I had to anchor outside. I never been this run before, but my people had some stuff they wanted to bring over here. Gray, d'you know him?"

"Yes, he's got a store a little way along."

"Well, there was a lot of canned stuff that he wanted over, an' he's got some copra. They thought I might just as well come over as lie idle at Apia. I run between Apia and Pago-Pago mostly, but they've got smallpox there just now, and there's nothing stirring."

He took a drink of his whisky and lit a cigar. He was a taciturn man, but there was something in Neilson that made him nervous, and his nervousness made him talk. The Swede was looking at him with large dark eyes in which there was an expression of faint amusement.

"This is a tidy little place you've got here."

"I've done my best with it."

"You must do pretty well with your trees. They look fine. With copra at the price it is now. I had a bit of a plantation myself once, in Upolu it was, but I had to sell it."

He looked round the room again, where all those books gave him a feeling of something incomprehensible and hostile.

"I guess you must find it a bit lonesome here though," he said.

"I've got used to it. I've been here for twenty-five years."

Now the captain could think of nothing more to say, and he smoked in silence. Neilson had apparently no wish to break it. He looked at his guest with a meditative eye. He was a tall man, more than six feet high, and very stout. His face was red and blotchy, with a network of little purple veins on the cheeks, and his features were sunk into its fatness. His eyes were bloodshot. His neck was buried in rolls of fat. But for a fringe of long curly hair, nearly white, at the back of his head, he was quite bald; and that immense, shiny surface of forehead, which might have given him a false look of intelligence, on the contrary gave him one of peculiar imbecility. He wore a blue flannel shirt, open at the neck and showing his fat chest covered with a mat of reddish hair, and a very old pair of blue serge trousers. He sat in his chair in a heavy ungainly attitude, his great belly thrust forward and his fat legs uncrossed. All elasticity had gone from his limbs. Neilson wondered idly what sort of man he had been in his youth. It was almost impossible to imagine that this creature of vast bulk had ever been a boy who ran about. The skipper finished his whisky, and Neilson pushed the bottle towards him.

"Help yourself."

The skipper leaned forward and with his great hand seized it.

"And how come you in these parts anyways?" he said.

"Oh, I came out to the islands for my health. My lungs were bad and they said I hadn't a year to live. You see they were wrong."

"I meant, how come you to settle down right here?"

"I am a sentimentalist."

"Oh!"

Neilson knew that the skipper had not an idea what he meant, and he looked at him with an ironical twinkle in his dark eyes.

Perhaps just because the skipper was so gross and dull a man the whim seized him to talk further.

"You were too busy keeping your balance to notice, when you crossed the bridge, but this spot is generally considered rather pretty."

"It's a cute little house you've got here."

"Ah, that wasn't here when I first came. There was a native hut, with its beehive roof and its pillars, overshadowed by a great tree with red flowers; and the croton bushes, their leaves yellow and red and golden, made a pied fence around it. And then all about were the coconut trees, as fanciful as women, and as vain. They stood at the water's edge and spent all day looking at their reflections. I was a young man then—good heavens, it's a quarter of a century ago—and I wanted to enjoy all the loveliness of the world in the short time allotted to me before I passed into the darkness. I thought it was the most beautiful spot I had ever seen. The first time I saw it I had a catch at my heart, and I was afraid I was going to cry. I wasn't more than twenty-five, and though I put the best face I could on it, I didn't want to die. And somehow it seemed to me that the very beauty of this place made it easier for me to accept my fate. I felt when I came here that all my past life had fallen away, Stockholm and its University, and then Bonn: it all seemed the life of somebody else, as though now at last I had achieved the reality which our doctors of philosophy—I am one myself, you know —had discussed so much. 'A year,' I cried to myself. 'I have a year. I will spend it here and then I am content to die.'

"We are foolish and sentimental and melodramatic at twenty-five, but if we weren't perhaps we should be less wise at fifty.

"Now drink, my friend. Don't let the nonsense I talk interfere with you."

He waved his thin hand towards the bottle, and the skipper finished what remained in his glass.

"You ain't drinking nothin'," he said, reaching for the whisky.

"I am of a sober habit," smiled the Swede. "I intoxicate myself in ways which I fancy are more subtle. But perhaps that is only vanity. Anyhow, the effects are more lasting and the results less deleterious."

"They say there's a deal of cocaine taken in the States now," said the captain.

Neilson chuckled.

"But I do not see a white man often," he continued, "and for once I don't think a drop of whisky can do me any harm."

He poured himself out a little, added some soda, and took a sip.

"And presently I found out why the spot had such an unearthly loveliness. Here love had tarried for a moment like a migrant bird that happens on a ship in mid-ocean and for a little while folds its tired wings. The fragrance of a beautiful passion hovered over it like the fragrance of hawthorn in May in the meadows of my home. It seems to me that the places where men have loved or suffered keep about them always some faint aroma of something that has not wholly died. It is as though they had acquired a spiritual significance which mysteriously affects those who pass. I wish I could make myself clear." He smiled a little. "Though I cannot imagine that if I did you would understand."

He paused.

"I think this place was beautiful because here for a period the ecstasy of love had invested it with beauty." And now he shrugged his shoulders. "But perhaps it is only that my æsthetic sense is gratified by the happy conjunction of young love and a suitable setting."

Even a man less thick-witted than the skipper might have been forgiven if he were bewildered by Neilson's words. For he seemed faintly to laugh at what he said. It was as though he spoke from emotion which his intellect found ridiculous. He had said himself that he was a sentimentalist, and when sentimentality is joined with scepticism there is often the devil to pay.

He was silent for an instant and looked at the captain with eyes in which there was a sudden perplexity.

"You know, I can't help thinking that I've seen you before somewhere or other," he said.

"I couldn't say as I remember you," returned the skipper.

"I have a curious feeling as though your face were familiar to me. It's been puzzling me for some time. But I can't situate my recollection in any place or at any time."

The skipper massively shrugged his heavy shoulders.

"It's thirty years since I first come to the islands. A man can't figure on remembering all the folk he meets in a while like that."

The Swede shook his head.

"You know how one sometimes has the feeling that a place one has never been to before is strangely familiar. That's how I seem to see you." He gave a whimsical smile. "Perhaps I knew you in some past existence. Perhaps, perhaps you were the master of a galley in ancient Rome and I was a slave at the oar. Thirty years have you been here?"

"Every bit of thirty years."

"I wonder if you knew a man called Red?"

"Red?"

"That is the only name I've ever known him by. I never knew
him personally. I never even set eyes on him. And yet I seem to
see him more clearly than many men, my brothers, for instance,
with whom I passed my daily life for many years. He lives in my
imagination with the distinctness of a Paolo Malatesta or a Romeo.
But I dare say you have never read Dante or Shakespeare?"

"I can't say as I have," said the captain.

Neilson, smoking a cigar, leaned back in his chair and looked
vacantly at the ring of smoke which floated in the still air. A smile
played on his lips, but his eyes were grave. Then he looked at the
captain. There was in his gross obesity something extraordinarily
repellent. He had the plethoric self-satisfaction of the very fat. It
was an outrage. It set Neilson's nerves on edge. But the contrast
between the man before him and the man he had in mind was
pleasant.

"It appears that Red was the most comely thing you ever saw.
I've talked to quite a number of people who knew him in those
days, white men, and they all agree that the first time you saw him
his beauty just took your breath away. They called him Red on
account of his flaming hair. It had a natural wave and he wore it
long. It must have been of that wonderful colour that the pre-
Raphaelites raved over. I don't think he was vain of it, he was much
too ingenuous for that, but no one could have blamed him if he had
been. He was tall, six feet and an inch or two—in the native house
that used to stand here was the mark of his height cut with a knife
on the central trunk that supported the roof—and he was made like
a Greek god, broad in the shoulders and thin in the flanks; he was
like Apollo, with just that soft roundness which Praxiteles gave him,
and that suave, feminine grace which has in it something troubling
and mysterious. His skin was dazzling white, milky, like satin: his
skin was like a woman's."

"I had kind of a white skin myself when I was a kiddie," said the
skipper, with a twinkle in his bloodshot eyes.

But Neilson paid no attention to him. He was telling his story
now and interruption made him impatient.

"And his face was just as beautiful as his body. He had large
blue eyes, very dark, so that some say they were black, and unlike
most red-haired people he had dark eyebrows and long dark lashes.
His features were perfectly regular and his mouth was like a scarlet
wound. He was twenty."

On these words the Swede stopped with a certain sense of the
dramatic. He took a sip of whisky.

"He was unique. There never was anyone more beautiful. There was no more reason for him than for a wonderful blossom to flower on a wild plant. He was a happy accident of nature.

"One day he landed at that cove into which you must have put this morning. He was an American sailor, and he had deserted from a man-of-war in Apia. He had induced some good-humoured native to give him a passage on a cutter that happened to be sailing from Apia to Safoto, and he had been put ashore here in a dug-out. I do not know why he deserted. Perhaps life on a man-of-war with its restrictions irked him, perhaps he was in trouble, and perhaps it was the South Seas and these romantic islands that got into his bones. Every now and then they take a man strangely, and he finds himself like a fly in a spider's web. It may be that there was a softness of fibre in him, and these green hills with their soft airs, this blue sea, took the northern strength from him as Delilah took the Nazarite's. Anyhow, he wanted to hide himself, and he thought he would be safe in this secluded nook till his ship had sailed from Samoa.

"There was a native hut at the cove and as he stood there, wondering where exactly he should turn his steps, a young girl came out and invited him to enter. He knew scarcely two words of the native tongue and she as little English. But he understood well enough what her smiles meant, and her pretty gestures, and he followed her. He sat down on a mat and she gave him slices of pineapple to eat. I can speak of Red only from hearsay, but I saw the girl three years after he first met her, and she was scarcely nineteen then. You cannot imagine how exquisite she was. She had the passionate grace of the hibiscus and the rich colour. She was rather tall, slim, with the delicate features of her race, and large eyes like pools of still water under the palm trees; her hair, black and curling, fell down her back, and she wore a wreath of scented flowers. Her hands were lovely. They were so small, so exquisitely formed, they gave your heart-strings a wrench. And in those days she laughed easily. Her smile was so delightful that it made your knees shake. Her skin was like a field of ripe corn on a summer day. Good heavens, how can I describe her? She was too beautiful to be real.

"And these two young things, she was sixteen and he was twenty, fell in love with one another at first sight. That is the real love, not the love that comes from sympathy, common interests, or intellectual community, but love pure and simple. That is the love that Adam felt for Eve when he awoke and found her in the garden gazing at him with dewy eyes. That is the love that draws the beasts to one another, and the Gods. That is the love that makes the world a miracle. That is the love which gives life its pregnant meaning. You have never heard of the wise, cynical French duke who said that with.two lovers there is always one who loves and one who lets himself be loved; it is a bitter truth to which most of us have to resign ourselves; but now and then there are two who love and two who let themselves be loved. Then one might fancy that the sun stands still as it stood when Joshua prayed to the God of Israel.

"And even now after all these years, when I think of these two, so young, so fair, so simple, and of their love, I feel a pang. It tears my heart just as my heart is torn when on certain nights I watch the full moon shining on the lagoon from an unclouded sky. There is always pain in the contemplation of perfect beauty.

"They were children. She was good and sweet and kind. I know nothing of him, and I like to think that then at all events he was ingenuous and frank. I like to think that his soul was as comely as his body. But I dare say he had no more soul than the creatures of the woods and forests who made pipes from reeds and bathed in the mountain streams when the world was young, and you might catch sight of little fawns galloping through the glade on the back of a bearded centaur. A soul is a troublesome possession and when man developed it he lost the Garden of Eden.

"Well, when Red came to the island it had recently been visited by one of those epidemics which the white man has brought to the South Seas, and one third of the inhabitants had died. It seems that the girl had lost all her near kin and she lived now in the house of distant cousins. The household consisted of two ancient crones, bowed and wrinkled, two younger women, and a man and a boy. For a few days he stayed there. But perhaps he felt himself too near the shore, with the possibility that he might fall in with white men who would reveal his hiding-place; perhaps the lovers could not bear that the company of others should rob them for an instant of the delight of being together. One morning they set out, the pair of them, with the few things that belonged to the girl, and walked along a grassy path under the coconuts, till they came to the creek you see. They had to cross the bridge you crossed, and the girl laughed gleefully because he was afraid. She held his hand till they came to the end of the first tree, and then his courage failed him and he had to go back. He was obliged to take off all his clothes before he could risk it, and she carried them over for him on her head. They settled down in the empty hut that stood there. Whether she had any rights over it (land tenure is a complicated business in the islands), or whether the owner had died during the epidemic, I do not know, but anyhow no one questioned them, and they took possession. Their furniture consisted of a couple of grass mats on which they slept, a fragment of looking-glass, and a bowl or two. In this pleasant land that is enough to start housekeeping on.

"They say that happy people have no history, and certainly a happy love has none. They did nothing all day long and yet the days seemed all too short. The girl had a native name, but Red called her Sally. He picked up the easy language very quickly, and he used to lie on the mat for hours while she chattered gaily to him. He was a silent fellow, and perhaps his mind was lethargic. He smoked incessantly the cigarettes which she made him out of the native tobacco and pandanus leaf, and he watched her while with deft fingers she made grass mats. Often natives would come in and tell long stories of the old days when the island was disturbed by tribal wars. Sometimes he would go fishing on the reef, and bring home a basket full of coloured fish. Sometimes at night he would go out with a lantern to catch lobster. There were plantains round the hut and Sally would roast them for their frugal meal. She knew how to make delicious messes from coconuts, and the breadfruit tree by the side of the creek gave them its fruit. On feast-days they killed a little pig and cooked it on hot stones. They bathed together in the creek; and in the evening they went down to the lagoon and paddled about in a dug-out, with its great outrigger. The sea was deep blue, wine-coloured at sundown, like the sea of Homeric Greece; but in the lagoon the colour had an infinite variety, aquamarine and amethyst and emerald; and the setting sun turned it for a short moment to liquid gold. Then there was the colour of the coral, brown, white, pink, red, purple; and the shapes it took were marvellous. It was like a magic garden, and the hurrying fish were like butterflies. It strangely lacked reality. Among the coral were pools with a floor of white sand and here, where the water was dazzling clear, it was very good to bathe. Then, cool and happy, they wandered back in the gloaming over the soft grass road to the creek, walking hand in hand, and now the mynah birds filled the coconut trees with their clamour. And then the night, with that great sky shining with gold, that seemed to stretch more widely than the skies of Europe, and the soft airs that blew gently through the open hut, the long night again was all too short. She was sixteen and he was barely twenty. The dawn crept in among the wooden pillars of the hut and looked at those lovely children sleeping in one another's arms. The sun hid behind the great tattered leaves of the plantains so that it might not disturb them, and then, with playful malice, shot a golden ray, like the outstretched paw of a Persian cat, on their faces. They opened their sleepy eyes and they smiled to welcome

z

another day. The weeks lengthened into months, and a year passed. They seemed to love one another as—I hesitate to say passionately, for passion has in it always a shade of sadness, a touch of bitterness or anguish, but as wholeheartedly, as simply and naturally as on that first day on which, meeting, they had recognised that a god was in them.

"If you had asked them I have no doubt that they would have thought it impossible to suppose their love could ever cease. Do we not know that the essential element of love is a belief in its own eternity? And yet perhaps in Red there was already a very little seed, unknown to himself and unsuspected by the girl, which would in time have grown to weariness. For one day one of the natives from the cove told them that some way down the coast at the anchorage was a British whaling-ship.

" 'Gee,' he said, 'I wonder if I could make a trade of some nuts and plantains for a pound or two of tobacco.'

"The pandanus cigarettes that Sally made him with untiring hands were strong and pleasant enough to smoke, but they left him unsatisfied; and he yearned on a sudden for real tobacco, hard, rank, and pungent. He had not smoked a pipe for many months. His mouth watered at the thought of it. One would have thought some premonition of harm would have made Sally seek to dissuade him, but love possessed her so completely that it never occurred to her any power on earth could take him from her. They went up into the hills together and gathered a great basket of wild oranges, green, but sweet and juicy; and they picked plantains from around the hut, and coconuts from their trees, and breadfruit and mangoes; and they carried them down to the cove. They loaded the unstable canoe with them, and Red and the native boy who had brought them the news of the ship paddled along outside the reef.

"It was the last time she ever saw him.

"Next day the boy came back alone. He was all in tears. This is the story he told. When after their long paddle they reached the ship and Red hailed it, a white man looked over the side and told them to come on board. They took the fruit they had brought with them and Red piled it up on the deck. The white man and he began to talk, and they seemed to come to some agreement. One of them went below and brought up tobacco. Red took some at once and lit a pipe. The boy imitated the zest with which he blew a great cloud of smoke from his mouth. Then they said something to him and he went into the cabin. Through the open door the boy, watching curiously, saw a bottle brought out and glasses. Red drank and smoked. They seemed to ask him something, for he shook his head and laughed. The man, the first man who had spoken to them, laughed too, and he filled Red's glass once more. They went on talking and drinking, and presently, growing tired of watching a sight that meant nothing to him, the boy curled himself up on the deck and slept. He was awakened by a kick; and, jumping to his feet, he saw that the ship was slowly sailing out of the lagoon. He caught sight of Red seated at the table, with his head resting heavily on his arms, fast asleep. He made a movement towards him, intending to wake him, but a rough hand seized his arm, and a man, with a scowl and words which he did not understand, pointed to the side. He shouted to Red, but in a moment he was seized and flung overboard. Helpless, he swam round to his canoe, which was drifting a little way off, and pushed it on to the reef. He climbed in and, sobbing all the way, paddled back to shore.

"What had happened was obvious enough. The whaler, by desertion or sickness, was short of hands, and the captain when Red came aboard had asked him to sign on; on his refusal he had made him drunk and kidnapped him.

"Sally was beside herself with grief. For three days she screamed and cried. The natives did what they could to comfort her, but she would not be comforted. She would not eat. And then, exhausted, she sank into a sullen apathy. She spent long days at the cove, watching the lagoon, in the vain hope that Red somehow or other would manage to escape. She sat on the white sand, hour after hour, with the tears running down her cheeks, and at night dragged herself wearily back across the creek to the little hut where she had been happy. The people with whom she had lived before Red came to the island wished her to return to them, but she would not; she was convinced that Red would come back, and she wanted him to find her where he had left her. Four months later she was delivered of a still-born child, and the old woman who had come to help her through her confinement remained with her in the hut. All joy was taken from her life. If her anguish with time became less intolerable it was replaced by a settled melancholy. You would not have thought that among these people, whose emotions, though so violent, are very transient, a woman could be found capable of so enduring a passion. She never lost the profound conviction that sooner or later Red would come back. She watched for him, and every time someone crossed this slender little bridge of coconut trees she looked. It might at last be he."

Neilson stopped talking and gave a faint sigh.

"And what happened to her in the end?" asked the skipper.

Neilson smiled bitterly.

Z 2

"Oh, three years afterwards she took up with another white man."

The skipper gave a fat, cynical chuckle.

"That's generally what happens to them," he said.

The Swede shot him a look of hatred. He did not know why that gross, obese man excited in him so violent a repulsion. But his thoughts wandered and he found his mind filled with memories of the past. He went back five and twenty years. It was when he first came to the island, weary of Apia, with its heavy drinking, its gambling and coarse sensuality, a sick man, trying to resign himself to the loss of the career which had fired his imagination with ambitious thoughts. He set behind him resolutely all his hopes of making a great name for himself and strove to content himself with the few poor months of careful life which was all that he could count on. He was boarding with a half-caste trader who had a store a couple of miles along the coast at the edge of a native village; and one day, wandering aimlessly along the grassy paths of the coconut groves, he had come upon the hut in which Sally lived. The beauty of the spot had filled him with a rapture so great that it was almost painful, and then he had seen Sally. She was the loveliest creature he had ever seen, and the sadness in those dark, magnificent eyes of hers affected him strangely. The Kanakas were a handsome race, and beauty was not rare among them, but it was the beauty of shapely animals. It was empty. But those tragic eyes were dark with mystery, and you felt in them the bitter complexity of the groping, human soul. The trader told him the story and it moved him.

"Do you think he'll ever come back?" asked Neilson.

"No fear. Why, it'll be a couple of years before the ship is paid off, and by then he'll have forgotten all about her. I bet he was pretty mad when he woke up and found he'd been shanghaied, and I shouldn't wonder but he wanted to fight somebody. But he'd got to grin and bear it, and I guess in a month he was thinking it the best thing that had ever happened to him that he got away from the island."

But Neilson could not get the story out of his head. Perhaps because he was sick and weakly, the radiant health of Red appealed to his imagination. Himself an ugly man, insignificant of appearance, he prized very highly comeliness in others. He had never been passionately in love, and certainly he had never been passionately loved. The mutual attraction of those two young things gave him a singular delight. It had the ineffable beauty of the Absolute. He went again to the little hut by the creek. He had a gift for languages and an energetic mind, accustomed to work, and he had already given much time to the study of the local tongue. Old habit was strong in him and he was gathering together material for a paper on the Samoan speech. The old crone who shared the hut with Sally invited him to come in and sit down. She gave him *kava* to drink and cigarettes to smoke. She was glad to have someone to chat with and while she talked he looked at Sally. She reminded him of the Psyche in the museum at Naples. Her features had the same clear purity of line, and though she had borne a child she had still a virginal aspect.

It was not till he had seen her two or three times that he induced her to speak. Then it was only to ask him if he had seen in Apia a man called Red. Two years had passed since his disappearance, but it was plain that she still thought of him incessantly.

It did not take Neilson long to discover that he was in love with her. It was only by an effort of will now that he prevented himself from going every day to the creek, and when he was not with Sally his thoughts were. At first, looking upon himself as a dying man, he asked only to look at her, and occasionally hear her speak, and his love gave him a wonderful happiness. He exulted in its purity. He wanted nothing from her but the opportunity to weave around her graceful person a web of beautiful fancies. But the open air, the equable temperature, the rest, the simple fare, began to have an unexpected effect on his health. His temperature did not soar at night to such alarming heights, he coughed less and began to put on weight; six months passed without his having a hæmorrhage; and on a sudden he saw the possibility that he might live. He had studied his disease carefully, and the hope dawned upon him that with great care he might arrest its course. It exhilarated him to look forward once more to the future. He made plans. It was evident that any active life was out of the question, but he could live on the islands, and the small income he had, insufficient elsewhere, would be ample to keep him. He could grow coconuts; that would give him an occupation; and he would send for his books and a piano; but his quick mind saw that in all this he was merely trying to conceal from himself the desire which obsessed him.

He wanted Sally. He loved not only her beauty, but that dim soul which he divined behind her suffering eyes. He would intoxicate her with his passion. In the end he would make her forget. And in an ecstasy of surrender he fancied himself giving her too the happiness which he had thought never to know again, but had now so miraculously achieved.

He asked her to live with him. She refused. He had expected that and did not let it depress him, for he was sure that sooner or later she would yield. His love was irresistible. He told the old woman of his wishes, and found somewhat to his surprise that she and the neighbours, long aware of them, were strongly urging Sally to accept his offer. After all, every native was glad to keep house for a white man, and Neilson according to the standards of the island was a rich one. The trader with whom he boarded went to her and told her not to be a fool; such an opportunity would not come again, and after so long she could not still believe that Red would ever return. The girl's resistance only increased Neilson's desire, and what had been a very pure love now became an agonising passion. He was determined that nothing should stand in his way. He gave Sally no peace. At last, worn out by his persistence and the persuasions, by turns pleading and angry, of everyone around her, she consented. But the day after, when exultant he went to see her he found that in the night she had burnt down the hut in which she and Red had lived together. The old crone ran towards him full of angry abuse of Sally, but he waved her aside; it did not matter; they would build a bungalow on the place where the hut had stood. A European house would really be more convenient if he wanted to bring out a piano and a vast number of books.

And so the little wooden house was built in which he had now lived for many years, and Sally became his wife. But after the first few weeks of rapture, during which he was satisfied with what she gave him, he had known little happiness. She had yielded to him, through weariness, but she had only yielded what she set no store on. The soul which he had dimly glimpsed escaped him. He knew that she cared nothing for him. She still loved Red, and all the time she was waiting for his return. At a sign from him, Neilson knew that, notwithstanding his love, his tenderness, his sympathy, his generosity, she would leave him without a moment's hesitation. She would never give a thought to his distress. Anguish seized him and he battered at that impenetrable self of hers which sullenly resisted him. His love became bitter. He tried to melt her heart with kindness, but it remained as hard as before; he feigned indifference, but she did not notice it. Sometimes he lost his temper and abused her, and then she wept silently. Sometimes he thought she was nothing but a fraud, and that soul simply an invention of his own, and that he could not get into the sanctuary of her heart because there was no sanctuary there. His love became a prison from which he longed to escape, but he had not the strength merely to open the door—that was all it needed—and walk out into the open air. It was torture and at last he became numb and hopeless. In the end the fire burnt itself out and, when he saw her eyes rest for an instant on the slender bridge, it was no longer rage that filled his heart but impatience. For many years now they had lived together bound by the ties of habit and convenience, and it was with a smile that he looked back on his old passion. She was an old woman, for the women on the islands age quickly, and if he had no love for her any more he had tolerance. She left him alone. He was contented with his piano and his books.

His thoughts led him to a desire for words.

"When I look back now and reflect on that brief passionate love of Red and Sally, I think that perhaps they should thank the ruthless fate that separated them when their love seemed still to be at its height. They suffered, but they suffered in beauty. They were spared the real tragedy of love."

"I don't know exactly as I get you," said the skipper.

"The tragedy of love is not death or separation. How long do you think it would have been before one or other of them ceased to care? Oh, it is dreadfully bitter to look at a woman whom you have loved with all your heart and soul, so that you felt you could not bear to let her out of your sight, and realise that you would not mind if you never saw her again. The tragedy of love is indifference."

But while he was speaking a very extraordinary thing happened. Though he had been addressing the skipper he had not been talking to him, he had been putting his thoughts into words for himself, and with his eyes fixed on the man in front of him he had not seen him. But now an image presented itself to them, an image not of the man he saw, but of another man. It was as though he were looking into one of those distorting mirrors that make you extra-ordinarily squat or outrageously elongate, but here exactly the opposite took place, and in the obese, ugly old man he caught the shadowy glimpse of a stripling. He gave him now a quick, searching scrutiny. Why had a haphazard stroll brought him just to this place? A sudden tremor of his heart made him slightly breathless. An absurd suspicion seized him. What had occurred to him was impossible, and yet it might be a fact.

"What is your name?" he asked abruptly.

The skipper's face puckered and he gave a cunning chuckle. He looked then malicious and horribly vulgar.

"It's such a damned long time since I heard it that I almost forgot it myself. But for thirty years now in the islands they've always called me Red."

His huge form shook as he gave a low, almost silent laugh. It was obscene. Neilson shuddered. Red was hugely amused, and from his bloodshot eyes tears ran down his cheeks.

Neilson gave a gasp, for at that moment a woman came in. She was a native, a woman of somewhat commanding presence, stout without being corpulent, dark, for the natives grow darker with age, with very grey hair. She wore a black Mother Hubbard, and its thinness showed her heavy breasts. The moment had come. She made an observation to Neilson about some household matter and he answered. He wondered if his voice sounded as unnatural to her as it did to himself. She gave the man who was sitting in the chair by the window an indifferent glance, and went out of the room. The moment had come and gone.

Neilson for a moment could not speak. He was strangely shaken. Then he said:

"I'd be very glad if you'd stay and have a bit of dinner with me. Pot luck."

"I don't think I will," said Red. "I must go after this fellow Gray. I'll give him his stuff and then I'll get away. I want to be back in Apia to-morrow."

"I'll send a boy along with you to show you the way."

"That'll be fine."

Red heaved himself out of his chair, while the Swede called one of the boys who worked on the plantation. He told him where the skipper wanted to go, and the boy stepped along the bridge. Red prepared to follow him.

"Don't fall in," said Neilson.

"Not on your life."

Neilson watched him make his way across and when he had disappeared among the coconuts he looked still. Then he sank heavily in his chair. Was that the man who had prevented him from being happy? Was that the man whom Sally had loved all these years and for whom she had waited so desperately? It was grotesque. A sudden fury seized him so that he had an instinct to spring up and smash everything around him. He had been cheated. They had seen each other at last and had not known it. He began to laugh, mirthlessly, and his laughter grew till it became hysterical. The Gods had played him a cruel trick. And he was old now.

At last Sally came in to tell him dinner was ready. He sat down in front of her and tried to eat. He wondered what she would say if he told her now that the fat old man sitting in the chair was the lover whom she remembered still with the passionate abandonment of her youth. Years ago, when he hated her because she made him so unhappy, he would have been glad to tell her. He wanted to hurt her then as she hurt him, because his hatred was only love. But now he did not care. He shrugged his shoulders listlessly.

"What did that man want?" she asked presently.

He did not answer at once. She was too old, a fat old native woman. He wondered why he had ever loved her so madly. He had laid at her feet all the treasures of his soul, and she had cared nothing for them. Waste, what waste! And now, when he looked at her, he felt only contempt. His patience was at last exhausted. He answered her question.

"He's the captain of a schooner. He's come from Apia."

"Yes."

"He brought me news from home. My eldest brother is very ill and I must go back."

"Will you be gone long?"

He shrugged his shoulders.

Neil MacAdam

CAPTAIN BREDON was good-natured. When Angus Munro, the Curator of the museum at Kuala Solor, told him that he had advised Neil MacAdam, his new assistant, on his arrival at Singapore to put up at the Van Dyke Hotel, and asked him to see that the lad got into no mischief during the few days he must spend there, he said he would do his best. Captain Bredon commanded the *Sultan Ahmed*, and when he was at Singapore always stayed at the Van Dyke. He had a Japanese wife and kept a room there. It was his home. When he got back after his fortnight's trip along the coast of Borneo the Dutch manager told him that Neil had been there for two days. The boy was sitting in the little dusty garden of the hotel reading old numbers of *The Straits Times*. Captain Bredon took a look at him first and then went up.

"You're MacAdam, aren't you?"

Neil rose to his feet, flushed to the roots of his hair and answered shyly: "I am."

"My name's Bredon. I'm skipper of the *Sultan Ahmed*. You're sailing with me next Tuesday. Munro asked me to look after you. What about a stengah? I suppose you've learned what that means by now."

"Thank you very much, but I don't drink."

He spoke with a broad Scots accent.

"I don't blame you. Drink's been the ruin of many a good man in this country."

He called the Chinese boy and ordered himself a double whisky and a small soda.

"What have you been doing with yourself since you got in?"

"Walking about."

"There's nothing much to see in Singapore."

"I've found plenty."

Of course the first thing he had done was to go to the museum. There was little that he had not seen at home, but the fact that those beasts and birds, those reptiles, moths, butterflies and insects were native to the country excited him. There was one section devoted to that part of Borneo of which Kuala Solor was the capital, and since these were the creatures that for the next three years would chiefly concern him, he examined them with attention. But it was outside, in the streets, that it was most thrilling, and except that he was a grave and sober young man he would have laughed aloud with joy. Everything was new to him. He walked till he was footsore. He stood at the corner of a busy street and wondered at the long line of rickshaws and the little men between the shafts running with dogged steps. He stood on a bridge over a canal and looked at the sampans wedged up against one another like sardines in a tin. He peered into the Chinese shops in Victoria Road where so many strange things were sold. Bombay merchants, fat and exuberant, stood at their shop doors and sought to sell him silks and tinsel jewellery. He watched the Tamils, pensive and forlorn, who walked with a sinister grace, and the bearded Arabs, in white skull-caps, who bore themselves with scornful dignity. The sun shone upon the varied scene with a hard, acrid brilliance. He was confused. He thought it would take him years to find his bearings in this multicoloured and excessive world.

After dinner that night Captain Bredon asked him if he would like to go round the town.

"You ought to see a bit of life while you're here," he said.

They stepped into rickshaws and drove to the Chinese quarter. The Captain, who never drank at sea, had been making up for his abstinence during the day. He was feeling good. The rickshaws stopped at a house in a side street and they knocked at the door. It was opened and they passed through a narrow passage into a large room with benches all round it covered with red plush. A number of women were sitting about—French, Italian and American. A mechanical piano was grinding out harsh music and a few couples were dancing. Captain Bredon ordered drinks. Two or three women, waiting for an invitation, gave them inviting glances.

"Well, young feller, is there anyone you fancy here?" the Captain asked facetiously.

"To sleep with, d'you mean? No."

"No white girls where you're going, you know."

"Oh, well."

"Like to go an' see some natives?"

"I don't mind."

The Captain paid for the drinks and they strolled on. They went to another house. Here the girls were Chinese, small and dainty, with tiny feet and hands like flowers, and they wore suits of flowered silk. But their painted faces were like masks. They looked at the strangers with black derisive eyes. They were strangely inhuman.

"I brought you here because I thought you ought to see the

place," said Captain Bredon, with the air of a man doing his boun-
den duty, "but just look-see is all. They don't like us for some
reason. In some of these Chinese joints they won't even let a white
man in. Fact is, they say we stink. Funny, ain't it? They say we
smell of corpses."

"We?"

"Give me Japs," said the Captain. "They're fine. My wife's a
Jap, you know. You come along with me and I'll take you to a
place where they have Japanese girls, and if you don't see something
you like there I'm a Dutchman."

Their rickshaws were waiting and they stepped into them.
Captain Bredon gave a direction and the boys started off. They
were let into the house by a stout middle-aged Japanese woman,
who bowed low as they entered. She took them into a neat, clean
room furnished only with mats on the floor; they sat down and
presently a little girl came in with a tray on which were two bowls
of pale tea. With a shy bow she handed one to each of them. The
Captain spoke to the middle-aged woman and she looked at Neil
and giggled. She said something to the child, who went out, and
presently four girls tripped in. They were sweet in their kimonos,
with their shining black hair artfully dressed; they were small and
plump, with round faces and laughing eyes. They bowed low as
they came in and with good manners murmured polite greetings.
Their speech sounded like the twittering of birds. Then they knelt,
one on each side of the two men, and charmingly flirted with them.
Captain Bredon soon had his arms round two slim waists. They all
talked nineteen to the dozen. They were very gay. It seemed to Neil
that the Captain's girls were mocking him, for their gleaming eyes
were mischievously turned towards him, and he blushed. But the
other two cuddled up to him, smiling, and spoke in Japanese as
though he understood every word they said. They seemed so happy
and guileless that he laughed. They were very attentive. They
handed him the bowl so that he should drink his tea, and then took
it from him so that he should not have the trouble of holding it. They
lit his cigarette for him and one put out a small, delicate hand to
take the ash so that it should not fall on his clothes. They stroked his
smooth face and looked with curiosity at his large young hands.
They were as playful as kittens.

"Well, which is it to be?" said the Captain after a while. "Made
your choice yet?"

"What d'you mean?"

"I'll just wait and see you settled and then I'll fix myself up."

"Oh, I don't want either of them. I'm going home to bed."

"Why, what's the matter? You're not scared, are you?"

"No, I just don't fancy it. But don't let me stand in your way. I'll get back to the hotel all right."

"Oh, if you're not going to do anything I won't either. I only wanted to be matey."

He spoke to the middle-aged woman and what he said caused the girls to look at Neil with sudden surprise. She answered and the Captain shrugged his shoulders. Then one of the girls made a remark that set them all laughing.

"What does she say?" asked Neil.

"She's pulling your leg," replied the Captain, smiling.

But he gave Neil a curious look. The girl, having made them laugh once, now said something directly to Neil. He could not understand, but the mockery of her eyes made him blush and frown. He did not like to be made fun of. Then she laughed outright and throwing her arm round his neck lightly kissed him.

"Come on, let's be going," said the Captain.

When they dismissed their rickshaws and walked into the hotel Neil asked him:

"What was it that girl said that made them all laugh?"

"She said you were a virgin."

"I don't see anything to laugh at in that," said Neil, with his slow Scots accent.

"Is it true?"

"I suppose it is."

"How old are you?"

"Twenty-two."

"What are you waiting for?"

"Till I marry."

The Captain was silent. At the top of the stairs he held out his hand. There was a twinkle in his eyes when he bade the lad goodnight, but Neil met it with a level, candid and untroubled gaze.

Three days later they sailed. Neil was the only white passenger. When the Captain was busy he read. He was reading again Wallace's *Malay Archipelago*. He had read it as a boy, but now it had a new and absorbing interest for him. When the Captain was at leisure they played cribbage or sat in long chairs on the deck, smoking, and talked. Neil was the son of a country doctor, and he could not remember when he had not been interested in natural history. When he had done with school he went to the University of Edinburgh and there took a B.Sc. with Honours. He was looking out for a job as demonstrator in biology when he chanced to see in *Nature* an advertisement for an assistant curator of the museum at

Kuala Solor. The Curator, Angus Munro, had been at Edinburgh with his uncle, a Glasgow merchant, and his uncle wrote to ask him if he would give the boy a trial. Though Neil was especially interested in entomology he was a trained taxidermist, which the advertisement said was essential; he enclosed certificates from Neil's old teachers; he added that Neil had played football for his university. In a few weeks a cable arrived engaging him and a fortnight later he sailed.

"What's Mr. Munro like?" asked Neil.

"Good fellow. Everybody likes him."

"I looked out his papers in the scientific journals. He had one in the last number of *The Ibis* on the Gymnathidæ."

"I don't know anything about that. I know he's got a Russian wife. They don't like her much."

"I got a letter from him at Singapore saying they'd put me up for a bit till I could look round and see what I wanted to do."

Now they were steaming up the river. At the mouth was a straggling fishermen's village standing on piles in the water; on the bank grew thickly nipah palm and the tortured mangrove; beyond stretched the dense green of the virgin forest. In the distance, darkly silhouetted against the blue sky, was the rugged outline of a mountain. Neil, his heart beating with the excitement that possessed him, devoured the scene with eager eyes. He was surprised. He knew his Conrad almost by heart and he was expecting a land of brooding mystery. He was not prepared for the blue milky sky. Little white clouds on the horizon, like sailing boats becalmed, shone in the sun. The green trees of the forest glittered in the brilliant light. Here and there, on the banks, were Malay houses with thatched roofs, and they nestled cosily among fruit trees. Natives in dug-outs rowed, standing, up the river. Neil had no feeling of being shut in, nor, in that radiant morning, of gloom, but of space and freedom. The country offered him a gracious welcome. He knew he was going to be happy in it. Captain Bredon from the bridge threw a friendly glance at the lad standing below him. He had taken quite a fancy to him during the four days the journey had lasted. It was true he did not drink, and when you made a joke he was as likely as not to take you seriously, but there was something very taking in his seriousness; everything was interesting and important to him—that, of course, was why he did not find your jokes amusing; but even though he didn't see them he laughed, because he felt you expected it. He laughed because life was grand. He was grateful for every little thing you told him. He was very polite. He never asked you to pass him anything without

saying "please" and always said "thank you" when you gave it.
And he was a good-looking fellow, no one could deny that. Neil was
standing with his hands on the rail, bare-headed, looking at the
passing bank. He was tall, six foot two, with long, loose limbs, broad
shoulders and narrow hips; there was something charmingly coltish
about him, so that you expected him at any moment to break into a
caper. He had brown curly hair with a peculiar shine in it; sometimes when the light caught it, it glittered like gold. His eyes, large
and very blue, shone with good-humour. They reflected his happy
disposition. His nose was short and blunt and his mouth big, his chin
determined; his face was rather broad. But his most striking feature
was his skin; it was very white and smooth, with a lovely patch of
red on either cheek. It would have been a beautiful skin even for a
woman. Captain Bredon made the same joke to him every morning.

"Well, my lad, have you shaved to-day?"

Neil passed his hand over his chin.

"No, d'you think I need it?"

The Captain always laughed at this.

"Need it? Why, you've got a face like a baby's bottom."

And invariably Neil reddened to the roots of his hair.

"I shave once a week," he retorted.

But it wasn't only his looks that made you like him. It was his
ingenuousness, his candour and the freshness with which he confronted the world. For all his intentness and the solemn way in
which he took everything, and his inclination to argue upon every
point that came up, there was something strangely simple in him
that gave you quite an odd feeling. The Captain couldn't make it
out.

"I wonder if it's because he's never had a woman," he said to
himself. "Funny. I should have thought the girls never left him
alone. With a complexion like that."

But the *Sultan Ahmed* was nearing the bend after rounding which
Kuala Solor would be in sight and the Captain's reflections were
interrupted by the necessities of his work. He rang down to the
engine room. The ship slackened to half speed. Kuala Solor
straggled along the left bank of the river, a white neat and trim
little town, and on the right on a hill were the fort and the Sultan's
palace. There was a breeze and the Sultan's flag, at the top of a
tall staff, waved bravely against the sky. They anchored in mid-
stream. The doctor and a police officer came on board in the
government launch. They were accompanied by a tall thin man in
white ducks. The Captain stood at the head of the gangway and
shook hands with them. Then he turned to the last comer.

"Well, I've brought you your young hopeful safe and sound."
And with a glance at Neil: "This is Munro."

The tall thin man held out his hand and gave Neil an appraising
look. Neil flushed a little and smiled. He had beautiful teeth.

"How do you do, sir?"

Munro did not smile with his lips, but faintly with his grey eyes.
His cheeks were hollow and he had a thin aquiline nose and pale
lips. He was deeply sunburned. His face looked tired, but his
expression was very gentle, and Neil immediately felt confidence
in him. The Captain introduced him to the doctor and the policeman and suggested that they should have a drink. When they
sat down and the boy brought bottles of beer Munro took off his
topee. Neil saw that he had close-cropped brown hair turning
grey. He was a man of forty, quiet, self-possessed in manner, with
an intellectual air that distinguished him from the brisk little doctor
and the heavy swaggering police officer.

"MacAdam doesn't drink," said the Captain when the boy
poured out four glasses of beer.

"All the better," said Munro. "I hope you haven't been trying
to lure him into evil ways."

"I tried to in Singapore," returned the Captain, with a twinkle
in his eyes, "but there was nothing doing."

When he had finished his beer Munro turned to Neil.

"Well, we'll be getting ashore, shall we?"

Neil's baggage was put in charge of Munro's boy and the two
men got into a sampan. They landed.

"Do you want to go straight up to the bungalow or would you
like to have a look round first? We've got a couple of hours before
tiffin."

"Couldn't we go to the museum?" said Neil.

Munro's eyes smiled gently. He was pleased. Neil was shy and
Munro not by nature talkative, so they walked in silence. By the
river were the native huts and here, living their immemorial lives,
dwelt the Malays. They were busy, but without haste, and you
were conscious of a happy, normal activity. There was a sense of the
rhythm of life of which the pattern was birth and death, love and the
affairs common to mankind. They came to the bazaars, narrow
streets with arcades, where the teeming Chinese, working and
eating, noisily talking, as is their way, indefatigably strove with
eternity.

"It's not much after Singapore," said Munro, "but I always think
it's rather picturesque."

He spoke with an accent less broad than Neil's, but the Scots burr was there and it put Neil at his ease. He could never quite get it out of his head that the English of English people was affected.

The museum was a handsome stone building and as they entered its portals Munro instinctively straightened himself. The attendant at the door saluted and Munro spoke to him in Malay, evidently explaining who Neil was, for the attendant gave him a smile and saluted again. It was cool in there in comparison with the heat without and the light was pleasant after the glare of the street.

"I'm afraid you'll be disappointed," said Munro. "We haven't got half the things we ought to have, but up to now we've been handicapped by lack of money. We've had to do the best we could. So you must make allowances."

Neil stepped in like a swimmer diving confidently into a summer sea. The specimens were admirably arranged. Munro had sought to please as well as to instruct, and birds and beasts and reptiles were presented, as far as possible in their natural surroundings, in such a way as to give a vivid impression of life. Neil lost his shyness and began with boyish enthusiasm to talk of this and that. He asked an infinity of questions. He was excited. Neither of them was conscious of the passage of time, and when Munro glanced at his watch he was surprised to see what the hour was. They got into rickshaws and drove to the bungalow.

Munro led the young man into a drawing-room. A woman was lying on a sofa reading a book and as they came in she slowly rose.

"This is my wife. I'm afraid we're dreadfully late, Darya."

"What does it matter?" she smiled. "What is more unimportant than time?"

She held out her hand, a rather large hand, to Neil and gave a long, reflective, but friendly look.

"I suppose you've been showing him the museum."

She was a woman of five-and-thirty, of medium height, with a pale brown face of a uniform colour and pale blue eyes. Her hair, parted in the middle and wound into a knot on the nape of her neck, was untidy; it had a moth-like quality and was of a curious pale brown. Her face was broad, with high cheek-bones, and she had a rather fleshy nose. She was not a pretty woman, but there was in her slow movements a sensual grace and in her manner as it were a physical casualness that only very dull people could have failed to find interesting. She wore a frock of green cotton. She spoke English perfectly, but with a slight accent.

They sat down to tiffin. Neil was overcome once more with shyness, but Darya did not seem to notice it. She talked freely and easily. She asked him about his journey and what he had thought of

Singapore. She told him about the people he would have to meet. That afternoon Munro was to take him to call on the Resident, the Sultan being away, and later they would go to the club. There he would see everybody.

"You will be popular," she said, her pale blue eyes resting on him with attention. A man less ingenuous than Neil might have noticed that she took stock of his size and youthful virility, his shiny, curling hair and his lovely skin. "They don't think much of us."

"Oh, nonsense, Darya. You're too sensitive. They're English, that's all."

"They think it's rather funny of Angus to be a scientist and they think it's rather vulgar of me to be a Russian. I don't care. They're fools. They're the most commonplace, the most narrow-minded, the most conventional people it has ever been my misfortune to live amongst."

"Don't put MacAdam off the moment he arrives. He'll find them kind and hospitable."

"What is your first name?" she asked the boy.

"Neil."

"I shall call you by it. And you must call me Darya. I hate being called Mrs. Munro. It makes me feel like a minister's wife."

Neil blushed. He was embarrassed that she should ask him so soon to be so familiar. She went on.

"Some of the men are not bad."

"They do their job competently and that's what they're here for," said Munro.

"They shoot. They play football and tennis and cricket. I get on with them quite well. The women are intolerable. They are jealous and spiteful and lazy. They can talk of nothing. If you introduce an intellectual subject they look down their noses as though you were indecent. What can they talk about? They're interested in nothing. If you speak of the body they think you improper, and if you speak of the soul they think you priggish."

"You mustn't take what my wife says too literally," smiled Munro, in his gentle, tolerant way. "The community here is just like any other in the East, neither very clever, nor very stupid, but amiable and kindly. And that's a good deal."

"I don't want people to be amiable and kindly. I want them to be vital and passionate. I want them to be interested in mankind. I want them to attach more importance to the things of the spirit than to a gin pahit or a curry tiffin. I want art to matter to them and literature." She addressed herself abruptly to Neil: "Have you got a soul?"

"Oh, I don't know. I don't know exactly what you mean."

"Why do you blush when I ask you? Why should you be ashamed of your soul? It is what is important in you. Tell me about it. I am interested in you and I want to know."

It seemed very awkward to Neil to be tackled in this way by a perfect stranger. He had never met anyone like this. But he was a serious young man and when he was asked a question straight out he did his best to answer it. It was Munro's presence that embarrassed him.

"I don't know what you mean by the soul. If you mean an immaterial or spiritual entity, separately produced by the creator, in temporary conjunction with the material body, then my answer is in the negative. It seems to me that such a radically dualistic view of human personality cannot be defended by anyone who is able to take a calm view of the evidence. If, on the other hand, you mean by soul the aggregate of psychic elements which form what we know as the personality of the individual, then, of course, I have."

"You're very sweet and you're wonderfully handsome," she said, smiling. "No, I mean the heart with its longings and the body with its desires and the infinite in us. Tell me, what did you read on the journey, or did you only play deck tennis?"

Neil was taken aback at the inconsequence of her reply. He would have been a little affronted except for the good-humour in her eyes and the naturalness in her manner. Munro smiled quietly at the young man's bewilderment. When he smiled the lines that ran from the wings of his nostrils to the corners of his mouth became deep furrows.

"I read a lot of Conrad."

"For pleasure or to improve your mind?"

"Both. I admire him awfully."

Darya threw up her arms in an extravagant gesture of protest.

"That Pole," she cried. "How can you English ever have let yourselves be taken in by that wordy mountebank? He has all the superficiality of his countrymen. That stream of words, those involved sentences, the showy rhetoric, that affectation of profundity: when you get through all that to the thought at the bottom, what do you find but a trivial commonplace? He was like a second-rate actor who puts on a romantic dress and declaims a play by Victor Hugo. For five minutes you say this is heroic, and then your whole soul revolts and you cry, no, this is false, false, false."

She spoke with a passion that Neil had never known anyone show when speaking of art or literature. Her cheeks, usually colourless, flushed and her pale eyes glowed.

"There's no one who got atmosphere like Conrad," said Neil.
"I can smell and see and feel the East when I read him."

"Nonsense. What do you know about the East? Everyone will
tell you that he made the grossest blunders. Ask Angus."

"Of course he was not always accurate," said Munro, in his
measured, reflective way. "The Borneo he described is not the
Borneo we know. He saw it from the deck of a merchant-vessel
and he was not an acute observer even of what he saw. But does
it matter? I don't know why fiction should be hampered by fact.
I don't think it's a mean achievement to have created a country,
a dark, sinister, romantic and heroic country of the soul."

"You're a sentimentalist, my poor Angus." And then again to
Neil: "You must read Turgeniev, you must read Tolstoi, you must
read Dostoevsky."

Neil did not in the least know what to make of Darya Munro.
She skipped over the first stages of acquaintance and treated him
at once like someone she had known intimately all her life. It
puzzled him. It seemed so reckless. When he met anyone his own
instinct was to go cautiously. He was amiable, but he did not like to
step too far before he saw his way before him. He did not want to
give anyone his confidence before he thought himself justified. But
with Darya you could not help yourself; she forced your confidence.
She poured out the feelings and thoughts that most people keep to
themselves like a prodigal flinging gold pieces to a scrambling crowd.
She did not talk, she did not act, like anyone he had ever known.
She did not mind what she said. She would speak of the natural
functions of the human animal in a way that brought the blushes
coursing to his cheeks. They excited her ridicule.

"Oh, what a prig you are! What is there indecent in it? When
I'm going to take a purge, why shouldn't I say so and when I think
you want one, why shouldn't I tell you?"

"Theoretically I dare say you're right," said Neil, always judicious
and reasonable.

She made him tell her of his father and mother, his brothers, his
life at school and at the university. She told him about herself. Her
father was a general killed in the war and her mother a Princess
Lutchkov. They were in Eastern Russia when the Bolsheviks seized
power, and fled to Yokohama. Here they had subsisted miserably on
the sale of their jewels and such objects of art as they had been able to
save, and here she married a fellow-exile. She was unhappy with
him and in two years divorced him. Her mother died and, penniless,
she was driven to earn her living as best she could. She was employed by an American relief organisation. She taught in a mission

school. She worked in a hospital. She made Neil's blood boil, and at the same time embarrassed him very much, when she spoke of the men who tried to take advantage of her defencelessness and her poverty. She spared him no details.

"Brutes," he said.

"Oh, all men are like that," she replied, with a shrug of her shoulders.

She told him how once she protected her virtue at the point of her revolver.

"I swore I'd kill him if he took another step, and if he had I'd have shot him like a dog."

"Gosh!" said Neil.

It was at Yokohama that she met Angus. He was spending his leave in Japan. She was captivated by his straightforwardness, the decency which was so obvious in him, his tenderness and his consideration. He was not a business man; he was a scientist, and science is milk-brother to art. He offered her peace. He offered her security. And she was tired of Japan. Borneo was a land of mystery. They had been married for five years.

She gave Neil the Russian novelists to read. She gave him *Fathers and Sons, Anna Karenina* and *The Brothers Karamazoff*.

"Those are the three peaks of our literature. Read them. They are the greatest novels the world has ever seen."

Like many of her countrymen she talked as though no other literature counted, and as though a few novels and stories, some indifferent poetry and half a dozen good plays had made whatever else the world has produced negligible. Neil was fascinated and overwhelmed.

"You're rather like Alyosha yourself, Neil," she said, looking at him with eyes that were now so soft and tender, "an Alyosha with a Scotch dourness, suspicious and prudent, that will not let the soul in you, the spiritual beauty, come out."

"I'm not a bit like Alyosha," he answered self-consciously.

"You don't know what you're like. You don't know anything about yourself. Why are you a naturalist? Is it for money? You could have made much more money by going into your uncle's office in Glasgow. I feel in you something strange and unearthly. I could bow down at your feet as Father Zossima did to Dimitri."

"Please don't," he said, smiling, but flushing a little too.

But the novels he read made her seem a little less strange to him. They gave her an environment and he recognised in her traits which, however unusual in the women he knew in Scotland, his

A A

mother and the daughters of his uncle in Glasgow, were common
to many of the characters in Russian fiction. He no longer wondered
that she should like to sit up so late, drinking innumerable cups of
tea, and lie on the sofa nearly all day long reading and incessantly
smoking cigarettes. She could do nothing at all for days on end
without being bored. She had a curious mixture of languor and
zest. She often said, with a shrug of her shoulders, that she was an
Oriental, and a European only by chance. She had a feline grace
that indeed suggested the Oriental. She was immensely untidy and
it did not seem to affect her that cigarette-ends, old papers and
empty tins should lie about their living-room. But he thought she
had something of Anna Karenina in her, and he transferred to her
the sympathy he felt for that pathetic creature. He understood her
arrogance. It was not unnatural that she despised the women of the
community, whose acquaintance little by little he made; they *were*
commonplace; her mind was quicker than theirs, she had a wider
culture, and she had above all a sort of tremulous sensitiveness that
made *them* extraordinarily colourless. She certainly took no pains to
conciliate them. Though at home she slopped about in a sarong and
baju, when she and Angus went out to dinner she dressed with a
splendour that was somewhat out of place. She liked to display her
ample bosom and her shapely back. She painted her cheeks and
made up her eyes like an actress for the footlights. Though it made
Neil angry to see the amused or outraged glances that her appearance provoked, he could not in his heart but think it a pity that she
should make such an object of herself. She looked grand, of course,
but if you hadn't known who she was you would have thought she
wasn't respectable. There were things about her that he could never
get over. She had an enormous appetite and it fashed him that she
ate more than he and Angus together. He could never quite get
used to the bluntness with which she discussed sexual matters. She
took it for granted that at home and in Edinburgh he had had
affairs with a host of women. She pressed him for details of his
adventures. His Scotch pawkiness helped him to parry her thrusts
and he evaded her questions with native caution. She laughed at his
reticence.

Sometimes she shocked him. He grew accustomed to the frankness with which she admired his looks, and when she told him that
he was as beautiful as a young Norse god he did not turn a hair.
Flattery fell off him like water from a duck's back. But he did not
like it when she ran her hand, though large, very soft, with caressing
fingers, through his curly hair or, a smile on her lips, stroked his
smooth face. He couldn't bear being mussed about. One day

she wanted a drink of tonic water and began pouring some out in a glass that stood on the table.

"That's my glass," he said quickly. "I've just been drinking out of it."

"Well, what of it? You haven't got syphilis, have you?"

"I hate drinking out of other people's glasses myself."

She was funny about cigarettes too. Once, when he hadn't been there very long, he had just lit one, when she passed and said:

"I want that."

She took it out of his mouth and began to smoke it. After two or three puffs, she said she did not want any more and handed it back to him. The end she had had in her mouth was red from the rouge on her lips, and he didn't want to go on smoking it at all. But he was afraid she would think it rude if he threw it away. It somewhat disgusted him. Often she would ask him for a cigarette and when he handed it to her, say:

"Oh, light it for me, will you?"

When he did so, and held it out to her, she opened her mouth so that he should put it in. He hadn't been able to help wetting the end a little. He wondered she could bear to put it in her mouth after it had been in his. The whole thing seemed to him awfully familiar. He was sure Munro wouldn't like it. She had even done this once or twice at the club. Neil had felt himself go purple. He wished she hadn't got these rather unpleasant habits, but he supposed they were Russian, and one couldn't deny that she was wonderfully good company. Her conversation was very stimulating. It was like champagne (which Neil had tasted once and thought wretched stuff), "metaphorically speaking". There was nothing she couldn't talk about. She didn't talk like a man; with a man you generally knew what he would say next, but with her you never did; her intuition was quite remarkable. She gave you ideas. She enlarged your mind and excited your imagination. Neil felt alive as he had never felt alive before. He seemed to walk on mountain peaks and the horizons of the spirit were unbounded. Neil felt a certain complacency when he stopped to reflect on what an exalted plane his mind communed with hers. Such conversations made very small beer of the vaunted pleasure of sense. She was in many ways (he was of a cautious nature and seldom made a statement even to himself that he did not qualify) the most intelligent woman he had ever met. And besides, she was Angus Munro's wife.

For, whatever Neil's reservations were about Darya, he had none about Munro, and she would have had to be a much less remarkable woman not to profit by the enormous admiration he conceived for

her husband. With him Neil let himself go. He felt for him what he had never felt for anyone before. He was so sane, so balanced, so tolerant. This was the sort of man he would himself like to be when he was older. He talked little, but when he did, with good sense. He was wise. He had a dry humour that Neil understood. It made the hearty English fun of the men at the club seem inane. He was kind and patient. He had a dignity that made it impossible to conceive of anyone taking a liberty with him, but he was neither pompous nor solemn. He was honest and absolutely truthful. But Neil admired him no less as a scientist than as a man. He had imagination. He was careful and painstaking. Though his interest was in research he did the routine work of the museum conscientiously. He was just then much interested in stick-insects and intended to write a paper on their powers of parthenogenetic reproduction. An incident occurred in connection with the experiments he was making that made a great impression on Neil. One day, a little captive gibbon escaped from its chain and ate up all the larvæ and so destroyed the whole of Munro's evidence. Neil nearly cried. Angus Munro took the gibbon in his arms and, smiling, stroked it.

"Diamond, Diamond," he said, quoting Sir Isaac Newton, "you little know the damage you have done."

He was also studying mimicry and instilled into Neil his absorbed interest in this controversial subject. They had interminable talks about it. Neil was astonished at the Curator's wonderful knowledge. It was encyclopædic, and he was abashed at his own ignorance. But it was when Munro spoke of the trips into the country to collect specimens that his enthusiasm was most contagious. That was the perfect life, a life of hardship, difficulty, often of privation and sometimes of danger, but rewarded by the thrill of finding a rare, or even a new, species, by the beauty of the scenery and the intimate observation of nature, and above all by the sense of freedom from every tie. It was for this part of the work that Neil had been chiefly engaged. Munro was occupied in research work that made it difficult for him to be away from home for several weeks at a time, and Darya had always refused to accompany him. She had an unreasoning fear of the jungle. She was terrified of wild beasts, snakes and venomous insects. Though Munro had told her over and over again that no animal hurt you unless you molested or frightened it, she could not get over her instinctive horror. He did not like leaving her. She cared little for the local society and with him away he realised that life for her must be intolerably dull. But the Sultan was keenly interested in natural history and was anxious that the

museum should be completely representative of the country's fauna. One expedition Munro and Neil were to make together, so that Neil should learn how to go to work, and the plans for this were discussed by them for months. Neil looked forward to it as he had never looked forward to anything in his life.

Meanwhile he learned Malay and acquired a smattering of the dialects that would be useful to him on future journeys. He played tennis and football. He soon knew everyone in the community. On the football field he threw off his absorption in science and his interest in Russian fiction and gave himself up to the pleasure of the game. He was strong, quick and active. After it was all over it was grand to have a sluice down and a long tonic with a slice of lemon and go over it all with the other fellows. It had never been intended that Neil should live permanently with the Munros. There was a roomy rest-house at Kuala Solor, but the rule was that no one should stay in it for more than a fortnight and such of the bachelors as had no official quarters clubbed together and took a house between them. When Neil arrived it so happened that there was no vacancy in any of these messes. One evening, however, when he had been four months in the colony, two men, Waring and Jonson, when they were sitting together after a game of tennis, told him that one member of their mess was going home and if he would like to join them they would be glad to have him. They were young fellows of his own age, in the football team, and Neil liked them both. Waring was in the Customs and Jonson in the police. He jumped at the suggestion. They told him how much it would cost and fixed a day, a fortnight later, when it would be convenient for him to move in.

At dinner he told the Munros.

"It's been awfully good of you to let me stay so long. It's made me very uncomfortable planting myself on you like this, I've been quite ashamed, but now there's no excuse for me."

"But we like having you here," said Darya. "You don't need an excuse."

"I can hardly go on staying here indefinitely."

"Why not? Your salary's miserable, what's the use of wasting it on board and lodging? You'd be bored stiff with Jonson and Waring. Stupids. They haven't an idea in their heads outside playing the gramophone and knocking balls about."

It was true that it had been very convenient to live free of cost. He had saved the greater part of his salary. He had a thrifty soul and had never been used to spending money when it wasn't necessary, but he was proud. He could not go on living at other people's expense. Darya looked at him with her quiet, observant eyes.

"Angus and I have got used to you now. I think we'd miss you. If you like, you can pay us for your board. You don't cost anything, but if it'll make you easier I'll find out exactly what difference you make in cookie's book and you can pay that."

"It must be an awful nuisance having a stranger in the house," he answered uncertainly.

"It'll be miserable for you there. Good heavens, the filth they eat."

It was true also that at the Munros' you ate better than anywhere else at Kuala Solor. He had dined out now and then, and even at the Resident's you didn't get a very good dinner. Darya liked her food and kept the cook up to the mark. He made Russian dishes which were a fair treat. That cabbage soup of Darya's was worth walking five miles for. But Munro hadn't said anything.

"I'd be glad if you'd stay here," he said now. "It's very convenient to have you on the spot. If anything comes up we can talk it over there and then. Waring and Jonson are very good fellows, but I dare say you'd find them rather limited after a bit."

"Oh, well, then I'll be very pleased. Heaven knows, I couldn't want anything better than this. I was only afraid I was in the way."

Next day it was raining cats and dogs and it was impossible to play tennis or football, but towards six Neil put on a mackintosh and went to the club. It was empty but for the Resident, who was sitting in an arm-chair reading *The Fortnightly*. His name was Trevelyan, and he claimed to be related to the friend of Byron. He was a tall fat man, with close-cropped white hair and the large red face of a comic actor. He was fond of amateur theatricals and specialised in cynical dukes and facetious butlers. He was a bachelor, but generally supposed to be fond of the girls, and he liked his gin pahit before dinner. He owed his position to the Sultan's friendship. He was a slack, complacent man, a great talker, not very fond of work, who wanted everything to go smoothly and no one to give trouble. Though not considered especially competent he was popular in the community because he was easy-going and hospitable, and he certainly made life more comfortable than if he had been energetic and efficient. He nodded to Neil.

"Well, young fellow, how are bugs to-day?"

"Feeling the weather, sir," said Neil gravely.

"Hi-hi."

In a few minutes Waring, Jonson and another man, called Bishop, came in. He was in the Civil Service. Neil did not play bridge, so Bishop went up to the Resident.

"Would you care to make a fourth, sir?" he asked him. "There's nobody much in the club to-day."

The Resident gave the others a glance.

"All right. I'll just finish this article and join you. Cut for me and deal. I shall only be five minutes."

Neil went up to the three men.

"Oh, I say, Waring, thanks awfully, but I can't move over to you after all. The Munros have asked me to stay on with them for good."

A broad smile broke on Waring's face.

"Fancy that."

"It's awfully nice of them, isn't it? They made rather a point of it. I couldn't very well refuse."

"What did I tell you?" said Bishop.

"I don't blame the boy," said Waring.

There was something in their manner that Neil did not like. They seemed to be amused. He flushed.

"What the hell are you talking about?" he cried.

"Oh, come off it," said Bishop. "We know our Darya. You're not the first good-looking young fellow she's had a romp with, and you won't be the last."

The words were hardly out of his mouth before Neil's clenched fist shot out like a flash. He hit Bishop on the face and he fell heavily to the floor. Jonson sprang at Neil and seized him round the middle, for he was beside himself.

"Let me go," he shouted. "If he doesn't withdraw that I'll kill him."

The Resident, startled by the commotion, looked up and rose to his feet. He walked heavily towards them.

"What's this? What's this? What the hell are you boys playing at?"

They were taken aback. They had forgotten him. He was their master. Jonson let go of Neil and Bishop picked himself up. The Resident, a frown on his face, spoke to Neil sharply.

"What's the meaning of this? Did you hit Bishop?"

"Yes, sir."

"Why?"

"He made a foul suggestion reflecting on a woman's honour," said Neil, very haughtily, and still white with rage.

The Resident's eyes twinkled, but he kept a grave face.

"What woman?"

"I refuse to answer," said Neil, throwing back his head and drawing himself up to his full imposing height.

It would have been more effective if the Resident hadn't been a good two inches taller, and very much stouter.

"Don't be a damned young fool."

"Darya Munro," said Jonson.

"What did you say, Bishop?"

"I forget the exact words I used. I said she'd hopped into bed with a good many young chaps here, and I supposed she hadn't missed the chance of doing the same with MacAdam."

"It was a most offensive suggestion. Will you be so good as to apologise and shake hands. Both of you."

"I've had a hell of a biff, sir. My eye's going to look like the devil. I'm damned if I apologise for telling the truth."

"You're old enough to know that the fact that your statement is true only makes it more offensive, and as far as your eye is concerned I'm told that a raw beef-steak is very efficacious in these circumstances. Though I put my desire that you should apologise in the form of a request out of politeness, it is in point of fact an order."

There was a moment's silence. The Resident looked bland.

"I apologise for what I said, sir," Bishop said sulkily.

"Now then, MacAdam."

"I'm sorry I hit him, sir. I apologise, too."

"Shake hands."

The two young men solemnly did so.

"I shouldn't like this to go any further. It wouldn't be very nice for Munro, whom I think we all like. Can I count on you all holding your tongues?"

They nodded.

"Now be off with you. You stay, MacAdam, I want to have a few words with you."

When the two of them were left alone, the Resident sat down and lit himself a cheroot. He offered one to Neil, but he only smoked cigarettes.

"You're a very violent young man," said the Resident, with a smile. "I don't like my officers to make scenes in a public place like this."

"Mrs. Munro is a great friend of mine. She's been kindness itself to me. I won't hear a word said against her."

"Then I'm afraid you'll have your job cut out for you if you stay here much longer."

Neil was silent for a moment. He stood, tall and slim, before the Resident, and his grave young face was guileless. He flung back his head defiantly. His emotion made him speak in broader Scots even than usual.

"I've lived with the Munros for four months, and I give you my word of honour that so far as I am concerned there is not an iota of truth in what that beast said. Mrs. Munro has never treated me with anything that you could call undue familiarity. She's never by word or deed given me the smallest hint that she had an improper idea in her head. She's been like a mother to me or an elder sister."

The Resident watched him with ironical eyes.

"I'm very glad to hear it. That's the best thing I've heard about her for a long time."

"You believe me, sir, don't you?"

"Of course. Perhaps you've reformed her." He called out. "Boy. Bring me a gin pahit." And then to Neil, "That'll do. You can go now if you want to. But no more fighting, mind you, or you'll get the order of the boot."

When Neil walked back to the Munros' bungalow the rain had stopped and the velvet sky was bright with stars. In the garden the fire-flies were flitting here and there. From the earth rose a scented warmth and you felt that if you stopped you would hear the growth of that luxuriant vegetation. A white flower of the night gave forth an overwhelming perfume. In the verandah Munro was typing some notes and Darya, lying at full length on a long chair, was reading. The lamp behind her lit her smoky hair so that it shone like an aureole. She looked up at Neil and, putting down her book, smiled. Her smile was very friendly.

"Where have you been, Neil?"

"At the club."

"Anybody there?"

The scene was so cosy and domestic, Darya's manner so peaceful and quietly assured, that it was impossible not to be touched. The two of them there, each occupied with his own concerns, seemed so united, their intimacy so natural, that no one could have conceived that they were not perfectly happy in one another. Neil did not believe a single word of what Bishop had said and the Resident had hinted. It was incredible. After all, he knew that what they had suspected of *him* was untrue, so what reason was there to think that the rest was any truer? They had dirty minds, all those people; because they were a lot of swine they thought everyone else as bad as they were. His knuckle hurt him a little. He was glad he had hit Bishop. He wished he knew who had started that filthy story. He'd wring his neck.

But now Munro fixed a date for the expedition that they had so much discussed, and in his careful way began to make preparations so that at the last moment nothing should be forgotten. The plan was to go as far up the river as possible and then make their way through the jungle and hunt for specimens on the little-known Mount Hitam. They expected to be away two months. As the day on which they were to start grew nearer Munro's spirits rose, and though he did not say very much, though he remained quiet and self-controlled, you could tell by the light in his eyes and the jauntiness of his step how much he looked forward to it. One morning, at the museum, he was almost sprightly.

"I've got some good news for you," he said suddenly to Neil, after they had been looking at some experiments they were making, "Darya's coming with us."

"Is she? That's grand."

Neil was delighted. That made it perfect.

"It's the first time I've ever been able to induce her to accompany me. I told her she'd enjoy it, but she would never listen to me. Queer cattle, women. I'd given it up and never thought of asking her to come this time, and suddenly, last night, out of a blue sky she said she'd like to."

"I'm awfully glad," said Neil.

"I didn't much like the idea of leaving her by herself so long; now we can stay just as long as we want to."

They started early one morning in four prahus, manned by Malays, and besides themselves the party consisted of their servants and four Dyak hunters. The three of them lay on cushions side by side, under an awning; in the other boats were the Chinese servants and the Dyaks. They carried bags of rice for the whole party, provisions for themselves, clothes, books and all that was necessary for their work. It was heavenly to leave civilisation behind them and they were all excited. They talked. They smoked. They read. The motion of the river was exquisitely soothing. They lunched on a grassy bank. Dusk fell and they moored for the night. They slept at a long house and their Dyak hosts celebrated their visit with arrack, eloquence and a fantastic dance. Next day the river, narrowing, gave them more definitely the feeling that they were adventuring into the unknown, and the exotic vegetation that crowded the banks to the water's edge, like an excited mob pushed from behind by a multitude, caused Neil a breathless ravishment. O wonder and delight! On the third day, because the water was shallower and the stream more rapid, they changed into lighter boats, and soon it grew so strong that the boatmen could paddle no longer, and they poled against the current with powerful and magnificent gestures. Now and then they came to rapids and had to disembark, unload and haul the boats through a rock-strewn passage. After five days they reached a point beyond which they could go no further. There was a government bungalow there, and they settled in for a couple of nights while Munro made arrangements for their excursion into the interior. He wanted bearers for their baggage, and men to build a house for them when they reached Mount Hitam. It was necessary for Munro to see the headman of a village in the vicinity and thinking it would save time if he went himself rather than let the headman come to him, the day after they arrived he set out at dawn with a guide and a couple of Dyaks. He expected to be back in a few hours. When he had seen him off Neil thought he would have a bathe. There was a pool a little way from the bungalow, and the water was so clear that you saw every grain of the sandy bottom. The river was so narrow there that the trees over-arched it. It was a lovely spot. It reminded Neil of the pools in Scotch streams he had bathed in as a boy, and yet it was strangely different. It had an air of romance, a feeling of virgin nature, that filled him with sensations that he found hard to analyse. He tried, of course, but older heads than his have found it difficult to anatomise happiness. A kingfisher was sitting on an overhanging branch and its vivid blue was reflected as bluely in the crystal stream. It flew away with a flashing glitter of jewelled wings when Neil, slipping off his sarong and baju, scrambled down into the water. It was fresh without being cold. He splashed and tumbled about. He enjoyed the movement of his strong limbs. He floated and looked at the blue sky peeping through the leaves and the sun that here and there gilded the water. Suddenly he heard a voice.

"How white your body is, Neil."

With a gasp he let himself sink and turning round saw Darya standing on the bank.

"I say, I haven't got any clothes on."

"So I saw. It's much nicer bathing without. Wait a minute, I'll come in, it looks lovely."

She also was wearing a sarong and a baju. He turned away his head quickly, for he saw that she was taking them off. He heard her splash into the water. He gave two or three strokes in order that she should have room to swim about at a good distance from him, but she swam up to him.

"Isn't the feel of the water on one's body lovely?" she said.

She laughed and opening her hand splashed water in his face. He was so embarrassed he did not know which way to look. In that limpid water it was impossible not to see that she was stark naked. It was not so bad now, but he could not help thinking how difficult it would be to get out. She seemed to be having a grand time.

"I don't care if I do get my hair wet," she said.

She turned over on her back and with strong strokes swam round the pool. When she wanted to get out, he thought, the best thing would be if he turned his back and when she was dressed she could go and he would get out later. She seemed quite unconscious of the awkwardness of the situation. He was vexed with her. It really was rather tactless to behave like that. She kept on talking to him just as if they were on dry land and properly dressed. She even called his attention to herself.

"Does my hair look awful? It's so fine it gets like rat tails when it's wet. Hold me under the shoulders a moment while I try to screw it up."

"Oh, it's all right," he said. "You'd better leave it now."

"I'm getting frightfully hungry," she said presently. "What about breakfast?"

"If you'll get out first and put on your things, I'll follow you in a minute."

"All right."

She swam the two strokes needed to bring her to the side, and he modestly looked away so that he should not see her get out nude from the water.

"I can't get up," she cried. "You'll have to help me."

It had been easy enough to get in, but the bank overhung the water and one had to lift oneself up by the branch of a tree.

"I can't. I haven't got a stitch of clothing on."

"I know that. Don't be so Scotch. Get up on the bank and give me a hand."

There was no help for it. Neil swung himself up and pulled her after him. She had left her sarong beside his. She took it up unconcernedly and began to dry herself with it. There was nothing for him but to do the same, but for decency's sake he turned his back on her.

"You really have a most lovely skin," she said. "It's as smooth and white as a woman's. It's funny on such a manly virile figure. And you haven't got a hair on your chest."

Neil wrapped the sarong round him and slipped his arms into the baju.

"Are you ready?"

She had porridge for breakfast, and eggs and bacon, cold meat and marmalade. Neil was a trifle sulky. She was really almost too Russian. It was stupid of her to behave like that; of course there was no harm in it, but it was just that sort of thing that made people think the things they did about her. The worst of it was that you couldn't give her a hint. She'd only laugh at you. But the fact was that if any of those men at Kuala Solor had seen them bathing like that together, stark naked, nothing would have persuaded them that something improper hadn't happened. In his judicious way Neil admitted to himself that you could hardly blame them. It was too bad of her. She had no right to put a fellow in such a position. He had felt such a fool. And say what you liked, it was indecent.

Next morning, having seen their carriers on the way, a long procession in single file, each man carrying his load in a creel on his back, with their servants, guides and hunters, they started to walk. The path ran over the foothills of the mountain, through scrub and tall grass, and now and then they came to narrow streams which they crossed by rickety bridges of bamboo. The sun beat on them fiercely. In the afternoon they reached the shade of a bamboo forest, grateful after the glare, and the bamboos in their slender elegance rose to incredible heights, and the green light was like the light under the sea. At last they reached the primeval forest, huge trees swathed in luxuriant creepers, an inextricable tangle, and awe descended upon them. They cut their way through the undergrowth. They walked in twilight and only now and then caught through the dense foliage above them a glimpse of sunshine. They saw neither man nor beast, for the denizens of the jungle are shy and at the first sound of footsteps vanish from sight. They heard birds up high in the tall trees, but saw none save the twittering sunbirds that flew in the underwoods and delicately coquetted with the wild flowers. They halted for the night. The carriers made a floor of branches and on this spread waterproof sheets. The Chinese cook made them their dinner and then they turned in.

It was the first night Neil had ever spent in the jungle and he could not sleep. The darkness was profound. The noise was deafening of innumerable insects, but like the roar of traffic in a great city it was so constant that in a little while it was like an impenetrable silence, and when on a sudden he heard the shriek of a monkey seized by a snake or the scream of a night-bird he nearly jumped out of his skin. He had a mysterious sensation that all around creatures were watching them. Over there, beyond the camp-fires, savage warfare was waged and they three on their bed of branches were defenceless and alone in face of the horror of nature. By his side Munro was breathing quietly in his deep sleep.

"Are you awake, Neil?" Darya whispered.

"Yes. Is anything the matter?"

"I'm terrified."

"It's all right. There's nothing to be afraid of."

"The silence is so awful. I wish I hadn't come."

She lit a cigarette.

Neil, having at last dozed off, was awakened by the hammering of a woodpecker, and its complacent laugh as it flew from one tree to another seemed to mock the sluggards. A hurried breakfast, and the caravan started. The gibbons swung from branch to branch, gathering in the dawn dew from the leaves, and their strange cry was like the call of a bird. The light had driven away Darya's fears, and notwithstanding a sleepless night she was alert and gay. They continued to climb. In the afternoon they reached the spot that the guides had told them would be a good camping place, and here Munro decided to build a house. The men set to work. With their long knives they cut palm leaves and saplings and soon had erected a two-roomed hut raised on piles from the ground. It was neat and fresh and green. It smelt good.

The Munros, he from old habit, she because she had for years wandered about the world and had a catlike knack of making herself comfortable wherever she went, were at home anywhere. In a day they had arranged everything and settled down. Their routine was invariable. Every morning early Neil and Munro started out separately, collecting. The afternoon was devoted to pinning insects in boxes, placing butterflies between sheets of paper and skinning birds. When dusk came they caught moths. Darya busied herself with the hut and the servants, sewed and read and smoked innumerable cigarettes. The days passed very pleasantly, monotonous but eventful. Neil was enraptured. He explored the mountain in all directions. One day, to his pride, he found a new species of stick-insect. Munro named it Cuniculina MacAdami. This was fame. Neil (at twenty-two) realised that he had not lived in vain. But another day he only just escaped being bitten by a viper. Owing to its green colour he had not seen it and was only saved from lurching against it by the Dyak hunter who was with him. They killed it and brought it back to camp. Darya shuddered at the sight of it. She had a terror of the wild creatures of the jungle that was almost hysterical. She would never go more than a few yards from the camp for fear of being lost.

"Has Angus ever told you how he was lost?" she asked Neil one evening when they were sitting quietly together after dinner.

"It wasn't a very pleasant experience," he smiled.

"Tell him, Angus."

He hesitated a little. It was not a thing he liked to recall.

"It was some years ago, I'd gone out with my butterfly net and I'd been very lucky, I'd got several rare specimens that I'd been looking for a long time. After a while I thought I was getting hungry so I turned back. I walked for some time and it struck me I'd come a good deal farther than I knew. Suddenly I caught sight of an empty match-box. I'd thrown it away when I started to come back; I'd been walking in a circle and was exactly where I was an hour before. I was not pleased. But I had a look round and set off again. It was fearfully hot and I was simply dripping with sweat. I knew more or less the direction the camp was in and I looked about for traces of my passage to see if I had come that way. I thought I found one or two and went on hopefully. I was frightfully thirsty. I walked on and on, picking my way over snags and trailing plants, and suddenly I knew I was lost. I couldn't have gone so far in the right direction without hitting the camp. I can tell you I was startled. I knew I must keep my head, so I sat down and thought the situation over. I was tortured by thirst. It was long past midday and in three or four hours it would be dark. I didn't like the idea of spending a night in the jungle at all. The only thing I could think of was to try and find a stream; if I followed its course, it would eventually bring me to a larger stream and sooner or later to the river. But of course it might take a couple of days. I cursed myself for being such a fool, but there was nothing better to do and I began walking. At all events if I found a stream I should be able to get a drink. I couldn't find a trickle of water anywhere, not the smallest brook that might lead to something like a stream. I began to be alarmed. I saw myself wandering on till at last I fell exhausted. I knew there was a lot of game in the forest and if I came upon a rhino I was done for. The maddening thing was I knew I couldn't be more than ten miles from my camp. I forced myself to keep my head. The day was waning and in the depths of the jungle it was growing dark already. If I'd brought a gun I could have fired it. In the camp they must have realised I was lost and would be looking for me. The undergrowth was so thick that I couldn't see six feet into it and presently, I don't know if it was nerves or not, I had the sensation that some animal was walking stealthily beside me. I stopped and it stopped too. I went on and it went on. I couldn't see it. I could see no movement in the undergrowth. I didn't even hear the breaking of a twig or the brushing of a body through leaves, but I knew how silently those beasts could move, and I was positive something was stalking me. My heart beat so violently against my ribs that I thought it would break. I was scared out of my wits. It was only by the exercise of all the self-control I had that I prevented myself from breaking into a run. I knew if I did that I was lost. I should be tripped up before I had gone twenty yards by a tangled root and when I was down it would spring on me. And if I started to run God knew where I should get to. And I had to husband my strength. I felt very like crying. And that intolerable thirst. I've never been so frightened in my life. Believe me, if I'd had a revolver I think I'd have blown my brains out. It was so awful I just wanted to finish with it. I was so exhausted I could hardly stagger. If I had an enemy who'd done me a deadly injury I wouldn't wish him the agony I endured then. Suddenly I heard two shots. My heart stood still. They were looking for me. Then I did lose my head. I ran in the direction of the sound, screaming at the top of my voice, I fell, I picked myself up again, I ran on, I shouted till I thought my lungs would burst, there was another shot, nearer, I shouted again, I heard answering shouts; there was a scramble of men in the undergrowth. In a minute I was surrounded by Dyak hunters. They wrung and kissed my hands. They laughed and cried. I very nearly cried too. I was down and out, but they gave me a drink. We were only three miles from the camp. It was pitch dark when we got back. By God, it was a near thing."

A convulsive shudder passed through Darya.

"Believe me, I don't want to be lost in the jungle again."

"What would have happened if you hadn't been found?"

"I can tell you. I should have gone mad. If I hadn't been stung by a snake or attacked by a rhino I should have gone on blindly till I fell exhausted. I should have starved to death. I should have died of thirst. Wild beasts would have eaten my body and ants cleaned my bones."

Silence fell upon them.

Then it happened, when they had spent nearly a month on Mount Hitam, that Neil, notwithstanding the quinine Munro had made him take regularly, was stricken with fever. It was not a bad attack, but he felt very sorry for himself and was obliged to stay in bed. Darya nursed him. He was ashamed to give her so much trouble, but she would not listen to his protests. She was certainly very capable. He resigned himself to letting her do things for him that one of the Chinese boys could have done just as well. He was touched. She waited on him hand and foot. But when the fever was at its height and she sponged him all over with cold water, though the comfort was indescribable, he was excessively embarrassed. She insisted on washing him night and morning.

"I wasn't in the British hospital at Yokohama for six months without learning at least the routine of nursing," she said, smiling.

She kissed him on the lips each time after she had finished. It was friendly and sweet of her. He rather liked it, but attached no importance to it; he even went so far, a rare thing for him, as to be facetious on the subject.

"Did you always kiss your patients at the hospital?" he asked her.

"Don't you like me to kiss you?" she smiled.

"It doesn't do me any harm."

"It may even hasten your recovery," she mocked.

One night he dreamt of her. He awoke with a start. He was sweating profusely. The relief was wonderful, and he knew that his temperature had fallen; he was well. He did not care. For what he had dreamt filled him with shame. He was horrified. That he should have such thoughts, even in his sleep, made him feel awful. He must be a monster of depravity. Day was breaking, and he heard Munro getting up in the room next door that he occupied with Darya. She slept late, and he took care not to disturb her. When he passed through Neil's room, Neil in a low voice called him.

"Hullo, are you awake?"

"Yes, I've had the crisis. I'm all right now."

"Good. You'd better stay in bed to-day. To-morrow you'll be as fit as a fiddle."

"Send Ah Tan to me when you've had your breakfast, will you?"

"Right-ho."

He heard Munro start out. The Chinese boy came and asked him what he wanted. An hour later Darya awoke. She came in to bid him good-morning. He could hardly look at her.

"I'll just have my breakfast and then I'll come in and wash you," she said.

"I'm washed. I got Ah Tan to do it."

"Why?"

"I wanted to spare you the trouble."

"It isn't a trouble. I like doing it."

She came over to the bed and bent down to kiss him, but he turned away his head.

"Oh, don't," he said.

"Why not?"

"It's silly."

She looked at him for a moment, surprised, and then with a slight shrug of the shoulders left him. A little later she came back to see if there was anything he wanted. He pretended to be asleep. She very gently stroked his cheek.

"For God's sake don't do that," he cried.

"I thought you were sleeping. What's the matter with you to-day?"

"Nothing."

"Why are you being horrid to me? Have I done anything to offend you?"

"No."

"Tell me what it is."

She sat down on the bed and took his hand. He turned his face to the wall. He was so ashamed he could hardly speak.

"You seem to forget I'm a man. You treat me as if I was a boy of twelve."

"Oh?"

He was blushing furiously. He was angry with himself and vexed with her. She really should be more tactful. He plucked nervously at the sheet.

"I know it means nothing to you and it ought not to mean anything to me. It doesn't when I'm well and up and about. One can't help one's dreams, but they are an indication of what is going on in the subconscious."

"Have you been dreaming about me? Well, I don't think there's any harm in that."

He turned his head and looked at her. Her eyes were gleaming, but his were sombre with remorse.

"You don't know men," he said.

She gave a little burble of laughter. She bent down and threw her arms round his neck. She had nothing on but her sarong and baju.

"You darling," she cried. "Tell me, what did you dream?"

He was startled out of his wits. He pushed her violently aside.

"What are you doing? You're crazy."

He jumped half out of bed.

"Don't you know that I'm madly in love with you?" she said.

"What *are* you talking about?"

He sat down on the side of the bed. He was frankly bewildered. She chuckled.

"Why do you suppose I came up to this horrible place? To be with you, ducky. Don't you know I'm scared stiff of the jungle? Even in here I'm frightened there'll be snakes or scorpions or something. I adore you."

"You have no right to speak to me like that," he said sternly.

"Oh, don't be so prim," she smiled.

"Let's get out of here."

He walked out on to the verandah and she followed him. He threw himself into a chair. She knelt by his side and tried to take his hands, but he withdrew them.

"I think you must be mad. I hope to God you don't mean what you say."

"I do. Every word of it," she smiled.

It exasperated him that she seemed unconscious of the frightfulness of her confession.

"Have you forgotten your husband?"

"Oh, what does he matter?"

"Darya."

"I can't be bothered about Angus now."

"I'm afraid you're a very wicked woman," he said slowly, a frown darkening his smooth brow.

She giggled.

"Because I've fallen in love with you? Darling, you shouldn't be so absurdly good-looking."

"For God's sake don't laugh."

"I can't help it; you're comic—but still adorable. I love your white skin and your shining curly hair. I love you because you're so prim and Scotch and humourless. I love your strength. I love your youth."

Her eyes glowed and her breath came quickly. She stooped and kissed his naked feet. He drew them away quickly, with a cry of protest, and in the agitation of his gesture nearly overthrew the rickety chair.

"Woman, you're insane. Have you no shame?"

"No."

"What do you want of me?" he asked fiercely.

"Love."

"What sort of a man do you take me for?"

"A man like any other," she replied calmly.

"Do you think after all that Angus Munro has done for me I could be such a damned beast as to play about with his wife? I admire him more than any man I've ever known. He's grand. He's worth a dozen of me and you put together. I'd sooner kill myself than betray him. I don't know how you can think me capable of such a dastardly act."

"Oh, my dear, don't talk such bilge. What harm is it going to do him? You mustn't take that sort of thing so tragically. After all, life is very short; we're fools if we don't take what pleasure we can out of it."

"You can't make wrong right by talking about it."

"I don't know about that. I think that's a very controvertible statement."

He looked at her with amazement. She was sitting at his feet, cool to all appearance and collected, and she seemed to be enjoying the situation. She seemed quite unconscious of its seriousness.

"Do you know that I knocked a fellow down at the club because he made an insulting remark about you?"

"Who?"

"Bishop."

"Dirty dog. What did he say?"

"He said you'd had affairs with men."

"I don't know why people won't mind their own business. Anyhow, who cares what they say? I love you. I've never loved anyone like you. I'm absolutely sick with love for you."

"Be quiet. Be quiet."

"Listen, to-night when Angus is asleep I'll slip into your room. He sleeps like a rock. There's no risk."

"You mustn't do that."

"Why not?"

"No, no, no."

He was frightened out of his wits. Suddenly she sprang to her feet and went into the house.

Munro came back at noon, and in the afternoon they busied themselves as usual. Darya, as she sometimes did, worked with them. She was in high spirits. She was so gay that Munro suggested that she was beginning to enjoy the life.

"It's not so bad," she admitted. "I'm feeling happy to-day."

She teased Neil. She seemed not to notice that he was silent and kept his eyes averted from her.

"Neil's very quiet," said Munro. "I suppose you're feeling a bit weak still."

"No, I just don't feel very talkative."

He was harassed. He was convinced that Darya was capable of anything. He remembered the hysterical frenzy of Nastasya Filipovna in _The Idiot_, and felt that she too could behave with that unfortunate lack of balance. He had seen her more than once fly into a temper with one of the Chinese servants and he knew how completely she could lose her self-control. Resistance only exasperated her. If she did not immediately get what she wanted she would go almost insane with rage. Fortunately she lost interest in a thing with the same suddenness with which she hankered for it, and if you could distract her attention for a minute she forgot all about it. It was in such situations that Neil had most admired Munro's tact. He had often been slyly amused to see with what a pawky and yet tender cunning he appeased her feminine tantrums. It was on Munro's account that Neil's indignation was so great. Munro was a saint, and from what a state of humiliation and penury and random shifts had he not taken her to make her his wife! She owed everything to him. His name protected her. She had respectability. The commonest gratitude should have made it impossible for her to harbour such thoughts as she had that morning expressed. It was all very well for men to make advances, that was what men did, but for women to do so was disgusting. His modesty was outraged. The passion he had seen in her face, and the indelicacy of her gestures, scandalised him.

He wondered whether she would really carry out her threat to come to his room. He didn't think she would dare. But when night came and they all went to bed, he was so terrified that he could not sleep. He lay there listening anxiously. The silence was broken only by the repeated and monotonous cry of an owl. Through the thin wall of woven palm leaves he heard Munro's steady breathing. Suddenly he was conscious that someone was stealthily creeping into his room. He had already made up his mind what to do.

"Is that you, Mr. Munro?" he called in a loud voice.

Darya stopped suddenly. Munro awoke.

"There's someone in my room. I thought it was you."

"It's all right," said Darya. "It's only me. I couldn't sleep, so I thought I'd go and smoke a cigarette on the verandah."

"Oh, is that all?" said Munro. "Don't catch cold."

She walked through Neil's room and out. He saw her light a cigarette. Presently she went back and he heard her get into bed.

He did not see her next morning, for he started out collecting before she was up, and he took care not to get in till he was pretty sure Munro also would be back. He avoided being alone with her till it was dark and Munro went down for a few minutes to arrange the moth-traps.

"Why did you wake Angus last night?" she said in a low angry whisper.

He shrugged his shoulders and going on with his work did not answer.

"Were you frightened?"

"I have a certain sense of decency."

"Oh, don't be such a prig."

"I'd rather be a prig than a dirty swine."

"I hate you."

"Then leave me alone."

She did not answer, but with her open hand smartly slapped his face. He flushed, but did not speak. Munro returned and they pretended to be intent on whatever they were doing.

For the next few days Darya, except at meal-times and in the evenings, never spoke to Neil. Without prearrangement they exerted themselves to conceal from Munro that their relations were strained. But the effort with which Darya roused herself from a brooding silence would have been obvious to anyone more suspicious than Angus, and sometimes she could not help herself from being a trifle sharp with Neil. She chaffed him, but in her chaff was a sting. She knew how to wound and caught him on the raw, but he took care not to let her see it. He had an inkling that the good-humour he affected infuriated her.

Then, one day when Neil came back from collecting, though he had delayed till the last possible minute before tiffin, he was surprised to find that Munro had not yet returned. Darya was lying on a mattress on the verandah, sipping a gin pahit and smoking. She did not speak to him when he passed through to wash. In a minute the Chinese boy came into his room and told him that tiffin was ready. He walked out.

"Where's Mr. Munro?" he asked.

"He's not coming," said Darya. "He sent a message to say that the place he's at is so good he won't come down till night."

Munro had set out that morning for the summit of the mountain. The lower levels had yielded poor results in the way of mammals, and Munro's idea was, if he could find a good place higher up, with a supply of water, to transfer the camp. Neil and Darya ate their meal in silence. After they had finished he went into the house and came out again with his topee and his collecting gear. It was unusual for him to go out in the afternoon.

"Where are you going?" she asked abruptly.

"Out."

"Why?"

"I don't feel tired. I've got nothing much else to do this afternoon."

Suddenly she burst into tears.

"How can you be so unkind to me?" she sobbed. "Oh, it is cruel to treat me like this."

He looked down at her from his great height, his handsome, somewhat stolid face bearing a harassed look.

"What have *I* done?"

"You've been beastly to me. Bad as I am I haven't deserved to suffer like this. I've done everything in the world for you. Tell me one single little thing I could do that I haven't done gladly. I'm so terribly unhappy."

He moved on his feet uneasily. It was horrible to hear her say that. He loathed and feared her, but he had still the respect for her that he had always felt, not only because she was a woman, but because she was Angus Munro's wife. She wept uncontrollably. Fortunately the Dyak hunters had gone that morning with Munro. There was no one about the camp but the three Chinese servants and they, after tiffin, were asleep in their own quarters fifty yards away. They were alone.

"I don't want to make you unhappy. It's all so silly. It's absurd of a woman like you to fall in love with a fellow like me. It makes me look such a fool. Haven't you got any self-control?"

"Oh, God. Self-control!"

"I mean, if you really cared for me you couldn't want me to be such a cad. Doesn't it mean anything to you that your husband trusts us implicitly? The mere fact of his leaving us alone like this puts us on our honour. He's a man who would never hurt a fly. I should never respect myself again if I betrayed his confidence."

She looked up suddenly.

"What makes you think he would never hurt a fly? Why, all those bottles and cases are full of the harmless animals he's killed."

"In the interests of science. That's quite another thing."

"Oh, you fool, you fool."

"Well, if I am a fool I can't help it. Why do you bother about me?"

"Do you think I wanted to fall in love with you?"

"You ought to be ashamed of yourself."

"Ashamed? How stupid! My God, what have I done that I should eat my heart out for such a pretentious ass?"

"You talk about what you've done for me. What has Munro done for you?"

"Munro bores me to death. I'm sick of him. Sick to death of him."

"Then I'm not the first?"

Ever since her amazing avowal he had been tortured by the suspicion that what those men at Kuala Solor had said of her was true. He had refused to believe a word of it, and even now he could not bring himself to think that she could be such a monster of depravity. It was frightful to think that Angus Munro, so trusting

and tender, should have lived in a fool's paradise. She could not be
as bad as that. But she misunderstood him. She smiled through her
tears.

"Of course not. How can you be so silly? Oh, darling, don't be
so desperately serious. I love you."

Then it was true. He had sought to persuade himself that what
she felt for him was exceptional, a madness that together they could
contend with and vanquish. But she was simply promiscuous.

"Aren't you afraid Munro will find out?"

She was not crying any more. She adored talking about herself,
and she had a feeling that she was inveigling Neil into a new interest
in her.

"I sometimes wonder if he doesn't know, if not with his mind,
then with his heart. He's got the intuition of a woman and a
woman's sensitiveness. Sometimes I've been certain he suspected
and in his anguish I've sensed a strange, spiritual exaltation. I've
wondered if in his pain he didn't find an infinitely subtle pleasure.
There are souls, you know, that feel a voluptuous joy in laceration."

"How horrible!" Neil had no patience with these conceits. "The
only excuse for you is that you're insane."

She was now much more sure of herself. She gave him a bold look.

"Don't you think I'm attractive? A good many men have. You
must have had dozens of women in Scotland who weren't so well
made as I am."

She looked down at her shapely, sensual figure with calm pride.

"I've never had a woman," he said gravely.

"Why not?"

She was so surprised that she sprang to her feet. He shrugged
his shoulders. He could not bring himself to tell her how disgusting
the idea of such a thing was to him, and how vile he had thought
the haphazard amours of his fellow-students at Edinburgh. He
took a mystical joy in his purity. Love was sacred. The sexual act
horrified him. Its excuse was the procreation of children and its
sanctification marriage. But Darya, her whole body rigid, stared at
him, panting; and suddenly, with a sobbing cry in which there was
exultation and at the same time wild desire, she flung herself on her
knees and seizing his hand passionately kissed it.

"Alyosha," she gasped. "Alyosha."

And then, crying and laughing, she crumpled up in a heap at his
feet. Strange, hardly human sounds issued from her throat and
convulsive tremors passed through her body so that you would have
thought she was receiving one electric shock after another. Neil did
not know if it was an attack of hysteria or an epileptic fit.

"Stop it," he cried. "Stop it."

He took her up in his strong arms and laid her in the chair. But when he tried to leave her she would not let him. She flung her arms round his neck and held him. She covered his face with kisses. He struggled. He turned his face away. He put his hand between her face and his to protect himself. Suddenly she dug her teeth into it. The pain was so great that, without thinking, he gave her a great swinging blow.

"You devil," he cried.

His violent gesture had forced her to release him. He held his hand and looked at it. She had caught him by the fleshy part on the side and it was bleeding. Her eyes blazed. She was feeling alert and active.

"I've had enough of this. I'm going out," he said.

She sprang to her feet.

"I'll come with you."

He put on his topee and, snatching up his collecting gear without a word, turned on his heel. With one stride he leaped down the three steps that led from the floor of the house to the ground. She followed him.

"I'm going into the jungle," he said.

"I don't care."

In the ravening desire that possessed her she forgot her morbid fear of the jungle. She recked nothing of snakes and wild beasts. She did not mind the branches that hit her face or the creepers that entangled her feet. For a month Neil had explored all that part of the forest and he knew every yard of it. He told himself grimly that he'd teach her to come with him. He forced his way through the undergrowth with rapid strides; she followed him, stumbling but determined; he crashed on, blind with rage, and she crashed after him. She talked; he did not listen to what she said. She besought him to have pity on her. She bemoaned her fate. She made herself humble. She wept and wrung her hands. She tried to cajole him. The words poured from her lips in an unceasing stream. She was like a mad woman. At last in a little clearing he stopped suddenly and turning round faced her.

"This is impossible," he cried. "I'm fed up. When Angus comes back I must tell him I've got to go. I shall go back to Kuala Solor to-morrow morning and go home."

"He won't let you go, he wants you. He finds you invaluable."

"I don't care. I'll fake up something."

"What?"

He mistook her.

"Oh, you needn't be frightened, I shan't tell him the truth. You can break his heart if you want to; I'm not going to."

"You worship him, don't you? That dull, phlegmatic man."

"He's worth a hundred of you."

"It would be rather funny if I told him you'd gone because I wouldn't yield to your advances."

He gave a slight start and looked at her to see if she was serious.

"Don't be such a fool. You don't think he'd believe that, do you? He knows it would never occur to me."

"Don't be too sure."

She had spoken carelessly, with no particular intention other than to continue the argument, but she saw that he was frightened and some instinct of cruelty made her press the advantage.

"Do you expect mercy from me? You've humiliated me beyond endurance. You've treated me like dirt. I swear that if you make any suggestion of going I shall go straight to Angus and say that you took advantage of his absence to try and assault me."

"I can deny it. After all it's only your word against mine."

"Yes, but my word'll count. I can prove what I say."

"What do you mean?"

"I bruise easily. I can show him the bruise where you struck me. And look at your hand." He turned and gave it a sudden glance. "How did those teeth marks get there?"

He stared at her stupidly. He had gone quite pale. How could he explain that bruise and that scar? If he was forced to in self-defence he could tell the truth, but was it likely that Angus would believe it? He worshipped Darya. He would take her word against anyone's. What monstrous ingratitude it would seem for all Munro's kindness and what treachery in return for so much confidence! He would think him a filthy skunk and from his standpoint with justice. That was what shattered him, the thought that Munro, for whom he would willingly have laid down his life, should think ill of him. He was so unhappy that tears, unmanly tears that he hated, came to his eyes. Darya saw that he was broken. She exulted. She was paying him back for the misery he had made her suffer. She held him now. He was in her power. She savoured her triumph and in the midst of her anguish laughed in her heart because he was such a fool. At that moment she did not know whether she loved or despised him.

"Now will you be good?" she said.

He gave a sob and blindly, with a sudden instinct of escape from that abominable woman, took to his heels and ran as hard as he could. He plunged through the jungle, like a wounded animal, not looking where he was going, till he was out of breath. Then, panting, he stopped. He took out his handkerchief and wiped away the sweat that was pouring into his eyes and blinding him. He was exhausted and he sat down to rest.

"I must take care I don't get lost," he said to himself.

That was the least of his troubles, but all the same he was glad that he had a pocket compass, and he knew in which direction he must go. He heaved a deep sigh and rose wearily to his feet. He started walking. He watched his way and with another part of his mind miserably asked himself what he should do. He was convinced that Darya would do what she had threatened. They were to be another three weeks in that accursed place. He dared not go; he dared not stay. His mind was in a whirl. The only thing was to get back to camp and think it out quietly. In about a quarter of an hour he came to a spot that he recognised. In an hour he was back. He flung himself miserably into a chair. And it was Angus who filled his thoughts. His heart bled for him. Neil saw now all sorts of things that before had been dark to him. They were revealed to him in a flash of bitter insight. He knew why the women at Kuala Solor were so hostile to Darya and why they looked at Angus so strangely. They treated him with a sort of affectionate levity. Neil thought it was because Angus was a man of science and so in their foolish eyes somewhat absurd. He knew now it was because they were sorry for him and at the same time found him ridiculous. Darya had made him the laughing-stock of the community. If ever there was a man who hadn't deserved ill usage at a woman's hands it was he. Suddenly Neil gasped and began to tremble all over. It had suddenly occurred to him that Darya did not know her way through the jungle; in his anguish he had hardly been conscious of where they went. Supposing she could not find her way home? She would be terrified. He remembered the ghastly story Angus had told them of being lost in the forest. His first instinct was to go back and find her, and he sprang to his feet. Then a fierce anger seized him. No, let her shift for herself. She had gone of her own free will. Let her find her own way back. She was an abominable woman and deserved all that might come to her. Neil threw back his head defiantly, a frown of indignation on his smooth young brow, and clenched his hands. Courage. He made up his mind. It would be better for Angus if she never returned. He sat down and began trying to make a skin of a Mountain Trogon. But the Trogon has a skin like wet tissue-paper and his hands trembled. He tried to apply his mind to the work he was doing, but his thoughts fluttered desperately, like moths in a trap, and he could not control them. What was happening over there in the jungle? What had she done when he suddenly bolted? Every now and then, against his will, he looked up. At any moment she might appear in the clearing and walk calmly up to the house. He was not to blame. It was the hand of God. He shuddered. Storm clouds were gathering in the sky and night fell quickly.

Just after dusk Munro arrived.

"Just in time," he said. "There's going to be a hell of a storm."

He was in great spirits. He had come upon a fine plateau, with lots of water, from which there was a magnificent view to the sea. He had found two or three rare butterflies and a flying squirrel. He was full of plans to move the camp to this new place. All about it he had seen abundant evidence of animal life. Presently he went into the house to take off his heavy walking boots. He came out at once.

"Where's Darya?"

Neil stiffened himself to behave with naturalness.

"Isn't she in her room?"

"No. Perhaps she's gone down to the servants' quarters for something."

He walked down the steps and strolled a few yards.

"Darya," he called. "Darya." There was no answer. "Boy."

A Chinese servant came running up and Angus asked him where his mistress was. He did not know. He had not seen her since tiffin.

"Where can she be?" asked Munro, coming back, puzzled.

He went to the back of the house and shouted.

"She can't have gone out. There's nowhere to go. When did you see her last, Neil?"

"I went out collecting after tiffin. I'd had a rather unsatisfactory morning and I thought I'd try my luck again."

"Strange."

They hunted everywhere round the camp. Munro thought she might have made herself comfortable somewhere and gone to sleep.

"It's too bad of her to frighten one like this."

The whole party joined in the search. Munro began to grow alarmed.

"It's not possible that she should have gone for a stroll in the jungle and lost her way. She's never moved more than a hundred yards from the house to the best of my knowledge since we've been here."

Neil saw the fear in Munro's eyes and looked down.

"We'd better get everyone along and start hunting. There's one thing, she can't be far. She knows that if you get lost the best thing is to stay where you are and wait for people to come and find you. She'll be scared out of her wits, poor thing."

He called out the Dyak hunters and told the Chinese servants to bring lanterns. He fired his gun as a signal. They separated into two parties, one under Munro, the other under Neil, and went down the two rough paths that in the course of the month they had made in their comings and goings. It was arranged that whoever found Darya should fire three shots in quick succession. Neil walked with his face stern and set. His conscience was clear. He seemed to bear in his hands the decree of immanent justice. He knew that Darya would never be found. The two parties met. It was not necessary to look at Munro's face. He was distracted. Neil felt like a surgeon who is forced to perform a dangerous operation without assistance or appliances to save the life of someone he loves. It behoved him to be firm.

"She could never have got so far as this," said Munro. "We must go back and beat the jungle within the radius of a mile from the house inch by inch. The only explanation is that she was frightened by something or fainted or was stung by a snake."

Neil did not answer. They started out again and, making lines, combed the undergrowth. They shouted. Every now and then they fired a gun and listened for a faint call in answer. Birds of the night flew with a whirring of wings, frightened, as they advanced with their lanterns; and now and then they half saw, half guessed at an animal, deer, boar, or rhino, that fled at their approach. The storm broke suddenly. A great wind blew and then the lightning rent the darkness, like the scream of a woman in pain, and the tortured flashes, quick, quick, one on the heels of the other, like demon dancers in a frantic reel, wriggled down the night. The horror of the forest was revealed in an unearthly day. The thunder crashed down the sky in huge rollers, peal upon peal, like vast, primeval waves dashing against the shores of eternity. That fearful din hurtled through space as though sound had size and weight. The rain pelted in fierce torrents. Rocks and gigantic trees came tumbling down the mountain. The tumult was awful. The Dyak hunters cowered, gibbering in terror of the angry spirits who spoke in the storm, but Munro urged them on. The rain fell all night, with lightning and thunder, and did not cease till dawn. Wet through and shivering they returned to the camp. They were exhausted. When they had eaten Munro meant to resume the desperate search. But he knew that it was hopeless. They would never see her alive again. He flung himself down wearily. His face was tired and white and anguished.

"Poor child. Poor child."

Other Works by W. Somerset Maugham

LIZA OF LAMBETH
MRS. CRADDOCK
THE MERRY-GO-ROUND
THE EXPLORER
THE MAGICIAN
THE MOON AND SIXPENCE
OF HUMAN BONDAGE
THE TREMBLING OF A LEAF
ON A CHINESE SCREEN
THE PAINTED VEIL
THE CASUARINA TREE
ASHENDEN
THE GENTLEMAN IN THE PARLOUR
CAKES AND ALE
THE FIRST PERSON SINGULAR
THE NARROW CORNER
AH KING
ALTOGETHER (*Collected Short Stories*)
DON FERNANDO
COSMOPOLITANS
THEATRE
THE SUMMING UP
CHRISTMAS HOLIDAY
THE MIXTURE AS BEFORE
BOOKS AND YOU
UP AT THE VILLA
STRICTLY PERSONAL
THE RAZOR'S EDGE
THEN AND NOW
HERE AND THERE (*Collection of Short Stories*)
CREATURES OF CIRCUMSTANCE
CATALINA
QUARTET (*Four Short Stories with Film Scripts*)
TRIO (*Three Short Stories with Film Scripts*)
ENCORE (*Three Short Stories with Film Scripts*)
A WRITER'S NOTEBOOK

The Collected Plays